Minga was aware of his dark Indian-like features dominating the flickering gloom.

"You fail to perceive a distinction," she told him.

"Distinction?"

"Yes. What has happened to me is my own concern. What you have done is the affair of the Crown. My duty to my King—"

"To hell with that stupid, Hanoverian glutton!" he blazed. His hand shot out as she dodged over to the window, but he only knocked her sidewise and she reeled on, put her head out of the window and screamed.

"Help! A spy! The watch! Here, the watch!"

"Damn your sluttish soul! Be still!" Frantically, he dove at her. He caught her, all right, and dealt her such a clip on the side of her face that her head whipped over onto her shoulder. She slipped down onto the floor, and crouched there panting, her skirts about her waist...

RIVERS OF GLORY

F. van Wyck Mason

A BERKLEY MEDALLION BOOK
published by
BERKLEY PUBLISHING CORPORATION

BERKLEY MEDALLION BOOKS are published by
Berkley Publishing Corporation
200 Madison Avenue
New York, N.Y. 10016

BERKLEY MEDALLION BOOK ® TM 757,375

Printed in the United States of America

Berkley Medallion Edition, JULY, 1976

To
DOROTHY LOUISE MASON
WHO SO WELL EXEMPLIFIES THOSE QUALITIES
OF AMERICAN WOMANHOOD FOR WHICH AMERICAN
MEN WILL ALWAYS BE READY TO FIGHT

*and to the memory of
the officers and men of*

**THE CONTINENTAL REGIMENTS OF THE
UNITED STATES ARMY**

WHOSE STEADFASTNESS IN VICTORY AND
IN ADVERSITY HAS EVER SERVED AS
AN ILLUSTRIOUS EXAMPLE TO THEIR
SUCCESSORS IN THE SERVICE.

CONTENTS

BOOK ONE — THE HUDSON

PART I—BOSTON, 1778

PART II—OCCUPIED CITY

PART III—THE *EVERGREEN*, BRIG

BOOK TWO — THE MONTEGO

PART I—CAICOS PASSAGE

BOOK THREE — THE SAVANNAH

PART I—HESPERIDÉE

PART II—THE *CONFEDERATION*, GALLEY

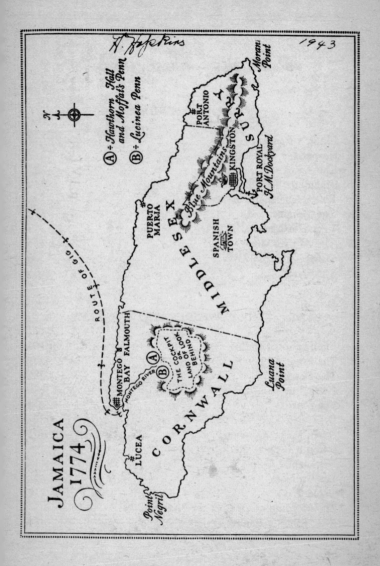

JAMAICA 1774

H. Hopkins   1943

Ⓐ = Hawthorn Hall
    and Moffat's Penn
Ⓑ = Lucinea Penn

N

Moran Point

SURRY

PORT ANTONIO

Blue Mountains

KINGSTON

PORT ROYAL
H.M. Dockyard

PUERTO MARIA

SPANISH TOWN

MIDDLESEX

ROUTE OF G^t°

MONTEGO BAY FALMOUTH

MONTEGO RIVER

Ⓐ

Ⓑ

THE "COCKPIT OR LAND OF "LOOK BEHIND"

CORNWALL

Luana Point

LUCEA

Point Negril

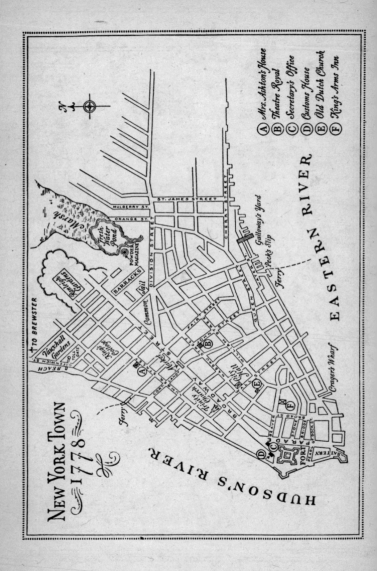

NEW YORK TOWN
1778

A Mrs. Ashton's House
B Theatre Royal
C Secretary's Office
D Customs House
E Old Dutch Church
F King's Arms Inn

EASTERN RIVER

HUDSON'S RIVER

TO BREWSTER

Marsh

Fresh Water Pond

Mulberry St.
Orange St.
St. James Street
Cherry Street

Galloway's Yard
Peck's Slip
Ferry

Powder Magazine
Common Jail
Division Street

Barracks

Vauxhall Gardens

King's College

Fair Street

Crager's Wharf

Ferry

Trinity Church
Broadway
Fort
Battery

SUNKEN SHIPS

FRIGATE

BRITISH PRIVATEER

COMET GALLEY

PRISON SHIP

BRITISH MERCHANT SHIPS

Huchinson's Island

MAC GILLIVRAY'S PLANTATION

BLUFFS

OGEECHEE CREEK

Yamacraw Swamp

MACINTOSH Woods

KING'S RANGERS

1ST BAT. GRENADIERS

71ST REG'T.

EBENEZER REDOUBT

ROAD TO AUGUSTA

SPRING HILL REDOUBT

SAVANNAH

GEN. PREVOST BRITISH H.Q.

15TH HESSIANS

BATTERY

BATTERIES

LINE OF

LAURENS *Swamp*

de STEDING

PULASKI

d'ESTAING

de SABLIERE

Woods

AMERICAN H.Q.

GEN. LINCOLN

RESERVES

BATTERY

FRENCH

COUNT PULASKI

de NOAILLES

MORTARS

d'EST

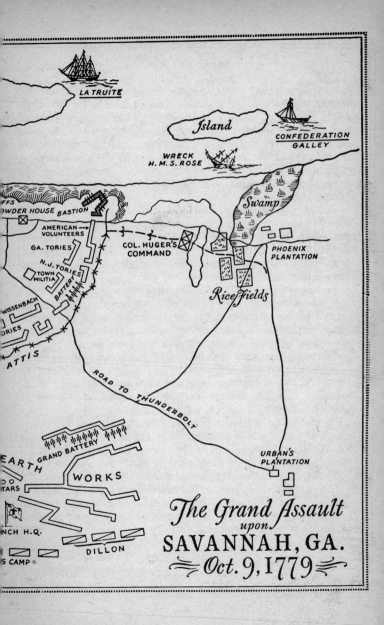

LA TRUITE

Island

CONFEDERATION
GALLEY

WRECK
H. M. S. ROSE

Swamp

FFS
OWDER HOUSE BASTION

AMERICAN →
VOLUNTEERS

GA. TORIES

COL. HUGER'S
COMMAND

PHOENIX
PLANTATION

N. J. TORIES

TOWN
MILITIA

WISSENBACH

ORIES

BATTERY

RiceFields

ATTIS

ROAD TO THUNDERBOLT

GRAND BATTERY

EARTH

WORKS

TARS

URBAN'S
PLANTATION

NCH H.Q.

DILLON

The Grand Assault
upon
SAVANNAH, GA.
Oct. 9, 1779

S CAMP

Author's Foreword

IN ATTEMPTING herewith to portray certain scenes, characters and events during the fourth and fifth years of our War for Independence, the author has had, unwillingly, to ignore a number of historically important occurrences. Among these are the Siege of Newport, the Evacuation of Philadelphia, Sir Henry Clinton's retreat across New Jersey and George Rogers Clark's memorable capture of Vincennes. Gladly he has avoided a recital of that long string of disasters which reduced to fragments the infant Navy of the United States.

The author has selected the Siege of Savannah as a background for a part of this book because, in the light of history, it appears that the results of this campaign indubitably prolonged the Revolutionary War by three terrible years. Had the Siege of Savannah ended differently, the British forces remaining in America would have found themselves confined to the vicinity of New York, dispirited and bereft of any real hope of victory.

It seems, therefore, that this critical, but inexplicably neglected siege is worthy of attention, not only because of its military significance, but because it so clearly demonstrates the folly of a nation's depending, primarily, on its allies to win a war for it.

The main characters, without exception, are fictional, yet representative of their class in the society of that day. The Warrens, the Proveaux, the Habershams and similar families did exist in the vicinities depicted, but the members portrayed in "Rivers of Glory" had no historical existence.

Careful research having failed to identify by name that South Carolina galley which participated in the siege, the author has allowed himself the liberty of christening her *Confederation*—a name popular enough in those parts to justify the selection.

The author is indebted in particular to Mr. Robert H. Haynes and his assistants at the Library of Harvard College for their invaluable assistance in the suggesting and locating of research material. To the Jamaica Library and to the Museum of Kingston, the author is indebted for much painstaking aid.

F. van Wyck Mason,
Riderwood, Maryland

BOOK I

THE HUDSON

I

THE NOAH'S ARK INN

INSISTENT, if cautious, knocking at his door caused Andrew Warren reluctantly to poke a tousled black head from beneath a pair of blankets topped by a distinctly shabby Jacob's ladder quilt. At the fierce nip of the air about his naked shoulders he flinched back like a box turtle into its shell. A plague on such unseasonable weather! From the fashion in which breath vapor lingered about his hair Andrew judged that the raw nor'easter must still be howling in over Boston Harbour.

"Andy! Mr. Warren, I mean. Mr. Warren." More knocking set the door to rattling in its frame. "Mr. Warren! Please wake." Anxiety entered a girl's hoarse but not unpleasant voice. "Be you ailing? I bin rapping the longest time."

Andrew shuddered at the contact of cold cloth as he straightened, cocked a reddened eye at the door and mumbled, "Stop that infernal pounding. My head's fit to burst."

"Please, sir, it's me, sir—Polly."

"Well, come, girl, come in. Don't stand there beating this condemned rat-trap of an inn to pieces."

The door opened a cautious crack. "Promise you won't buzz nothin' at me, Mr. Warren?"

"No."

A pretty head in a mob cap peered through the door. "Yer won't be playin' none of yer pranks, sir?" Polly's full, rather sullen-looking mouth relaxed, but apprehension lingered in her round blue eyes.

Shivering under the thin blankets, Andrew stared about the bare gray walls of his room. It looked bleaker than ever this morning. Its dresser, its flawed mirror, bent brass candlestick and trio of gaunt rush-bottomed chairs had never appeared more repellent. The lead-mended earthenware pitcher would require still more mending. Someone had knocked off its lip.

An insistent throbbing at Andrew's temples made the room tilt a little. "You need entertain no fears, Polly. Before you lies but the shattered hulk of a naval officer. One who could not offer affront to a stunted cockroach."

He grinned, settled back among the covers, a day's growth of beard brown-black on a wide jaw which was leaner than it should be.

Giggling, her blue and white striped petticoat a-sway, the chambermaid came sidling into the room, closed a well-scarred door behind her. She gathered a faded blue shawl about sturdy shoulders and remained, looking curiously on the figure in bed.

"I hope as how you don't feel too rocky, Andy—er, Mr. Warren. You was wonderful. Never have I seen a gent'man down hard cider way you did." In her tone awe was mingled with admiration.

"And, pray God you never will again."

Not a bad-looking girl was Polly. He wished he could remember more of last night. Must have been rattling good fun. Good old Tom. First fun he'd had in a month of Sundays.

It was hell being out of a ship like this. Did things to one's self-respect, it did. No pay, no duties, nothing to do but go hungry waiting for orders that never seemed to come. Six weeks now he'd been watching for the post rider's arrival, standing by while that beery old rascal was emptying his calfskin-covered saddle bags on Mr. Willard's bar. Jerusha! He knew the brown and white calf hide's design to the least detail.

When Andrew opened his eyes Polly had begun setting the room to rights. Not a bad-looking wench. But last night he'd not noticed the torn hem of her petticoat sagging so untidily, the raw, red chapped state of hands that could snap a faggot like a twig. He noticed, too, a long golden hair curling from a mole on one side of her chin. A good wash wouldn't hurt her neck any, either. Poh! Polly's bodice was stained yellow at arm-pits with sweat. No excuse, either. She slept on a bed let into the kitchen wall. Daytimes it was drawn up, concealed by a curtain of homespun. Scarcely private, still it was warm in the kitchen and one could wash in comparative comfort—if one had a mind to.

Because Mr. Warren's dark blue uniform tunic, red waistcoat and blue breeches lay across the foot of his bed and because his cambric shirt and jabot were draped over a chair, Polly guessed that this romantic, if impecunious, young naval officer wouldn't be wearing much by way of night clothes.

A pity Mr. Warren had got jingled so blamed quick. In an ill-covered bed two slept a sight warmer than one. She figgered it was a case of too much applejack on an empty stomach. Andy—Mr. Warren hadn't been eating hearty of late despite his careless laugh and confident airs. Must be down to near his last farthing. A pity, a cryin' shame, and him so generous and gay.

As she tidied up, Polly covertly considered Mr. Warren's lean outline clearly revealed by the grimy quilt. She felt more than ever aggrieved. Fancy missing such a fine buck! He must be uncommon strong. Why, he'd hefted that watchman as if he'd been a lad, had hung the officer by his belt from a hook let into the wall. Lord! She'd fair laughed herself sick at the watchman's vain threats and purple face.

"Watch out now—Andy." Boldly, she used his given name, sighed and looked hopefully in his direction. In the morning some men—

But Mr. Warren only closed his eyes against the light she let in by pushing back the shutters. Disappointed, she considered sullenly his strong brown-black hair dispersing in crazy rivulets over the dingy pillow-slip, his bold, straight black brows and a chin which could, all in a trice, take on a peculiarly reckless and devilish angle.

The mouth was wide, genially set in good-humored lines and forever quirking up at its corners. Polly liked wide mouths. She'd learned it was very seldom you came across a mean person who'd a wide mouth. Then, too, his hair was so soft and wavy and there was a mysterious scar near the point of his jaw—like a little white new moon as a rule, but it turned red when he grew angry. She wondered where he could have suffered it.

Most of the serving wenches deemed Mr. Warren prodigious fine looking, even if he wasn't exactly handsome—not up to some of the younger British officers in garrison during the Occupation. At times he suggested an Indian, what with that high-bridged nose, dark hair and skin so deeply sunburnt that not even winter had faded it.

Busily turning right-side-out his white thread stockings, Polly stole another look at the long figure beneath the faded red, green and white quilt. His eyes were shut, or nearly so, and there was a tired half smile on his lips. Godfreys! Mr. Warren certainly wasn't easily cast down. A body would think, what with being out of a ship, poor as Job's turkey and in some sort of disgrace with the Naval Commissioners, he'd act downhearted. But he didn't. Andy—Mr. Warren was always full of fun and devilment.

For all her cornstarch airs Polly, who'd been Colonel Foster's leman and knew quality when she smiled at it, doted on him, penniless or not.

She was recalled to actualities by a muffled groan. Turning, Polly realized that the early morning sun, glancing off the golden cap of Mr. Warren's epaulet, was striking him in the eyes. As she swung a creaking wooden window blind into place, she demanded,

"Your head, Mr. Andy—" she had compromised on that form of address—"is it very bad?"

"To call it bad, Polly, is a horrific understatement. By the bye, how did you survive our—er—celebration of Mr. Hadley's appointment in the *Active*?''

Polly giggled, wriggled under her shawl as if to hitch it higher. As she had calculated, her full breasts undulated a little, but he paid not the least heed. Said she, '' 'Twere a rare fine 'rouse, that it was. My bottom's checkered like a India print what with the pinching it got. You can see yourself.''

Unconcernedly Polly hauled up a trio of petticoats, displayed a series of livid finger marks mottling the bluish-white sheen of her thigh.

Gingerly Andrew pressed fingertips to his temples. ''My dear, if your bottom aches but a fraction as much as my head, I am truly contrite. And now, be a good lass, and kindle a fire. 'Tis colder than Christian charity in here.''

''Indeed it is.'' The girl huddled deeper into her shawl and looked away. ''Mr. Warren, I—I wish I could—but—''

''But? But what?'' Forgetful that he wore no nightshirt, Andrew sat up suddenly, dark eyes narrowed. ''Hell's roaring bells, Mistress, am I condemned to die of cold?''

''Oh no, sir—I—I trust not.'' Polly backed away, clutching his shirt retrieved from a corner. Her uninspired features flaming with the cold, she shrugged. ''Mr. Willard has given orders—''

''Well, go on!'' Andrew felt a flush of shame warm his chilled skin. He knew well enough what was coming.

''I'm dreadful sorry, I am—but he's told the help you're to have no more credit, sir, at the Noah's Ark.''

She came closer to the bed. ''If you—you want 'em, Mr. Andy— why I got a few shillin's put—''

''God's heart, girl! D'you fancy I'm so hard put—!''

Before his furious gaze, she flinched, clapped a startled hand to her mouth and went scarlet.

''W-why—why, I didn't mean to harm.''

All at once his hard brown body relaxed, shrank back under the covers. He gave her one of those surprisingly boyish smiles of his.

''Of course not—I fear I've been boorish. Pray forgive me, though I deserve no such consideration at your hands.''

''Then you—you'll take the silver?''

''My thanks, Polly, but I can't accept your offer.'' Bitterness reentered his voice as he continued, ''So that old rumble-gut Willard's stopped my credit? All on account of a beggarly shot of not over three pound.''

The girl stared as she brushed plaster dust from the uniform's sleeve. ''Three pounds—hard money—is a sight of cash these days.''

He nodded carelessly. "So it is, when our poor damned Navy freezes its parts off running blockade, fighting duty frigates and privateers, and never getting paid. And why do we do it? Why, to keep fat-bottomed innkeepers and such safe from Lord Howe's and Sir Henry Clinton's tender clutches."

Precisely, the girl's chapped red hands folded his blue and scarlet uniform coat across the dresser. Over her shoulder Polly said seriously, "Me and the rest o' the help know how 'twas during the Occupation. Godfreys! Us plain folks figger our ships is doing the best they can—and then some."

"Do you? Do you really now?" Andrew propped himself on a forearm covered with fine black hairs and marred by just such a jagged red furrow as an oaken splinter slashes through a man's flesh.

"Aye, we do, sir, indeed. Any God's body knows 'tis only Continental men-o'-war tries to drive off the Britainers. Shippers of private-owned war vessels," she sniffed audibly, "will always run from a bulldog, my brother claims, no matter what her size. He was 'listed in the *Hancock* when she was took by the *Rainbow* last year. Lord alone knows what's befallen poor Billy."

Andrew knew. If Billy weren't already dead, he would be freezing, half-starved and despairing up in bleak, gale-lashed Halifax. But he didn't say so.

Br-r-r. It was cold enough right here on the waterfront of Boston Harbour. So he'd been denied further credit? A pretty pass for a lieutenant of the Continental Navy. Damn. Of course Polly's money couldn't be touched but—

"Polly, my dear," he grinned suddenly. "Pray, draw near."

Polly giggled, clapped hands to her rear, sidled forward. "No pinches?"

"Never a pinch. I feel a most ungrateful dog. Should have thanked you more handsomely for your offer of assistance. Permit me now to express my gratitude with a chaste salute upon your lips."

Flushing, her mob cap's edge falling forward, Polly bent over the bed and remained so after a jaunty kiss had sent pleasurable little impulses rioting down her back. La! Mr. Andrew smelt fresh and clean for all his having raised the old Harry most of last night. He must be mighty cold, though, the way he trembled and chattered his teeth.

Dark eyes dancing, he sank back, patted her hand. "Pleasurable, Polly, most pleasurable. Were this sumptuous apartment warmer, why—"

The girl's features lit and eagerly she commenced tugging at her

shawl. "Don't you worry none, Mr. Andy. I'll come by a few sticks
of firewood in the stable yard, shouldn't wonder."

Her wooden pattens went clacking hurriedly towards the door.
Suddenly she halted.

"Lord's mercy. Mr. Warren, now ain't I the great goose?"

"Say rather a swan. What prompts the query?"

"Why, I clean forgot what I come here for. There's a letter for
you."

Shivering violently, Andrew wondered. A wild hope surged
through him. An appointment to a man-o'-war. At last. At last!

Polly bobbed like a duck at the edge of a pool as she fumbled in
the pocket of her none too clean "show" petticoat. "A lad brought
this for you."

"Were wits a burden, *ma petite*, I fear you would scarce bend
your pretty back."

"Godfreys, Mr. Warren, how you do go on."

Andrew Warren extended a wiry arm, felt the chill air bite on it.
His hopes sank. There was no official air about this plain, square
envelope. After breaking the paper wafer securing its flap, Andrew
rubbed eyes which felt retrieved from a sandy beach and read:

                                   Saturday ye 14th of March, 1778
Lieuten't Andrew Warren, U.S.N.
Noah's Ark Ordinary,
Ship Street, Boston.

My dear Nephew:
    I desire that you come to my Counting House this morning
with all Speed. I have the intelligence of an Opportunity to yr.
advantage.

                                        Yr. affec. Uncle
                                          Hosea Warren

Intelligence to his advantage? Andrew's straight black brows
climbed an incredulous half inch. Disbelief thinned his lips. An
overlong succession of disappointments, heartbreaks and disillu-
sionments taught one wariness.

Still—Uncle Hosea wasn't one to go off at half-cock. Maybe—
Andrew didn't dare be sure but maybe a turning point in his fortunes
had been reached? A possibility, no more. His naturally buoyant
spirits soared.

"*Enfin un miracle, ma petite.* I have, I trust, good news at long
last. Now, out. Out with you!"

"Yes, sir, but—please Mr. Andy, mayn't I first take your

chamber pot? Our leeching barrel ain't near filled this week and the Ordnance Department Collectors will be calling any minnit.''

Andrew laughed to cover his embarrassment at her matter-of-fact manner when she stooped and retrieved the chamber from its conventional situation.

"Of course, my dear, and may this patriotic piddle refine into superb nitre to make the finest gunpowder for the deadliest broadside ever fired by American cannons. Now out with you.''

II

WARREN, WHITTIER & CO.

ANDREW WARREN, Lieutenant, United States Navy, sensed but little of the savage wind leaking through the Ark's thin walls. "An opportunity to your advantage,'' Uncle Hosea had written. Did that mean Old Moneybags had secured him an appointment? He prayed God it did.

A long farewell to shore life would mean restoration to his career, to his self-respect and, most opportunely, to his purse. Wouldn't it be elegant to be at sea once more? To feel face and body buffeted by clean wind and flying spray? It would mean everything to sense a live deck beneath his feet again, to see for miles and miles in any direction, to know that politics, self-interest, jealousies lay long leagues astern. Lord above, it had been six eternal months since last he'd heard canvas snap and blocks rattle aloft.

Carefully he tied his plain leather neckcloth, then polished his blunt-toed pumps on his breeches' leg turned inside out. Well, he was glad now he hadn't swerved from his set course, hadn't given up the Navy to officer aboard some privateer. The temptation had been great. Some of his ex-fellow officers now were fairly rolling in gold. He'd been envious of their high times. The girls flocked to them, the citizens praised them—and who more than he, Andrew Warren, enjoyed girls and admiration?

While burnishing his brass shoe buckles Andrew smiled. Maybe in the long run it paid to abide by one's principles? Lord knew he'd few enough to adhere to.

His chilled fingers made slow work of setting straight his

stockings—aboard the *Boston* Captain Manley had insisted that his juniors turn themselves out neat to admiration.

To which man-o'-war had he been appointed? To the *Boston?* The *Raleigh?* The *Ranger?* No, couldn't be the *Ranger.* She was at sea. Maybe—his heart checked at the possibility—could Uncle Hosea have secured him command of one of those fast light cruisers like the *Independence,* the *Wasp,* and the *Sachem,* which recently had begun coming off the ways?

Damn the luck! During the frolic of last night he'd torn a small rent above the knee of his blue knee breeches.

Teeth chattering, he clumped over to a piggin standing beside the cold ashes of the hearth, but the water in it had frozen. Should have waited for Polly to kindle a blaze. Using his heel he broke through.

Whew! The water burnt his skin like a white-hot iron, but he scrubbed doggedly, then bathed his face. Wouldn't do to confront Uncle Hosea, that God-fearing elder of the Presbyterian Church, with eyes resembling brandied cherries.

During a full minute Andrew combed hair which, in strong jet strands, fell almost to his shoulders; then he clubbed it and secured the resultant queue with a frayed black ribbon. Next he instituted a search for his whalebone hair pins and found them under the bed. Skilfully, he utilized them to secure the hair away from his ears.

Polly's vigorous brushing had indeed improved the appearance of his turkey-red waistcoat, and his blue uniform coat looked almost brave with its epaulet, its flat yellow buttons, its round red cuffs and revers.

To sea once more! He quivered in anticipation of the details. On this cruise he vowed he'd not be over-eager, headstrong or tactless. Mistakes made aboard the *Boston* weren't going to be repeated. Even if he were not granted independent command, he'd plan just how best to put into practice certain notions concerning gunnery evolved during these long, lonely hours.

Um. If he got ahead and earned prize money, he'd soon be in a position to marry Belinda Dawson. Um-m. Perhaps Dorothea Holingshead would be more fun? On the other hand, Nancy Monks would make a man a rare fine wife.

From a nail driven into the inn's greasy bare wall beside the door he removed a greatcoat contrived in effective rough and ready fashion from a blue and white Dutch blanket. After righting the red, white and blue cockade stitched to his weatherbeaten tricorn, Lieutenant Warren buckled on his sword, a slim French affair with a guard shaped like a sleeping nymph. It served very well for shore duty and ceremonies, but for sterner assignments he'd a heavy British hanger Uncle Isaac had given him years ago.

It was odd to think of Uncle Isaac as an enemy, as Captain of H.M.S. *Niger,* 32-gun frigate. His name was never mentioned about home—Portsmouth—nowadays.

Downstairs Polly was waiting. A little fearfully, she indicated a cloth-draped salver reposing in a nook under the stair. She caught up her birch-splinter broom and, with the air of a deep-dyed conspirator, whispered, "There's a bun yonder, Mr. Andy, and a morsel of salt fish and a cup o' raspberry leaf tea—Liberty tea as some calls it."

"My earnest thanks, Polly."

"You're welcome, Mr. Andy. I wisht I could ha' snitched real sugar, 'tis just ground dried pun'kin ye'll find there."

With long gulps of Liberty tea he washed down a strip of tough salt mackerel then, putting the roll in his pocket for later consideration, pinched Polly's bottom through force of habit and stepped out.

Warren & Whittier's counting house lying a good third of a mile distant, he struck briskly off southwards along Ship Street. The counting house, the red brick façade of which Andrew had first seen as a child on a visit to the great town of Boston—all of 25,000 souls, even in those days—stood on Hanover Street directly opposite the end of Gallop's Alley and facing the Great Cove.

Whew! For March, this day was extraordinarily cold. A sprinkling snow, fallen during the night, eddied restlessly about gutters and doorways and tidily veiled little mounds of rubbish and refuse still undiscovered by foraging pigs and chickens.

Great Cove, nonetheless, was busy under the lowering gray clouds which scudded by so low they seemed to scrape the topmasts of the vessels. Bluish wood smoke was bent earthwards by the gale the instant it escaped blackened flue or sooty chimney pot. Everyone was muffled to the ears and bent his body into the wind. Through watering eyes Andrew could make out the masts and rigging of vessels tied up to Scarlett's Wharf etched black against the yellow-gray skies.

Against the outer rim of the barricade—that great stone and timber breakwater which for years had enclosed Great Cove and protected Boston from attack by fireships—waves hurled themselves in an insistent lathery fury, flung their spray yards high into the air. Within the barrier small boats scurried to and fro on their various occasions, quite unconcernedly. Few would have guessed that the King's tall frigates were cruising on blockade duty in Massachusetts Bay, not twenty miles to windward.

Evidences of the siege of '75 and '76 and of the Occupation were plentiful. Within the limits of Boston town scarce a tree had survived the British garrison's desperate need of fuel. The few fences which had been restored protruded raw and yellow above the dirty snow. There were telling gaps among the gray, weather-scarred fishermen's shanties hemming in the shores of Great Cove.

"H'dqu'ters, 2nd Batt 52nd Reg't," read an inscription done in red lead above the entrance to a solidly built cooperage. A shutter banged noisily, insistently, from the second storey of a ship fitter's loft.

The inevitable knots of sailors wearing long red stocking caps, canvas breeches and greasy leather coats were augmented by soldiers in a weird miscellany of uniforms and parts thereof and a goodly number of tradespeople. In striding down Ship Street Andrew hurried his paces. Jerusha! This wind was boring into him like an auger honed on an icicle.

A chapman bent under a load of pots, brooms and cutlery came plodding by, his bell tinkling thinly. A sooty chimney sweep, ladder on shoulder, bawled out, "Swe-e-ep! Swe-e-ep!" but his stunted, miserable-looking apprentice boy only snuffled and clutched his ladder and brushes when Andrew bade him good morning.

At the entrance to Fleet Street, the progress of a plodding span of liver-and-white-colored oxen forced him to stand clutching at his tricorn. They were drawing a chebobin loaded high with grayish beech logs. In the narrow street, the crude vehicle loomed importantly. Across the street the gale was making a pretty play with the petticoats of a young woman hurrying home with a basket of bread on her arm. Andrew watched her out of sight.

Children, glimpsing the red waistcoat of his naval uniform, paused in their construction of slides to jeer, "Red belly! Red belly! When do you sail?"

Andrew merely smiled. He'd sail soon enough. So would many another Continental Naval officer, if only Congress would supply guns, provisions and find commodores who knew what they were about.

By the time he had reached Martin Brunne's store, he was beginning to warm up and the remnants of last night's fogs were lifting ere the cranes, derricks and ways of Joshua Gee's shipyard loomed on his left. He cast the shipyard a second glance. They were all-fired busy yonder. Hammers were ringing, saws rasped and whiffs of heated pitch and the smell of oakum were brought by the wind.

Considering the blockade, there was a surprising variety of goods and foods displayed in various window fronts. Still, they were as nothing compared to what had been on sale four short years ago.

What a monumental, what an incredible, change the passage of those years had wrought! Pa gone, fallen at Freeman's Farm, with a Hessian bayonet through his strong, steady heart. Uncle Hosea, a merchant prince in '74, now was barely able to keep above water financially. Uncle Isaac, sailing under the Royal Pirate's Flag, would never return to that serene old home on Ladd Street—not if the new nation won out.

His heels creaked briskly over manure-stained snow muffling the lumpy cobblestones of Fish Street. Odd to see so few dogs and cats about; but then, during the Occupation a prime plump tom had often fetched five silver shillings, a fat rat a third as much. The Lobster-backs must have been all-fired hungry that winter of '76.

The harbor, which he could now see more clearly, had never looked more utterly cheerless. It seemed as if Spring was indeed very remote. The on-shore wind had piled rubbish-spotted drift ice along every indentation of the shore. Miniature floes drifted and bumped among a heterogeneous collection of snows, brigs, sloops and schooners sawing and swinging to their moorings off Colonel Hancock's long wharf. Most Bostonians continued to call John Hancock "Colonel" for all that he had risen so far in the affairs of the new nation.

Of the harbor proper, beyond the barricado, Andrew got blurred glimpses of the islands, Deer, Apple, Spectacle and the rest. They showed as rounded smears of white rising reluctantly above the gray of the water. Black specks revealed all that remained of farms which once had thrived on them. They had all been burned by one army or the other.

Absently, the solid figure in the blanket coat noted gray gulls wheeling above the bare topmasts of a big Indiaman. She had been captured quite recently as ragged, raw yellow holes in her black bulwarks testified. He remembered her now. She'd struck her colors to a vessel from home. The private-armed ship *Pilgrim*, 20 guns, Captain Jonathan Haraden.

A sigh escaped the lieutenant's chilled lips. Waterfront gossip claimed the Indiaman's cargo would fetch nigh on one hundred thousand dollars at vendue. That would give every man-jack of her company a small fortune. As so often previously, he began to wonder whether he was not a great, blind fool? A plague on that stubborn streak born into all the Warrens!

At the foot of the pier to which the *Pilgrim* lay charging stores and magazines, a drum began to thump. A lantern-jawed individual in a fine serge pea jacket raised a leather speaking trumpet and began to intone. Though somewhat distorted by the wind, his words were quite intelligible.

"Come all you jolly mariners, with courage stout and bold,
Come all who value venture as a miser doth his gold."

The drum rolled loud, louder, until the doors of various ordinaries and taverns commenced to open. Loafers, dock hands and fine solid-looking seamen wandered out into the street followed by a faint fog of tobacco and wood smoke.

From his post on an up-ended pork barrel, the lantern-jawed privateersman noticed Andrew.

"Hi! Hark ye, Cap'n!" he bellowed and a dozen bearded and shaggy faces turned. "How's about goin' to sea fer a change? Ye'll git a real chance at them Britishers."

Andrew shook his head. Damn the fellow's impudence to hell and back! The crowd commenced bellowing with derisive laughter.

" 'Tis short a lieutenant we are," insisted the gangling fellow on the barrel. "And ye can name yer terms I expect. Come aboard. We've a fine vessel, a bully lad of a captain and generous owners. What say?"

But for Uncle Hosea's message, Andrew might have yielded. As it was he shook his head, called back, "I sail soon in a Continental man-o'-war."

A gale of raucous, incredulous laughter sent blood streaming into Andrew's dark features.

"Continental ship? Ain't any!" "What's one look like?" "How's that froze-spit Esek Hopkins these days?" "Red belly!" "To hell with the Navy—the shirker's paradise." "Yah-h-h. Red belly!"

Andrew halted, but the crowd was too many. A stick sailed over his head, but the man on the pork barrel called out sharply, "No more o' that!" and no more missiles were flung.

Gibes followed the solitary figure in blue and red all the way to the entrance to Richmond Street. Andrew was boiling mad. Damn these yapping louts to Tophet. It wasn't just, so to torment men of the Continental Navy. Was it their fault that, through the incapacity or neglect of Congress and the Marine Commission, not even a dozen American men-o'-war showed their flag on the seas?

It was all of a piece with the stupid, cruel and unjust treatment meted out to poor Captain McNeill. When he remembered certain phases of that court-martial, his blood surged like a comber up a shale beach.

Because the Massachusetts people had demanded a scapegoat for the loss of their beloved *Hancock*, bluff, capable Captain McNeill had been dishonorably dismissed. It was a crying injustice, said everyone who knew the rights of the matter.

Andrew began to feel a trifle better when, up Hanover Street, loomed the grimy but still handsome red brick fronted building of Warren, Whittier & Company, Shipping Ag'ts, Import'rs & Commi'n Merch'ts. Though a swingboard displaying the firm's trademark had disappeared, its support arm of rusty wrought-iron remained and only a few of the heavy, purplish panes of glass in handsomely leaded windows had been shattered. Not a trace remained of the two-storeyed structure's heavy white pine window shutters.

Warren, Whittier & Company. Ever since he could remember, those names had sounded in his ears. Pa had spoken of the firm with a military man's kindly tolerance for mere civilians; but Mother, well, she'd always had a sort of awe in her voice. Weren't many firms around Boston doing £20,000 of business a year. The Warren and Whittier ships were all well found and fast. Had to be, or Hosea Warren would dispose of them quicker than quick.

As he swung up to the battered granite doorsteps, he saw that the words, "Strike Britons Home," had been painted in tar on a level with the street. They had been done over with whitewash but the wet weather had let the lettering come through.

What could Uncle Hosea have to offer? Andrew felt inexplicably annoyed that his heart had begun painfully to pump.

Inside the firm's counting house it was only a trifle warmer than outdoors, but it certainly brought back old times to recognize the odors of turpentine, salt fish, oakum, wet wood and wood smoke. Bezeliel Edson and Edward Leeson, efficiently dried husks of men, crouched above a high desk, working short-sightedly over huge calf-skin bound ledgers.

Just as it always had, a pellucid drop was trembling at the end of Bezeliel's pointed red nose, threatening to fall and blot the page. But as always he sniffed at the last instant, averting the disaster. Splashes of snuff marked old Leeson's rusty dark brown waistcoat, and his ancient wig was black above the right ear with ink from the quill he tucked there between entries.

Without looking up, Edson mumbled, "Pray, close the door," and kept on working over a pathetically lean sheaf of invoices.

"God's blood! My welcome is even chillier than this room," Andrew remarked, crossing to a very tiny fire smouldering on the hearth.

Leeson gasped, peered over his heavy steel-rimmed spectacles, then slid from his high stool. "God bless my soul, Mr. Andrew," he choked. "Look, Edson. He's come back, an officer and all." Jamming his pen over his ear, the clerk pattered forward, bony hand outstretched.

Old Edson grinned and scrambled down too. His hand felt dry, hard and cold—rather like a chicken's foot.

"My, my. And how do you fare in the Naval service? I vow you look very fine."

"If I do, Edson, I am indeed astounded. Since yester evening a flock of swifts have taken up their abode in the pit of my stomach." Andrew revealed white, but not wholly regular, teeth in a quick smile. "At this moment they are beating their wings with confounded insistence."

Edson's withered apple of a face contracted and he cackled briefly while Leeson relieved Andrew of the blanket coat.

"I'd like to—er—forewarn you, Mr. Andrew. Your Uncle has learned of certain of your—ahem—escapades, no doubt exaggerated. I venture Mr. Warren ain't overly pleased." Head wagging like a mechanical toy, the clerk winked at his colleague. "But me, I say life at sea is no green pasture, so a sailor ashore has the bounden right to—to—raise the—ahem—old Ned."

So Uncle Hosea had heard the gossip? Andrew drew a deep breath. Um-m. How much? That was the rub.

One cold night when the port had been mulled extra long, Pa had let drop that, for all his psalm-singing, younger Brother Hosea had, in his time, fancied a neat-turned ankle and a well-filled bed as much as the next man. At the same time he recalled another of Pa's sayings:

"When the Devil was young a Devil he'd be,
When the Devil grew old, a Saint was he."

Andrew drew himself up and faced the set of circular stairs leading up to his uncle's office. He hesitated when Leeson gave him a timid look of concern.

"Mr. Andrew—?"

"Yes?"

"Pray be patient with Mr. Warren," the clerk pleaded, his watery eyes narrowed under shaggy, frosty brows. "It ain't two days since we've heard that the *Sycamore* has been lost."

"Lost?"

Leeson nodded his dry old head. "Aye, sir. Went down off Hatteras with all hands—and no insurance. There's the real pity. Rates is out o' sight these days."

What small measure of elation Andrew possessed was dissipating faster than the snow melting on a roof across the street. Maybe this

interview wasn't going to prove such a cheery affair? Setting foot to
the stair he could feel the old clerks' eyes following him. One of
them clucked softly in his throat. To the devil with them! People like
Edson and Leeson were born half scared to death and grew worse as
they got older.

III

THE OFFER

HOSEA WARREN, ESQUIRE, feet braced apart, stood before a bed of
sea coal glowing fitfully in a Carron grate. A somber, squarish
figure in dark blue, the merchant nodded to his nephew and continued to fumble at the five or six seals attached to his watch fob. For
so solid a body Hosea's features were surprisingly sharp, angular
and alert. From the way Uncle Hosea's waistcoat hung loose along
its lower edge, Andrew could tell that his uncle must recently have
lost quite a deal of weight.

At first glance, Andrew realized that Hosea Warren must have
been making efforts to restore offices which had once been reckoned on a par with those of Colonel Hancock and the Adamses.

Today, instead of a deep-pile, pale brown rug imported from
China, only a mildewed scrap of Turkey carpet graced a floor
hopelessly marred and pitted by the hobnails of His Britannic
Majesty's 52nd Regiment of the Line. On the cruelly knife-scarred
mantelpiece a small blue and white Dutch clock was ticking nervously, metallically; not sonorously, complacently like the glossy
"grandmother" clock which, in the old days, had stood against the
far wall.

Behind a wide table-desk, however, glistened a handsome
mahogany chair of a design originated by a certain Mr. Sheraton in
England. Uncle Hosea must have brought it into town from his
summer dwelling near Milton. This, fortuitously, had escaped the
ravages of the Occupation.

Inadequately attempting to conceal faded patches on the hurriedly whitewashed wall, hung damp-speckled water-color
sketches of schooners and sloops dating away back to the firm's
early days. Their stiff old-fashioned lines were a thing to smile over.

The merchant's tall pewter inkwell, sander, paper knife and seal-ing-wax set, however, glowed with polish. When a man was sixty and more, such efforts to restore past glories must come hard, Andrew reflected. While waiting for his uncle to speak, he straight-ened his black silk stock and felt the cold begin to leave his tunic, but the epaulet kept the chill in his left shoulder.

For a moment longer the two men regarded each other across the dull bare boards of the floor—the small carpet only seemed to emphasize the emptiness. For his part, Andrew beheld a solid, thick-legged figure in decent dark blue broadcloth, damask and linen. From behind square-lensed spectacles peered shrewd gray-blue eyes which seemed always to be peering beyond the confines of the room—a hold-over, no doubt, from those distant days during which Captain Hosea Warren had walked his quarterdeck in such remote ports as Algiers, Teneriffe, Bahia, Calcutta and the River Plate. The commission merchant's complexion still was ruddy, but mottled now with white about jaws that argued firmness without stubbornness. Under an old-fashioned box wig, Hosea's heavy black brows flared aggressively above his strong nose.

Surveying his nephew, Hosea Warren was thinking, "He's grown to look uncommon like poor Horatio. Same forehead, same twinkle at the backs of the eyes, same long nose and be-hanged-to-you set to the mouth. But he's a replica rendered in somber tints. His black hair and eyes, his romantic flights of fancy, his flair for the opposite sex—he's inherited all that from that plagued French mother of his." Tarnation! Why had Horatio had to fall in love with Marguerite de Civray? She'd been a foreigner and unwelcome in the Warren family even though a member of the lesser nobility and, wonder of wonders, a Huguenot.

That Canada campaign during the Old French War had brought about altogether too many such marriages. Grudgingly, Hosea had to admit that Marguerite de Civray had made Horatio happy—she'd been an uncommon clever and capable wife. It was a crying shame that Marguerite had never been quite right aloft since her twin girls had been born deader than Chelsea mackerels.

Expressionlessly, Hosea studied his nephew standing so tall and lean just inside the entrance. A queer mixture, mighty queer, this nephew. God alone knew what would likely become of him. Impul-sive and smart and loyal to a fault. In his sight the amenities, the good things of life bulked larger than they should on a sound New Englander's horizon.

Hosea forced shiny, newly shaven features to thaw, held out his hand.

"Good morrow, Andrew. Pray be seated." He crossed to the

mahogany arm-chair, seated himself in it and crossed his legs. He made an effort, too, to relieve his nephew's wary manner. "Pray confide in me how you have evaded the debtor's prison so long? 'Tis a minor miracle, I'm thinking."

Andrew grinned, eased his slender French sword—it had been Pa's, given to him as a wedding gift by Mother's sire, the Chevalier de Civray. "Even sheriffs are reasonable folk, sir, if you flatter 'em."

The merchant nodded, toyed with his seals. "Precious few men have been hanged for flattery, and that's the plain truth. On the other hand, flattery buys few friends."

Aware of penetrating attention in his uncle's pale blue eyes, Andrew felt a flush creep up over his frayed uniform collar and spread hotly over his neck and forehead. The older man clucked deep in his throat once, twice.

"No, Nephew, we're not extra well-turned-out—either of us."

Grimacing, he waved about the office, mourning the loss of the fine scale models of his firm's vessels. The *Locust* brig had been hung over the mantel; the *Maple*, brigantine, yonder, and the full-rigged 200-ton ship *Oak* no longer glistened above Hosea's desk chair.

"We shall mend matters," he said heavily. "We must—both of us." He shot his cuffs. "Well, sir, how do you enjoy your Naval career?"

"I could not wish for anything finer," Andrew's voice rang out.

"I had feared so," the older man commented. " 'Like father, like son.' This passion for fighting will undo you also, I fear."

Andrew shifted to the edge of his chair, fired right up. "My father died for this country, sir. His memory is respected by his superiors and beloved by his men."

Hosea held up a hand mottled with big brown freckles. "You mistake my meaning. My brother Horatio was fine and honorable. I was simply wishing he had never followed the course of arms. Too many of us Warrens have. No, lad, there is small profit in the pursuit of arms."

Andrew bit back an angry retort and sat with lips thinned. All he said was, "No doubt, but has not someone to protect our valiant merchants?"

At his nephew's implication a flush tinted the older man's shiny cheeks.

"Yes, yes, so they must. But plague take it, Andrew, we Warrens have been shot down to nothing. Remember, I am a bachelor and your Uncle Isaac has only two children."

Uncle Isaac! Andrew felt certain resolutions anent keeping a rein on his temper begin to weaken. Dark eyes gone hard and bright, he gripped with both hands his sword scabbard and scuffed and scratched dark blue morocco.

"No damned King-loving Tory is an uncle of mine!"

Hosea bit his hard nether lip, stared across the desk on that sinewy figure in the faded blue tunic and spotted scarlet waistcoat. "That will do! Employ moderation in the mentioning of our kin." A quarterdeck ring made the older man's voice fill the whole office and, when he had done talking, his jaw shut with a little *click!*

"I admit no traitor as kin."

Andrew made a great effort and kept his seat instead of stalking out. To the Devil with this coldly superior old man. Ice water must long since have supplanted blood in his veins.

Stubbornly, but in a lower voice, he insisted, "Captain Sir Isaac Warren's people have killed my friends at my side. It was a British bayonet that—"

Hosea surged to his feet, his thick neck swelling over a simple linen stock.

"Silence! Don't you dare use such a tone to me. Think twice." The merchant's dull silver shoe buckles glinted as he took a short turn down the room. "Suppose we lose this war? We very well may. In that case, your Uncle Isaac—"

"—While we have a navy we will not lose it!" The force in Andrew's voice startled from its slumbers a large, tortoise-shell cat which had been drowsing comfortably in a square of sunlight. The creature treated him to a look of infinite annoyance mingled with disdain, then yawned and stretched.

Hosea Warren's plump shoulders straightened. "Were you not purblind or ill-informed, you would realize that, saving Captain Jones and his *Ranger,* this navy you speak of has been swept from the seas. Where are the *Hancock,* the *Delaware*, the *Lexington* and dozens of others?"

"Lost, burnt or captured." The words fell with a leaden heaviness from Andrew's lips. There was no dodging facts, no use telling how hard men had fought and died to save those same ships.

"What hope is there for a navy of our own when its best vessels are sacrificed to the incompetence or cowardice of knaves like Hoysted Hacker, Thomas Thompson and Hector McNeill?"

It was that mention of McNeill, of his own ex-captain, which touched off the mine of Andrew's resentment. Quivering, he reached for his tricorn hat.

He'd not listen to another word. Somehow he'd not expected Uncle Hosea to join in the outrageous clamor for Captain McNeill's disgrace. Not a man aboard the *Boston*, frigate, but had spit to windward and crossed fingers at the way Commodore Manley, with the blind assurance of a lunatic, had ordered his weak little squadron into the teeth of the British base at Halifax.

None but a purblind fool would have dreamed that the *Hancock*, 32 guns, the *Boston*, 34, and the new prize frigate *Fox*, 28, could for even a moment stand up to the tremendous naval power known to be concentrated in that bleak Nova Scotian port.

Ever so clearly Andrew recalled every detail of the three-day chase which had ensued. In his ears sounded once more the devilish scream of British round shot expertly seeking the range. He saw again the hard line of Hector McNeill's jaw as, coolly, calmly, when it had been all but too late, that hard-bitten commander had drawn on his stock of experience and seamanship. How desperately the handy little *Boston* had clawed up to windward when Commodore Manley's signal flags finally had told his consorts to run for it.

Andrew swallowed once, twice and felt his thighs grow hot but spoke in a voice which he hoped sounded controlled.

"Sir, either you have been grossly misinformed or hold some private grievance against my captain. I have the honor to bid you good day."

A peremptory gesture of Hosea Warren's broad hand checked his progress towards the door. "Such a temper, Andrew, will earn you small advancement in this world. I did just now but voice a general opinion and reflect the verdict of the court-martial. You did your prospects of advancement small service during Captain McNeill's trial—though 'twas through a sense of loyalty, no doubt."

Andrew began to cool down. Why couldn't he bridle his temper? Well, he intended to learn. Captain Biddle and Captain McNeill and a good many others had warned him on that score.

Uncle Hosea's succinct accents were crackling now like ice in a pitcher. "And where are you going in such a hurry? To pay your debts?"

Andrew winced, checked his stride towards the door. "Need you remind me of them?"

"It appears so," came the dry retort. "Surely, Andrew, you are not such a fool as not to surmise why the Navy Board has left you unassigned to a ship?"

His dark chin hardening its outlines, Andrew reseated himself, swung the slim French sword across his lap. "Rather than help make a scapegoat of a brave and an honest man, I still figure I'll walk the streets and—and wait."

"Such loyalty is commendable, but unfortunately it butters no parsnips,'' murmured Hosea Watren. The merchant frowned, commenced to finger the fob seals at the end of a heavy black grosgrain ribbon. ''How much cash have you?''

The lean young man grimaced. ''All of ten dollars.''

''I said cash—hard money, that is. How much?''

A lot of the starch went out of Andrew's back. Damn. Money was such a nuisance. ''None. I've only Continental scrip.''

''In other words, you haven't a penny—real money.''

Andrew nodded, shrugged and, looking out of the window, watched a fishing schooner make sail towards the entrance to Great Cove. From the way breakers were frothing all along the barricado, he calculated the wind must be freshening. Time and again the fisherman heeled 'way over showing her slimy green bottom to the pale yellow sunlight. Andrew's dark eyes refocused themselves on his uncle.

''You wish me to sign onto a privateer?''

Andrew didn't really think so. He was dead-sure the old merchant had found a Naval post for him but, characteristically, intended to have such a favor duly appreciated.

''A privateer?'' Uncle Hosea's frosty, bushy brows went up. ''I had thought you dead-set against service in a private-armed vessel.''

''I am.'' Andrew, studying that solid, self-contained figure across the desk, experienced sudden misgivings. ''I'm a Naval officer, not a damned sailor-of-fortune.''

''Um. Fine words, Andrew, but, like fine clothes, can you afford them?'' Granting his nephew no opportunity to interrupt, Hosea Warren arose, commenced to pace, moving with that sea captain's rolling gait he had never quite lost.

''I am about to put you a question—''

''If it's—''

''Pray listen and do not answer ill-advisedly,'' the merchant warned. ''You have tried my patience already.''

''I regret that, sir,'' Andrew said. ''I need every friend I can find these days—but—''

''I can secure for you the command—''

''—Command!'' Andrew's exclamation made the big bare office resound, and the cat started. The gaunt young officer's heart leaped like a speared fish. Then he had guessed a-right. He would have one of the fine new brigs!

''—Of a fine, well-found merchantman.''

''A—a *merchantman!*''

''Aye, and why not?'' Against the whitewashed wall Hosea

Warren stood, his chin out-thrust, his small eyes hard and bright. "I repeat, why not?"

"I? A merchantman?" Andrew went red as any turkey cock's wattles. The brilliant edifice of his hope swayed, toppled in disastrous ruin. "Oh, no. Not I. Never!"

Great God, hadn't this owl-eyed, pickle-faced old fool a whit of human understanding? How absurd to imagine that an officer who had helped old Esek Hopkins to raid the Bahamas, who had fought in the long, deadly duel betwixt the *Andrew Doria* and H.M.S. *Race Horse,* who had led the *Lexington's* shouting boarders over H.M.S. *Edward's* rail would sink to accepting the command of a double-damned floating hogpen of a merchantship?

"I thank you," said he heavily. "But I cannot accept. You can never understand. Once a man has served as a Naval off—"

"—His friends pity him and his family starves," cut in Hosea and, opening a small brass box, helped himself to a minute pinch of snuff. Moodily he considered the scarred floor, the pitiful substitutes decorating the walls, then spoke gravely, "Andrew, I fear you are not as intelligent as Captain Barry and others have led me to believe.

"Again let me ask you this. Is it pure accident that you, a trained and capable officer, should be kept cooling your heels week after week?"

"But, sir, there are some regular Naval vessels nearly ready for commission," the dark young man pointed out stubbornly. "There are the new brigs, the *Independence,* the *Ranger,* the *Saratoga,* the—"

"—Enough! There are six men waiting for every post. And by the bye," the older man's pale blue eyes wandered off, came to rest on a gouge dug by some British bayonet in the fluted pilaster to the left of the fireplace, "whatever prompted you to attempt elopement with that—that female?"

Andrew relaxed his taut attitude. "I presume you refer to Mrs. Seddon?"

"God's patience, who else? Surely you haven't attempted other elopements?"

"No." The sea coal crackled softly and an ash fell to the hearth beneath the grate.

"Whatever prompted you to such folly?"

"Why, she was young and uncommon pretty, I suppose." Andrew smiled and, stooping, began to scratch the chops of the cat which had come over to undulate against his muddied white stockings. "Besides, I'd not the least notion she was not the widow she

assured me she was.'' Andrew grinned. ''I vow I was mightily
taken aback when Captain Seddon burst in waving a confounded
huge horse pistol. If I'd not been so startled, I'd not have struck him
so hard.''

The merchant sighed, held short-fingered hands to the oily-
yellow flames. '' 'Tis no laughing matter. Seddon has friends in
Philadelphia. Nor does it improve your situation to play so high and
free with the Holingshead girl at home.''

Hosea Warren, for all he had lived in Boston for nearly twenty
years, invariably referred to Portsmouth, New Hampshire, as
''home.''

Had he not been so confounded perplexed Andrew would have
laughed the matter off; as it was he frowned and spread his hands.
''Am I to blame if a girl becomes dazzled by a Naval uniform?''

So *that* was it. Because he'd passed Belinda Dawson up for
Dorothea Holingshead, Belinda must have tall-talked about Ben
Ackland's bundling party back in December. This was odd because
such gossip could not but have touched her, too. Lord! Even
Solomon's wisdom could not predict a female's notions.

''Saving a miracle, Andrew,'' the older man spoke slowly, ''you
may as well give up the Navy. There will be nothing more for you
there. I have that on excellent authority.''

Give up the Navy? Nothing more for you? Like heavy hostile
fists the words pounded on Andrew's incredulous ears. This must
mean that even his most modest hopes were groundless. What a
fool, what an arrant imbecile he'd been to calculate on commanding
a brig. Fancy deluding himself into the illusion that the *Sachem*
might be his.

Intently Andrew considered his uncle and tried to read below the
surface of his grim, yet not intolerant, expression. Was this a
dodge? Instinct prompted that it was not.

Give up the Navy? Well, he wouldn't, not any more than he'd
part with his right leg. The Service during these last two years had
become an integral part of his life. He'd never again be happy if
completely deprived of the precise, well-ordered existence aboard
ship. It was curious how perfectly ship, sails, lines, guns, officers
and men integrated themselves into a perfect unit—under the right
command, of course.

What a pitiable sight it was to see sloppy, private-armed vessels
masquerading as men-o'-war. Captain McNeill's men had had
nothing but contempt for the ill-equipped, poorly disciplined men-
o'-war out of Spain, Portugal and dozens of little Italian states.

A slant of sunlight touched with fire the scarlet lapels to

Andrew's waistcoat, drew dancing flashes from his single epaulette as he said soberly, "I can't and I won't resign from the Service. Sooner than do that I—I'd—"

There was something compelling about the way the ex-sea-captain's hand rested on Andrew's shoulder. Hosea lowered his voice and looked his nephew squarely in the eye.

"Have I advised your resignation? No. I would go far to prevent that. We Warrens—well, we ain't used to calling quits when the going's poor."

"What then—what is your meaning, sir?"

"If you will heed my advice on a certain matter," the other began to talk more rapidly, "you may preserve this Naval career of yours—may even enhance it in great measure."

The room gradually became real once more and Andrew ceased to exist in some uncanny fourth dimension.

"Yes, sir. Pray continue." Uncle Hosea had gained his point all right; nobody could have listened more respectfully, more intently than Lieutenant Andrew Warren.

Hosea's little eyes sought the Cove, attracted no doubt by the sight of three small vessels—a brigantine, a brig and a schooner—surging into port under reefed topsails. All three were flying the new-fangled striped and starred flag the Congress had finally decided on. Two of the vessels, however, displayed ragged red ensigns under the American flag, thus advertising to those interested that still another privateer and her prizes were making port.

Bom-m-m! Once, twice, three times the brigantine saluted the port. In a twinkle the blue-gray smoke of her guns was whipped away.

The solid figure in dark blue plucked a yard of clay from the mantelpiece, prepared to load its bowl with Virginia bright tobacco.

"I am gratified that you display a more reasonable attitude," Hosea observed. "For, as I have said, I desire you to succeed in your career—very earnestly, indeed."

"Thank you."

"Since your mother was Canadian you are familiar with that horrible language called French?"

"I learned it as a child." Andrew knew his uncle had never cottoned to a foreigner's having been brought into the family—even a lovely and talented one.

"How much of it do you recall?"

His interest rising, Andrew unhooked his sword, stood it in a corner. "Well, nearly all I ever knew. Back in '74 Pa made me study in Toulon 'til I had learned something of the writing of the language.''

''That's good.''

''Why?''

''Pure curiosity, Andrew. The knowledge may come in handy before long.''

Enthusiasm animated the younger man's dark features. ''If this projected alliance is accomplished, the war will not endure six months.''

Hosea grimaced over the stem of pipe. The snap of a tinder pistol in the merchant's hands sounded staccato. ''Now do tell!''

''You don't believe it?''

''No.''

''The French are fine people. I—''

''—In France no doubt they are.'' Puff, puff. ''But in my experience,'' puff, puff, ''which ain't inconsiderable,'' puff, ''I've set 'em only a small smitch above other foreigners. Of all the self-seeking, weather-cock-minded, braggart and corrupt races God ever put on the face of the earth, they rank near the top.''

''But—but they're very sensible of their honor.''

''In a drawing-room where the ladies will hear. Bah! The Crapauds will shovel out a deal of fine words when it suits, then forget their promises as readily.''

Andrew started to interrupt, yet subsided. It would boot nothing to argue. Ninety-nine of a hundred New Englanders would agree heartily with Hosea Warren. Southerners, though, held the French in mighty high esteem.

''You don't like the French much.''

''No, I don't,'' the sturdy figure continued between hard puffs at his pipe. ''My half-brother Oliver and your Cousin Obadiah were skinned alive by Hurons near Trois Rivières while the Frenchmen who had captured 'em looked on and laughed. At Deerfield 'twas Frenchmen who led those hellions who scalped your grand-aunt, then split her baby open like a cod on a rack.''

The merchant's lips tightened and a tinge of color brightened the smooth curves of his cheeks. ''Near a dozen of our people have perished fighting the French and, twixt you and me and the anvil, I wish to God we were fighting 'em now, 'stead of killing our own flesh and blood.''

If he knew what was good for him, Andrew mused, Uncle Hosea had better not hold forth in public like this. Most everybody was getting optimistically heated up over the help the French king was going to give America. Old-fashioned and extra hard-headed was

Hosea's generation, and they never *had* understood foreigners. That was plain as a pike staff.

"Mark my words, Andrew. An alliance with the French, *if* it comes about, will more likely prolong, rather than shorten this war."

The senior partner of Warren, Whittier & Co. drew several deep puffs from his pipe, sent woolly smoke drifting about the room in long gray tendrils. "However, I digress, Andrew, I digress; and in these times one must keep one's eyes on the mark."

Andrew's hands tightened on the none-too-clean fabric of his breeches.

"This command I offer, while not Naval, nonetheless calls for an officer of uncommon wit, hardihood and resolution. Should you succeed in this mission you will have gone far in mending this damaged career of yours, and you will have aided our country. That is what you want, is it not?"

"Of course." For the life of him Andrew couldn't penetrate the old man's intention.

"I have been assured that *if* you bring to a successful conclusion the mission I will mention, you will be appointed lieutenant in the *Trumbull*, frigate—" he sniffed, "—provided those Connecticut blockheads can devise some means of transporting her across Thames River bar."

The young lieutenant went over to stand beside the fire and the shabbiness of his uniform was more fully revealed by brilliant sunlight pouring in a south window. He tried hard to remain impassive. After all, there remained a proviso, and a stiff one, if he knew his uncle.

Hosea Warren's speech quickened. He jerked a nod to a bare spot just above Andrew's head. The rusty nail there looked very poor and forlorn. "Do you recall what used to hang up here?"

"I think it was a model of your brig, the *Evergreen*."

The old man's pale blue eyes again sought that faded oval spot above the fireplace. "How well do you recall the *Evergreen*?"

"She is new and of about one hundred tons' burden." He hesitated, frowned. "But I thought the Britishers took her late last fall?"

"Quite correct. The *Augusta's* tender ran her down, carried her into New York for condemnation by the Prize Court. She was sold at auction last month."

"Who bought her, sir?"

"I did," came the quiet assurance, "through a dummy in New York. It was arranged through the good offices of a patriotic merchant—one Isaac Roosevelt. The actual dummy was a fellow named Henry Oakman. Mark that name well.''

Andrew nodded. God, but he was hungry. That snack the chambermaid had found him had been utterly inadequate. He did not let on to be too interested. He wasn't, but he'd made too many hasty decisions in the past. Um. Go slow, that was what he'd better do. Uncle Hosea would respect him for it.

''I will remember the name, Henry Oakman. What is it you wish me to do—if I agree?''

The old merchant batted his eyes over the ''if.''

''You will proceed immediately to New York, proclaiming yourself a Tory refugee. It is fortunate you have lived in foreign parts so much there must be small danger of recognition.''

Hosea was wrong there, Andrew knew. In those same foreign parts he'd gone about ashore quite a bit, socially—and otherwise. For a sailor he had met, during the past years, an uncommon number of people of importance—not to mention a very fetching female or two. No call to mention this, though.

''You would seek this Mr. Oakman and present him with certain letters of identification and instructions.''

Andrew's interest warmed a trifle. In New York he supposed a smart observer could learn or deduce quite a lot about the British there. The state of their ships and the condition of their crews, for instance.

''Mr. Roosevelt, I am informed, already has secured the necessary cargo clearances as well as a sailing permit from General Pigot—at present Commandant of the Port. Upon your arrival he will find some identification papers for yourself.''

''What of the crew?''

''Your crew will be entirely Tory,'' the merchant explained and, drawing hard on his pipe, made a small bubbling noise. ''Your ship's company must be convincing.''

''And then?'' Andrew's finger crept up and loosened the black leather stock about his throat—his Irish linen one had fallen apart two weeks ago.

''You will shape a course for Montego Bay on the north coast of Jamaica. There you will pick up a cargo for me; among other things certain medical supplies—''

''—Jamaica?''

Jerusha? That, sure enough, would be sailing into the Lion's jaws. It was from that island's many, well-protected harbors, whence sailed those stinging fleets of frigates, light cruisers and patrols which daily were snapping up American ships, severing the line of illegal traffic with North America.

Here was risk and adventure to spare, yet, yet— All of his old
resolution returned with a rush. Hosea was a neat talker, always had
been, as his business rivals knew to their sorrow. Most likely this
talk of his being blacklisted by the Marine Committee was tootle—a
shrewd dodge to secure a man-o'-warsman to captain Warren &
Whittier's last remaining vessel. He felt sure of it, was pleased with
himself for having smelt the trap. That bait about danger had been
smart on the old man's part.

Beyond the desk Hosea must have sensed a change as he looked
up under his heavy brows.

"Will you undertake this voyage?"

"No."

"But the medical supplies? They are sorely needed—"

"That's the business of the Hospital Board—I'm no sawbones.
I'm a fighting man. No, I won't accept and that's flat."

Hosea Warren's expression changed not at all as his hand sought
a small brass bell. "I see. I wonder whether Dr. Blanchard has
arrived?"

IV

DR. BLANCHARD

OLD EDSON, grayish jowls gone mottled crimson with effort, came
shuffling up from below the corridor.

"Yes, sir. Dr. Blanchard is below," he puffed. "I hope, sir, I did
right in showing him into Mr. Whittier's old office?"

"You did quite right. Send him up, Edson, and be confounded
quick about it." Hosea Warren's anger broke through his words if
not through his expression.

Big, hearty Mr. Whittier was dead, carried off by the terrible
smallpox epidemic of the winter of '76; hardly a home in Boston had escaped paying some measure of tribute to that dead
scourge.

A quick, light step sounded on the carpetless stairs, the door
swung open and there entered a solid, large-framed figure. The
newcomer could not have been much over thirty, but his eyes
looked older by ten years.

He was painstakingly neat in his well-cut black suit and a triple-caped riding coat of the same sober hue. By contrast, the simple lace at his throat and wrists sparkled. He was carrying a walking stick equipped with a curiously heavy head of silver.

"Dr. Wallace Blanchard, my nephew, Lieutenant Warren," grunted the merchant.

The newcomer's ruddy, attractively homely features lit as he clasped Andrew's hand between both his big, clumsy-looking ones.

"A pleasure, I vow, to meet a real officer. One wearies of these roistering privateersmen."

"Ha-r-umph." Hosea Warren arose and went over to prod the sea coal to a brighter effort. "Nephew's no better—lived in France too long."

The young surgeon grinned until clear, dark blue eyes almost became lost. "I had hoped to study at the Hotel Dieu, but," he shrugged, "Messrs. Hancock, Adams and the rest arranged to the contrary. You have broached the—the matter to Lieutenant Warren?"

The merchant flushed and fiddled pettishly with his seals. "My nephew has—er—reserved judgment."

"I refused," Andrew corrected shortly. "I am a Naval officer—"

"I see." Dr. Blanchard glanced at first one, then the other of the two. One could see that they were much alike about the eyes though the younger man was darker; about the mouth, too—stubborn, self-determined and proud. Curious thing, New England pride, Blanchard mused; it didn't take outward expression, no elaborate homes, no expensive horses or clothes, no fancy "Stab me's" or "I do protest's." Yet it was ingrained, ineradicable. To be mistaken in one's considered judgment, in New England, was a disgraceful thing.

Um. These two had certainly been rubbing each other's fur the wrong way. A pity. Lieutenant Warren looked capable, determined.

Mildly Dr. Blanchard inquired, "And why have you decided against this cruise to Jamaica?"

Impatience broke through Andrew's voice. "Why? Dammit, can't you civilians realize a Naval officer's a man-o'-warsman, not a damned pick-nose merchantman or piratical privateersman?"

"I do realize the difference," Dr. Blanchard declared and with a covert gesture checked an outburst on the older man's part. "That is just the reason why we—well, all of us—wanted you. We have heard of your enviable record aboard the *Andrew Doria*—of your courage aboard the *Lexington.*'' There was a brisk, yet soothing, quality to the medical man's speech. ''I have envied you greatly, sir. We chirurgeons must labor incognito.''

To Wallace Blanchard it appeared not only unfair, but ill-advised, that the Army Medical Board had refused uniforms to its surgeons, physicians and apothecaries.

''We all have our disappointments. Believe me, Mr. Warren, I do admire your constancy towards your chosen endeavor,'' the doctor declared. ''I am indeed proud to greet a member of our Navy—sadly unappreciated thus far, I fear.''

Andrew's heart began to warm a trifle. It wasn't often these days a Navy man met with open appreciation.

The surgeon rubbed big clumsy-appearing hands, held them towards the grate. He seemed to be seeing something in the depths of those little yellow flames spurting out of cracks in the sea coal—something by no means cheering. Andrew noticed again a dull, red-brown smear on his cuff.

''Yes, greatly I lament your decision—''

''—He'll regret it more than you,'' rasped Hosea's voice. ''And you may lay to that! I regret, Doctor, I apologize at having failed you.''

When the old man tried to secure the lower buttons of his waist-coat his fingers fumbled; they quivered so with anger. ''As for you—'' the merchant directed a baleful glare at his nephew—''I despair of your future. Apparently there is no standing betwixt a fool and his folly. You may, my dear nephew, go to the devil on your own course.''

''I intend to,'' Andrew replied evenly and, stalking over to the corner, buckled on his sword, ''and it won't be aboard a stinking bull-nosed barge of a merchantman!''

''S-stinking, bull-nosed!''

That fetched Uncle Hosea's dander, all right. The clean lines of his ships were his especial vanity.

''Out!'' he bellowed. ''Out of my office with you! Of all— Why you slab-sided, snotty-nosed whelp! By God, I'll—I'll—''

He fell silent from sheer lack of breath; whereupon Dr. Blanchard broke in with professional adroitness.

''A thousand pardons, Mr. Warren, if I leave you for the moment. I have an appointment of first importance—I will return as soon as may be.'' He placed a hand on the chill gold braid of Andrew's epaulette. ''Would you care to walk with me? I fancy we are headed in a similar direction.''

V

"DRYDOCK"

A SEAMAN was standing all huddled up in the scant shelter of Warren & Whittier's doorway. Here watery winter sunshine was doing its best to supplement the doubtful warmth of the vagrant's threadbare gray peajacket and petticoat breeches of tar-stained canvas.

In the strong sunlight the lurker's pinched features gave the impression of old, old parchment and his blue eyes, sunk deep in his head, were encrusted with little yellow granulations. As he ducked his head, his tarred pigtail, stiff as a poker in its wrinkled eelskin case, swayed like the tail of a dog attempting to be friendly.

"If yer please, yer Honors, I've not a copper and I—well I've had not even a smell o' vittles since yesterday."

Instinctively Andrew searched his pockets but found not a thing beyond a clasp knife, a lump of sewing wax and a bronze religious medal a girl back in St. Malo had made him promise to keep. Dr. Blanchard, however, found a silver sixpence.

"Thank 'e, sir. Gawd bless 'e, sir," babbled the seaman through teeth which chattered in the bitter wind. He glanced about hesitantly, straightened a trifle, then looked at the dirty snow under his feet. "Yer mayn't believe me, yer Honor, but this is the first charity I've ever begged, sir, honor bright. I really hadn't intended so but—but this here wind blows clean through a man."

Dr. Blanchard bent forward and sniffed. His strong red face contracted. "You've been sick?"

"Aye, sir. Two long months. If I hadn't have took the jail fever I'd be to sea." He shot a hopeful look at Andrew. "I'm a gunner's mate I am, sir."

"When last have you had a bath?" Blanchard demanded in brisk, dispassionate tones.

The seaman rubbed his chin, cocked his head to one side. "Why, sir, I allow it must ha' been last Fall, sir. Water's killin' cold now." He scratched at his armpit. "I've got used to the little bastards."

Dr. Blanchard nodded. "I expect so, but the sooner you clean yourself, the sooner you'll mend."

"Aye, aye, sir," the man-o'-warsman agreed and snuffled noisily. "Me, I don't fancy a winter-stink like some."

"Tell me," the surgeon demanded, "were you given Peruvian bark for your jail fever?"

Suspicion mingled with resentment, the seaman eyed his questioner, looming very solid in a bottle-green riding cape.

"Bark? Lord love yer, no sir. Yer don't get bark in a almshouse—nor nothin' else neither but hard words and harder treatment."

"Almshouse?" Andrew demanded, gathering his blanket coat against the wind's insistent tugging. "Why weren't you in a hospital?"

"Hospital?" A surprised stare was Andrew's reply.

"Why, yes. There's the Boston Marine Society—"

"—Not for a man-o'-warsman—"

"Well, then, there's one over in Cambridge—"

"Vassall's," the doctor supplied. "Full up and short of supplies of all kinds."

The beggar's breath went whipping off as, with a sly look, he delved into his old peajacket's pocket. "I ain't going to take no more fever though, sir. I got this." Proudly he held forth a short length of twine so heavily tarred it was lumpy half its length. "Worn about the wrist it'll ward off fevers o' all sorts."

Andrew spoke up. "You say you're a man-o-warsman?"

"Aye, aye, sir. I'm Joe Atherton, sir," the beggar mumbled, plunging purplish hands into his pockets. "I were gunner's mate in the *Randolph*. Soon's I get rigged and fit for duty I'll 'list up. Still I might go as a soldier—Navy ships is turrible scarce."

"I know it. I'll lend you a hand, Atherton," Andrew burst out. "It isn't right you should drift about like this. Come and see me at the Noah's Ark—tomorrow." He sensed, rather than saw, Blanchard suppress a smile. Well, he'd a right to. As if he, Andrew Warren, could help anyone! Couldn't even set a sound course for himself.

The fellow's unshaven jaw commenced to twitch. "Gawd, sir, d'yer mean it? Them's the near first kind words I hear spoke since the *Randolph* sailed away—and me on my beam's end with the yellow janders."

"By your speech, Atherton, you are English-born?" Blanchard demanded, his eyes deceptively indifferent.

A worried look wrinkled Atherton's eyes and his gaze shifted to the gray harbor. Out yonder the newly-arrived privateer and her prizes were snugging down; their crews, lying out on the yards, were trying desperately to secure weatherbeaten topsails against the whistling wind.

Already a disorderly flotilla of barges and bumboats were putting out from shore, eager to bargain for odds and ends of food and merchandise. The bulk of the cargoes, however, would have to await a Prize Court's verdict.

"Aye, aye, sir. English I was born. But me, I've precious small use for the Bloodybacks." Atherton blew hard on grimy fingers. "Press gang jumped me in Bristol, they did, and I were scarce fourteen. In the Carolinas an officer had me flogged for findin' one o' his handkerchiefs—'tweren't marked so I kept it." He lowered his voice. "Well, I jumped ship."

The man-o'-warsman's malevolence was impressive. "That's why I likes service in reg'lar Navy vessels. Ain't nothin' to touch 'em when it comes to standin' up to a Britisher."

Andrew's heart warmed to the pinched, faded figure that yet held such a pride. "The Noah's Ark then—remember."

"Aye, aye, sir."

Atherton knuckled his forelock and, holding a battered, black-painted straw hat hard to his head, shuffled away.

The doctor watched him go, sighed. "Poor devil. Bark or even jalop would have halved his sickness. Would to God he were the only one in like case. There's so little we can do lacking ipecac, camphor, coriander, even epsom salts."

Dr. Blanchard, it appeared, knew home, Portsmouth, well. He'd visited the Buckmasters there several times and was familiar with the countryside. He had, Blanchard explained, paid Portsmouth a visit not two months back—on a matter of official concern.

He set off down Hanover Street to his left and Andrew kept pace though scarcely knowing why. To his surprise, Dr. Blanchard asked, "What say to a hot toddy at the Two Palaverers'?"

Andrew looked his gratitude. A hot buttered rum would go far towards making him forget the void in his stomach.

Windows rattled about the two men, tradesmen with flaming noses and watery eyes stumped by muffled to the ears as they led horses whitened by frost. The creaking of sleigh runners told how cold it was.

Side by side the two hurried along, speaking of skating parties on South Mill Pond back of the fast-growing port, of deer and duck shooting, of bundling parties, quilting bees and small boat races on the Piscataqua—out to Badger's Island and back.

It was mighty fine, Andrew decided, to hear once more familiar names such as Stiles, Bell, Langden and Cutts. And how was Faith Merserve?

"Well," Blanchard said, "folks say she's setting her cap for Johnny Newmarck, the minister's son. Dorothea Holingshead's growing prettier than ever." The surgeon cast a curious glance at the gaunt Indian-like figure at his side. "I remember now, she inquired what's become of you—and more than once."

Major Sherbourne, the surgeon continued, had been killed in a battle near Germantown, a place near Philadelphia; Colonel Joe Hackett had built the new Continental cruiser *Ranger*. The Marine Committee had given her, though only God in His wisdom knew why, to a crabbed, belligerent, renegade little Scot who called himself John P. Jones. There was a mystery about the man; a heap of folks claimed Jones wasn't his right name at all.

As, briskly, Dr. Blanchard led along Ship Street, they could make out the new flag, its stripes and stars streaking out stiffly from a tall staff on the North Battery.

"A neat design," Blanchard commented, wiping streaming eyes on the heel of his mittened hand.

"The handsomest ever," Andrew agreed. "We always did despise that damned slimy rattlesnake on its sickly yellow field— Captain McNeill always claimed it put him in mind of a bilious complaint."

Shorter by half a head than his dark-faced companion, the surgeon kept on until, at the foot of Unity Street, he slowed his gait and led across the street, adroitly dodging pigs and a flock of big gray geese on the lookout for offal.

They now found themselves in an uninviting section of the waterfront. Here thin, acrid-smelling wood smoke beat down from cracked and blackened chimney pots; windows were mended with paper or stuffed with dingy rags. Gutters overflowed and frozen filth stained the ground. Again and again they encountered children who, with ferret-like faces set in dull, weary lines, trudged along under burdens too great for them.

"If you don't object, I'll stop in for a look at my drydock," Blanchard announced. "It's directly on our way and I've a moment's business there."

Andrew was puzzled. He knew Boston from end to end and though wharves and a construction yard lay near by, he knew there was no drydock in the vicinity.

"Drydock?"

"It's yonder," the doctor informed quietly and inclined his head towards a dilapidated brick structure.

He wondered whether Lieutenant Warren would balk. He was

looking annoyed. To cover his anxiety, Blanchard went on hurriedly, "It's a drydock of an unusual sort, Mr. Warren. In it, Dr. Wright and I do what we can to patch and repair the shattered hulks of sailors and mariners. Because the Congress has made no provision for sick and wounded Naval seamen, we give them preference. We've made but a pitiful start, I confess it, but still it is a beginning."

The instant he passed under a blistered and faded sign reading, 'Wm. Mahoney, Sail Loft & Chandler's Goods" and set foot in the door there beat into Andrew's nostrils a stench so revolting, repelling it was like a blow in the face.

Standing in the sudden gloom Dr. Blanchard summoned a tight smile, unhooked his triple-caped cloak, apparently unaware that, from above, was sounding an unchecked series of lowing noises. To Andrew the noise suggested the piteous bawling of milch cows long left unmilked by some shiftless farmer.

"I must go upstairs," Blanchard explained, producing a small green bottle. "Will you come up or wait here? After all, it's the other end of this business that's your affair." His words were polite yet conveyed an unmistakable challenge.

Before he knew it Andrew had said, "I'll go up." Damned if he'd let any bloody saw-bones face him down. Aboard the *Andrew Doria* during the fight with H.M.S. *Race Horse* he'd seen sights worse than anything Blanchard could produce.

The doctor offered the green bottle. It was vinegar. "Better use this." He sprinkled the fluid liberally on Andrew's handkerchief; next he fiddled momentarily with the heavy head of his walking stick.

"Your weapon." Lightly he touched Andrew's sword hilt. "—And mine." Plain as a Quaker in his black suit, he pulled a worn leather scalpel case from the pocket of his cloak. "Thus armed, let us proceed."

" 'Lead on, MacDuff,' " quoted Andrew and raised his handkerchief. "What is this? A charnel house?"

Dr. Blanchard looked more nearly fifty than thirty years of age. "You are fortunate. Today it is cold, and the—er—odors are not strong."

An unfamiliar tension keyed Andrew's nerves—it was reminiscent of his sensation when he had heard the first of H.M.S. *Glasgow's* shot go smacking through the *Andrew Doria's* main course. A series of shivers, generated in his shoulders, shot down his forearms and dispersed into his fingertips when, after they had climbed the gritty steps, he heard a voice wail,

"Kill me! Won't somebody kill me? Lend a hand, mates. Dear Christ, I can bear no more of this—"

The cry, edged with agony, was beating through a battered door opposite the landing above. On it a figure six had been daubed in crude red paint.

"*Ai-e-e*. Doctor! Doctor! I can't stand no more. Give me some laudanum—why must you torture me so? Ain't there nothing?"

"Ah, shut yer trap—why can't yer die quiet-like?" snarled a hoarse voice. "Stow it, ye screechin' catamount, er we'll give yer the same as Tom—"

"But my side hurts—I bin quiet, ain't I, ever so long? And now—oh, God in Heaven—the stump, it—it's afire."

"Shut up! I warned yer!"

A smacking sound penetrated the hall, a pitiful whimpering and broken sound.

"That'll be Thompson. Came off a beaten privateer which made port last week," Dr. Blanchard stated mechanically. "Lost his left hand and he's got a splinter through his side to boot. We can't dose him because we've no laudanum, so the poor devil gets no rest. He'll die soon. He keeps tearing his bandages away in delirium, you see."

Chills commenced to cascade over Andrew's shoulder blades, his throat felt as if it had been grabbed in a free-for-all. There was something incredible in the fact that this poor devil must die. It was sickening.

"Had we some laudanum, Thompson might rest and leave his dressings alone. He'd recover, most likely. This patient is strong, strong as any bull." Blanchard shrugged. "But—well, the fact is we've no laudanum at all, nor has any hospital around Boston I know of."

Through another door marked with a figure four moaned a voice, "Water! Water! I'm burning—burning. In God's love, dear friends, fetch me a drink of water."

A loose-jointed Negress appeared, her gray kersey dress sagging, half revealing massive, pendulous breasts. Her wool was carelessly secured by bits of vari-colored rag. In one hand she carried a sponge, a bucket of pinkish liquid in the other. When she saw Dr. Blanchard, the slattern grinned, waved a lax hand.

"Mawnin', Mista Doctah. Glad you's come, suh. Doctah Wright he bin askin' where you done got dat calomel?"

"I begged a little, Suzy. How is the putrid-fever patient?"

"Tchk! Tchk! He de contrariest man I evah see." The stupid black face swung away, nodded at the door marked with a three.

"Aftah all dat trouble you and Doctah Herbert done took—why dat pernickety cuss done die jus' now."

"So he's dead—" Blanchard shrugged, eyed a little bottle in his hand. "If only I'd found some of this earlier."

"Whut we gwine do, suh, wid dat deader?"

"Send word to the coroner's." He turned with a small apologetic smile. "Fractures and amputation cases are here. I'll look in and then we'll go and have that toddy."

"I'll need it," Andrew admitted. God above! The noises and smells in this dim and chilly structure were like a page out of some Presbyterian preacher's description of hell. He felt strangled, disoriented, enveloped by a sense of futile despair.

When Blanchard lifted the latch of a door hanging loose on leathern hinges, dust came eddying out into the corridor. Twice, thrice the surgeon waved his walking stick, briefly filling the air with a fine powder cast from holes let into the cane's head. The smell of verbena and cloves stuck Andrew's nostrils like a soothing balm—but only ineffectively. Atmosphere, fetid beyond description, came pouring out into the corridor. The stench from within grew so bad Andrew bent forward like a man walking into a gale.

By the light of a single grimy window, he could see nearly a dozen wretches, gaunt and unshaven in their rags. They lay huddled on trusses of straw, their naked feet extended towards a single charcoal brazier.

In places three shapeless figures often lay together under a single set of blankets. When a man was seized by a sudden paroxysm of coughing, his spittle fell unheeded on the faces of those in the next pallet.

Bending low over the nearest unshaven and malodorous wretch, Dr. Blanchard pointed in silence to the neck of the patient. There a line of lice had attached themselves. Andrew's stomach heaved. Angrily he demanded, "You are a doctor?"

"I am."

"Then why in God's name do you tolerate such abominations?"

"There is no provision for a Naval hospital, let alone a Medical Board. There are no funds. The people are sick of demands. The Navy—well, you know what they think of it these days."

"But is there no lye, no soap; are there no drugs in Boston?"

"As to the first two, yes," came the imperturbable reply. "But the Marine Board has appropriated no funds—"

"—But the local people? Surely—"

Blanchard shook his head. "These men all hail from other colon—er, States."

Something grasped Andrew's ankle so hard he turned sharply. A pair of hollow, preternaturally bright eyes were staring up out of the gloom like some animal's out of a den.

"Mr. Warren—please—for God's sake—"

Shakily, an indescribably unkempt figure raised bony, talon-like hands.

"What—how do you know my name?"

"Don't yer know me—"

Andrew suppressed an almost overwhelming sense of repulsion. "I recognize your voice," he lied and peered intently at the appari-tion. "But the light—I—"

"It's me, Reuben Young," croaked the voice as, gradually, the patients roused; a few heaved themselves up on their elbows. A rag stopping one of several broken window panes fluttered feebly. "Captain Number Two gun in the *Boston*."

"You, Young? Can't be—" he gasped, shocked beyond expres-sion. "God above!"

Feebly, fingers picked Andrew's white yarn stocking. "My leg's been off a week and it's beginnin' to stink fierce. Please, Lieuten-ant, we—we wuz shipmates once, wasn't we? Get me out of this!"

The shaggy head sagged from weakness. "If I was gettin' better, sir, I'd not complain. Dr. Blanchard has been wonderful good. Even heated the saw when they took my leg off, even got a nigger to bang a kettle in me ear to take my mind off the pain. Gave me the last of his spirits, he did. Ah, me, I'm lousy now and I'll catch the jail fever sure. I'd liefer die or freeze in the open."

His fingers tightened on Andrew's leg. "Please, sir, why don't they find us medicines, sir? Why don't they detail a few waisters to this here sick bay?"

Andrew sank onto his heels, placed a hand on the crippled seaman's shoulder. "You were—are—a fine gun captain, Young, and we need fine gunners. I'll see you get help. Depend on it."

When the man held up the bandaged stump of his left leg, Andrew's stomach heaved. The linen covering was splotched with dark pus, smeared with dirt from the gritty plank flooring.

"Thank 'ee, sir." Tears began tracing pale, erratic courses down the wounded man's hollow cheeks. He turned to his dully wonder-ing companions. "See? What did I tell yer? Service officers ain't like bleeding privateersmen what don't care a fig for a man once he gets stove in."

The other patients began to plead and beg for help. Nonetheless, one and all seemed numbly to realize there was little or no hope. Neither did they blame the grim-eyed surgeon who busied himself briefly and promised to return. Out once more in the fetid gloom of the hall, Andrew passed his cuff over a brown forehead speckled with perspiration.

"Good of you to cheer poor Young. Whatever you can do—"

"—What can I do, you mean," Andrew corrected bitterly. "You must have seen a while back that I haven't a penny. But, so help me, I won't let Young die for want of aid."

"Yours is a noble impulse, Mr. Warren," came Dr. Blanchard's earnest comment, "but drugs cannot be made out of wishes and moonshine."

From a door marked with the number three emerged such a poisonous reek Andrew felt ready to vomit.

"Gangrene cases in there," the doctor explained, sniffing hard at his handkerchief.

"Wallace! I say, Wallace, that you?"

"That'll be Wright, my colleague," Blanchard explained. "Very sound fellow except he believes in bleeding. I don't."

Andrew was startled. "What? Is not bleeding the cure for nearly everything?"

"It isn't!" The words fairly exploded from Blanchard's lips and his eyes glittered. "If Nature had intended bleeding as a relief, she would have made some natural provision for it."

"Damme, Wallace. Come in here, will you?" demanded a high, almost shrill voice. "This suture's about to come free."

"You'll excuse me?"

Before Andrew could answer, the door marked "three" swung back and there emerged a little sparrow of a man in a blood-stained apron. Behind heavy glasses he blinked.

"Eh? Oh, sorry, Wallace. Didn't know we'd visitors."

"Dr. Wright," Blanchard said. "Mr. Warren, a lieutenant of our Naval establishment."

"Servant, sir."

The black ribbon securing Dr. Wright's wig fluttered to his bow—a really elegant bow.

"Can't help showing he's studied in Edinburgh," Blanchard thought. "Wonder if he bled Peterson. We've got to have that out soon. If only I were as sure with the knife as Herbert Wright."

"Speaking of knives, I wonder why I get better results when I heat knives and saws? Um. Maybe warmth injures the nerves, the severed blood vessels less? The hotter the water the better the result. Queer, queer."

He glanced at the Naval officer. "I'm fetching young Warren a bit," he decided. "Luck, pure luck about Reuben Young. Like to have him go. We've got to get those drugs out of Jamaica—if it isn't Warren someone else must go. *I will have those drugs.*"

"Did you find the calomel?" Dr. Wright's voice broke in upon Blanchard's thoughts.

"Yes. But Suzy says the patient's dead."

Dr. Wright's small figure sagged briefly, straightened. "Give it to me, Wallace—there are a dozen others need it. Find any Sal Polychristus?"

Blanchard summoned a wry smile. "Old Dr. Meade's got some, but the beggar won't release it from his Army stock."

"What about Abrahams?" Wright demanded, mechanically retying his apron.

"Wants ten dollars the ounce. Might as well ask a hundred."

Andrew knew how Blanchard felt, recognized that blank look of bafflement.

The two surgeons went down the hall, talked together in undertones as if the smells and sounds all about did not exist.

"I'll try old Mrs. Stoughton again," he heard Wright say. "Took the last sixpence to buy charcoal last night—"

"Water! Water!" wailed a voice. "I'm fair perishing of thirst."

Gasping for breath, old Suzy came up the worn unpainted stair. "Hush yo' fuzzin'. I ain't no centipede." Snuffling, she passed Andrew, a wooden bucket and dipper in her gray-black hands.

A male attendant, dirty and toothless, appeared carrying a pitchfork of straw and slunk by leaving a miasma of gin in the poisoned air.

"Kill me, won't somebody kill me?" the delirious man began to shriek with a rising inflection.

Blanchard came up. "Suppose we go for that drink now?"

"Yes," Andrew choked. "Let's get out of this."

The roar of broadsides, the eerie screams of flying shells and splinters, the shrill cries of men freshly wounded—such trials, though often soul-searing, were endurable. But this—!

Once outdoors Andrew drew a series of whistling breaths of clean cold air.

"The Two Palaverers is near. Will that do?"

Andrew looked at the surgeon steadily an instant. "Any place will do, Doctor, where we can toast my coming cruise to Jamaica."

VI

SAILING ORDERS

REACHING into his desk, Hosea Warren produced a thin portfolio of documents.

"I am pleased, vastly pleased over this reconsideration, Andrew," he murmured. "The more since I had scarce expected it from one of your er—unruly—disposition." The merchant's pink lips tightened in a faint smile. "You will do well to listen carefully to what I am about to impart. Your first mistake may be your last."

It was like listening to Captain Biddle describe the plan of action off Fort Nassau in the Bahamas. Andrew prepared to engrave every word into his memory. He was thinking more clearly now, thanks to Dr. Blanchard's buttered rum and hot soup at the tavern.

He'd be a long time forgetting the relief which shone in Wallace Blanchard's eyes when he became convinced that the *Evergreen* would indeed sail.

Come to think of it, those two doctors were doing a large task. They'd given up comfortable, fashionable practices, had literally beggared themselves in the interests of their pathetic little "drydock." No glory, no uniforms and very few thanks were theirs for long hours of disgusting, perilous toil. Faugh! Even to set foot into that noisome structure on Hanover Street was an ordeal.

"When you reach New York," Uncle Hosea was saying, "you will make discreet inquiry for Henry Oakman—go to his home, not his place of business. He lives near Queen Street."

"Very well. And when do I sail?"

"Tomorrow at six aboard the *Swan,* a small coasting pink. She'll not excite a British patrol boat, I warrant. She lies to Scarlett's wharf." Frowning, the merchant rearranged a sheaf of papers before him. "Always remember this, Andrew; a closed mouth catches no flies. The less others know of your plans the better. A great many 'Ichabods' lurk around our waterfront these days."

This was but too true, Andrew knew well. Almost every morning that ill-favored name appeared scrawled on some wall or fence. It gave one some notion of how many loyalists, spies and Royal agents still remained in Boston.

The way the old merchant's eyes snapped when he began to finger the cargo manifests and various bills of lading betrayed how much such matters meant to him.

Precisely he separated the documents, handed his dark-featured nephew a scroll of parchment. It was very tastefully ornamented. Lips pursed, Andrew read, then cast his uncle a quizzical glance. "May I compliment you on a tidy bit of forgery? Whoever would suspect Messrs. Warren, Whittier & Company of such artfulness?"

Uncle Hosea cleared his throat, looked severe. "In times of war—ahem—one must become er—adaptable." Smoothly, he continued, "And these are the papers of a Tory sea captain captured off Portsmouth last week by the *Amphitrite*, privateer. They have been altered to your name."

The shrill laughter of children sliding down an icy walk beat in the window. Downstairs, old Edson kept on coughing. With a quick movement the merchant passed over a portfolio.

"Here are your second set of papers for the *Evergreen*— American ones. They are complete: letter of marque, commission, good-conduct bond, insurance coverage—everything." He sighed, rubbed his chin. "They are exact copies of those papers under which the *Evergreen* brig last sailed."

Relieved to find himself on familiar ground, Andrew leafed through the printed forms. Critically, expertly, he studied them for such a minor error as might precipitate a major calamity. Under the heading "IN CONGRESS," he read:

The Delegates of the United Colonies of New Hampshire, Massachusetts Bay, Rhode Island, Connecticut, New York, New Jersey, Pennsylvania, the Counties of New Castle, Kent and Sussex in Delaware, Maryland, Virginia, North Carolina, South Carolina, and Georgia. TO ALL unto whom these Presents shall come, send Greeting, KNOW YE

That we have granted, and by these Presents do grant, Licence and Authority to Andrew Warren, Mariner, Commander of the brig called EVERGREEN of the burthen of One Hundred tons, or thereabouts, belonging to Hosea Warren of Boston in the colony of Massachusetts Bay, mounting six four-pound Guns and navigated by 21 Men to fit out and set forth the said brig in a warlike Manner, and by and with the said brig and the Crew thereof, by Force of Arms, to attack, seize and take the Ships and other Vessels belonging to the inhabitants of Great Britain, or any of them, with their Tackle, Apparel, Furniture and Ladings, on the High Seas, or between high-water and low-water Marks, and to bring the Same to some Convenient Ports in the said Colonies, in order that the Courts, which are or shall be there appointed to hear and determine Causes civil and maritime, may proceed in due Form to condemn the said Captures, if they be adjudged lawful Prize; the said Hosea Warren having given Bond with sufficient Sureties, that Nothing be done by the said brig or any of the Officers, Mariners or Company thereof contrary to, or inconsistent with, the Usages and Customs of Nations and the Instructions, a Copy of which is herewith delivered to him. And we will require all our Officers whatsoever to give Succour and Assistance to the said Hosea Warren in the Premises. This Commission shall continue in Force until the Congress shall issue Orders to the Contrary.

By Order of the Congress
(*signed*) JOHN HANCOCK, PRESIDENT

    Boston
Dated at ....
    March 2, 1778

(This is copy of a Privateer's Commission taken from page 58 of the COMMONWEALTH HISTORY OF MASSACUSETS (Hart) Vol. III. (IQG—1929).
I have filled in such names as "Evergreen" "Oakman" for owner, Warren for Master, etc. This particular Privateer's Commission designates a schooner, rather than a brig and was dated, if memory serves correctly, some time in 1779 or thereabouts.)

Everything was in perfect order. Hosea Warren had always been careful. The older man's chair creaked as he settled back in it and shoved a pair of square-lensed iron-rimmed spectacles up onto his forehead.

"You will have to secure through Mr. Oakman your New York clearances, and your sailing permit from the British port commandant. The enemy alter their plagued regulations so often nothing can be accomplished from this distance."

Hosea Warren commenced to drum on the arm of his chair, then leaned forward and spoke with incisive earnestness.

"From the moment you quit Boston, my boy, you must think, look, *and act* like a Tory. You were born a King's man, always have been one, always will be. You hate the damned penny-pinching rebels. Rehearse the tale you'll tell in New York, time over time—test it for flaws. We Warrens don't make extry good liars. You are aware, of course, you'll be hanged as a spy should you be discovered?"

"That is obvious," Andrew observed quietly.

The older man pulled off his spectacles, leaned forward. "You will sign on a *completely* British or Tory crew. Personally, I'd chose Britishers—they ain't overbright and wouldn't be so apt as Tories to notice a slip on your part."

Andrew nodded, fixed full attention on the strongly lined features opposite him.

"Reposing especial confidence in Dr. Blanchard and his associate, Dr. Wright, and the work they are undertaking, certain gentlemen of this town and—ahem—myself," Hosea Warren continued, "have, at considerable pains, collected a sum—"

"To buy what is needed?" Andrew said. "Capital! How soon—"

"One moment—" The merchant's heavy shoulders sagged an instant. "True, we have a modest sum, but I doubt whether you have any conception of conditions, medically speaking, in these colonies today."

Toasting his shins before the grate, Andrew confessed he had not thought much on the subject.

"Dr. Shippen told me, not a fortnight ago, that the entire medical establishment of the Armed Forces stands in dire need not only of drugs and medicines but also of instruments: scalpels, needles, cuppers, knives, lancets, saws—everything. In your own Service you know how ship after ship puts to sea with her surgeon or surgeon's mate wanting the most elementary supplies."

"Yes, I know that. Blanchard declares some day the Navy will have to set up its own hospitals, its own surgeries and dispensaries."

"Once clear of New York," the merchant resumed, "you will shape your course for Montego Bay. You are familiar with that port?"

"Yes. It lies on the northwestern coast of Jamaica."

"Good. Once arrived, you will inquire for a Mr. Allerdice of Winde, Allerdice and Company. Before this trouble they were my factors there. He will be glad of this cargo," Hosea glanced at the sheaf of bills of lading, "and, I fancy, gladder still to ship some Manchester goods. He's bound to have a surfeit."

"With Mr. Allerdice, am I to appear as a Tory?" Andrew inquired quietly.

The merchant rubbed his chin deliberately, momentarily. "Well now, as to that you'll have to judge how the wind blows. Most Jamaica merchants hate and despise the King and his Ministers as much as we."

"What of the medicines?"

"I am coming to that." Uncle Hosea went to the door and stood listening awhile. "Pays to be careful," he muttered. "Now listen well."

"Yes, sir."

"In the hills near Montego Bay dwells a Portuguese Jew—name of Cardozo, Carlos Cardozo. Dr. Blanchard and his colleague have learned—God knows how—that this Israelite has, of late, received from Spain a rare supply of medicines and surgical supplies. We must secure these. That is all I know. This information may be wholly, or partially, false. I trust it is not. But of this I *am* sure." Hosea Warren wagged a warning finger. "Proceed with care. I know this Cardozo of old. He is, to put it bluntly, slippery as an eel dipped in butter and will betray you to the English in a twinkle should it suit his purse or purpose."

"I understand," Andrew said slowly.

"Here—" the older man fumbled in the bosom of his blue broadcloth coat—"is a draft on certain merchants in New York. Mr. Isaac Roosevelt should be able to negotiate it for you. With five hundred pounds you should buy a really fine stock of drugs and such. In this envelope are directions from Dr. Blanchard on how much to pay and what to purchase."

The merchant shook his head and the side curls of his wig fluttered. "I mistrust Cardozo—indeed, I wish there were some other person to deal with. As for my own traffic, Mr. Allerdice will handle that—"

It was like his uncle, like most New Englanders for that matter, to realize some profit out of a patriotic move. Probably the old man would make a small fortune out of this venture to Jamaica. Lord knew there was a terrific demand for Manchester and Birmingham goods the whole length of the Atlantic Coast.

Slowly the merchant rubbed hands splotched with big brown freckles one against the other. "Your real trouble, I fear, will be encountered on the voyage home, Andrew. But—" he shrugged— "that is your concern."

Andrew smiled. "That, sir, is indeed in my soundings and you'll have no cause to be uneasy. I will bring home the *Evergreen*."

It was fine to have made the decision. No more lying about in wretched, time-wasting idleness, no more dogging the post rider's steps, no more bitter conjectures on the meanness of human nature. Action—sails and sea again.

Jerusha! It would mean much once more to behold the pale green and aquamarine water of the Caribbean, to sniff again the rotten-rich but subtly seductive odors so characteristic of the Antilles. He laughed happily within him. After this grim, cold winter how he'd welcome the carefree—if senseless—merriment of the blacks.

A tide of memories set in, flooded his being. Ever so clearly he recalled that cruise to Antigua and St. Kitts in '72. He wouldn't soon forget the bold tendernesses of Anita. Um. Wasn't much about love a Creolian did not know or want to learn about. Then again on the second raid on New Providence in '77, the foray under ungainly John Rathburne—he who had fished out of New Bedford until the war began.

That was when he'd met Winifred on a balcony all flaming with flamboyants and silver moonlight. There were yet scars on his palms traced by broken bottles set into the summit of a certain garden wall down in drowsy, languorous Guadaloupe. And now he'd be sailing for those latitudes again. A consuming impatience seized him.

"What the old Harry is that moon calf grin of yours about?"

"—A twinge from an old wound."

"One hears you have uncommon hardihood in battle," Hosea Warren remarked with elaborate casualness. "I envy you this courage."

Followed by the yellow and white cat which labored under the mistaken impression it was about to be fed, the older man stumped across his office. He paused before an iron-clamped chest, secured with a heavy padlock and chain to an eye let into the wall. Employing a small brass key and breathing a trifle louder, Hosea raised the lid. When he straightened he'd a small canvas sack in one hand and his expression was bleak as a winter hillside. It was clear he loathed this parting with metal money.

"Here," he stated, "is your ship's money. It should buy her stores and pay port dues. In this," he held up an envelope, "are funds to clear your expenses here in Boston. It is not much, Andrew. With the *Oak*, the *Pine,* the *Elm* all fallen into enemy hands and the *Sycamore* sunk, I am become a poor man."

Hosea shrugged, showed his real age for the first time by fidgeting with his spectacles. "I might add, Nephew, that the profits of this cruise—er—well—are urgently needed by this firm—"

The admission was a sobering one. Abruptly banished were those delicious, subconscious anticipations of a moment before.

"During this cruise," Andrew promised quietly, "I shall not expose your brig to the least unnecessary hazard. You may rely upon it."

The old merchant placed a hand on Andrew's shoulder—the one lacking an epaulet. "I am vastly relieved to hear you vouchsafe so. To date, your career reads of impetuosity, impulsiveness and hardihood, rather than of prudence and deliberation. Always tackle a problem from the right end—like in making friends with a skunk. God speed you, Andrew—" Then in a bit of dry humor typical of the man, he added, "You will do well to steer clear of your dear Uncle Isaac and his British men-of-war."

Fingers a-quiver with eagerness, Andrew broke a pale blue wafer on the envelope containing his expense money. He frowned. Uncle Hosea indeed had been anything but lavish; there was enclosed a sum just adequate to settle his debts and to get him to New York.

On the edge of the clam-shell sidewalk he lingered, debating his next step. To be doing something again, to be clear of the doldrums of inactivity seemed strange—and delightful. For one thing, he'd have to find civilian, Tory-looking clothes. Most likely Bob Kinnicut, ex-lieutenant in the Continental cruiser *Cabot*, would have some garments left over from civilian life. Bob and he were about of a size, and Bob would not drive too hard a bargain.

Lieutenant Kinnicut was not at home; his landlady stated darkly that she was wanting to come up with him. Yes, she would tell him to repair to the Noah's Ark and sniffed as if she were promising to direct someone to the decadent court of Belshazzar. Nor had he any better luck with his other boon companion. Lieutenant Jewett had gone over to Dorchester, his sister said with a slow smile, to talk with the owner of a privateer.

Time being short, Andrew perforce spent the balance of the day getting together his kit. His chronometer and sextant he rescued from a pawn shop and then set about filling a small, brass-bound sea chest. He packed serviceable kersey breeches, woolen and cotton jerseys, even some white duck trousers and bandannas against tropical heat. A few shirts and a decent blue serge mariner's coat completed his meager wardrobe.

The instant Andrew entered the Noah's Ark taproom, Mr. Willard heaved himself to his feet and came waddling across the freshly sanded floor. He puffed out his cheeks, expanded like an angry frog, and assumed a severe expression.

"Mr. Warren," he boomed, "already I have extended you credit beyond—"

"Tut! And again tut, my dear sir." Andrew produced his small supply of pound notes and by doubling them back contrived to make them into an imposing sheaf. These he flourished gently under the publican's purple-red nose. Mr. Willard blinked, deflated himself and showed a pair of resplendent gold front teeth.

"Well, now, may God bless my soul!"

"He won't," Andrew said lightly. "Not even the Almighty can bless that which does not exist."

"Ha! Ha! You've a nimble wit, sir, but frankly I am at a loss to understand this happy change in your affairs." He winked, looked slyly about, then suggested, "A fortunate turn of the cards, eh?"

The words escaped before Andrew realized it. "No, Willard, 'tis better than that. At last I've me a ship."

Two patrons seated in a far corner had looked up and were considering him curiously. He could have bitten off his tongue.

"You'll be sailing in the *Rainbow* Privateer I take it?"

"It's possible," he mumbled, belatedly cautious, then passed over twenty silver shillings. "This is for the moment. I want a fire in my room and hot water—a great store of it."

Willard clapped pudgy hands. "Lucy! Oliver! Freshen up Mr. Warren's quarters." He bent unctuously, massaging perpetually moist palms against each other. He seemed, though, to be thinking about something other than the matter at hand; his little fat-lidded eyes had narrowed unconsciously.

"Polly, fetch up a bottle of Madeira." The innkeeper winked. "We'll have a drink or two—compliments of the Ark."

A voice, deep and unusually soft, spoke from the bar across the room. "Your pardon, sir, but I'd be delighted to stand the first round. 'Tain't often I'm privileged to treat a Naval officer."

Andrew was suspicious of irony, but he detected none. From his accent this big, solidly-built stranger must be a Southerner, a Virginian if Andrew judged aright.

Mr. Willard's round florid features beamed like an August moon. "Why, of course, Cap'n, of course. Just as you say. Lieutenant Warren, this is Cap'n Ashton, master o' the *Grand Turk II*, the privateer which made port this morning with them two fine prizes."

"An honor, sir," Captain Ashton declared bowing with a grace one seldom found in New England. "I was hoping that possibly you might consider a—"

"—Lieutenant Warren has just had the good fortune to be

assigned a ship," Mr. Willard cut in. "By the bye, I didn't catch her name?"

Andrew ignored the hint. What damned Nosey-Parkers inn-keepers were; worse even than barbers.

He ran an eye over this big, gray-eyed Virginian; curious, that indefinable expression which continual looking out over wide spaces imparted to a man. The privateersman wasn't old, not much over thirty. Must have been through some bad times, though, if those practical, almost severe, lines about his mouth meant any-thing.

Captain Ashton looked prosperous from spotless stock of hand-some French lace to dark green coat cut on semi-uniform style, tan waistcoat and brown knee breeches and silver buckled pumps. He carried a slim dress sword—a French one rather like Andrew's—its guard was fashioned like a lively leaping dolphin. On a clear space the name "Rob't Ashton" was engraved in a very elegant script.

"One sees you've had luck this cruise. My congratulations, Captain," Andrew commented as the privateersman indicated a table and Mr. Willard waddled off to draw the cork of a Madeira bottle.

A quick smile relaxed the Virginian's expression. "Reckon so. Just about time, though. We'd been cruisin' about nine weeks and the only sail we raised was that of a damned fast man-o'-war, the *Albany* sloop. Watch out for her if you ever raise her tops'ls."

There was a quality uncommonly grave and courteous bearing to this ship captain, Andrew felt, something at sharp variance with the general run of privateersmen one met around Boston. As a rule they were braggart, swaggering, insensitive; over-eager to squander the profits of a successful cruise in brutish pleasures.

The Virginian smiled, smoothed wavy brown hair clubbed with a swallow-tailed grosgrain ribbon, suggested, "Shall we sit in this corner?"

Polly, hustling in beaming, gave the stranger an arch glance as she set down the glasses and flapped away crumbs remaining from some previous repast. Captain Ashton only smiled absently.

They raised glasses, solemnly toasted the Congress.

The Virginian was big, Andrew noted, wide at the shoulder and heavy in the bone; suggested a merchant rather than a fighting man. Probably he'd never arrived at a hasty judgment in all his life. For his part, Captain Rob Ashton was deciding that here, at last, was something raw—a Naval officer who talked and bore himself like one. Something like the British he'd seen in Norfolk—yet set in less of a pattern.

Lieutenant Warren didn't in the least resemble those rum-fuddled, loud-mouthed ignoramuses who had first appeared in the blue and scarlet of the Continental Navy and had blundered so disastrously. The sooner the Service got rid of poltroons like Hoysted Hacker, Thomas Thompson and James Nicholson; of wind-bags like Dudley Saltonstall and James Robinson and of political bootlickers like Elisha Herriman and Thomas Simpson, the better it would be for America. Yes, Lieutenant Warren well might know his duties; the Yankee looked as if he had been through a hard schooling.

Said Ashton, "May I offer congratulations? Our host observed that you are newly appointed to a vessel?"

"That is true," Andrew evaded. His embarrassment was intense. For the life of him he *could not* confess that he was only to skipper a goddamned merchantman—no matter how worthy the reason. "You are a Southerner?" he hazarded.

"What makes you think so?"

"You talk so—so—well, so damned polite."

Ashton's eyes crinkled at their corners. "Thank you. I am, that is, I was." A weary twist dominated his broad, wind-darkened features. "I hail from Norfolk. But the bloody Redcoats drove us out; my wife and I then settled in Philadelphia." The *Grand Turk's* Captain's strong shoulders rose a trifle beneath sturdy green broad-cloth. "Alas, we Ashtons appear doomed to be uprooted."

Andrew swallowed another sip of his toddy. He hadn't realized a Southerner could be so companionable—even if he did drawl in his speech. "I am glad you escaped before the British seized the capital."

It made him boiling mad to think of Lord Howe occupying the nation's capital, parading his lovely young mistress, Mrs. Loring, and giving theater parties. His younger officers were reported to be achieving a great success with the belles of the town.

There had been no theater parties, no pretty mistresses at a place called Valley Forge, somewhere in Pennsylvania. Folks rumored that the remnant of General Washington's Continental troops there were suffering the most appalling privations.

Ashton's wide mouth quirked up at its corners. "Yes, sir, we sailed out just in time. One advantage to being a seafaring man, you know. My wife and daughters just came aboard the *Grand Turk* and we sailed down the Delaware through a fog thicker than a Yankee—er—Hessian's head."

Captain Ashton's eye wandered out of the taproom's heavily leaded windows and across the frozen ruts of Water Street. Out yonder, very trim and dangerous of appearance, his brig was swinging to her anchors. Did him good to see those captured Red Ensigns flying from her signal jack.

"Now I'd hazard she's French built," Andrew said admiringly.

The Virginian laughed and unhooked his sword to place it on the greasy-looking bench beside him.

"It's no wonder you think so; but my *Grand Turk*—second of her name, by the way—is Bermuda built on French lines," the Virginian explained. "As I was saying, Mrs. Ashton and I made it into Wilmington two gunshots ahead of a damned handy British sloop-o'-war." The lightness departed from his manner. "Tried to make my crew stand and fight—but they wouldn't. None of them will, sir. I can tell you, 'tis a rare privateer's hand will willingly stand up to a bulldog."

Andrew raised his glass, studied its depths, said carefully, "No offense, Captain, but since you feel that way, why not serve the Navy? Weak as we are, our men-o'-war have tied some true-lover's knots in the Lion's tail—would tie more if private-armed—" He broke off, his Indian-like features tinted with embarrassment.

Andrew hadn't meant to be rude, really, but it gravelled him, and all the younger Naval officers, to meet secure, well-fed letter-of-marque and private captains like this. They'd never had to study, to bow to the whims—just and mostly unjust—of a Marine Committee.

The privateer captain held up a broad, brown hand. "I know what you mean, sir. I have heard it before, but—well, in my case I am not really a fighting man. We Ashtons, here and in Bermuda, have always been merchants and tradespeople. I, also, want to be one. To win fortune, security for my family—for a son, some time. The British won't let me trade so—well, I traffic as best I may; sometimes in the vessels of the enemy."

Andrew found an elusive twinkle in the depths of this Virginian's eyes.

"But isn't privateering—in a way—selfish? You'll pardon the question?"

For a little the privateersman stared ahead, powerful fingers drawing short parallels on the table. Presently Captain Ashton flicked a crumb away, said gravely, "I have no doubt, sir, that it must seem so to a Naval officer." The ruddy, wind-seared oval of his face grew older all in an instant, and he loosened the sparkling lace of his stock. "Yet I ponder whether privateers are not the answer to this war? Each month private-armed vessels sink, burn and capture more and more British commerce. Their commerce is being swept from the seas. We learn that insurance rates at Lloyd's have soared higher than a kite. Sugar, rum, West India goods are at a rising premium. Louder and louder planters and merchants cry out to Parliament for an end to this war.''

Thoughtfully Rob Ashton studied the New Englander's dark and intense features—odd that they should so remind him of David. David—he who had fought at Breed's Hill, who died in this very town of Boston, who lay buried God knew where—within a few hundred yards, perhaps.

That had seemed a long time, a whole lifetime away. Johnny Gilmorin, too, had perished over in Charlestown. Captain Ashton didn't like to think of Virginians lying in this frozen foreign ground—they wouldn't rest easy. What had become of David's wife—no, she hadn't had time to marry him. Farish, dour old Farish, who'd captained a vessel of his, once had spoken of a child. Well, that was what war did. He might have walked past his own nephew—or niece—today and hadn't known it. That was bad. Such things affronted his naturally orderly soul.

He returned to the present, went on seriously, "After all, Lieutenant, the British are not a war-like nation at bottom. It appears to me they rarely fight for the sake of fighting—like the Irish and the Germans—but only to enhance, to promote their trade. 'Twas an excess greed in that direction brought on this damned, useless war.''

Here was an angle Andrew had not heretofore considered. He listened with a rare degree of patience.

"Pray continue, Captain.''

"Saving your presence, sir, I think we are fools to attempt to stand up to the British with such a Navy as we poor, bankrupt people can put to sea.'' The Virginian leaned forward, spoke so honestly one couldn't take offense. "We simply have not the guns; we have not sufficient wealth and, worst of all, we lack the trained Naval officers.''

The epaulet on Andrew's shoulder shimmered when eagerly he leaned forward. "But, Captain, I know we possess capable officers and crews. We'll have more if only the nation will have confidence and patience. We can never have a Navy unless we put a fleet into being. Fighting men are not to be fashioned out of textbooks and old men's tales. Fight we must.'' His voice rang out so loud Polly turned and stared.

The Virginian offered a very elegant brass snuff box. When Andrew declined, he took a pinch of the dark brown powder and absently flicked a few stray grains staining the dark yellow revers of his semi-uniform.

Captain Ashton frowned, spoke deliberately. "I would I could believe you right. Alas that I have been wrong so many times."

There was nothing bumptious about his manner so Andrew lingered, twirling his toddy between reflective fingers.

"You are familiar with Jamaica?"

The Virginian chuckled softly. 'Reckon I might claim so. Made three prizes in the Windward Channel last autumn.''

"But isn't that considered a most perilous cruising ground?" Andrew queried.

The privateer captain sighed, thrust neatly-shod feet far out and in so doing sketched twin grooves in the sawdust.

"Another time I expect I'd prefer the Caicos Channel—runs almost parallel, you know. Not that there are not dangers there. Caicos Passage is most imperfectly charted and—well, of late the picaroons have grown confounded bold."

For the best part of an hour Andrew drew out a number of pertinent facts; the approximate schedules and cruising grounds of various duty frigates working out of the great naval base at Kingston on Jamaica, the approximate dates of departure of convoys for England.

" 'Twas us privateers drove the Bloodybacks to convoying," Ashton observed, comfortably easing the buttons of his buff satin waistcoat. He beckoned Polly, ordered a pair of toddies.

"Two more, you mean," the girl corrected. She wasn't pleased at being so completely ignored.

The Virginian shook his brown head and, smiling, said, "The word 'more' don't occur in a drinkin' gentleman's vocabulary—not in the Southern col—er—states, at least. Therefore we will have a pair of toddies. As I was saying, Mr. Warren, many's the man-o'-war detached to convoy duty which would at this very instant be harrying our shores."

His companion had there a real point in favor of privateering, Andrew saw. Still he could not help adding, "Quite true, Captain, that is so. However, had our Navy a squadron of light cruisers at sea, it could seize the whole convoy and destroy the protectors. Then, indeed, the Lloyd's underwriters in London would go into mourning."

Captain Ashton nodded, rubbed his gale-reddened chin and considered his companion with a mounting respect. There was a good deal in what this officer was saying—even if he was a Yankee.

"You said you are married?" Andrew, warmed by the first toddy

and cheered by the prospect of a second, attempted to lighten the
tenor of the conversation.

"Aye—and to an English girl." Ashton chuckled. "Nay, there's
no call to raise an eyebrow. My Andrea has become as red-hot a
patriot as you'll encounter from the Penobscot to St. Augustine. She
has small use for Jemmy Twitcher, George Germain and parasites
of their ilk. Were I killed tomorrow I know that the Geminae—my
twin daughters—" he amplified; his reserve was thawing rapidly,
"will be brought up as uncompromising—and I trust charming—
rebels. Indeed, sir, it is a vast comfort to think of a loyal wife in the
home port."

Captain Rob Ashton raised a glass. "Your health, sir, and speedy
victory in your new vessel. May she bring undyin' glory to the
Continental Navy."

There was a quaint courtliness to the way the Virginian raised his
glass, to the little bow he made.

In his turn Andrew made the other stare by rising, making a
"leg" any courtier at Versailles could have envied. In excellent
French he murmured, "*Mille remerciements, mon ami,* and to your
charming wife."

"Well, suh, I'm sho'ly damned," was all Ashton could find to
say. For a fact, Yankees were sometimes the damnedest surprising
people.

I

THE NEUTRAL GROUND

THE Continental officer, a lieutenant by his single epaulet, made no effort to dismount but bowed mighty stiff in his saddle. It was inescapable that he wasn't relishing this business of protecting Tories one little bit. His sentiments were written plain all over his thin, scholarly features.

"Detail, ha-a-alt!" he yelled, whereat Mistress Minga Allen's driver checked his team—big placid geldings, bays with black manes.

During the afternoon dust had settled along their backs, had become speckled when a shower passed. It created a dappled effect. Briskly, the lieutenant's men, a half dozen variously uniformed troopers, reined in also. They must be veterans from the way they kept turning their leathery faces now left, now right. Mostly their attention centered on a clump of silver birches just ahead. It looked, the lieutenant was thinking, just the place to harbor a party of Redcoat or Cowboys, their savage allies.

Mistress Minga Allen straightened as a lady should, forced a meaningless smile and said, "Lieutenant, I think my man and I shall manage very well to the British lines. You have been very kind."

The lieutenant frowned and rubbed his chin.

"We are in British Territory, are we not?"

"We-ell, not as *we* admit," he explained, red-rimmed gray eyes always on the move. "This is part of No-man's-land—er, the Neutral Ground."

"Then let me go on—"

"I wish, Ma'am, it were possible for us to escort you straight into the Lobsterback lines, but my orders—"

"Lobsterback!" Indignantly, Minga Allen turned away her head. "Do your orders include license to insult a loyal subject of His Majesty?"

At that the cavalry officer flushed. He started to say something but put it off and, instead, pushed onto the back of his head a dragoon's black leather helmet. It sported a forlorn little crest of

56

faded blue horsehair. Though he must have inherited his uniform
coat from a much larger man, his weather-stained breeches fitted
very well indeed.

"Can't say as I blame you much, Ma'am. Form up, you men,"
he added over a threadbare, gray-blue shoulder. "Aye, most decent
Americans are grieved to learn of the ill treatment certain Tor—er,
Loyalists have experienced."

"Ill treatment!" Minga's dark brown eyes narrowed, but at the
same time she recalled she wasn't yet quite clear of Rebel-held
territory. Ill treatment! A weak term for arson, murder and theft.
For the hundredth time she glanced over her shoulder, conducted a
hasty inventory. Praise the Lord, all her boxes and barrels still rode
the wagon body—dust-sprinkled and rather spotted, but securely
lashed down with cords.

The American lieutenant's rather severe countenance tightened,
and his mouth thinned into a straight brown streak. "You'll find not
even a pickle jar missing. I trust you will have as good fortune with
certain of His Majesty's loyal followers."

Under her uncommonly white skin Minga felt hot. The insolence
of this country Jack masquerading as an officer and a gentleman!
"You trust—and why?"

"Because, Ma'am, you appear to hate us poor Patriots so much,
would it not prove a grievous disappointment if the Redcoats proved
not all paragons of valor and virtue?"

The American lieutenant turned his mount with care. Minga
Allen noted that he did not use the clumsy brass spur strapped to his
boot heel at all. Curious, most young officers were prone to punish
their mounts just to make them appear spirited, to make them curvet
in the eyes of a girl.

"By the right and left, to the rear, whe-e-el," the lieutenant
commanded in a powerful but somewhat nasal voice.

"Farewell." Straightening his long frame in his saddle, the
American shortened the reins of a gaunt, ungainly charger. In a
gesture at once clumsy and stately, he raised fingertips to the visor
of his weather-beaten leather helmet.

For the first time Minga noticed the tarnished and verdigris-
flecked brass emblem upon it. "Liberty or Death!" was the motto.
About the "Liberty" part Minga wasn't sure; but concerning the
"Death" part she knew too much, by half. The cavalryman looked
very tired and shabby as he said, "I have the honor to bid you
Godspeed, Ma'am."

"Thank you for an unexpected courtesy." Minga nodded stiffly.
"You may drive on, Tobias," she added to the frightened, fat old

man on the seat beside her. "His Majesty's troops will meet us soon."

"Yes'm. G'up!" Tobias clucked, extracting small puffs of dust from the broad backs of his team by smacking them with the reins. The axles creaked as again the strong farm wagon commenced to bump and lurch southward along this road running parallel to the distant Hudson.

Rapidly the *clip-clop* of the American escorts' hoofs dwindled, faded and became lost. The riders in their faded semi-uniforms blended into the bare beech and oak woods and were lost to sight.

With chilled, suddenly unsteady, fingers Minga Allen tightened the hood of her gray and scarlet riding cape, the one Papa had given her for Christmas a whole life-time ago—actually it had been the Christmas of 1774—only three years ago. She stole another glance to the rear. Away back there lay home. A series of small chills darted up under her ribs. Never again in this life would she see Millwood's lovely white façade all dappled by sunlight slipping through the green and black majesty of those huge oaks which stood sentry guard over it.

Yonder, miles away in drowsy, comfortable Brewster remained most of her friends—yes, precious few had understood the iniquity of defying one's rightful sovereign. In silence they had watched her drive away from the little town, those young men and women she had known since Minga Allen had first been able to follow her round little stomach down the long bricked walks towards Main Street. It was there dusty coaches for Boston and Hartford used to go rolling by. She still could hear the well-soaped harnesses creak and steel wheel tires grate over the cobbles before the Hen & Chickens, or against stone outcrops in the road. It was strangely depressing to think that all Brewster had meant was done with forever.

"You'd better whip up," she told Tobias. "I won't feel safe till we're behind the King's lines."

"Aye, Mum, as you say, Mum. G'up!" the old gaffer grunted. In a purely mechanical effort to smile he bared a pair of lonesome yellow teeth, standing like the last survivors on a stricken battlefield. "The team is tired, Mum. If yer figgerin' on beddin' in White Plains tonight it's best not to press the critters. G'up!" He clucked deep in his throat. "What ye can have in them trunks and boxes stumps me. They're heavier nor sash weights."

"Books, just books," Minga replied briefly and, she hoped, casually.

Those three trunks, four chests and five barrels contained the last pitiful remnants of Judge Edmund Allen's fortune. Among them in the No. 1 trunk, was some fine old Sheffield. Candelabra, ladles, saucers and the silver service were in that chest with the black horsehide cover. The other boxes and trunks held salvers and goblets, some fine linens, ivories from far China and glassware from the Italian Kingdom of Naples.

Scattered through the luggage were laces and brocades and carvings and certain immoral-appearing works of art which Papa had brought from Europe, relics of Edmund Allen's early days in His Majesty's diplomatic service.

His Honor Edmund Allen was dead. Resolutely, she diverted her thoughts from Papa and his dreadful death. She kept telling herself it was good indeed to leave forever this brutal land. Never, never would she wish to see America again; the sound of a pane of glass breaking, the sudden glare of a torch still made her want to scream.

The sun was swinging lower. After all, it was only April and early April at that, and it must be all of four of the afternoon. Minga Allen sat straighter on the plain board seat and kicked chilled feet against the dashboard. Tobias, floppy gray hat canted over his rheumy gray eyes, had settled into a great brown muffler and was staring straight ahead when he wasn't snuffling in his nose.

The horses had settled themselves into their collars, were pulling steadily up a low rise in the highroad. She looked about. Bereft of foliage and streaked here and there with snow, the country looked indescribably bare and forlorn.

Far off to the left stood the charred remains of what must once have been a sizeable house and an even larger barn. An orchard standing behind the ruins had been hewed down. In the mud beside the road the bones of several animals—Tobias allowed they were cows—lay scattered and half buried.

The world seemed infinitely empty except that, in the distance, a crow had begun cawing excitedly. Others swelled the chorus. First one, then the other of the team cocked furry ears in the direction of the woods from whence came the cawing.

Old Tobias looked up. "What in tarnation's disturbin' them corbies?" he snuffled at the world at large. "Hadn't oughter raise such a racket over a fox or a dog."

Minga drew her riding cloak closer. She was getting mighty hungry and what with the sun's starting down, it was growing cool, almost cold. Surely they must encounter the British outposts soon. There couldn't be such a great distance between the lines. She'd be immeasurably relieved to see a scarlet uniform once more; scarlet and gold meant a return to life under law and order.

During '77, while the Saratoga campaign was being fought, loyal people had had a pretty bad time in Putnam County and around Brewster especially. The so-called patriots had developed a positive genius for appointing crude, heavy-willed officials.

All his life Papa had held law and order in deep respect. So had Mamma. She had always agreed with Papa. Yes. Perhaps it was as well that Mamma had gone to rest beside Papa in the churchyard— after the war Minga would see that tombstones were raised. Now it wouldn't do. The patriots had scrawled all manner of obscene epitaphs on old Major McHenry's headstone.

When the road made straight towards a line of hardwoods barricading the horizon, old Tobias began to blink and to peer about.

"Where's the King's people, Mum?"

"The British outposts must be very near now," Minga heard herself saying. "So whip up. We can't take all day."

"G'up! You Joe! G'up! Tom!" With a bull's pizzel whip the old coachman stirred the clumsy-footed bays into a jolting trot that set the wagon swaying and clattering until it seemed to jar the whole road.

As the bluish shadows of beech, oak and birch boughs began to throw a lace-work over the highway, Minga, too, began to peer about. She shouldn't have felt uneasy—she'd been through too much the past three years and yet—yet—the Yankee lieutenant had guessed that the King's outposts rode less than three miles distant, and she had driven twice as far. He must have been lying. Truth wasn't often to be found in the mouth of a Rebel.

Distinctly, she could remember the first time she had travelled this road. Papa had taken all the family, Mamma, Ned—it didn't seem possible he was dead, killed by his own neighbors at the battle of Freeman's Farm—Grandma, Ruth and herself to visit Aunt Julie who lived 'way on the other side of Hudson's River in Jersey. It had been wonderfully—

The thing happened with uncanny suddenness. Before Minga could even catch breath to scream, a pair of wild figures in shabby green uniforms sprang from behind a pair of boulders and grabbed at the team's bridle. The bays reared, snorted their fright but came to a halt, harness rattling and trace chains jangling.

A lanky individual astride a pale yellow horse burst out of an ash thicket and, brandishing a horse pistol, bellowed, "Halt, in the King's name!"

"Don't ye shoot! Fer God's sake, don't ye shoot!" Tobias' arms shot up as he dropped whip and reins. From behind, the dust caught up and eddied over the farm wagon.

More figures in a weird collection of caps, coats and equipment came riding out of the woods. In no time at all the farm cart became the center of a circle of the most vicious-appearing men Minga had ever beheld—worse even than the Liberty Boys who'd wrecked Millwood that awful night last autumn.

The leader, a gray-haired fellow lacking a good part of his left cheek, rode closer. He was utterly calm.

"Keep quiet and you wunt get hurt."

"B-but you used the King's name," Minga protested.

"So I did—we're King's people. Partisans, you might say." He displayed yellow teeth speckled black with decay. "Briskly now," said he to his followers. "Get them bar'ls and chests outer there. And you—" He levelled a brass-bound pistol at Minga's stomach. "One peep out of you and you're a dead goose. It's our duty to search fer contraband."

Minga rose to her full height on the wagon front. "You dogs! You dirty dogs to use the King's name. You're Rebels! Well, look at this!" She fumbled in the front of her dress and so drew the interested stares of several horsemen. "See? I've a safe conduct from General Arnold himself."

"A safe conduct from Arnold, ye say?" growled one of the bandits. He turned to the leader. "Say, Enoch, ain't we glad to hear that?"

The man Enoch motioned his followers to dismount. They did, all except two who held the bridle reins for the rest. They must be troops of some sort, if one went by the precise execution of the man Enoch's orders. The leader kept his small dark eyes on the front of Minga's gown.

"First ye call us 'Rebels,' then you show a safe conduct from the American commander. Looks mighty suspicious; what say, boys?"

Beyond curses that the luggage had been so securely strapped down, he got no answer.

Already, his men had begun to claw aside the tarpaulin cover. To Minga it became dreadfully apparent that her property, her precious property, was about to be looted.

"We are King's people," Minga said coldly. "If you are indeed a Loyalist, warn your men to let my property alone."

"So yer loyal?" queried Enoch easing a bandoleer bisecting his faded green uniform.

"Yes, never was anyone more so!"

"Then if yer the red-hot Loyalist you make out, ye won't begrudge yer partisans a share o' what you got in yer cart. 'Share one, share all.' That's our motto on the Neutral Ground."

Sabers were swinging, gleaming in the sunset as the shaggy

riders hacked through the canvas covers, sawed at the baggage
lashings. At this rate, they'd be into those trunks and chests in no
time. They mustn't. All she had left in the world to begin a new life
with was in her baggage.

"Stop them!" she cried.

"Stop them!" mimicked a young, sickly-looking partisan.

His insolence fired Minga to action. Catching up the whip, she
lashed full across the face of a small, leathery individual who
was hacking industriously at the lines securing her clothes hamper.

Squalling in hurt surprise, the looter reeled back, hands clasped
over a purple-white stripe. Encouraged, Minga scrambled out on
the load. She wasn't sure what would happen next, but she did know
that if those trunks, if those chests ever got dragged off the wagon—
well, she'd be penniless.

"Let my things alone!"

Again and again she slashed at various ragged fellows but nearly
fell from the seat when the horses, frightened by the whistling of the
lash, commenced clumsily to rear and plunge. The men laughed,
leaned their musketoons against nearby trees to leave themselves
freer. They tried to catch the lash.

"Get on with it, you bloody fools," panted a tall Cowboy trying
to hang onto the team's bridles.

The leader stopped guafawing, "Aye. Stop yer playin', Miss.
Now I'll show yer some real sport."

Drawing a whining rasp from steel on brass the irregular freed a
heavy saber. When, outraged, Minga slashed at him with her whip,
dexterously he parried the blow, then spurred his horse up alongside
the cart. It was a big brute the man Enoch bestrode so he rode nearly
on a level with her. She couldn't strike surely at him because the
team's plunging and stamping threatened momentarily to pitch her
over the front wheels.

Leaving his saber to dangle from a rawhide thong securing it to
his wrist, suddenly the leader flung an arm about her legs, forced
her knees to give until she toppled awkwardly sideways across a
barrel head. Outraged, she had a vision of his maimed powder-
blued face looming near.

A horse's head brushed her cheek when he grabbed her about the
waist and hauled her bodily out of the wagon.

Meanwhile the Cowboys uttered fierce little cries when the ropes
securing her luggage began to give. One bag had been hacked open
and a grinning unshaven rascal in a stained, bottle-green uniform
flourished her best cerulean blue petticoat.

"Rest easy, Chicken" the leader panted. "Me, I allus allow the finest goods ain't far off a traveller."

With petticoats swirling high about her thighs, Minga clawed, twisted and tried to bite, but the man Enoch's grip was vise-like. He backed his mount away from the cart while the irregulars bellowed delightedly at the exposure of pink ribbon garters and long slim legs in white silk stockings.

"Let me go!" she choked. "You mistake us. I tell you we're King's people."

"King's people? Haw! Haw! So are we, honey bird. Nacherally you won't begrudge a few jools and trinkets to comfort our noble King's fighting men?"

In savage haste Enoch wrenched a ring from her small finger, then snapped a necklace of fine gold links from her neck but he disdained to trouble her cleverly wrought silver bracelet. Though Minga struck at his eyes with all her strength, the irregular thrust horny fingers deep inside the front of her bodice. At the contact of his cold fingers on her breast she winced.

"No! No! You mustn't. It's all I—"

"Ha! I *thought* so!"

To her chemise she had pinned the necklace of pearls which had been Grandma Jennifer's wedding gift to Mamma.

When he delved deeper, the yellow-green fabric of his sleeve and a hairy wrist loomed before her eyes. Minga bit, bit as hard as she could.

Her captor vented a breathless squeal and relaxed his grip just long enough to permit her to wriggle off the pommel. She fell flat on the ground, legs waving ridiculously, and lost one of her slippers. Though her hair was tumbling over her eyes, she scrabbled at the hard ground to recover her footing.

A burst of laughter rang in the narrow space between the woods. It made the leader furious. He sucked at his skinned wrist an instant before wrenching his horse about.

"So you'd bite, you bloody slut?"

A pair of furious blue eyes veined with red charged at her: she thought she'd be ridden down but the horse, at the last instant, threw its head out of harm's way and veered aside.

Incisively as an acid, a yell bit into the situation. "Enoch! Enoch, leave be!"

The raiders stopped whatever they were doing, and froze in their tracks. Enoch wheeled in the direction of the speaker. He was gesticulating to the left, towards a birch grove. From it came a shrill whistle. Lying prostrate among some sere dead ferns beside the highway, Minga struggled for breath, watched the frozen figures spring into action. When, in headlong haste, the tatterdemalion pillagers began scattering, the bay team, their bridles released, began bucking and lunging back and forth.

Tobias made no move to control them, lay white and motionless across the front of the cart, dripping a trickle of claret-colored blood onto the manure-stained whiffletree of the off horse.

Raising cautiously on an elbow, Minga Allen realized that the ground was littered with rope ends, that shreds of torn canvas were streaming from the wagon's sides. The man in the green coat was standing up in his stirrups, casting a quick look down the road. Suddenly he leaped agilely off his horse and came running over to her.

"Give me them jools!" he commanded, "or I'll stretch yer out! Quick now."

"No."

Minga tried to rise but the shock of her fall to earth seemed to have numbed her. The irregular cast another swift look over his shoulder, then, gripping the front of her dress, ripped out the bodice, fabric, oiled-silk bag of pearls and all. Cold air rushed over her breasts and down over her stomach, but not faster than a sense of desperation. She mustn't, *couldn't* let that necklace go.

With the evil, sinuous grace of a lynx, the partisan recaptured his horse, vaulted into the saddle.

Somehow Minga got to her feet. Her pearls were escaping. *Her pearls!* Her stake in the future. She tried to catch the leader's bridle, but the missing shoe threw her off stride and instead she lurched violently sidewise and struck against the side of the wagon.

When a ragged but deafening fusillade shattered the evening's calm, her team, no longer restrained, started down the road. The man Enoch uttered a resounding curse and grabbed at his reins in an effort to turn his mount towards the river.

"Ah-h," he yelled, then stiffened in the saddle and hunched awkwardly forward until he was clinging to his horse's neck. Minga guessed the partisan couldn't have known what he was doing because he pulled so hard on his left rein that his ribby bay mount swerved violently.

The leader fell, lay limply across the deep ruts of the highroad, but even in his fall he never lost his grip of that section of loose cloth and the yellow oiled-silk bag pinned to it. Face down, he shuddered violently, then tried to lever himself upwards, but couldn't.

Because in all the world there was nothing more important than that bag and its contents Minga Allen kicked off her other slipper and ran for the slowly twisting figure in green. Only dimly was she conscious of hoofs coming near, nearer. She was sharply aware, however, that her would-be despoiler had managed to turn over and now lay on his back. A vivid smear of scarlet was oozing slowly from between his flattened lips. Inexplicably he grinned, gasped; then, lunging, caught the hem of her skirt.

"Almost, little Chicken. Almost—"

"You—you thief. Give it back! I want my necklace."

Minga set her foot on the man Enoch's wrist and tried to wrench free the shredded front of her dress; but the dying partisan hung on. The staccato rattle of hoof beats sounded immediately behind her, made her turn, utterly unaware that her gown now fluttered open to the waist.

"Halt! Halt there, you damned rogues!"

Minga caught glimpses of flashing silver, of crested helmets, of black and brown horses surging near and of sabers in the fading light. The riders, she realized with infinite relief, wore brilliant scarlet.

II

RIDE BY NIGHT

"SERVANT, Ma'am. Leftenant Geoffrey Petersham, His Majesty's 17th Dragoon Regiment, at your service."

As the long-legged cavalryman bowed from his saddle, the silver death's-head device affixed to his helmet of black leather glowed copper red in the sunset.

Minga Allen, however, paid him no attention. She had replanted her stockinged foot on the man Enoch's wrist and was wrenching free the piece of her dress and the pearls.

She wasn't a bit sorry the partisan was dying, not after what he'd done. She wanted to kick him; he was so dirty, vicious and common-looking, just like those men who had come storming into Judge Allen's home not two months back, yelling "Liberty forever!"

The most incredible part of this sorry business was that Enoch and his fellow plunderers had declared themselves for the King. How absurd of them to attempt so pitiful a deception. Why, even the village idiot knew that on the King's side fought law-abiding, well-disciplined, decently-behaved troops; true soldiers. Quite a contrast to the raggle-taggle State militias, to the lean, threadbare soldiery who called themselves Continentals and kept their arms bright, but argued with their officers whenever they felt disposed.

Curious, that the sight of blood no longer made her stomach tighten, the lining of her mouth pucker inward. There was a smear of red on her dress when she straightened; her hand, too, was wet and sticky. The lieutenant sat his horse, stared down on her in wide-eyed amazement.

An orderly ran up, caught the officer's bridle and spoke soothing words to his black charger.

"Well," she snapped, "well, what are you staring at?"

When he had dismounted, Minga realized that this young Englishman stood surprisingly tall in his short, gold-laced jacket and buff breeches. His bold brown eyes were very clear, their whites blue-white like those of a young child. He wheeled as a series of shots snapped in the distance.

"Judson! My watch cloak. Smartly now!"

After undoing a strap the orderly ran forward with a cloak of black serge lined with scarlet. Both the horses he held trotted after him, stirrups clanking.

Warned by the stares of troopers returning from patrol, Minga realized at last that she stood all but naked from throat to waistband, her small, softly-rounded breasts quite exposed. A furious heat warmed her skin from the waist upward.

Heavens! What *would* these Englishmen take her for? Defiantly she pulled together her dress. After all, she still had her pearls and she would have lost them if she hadn't delayed the partisan leader. How much of her property remained in the wagon?

"Permit me, Ma'am," Lieutenant Petersham muttered and dropped his cloak over her shoulders. It was surprisingly heavy and reeked of horses.

A gruff, flat-faced, ruddy fellow came trotting up, saluted and puffed, said, "Henemy's dispersed, sir, and hoccupying a wood. Shall we attack, sir?"

"No, Sergeant. Inspect the harness and take a look at the old bumpkin."

Tobias lay on the side of the road breathing stertorously, a livid lump rising on his shiny scalp.

" 'E'll be right as rain in 'arf a moment, sir," reported a

fox-faced corporal. '' 'Ere, my lad.'' He emptied the contents of a flat wooden canteen over the old hostler's face.

Water clung to Tobias' three days' whiskers and the wind, chilling it, brought him about in a hurry.

Two troopers came trotting up. They were busily reloading their carbines and escorting a third man who was driving Minga's farm cart. Two or three shots sounded in the deep sunset.

"Oh, Lord! Lord!" Tobias commenced to moan. "I'm an old body, friends—old and I ain't never hurted no one. Don't kill me—"

"Lord love yer Gramper, them others has gone," a sergeant told him and, his saber trailing, dismounted to tie a grimy shirt sleeve about the old man's bloodied scalp.

On closer inspection Minga became aware that though Lieutenant Petersham's uniform fitted, its brilliant fabric was singed here and spotted there. Sections of the tunic's silver frogs and lace work had been ripped, then clumsily repaired with coarse brown thread.

The officer, too, wore that lean, hard-bitten expression she had come to recognize in those who spent long hours in the saddle or who endured the weather as Providence sent it.

A trio of troopers, to her surprise, commenced going through the pockets of the dead partisan. Because others of the red-coated dragoons clustered in the underbrush, she suspected that some other raider had been killed.

Fingers flying, Minga hastened to fasten two frogs securing the front of this hatchet-profiled lieutenant's cloak. Lord's mercy! That dead rogue had spoiled her gown for good and all. What a stupid waste. Such material wasn't to be had any more.

Indignation flamed within her and, angrily, she glanced at the dead partisan. He had been bereft now of coat, new boots and pistols. His half-undressed body now sprawled ungainly across the frozen ground with fingers curled and eyes glassily wide. She was gladder than ever that he was dead.

The lieutenant helped her up on her cart's seat, then ordered a corporal to take up the lines. Two captured horses, hitched to the wagon's tailboard, fidgeted beside the corporal's mount. Tobias, semiconscious, lay on some sacks among her still undisturbed boxes and chests of household effects.

Odd, what three and more years of war could do to one, Minga thought. There was no time nowadays for the polite niceties. Whether you got enough to eat, or kept warm, had become the only consideration.

She cast Lieutenant Petersham a quizzical glance, inclined her head towards the troopers engaged in searching the dead.

"Is—is that usual?"

"Oh, quite," he told her, "quite. Necessary, you know. Commissaries don't get this far very often."

Presently the troopers remounted, their pockets bulging. The corporal clucked at Minga's team and the cart resumed its jolting. The convoy set off through the deepening twilight.

"It's utterly abominable that those villains you drove away should have dared claim themselves in the King's service."

The gaunt line of Lieutenant Petersham's rather long jaw tightened. "Odd part of it is, Ma'am," said he as his horse felt for the bit and, stretching its neck, pulled the reins until it had gained a comfortable slack, "that in a way the beggars *are* on our side."

"What! Highwaymen, common robbers serving the King!" Her eyes grew so round he laughed.

"Skinners or Cowboys, Ma'am, are all the same though one lot cries for the King, the other for Congress. Such jackals prowl the edges of every fight."

"Skinners? Cowboys? I fear I don't comprehend." Minga peered through the dark, as the British patrol closed up and rode with handy little carbines balanced across their pommels.

"Ma'am, those are the nicknames for partisans. Cowboys affect the King's side. Skinners are the same type of rogue, who support Congress."

"Who support the Rebels!" Minga corrected fiercely.

Lieutenant Petersham eased a muddied boot from his stirrup, let his leg dangle to relax its ankle muscles. He gave her a deliberate look.

"It's as you say, Ma'am," he agreed presently. "From a legal point of view I daresay the Americans *are* Rebels and you'll find plenty of elegant folk about New York who will still term them so." He looked about carefully; just ahead loomed another thicket. "Those of us in the lines, however—well, we've come to consider them as lawful, legal enemies. Got to, you know."

He sighed. "I've fought in three countries, Ma'am, and these farmers and peasants and merchants have stuck to their fight better than any Don or Johnny Crapaud I've seen. They've the strength of their convictions, wrong-headed no doubt, but—"

"—Wrong?" Minga's voice took on an edge. "Wrong? Of all the murderous, hypocritical, treacherous rogues, the rascals that follow this charlatan who dares call himself 'General' Washington are the worst. I—I— Don't you ever speak well of them to me—"

"—I shan't," Lieutenant Petersham said shortly. "No doubt you've been afforded ample grounds for your views."

It had grown quite dark now and the horses were stumbling frequently. In the cart Tobias moaned every time the wheels passed over a boulder. Amid some woods, shadowy off to the left, an owl's eerie cry punctured the dead stillness of the background.

"I believe we'd best take up the trot, Ma'am. Our bivouac is still some distance off and those bestial Rebels of yours may be on foray."

His sarcastic use of the words "bestial Rebels" was unmistakable. Minga could hardly believe her ears. Could this Englishman be typical? How could one of His Majesty's officers talk like this? Although he had not uttered a word which was not perfectly correct, she knew she stood rebuked. A pox on Lieutenant Petersham! If he'd the least notion of what loyal King's folk had suffered in Putnam County, well—well, he wouldn't speak like this.

Trace chains jingled, leather squeaked, and the wagon jolted and rattled down a hill as the bay team took up a heavy-footed trot. When the woods in which the owl had hooted crowded the highway, Lieutenant Petersham rode out in advance. The patrol came in still closer about Minga's cart, their carbine butts steadied against their hips.

Now that the sun had drowned itself in the not-too-distant Hudson, the horses forgot how tired and hungry they were and sharpened their ears.

Minga had never felt more fatigued. Her wrist, where the partisan had grabbed her, ached and her left breast had been bruised in squirming off the leader's pommel. She hoped she wasn't going to have trouble. Young Mrs. Gray had perished slowly, miserably of a decay in that way. An axe handle had slipped, struck her across the chest.

Lord's mercy! How ever could she repair this dress? A lace insert perhaps might do the trick? The night wind began sifting in over the tops of her sturdy, home-pegged shoes.

Covertly, she examined her hands. There was still blood on them. What a termagant she must have apeared to Lieutenant Petersham! He'd found her stepping on the leader's wrist! Yes, war certainly did strange things to people.

Lieutenant Petersham was reining in now, mighty stiff and straight in his saddle, a real officer. She coughed, caught his eyes. "Pray, inform me, sir, from what part of England do you come?"

He smiled. "Why, Ma'am, I come from Wilts, from Cricklade. It's a pretty little town."

"Have you ever been to London?"

She wasn't really interested in London, but conversation took her mind off Tobias' groans, off her own chilled, bruised body. What kind of a bivouac lay ahead? A comfortable farmhouse, she felt sure.

"Sorry to say I haven't, Ma'am," Petersham replied, his horse-hair crest stirring under the night wind. "My brother lives there. On Half Moon Street. Tom inherited the title, you know."

Minga felt relieved. "And tell me, what do you make of New York?"

The lieutenant's weather-stiffened features contracted in a grin, and he eased the heavy, curved sword that clanked from his belt. "Why, I think it's rather a jolly spot, exciting and overcrowded, no water, too many traitors, but still fun. The theatre's uncommon good—or was last winter." He glanced curiously at her. "Do I presume correctly, Ma'am, that you have relatives there?"

"No relatives," she admitted, "but perhaps a few friends. I don't know how many of them are still in New York. The war shifts people about so."

"Aye, war has a way of doing that." He couldn't understand such remarkable self-possession. Not an hour ago this young woman had been looted, had been manhandled and had witnessed the violent death of the man whose blood yet marked her hands. Yet was it so strange? Revulsion against violence lost impact very swiftly. Human nature was so appallingly adaptable. He'd found that out while campaigning in India.

It was almost dark now; but as the night wind from the west began to finger the faded horsehair crest of his helmet, he considered the fine clean lines of this tall young woman's body. How very tired she appeared slumped there on the seat. It was growing colder and the sound of hoofs and equipment came clear, staccato.

"Not in five years have I been in New York," she remarked. "Not since that odious town of Boston brought all this misery upon us."

"Then I fancy you'll discover great changes," he predicted. "Everywhere ride generals and their staff officers, country gentlemen and ladies and a great many merchants who have refugeed from the back country. Yes, Ma'am, New York is monstrously, dangerously, overcrowded, prick my vitals if it isn't. Too many pickpockets, rascals, clippers, scaw-bankers and undisciplined provincial troops about. A good quarter of the inhabitants live in tents, you know, in hovels or in the hulks of old vessels. 'Tis a great demonstration of the power of human ingenuity. I trust, Mistress Allen, you've a place to bide?"

The way her hands tightened on her lap told him instantly she hadn't.

"Why—why, I had no idea."

Lieutenant Petersham gathered his reins and slipped his patched boot back into the iron stirrup.

"You had best be wary, Ma'am, when you reach New York. Pardon my suggesting it but beware teamsters, porters and barrow men. They'll rook you, lead you astray and do you in the eye at every turn."

Weariness enveloped Minga. Fatigue dulled the impending thrill of reaching the city.

"What of the Chequers Tavern, Mr. Petersham? Surely I shall find accommodations there?"

"The Chequers? Hardly. Nor at the King's Arms, nor even the Lion and the Unicorn. I tell you the town teems with troops, refugees and rogues."

She looked at him in rising dismay. Here was a possibility that had never occurred.

"But, sir, whatever am I to do? I—I can't camp out."

The rangy, half-seen figure shrugged, then picked up his mount's bit as the animal stumbled on a frozen lump of mud.

"Let's see. Mayn't help a trifle, but—why you might look up my raffish cousin, Jerry Vaughan. Captain in the 17th Dragoons. Sound fellow, very steady to hounds. Might still be there. Jerry boards with a Mrs. Ashton, very glum because he ain't been sent down to beau the girls in Philadelphia, along with the rest of our noble commander's *petits maîtres*."

Lieutenant Petersham broke off, considered a distant hillside over his shoulder. Upon it the remains of still another burnt farmhouse stood etched a funereal black against the bare earth.

"In Mrs. Ashton, Ma'am, you will meet as sweet a body as ever took the breath of life," he predicted quite gravely. "Lives on Exchange Street. A widow," Lieutenant Petersham continued. "Bit of a mystery, too. Claims she lost her husband in the Boston siege, at the Breed's Hill battle."

"Claims?"

The officer nodded. "We-ell . . . Furness, he served as a subaltern in the 23rd in Boston, claims her husband wasn't exactly— well, Major de Vaux brought—er—well, it's all gossip, I daresay."

Minga was too weary to care much about Captain Jerry Vaughan, the 17th Dragoons or Mr. Ashton, but she inscribed the names upon her memory. Curious, how much she had learned to remember. A few years back she could never be sure where she had left her gloves.

Without command, two of the troopers all at once spurred forward, went *clip-clopping* down the road. The other closed in about the cart.

"Oh God, my head!" mumbled Tobias. "What's happened?"

"Yer've 'ad a pot too many," the sergeant grunted, "so stow yer gab, old loon."

"But my head—"

Uncertainly, the old man struggled up among the uncovered chests and peered stupidly at a vista of naked shrubs and trees. When Lieutenant Petersham set his spur gently into his charger's side, Minga noticed that his boot, like the Yankee's, was patched on one side. The leather was really very worn.

"We are nearing our lines, Ma'am," Petersham explained over his shoulder. "Our quarters are a barn we've altered after a fashion." He looked embarrassed. "They are scarce fitting for a lady but—well, Ma'am, your horses are done in. When they've baited and rested, they'll be fit for further travel."

"What is good enough for the King's officers," Minga told him quite seriously, "is good enough for my King's subject."

All the same she wondered how it would be to be quartered with a troop of cavalrymen. There would be precious little privacy.

III

THE KING'S STRONGHOLD

MINGA ALLEN lay half awake. Like most people, she enjoyed that period of delicious unreality which descends just before sleep or appears just before wakefulness. It was a wonderful interval, she'd always felt, when one could discount realities.

This Lieutenant Petersham was indeed an odd duck, as Papa would have put it. Though English to the marrow of his bones, he had, after supper, voiced some of the oddest opinions concerning the Rebels; they had all but bordered on sedition. And *he* carrying the King's Commission! He'd been pulling her leg, most likely— some English were deucedly clever at it, and thought it funny, especially with colonials.

She sighed softly, turned on her truss of hay and laxly poked a sleep-dampened curl away from her cheek. Hadn't seemed worthwhile to bother to unpack her luggage in search of that feather bed Mamma had bought from a German woman down in Pennsylvania. When had that been? Mercy, all of six years ago during the family's unforgettable visit to gay, worldly, wicked Philadelphia—a huge place boasting all of 23,000 inhabitants.

A fine thing that General Howe had captured the Rebel capital last year so now Philadelphia belonged to the King once more. Oh, why wouldn't the Rebel leaders, Greene, Moultrie, Washington and the rest, admit they were whipped? By every rule of sense their cause was undone. Aside from their capital, New York was held by the King's men, not to mention near half a hundred lesser ports.

Minga guessed it would call for a lot of thinking on her part to understand what Lieutenant Petersham had meant by saying, "Hold what you will, Ma'am, these Rebels believe, and believe stronger than the fear of death, in something I don't think many of us perceive. Of course, the poor beggars are mistook, Mistress Allen. This spring Sir Henry Clinton will jolly well convince them of it." He had frowned into the wavering camp fire, his eyes looking preternaturally deep and sombre.

"Odd. We've discovered that it's when the enemy seem the most wrong that they prove the most dangerous. For all the whippings they've suffered the beggars ain't afraid of us. Do you know, Ma'am? If the Americans ever lose a war it will be because life has been too easy, not too hard for them."

On that she'd wondered if Lieutenant Petersham really were in earnest. She considered him curiously across the bitter-smelling campfire. Behind a well-gnawed partition had sounded the *crunch crunch* of many horses tiredly chomping their ration of grain.

"I vow, Mr. Petersham," she'd said at length. "Am I mistaken, or do you not find a deal to admire in these wretched brutes of Rebels?"

The lieutenant had run fingers through brown curls crushed flat by the weight of the brass helmet he had finally pulled off. He had vented a small laugh. "It's odd, but I do admire the Americans—with qualifications, of course. For example, I like the French individually and detest 'em collectively; with the Americans, 'tis the other way around."

Oh, bother! Mr. Petersham's thinking was too complicated for words. The Rebels were uncompromising scoundrels and that was all there was to it.

It was nice to lie here on the hay, Minga found. On opening her eyes she could see, by the firelight, troopers lying huddled in their blankets, their booted feet towards the embers. The lieutenant and his sergeant lay beside another, their swords stuck point down in the earth near their heads. Ugh! Those fragile cross-like outlines suggested headstones in a cemetery. One thing she'd noticed about real soldiers; they slept any time they were granted half an opportunity. During a campaign, they preferred slumber to almost any other pleasure.

Lieutenant Petersham was snoring softly, like a gentleman, though his N.C.O.'s and men were bugling away like a pack of hounds in full cry.

To think that tomorrow she would be in New York, and, thank Heavens, with her little fortune intact. The way those Cowboys had boasted of riding in the King's name gave her a nasty memory. When she recalled how she must have appeared to Mr. Petersham with her bodice ripped and her breasts bared to the wind—she went hot under the rough horse blanket.

Her eyes were wide open now and her jaw set itself. Well, what if she had—er—been seen? She'd got her pearls back; besides, no girl had ever died through man's only staring at her.

Turning again on the hay she considered the immediate future. No matter what people said, she *would* find a ship bound for her destination—Aunt Adelina's romantic sounding plantation.

When a fox barked not far away, several of the troopers' mounts began to stamp and snuffle under a giant oak which stood just behind the barn. Minga drew a deep breath and discovered that in her nose lingered the smell of fried salt pork. Horrors, her mouth and chin must look greasy! Oh, the devil with it; there hadn't been any hot water to wash with. Besides, which of these weary, wind-burned men gave a hang how she looked?

Curious . . . in a deal of ways that Rebel lieutenant and Mr. Petersham . . . ridiculous, but they were in a way similar . . . rode alike . . . talked much in the same vein. . . .Mr. Petersham handsomer, though. . . .King's man. Scarlet, gold. Not Enoch . . . incredible to think . . . Cowboys as King's people . . . really could . . . be so beastly.

The campfire, smouldering in the center of the barn on the dirt floor, flared as a stick burned through. Minga's grayish-green eyes opened wide enough for her to make out a guard at the barn's entrance. He was bent far over his carbine and was all huddled into a horse blanket draped Indian-like about his shoulders.

Stupid business, war . . . so much energy wasted . . . so much building for destruction. . . .New York . . . great fire must have burnt James Caldwell's house. . . .It had stood on Exchange Street. . . . Fire . . . fire.

The next morning a slow, undramatic but drenching rain spread inches of stiff mud over the dirt roads of Westchester County. Big, white, chilly drops dripped monotonously from the bare twigs of trees lining the highroad into New York. Every now and then a squall tapped with impatient fingers at the canvas tarpaulins which once more protected Minga Allen's meager possessions.

Long since, Lieutenant Petersham had turned back. That angular, caustic young man had, after an hour's progress through the sifting rain, drawn his drenched and blue-lipped troopers up on the side of the road. He had then saluted precisely and in essence repeated the Rebel lieutenant's words.

"I trust, Mistress Allen, that in New York your good opinion of our cause will suffer no disillusionment."

As she had rearranged the hood of her calash, Minga had smiled confidentially. "I am confident that I shall not."

The lieutenant had been very kind about leaving for old Tobias a threadbare cloak. The old ostler had had a bad night with his hurt head and there were purplish rings under his eyes.

"G'up! G'up! Ye lazy crowbaits," Tobias mumbled, slapping his reins against the team's broad backs as the patrol trotted back towards that desolate and treacherous expanse of disputed territory otherwise known as the Neutral Ground.

The stout brutes responded, quickened their stride, sinews rippling under their rain-brightened skin. The ostler snuffled, reset his wide-brimmed felt hat. Twice a squall had sent his faded old beaver rolling onto the roadside so he had secured his headpiece with a length of line tied under his chin. It lent him a grotesquely childish look.

One of the farm cart's axles had begun to need greasing; it complained like a querulous child. Through the drizzling mist Minga now could discern the Hudson, flowing far off to her right, a dreary slate blue today—the same hue as the sky. Heavens! Wasn't there even a mite of color in all this cheerless world?

As if in remedy to her complaint, movement appeared on the great gray river.

"Oh, Tobias, look! Look! There's a war ship—one of *our* men-o'-war!" She pointed to a slim brown-and-yellow painted sloop heaving into sight beyond a wooded knoll. The vessel was cruising leisurely upstream, with her yards squared to the chill

nor'west wind. Her master had set tops'ls and royals and jibs and a
White Ensign almost as big as the sloop herself.

Being occupied with avoiding a bog hole on one side and a jagged
boulder on the other, all the old ostler said was, "G'up!"

Minga's heart lifted. Oh, but it was fine, inspiring to behold the
emblem of Royal authority whipping out clean, straight and proud
in the breeze. It convinced her that she was back once more under
the shelter of the King's laws.

Order, was what she yearned for and would always crave; she
aimed to shape her life into regular, predictable and well-bred
patterns. As a judge's daughter, she held law in high respect.
Among the Rebels everything that was supposed to be legal was
crazy, topsy-turvy. Laws regulating their every-day life were
changed near as fast as these raindrops dripped off Tobias' hat brim.

Gracefully, the distant cruiser slid out of sight behind a hill; first
her hull became lost to view, then her shrouds and finally her
topmasts. The horses splashed on, clumsy hoofs splattering mud
under their bellies.

Tobias flapped the reins half-heartedly. New York seemed still
half a world distant. "G'up!" he grunted.

Minga surprised herself by snapping, "Tobias, say 'git up!' 'git
on!' 'go!' but if you say 'g'up' just once again, I'll surely push you
off this seat."

Silver-gray bristles on his jaw glistened as Tobias turned his head
in heavy surprise. "Yes'm, it's as you say, but there ain't no call to
be so short about it."

On the outskirts of New York appeared an apparently limitless
pattern of earthen redoubts, embrasures and entrenchments. Some
sappers in dirtied white aprons were supervising the lackadaisical
efforts of a gang of prisoners to construct a number of abatis.
Further away several crows were foraging about an old gun em-
placement—probably built by the Americans before the city fell.

When a red and white swing barrier rigged across the road
brought the farm cart to a halt, Minga Allen shivered, wiped the
mist from her eyes. What *was* the name of that rooming house
Lieutenant Petersham had suggested? Mrs. Anton? No. Ashley's?
No. Mrs. Ashton—yes, that was it. Ashton.

The rain now was beating down in steady, driving squalls which
momentarily obliterated all view of three tall steeples towering over
New York. For some time now water had been trickling down
Minga's neck and over her shoulder blades. The riding cloak had
admitted water in front, too. A small chill ribbon of damp had
persisted in descending the *val* between her breasts.

She saw now that, to the left of the barrier, stood a small building which must be a guardhouse. Greasy-looking smoke was pouring out of its blackened chimney pot. A hoarding, standing beside the road, was plastered with illegible and sodden proclamations, warnings and recruiting posters. Nobody, not even a sentry, was in sight, only a couple of gaunt curs sniffing hopefully at the door to a blacksmith's shop.

"Hi!" Tobias called. "Hi, in there! Raise this confounded toll bar!"

Tobias' thin old voice, however, was inadequate to penetrate the sound of wind and hard-driven rain drops. He sat huddled with the starch gone out of his spine and his head bandages soaked. A dull reddish-brown line escaping them stained, then disappeared beneath his greasy linen stock. The horses stood patiently. No one appeared from the guardhouse.

She couldn't order the old man to get down, Minga realized. He was pretty shaky; the way his hands trembled told her that.

"Wait here. Let me see if I can rouse somebody. There ought to be a guard. The idea of their keeping us waiting in the rain."

She was angry. Soldiers were supposed to ignore the weather—the King's soldiers at least. They weren't like the undisciplined levies from up-state and New England.

Before she got down Minga glanced over her shoulder to make sure the canvas cover was still snug over her goods. Wouldn't do for the rain to get into her linens and clothes. They'd mildew and then she mightn't be able to sell them when—well, when she'd need to.

Minga was angrily aware that her change of position had permitted moisture even more intimately to seep down her body. She did not even knock on the door, just lifted the latch and flung it back with a crash.

"You guards! Is this your idea of duty? For what does His Majesty pay you?"

"*Ach, du lieber Gott!*"

"*Himmel, August. Ist hier eine Mädel!*"

A huge figure in a blue uniform turned up in dull orange arose, came lumbering toward her through a fog of the rankest tobacco smoke Minga had ever smelled.

"*Was wünschen Sie?*"

Enormous, carefully waxed mustache ends alternately moved up and down. Orange worsted epaulettes, fat as English muffins, lent this giant a round-shouldered effect.

"Talk English, you lout."

"English? *Nichts verstehe.*" The huge fellow shook his head and grinned. She guessed that this must be one of His Majesty's

German mercenaries. People repeated all manner of curious tales concerning them.

Exasperated, Minga stamped her foot, felt the wet leather of her shoe squelch softly.

"Oh, you idiot! How dare you keep me standing out in the rain?"

The foreigner twirled his mustaches. "*So? So? Gut, Liebchen. Kommen Sie mit Willie.*"

While the two other guards uttered guttural comments and stood toasting steaming uniforms before the fireplace, the colossus took Minga by the elbow and put his arm around her so quickly she was taken utterly aback. She got over her surprise in a hurry when his fingers closed, cupped themselves over her right breast, and she dealt him a resounding slap.

"*Gotthimmelkreuzen!*"

From the rear of the guardhouse came a shot. "*Was ist los?*"

An immensely corpulent non-commissioned officer came stamping out.

"*Vot schweinishness iss dis?*"

"*Aber ich—*"

"*Schweig!*"

Right and left the N.C.O. dealt his huge subordinate half a dozen crackling slaps, then kicked him so hard in the rear that Minga couldn't help laughing at the way he yelped.

Breathing thickly, the sergeant turned, bowed profoundly while offering apologies in broken English. Minga was so glad to be back in the King's territory she accepted them.

Hurriedly the three privates put on high, brass-fronted hats and, like automatons, tramped out into the rain after their sergeant.

Respectfully, the sergeant saluted. It was unfortunate but orders were that all goods entering the town must be examined.

"But I'm a Loyalist."

"Forgiff, *Fräulein*, but do not difference makes. Der orders so say. All goots examined must be."

In vain Minga pled for the summoning of a British officer; it appeared none was on duty. So, rain or no rain, examine her goods the Brunswickers did.

For all his blunt, red nose, stupid-looking eyes, the sergeant in charge was smart. He sensed that here was no common traveller and accordingly expedited a search. Nonetheless, not a dry stitch remained on Minga's back by the time the barrier was raised and, lugubriously, the three drenched mercenaries presented arms. The wheat flour dressing their hair had turned lumpy and was staining their high yellow collars.

Once Tobias had flapped his reins and said, "G'up!" the sergeant cursed and began kicking his men. The horses leaned into their collars and the cart shivered and rolled into New York.

Fortunately it was no great distance to Mrs. Ashton's home on Exchange Street; it stood right on the edge of a great area which had been ravaged by fire not very long before. Like blackened claws, a long series of chimneys towered up out of heaps of tumbled masonry, rubble and charred beams. The distinctive smell of charcoal was strong in the air.

The widow had a ready smile, was soft spoken. "A friend of Mr. Petersham? Oh, do come in." In Mrs. Ashton's large and dark blue eyes Minga read such a compassion as she had not met with in many a blue moon.

Mrs. Ashton was small, her features and figure delicately fashioned—rather like one of those procelain pieces Papa's friends had brought back from Saxony, or one of those German Principalities or Kingdoms. She could not have been more than two or three years older than Minga, yet she spoke crisply and with authority.

"There is a fire in my room—it's at the foot of the stairs. Go there and warm yourself. Buff—" she nodded to a huge, sombre-looking Negro bearing curious chevron-like scars on either cheek "—will care for your team and things."

"No, no, I must see my property safe." Fatigue sharpened Minga's voice. "The rain has got into my linens."

Mrs. Ashton's narrow, black brows flickered upwards. "You are—from up-state?"

"Yes. I—I—These trunks are all they—left me." Yes. They held all that remained of Millwood.

"I understand. Which boxes shall you want in your room?"

"You are very kind, Mrs. Ashton," Minga said heavily. She was shivering, plain "tuckered out," as they would say in the rebellious state of Massachusetts. "But can my man find lodging, too? Tobias has been hurt, and he—well, he's quite old."

Mrs. Ashton considered her new lodger with a curious, wise little smile on lips warmly red and wide.

"From the first I had deemed you gently bred. Now I see I am right. Rest assured, your—er—coachman will be well attended."

Captain Jerry Vaughan

"DR-R-Y pine wood for sale!" a voice was intoning outside of Minga's leaded and curtained window.

Br-r-r! She found the morning not really cold but just a trifle raw. She felt fine, fine as satin, after such a good night's sleep. Guiltily, she realized she had stayed abed disgracefully late. Right now the clock on the Dutch Reformed Church had boomed seven deep shivery notes. Further down Manhattan's Island another bell, a few instants tardy, was supporting the first chimes' accounting.

"Buy my-y dr-r-y wo-o-od! Prime dry walnut. Five pound the cord."

Minga huddled further under the quilts. M-m-m. Mrs. Ashton's beds—this one at least—were uncommon comfortable and smelt faintly of pot-pourri.

As the first hawker's voice faded off down the street a second peddler began to bawl. "Wa-ter, wa-a-ter, fresh wa-a-ter from the Tea Garden pump."

With that Minga knew for sure she was back in New York. Everybody knew that the greatest drawback to living on Manhattan's Island was the perpetual shortage of pure water there. What with the increasing number of ducks, geese and cattle drinking from it Fresh Pond had grown so foul it tasted poisonous.

Minga stretched lazily, dug knuckles into her eyes. La! This *was* a comfortable bed. She had wiggled down so far into it her night dress had ridden up clean under her armpits. Slowly she passed hands over her long, straight body. It was elegant to be clean once more. Usually one bath a week was considered pretty high-toned in Brewster. But until last night she'd missed bathing for nearly a month. Lots of the doctors claimed too much bathing took a body's strength away. They were certainly right in one interpretation of that theory.

Slowly she flexed her knees upwards into the covers, heard sinews crackle softly. M-m-m. Luxuriously she rubbed the softness of her breasts upwards. She guessed she must possess an uncommon fine figure. Must be the explanation why the local boys stared so hard. A French nobleman visiting the DeWitts had made bold to say, "Mademoiselle has been designed by *le bon Dieu* to make some man a very pleasant bedfellow." She'd blushed clean down to her bodice and would have struck the old rake-hell with her fan if she hadn't perceived he intended no offense. Privately, she'd been just a little flattered—and puzzled.

Staring unseeingly at the ceiling she realized abruptly that a lovely, serene chapter in her life was closed. Another would begin when she went down to breakfast with Mrs. Ashton. Already she had heard the other guests go below, coughing, clearing their throats as they clumped down Mrs. Ashton's very steep and narrow staircase. The house, like its owner—if Mrs. Ashton was the owner—was small and neat and well-built.

Mrs. Ashton, from what she had seen of her, seemed a sweet person, yet capable. She had a little boy named David. A while back she had heard some Irish officer playing with the lad, calling him, "Davey, me foine lad."

Yes, it was wonderful to know herself back under the King's protection once more, safe from disorder, injustice and bodily peril. Triumphantly she assured herself that there could be no substitute for such a sane, orderly life as this. Why, the very clumping of those heavy boots, the clatter of a sword in its scabbard and that jingling of the spur chains lent a wondrous sense of security.

And yet there was that matter of Enoch and his Cowboys. She must try to pretend that had never existed.

"Up with you, you lazy baggage," she cried aloud, and startled into flight a blue-gray pigeon perched below her window sill.

Even though her window had been shut tight as could be, it was chilly in the room. She hurried over to the fire, snatched up a handful of tinder shavings. From a bronze box on the mantelpiece she selected a piece of tinder, linen scorched brown on this occasion, and kneeling, poked among the soft gray ashes until she found a live coal.

Instantly the tinder took and the kindling flared. After she had got a blaze she hiked up her nightgown quite shamelessly, to warm her legs and backside. M-m-m. The heat began to beat up under the linen until she could feel warm currents eddying over her stomach. Sunlight beat in and glowed on the little bedroom's pale yellow walls and flooded it with spring glory. Minga's naturally buoyant

spirits soared; and as she stepped out of the nightgown and into a
fresh chemise, she commenced to sing:

> "Oh, never say that I was false of heart,
>   Though absence seem'd my flame to qualify!
> As easy might I from myself depart,
>   As from my soul, which in my breast doth lie."

In a luxurious deliberation she combed out her mane of hair,
laughed to see a twig and several blades of hay flutter to the floor.

All at once impatience seized her to go downstairs and see what
Mrs. Ashton's other lodgers might be like. It would be curious to
learn whether she would recapture an elusive impression that, at
some time, this handsome, young widow must have seen, or done,
things she would prefer not to recall.

She had tied on the third of her four petticoats and was knotting
some pale blue ribbons to secure her stockings when, without
warning, the latch to her door lifted. Scarlet, she whirled.

"How dare—" She broke off when around the door's worn edge
appeared a small head topped with riotous tawny curls.

At the harshness of her words the child blinked, prepared to
shrink back into the gloom of the hall.

"No, no, don't go away," she begged smilingly. "Come in,
do."

The boy could not have been over four years of age.

The lad entered quite solemnly. In his tan knee breeches, ruffles,
buckled slippers, and coat with modishly blue waistcoat and flaring
skirts, he looked like a miniature of some buck out of White's.

"My name is David," he announced. "Are you going to stay
with us?"

"I hope so," Minga replied; and, being wise in the ways of small
boys, made no effort to pet him. Instead she talked over her
shoulder and went on tying her garters.

"I hope you are going to like me, David."

The child's large and deep blue eyes appraised her quite frankly.
"You *seem* like a nice person," he answered. "Do you like
rabbits?"

"Yes," she said. "Perhaps because there are so many of them,
one right after another. I had a rabbit once. I called him Archibald."

Her smile faded a little. Archibald had been named after Papa's
best friend, the King's counsel of Putnam county. Squire Quacken-
boss had died of a stoning some of the noble patriots had given him
by way of revenge for the disastrous American defeat on Long
Island in the Spring of 1777.

David stepped inside but, taking no chances, left the door open a little. Through it from below came the smell of coffee. Also the succulent odors of baking and the sound of hearty English voices. "Stab me, sir, if I do." "Egad! Is that indeed so?" "I vow." She caught all those familiar phrases.

Asked David unexpectedly, "Are you for the King, or against him?"

In that moment, the child looked ridiculously old. He was so deadly serious, his small firm chin raised just a little.

Quite as seriously as if she had been addressing an officer of the Crown, Minga replied, "I am a very loyal subject of his Majesty."

David seemed not particularly impressed. "I see."

Minga slipped on her bodice and commenced to tighten its velvet laces. "And you, which side do you support?"

"I don't know. You see, my papa was a Rebel," he answered sturdily, "but my Mamma is for the King."

The boy wandered deeper in the room, smiled in pleasure at the smoothness of a velvet cape flung across the foot of the bed.

"Mamma says I am to be for neither side. It's difficult." He sighed.

"That makes things easier," she told him over the creaking of a wain passing below. "We shall become friends, and then I shall make you into a real King's man."

To her surprise the child started for the door. "No. My Papa was killed fighting for the Colonies. My Mamma says I'm not to take sides until I'm grown up."

The pronouncement gave her pause. Seriously she said, "Then we'll not go against your mother's word. And now, David, please tell your Mamma she can expect a ravenously hungry guest in two shakes of a lamb's tail."

"Do you think you would get there so quick?" David objected. "I have seen lambs. They wag their tails very fast."

Whatever the late David Ashton's political convictions, Minga decided as she made her way down the stairs, he must have left his widow reasonably well-fixed. Her house was clean to admiration, and revealed a taste in the matter of furniture, china and draperies, none of which were inexpensive.

The click of china and the clink of silver grew louder. Halfway down the almost perpendicular staircase, Minga paused to readjust a blue bow which, for some unexplainable reason, she had decided to set in her hair. It had been a long time since she had indulged in such frivolities; but since today was undoubtedly the beginning of a new phase in the life of Minga Allen, why not start in on a brave, cheerful note?

From the foot of the stair David spied her in her pale blue callimanca and, pursued by a fuzzy puppy of uncertain ancestry, went scampering out of sight.

"Mamma, Mamma! She's coming."

At the foot of the stairs the puppy returned suddenly and dashed between Minga's feet. To avoid treading on him, Minga took a hurried extra half stride, so stumbled, then reeled headlong into a tiny sun-dappled dining-room. While steadying herself frantically on the door frame, she heard a chair scrape back.

" 'Pon my word!'' someone burst out, came running towards her.

One hand on the door frame, Minga looked up through the tumble of chestnut strands fallen over her eyes into a young man's ruddy face. This must be Jerry Vaughan! He too, like Lieutenant Petersham, was a dragoon. She could tell that by his short, liberally gold-laced jacket, tight white breeches and jaunty black leather boots edged along the top with gold braid.

Handsome in a bluff, hearty way, he bent, freed her skirt hem from her heel. Golden epaulets, transfixed by the sunlight, created such a blinding glory that Minga Allen's heart gave a big, resounding thump. There were no other figures about the oblong table but two places in disarray revealed that earlier breakfasters had gone.

"Animals should not be kept indoors," he smiled. "I've said—"

When the dragoon officer sensed that she was looking at him in a sort of speechless intensity, he flushed; then, his well-powdered head gleaming bright as freshly polished silver, he made as graceful a leg as Minga had ever beheld. "Servant, Ma'am. May I presume to persent myself?"

"P-pray do." Lord above! There couldn't be browner, steadier eyes in the world. She felt as she had that time when Tommy Schuyler had kissed her under the old crabapple tree. Poor Tommy.

"Captain Jerry Vaughan, very much at your service, Ma'am," he declared in one of those crisp precise English voices she so vastly preferred to the drawling speech so many Britishers affected.

Mrs. Ashton appeared, petite and dainty in a lace-trimmed mob cap. Like swallows darting about a barn her deep blue eyes flickered from one to the other of her two guests. An understanding person, this, and brimming with vitality.

"One perceives presentations are tardy, Mistress Allen. I trust my little dog did not—?"

"I fear it was the thought of breakfast that threw me off gait," Minga explained, attempting to regain her pedestal of poise. "I'll admit I'm vastly hungry—"

She choked off the remark in a hurry. Elegant ladies were not supposed to possess appetites. Captain Vaughan must secretly be laughing at such a disgustingly healthy Colonial. Maybe, maybe not. He was applying himself rather industriously to a rasher of bacon. He used his fork prettily.

Primly, Minga unfolded her napkin, glanced at herself in a mirror set above a mahogany hunting board. She looked flushed, better than in a long time.

Tactfully, Mrs. Ashton suggested, "Would you care to go marketing?"

"Why—why yes."

All the time she spoke she was conscious of Captain Vaughan's look. Heavens! How straight he sat, how palely gold his buttons shone; and there wasn't even a speck on his white waistcoat. The lace at the cuffs and buttons fairly sparkled. A faint smell of horses, however, permeated that of coffee and baking.

Mrs. Ashton had just seated herself as a yellow-skinned colored girl slouched in uncertainly bearing a tray.

"Colonel Saunders and Major de Vaux have already departed to their duties," Mrs. Ashton observed, a small silver coffee pot poised. "The penalty of not bearing a title, I presume," she added with a slow laugh.

His indefinable glance at Mrs. Ashton put Minga on her guard.

"You are not just plain Captain Vaughan, I gather?"

The young officer laughed, shrugged. "I do protest I've had nothing to do with it—beyond getting myself born. Well, Ma'am, if you must have it, the rolls carry me as Captain Sir Gerald Augustus Andrew Henry Vaughan. I've a whole covey of uncles, you see; my mother wished to make sure I would inherit something from each and every one of them.

"By the bye, Mrs. Ashton," he arose and flicked a crumb from his stock, "in your marketing do not venture too deep into Canvas Town. Some ugly happenings chanced there yesterday afternoon."

"Canvas Town?"

"Aye. 'Tis where the refugees, shipless sailors, troll—ahem—homeless women and rogues, cut-purses and the like dwell in improvised shelters of sail cloth or scantlings."

V

WATERFRONT

AFTER the quiet desolation of winter, after the bucolic silences of Brewster and the lifelessness of the country through which she had travelled, New York to Minga Allen appeared a veritable hive of activity. Sight of so many uniforms lent her a fine sense of reassurance.

Mrs. Ashton was familiar with all the regimentals they encountered as they started down Exchange Street.

"Yonder sergeant wearing the sky-blue revers to his tunic," she explained, "belongs to the 10th of the Line, otherwise the Royal Irish. I think that young cornet with the yellow facings must belong to the 38th—a detached officer since the 38th isn't serving here."

"And what in the world is he?" Quite shamelessly Minga stared at an individual in pale buff, skin-tight breeches. A veritable battalion of silver braids paraded down his chest, rank on rank. Above this stroller's wig was a casque set at a rakish angle. A brazen ornament consisting of a death's head and cross-bones flashed bravely in the morning sunlight.

" Yonder *petit maître*," Mrs. Ashton explained, her color rising as the young officer ogled them in passing, "is a leftenant of the 17th Dragoons—Captain Vaughan's regiment, you know."

Never had Minga beheld such a bewildering variety of tunics. The preponderance, of course, was the King's scarlet, but there were many unfamiliar regimentals. Mrs. Ashton, in her sweet and undisturbed low voice, explained them.

"The green coats, for the most part, mark men from Loyalist regiments such as De Lancey's, Colonel Rogers' Royal Americans and Colonel Christopher Billopp's Tories from Long Island. Those three men over there are out of Turnbull's 3rd American Regiment, the sergeant in orange is from the Jersey Volunteers."

Minga felt the widow's fingers tighten on her arm, and her voice went flat as, staring straight past a party of towering infantrymen in tall brass-fronted caps, she said, "These are Hessians."

Advancing with a ponderous, exact stride, was a quartet of broadshouldered privates in bright blue coats, yellow vests and black gaiters. When they drew nearer it became obvious that their heavy, fiercely flaring mustaches had been dyed black.

Minga fired right up at the way they jostled her and her companion and winked. They passed so close one of them rubbed his elbow across her breast. She would have said something pretty crushing if only she'd known what to say. As it was, the mercenaries broke into guttural guffaws as they tramped on, brass-hilted sword bayonets aswinging.

"I don't like these foreigners," she burst out. "There were some others last night at the customs barrier. They were—well, they were rude'."

"These Germans are child-like," Mrs. Ashton explained drawing aside lest mud flying from the wheels of a passing sulky splash her gown. "But they are bad children, of the sort which plague cats, dogs and fledgling birds."

The widow's gentian eyes swung to her companion. "They make a great fuss over children, Miss Allen, and are forever sighing for home; but these Hessians and Brunswickers are to be feared.

"The King's ministers never made a greater mistake than to unleash such brutes on fellow Englishmen." She studied her companion as she added, "Captain Vaughan claims they are even more brutal than Walter Butler's Iroquois."

On Lumber Street they came upon the fringes of Canvas Town. Here hastily-improvised board shacks, tents and canvas hovels stood huddled among the charred ruins of once-fine houses. Several chimney places, rising solitary above the sooty debris, had been restored to their original purpose; and ragged people were busy cooking. Before some of these wretched abodes trunks and rope-bound chests stood in rows. Here and there an occasional piece of fine furniture warped and rotted in the weather.

"Yes, New York is not a pretty place these days," the widow explained. "We all fear that a terrible pestilence will break loose. Many of the Irish drafts are utterly undisciplined; with no fighting going on, Major de Vaux says the Provost-Marshal is hard put to keep them in hand. Hardly a week passes but there are many hangings for murder, robbery, or rape."

Minga could hardly believe this was the New York she had known, the New York of the Vaux Hall Gardens where the catalpa trees flowered. Still, there remained a few familiar sights and sounds. Hucksters were everywhere. One of them, pushing his barrow, drew near chanting not unmelodiously,

"Sturgeons, drums and frost fish! Buy me fine oysters, breams and periwinkles!"

The day was fine and the wind had shifted to the west, tinting the sky a blue so brilliant it almost hurt the eyes. They drew near a house on the door of which the letters "G.R." had been painted in red and with some skill. Mrs. Ashton explained that the doors of professed Rebel sympathizers were so marked.

When a gentleman strode by wearing a brilliant red ribbon in his buttonhole, the widow stated that he wore it as a true King's man—else the public might deem him one of the many Rebel officers on parole and free to wander about New York.

Pasted to shop fronts, ruins and nailed to trees were an abundance of placards and posters, most of them mud-splashed and faded. One, however, Minga saw was spandy new. It read:

For One Night Only
By Permission of His Excellency Major-General
Valentine Jones, Commandant, Port of New York
On Monday Evening and on Thursday Evening
THE CELEBRATED MRS. TURNER
WILL DEPICT DESDEMONA
The Theater Royal Company will
Present a Tragedy called

OTHELLO

The Duke of Venice
Brabantio, a Senator
Othello, a nobleman in the service of
    the Venetian State
Cassio, his lieutenant
Iago, his familiar
Desdemona, daughter to Brabantio
Bianca, mistress to Cassio

Mrs. Ashton laughed and nodded at the broadside, so new the paste had not yet dried. "I see you are curious. For all our troubles, we still have our plays."

"The Lying Valet," it appeared from an older poster, would be offered the next week following. Among the actors would be a Major Moncrieff of the Engineers, a Lieutenant Spence of the Queen's Rangers, and the actresses, one Jane Tomlinson and a Margaret Shaw. Entrepreneur of this production was Major John André of His Majesty's Brigade of Guards.

"I have never seen a theater," Minga was surprised to hear herself saying. "In Brewster play acting is considered—well—" she hesitated and dropped her gaze "—lewd."

As if reading her mind, Mrs. Ashton observed very casually, "Sir Jerry—or Captain Vaughan as he prefers to be called—is devoted to the theatre and has asked me to attend 'Othello.' Alas, my David is having his birthday fête. Perhaps you—?"

"Should Captain Vaughan invite me, I—well, I shall deliberate."

That sounded silly and affected, Minga thought as quickly as she had said it—and, of course, it was.

A breeze, beating in from Hudson's River, gave her stomach a turn. Utterly nauseating was a sudden stench.

"*Pfui!* Is there a slaughterhouse near by? Mrs. Ashton—"

She broke off, puzzled by the sudden haunted look sweeping over the widow Ashton's smoothly pink face. Madelaine Ashton's mind was racing back one, two, three, four long years ago to Boston. Ever so clearly this fetid reek resurrected every last detail of the jail there.

In her imagination she could recall the malodorous street leading to that gray stone structure, the buckets of festering bandages in the halls, the whimpering, sad cries of hurt prisoners. She recalled that ward where her David had lain, his nervous dark features refined by the suffering he made light of.

"David Ashton." The widow thought as they descended the street, "David. My soul's own, my adored David. You, only you I'll *ever love*—truly love, that is."

The thought of him was enough to force her to halt and to pretend to consider some vegetables she had not the least intention of purchasing.

"Of course, David, you understand why I took up with Major de Vaux? There wasn't a shilling to my name—or yours. I'd no choice, had I? Small David, your son, was soon to be born. Tom de Vaux's a gentleman, generous and so discreet. A lesser man would parade his mistress.

"The good Lord knows, Lord Howe, Gentleman Johnny Burgoyne and the rest fairly flaunted their lemans in the face of decent society; but I'm sure no one knows of our—our relationship. Besides, Tom's prodigious good and patient with Davy. Not like you, of course, sweeting. I hope this Allen girl won't guess. She puzzles me, so hard and determined, so bitter and so—so frightened."

Oh, if only David had lived, instead of bleeding quietly to death in the prisoners' ward in Boston jail! She'd have become his true wife. Madelaine guessed she'd never forget the first time she'd seen David Ashton, drunk as any lord, but oh, so gentle and dignified that spring evening before the battle on Breed's Hill.

It dimmed some of this tumultuous April sunshine to realize that she, Madelaine, was no "Mrs." at all, that Davy was by law entitled to just that part of his name.

Oh, this war, this rotten, damnable, interminable war! Four years now of blood and tears and privations. Wouldn't it *ever* end?

With each stride, Minga decided that the evil odor was growing stronger. "What makes that—that horrible smell? A slaughterhouse?" she repeated.

"Yes, of a sort," Mrs. Ashton murmured, tightening the strings of a jaunty little Leghorn hat. "There it is." She nodded at a solid three-storey, red brick building. "It used to be the Middle Dutch Church. Now it is but one of too many prisons here on Manhattan's Island."

"Alms! Alms! Have pity, friends."

Quite a crowd of people were congregated on the brick foot walk separating the former church from the muddy ruts of the street. Below the rusted bars of the window loafed carters in leather breeches and muddied boots, websters carrying bolts of cloth under their arms, farmers in long linen smocks, grubby children and hucksters, with their full-bosomed wives munching bread and cheese. A pair of slovenly sentries stood scratching themselves before red-and-white-striped sentry boxes, eyeing the crowd with bored indifference.

Into the clear sunlight wan, bearded faces peered from the windows of the first and second floors, hollow-eyed, all of them. Their gray features pallid in the daylight, the prisoners crowded for the fresh air.

A few downcast women holding cloths over pitifully small baskets waited patiently before a postern. Some time it might open and they would go in.

From the windows, ragged arms were extended holding out for inspection bits of wood carved into the shape of ships, houses, hobby horses, nigger heads, and boxes.

"Buy! Buy, kind friends!" voices wailed. "Only a few pennies for this elegant box!" "Look, what an elegant necklace o' fine carved beef bone."

When Minga got a good look past the greasy bars her stomach turned as it had not since the night she had come down of a strangary.

"Hi! Look 'ere, fellow, 'ere's a bonny peach." "Give us a kiss, Dolly!"

More faces began looming up out of the inner dark, waxen, yellow or unhealthily flushed. Dirt caked outstretched arms and wrists. The imprisoned wretches tugged each other aside, cursed and fought for a place at the bars. None of the people outside paid much attention.

"What sort of criminals are kept here?" Minga queried.

Mrs. Ashton quickened her pace, would not look up. She was clutching her market basket so tightly that her knuckles showed blue-white.

"They are *not* criminals, Miss Allen! Only poor wretches of Rebels; mostly soldiers captured in Fort Washington, or at the battle on Long Island."

"But—but they can't be. British are always generous victors. Papa said so. Papa was seldom wrong."

"He was right in part," the widow admitted in a curiously low voice. "Parliament *does* send money for their decent care; but William Cunningham, the Commissioner of Prisons, and his fellow devils embezzle nearly all of it."

Long after they had left the prison behind, a poisonous smell lingered in Minga's nostrils. She stole an occasional look at Mrs. Ashton and began to wonder. Why should those always-present sad lines about her mouth and eyes have become engraved so much deeper?

A poorly dressed man of middle age with fine eyes and a generously wide mouth advanced hesitantly, a cleverly designed bird house in his hands.

"Please, ladies, will you not assist an unfortunate officer on parole?" he began in that precise hopeless monotone born of constant repetition. "I—I need to sell this. Unfortunately, even an American must eat. To you perhaps—Why! It—"

Minga saw the shabby figure in patched and shiny red-and-blue stiffen. His pitiful offering was suddenly wrenched aside.

"Why, you—you're Mr. Swazey!" She'd not immediately recognized her old schoolmaster. "Please—" Her fingers dove into her pocket, fumbling for the coins there.

The paroled officer's lean, lanky figure straightened still further, chin sharply outlined. "Well, Mistress Allen?"

"I will buy your bird house, Mr. Swazey. Please, I—"

Mrs. Ashton looked on curiously as the schoolmaster cut Minga short with a sidewise gesture.

"Mistress Allen," he spoke succinctly, "I will sell and *have* sold to the English—they are honorable, if mistaken, enemies— but—" His sombre eyes lit, fairly blazed. "I'll not sell to a Tory! A plague on you and your traitorous sort, Mistress Allen."

Before Minga could catch her breath, Mr. Swazey had turned and had lost himself in a crowd of women buying vegetables from a huckster.

"Well, I never!" Minga's face was hot as fire. "I only meant—"

"Of course, my dear," Mrs. Ashton said. "But Loyalists here are ground between the indifference and the contempt of the British garrison, and the fear and hatred of the Rebels. It is not a pleasant lot. Come, let's get on before the stalls are cleaned out."

A scroll, neatly lettered in gilt paint, presently captured Minga's attention. It proclaimed that within were offered for sale such wonderful mysteries as "Parfum Eau des Fleurs de Venise," "Bloom of Circassier Face Powders," and "Lady Molyneux's Italian paste for Enameling ye hands, Skin, Neck a lovely white. It makes ye roughest Skin like Velvet."

"Oh, look! Let's stop here."

Sober second sight having overriden first impulses, Minga emerged, after a long and delightful hesitation, with a single tiny parcel.

The Old Ship Market whither Mrs. Ashton was bound stood on Peck Slip near Queen Street. As the widow and her tall, young companion neared the waterfront, they drew frankly appraising glances and the audible approval of Naval officers, marines and dock workers crowding the district.

Now the yards and rigging and masts of various vessels commenced to tower almost directly above the housetops, sketching weird designs in shadow. The clean, distinctive odor of melted pitch became mingled with the damp reek of tidal flats exposed by an uncommonly low tide.

The crowd stirred and shopkeepers ran to their doors when the thudding rattle of a drum sounded from the direction of the Battery and of Fort George, which guarded the very lowest tip of Manhattan Island. Arms glistening, a detachment of Royal Marines appeared, swinging up Queen Street behind a single little drummer. Their bayonets sparkled in the brisk April air. Among them shambled a short column of grimy individuals, the clashing of whose chains commenced to penetrate the drum's clatter.

Someone in the crowd called, "Here goes another pack o' rascals took last month in a Rebel sloop off Hatteras. It's a wonder they weren't sent to the hulks."

Though she didn't wish to, Minga couldn't help looking at the captured seamen. To her surprise, one of them in the second rank couldn't have been much over seventeen years of age. An untidy wad of brown-stained bandages had been tied, any which way, about his right shoulder and he was being half dragged, half carried by a big, square-jawed sailor in a striped red and white jersey. He kept muttering,

"It ain't much further, lad. Just keep puttin' yer feet down. It ain't much further, 'fore God it ain't."

When the stricken boy's hollowed eyes chanced to meet Madelaine's, he managed a wan, impudent grin. It dealt a small stab to Minga's composure.

"Pick yer bloody feet up!" A red-faced marine corporal snarled. "Keep moving, ye Rebel dogs!"

There seemed nothing much to say as guards and prisoners tramped on, cleaving apart the onlookers. Up in Brewster, once, a column of captured Highlanders had been marched past Millwood, and the country people had just stood staring until Jameson, the local hog reeve, had picked up a handful of manure and flung it. The Highlanders had tried to fight back but the guards hadn't let them.

"Well, my dear, here we are," Mrs. Ashton remarked. "I do hope the plaice is not all gone. Major de Vaux has conceived a positive passion for it."

"And what does Sir Jerry—er—Captain Vaughan prefer?"

A sparkle shone in the depths of Madelaine Ashton's liquid eyes. "Prefer? Why thoroughbred horses, blond wenches and Yorkshire puddings."

Blonde! Minga felt inexpressibly annoyed. Blondes! Most all of them looked so wan and washed out in the morning hours. A pox on Sir Jerry Vaughan.

VI

INVITATION

MAJOR CLARENCE DE VAUX of the Royal Irish Regiment—otherwise the 18th of the Line—customarily sat directly across the table from Minga Allen. The facings of his tunic were of royal blue and its lace work of white, striped with blue, went very well with sharp, fiery red features. With an Irishman's characteristic independence, he disdained to powder black hair beginning to show silver above the ear.

It didn't take Minga long to notice how Major de Vaux's wind-reddened features relaxed whenever Mrs. Ashton was about, how solicitous he was of her comfort. But he gave her his attention in an easy, confident way—suggesting a good husband rather than an impasssioned swain.

The third of Mrs. Ashton's military guests was a choleric lieutenant-colonel of the Royal Welch Regiment. Colonel Saunders, Minga soon learned, had served many years in the Tropics, in India, Jamaica, the Cape Colony and in Mauritius.

He looked it. The whites of the colonel's eyes were yellow as a canary. Perpetually parched-appearing skin was drawn tight over chin, forehead and cheek bones; he was given to unexpected fits of tremblings, Mrs. Ashton had confided, and on even the hottest days the veteran's teeth would chatter and he would shiver like a frightened colt.

Nearing fifty, Archibald Saunders was one of those unhappy career officers who, had he possessed means or influence in Whitehall, might have had his own regiment. His temper, Minga soon discovered, was as uncertain as it was explosive; but during the first few days of her stay he achieved a gruff fondness for her.

"Damme," he'd growled one evening as he sat sipping a mulled port, "you've got a back-bone to you, Ma'am. No silly simpering airs and vapours. I fancy girls with decision; always have, fact."

"Capital fellow," Captain Sir Jerry Vaughan murmured as the veteran got up, pushed back his chair and stamped out muttering a perfunctory, "Your servant, ladies," which sounded more like a challenge than a salutation.

"Old Saunders has fought the Spanish and French more times than I've fingers and toes."

"Sure and the Colonel's knowledgeable, too," Major de Vaux put in, lighting a long-stemmed yard of clay, "And it's thanking God I am he speaks the language of these heathen Germans."

Sir Jerry looked a little sober, but sang in soft baritone,

> "Oh, to Hesse, Brunswick, Hanover they run
> To fetch across the Atlantic every Mother's son
> Or that poor Milch cow, Britannia, is undone."

De Vaux drew hard on his pipe. "And well may ye sing so, Jerry, me lad. There was the most tremenjous shindy down in Canvas Town last night. Seems some o' them Loyalist refugees are fearful o' our mercenary friends and stole every last musket out o' the guard house on William Street. The dumb-lock Hanoverians there thought 'twas some o' my lads had 'em. Arragh! 'Twas an elegant fight whilst it lasted.

"They say the ould German commandant was down to Headquarters raging this morning. Watch out for trouble. Thim foreigners hate the civilians near hearty as the civilians hate thim."

Sir Jerry Vaughan looked across at Minga sitting very serene and confident, thought her new cerise and rose lutestring gown was mighty modish and becoming.

"With New York so vastly overcrowded, Ma'am, this matter of the mercenaries is bad, very bad indeed."

Colonel Saunders' precise tread sounded in the corridor and he reappeared, very stiff and correct, his French lace jabot sparkling.

He bowed profoundly. "Mistress Allen, I ain't much of a playgoer but—ahem—should you care to attend the play tomorrow—why, there's to be presented a piece by Messer Shakespeare." He glared at her as if on some guilty recruit. Those bright blue eyes, set in yellowed whites, lent him an odd, unreal expression. "Will you—er—do me the vast honor of—ahem—of accompanying me?"

While Minga was still catching her breath, Sir Jerry turned with a quick disarming smile. "You are a trifle late, sir. May I offer my condolences?"

"Eh? What's this?"

"Mistress Allen has already condescended to accompany me to 'Othello.' "

All at the same instant Minga wanted to kiss and to slap Sir Jerry's pleasantly tanned cheeks. The idea! How dare he anticipate her acceptance?

"Why, Colonel. Captain Vaughan is—"

"—Is breathless with impatience," Sir Jerry drawled. "Or did I misunderstand?"

Colonel Saunders blinked. "Eh, what's that?"

Indecision shook Minga. A plague on Sir Jerry! Why couldn't he have asked her before now? She wavered, but ended by giving the straight-backed veteran in the doorway a smile intended to be ravishing.

"Alas, sir, Captain Vaughan has anticipated your kind invitation. I trust, however, you will honor me on another occasion."

Major deVaux commenced to grin when Colonel Saunders' tread faded, his gilded gorget very bright in the candlelight. "Faith, Jerry, 'tis the most gorgeous liar you are," he observed amiably. " 'Twas Molly Moncrieff you invited, and she couldn't come."

"Nonsense!" Sir Jerry said hurriedly, "like all Irishmen you're a trouble-maker, Tom."

Major de Vaux sighed and tapped the dottle from his pipe. "Be that as it may, I'm wishin' ye both a pleasant evening. I'm officer o' the guard tonight, so mind yer ways.'' He nodded, and when he went out into the hallway Mrs. Ashton came hurrying out of the kitchen to superintend the buckling on of his sword.

Together they went to the front door and their voices grew soft and indistinct before he said, ''Good night, Macushla—'' and marched away.

''And what, sir,'' Minga Allen demanded, facing Captain Vaughan with what she hoped to be a look of severe disapproval, ''lent you the temerity to assume that I would care to attend the theater with you?''

She knew very well she shouldn't go to a play, not with Papa dead less than a year and Mamma having departed this world not four months ago. And yet, and yet—when would such an opportunity again present itself? A play wasn't to be seen in America every week, or month, or year, for that matter. Congress, 'way back in '74, had forbidden ''shews or conjuring or play acting of any sort.''

In other times such conduct would have been downright scandalous, but nowadays Violence, Death and Heartbreak were so commonplace that few, especially the young people, set store by the old rules any longer.

''Temerity, my dear?'' The way Sir Jerry—she would always think of and privately recall him so—smiled shortened her breath.

'' 'Tis no temerity,'' he told her with a curious steadiness, ''because, here's an odd fact, the instant I laid eyes on you, I knew that I am going to marry you, Mistress Minga Allen.''

Full skirts gently a-rustle, Minga arose, bent a little over the deserted supper table.

She tried to find the courage to say, but could only think, ''I have felt so too, Jerry. For me you are just the man I have yearned for. Your wide-set blue eyes, your ruddy cheeks with the little scarlet veins in them, your high-bridged nose and wide, sensitive mouth. You represent all that's best and finest in England. Really, dear, the one thing in the world I crave is to be held close against that broad chest of yours. I want you to kiss me until—well, until—well, I want you to kiss me.''

Instead, she heard herself saying, like any silly schoolgirl, ''La, Captain Vaughan, you are indeed impetuous.''

He arose, disconcerted, which rendered him all the more appealing. ''Your pardon, Ma'am. I spoke without thinking, but 'tis true nonetheless.''

Then he reverted as quickly to his former gay, half-mocking manner. ''Perhaps you would care to dine at the Sign of the Lion & Unicorn? Some of our leading lights may be seen at their meat.''

''I shall be charmed,'' Minga smiled and experimentally held out her hand. When Sir Jerry kissed it skillfully, but not too expertly, she felt a lightness of spirit which banished, for the moment, all memory of the Liberty Boys and of Enoch's fierce partisans.

"Tomorrow night," he predicted, catching up his black leather helmet, "I venture will be a night that neither of us will ever forget."

Inexplicably, Minga knew that this would be so.

VII

THEATER ROYAL

THE Tavern's orchestra—two flutes, a harp and a violin, no less—played tirelessly. The exciting odors of many perfumes, of pomatum and snuff and tobacco, the continual glinting of gold buttons and braids adorning a multitude of vivid uniforms, plunged Minga Allen into a delicious haze. Sir Jerry's choice of foods proved imaginative. They sampled green turtle fresh from the Indies, mallard duck, roast suckling pig, savories, trifles and puddings galore.

The two slender glasses of Canary Minga drank heated her cheeks, but she hoped, not to an unladylike redness.

In prodigal profusion, tapers glowed in great clusters; real tapers they were; no common tallow dips which reeked of roasted beef when they guttered.

Sir Jerry pointed out various great personages: Surgeon General Beaumont, who took a deal of interest in the theater and certain of its fairer Thespians; gigantic, beetle-browed Major Robert Rogers, defeated and embittered seeker for a Northwest Passage, was well gone in drink already. Somehow Rogers didn't look in the least happy in his rôle of Tory officer.

Sir Henry Clinton was present for a moment, lean, waspish and fairly bent under all the decorations and orders flashing on his tunic. The officer with him was Major General Valentine Jones, a heavy, good-humored appearing soldier who was, so Sir Jerry said, Commandant of the Port of New York.

"Not a ship enters or leaves New York but by General Jones'

permission. Not a person sails without the endorsement of his office.''

A few lesser celebrities, attracted by the tall and refreshingly healthy young woman at Sir Jerry's side, paused by the table.

''Fancy meeting you here, Jerry, old boy. And how are those wretched nags you dignify by the term of horses?'' ''I say, Captain, do stop by tomorrow for a game of pharo.''

A middle-aged officer wearing a brilliant green tunic turned up in orange drew near. ''Evening, Sir Jerry. I'm told there's to be a little hop at Mrs. Hobson's. Perhaps you'll bring—'' He broke off. ''Why, 'pon my word. 'Tis the lovely Mistress Allen.''

He was Lieutenant Colonel Oliver de Lancey, famous Loyalist and founder of De Lancey's Brigade of Cavalry. Minga remembered meeting him on her last visit to New York; the time she'd visited with Peggy Shawkirk.

'' 'Tis a prodigious pleasure, sir, to encounter you once more,'' Minga declared.

Though Colonel de Lancey obviously felt inclined to linger, Captain Sir Jerry Vaughan made no motion towards a vacant chair. Presently the Loyalist leader shrugged just a trifle and bowed. ''I will be calling on you soon, Mistress Allen. After all, we King's people must stick together.''

''A special friend of yours?'' Sir Jerry drawled after the Loyalist's compact figure had moved on.

Barely in time, Minga recalled it was ever a wise scheme to keep an understudy for every beau a-hovering in the wings. ''I deem Colonel de Lancey most attractive. The last time I visited here he was—well, quite attentive.''

The way Captain Vaughan's lips thinned indicated that he had really meant what he'd said the night before. ''Oh, I fancy Oliver would do for many; but not for you, my dear.''

''Why?''

''He's a good sort, I presume, but still, he's just a common Colonial.''

''A common Colonial!'' Minga stiffened as if she'd sat on a sand burr.

''Eh, what?'' Sir Jerry looked a trifle perplexed. ''But he's not English, y'know. A sound fellow, just the same.''

There was an unexpected tremor in Minga's voice as she demanded, ''So you hold Colonials as inferiors?''

''Oh, stab me, Mistress Allen. I only spoke in jest,'' he hastened to assure her.

Though she knew that really he hadn't, the occasion was far too memorable to be marred by a quarrel.

A trifle hurriedly, Captain Sir Gerald Vaughan dispatched his orderly to fetch up a sedan chair and when the bearers—a pair of towering Brunswickers out to pick up a bit of easy money—halted before the tavern's door, the dragoon captain had become the soul of solicitude. She forgave him, even smiled radiantly, when he opened the chair's glass-mounted door. Standing there in a rich yellow glare from the tavern's windows, Sir Jerry created a picture she would be long years in forgetting.

Carrying his scimitar—or so he called his curved dress sword—Sir Jerry stalked along beside the conveyance, talked light-heartedly through the open window, for the night was unseasonably warm and fine. Probably it was this unexpected balminess which overflowed the streets with strollers; shays, carts, and top-heavy mail coaches lumbered by. More and more sedan chairs hove into sight, mostly travelling in the same direction.

It lent Minga a delicious sense of importance to be riding along like this over the muddy cobblestones and escorted by so commanding a figure. The slow *creak-creak* of the military porters' neck straps sounded a triumphant paean.

At the entrance to John Street the chairmen prepared to swing left in the direction of the theater, but halted when a Scottish sergeant barred the way with a ponderous espantoon.

"I say Sergeant. What the dev—er, the deuce is the meaning of this?" Ice tinkled in Sir Jerry's accents.

"Beggin' yer pardon, sir," said he, saluting like an automaton, "John Street taenight is tae be travelled in one direction only. Or-r-der o' the Provost Marshal, sir."

Vaughan's epaulets shook in a shrug as he turned to the chair's window. "Split me, Mistress Allen, what are we coming to? Who in creation ever heard of a one way street?"

In the narrow street the Theater Royal, as the old John Street theater had been re-christened, caused activity bordering on confusion. All New York, it seemed, was intent on watching one Major Moncreiff portray Othello, the Moor of Venice; or possibly—as Sir Jerry hinted—it was the undeniably attractive features and "figgers" of Maria Turner and Mistress Storer which constituted the real magnet.

On alighting from the sedan chair, Minga experienced the not unpleasant realization of having created a mild sensation. In all directions people were raising quizzing glasses and studying her with an almost insolent deliberation. She did not like such rudeness.

A grizzled officer with canary yellow revers to his tunic said quite audibly, " 'Pon my word! She's a stunner, a positive Venus! Trust Vaughan to flush the really pretty birds."

If Sir Jerry heard the remark, he ignored it by giving succinct directions to the chairmen.

Other ladies were alighting, some of them bony, some of them fat, some of them dressed in the *dernier cri*. Some were wives of officers in the garrison; others, considerably more lithe and merry, obviously were not.

A crier making a clangorous uproar with his brazen bell was endlessly intoning, "In the pit, me lads, 'tis but two shillings; in the gallery, my lords, 'tis a paltry four. This way for the gallery."

The theater's attendants, it appeared, were nearly all from the German regiments and smelt of sweaty leather and rank tobacco. "*Aus*," one usher warned the pair of orderlies Sir Jerry had dispatched early in the afternoon to hold for his occupancy a pair of choice box seats.

The two troopers arose, saluted precisely. "Yessir. Glad you've come, sir," one of them said. "A bleedin'—beg pardon, Ma'am— Marine hofficer tried to scoff 'em."

"Capital! Capital. For the Marines it's *per terram, per mare* perhaps, but never *per egrius*. Ha! Ha!" he laughed quietly, and Minga laughed, too, though she'd no idea what over.

The trooper stood ramrod straight. "Here are two shillings apiece, my lads. You may be able to squeeze into the pit."

Grinning, smelling strongly of horses, the orderlies saluted and tramped out.

Rows of candles wavered and fluttered from four great candelabra illumining two rows of boxes built in front of, and below, the gallery. To Minga's curious eyes the theater seemed huge beyond conception. Excitedly she thought, "When everyone's seated and the pit is jampacked, this theater will hold near on to eight, or maybe nine, hundred persons!"

"Well, my dear," Sir Jerry said, "thank God we've not much longer to wait. Boy!" He beckoned a small Negro garbed in an enormous turban and faded pantaloons of silver cloth, and purchased a pair of oranges. They cost two shillings apiece. Teeth gleaming, the boy produced a knife and nicked off a slice of each. Minga could have eaten hers but Sir Jerry merely held his to his nostrils, in a measure dispelling the sour reek of the populace standing just below and perspiring like plow horses.

The footlight candles were being lit by another of the German attendants, when a stolid orchestra of soldiers in lumpy green chasseur uniforms tramped in and commenced to tune like fifty lovesick tomcats. Flutes, horns, hautboys, trumpets, bassoons, and clarinets squealed deliciously. In a far corner of the orchestra pit a harp was being twanged by a dumpy blond woman.

Presently the orchestra stilled its caterwauling and commenced to play a sprightly tune—the program said it was "a Sinfonia by Toeschi"—that set Minga's best green satin slippers to twitching. None of the tall wigged officers or officials or their ladies paid the least attention; so, to avoid appearing unstylishly fascinated, Minga considered her program.

By the uncertain candlelight she learned that presently, and before the tragedy commenced, Mrs. Hyde would sing a Prelude, "Soldier Tired of War's Alarms." The managers of the theater, it appeared, were Surgeon-General Guy Beaumont and a Captain Delaney.

By the kind permission of Major General Valentine Jones, Commandant, the players would, for the benefit of soldiers' widows and orphans, present "Othello, or The Moor of Venice," by Messer Wm. Shakespeare. Next month, on April 26th, the company would present "The Rivals."

"Here's luck," Captain Jerry drawled. "Seems Moncrieff's sobered enough to play Othello. Fellow's not up to London standards, of course, but still capable, definitely capable."

Completely captivated by her first theater, Minga studied her program, read, among other things, that the scenery had been rendered by a Major John André of the Guards.

"You are creating quite a stir," Sir Jerry observed. Sitting very straight on his seat, he was obviously delighted with the realization.

There were present many prominent Loyalists. All in a moment Minga recognized Pastor Shawkirk; her father's old friend, Nicholas Remind; the printers, Elias and James Desbrosses and Aaron Cohn; and 'way over yonder Katrina Brevoort, as pretty and round-eyed as a month-old kitten—and as stupid, if you asked Minga Allen.

As Mrs. Hyde's song ended, whistles, shouts, and stampings broke out among the tradesmen, seamen, soldiers and artisans in the pit. "On with the show! On with the show!"

Servants commenced to snuff candles in the huge candelabra as, restlessly, Sir Jerry shifted his scimitar, laid it across white-clad knees. "Now that that wretched female is done squawking, let's pray that the tragedy will prove amusing."

VIII

THE BRUNSWICKERS

"Is IT too late for a wee *doch-an-dorrach*?" Captain Sir Gerald Vaughan demanded as they pushed their way through a perspiring but good-humored throng in the theater's lobby.

"Another time," Minga said softly. "Fresh air, I'd quite forgotten how good it is." She didn't think it fitting or good tactics to be seen too intimately in Sir Jerry's company. Besides it wouldn't do to say "yes" to everything he suggested, and she really didn't much care about drinking.

"Very well." Entirely good-humored, he dispatched one of his orderlies, who had stood waiting patiently, in search of the sedan chair.

Under the street lights Sir Jerry's carefully powdered wig looked extra frosty with its black grosgrain hair tie gently fluttering its swallow-tail ends. His features, large-boned but well formed, certainly were windburned.

Minga's heart gave a little squeeze. What an odd, fascinating, unpredictable blend of sophistication and simplicity Captain Vaughan was proving. Why, he'd actually grown wet-eyed over some of the play's more tender heart passages. Here, she felt, was the sort of a man who'd sire lusty small boys who'd grow and grow until they, too, exemplified the strength and grandeur of an England which had endured now for nigh on a thousand years. It must have been men who looked and walked very much like Jerry who had evolved the kingdom's laws, had fashioned her solidity.

Pretty soon Minga's chair appeared, stalwart, blue-uniformed, fierce-mustached Brunswickers and all. Sir Jerry was glaring coldly on a portly colonel of Loyalist troops who seemed almighty put out that a mere British captain should demand—and receive—precedence. Minga felt a moment's qualms. That colonel was peppery old Christopher Billopp. What he had to say went a long way among the Tories on Staten Island—so Papa had said.

When the broad black straps slung over their shoulders began creaking gently, the bearers set off down Queen Street.

Had her life depended upon it, Minga couldn't have said "no" when Jerry observed, "You're right, the night is too uncommon fine to waste indoors, my dear, and it's still early. Shall we ascend from the Bowling Green and view Hudson's River?"

Jerry walked alongside, as before, spoke of his "Grand Tour" through France, Spain, and finally through the Kingdom of Naples and of the two Sicilies.

What wind there was proved mild and fickle and, just as they commenced to avoid the tumbled, fire-scourged ruins of Trinity Church, Minga glimpsed a fragile new moon.

"There's good luck," she thought. "I saw it first out of the chair's right-hand window."

The bearers were sweating, breathing hard by the time an increased chill warned of the river's proximity. Presently their footing grew less secure on the sand of a wide beach and the chair swayed past a series of leafless shrubs and clumps of beach grass.

"That will do, my lads," the dragoon said presently. "Here's sixpence apiece and I shan't want you back within an hour."

"*Danke sehr, Herr Hauptmann, danke bestens!*" the guards rumbled and saluted, fingertips touching towering, mitre-like brass caps.

The taller bearer, a big-featured lout who spoke a little English, said, "At eleffen und vun half, sir, we come back?"

"Correct."

For all her country upbringing, Minga knew better than to leave things that way. "They're to return in half an hour," she revised primly, though it cut her to the heart to think of thirty minutes less with—with Captain Sir Gerald Vaughan. She recalled a line from one of Mr. Shakespeare's plays. "Why, man, he doth bestride this narrow world like a colossus—"

"Very well. A half hour, then," Jerry spoke shortly. Dashed if he was accustomed to being dictated to, although the local blades never took it amiss if the girl were really attractive. Odd. Anything a pretty girl said to an American seemed to stand as law.

The intimate, characteristically masculine smell of pomatum came into the chair with a mild breeze from the direction of Jersey. Jerry put his head in the window and pointed to the river.

"Well, there it is. A vast satin ribband studded with angels' tears all unrolled for my dear lady."

Minga felt her stays all at once grow unbearably tight. She tried to think of something to say but couldn't, only held her hand to the window. Sir Jerry pounced on it like a falcon on a white rabbit; but his hold was warm, not a bit severe or cruel. The tide was running out. Minga could tell that from the flotsam drifting so silently by.

After a little he unhooked his watch cloak—red, with a powder-blue lining—laid it on a conveniently flat rock.

"Shall we—shall we consider the river?"

"I could imagine nothing more delightful," Minga murmured, and never had she spoken truer words.

Though the new moon had dipped out of sight beyond the heights over in Jersey, Minga Allen was not aware of it, nor, for that matter, was Captain Sir Jerry Vaughan. He was deciding that never before had he met a girl even a little like this. For all she was well-bred to her fingers' tips, Mistress Allen affected no silly parlor graces, no fainting airs, and she handled a fan in a fashion reminiscent of young subalterns handling their swords—with an instinctive feeling, yet lacking grace.

He knew now that, in all the span of his life, he could never love another as he loved Minga Allen. A pox on old Uncle Joseph and those estates he'd never leave to a nephew who'd marry a Colonial with never a title to her name. The devil fly off with crabbed, purseproud Uncle Roger and his damned seat in the House of Lords. His hand tightened on Minga's. Aye, let a plague take everything which stood in the way. What if Minga were a Colonial? Let the London people laugh, stare down their silly snobbish noses. Damn it all! This girl was divine.

"Curious," he was thinking, "I love her and I really know so little about her, beyond her father was a country squire, a barrister and a judge of some note. She's been through a ghastly experience of some sort. Come to think of it, she and Mrs. Ashton have much the same look in their eyes at times."

The tide was commencing to turn. The currents made a gentle gurgling among some barnacled rocks down the beach. He hoped those cursed chair bearers had sensed his desires in the matter of staying away; at the same time he prayed they weren't getting royally drunk.

He realized Minga was looking at him, her eyes wondrously large in the half light. They looked like faintly oblique smudges in the delicate pattern of her features.

Jerry Vaughan's hair ribbon fluttered gently as they sat on the rock there in the warm, live darkness. She could feel his silent inspection and that side of her body which was next him seemed to glow. Her breasts filled, rose when his fingers, roughened by recent field duty, closed over hers.

"Minga—my dear, you are indeed wondrously lovely. So utterly, so utterly—fresh and sweet and real." He leaned towards her.

For the life of her Minga couldn't find voice. She just smiled, peered at him, her lips parted a trifle.

He thought of something both tender and clever to say. "My dear, whatever—" but his habitually clear voice became oddly thickened and throaty.

"Oh, Jerry, Jerry darling!" An irresistible impulse drew her towards him and, as naturally as if she'd done so a thousand times, she slipped into his arms. When the hard warmth of his mouth descended on her lips, Hudson's River, the sky and all the stars blended into delicious, undreamt of patterns.

"My heart—" he murmured. Jerry drew her closer. She was, he found, surprisingly solid for all her grace and soft lines; not spongy and flabby like so many of the fine ladies.

Ecstatic instants merged into an indescribable blend of sensations until at length Minga drew back a little. "Please, sweeting—I—I really must breathe."

"Minga—What a wondrously savage name!" he said softly. "Whence did it come?"

"From a friend of my father's, a fine old Indian, named Mingo." Her voice was so faint it sounded like a whisper above the increasing rush of the river.

They kissed again, lingeringly, blissfully, but then he disciplined himself. "Steady on, my boy, mustn't rush the jumps," he thought. "Minga is not to be spoilt."

Damn! The chair men were coming back. He had learned to use his ears here in America. Even a year ago he'd never have noticed the sound of one pebble clicking against another, even less the faint sound of a dried reed breaking.

Something was wrong with British Army regulations, he had learned, too stiff, hopelessly antiquated. Marlborough's dictums might serve to whip the French, perhaps the Dutch too; but these Colonials were a different sort.

Oh, curse it, those chair men had been drinking. They were walking heavily. Never should have given them spending money. He straightened and stood up.

"I am sorry, my dear, I fear me our divine interlude is over."

For weeks, months afterwards, Minga was to recall those words.

The sound of feet grew louder. To Jerry's annoyance the bearers had been joined by two other mercenaries and all of them were jingled.

"Where the devil have you been?" he hailed in his iciest tone.

One of the dim shapes advancing through the beach grass stumbled and fell. Laughing uproariously, two of the Brunswickers hauled their companion to his feet.

"*Grüss Gott!*" The foremost mercenary waved a loose hand.

"Salute, you drunken dog!" Sir Jerry snatched up his tricorne hat, clapped it on his head and, straight as any ruler, stalked towards the offenders.

Minga could see them quite clearly now. One had lost his pointed metal cap, but the starlight shone dully on the little brass balls topping the other three. Swaying and puffing, they lumbered up through the gloom.

"Attention!" Sir Jerry, though of more than average stature, seemed quite small by comparison with these foreign giants. Minga's pulses commenced to throb when the four Germans paid not the least heed to Sir Jerry's command.

"*So, Ernst, Du hast recht ist hier die Mädel—ja—und sehr schöne.*"

"Stay where you are, you sodden swine!"

"*Ho! Ho! Der kleiner Englander sprecht schwer!*"

Fingers closing over sword grip, Sir Jerry Vaughan walked up steadily towards them. How sickly green-yellow the brass on their dark uniforms shone by the starlight.

"*Geben Sie uns das Mädchen.*"

The mercenaries were indeed drunk, Minga realized, dangerously so, and very, very large.

"Hello, Miss. You come mit us?" The chair man who spoke English beckoned, his eyes rolling. One of the others kept sucking in his breath. "You tell Captain to go avay—ve good fellows are—"

"Silence!" Making a soft hissing sound Sir Jerry's dress sword left its scabbard. The blade caught the moonlights, betrayed how pitifully inadequate it was. The dark uniforms looked enormous. The quartet hesitated, conferred briefly in German, then, crowding out acres and acres of starlight, the four mercenaries advanced through the weeds at a lumbering trot.

"Stand back, you dogs! Stay where you are!"

Trouble was not to be avoided so, characteristically, Minga stooped swiftly, caught up a stone from the beach.

"By God, your backs will smoke tomorrow."

Minga glimpsed the leader whip out his heavy sword-bayonet and surge forward— a giant with a thick queue standing out stiff from the back of his neck.

Minga saw Jerry's slight figure lunge suddenly. A hoarse scream, "*Ach! Mein Gott!*" A great dark shape loomed right in front of her. She threw the stone as hard as she could, but awkwardly and with a stiff arm.

"I've missed—" she thought when the missile went *thump!*

against the sedan chair.

The next instant the foreigner had her by the waist. She screamed. Two of the mercenaries were slashing at Sir Jerry who was giving ground but making desperate play with his walking sword. The leader was reeling in the background, cursing and clutching a side that was spattering the starlit sand with big black splashes.

Before she could scream again the Brunswicker clamped his hand down over her mouth cruelly hard. She bit as deep as she could, then she and her captor swayed back and forth. Blood gushed into her mouth, but she was in such mortal peril she never realized it. The mercenary groaned but squeezed her so tight her breath left her and bright streamers of light spiralled before her eyes. This devil—he was tearing at her dress!

As from a great distance, she heard Jerry's pain-stricken voice gasp. "Oh, my God!" Though her vision was gorged and distorted, she perceived vaguely that that shifting pattern of figures struggling down the beach was gone.

"*Verdammte Teufelin!*" snarled the soldier whose hand she had bitten, and threw his weight against her equilibrium. The odors of sweaty wool of some unfamiliar liquor, of rank tobacco filled her nostrils.

"Oh, damn you for—bloody—" Jerry's gasping voice laden with amazed outrage became lost. Fingers were fumbling at her breasts, she could feel nails scoring her skin, as had once a fence rail when she'd lost her balance while walking it tomboy fashion.

The roar of a great gale began to sound in Minga's ears but still she fought frantically, used her knee in a vicious upward drive which drew a whistling gasp from her assailant. She had all but broken loose when another mercenary ran up, wound fingers in her hair and wrenched her head violently backwards.

"*Du! Schnell, Kurt, ihre Füsse!*" A face hideous as a caricature blotted out the sky, a series of buttons rasped across her cheek as she was shoved violently forward; simultaneously her feet were pulled from under her and apart. Her head struck a smooth river rock; a thousand white hot stars came hissing down from the sky to pour into her eyeballs and, amid a dazzling sheet of greenish-yellow lightning, Minga Allen's consciousness departed.

IX

SHARDS

UP HUDSON'S RIVER the tide had run almost full. Now it was lap-lapping up an expanse of slimy mud toward a little, disorderly peninsula of reed roots.

Minga Allen's consciousness returned with terrifying swiftness. How very cold it was! Why? Opening her eyes she saw that stars—not a bed's canopy—were above. What?—When? She tried to raise her head to see where she was, but the effort set everything to wheeling, reeling about.

This must be a singularly vivid nightmare. No, it wasn't. Her head was aching with a steady pounding pain. Yes, and Merciful Heaven, her face, wrists, calves—so much of her was smarting, quivering. She realized now she was cold because her clothing was twisted, torn asunder.

A bewildering congregation of perceptions briefly throttled her reason. The only occurrence faintly like this was that time when, very young, she'd fallen out of an apple tree and had knocked her wind out, or so Dr. Archibald had said. Then, too, nothing had seemed real for a time. Her whole body ached, hurt. Surrendering to a vast fatigue, she didn't try to think. The water purled up, up towards a broken spar she could see lying a foot or two below her. Where had all this begun?

Confusedly, she imagined that the Liberty Boys were again looting Millwood. No. Couldn't be that. That had happened a long while ago and there had been fire then. Now there was only darkness.

Slowly she picked up her mental feet, stopped stumbling. A theater—sedan chair with musty smelling upholstery. She blinked, looked for the conveyance. There it was, sure enough, standing with windows dulled by a mist which came coasting in from the river. What river? Hudson's River. Suddenly she remembered.

"Jerry! *Jerry!* JERRY!"

No sound except from away behind the ruins of the burnt houses. Quietly a sentry called, "Two o'clock and a-a-all's well."

But all wasn't well. Not with Captain Sir Jerry Vaughan. She saw him now, lying crumpled on his back, arms out-flung. A dark irregular pattern marred the sheen of his white waistcoat.

"A-a-all's well!" Like a tiny drop of sound, another sentinel's hail beat through the dark. It wasn't true. All was not well with Minga Allen, either.

Across the blue-black river some farmer's dog began barking, at a cat or perhaps at a muskrat feeding among the great fens guarding the Jersey shore.

Minga's memory commenced to serve her, slowly at first, then more rapidly, more terrifyingly clearly. She could reconstruct that furious struggle during which Jerry's thin blade had woven so deadly a pattern. She could see another crushed-looking outline sprawled among the dead reeds. She began to shiver, dug knuckles into her eyes and twisted her head slowly from one side to the other.

Jerry wouldn't want her now, nor would any decent man. She felt immeasurably unclean. A line from "Macbeth"—a tragedy by Messer Shakespeare—recurred. "All the perfumes of Arabia will not sweeten this little hand." True enough. Only she'd more to sweeten than a hand.

"Jerry!" Her anxiety lent her breath. She was immeasurably surprised to hear his voice answer ever so faintly.

"My poor—they didn't—kill—"

She commenced crawling slowly on hands and knees over coarse water grass, over towards the sound of his voice. Jerry was lying face up. She tried to draw his arms towards him to make him warmer. He stifled a groan. "Don't, sweeting! But—cold—like winter," His eyes were only half open, peered straight ahead, like a blind person's.

"Of course, it's very cold, Jerry. Terribly cold. What can I do?" She had to fight to get the words out when she saw what had happened to his left shoulder.

"Nothin', 'cept—except—"

"Except what—" She lifted herself onto her elbows, batted her eyes in a desperate effort to completely recapture consciousness.

He stirred. An epaulet glistened dully, the other lay some feet away down the beach. Towards it was meandering a dark stain.

"I'm going for a doctor," she said presently.

"Mustn't—people aren't—see you like this." The unexpected strength of his voice was as astonishing as it was encouraging.

"What do people matter? Dearest, you're hurt." How silly to talk thus. As if he weren't near to dying.

"Aye, my dear."

"But you'll live." Minga heaved herself up into a sitting position, found a torrent of words pouring from her lips. "I couldn't help—I fought—like you. Oh, Jerry—Germans are horrible! You see—only you can understand and—and forgive that— You must live, Jerry, I— Oh, dear God!—I love you so!"

Jerry's eyes opened wider, and his hand crept towards her sidewise jerking, like a hurt crab. "Do you, do you?"

Quickly Minga took it between hers, pressed it to her cheek. "I'm going, I don't care what people think."

Jerry Vaughan whispered, "My poor chick. Those foreign swine—they must have hurt you so."

Hurt! It took a bit of courage to lie convincingly: "Heavens, no, Jerry. Oh, I'm a bit bruised, but they ran off."

"Oh, thank God!" he spoke just a little too eagerly. "I was afraid—out for a stretch. Silly. Imagine getting pinked by a couple of—King must be mad—hire such butchers."

Said she, "His Majesty has been deceived. He couldn't have known what these Brunswickers are like." More and more strength came welling back into Minga's body until she was able to straighten her hair and pull together her dress.

"Good girl. I—I love you, my sweet American."

"*I am not American!*" Minga burst out. "I hate America! I'm English."

Jerry Vaughan's clearly defined head rolled on the grayish sand. "There you—wrong, m'dear. Wrong indeed."

"Wrong?" It was frightening to feel his fingers so feeble against her palm.

"Room in your soul—strength in your body—so much distance in your glance—no small island can ever breed that."

Beyond the dead Brunswicker she found Sir Jerry's watch cloak, pushed it under his head. He seemed unaware of her proximity, only breathed heavily.

Like some woman of primeval days, Minga got to all fours, struggled up—up. Erect at last, she swayed. Why was there no tree or fence post within reach? She needed steadying. When a man got drunk, he must feel something like this. The scratches across her body felt like cold wire while, laboriously, she toiled to return her clothing to some semblance of order.

He instructed her to seek the nearest sentry post, Number Ten. The sentry must quietly fetch the sergeant of his guard, and the sergeant was to send for a Leftenant Holcomb who lived on Broad Way.

Though Minga needed her last pittance of strength for other things, she dropped to her knees, kissed him tenderly, tried not to notice the smeared, sodden cloth so oddly distorting the normal outlines of his shoulder. Walking stiffly and staggering a bit, she started off past the overturned sedan chair. God's curse must surely fall heavily on the Brunswickers.

The further she walked, the more she recovered strength. At length she felt able to consider the future; to reassemble the scattered shards of her integrity became a stark necessity. But it wasn't going to be easy. If the folks back in Brewster ever learned about this terrible thing that had happened!

She guessed she wasn't respectable any more. Just imagine Judge Allen's daughter shamed, deflowered. Just a common whore. She halted, covered her face with her hands, and wanted to break out in a wild torrent of tears. No! No, she wasn't; it wasn't right for people to deem her so. Hadn't she fought with every ounce of strength? Fought until—until—

Oddly enough, a remark made by an old colonel who had fought many, many battles in India and Canada and in France returned to her. He'd said to Papa, "I've never yet served under a real general who ain't sometime lost a battle. Only the real soldiers can survive a set-back. Always bear it in mind."

And she had borne it in mind—though she couldn't have been above eleven years of age when Colonel DuBois had visited at Millwood.

Well, it seemed that Minga Allen had lost a battle. What to do? The wind, beating in her face, restored her faculties still more. Good thing Jerry was such a gentleman. He'd pretended he didn't know what those two mercenaries had done with her—or had there been three? It really didn't matter much.

If only Jerry could be saved! She'd be hanged if she was going to live out her life moping and pining like a fowl with the roup. No. What had occurred on the cold sands of the beach must remain a secret which would descend to the grave with her. But would it?

Of course, now she could not marry—ever. Not unless Jerry lived—and still wanted her The more she thought on it, the surer became her conviction he really had been unconscious.

From behind the twisted trunk of a willow a voice thick with drowsiness rang out, "Halt! Who goes there?"

"A—a friend."

"Lor' luv me, a wench!" A British soldier, a light infantryman from the short skirts of his tunic, stepped into sight, his white crossbelts gleaming faintly. "The password?"

"Blenheim. Quick! Send for the sergeant."

"Counter-sign?"

"Quebec! In Heaven's name, fetch your sergeant!"

X

———

Aftermath

On the second day after suffering his wound, Captain Sir Gerald Vaughan took a turn for the better. He felt well enough to clasp hands with some of the many officers who, with concern badly concealed on their weatherbeaten faces, had appeared time and again to inquire how Captain Vaughan was making out.

Invariably Mrs. Ashton told them, "He is progressing as well as can be expected."

And this was indeed truth. General Sir Henry Clinton had detailed to the patient's care his personal surgeon, one Dr. Bolton, who had cupped and bled his patient as consistently as the best physician in England.

If it hadn't been for Madelaine Ashton, who seemed to know exactly what to say—and when—Minga couldn't imagine what she would have done that first night after he'd been brought home, when the candles were guttering out.

Minga stitched mechanically on her tambour frame. She fetched a slow sigh. Poor Jerry. He'd never have the use of that left arm again. The Brunswicker's heavy blade had not only severed many muscles but also had crushed some bones.

Without looking up, Mrs. Ashton said quietly, "I sense your feelings. You see, my—my husband was wounded once—very badly—at the battle of Breed's Hill back in '75." The widow stared into the sleepy little fire on the hearth and must have relived those days which had etched the first tragic lines about her eyes, mouth, and her smooth cheeks. "Mr. Ashton—David—would have recovered if only the hospital orderlies hadn't dropped him and so reopened his wound. His death was so needless."

When Jerry commenced mending on that second day, Minga lost

some of her anxiety, felt so happy it hurt. Though he looked decidedly wan and his eyes were bluish about their sockets, his fever was gone and that great lump of bandages about his wounded shoulder was no longer pink-stained.

When she came in bearing a bowl of gruel, he smiled, waved the food away. "My dear, I am glad you've come. I've been wanting to talk."

"But you mustn't," Minga objected dutifully. "The physician said so." She'd have given her hand for the opportunity to talk for hours; it was so necessary to try to convey to him how very dearly she loved even the least hair of his sturdy red head.

"Minga, sweeting, here's enough of that confounded doctor's meddling." His fingers closed over her wrist, dragged her with feeble strength to sit on a chair beside his bed. "You see—I must talk to you. What with that idiot doctor and his venesections, I—I—well, I shan't leave this bed, ever."

"Oh-h!" She could only stare at him, gray-green eyes gone very round. "Oh, nonsense! You mustn't say such things." She felt sure he was fooling, for he possessed that knack of teasing on the very edge of truth, which renders so many English infuriating at times. "Let me make you more comfortable."

Half amused, he let her fuss about, straightening the cushions on the chair, readjusting the window shutters, refilling the water glass at his side, glancing critically at the imposing row of bottles on the table beside the bed. To cover a sudden sense of deep disquiet, she read some of the labels. Dr. Saxnay's Imperial Golden Drops, Sal Polychristus, Turlington's Balsam, and a bewildering list of others. Everywhere his eyes followed her. In an effort to straighten the puff she bent half-way over the bed and, of course, ended by kissing him.

"Minga, my adored red Indian princess. Come here, dear—and pray don't interrupt. There."

Awed by his almost perceptibly increasing pallor, she seated herself.

His lips, purple blue, tightened a trifle. "I lied to you the other night. I—I knew what those German swine—"

She nodded. "It was sweet—like you—to pretend the opposite."

"Did I entertain hopes of—" he paused, fetched a long, long breath, "of recovering, I'd perish rather than speak of this—but as it is—"

A bad sign, that sigh. Minga knew it. Back in Brewster Dr. Alderson once had explained that that meant a patient's heart was getting tired.

"What—happened there makes no difference in—in my wanting

you,'' Jerry said. ''Even if a—a child—but there won't. Fate couldn't—be so cruel.''

As if his quickened breathing made it imperative, he struggled up higher on the bolster.

''Remember this, dear Minga. From now on—always reach at life with both hands.'' His gaze wandered away, out of the room into the glorious afternoon in the street.

''What is it, Jerry dear?''

''I am recalling those things which I've always wanted to do— and haven't, through fear of one sort or another. Fear, you know, of not inheriting the estate. My father . . . was very strict and often . . . in the spring when I'd wanted to live . . . in a dozen ways . . . I didn't. I wanted to go barefoot like the village children. I wanted to paint landscapes. . . .I wanted to strip to the waist, ride hell-for-leather over the hills; and I didn't do that. I fell in love, wanted to marry the parson's daughter . . . and I didn't do that. Another time I fell in love with my cousin's wife—really in love, you know, and she with me, but—well, I didn't take Camilla. Should have—we'd have been so very happy together.''

He drew a slower sigh and the veins in his half-closed eyelids seemed to go bright blue. ''And now—all over and done with. Now I'll never know—how life would have been had I done any of those things.''

''Jerry! Jerry! For heaven's sake, don't talk so. I—I—You've *got* to live.'' She sprang up. ''I'm going for the doctor.''

''Don't!'' His eyes opened wide, wide. ''No time—believe me, I know. Sit, please, and take my hand.'' When, trembling a little, she obeyed, he continued, ''Yours, my sweetheart, is a vast courage. I know you are brave and, I think, true.'' His voice grew entirely normal in volume. ''Minga, please to remember this, if nothing else. Never marry a man *you can make come to heel.* That's a point . . . necessary among you Americans.''

''But, Jerry, I'm not an American—''

''Ah, but you are,'' gently insisted Captain Sir Gerald Vaughan. ''Try as you will, you'll remain as American as the great forests, the clear wide rivers—the mountains. And now, my dear, kiss me . . . then open the . . . shutters wide. Always said . . .I'd like to go out . . . in a blaze of light, you know.''

Because, indefinably, she knew Jerry was right, she ran to obey. As she let in a great flood of sunlight, his spirit rushed to greet it.

XI

THE CAISSON

THREE o'clock the afternoon of Saturday, April 17th, 1778. The widow Ashton carried herself as usual; gently, quietly efficient. To the observant her great, dark-lashed blue eyes, however, seemed more than ever to speak of ghosts. Sometimes it appeared that Madelaine Ashton must be merely re-enacting a familiar rôle.

As for Minga, she considered, with deceptively impassive eyes, a procession of callers. Staff officers resplendent in trim gold, white, and scarlet regimentals and glistening boots. Two distant cousins out of H.M.S. *Niger*, a major of Marines who'd won a race horse from the deceased at pharo and was genuinely distressed to see so sound a sportsman go. General Clinton's own aide appeared at the last moment, very correct and wearing the Order of St. Andrew.

Colonel Saunders donned all his decorations and remained as a self-imposed guard of honor at his casket. Major de Vaux couldn't have been more overwhelmed and made a great effort to relieve Mrs. Ashton of every possible responsibility.

Major de Vaux entered the withdrawing room in which the two women sat looking blankly out on a caisson sent by the Corps of Engineers. It was drawn by four rangy bays never designed to draw a military equipage.

Dully, Minga realized that a full troop of the 17th were drawn up in Exchange Street. Also attending by courtesy were platoons from the 42nd, the 18th, and the 60th, their regimentals freshly cleaned. Spatterdashes, crossbelts and slings shone white as snow and the brass work on the tall grenadier caps glowed as if heated.

A quartet of sergeants from Jerry's regiment, solemn, perspiring freely, and smelling of horses, guided the coffin down the crooked staircase.

"Ahem." Major de Vaux was biting his lips. "The—the cortège is forming."

Minga Allen rose to her feet. Jerry, she knew, was coming closer

115

as they bore the casket toward the entrance. Close, close. Unbelievingly, she stared on that ugly coffin muffled beneath the dragoon colors.

"He'll never in all this life ever come so near to me again," she told herself. "They're taking him away from me—forever. Oh, Jerry, Jerry! Why?—There was so much for us to share—successes, disasters, glory, children—"

Rigid, erect, Minga remained in Mrs. Ashton's withdrawing room. This was war. First, Uncle Philip. Then Papa. Then poor, sweet, silly Mamma. And the Holden twins. She'd felt terribly about their death in an Indian ambush—even though they had fought on the American side.

She wanted to burst into wild sobs, but she couldn't. This grief was too great, too poignant, for so simple a balm.

Buff, the scarred gigantic Negro who watched over his mistress day and night, looked mighty solemn.

Swaying just a little, she heard the thump of boots dwindle in the hallway. Outside, sounded the sibilant distinctive rasp of swords leaving their scabbards.

A voice seemed to explode—silenced the crowd, which stood gawping, babbling behind the regular patterns of soldiery. "At—ten-shun! At—ten-shun! Reverse—arms!"

Aye, reverse arms for Minga Allen.

Some drums commenced to roll, softly because their snares had been loosened. She felt Mrs. Ashton's fingers dig into her wrists. Startled, she turned. The widow's complexion was colorless.

"Stop them, stop those drums!" she choked. "It was like that—before. I—I— Oh—I *can't stand it!*"

Out in the kitchen little David, outraged because Buff was denying him a part in all this brave show, commenced to whimper. Horses trampling, drums beating, troops parading just outside, and he was being told to "Hush yo' fuss, Mastuh Dave. Yo' Pa would'n' like it."

Colonel Saunders, his beak of a nose redder than ever, appeared, very erect. "We'll be leaving for the church directly—" He broke off suddenly. "Here, here, this won't do."

Before Mrs. Ashton's eyes swam visions of another church, of a rude, unpainted coffin trundled into the church from a huckster's cart. Another funeral—that of a British colonel who had died, name of Fortescue—had come up behind drums—thud-thudding ever so mournfully through the streets. Her hand pressed itself to her throat and things started tilting before her gaze.

Not in the three years and more had she mourned David Ashton so poignantly as this instant. Not that Tom de Vaux hadn't been kindness itself, but daily the child grew more and more like his father—who wasn't Tom de Vaux.

If *only* she and Davy'd been granted the time to marry as they'd planned—but they hadn't been. David, gay, reckless Virginian! From her memory she heard speaking that soft familiar voice—and, amid a swirl of skirts and petticoats, fainted dead away.

"Go with—with Captain Vaughan," Minga cried. "He is—he belongs to you—to his comrades. It may be some time before Mrs. Ashton is restored."

The hall emptied; and hands slapped briskly at muskets when Colonel Saunders tramped out. In the darkened parlor, Minga bent over Madelaine Ashton, waved out Buff and set about loosening the widow's stays. Heavens, what a tiny thing she was. She had kept her figure well, too, and her hair was sweet with the fragrance of pot-pourri.

Minga stooped, lifted the unconscious woman, and quite easily carried her up the stairs. Until this moment she hadn't even suspected how strong she was.

Strong. Aye. She *was* strong now. America had dealt her this final cruel blow. As Minga laid Mrs. Ashton out on her bed and undid her garters, an insensate impatience, a well-nigh unbearable craving to board a ship came upon her. Yes! Yes! She'd sail on and on, far away from America. . . .

An inspiration germinated, sprouted and flowered. Two years back, Aunt Adelina Moffat, Papa's almost unknown youngest sister who lived in the Sugar Islands, had written a curious, misspelled invitation replete with deliciously mysterious implications. She'd go to visit, perhaps to remain forever, with Sir Thomas and Adelina Moffat. In the Sugar Islands surely nobody would know, not even suspect who Minga Allen was—and what she wasn't.

I

The East River

THE MORNING of Monday, April 6th, broke gray and cheerless but not quite so raw as it had been farther north. Over the East River hung such a low mist, it was only with difficulty that one could discern a series of low hills rising to starboard.

In another hour, if the tide kept running as it had, Andrew Warren would, for the first time, behold New York, British stronghold and Loyalist sore-spot.

The mate, a gnarled old man with hands the color and shape of oak roots, came stumping forward, his frayed duroy jacket pearled with mist.

"Ef ye keep yer eyes peeled," he predicted, "we orter make out some men-o'-war a-lyin' in Kip's Bay. Over yander is Horn's Hook."

The steady rhythm of Andrew's heart beats checked when, like some ghostly apparition, a patrol boat loomed up through the fog. The enemy! Her white-painted rail glimmered silvery in the dim light. She'd half a dozen Royal Marines aboard under the command of a tall sergeant who crouched beside the steersman in her stern.

It gave the Indian-faced voyager quite a turn. Last time he'd seen scarlet, short-skirted tunics, black gaiters and cross-belts he'd had to fight for his life. They were hard customers, those fellows who wore "*Per Terram, Per Mare*" on silver plaques set on the front of their low scarlet caps.

One or two of them craned their necks at this insignificant ship, but the majority only huddled into their collars, protected the priming of their short-barrelled fusils under the pits of their arms.

The sergeant arose, cupped his hands and, swaying to the barge's motion, bellowed, "Vessel ahoy! where d'you come from, where you bound?"

The pink's master parted a patriarchal beard, shouted convincingly enough through a leather speaking trumpet, "Pink *Jeanette* Cap'n Crane, out o' Newport."

Newport having been in British hands since the past year, it was logical that this loyalist pink should be putting into New York.

118

"Heave to," ordered the petty officer in the barge and, presently, that ungainly craft bumped alongside and its crew tossed dripping oars in uninterested fashion.

Scowling, the sergeant clumped aboard and scanned without care the vessel's clearance forms, bills of lading and manifests. The pink's crew grinned. This was a familiar routine. Was not the *Jeanette* among certain craft favorably listed with one Captain Cubitt, an officer who enjoyed an income greatly in excess of his pay? That he held a post in the port-commandant's office might have gone far to solving the question.

Joe Atherton came up on deck looking vastly relieved. His blunted features still lacked a good measure of their normal color as he came swinging up to his new captain. There, by God, was an officer with the juice of command in him—a real Navy man. Last month he'd said—a bit jingled to be sure—"Come with me, Joe, and you'll wind up a petty officer or my name ain't Warren."

Joe had been mighty curious until Mr. Warren explained he needed someone as could talk like a Britisher, and act like one, but who could be trusted to go along on a very secret mission.

"My Uncle has forbade my fetching anyone along from Boston," the lieutenant had said, "but *I'm* commanding this cruise; it'll do me well to have another man-o'-warsman along."

He wondered why the bleedin' 'ell Cap'n Warren, as he'd taken to calling himself, had said they must both of them talk and act like Tory refugees. He was pretending to be a Loyalist out of the Maine district of Massachusetts. The patriots had been extra busy up there of late.

Well, it wasn't for a rating to question the quarterdeck so Joe had kept his lip buttoned. Right now he was praying to God none of his old shipmates would be in port.

A gull, ghostly in the thinning mist, coasted by the bowsprit, mewed and let go a load of lime right over the patrol boat. The whole crew of the pink roared at the futile curses and fist shakings of the marines. Their scarlet jackets weren't nigh so pretty now. Captain Warren was laughing, too, when he beckoned.

"Yes, sir, Mr. Warren, sir."

"*Captain* Warren, you chuckle-head," Andrew corrected in a savage undertone. "And for the love of God don't knuckle your forelock like that. You're not a man-o'-warsman any longer."

At length the frowsy little coaster dipped her frayed red ensign and proceeded on her course down the East River.

Flocks of black and red-headed ducks, migrating northwards after their long, sleepy sojourn in Georgia and the Carolinas, arose reluctantly when the coaster bore down on them, went speeding off on wings which whispered softly above the moisture-speckled rigging.

Fishing boats manned by ragged, hungry-looking crews began to pass, beating their way upstream. They gave the *Jeanette* hardly a glance.

Presently, the mist lifted. Captain Crane came clumping forward, his tobacco-stained beard beaded with tiny drops. Beneath his air of boisterous good fellowship, he was nervous. Well he might be. Under the cargo and unlisted in the manifest, lay two dozen sacks of wheat and corn, six tubs of butter and sundry other foods. Such were greatly in demand by the hungry garrison and troops of occupation. Captain Cubitt would provide them with such extra luxuries—at his price. Two-thirds for Joshua Cubitt, one-third for Abezeel Crane—that was the arrangement.

It wasn't fair, though, Captain Crane was thinking. Suppose he got found trafficking with the enemy? The Continental authorities at Boston would surely stretch his neck four inches and no mistake.

"Well, sir," he predicted, "inside another glass we'll be made fast to our docks." He spat scornfully. "And don't be expecting too much of New York. Of all the pox-ridden, thief-run, Tory-infested hell-holes along this hull coast, New York is the worst. A plague out o' Egypt on it!

"Take New Haven, now, where I hail from. *There's* a town with a future. Wouldn't wonder if it grew to be near as big as Philadelphia, some day. But New York? Hell, 'twon't never amount to shucks. Too hard to get to the mainland. What's more, the plagued place can't be defended."

There was some justice in this last remark. Even the great General Washington, for all his painfully contrived fortifications, had been driven out, and roundly trounced by a force little greater than his own. That the Americans must have made serious efforts towards defense, Andrew saw at a glance. Along both shores of the East River raw earth and embrasures appeared among the woods and fields, marking the existence of batteries, flêches and demilunes.

"No, Cap'n Warren," Captain Crane persisted, "if you asked me my say, I'd set a torch to yonder Tory rat's nest and burn what's been left after that fire of two years back."

"Fire?"

"Aye," the skipper said, wiping a button-shaped nose on a cuff which had served for that purpose all too many times. " 'Twas quite a fire; burned nigh on a third of New York."

"Who set it?"

Captain Crane squirted tobacco juice over the rail to leeward. "Well, friend, the British claim 'twas the Americans, and the Americans claim 'twas the British; so it's a fair swap." He nodded to himself. "If you ask me my say, I'd bet it was some o' them plagued Tories. Yessiree, 'twas quite a fire. Flames leapin' two cables' length into the air, the British cursin', the people prayin' and the rabble looting. I was in port then. Greatest sight o' all was when the spire of Trinity Church fell. Sparks flew nigh half a mile into the wind. Pity the whole durned place didn't burn."

Queer talk, Andrew mused, for a man who at the moment was fetching aid and succor to the enemy. Most likely Abezeel Crane didn't see it that way. Almost nobody did. Anyone who could garner in a few odd pounds and shillings in these days did it. Besides, both sides indulged in smuggling.

Every few nights quite a store of British powder and shot went sailing out of New York in whaleboats which sped down the Sound and were out of sight before dawn. They came by the dozens from Fairfield, Mystic, Milford, New Haven. Of course, the powder was later returned—from guns and muskets fired at the Ministerial troops and King George's well-hated German mercenaries.

They neared a stately brown and white frigate. One could see the neat, scarlet bands encircling such of her guns as were run out. The greater part of the man-o'-war's battery was behind ports painted gray.

"Look there, sir," Atherton cried in quivering tones. "There they are, the bloody man-killers. Gawd, how I wish this was a ship o' the line!"

Blood commenced to pump and thump at Andrew's wrists when, by the gray light, he discerned the awe-inspiring silhouette of a towering three-decker. The *Asia,* 64 guns, was a third-rater of the line of battle.

Lying to her moorings also loomed the *Roebuck* frigate. Downstream lay the *Brune*, 32 guns, her blue and yellow sides glistening with moisture.

The sensation of passing peacefully under the very guns of ships such as he had only seen previously through battle smoke was disorienting, grotesque. Anchored at intervals along the Long Island shore were more of the King's Navy, an impressive, and a disheartening, array when one paused to remember that this was but a fractional part of that power against which was pitted the feeble and disorganized Continental Navy.

"Nao that one nearest the shore," Crane pointed out, "is the

Experiment. Folks claim the Southerners near blew her to bits down to Charleston. Allow they're tellin' the trewth fer once. You kin see her masts and top hamper are spandy new.''

As the sun came out, the windows of farmhouses around the village of Harlem materialized to reflect its glare. Occasional rickety docks with tall stands of trees behind them began to line the water's edge. Off to the *Jeanette's* port side Long Island was displaying such hints of greenery as were becoming to early April.

Wind, beating in from the south, was commencing to convey an odor which grew stronger and less pleasing each instant the *Jeanette* descended the East River. Several of the crew commenced to sniff. One of them pinched his nose.

"Gawd, what a stink. It's worser'n Gloucester in July.''

Curiosity piqued, Andrew turned to Captain Crane.

"Slaughterhouses?''

The pink's captain nodded and the prominent lump of his Adam's apple worked twice, thrice. "You might say so, only 'tis humans, not beasts, that perish on them Christ-cursed prison hulks in Wallabout's Bay.''

Like a pall which erased the last traces of pleasure at concluding the cruise, the reek of rotting flesh and the stench of hundreds of unwashed bodies enveloped the pink. Presently, the prison hulks became visible, weatherbeaten, riggingless, their many-decked hulls ominously black against long rows of sandspits and the freshness of meadows on Long Island.

A boat bearing a tattered blue ensign was pulling out to the nearest prison ship. Musket barrels glinted bravely in her bow and stern, but in between crouched a dun-colored group of men—prisoners.

With half an eye Andrew could tell that for size New York wasn't a patch on Boston, but the place looked more elegant and was at least as busy. During the past half hour all manner of chips and bits of lumber had come floating out from a series of shipyards hard at work above the town itself. On a pier close by, a detachment of troops in blue and orange stood patiently awaiting transportation to a chunky brig lying close inshore.

"There's them Goddam' Hessians,'' remarked the boatswain and spat resoundingly towards them. "Heard tell they wrapped a prisoner—a sharpshooter it was—in a blanket, soaked it with rum and set him ablaze.''

"Aye. They're hard people whether they're Waldeckers, Brunswickers or Hessians,'' agreed another.

At length Captain Crane took the tiller himself and headed straight for shore. There, smoke from hundreds of chimney pots was climbing slowly into the sky. Off to the right some geese and goats and a few cows were foraging in a field.

"Where are we headed for?" Andrew demanded.

"Beekman's Slip."

It was quite a moment; within a few minutes he would be ashore, in the heart of the enemy's main base in America. One mistake and he'd be dead.

"Way enough!" yelled the mate, and the pink's mainsail banged down any which way, as the *Jeanette* nosed into a wharf stacked high with bright yellow lumber, black barrels and brown cases.

"Ahoy, there!" A sentry in a short red tunic removed hands clasped over the muzzle of his King's Arm musket and started forward. A burly individual in patched brown breeches and a watchcoat also came stumping out.

"Let be! Let be! This vessel's expected."

The guard stared suspiciously a moment, then nodded and returned to the lee of a stack of yellow pine planking.

II

HENRY OAKMAN

SPRAWLING, raw and raucous, New York town appeared badly overcrowded this softly warm April morning. A rain squall, passing earlier, had glossed hundreds of roofs a dull silver, had left puddles behind in the rutted street—to the great delight of sundry hissing gray geese and white ducks. Dogs lapped eagerly at these muddy little pools. Fresh water was hard to come by in New York, a fact attested to by the presence of peddlers driving carts or hauling barrels.

"Water!" they bawled. "Sweet fresh water! A penny the gallon!"

"Where away, sir?" Joe Atherton was grinning, staring delight-edly once they had passed over the *Jeanette's* rail and had set foot on the dock.

"King's Arms." Andrew had selected that hostelry on purpose as the most out-and-out Tory tavern in town.

Crikey! thought Atherton. This *was* a town. Reminded him a bit of home, of Hull, and of Bristol where the weatherbeaten merchant ships came in to rest and to heave down. To recruit their crews, too. Lord, it seemed like an age ago that a press gang had cornered him in Prince Street.

It seemed familiar and, strangely enough, not unpleasant to behold scarlet-coated soldiers and marines swinging by, to hear the clean-clipped accents of the officers who stalked along the muddy footpaths like the lords of Creation.

The sight of blue and brass gave Joe a nasty turn, though. Suppose H.M.S. *Niger* or the *Ariel* were to make port? In the eyes of dozens of their officers and ratings he undoubtedly stood as a deserter. Some of the warmth went out of the sunlight and, bending his head under his meagre sea bag, he moved close as Cap'n Warren beckoned a shiny black barrow man who lacked an eye and three fingers of his left hand.

"To the King's Arms—how much?"

"Dat long weh, Baas, berry long weh," sighed the Negro, scraping mud with the side of his bare foot. "T'ree shillin'."

"Two—"

"Yassauh, Baas." And the black dumped Andrew's sea chest onto his barrow.

"*Baas*?" Andrew tested the word.

"Meanin' no disrespect, sir, that's Dutch for 'master'!" Joe supplied. "Heard the word at the Cape when we sailed for India in '73."

"Good. Well, let's shove off and avoid this mess."

A swarm of barrow men, carters and porters, spying the vessel making fast, were converging on the wharf, with a swarm of beggars, venders and runners for various taverns and brothels at their heels.

Clutching under his sea coat a portfolio containing the ship's papers Hosea Warren had procured, Andrew started after the barrow man. A few paces in his wake he was followed by the increasingly uncomfortable-appearing Joe Atherton. He'd best keep a lively look-out, too. Some of the *Andrew Doria* and *Lexington's* prisoners must have been exchanged, and it wouldn't enhance the *Evergreen's* chances of reaching Montego Bay were he to be recognized. Pigs, flocks of geese and innumerable stray dogs explored the muddy expanses of Water Street.

In a shipyard to the little column's right a detail of British sappers, stripped to their gaudy scarlet coats, were hewing away at the ribs of a hulk drawn up on the beach.

"What are they up to?"

"Dey's huntin' fiah wood, suh," explained the porter. "It's skercer than a kind word in dis town."

A cart appeared, creaking along at a slow walk. The horse between its shafts was struggling for the bit. Obviously, it was in good spirits and wanted to run.

"Can't you move that damned cart faster?" demanded a gentleman riding a tall black horse.

The carter, leading his horse through the noisome ooze of the street, turned a sullen, bruised-looking face. "Naw. It's agin regulations. Ain't no waggin 'lowed to travel faster'n a walk. Next thing the British will be tellin' us how to pick our noses."

There were trenches at the end of nearly every street, Andrew noticed, and little demi-lunes and flêches at every strategic point. The British, it seemed, had added to the already elaborate system of defenses erected during Washington's futile defense of the island. Water Street presently became Dock Street and wound its malodorous way past a succession of dingy sail lofts, chandlers' stores and warehouses.

At the foot of Beekman Street a sail ferry was loading passengers and freight. Soon it would go tacking over the Sound River to a scattering of houses which had been called Brookland but now was becoming known as Brooklyn.

The Negro settled his shoulders under a greasy strap joining his barrow's hands and wheeled past Burnette's Key and a small slip-shod brick building marked "Brownjohn & Son."

Presently, several squads of scarlet-clad dragoons wearing caps boasting skull and bones insignia came clattering up. Heedlessly, they scattered pedestrians, livestock and commercial traffic.

"I heard there was a great fire here. Where is the burnt section of town?" Andrew inquired presently.

"Hit's on de west side ob dis heah Island," the barrow man said and halted, glad of the excuse to run a frayed jacket cuff over his forehead. "Dat wuz sho' a sight, dat fiah. Smoked near a week and wiped out lots of folkses' livin's."

The further the little party advanced into New York the more crowded it appeared and the more poverty-stricken. Huddled beside the stable of an abandoned warehouse a woman crouched, cooking something over a badly-made open fire. Under one arm she clutched an infant. Three ragged young children stood about.

From the door of a wretched hutch contrived of cases and a

condemned topsail, a man, wearing what had once been well-cut garments, stood staring out over the river with anxious, discouraged eyes. The children were whimpering with cold and hunger.

"I say, Snowball, wot's the matter with them?" Atherton demanded of the porter. "Why don't they go somewhere?"

"Dey cain't," the Negro announced. "Nossah. Dey's King's people drove outer Jersey by de Rebels. Dey's a mint ob dem heah in N'Yawk, suh. Hundreds and hundreds ob de King's people all de way fum Albany an' Noo London."

There seemed to be any amount of these hopeless, wretched refugees. Groups of them lived in crude plank cabins, camped beneath old cart bodies or under old tarpaulins stretched across broken yards and bowsprits.

It commenced to rain again, gently at first, then harder until the backs of passing horses began to steam. The barrow man dodged into an archway, and there the three waited until the downpour ceased lashing and whitening the surface of the Sound River.

The King's Arms, it appeared, stood between Crown and Little Prince Streets and was a favorite rendezvous for the officers from Fort George. Fraunce's Tavern, located not far away, seemed a jollier spot by far and Andrew was tempted to go there, but Uncle Hosea's injunctions remained engraved large on his memory: "You must act a King's man through and through. Remember, you were born, bred Loyalist and stand ready to die for George the Third and his Crown."

Striding along the steaming brick footway under some budding catalpa trees, Andrew Warren swallowed hard. It wasn't going to be easy for the *Lexington's* former lieutenant to parade as a dyed-in-the-wool Loyalist.

The impostor kept his eyes about him as he followed the barrow man. Not since he'd been in Toulon had Andrew beheld such a galaxy of uniforms. Hulking, dull-faced German mercenaries plodded by in dark blue turned up in red or yellow. Because of high mitre-like hats, faced with gleaming brass, they seemed gigantic.

There were also green-uniformed Tories boasting dirty white facings and cuffs to their tunics, a few orange-coated Tories belonging to the King's Loyal Orange Rangers, and men of the Jersey Volunteers wearing green and black with white crossbelts. Somehow, none of the provincials seemed really at home in their regimentals; by comparison, the scarlet-coated officers and men of the regular establishment appeared positively dashing.

Andrew recognized, as the barrow creaked into Crown Street, the 18th and 60th Regiments of the Line, the former swaggering and very proud with their pale blue facings, white waistcoats and lacework of white with a blue stripe. Atherton now was walking very close and said nothing.

What chiefly interested Andrew, however, were the foreign troops—men from Hanover, Brunswick, and Hesse-Cassel. Though their uniforms were superficially neat, when one walked to leeward one could tell with half a breath that their bodies must be long unwashed.

Andrew got a bit of a turn to read a mud-splashed placard.

Now for St. George! All gentlemen
VOLUNTEERS
that are free, able and willing to serve
His Majesty King George
in His Majesty's American Regiment which is now on
immediate Service and commanded in Person by their
gallant Colonel Edmund Fanning
Let them repair to the King's Head Tavern at 45 Brownjohn's
Wharf where 2 sergeants with recruiting Parties, very lately
from the reg't constantly attend. Bounty 3 guineas
No militiaman shall be taken or any apprentices without
their Friends' consent.
Boys wanted for Drummers.

"Here yo' is, Baas," the Negro announced, scraping mud and manure from his bare feet against the curbstone. "Sho' is a mighty elegant hostelry, suh, Baas."

His hopeful smile widened when he saw the extra sixpence Andrew dropped onto his pink-skinned palm. "Thank you, Baas, thank you. Hope yo' lives long time, Baas."

"Say no more. It was a longer trip than I'd imagined, my good man," Andrew mimicked the drawling accent of those British officers captured aboard the *Racehorse*. He guessed he must have a good ear for language, perhaps to compensate for his woeful clumsiness with figures.

"Mornin', Baas, mornin'. Carry yo' chest, suh?"

Two colored boys came running out of the King's Arms and grabbed up Andy's sea chest. A moment later he found himself haggling with the proprietor, a huge, pimpled individual whose nose was reminiscent of a rather hairy and overripe radish.

The publican, so bent by some racking disease that he resembled a hunchback, wore a spotted blue-and-yellow-striped waistcoat and

a wig which looked like a last year's bird's nest knocked out of a tree
by a gale.

"For two shillings what sort of a suite can you give me?"

Andrew stood on his dignity while Joe Atherton gawked nervously about.

"Suite? Two shillin'?" The landlord sniggered, blew his nose
with his fingers. "Why, Mister, that's for only your meals. Your
bed's that again."

"What! Four shillings for bed and board?"

The innkeeper shrugged, started back indoors after a brace of
Highland officers who came swinging by.

"Aye, and mark you, there'll be only two others sharing the
bed."

"Two! Are you mad?"

"Nay," grunted the publican, pausing on the steps. "We've
often had four in the bed and they been mighty grateful for the
shelter. Sir, you must take it or leave it."

He had, Andrew perceived, to take it. Still, the situation might
get him acquainted, in an innocent way, with some British officers.
Possession of general information would be a necessity. When he
applied for clearance and sailing permits the mentioning of a good
name or two should expedite matters.

Curious, this business of entering an enemy town, Andrew
reflected as he followed the Negro up a wide, resounding staircase.
One held the impression that every passerby knew him for what he
really was, that any minute the provost guard must come circling up
to pounce on him. Tomorrow the bell on the New Gaol might toll as
another hanged Yankee spy kicked out his life, perhaps for the
especial amusement of the monstrous Commissioner of Prisoners,
his mistresses and friends. The whole length of New England it was
common gossip that William Cunningham frequently indulged in
what he facetiously termed "necktie parties."

Joe Atherton meanwhile made his apprehensive way to a sailor's
rooming house, recommended by the Negro barrow man.

"I'll report morning and evening, sir," he promised. "And I'm
'oping we'll not delay long in sailing, sir."

The room offered Andrew proved reasonably clean and its bed
was all of five feet wide, so if his bedfellows weren't too portly,
three of them should be able to sleep. He saw his sea chest stowed,
and departed in search of Henry Oakman.

"So old Hosea Warren's finally found him a captain, has he?"
Henry Oakman muttered, scratching his nose but skillfully avoiding
a wart on its end.

Peering out from behind a stock of horse collars, he looked like nothing so much as a groundhog. The harness-maker's eyes, when he raised them from Andrew's credentials, were like a rodent's, small, beady and very alert.

Andrew fired up right away. "You refer, I believe, to Mr. Hosea Warren. I'll trouble you to mention my uncle with more respect."

Henry Oakman's prominent ears quivered. "Well, now I never!"

Abruptly Andrew remembered, changed his tone. This cruise he was damned well going to mind his tongue. Smilingly, he resumed, "It is indeed a pleasure to make your acquaintance, Mr. Oakman. My uncle sets quite a store by your good opinion."

"Your uncle, eh? Oh, whyn't you say so?"

The chandler emerged from behind the counter, hands clamped over a big, half-globe of a belly. Over it a knitted gray woolen waistcoat was stretched so tight it had shed two of its greasy wooden buttons.

"So, you're his nevoo. What's all this about the *Evergreen?*"

Andrew looked about, found the shop deserted save for an old beagle bitch nursing a litter of puppies in a box set next to the mantelpiece.

Andrew told him. "The main thing," he concluded, "is that I get to sea as promptly as may be."

Henry Oakman dug a long fingernail into his ear, briefly inspected the gleanings, then tugged his breeches' top up and over the half-globe. "Shouldn't wonder but you'd b'tter. Your way o' talkin' may fool a Britisher, but it won't a smart Tory. You'd better lay mightly low 'til you sail."

He cocked his head to one side, tugged meditatively at his ear lobe. "Mister, fer your own sake, try to walk more like a merchant-man. You ain't parading no quarterdeck now, best remember that. The Provost hanged some fellers from Maryland last week; tried to cut out a schooner, they did, but a contrary wind came up."

The harness-maker sighed, commenced coiling a trace. "Lord, Cap'n Warren, that were a pretty hangin'! Nice and warm—the folks took their suppers along. First man condemned must ha' been a lawyer once; he made such a pretty speech about what the Frenchmen are goin' to do to help us drive the Britishers away."

Andrew nodded, said, "The French king's fleet is near as big as the British."

Henry Oakman gave his caller a shrewd glance. "So? Then I wish his was twice as big."

"Why?"

The harness maker winked. "On account of what ships the French King's got ain't half so good as King George's and don't mistake me; I want the English and their Lord High This and the Admiral Sir That to get knocked to hell out of America—and their fancy whores, too. Still, I tell you, Cap'n, them there French— well, me and a lot of folks here figger them furriners ain't to be trusted. Me, I'd liefer see us hang or win, as the case may be, in our own way."

Andrew wanted to speak right out. People in these latitudes were so damned ignorant about the French. *Nom de Dieu!* Why, in Toulon harbor alone he had seen *ten* great 74-gun ships of the line, swinging to their moorings. Any two of them had mounted more guns than the whole United States Navy.

Nor were these great high-sided sea-going castles all. Louis the Sixteenth possessed a vast fleet of fast frigates, razees, brigs, sloops and corvettes designed with a grace of line no Englishman could approximate.

In his mind's eye Andrew saw again the parade ground below the Vieux Port at Marseilles. There had been a big review that day—it was the little Dauphin's birthday—steady marching troops, breath-takingly impressive, swung by, regiment by regiment, their white uniforms turned up in claret, scarlet, green, azure, and orange.

Even now he could recall how their muskets and side-arms had shone like the prisms of a chandelier in sunlight. Along the Champ de Mars had rolled dozens of great cannon drawn by such sturdy horses as were bred in the north, in Picardy, Normandy and along the border of the Low Countries.

Oh, what obstinate fools were Americans like Hosea Warren and Henry Oakman. Couldn't they realize that the French Alliance had secured for the struggling new nation the services of whole armies of seasoned soldiers fit to stand against England's best? The answer was, of course, that in the old Colonies one had never heard of French victories—only about the British successes. Well, there was no use arguing. In due course America would learn how much the French Alliance would go towards defeating the British.

"You've a crew waiting," Oakman said, stitching busily at a breeching.

"And have I really?" Suspicion started at Andrew's mind. Why should anybody take on readily so onerous a task? He didn't like this, not at all; but he wasn't going to show it.

Oakman rubbed a length of flaxen thread with a scarred black lump of beeswax.

"Mr. Isaac Roosevelt got 'em together. He's a main smart one, is

Mr. Roosevelt—sharp, gets his own way even when you figure he is giving you yours.''

''I would like to see the *Evergreen*.''

He was damned if he knew what to make of Oakman, Mr. Roosevelt and this town of New York. Boston, Portsmouth, Charleston, and half the ports of Western Europe he understood, their smells, sights, customs—and women.

''At Galloway's yard.'' The saddler glanced at a battered, dusty old Dutch clock, then from a rusty nail removed a rabbit-skin cap which lacked most of the fur along its edges. From a drawer under the counter Oakman produced a brass door key big enough to stun a calf with.

''Well,'' said he, ''since you're set on the idee, let's go take a look at the old girl.''

III

GALLOWAY'S YARD

TO SEE the *Evergreen* once more gave Andrew quite a turn. He'd have recognized her anywhere for the trim craft he'd watched being launched in Boston only six years back—a whole life-time ago by some reckoning. His uncle's vessel wasn't pretty now. She had been re-painted chocolate brown with a sloe-green streak, and, unimaginatively, some British rigger had shortened the little brig's topmasts. This was a real pity, Andrew thought, because the alteration must certainly hamper the *Evergreen's* handiness to windward. It was encouraging, though, to note that her bottom, seen through a clear flood tide, was sweet and clean.

A gang of Negroes was busy caulking her decking. In the tall young officer's ears the *clink-clank* of the hammers on the caulking irons played like the tinkle of heavenly harps.

''Well, Cap'n, there's your vessel,'' Oakman observed in an undertone. ''And if only her canvas was as sound as her hull, I'd not worry a mite about your cruise.''

Andrew hardly heard the comment. His fingertips were beginning to tingle. There, lying to Galloway's wharf, was *his ship—HIS SHIP*. This vessel was his to command. He could sail her to the East Indies, to Chile, to Europe or Africa if he so chose! Free again! Yes,

independent. He drew a deep breath. *This* was *his* command. He
was her captain—sole arbiter of her destiny.

In two, or at most three, days now, he'd be taking her down the
river into the lower harbor, then through the Narrows, out to open
ocean. Andrew Warren paused at the lower end of the wharf looking
at his ship. What pages would the *Evergreen* write in his life's
history? Would this brig fetch him back to Boston comparatively
rich, re-established, and with a future?

Suppose matters went against the brig? He guessed most likely
he'd dangle and choke from the main-yard of some British cruiser.

"Yes, Cap'n, this here brig's sound as a sovereign," Oakman
chuckled, leading out onto the wharf. "Wait 'til you spy the prime
cargo you've got. Heh! Heh! It'll bring you a small fortune in
Jamaica. Saving some firkins o' butter that's over-due from Long
Island, yer cargo's all aboard."

With half a dozen silver-gray gulls wheeling and chortling just
above their heads, the two men walked out along the pier, past
disorderly coils of cordage, blackly bubbling tar pots, and raw
yellow plank ends.

When he actually set foot on the brig's deck, Andrew looked
about smiling. Suddenly his breath went out with a rush. "Good
God!" he burst out. "What are those overgrown squirt-guns doing
aboard?"

"Your cannon you mean?"

"*Cannon?*"

Oakman frowned. "Easy on, Cap'n. Don't talk so high and
mighty. Them four-pounders cost yer uncle a pretty penny. And
me, I've risked my neck and fortune to find 'em."

"But four-pounders, man! Such popguns ain't able to blow the
lid off a teakettle!"

The fitter's men gazed dully at the new captain staring resentfully
at the six guns ranged behind as many red-painted gun ports. They
looked sound, to be sure, but their cannonballs weren't the size of a
good mock orange.

Oakman insisted in an undertone, "Yer lucky to get these,
Cap'n. Believe me. Cannons are mighty hard to come by, especially good sound pieces. There's been a mort o' Tory privateers
fitting out this spring. Ain't none of *these* cannons going to blow
up. You Massachusettsers are a sight too choosey to suit my
notions."

"Hi, there!" Some soldiers on guard on a neighboring pier began
waving a newspaper. "Hi, Galloway. Heard the news?"

Galloway, a thick-bodied, bull-necked fellow, set down the

marlin spike he'd been plying and flicked an irregular pattern of
sweat drops on the bright yellow planking of the deck. "Ef you
mean that rascal Boone's being took by the Injuns, I've heard about
it."

"Hell, no! Bloody Rebels have lost their best ship."

Oakman, with admirable presence of mind, yelled, "Which
one'd we sink this time?"

The guard's red face gleamed in the sunshine as he cupped hands
about his mouth and bellowed, "Why, 'twas some frigate called
the *Randolph*. Our *Yarmouth* blew her clean out o' the wat-
ter."

All uncomprehending, the black laborers paused to peer stupidly
out over the rubbish-littered water.

Galloway held a hand to a hairy ear. "How's that again?"

"Fact. First broadside, the ruddy rebel ship's magazine blew up.
Took her crew to hell with her, saving only four."

A sour-tasting spring welled up in Andrew's mouth when the
import of the news came home. So handsome young Nicholas
Biddle, one of the few real officers in the Continental Naval service,
had been lost to the country which needed him so badly.

"Come on," he said harshly to Oakman. "Come on, let's go
ashore. I want a drink."

Oakman drove his wrist against Andrew's elbow. "Careful!
Galloway's suspicious. Tell him the news, quick—*and sound
glad.*"

Tell them? The bitter taste in Andrew's mouth was almost overpowering. "Hear that?" he was surprised to hear himself calling.

"No. I'm a wee bit hard o' hearing," Galloway explained.
"What did he say?"

Andrew told him, but it was hard to conceal his grief. He had
known or served with half the officers on the *Randolph*, smartest
frigate in the terribly diminished Continental Navy. Yes, the French
alliance had been negotiated not a moment too soon.

Said he quietly, "Come, Mr. Oakman, I'll chance the four-
pounders. Let's see about permits and clearances." He needed to
get to sea in a hurry.

A nondescript cur was crimping at his flank on the sunlit stoop
before Mr. Kennedy's fine house at Number One Broad Way.
General Valentine Jones, Commandant of the Port of New York,
certainly believed in the importance of creature comforts even in
war time, so it seemed.

Superbly aloof, two Highlanders stood guard at either side, their
high bearskin hats and rakish red plumes looking a bit weatherworn

in the pitiless daylight. Andrew was impressed in spite of himself.
Not a speck marred the white of their spats or crossbelts, and their
kilts, green crossed with yellow and blue, were as neatly pressed as
a girl's Sunday-best frock. The long hair of the two Scots,
moreover, had been freshly floured and curled. When he drew near,
Andrew could see the big bone hairpins tucked above their ears. The
two sentries, eyes bright blue in their red faces, swung to meet the
visitors.

Andrew was drawing himself up, preparatory to plunging into
that atmosphere of officialdom which had always held terrors for
him, when a big Tory officer, a wild, brutal-appearing fellow, in a
rusty green tunic, came swinging out in company with an Indian. By
his pale skin Andrew judged him an Iroquois. The aborigine presented at once a grave and a ludicrous figure in a British colonel's
cast-off jacket, a gleaming silver gorget and a beaver hat impaled
with half a dozen peacock feathers. In a frayed belt which must once
have belonged to a woman were tucked a pipe, a greasy-handled
war axe, and a pouch of either food or tobacco. The savage was
wearing no breeches whatsoever, just a buckskin clout sketched
with erotic designs. Like those of most Indians, his bowed legs
showed no calves at all. Absurdly, the Iroquois had thrust his feet
into the depths of a pair of hussar patent-leather riding boots
garnished with the most tremendous pair of brass spurs Andrew had
ever beheld.

When Mr. Oakman stepped politely aside, Andrew followed suit
though, instinctively, he was prepared to defend his share of
the sidewalk. Talking in some Indian dialect, the unsavory pair
swung past. Whew! That Indian smelt like a dog fox during his
rut.

Mr. Oakman had started forward when a pair of sea captains
emerged from the Commandant's quarters. One was a weazened
little fellow whose face was brown and wrinkled as any winter
apple.

"Now we're in for it!" he was saying. "Goddamn those frog-
eating Mounseers. Plague take it, Jarrold, it's been difficult enough
with those accursed New England privateers snapping at our convoys and those jaundiced mothers' mistakes of Cubans plundering
every vessel comes their way unguarded. But now! Ye'll hear bad
news from Lloyd's and plenty of it, I'm thinking."

The other captain, as long and gaunt as his companion was short
and fat, nodded. "Aye, this alliance is a fashing business, but yon
French—Auld Clootie singe their souls forever and aye—will rue
the day they joined wi' the Rebels."

Oakman shot his companion a quick glance as the two captains made off under a row of horsechestnuts which had begun to leaf out a little.

"Come, Captain, let's get on with this." So saying Oakman led him into the musty smelling gloom of Number One Broad Way.

IV

THE COMMANDANT'S OFFICE

CAPTAIN CUBITT, please." Mr. Oakman had doffed his rabbitskin cap and was bowing almost servilely to a hatchet-faced clerk posted at a desk just inside the entrance.

"Name?" snapped the clerk, without interrupting the re-pointing of a goose quill pen.

"Oakman—Henry Oakman, sir, and please—this, this is Cap'n Warren."

"Business?" Still the clerk never so much as glanced up, blew on the point he had made.

At the fellow's rudeness Andrew commenced to steam under the collar. Damn it, he was a public servant, paid for by taxes. "I need clearances for my brig, and, my good man," he added in acid accents such as he had heard used by Britishers in Leghorn and at Gilbraltar, "I don't propose to be kept waiting."

The clerk started, peered up from behind square-lensed spectacles. "Hoity toity! You'll wait your—"

"That I will not! Not an instant!" Andrew snapped, his jaw widening. "On your feet, you sluggard. I must see Captain Cubitt immediately."

The clerk sprang up babbling, never heard Oakman's frightened, "Please, sir. My friend's a bit impatient, but—"

Andrew remained bolt upright, glowering down his nose. He'd seen how English officers handled underlings.

"Yes, sir," the clerk said, and bobbed a hurried bow. He hurried off through a narrow door to his left.

"Don't be an idiot," Oakman whispered. "If you play the grandee, they'll never grant you clearance."

"Not with these?" From his breeches pocket, the merchant captain produced a handful of broad gold sovereigns. "I've heard of Captain Cubitt." This was true. All New England knew about the sordid peculations of General Jones' deputies.

"Yes, sir. Please, sir, this way. Cap'n Cubitt, sir. A caller." The clerk, all of a twitter now, led them into a spacious green and white painted apartment; it must have once been a dining-room if one were to notice the dish racks about the walls. Quietly as an abashed mouse the clerk slipped behind a desk and produced some forms.

"Ha—brumph! What the devil d'you want?" Andrew found himself facing one of the most remarkable figures he had ever encountered.

Captain Cubitt suggested nothing so much as a fat-faced and very obese old seraph. By contrast with his scarlet features his functionary's stock of Flemish lace was positively pristine. Valiantly, his buttons tugged at their buttonholes to contain a truly Homeric belly.

The deputy Commissioner set down a glass of what seemed to be sherry, and puffed out reddish mottled cheeks. "So? So you want clearance, eh, Captain?"

Surprised at his own temerity, Andrew pursued his tactics. "Aye, sir, and as speedily as may be."

The gross, scarlet-and-white-clad figure ensconced behind a delicate mahogany desk remained impassive save for a quick batting of the eyelids.

Andrew thought, "The deputy commandant's piggy blue eyes wouldn't wash well."

"Begging yer pardon, Captain Cubitt—I—"

Only the heavy figure's full and shiny lips moved. "Mind your stupid business, Talcott! One perceives that, at last, one has a gentleman to deal with."

"Thank you, Captain. I wish to secure clearance for Jamaica for Montego Bay."

"And do you so?" Captain Cubitt's vividly red lips parted. "Lovely spot, Jamaica. Tell me, Captain, what leads you to believe so readily that I shall issue these clearances?" The deputy commandant wasn't stupid, for all his ponderous lethargy. Not a bit of it.

"Because," Andrew said smiling, "I'll wager you five gold sovereigns that you won't write them."

"Eh? Won't write what? What's that again?"

Andrew felt immeasurably pleased at the unexpected cleverness of his maneuver. "I said, Captain, that I'd venture five sovereigns you'd not issue clearance for my vessel."

Captain Cubitt still made no movement. His plump puffy fingers remained splayed across a litter of official documents—a pink pattern dividing quantities of red wax seals.

"Talcott!" he wheezed. "Dammit, Talcott, am I to stifle here? Go open some windows in the front office!"

"Yes, sir. Directly, sir!" Pallid features expressionless, the clerk arose and pattered out, thin, black-stockinged shanks moving stiffly.

Andrew grinned to himself. The British in New York then *were* as corrupt as rumor had them. Best be careful though. Captain Biddle had always held that you must never be more wary of a Britisher than when he acted the perfect fool.

"Ahem! You are a careless bettor." Captain Cubitt closed his eyes tight. "Your clearance will be arranged."

"I never was a lucky gambler," the New Englander complained. Solemnly Andrew Warren placed five gold coins on Captain Cubitt's desk; tactfully placed a tortoise shell snuff box upon them.

"Well, I'll be hornswoggled!" Henry Oakman was saying to himself. It was a revelation to witness how cleverly this young whippersnapper worked. Hadn't suspected it of Andrew Warren, for a fact. But then, no good New Yorker should ever trust a Yankee—no more than a Jerseyman or Pennsylvanian.

In the gracefully proportioned dining room of Mr. Kennedy's former residence silence reigned. Out on the river a frigate's jolly-boat was pulling in toward Fort William, its well-pumiced oar blades flashing rhythmically.

Captain Cubitt moved suddenly, bellowed, "Talcott! Where in hell are you? Talcott, damn you, why must you forever keep me waiting?"

"Yes, sir! Right away, sir." Talcott's voice was reedy, nervously obsequious. It grated on Henry Oakman's nerves, too. No one had the right to make a man quail like that.

Andrew Warren was vaguely aware of the Highlanders on guard at the entrance. Briskly they were slapping their muskets, must be presenting arms. Then voices sounded in the outer office. A man's gruff accents, an officer beyond a doubt. Also a girl's voice, rich and musical. Damn. He didn't want this business interrupted. In a few minutes more he'd have leave to take the *Evergreen* to sea, down to the Sugar Islands, for those medicines Carlos Cardozo was holding for a goodly price.

Captain Cubitt was puffing, "Damn bad news, this alliance, 'twixt the French and these plagued rebels. Fancy, though, we'll whip the Mounseers still another time. Always have, you know.

Shocking bad sailors, the French. Eh what? Ought to have learned better than to stand against us.''

The speaker's swollen eyelids rolled. ''But betwixt the two of us, you'd best look sharp below Hatteras. Blasted privateers, Yankee or French, ain't to be trifled with; stab me, if they are. Clever sailors, the privateers. No pox-ridden nobles in command.''

A voice outside demanded loudly, ''We must see General Jones. Immediately, understand? Mistress Allen is under the protection of Colonel Saunders.''

Andrew smiled privately. Colonel Saunders' protection, eh? A polite term, that, for some staff officer's ammunition wife. He was curious to see what a British officer's mistress would be like. Pretty, no doubt, and Tory to the core—like Mrs. Loring.

''Yessir. Your pardon, sir. I'll return in a moment.''

The clerk, Talcott, pattered in, some printed forms in his hand. He spoke in a hoarse whisper, ''There's a colonel of the Royal Welch outside, shall I—?''

''Just a damned Whitehall hero,'' the Captain grunted. ''Let him wait. Arrange Captain Warren's papers.''

The clerk nodded, slipped in behind a table desk, was pleased to discover a shilling Andrew had placed beside his leaden inkpot.

''Here, sir, is your permit to charge your vessel. Sign here. Your sworn enumeration of cargo comes next. This, sir, is your certificate of non-fraud.'' Andy sensed, rather than recognized, a mocking gleam in the clerk's doleful brown eyes. ''There will be charge of three shillings the ton due for dockage tax. You have your town dues and bond?''

''Here.'' Andrew opened his portfolio. He experienced a sudden anxiety. What if they weren't as they should be?

The clerk sniffed, poised heavy, iron-rimmed spectacles. Laboriously Captain Cubitt opened the tortoise shell snuff box and measured out a pinch of the fine brown powder. His hand faltered on the way to his nose as in the hall sounded the determined advance of heavy boots.

''Cubitt! Confound it, Cubitt, where are you?''

Captain Cubitt's enormous figure stirred, heaved itself majestically upwards as the door swung back. '' 'Pon my word, Colonel, I never recognized your voice. Stab me, if I did!''

A tall, bony officer with whitening hair appeared in the doorway. His nose was a regular beak, thin and netted with tiny red veins. His tunic turned up in the dark blue of the Royal Welch fitted with calm precision. A real fighter, this chap, Andrew thought, but lost further interest when he glimpsed a young woman behind him. Jerusha! Here *was* a handsome filly. Chestnut hair, wide-spaced gray-green eyes and a complexion that spoke of fresh air, sunlight—and soap. So many fashionable misses had taken to substituting weird foreign lotions and perfumes in the Continental fashion.

In a gray taffeta gown garnished with many little emerald green silk bows she was indeed a sight to take to sea in one's memory. No wonder Colonel Saunders was according her his protection. Yes, sure enough, this girl's eyes were unusually large and shaded by lashes which did much to set off the strong yet delicate contours of her brows.

The new arrival came stalking in and brushed by Andrew and Henry Oakman as if they'd been a pair of footstools. A frozen sort of smile appeared on his slash of a mouth. "Dashed glad to find you here, Douglas. Come for a favor."

The color mounted slowly into Andrew's cheeks. Here was a dangerous mischance. Involuntarily he had stiffened at the gold lace and epaulets. Though Captain Cubitt addressed Colonel Saunders, his piggy blue eyes were fixed on that supple young woman who still stood hesitatingly in the hallway.

"A vast pleasure, Colonel. Your servant, sir. You'll be off to join Lord Howe in Philadelphia very soon, I expect?"

"Or maybe further," Colonel Saunders snapped. "Those accursed French will begin raiding our Indies. We'll have to consolidate, you know, before giving the Johnny Crapauds another basting."

"Ahem. May I have the honor? Er—this young lady?" Captain Cubitt was tugging at his yellow-and-white-striped satin waistcoat; delicately he flicked the slightly grimy Valenciennes lace at his wrists.

"Oh yes, of course, of course!" While Andrew looked on, torn between apprehension and amusement, Colonel Saunders bowed stiffly in the direction of the tall young woman.

"Captain Douglas Cubitt of the 18th of the Line," his clipped accents rang out. "Mistress Minga Allen, daughter of the late Judge Allen of Brewster, New York."

Some of the elegance departed from Captain Cubitt's manner. So, for all her fine looks, this pretty creature was only a colonial? Her bearing had fooled him, quite. That chip hat wasn't bad, nor was her coiffure; the green taffeta pocket she dangled from her wrist was distinctly modish.

"Yours to command, Ma'am," puffed the deputy commandant, making a leg in her direction.

"I am honored, sir," the girl replied with the briefest of curtsies. Pah! What a bloated old satyr this was.

Producing a snuff box, Colonel Saunders tapped its lid with brisk

precision. "As I told that ass of a clark of yours, Mistress Allen is
under my protection. She was affianced to the late Captain Sir
Gerald Vaughan of the Dragoons."

Captain Cubitt stared. "He wasn't that poor chap who was
murdered last week by the Brunswickers?"

"The same," Colonel Saunders nodded. "Pity—"

"Pray—let's not discuss the matter." The handsome young
woman's eyes had suddenly wavered and the bright line of her softly
curved lips had contracted as if under the pang of a sudden hurt.
Andrew wondered.

Colonel Saunders commenced to sniff. "Who are these?"

Captain Cubitt waved a pudgy hand. "That one's Oakman, a
merchant of the town. Yonder's a sea captain and a Loyalist.
Captain Warren was the name, wasn't it?"

"It was, and is."

Colonel Saunders put an eyeglass to his left eye and stared as if he
were inspecting a doubtful colt. "So you're a Loyalist, eh? For how
long, I wonder?"

Andrew's dander commenced to rise, but he remembered in time
and schooled himself enough just to say, "As long as you, sir."
Then, deliberately, he shifted his gaze to the girl. She, of course,
must be a Loyalist. Hum! Seemed a sight too attractive to be a real
Tory. She wasn't bad looking at all and those flared brows of hers
were something to remember; bigger than most women, though.
Must be all of five feet two inches.

"Well, sir, how can I be of service?" Captain Cubitt demanded,
swaying on lumpy legs as thick as newel posts.

The red-faced officer seated himself, adroitly shifting his dress
sword diagonally across his lap. "Mistress Allen is desirous of
securing passage to Jamaica with all possible speed. His Excellency, Sir Henry Clinton, requests that you arrange the matter."

"Indeed? Where in Jamaica?"

"Either Kingston or the North Shore will do." The girl had
seated herself on the far side of the green and white room, feet
together, hands on purse, all attention. Apparently she had not so
much as noted the existence of either Mr. Oakman or the straight
young merchant captain standing before the clerk's desk in homely
duroy breeches and well-worn serge jacket.

Andrew's pride was stung. Damn it! If he'd only been wearing
his lieutenant's uniform with its scarlet waistcoat, she'd have
noticed him quick enough. A plague on her and another plague take
that snotty red-faced, eagle-beaked Colonel. His stream of thought
was rudely interrupted by a roar of laughter from Captain Cubitt.

"Jamaica? Why, blast my vitals! Ma'am, you've come in good season. Stab me, if you've not." He waved a fat, be-ringed hand in Andrew's direction. "Captain Warren here is clearing for Jamaica tomorrow. You'll go aboard of him, Ma'am."

"Capital!" Colonel Saunders clapped himself on the white satin knee of his breeches. "What uncommon luck. Eh, Mistress Allen?"

Andrew stiffened. "I regret, sir, and Madam, that there are no passenger accommodations. I cannot take a woman aboard my brig."

Lord above! A woman aboard his ship on a cruise of this sort? Never. It augured the worst possible luck to have a female around—aboard ship woman and preachers and rabbits were unlucky.

"Eh? What's that? Can't take her aboard?" Captain Cubitt's naturally prominent jaw achieved an aggressive angle.

Andrew was aware of the Allen girl's cold attention. "The *Evergreen* is small, sir, only a hundred tons' burthen. She's not really fit for so fine a lady."

"Fit?" snapped Colonel Saunders. "That's for *her* to say, not you, my man."

"Mistress Allen," Captain Cubitt said, "the brig, as Captain Warren states, is indeed very small. However, if you choose to chance a voyage in her, we'll see to it she's clean."

Andrew shook his head. "Since you force me to it, gentlemen, may I remind you that the *Evergreen* is my vessel. I want no passengers and I'll take none."

Cubitt's blotched features went a rich plum color. "God damn it, keep a civil tongue in your mouth," he bellowed. "Who asked you what you want? You beastly Colonials are too confounded free with your opinions. If this lady desires accommodations, by God you'll grant them or I'll know the reason why."

Mr. Oakman signalled urgently from the corner into which he had retreated. Almost gray with fright, he nodded several times.

Since the start of the controversy Minga Allen had sat rigid, fingertips laced on her lap. She couldn't quite make out this black-haired, black-eyed young merchant captain. Looked a reckless, thoughtless sort who probably held women as an amusement but a shade more refined than horses, dice, and brandy.

"I hesitate to force myself upon so gallant a gentleman," she told Captain Cubitt, "but it is urgent that I reach Jamaica as quickly as possible. My aunt owns an estate there."

It *was* important that she get clear of New York. Until she did, the memory of Jerry, of that hideous night beside the Hudson, would not cease racking her peace of mind. There were other memories, too, to be left behind: of Brewster and the Liberty boys and Pa carted half-naked through a January snowstorm, the tar hardening on his withered shoulders.

"I don't care about discomforts," she quietly said. "I am accustomed to them. I will go if—if Captain Warren can be persuaded."

Hell's booming bells! Dismay flooded Andrew. If there was any complication he wished to avoid, it was the presence of a Tory, and a shrewd young woman, to boot.

"Well, sir?" Colonel Saunders arose, levelled a chilling stare.

Andrew Warren laid his already-counted money beside the papers on the clerk's desk. "May I remind you, sir, that my vessel is not a military transport; therefore, I'm not subject to your orders. I take no passengers on this voyage."

His lean features scarlet as any turkey cock's wattles, Colonel Saunders marched over the bare plank floor. His hand perhaps subconsciously sought the gilded grip of his sword. "Since when have the wishes of a wretched merchant seaman been of any importance in time of war?"

Captain Cubitt's clerk squeaked and Oakman slipped quietly through the half open door. As for Captain Cubitt, he moved with that surprising agility of the very corpulent.

"A moment, Colonel. Just a moment." He plucked the *Evergreen's* papers off the clerk's desk.

"I'll take a look at these." He pursed his thick lips. "Dammit, Talcott, you're forever making errors. Look—here's one, here's another."

"Beg pardon, sir—I—I—"

"Silence! You'll likely have to do them over—"

A turmoil raged in Andrew's soul. Damn! Colonel Saunders' every accent riled him but he'd never sail in a month of Sundays if Cubitt held up his papers.

Though it came hard, he forced a smile. "Your pardon, Colonel. I had not perceived how really urgent it is for Mistress Allen to sail." He fixed the girl in gray with a blank, non-committal look. "My brig is at your disposal."

Their gaze met, clashed like the épées of engaging fencers. Icicles tinkled in her accents as Minga Allen smoothed her skirt and murmured, "You shall not receive me under duress, Captain. I shall make other arrangements."

"Damme, there is no duress in this!" roared Captain Cubitt. "You'll sail in the *Evergreen,* by God, and welcome!" Puffing, he waddled over to confront Andrew. "If you're a loyal subject of His

Majesty—which I am beginning to doubt—you will oblige this lady—and graciously, too.''

There was nothing else to do. Andrew bowed stiffly in the direction of this straight young woman in gray. Why the devil hadn't she taken "no" for an answer? Suddenly the perfect explanation offered itself. This young woman was clearing out of New York *because she had to!* Of course. Such imperative departures were far from uncommon among the protégées and ammunition wives of officers. Colonel Saunders wanted no bastard of his born where fellow officers could sneer and manufacture crude humor.

"You will be welcome." Andrew actually grinned. If this hawk-billed old goat of a Colonel could— Well, something told him Mistress Allen would have cause to remember this voyage to Jamaica as long as she lived. Aboard ship the captain's word was law, was it not?

"Galloway's wharf, Madam," said he. "We sail on morning tide, six o'clock. Your humble obedient servant, gentlemen," and, plucking his papers off Captain Cubitt's desk, Captain Andrew Warren walked firmly to the door and disappeared through it.

I

OFF LITTLE INAGUA

IN SHIMMERING streamers heat-waves rose from the oil-slick Caribbean to distort a row of palms fringing a scattering of islets off to port. In the distance sounded the sullen boom of swells creaming over a long succession of coral reefs.

The *Evergreen,* merchant brig, rolled wearily, heavily to an endless succession of dark blue swells, relics of some gale risen somewhere far below the horizon. Like inverted pendulums the chunky little vessel's tops swung back and forth, back and forth, across a brazen blue sky.

Captain Andrew Warren sighed as a kettle, unsecured in the galley, continued to clank at each heave of his brig. Jerusha! There wasn't even a suspicion of wind in this blistering noonday air and it was hotter than ever despite the shade of an old jib, rigged awning-wise across the quarterdeck. Opening his faded blue shirt, he stanched a trickle of sweat which had begun to creep down over his ribs.

Irritated by the sting of perspiration salt on his kips, he cocked a disapproving dark brown eye at the fore royal. Damn! The brownish canvas was slatting up there, just as limp and useless as it had been during the past three days.

At this rate Hosea Warren's brig was getting nowhere. Momentarily his lips compressed themselves. Could the *Trumbull's* builders in Gildersleeve's yard up to East Middleton, Connecticut, possibly complete and commission the frigate before he got back?

Absently, Andrew rested wiry forearms on the rail but flinched away when the fierce heat bit into his skin. Damn! He should have raised the jagged azure outlines of Jamaica a week back. Right now he should be in Montego Bay discharging cargo at Winde & Allerdice's wharf.

He passed the tip of his tongue over lips so burnt they felt like the crackling on the outside of well-roasted beef. Um-m. What was going to happen there in Jamaica? He felt his heart lift a little. After all, it wasn't every day one ran into an enemy port under forged papers and with the outline of a gibbet casting its shadow across the whole adventure.

Hadn't Henry Oakman soberly predicted that if he got recognized or found out in Jamaica, he could count on being taken to Port Royal and hanged?

Running an experienced eye along the brig's deck, he decided the *Evergreen* was a sight cleaner than any other merchantman he'd seen. Um-m. Would it arouse suspicion if he kept her so man-o'-war style?

He'd found the *Evergreen* a trim and handy vessel, well—if unimaginatively—built. Moodily, Andrew considered his little starboard battery. She should, in all reason, mount much heavier guns than the ineffective little four-pounders Henry Oakman had procured.

Old Scratch take this infernal calm! Through the open gun ports he saw a big patch of yellow-brown Gulf weed still where it had been half an hour ago. He wasn't an overly patient man and he knew it, but he'd have to cultivate self-possession if he were to succeed.

In dull disinterest he glanced at the brig's half-Indian quartermaster. The Penobscot's flat, brown face was turned to port, considering a cluster of low-lying islands which, since dawn, had remained some two miles distant.

The sound of heavy brogans clumping up the companion preluded the first officer's appearance. Mr. Jared Beetle, carrying a heavy brass spyglass, shambled forward, his shadow a bluish splash at his feet.

"Glass has fallen a mite, sir," he grunted and blew sweat from the tip of a nose which had suffered severe alterations from its original design. "Come sundown we might catch a breath o' wind."

He lifted the spyglass and trained it on the group of palm-crested islands. After a long study he closed the instrument and rubbed at his eye. "Fancied I spied a spar amongst them coco palms—must have only been heat waves, I allow."

"I fear, Mr. Beetle, you are over-apprehensive."

A small gold ring set in the mate's left ear flashed like a point of flame and he flushed quickly.

"Maybe so, sir, but I wish to God you had elected to descend the Mouchoir Channel like the Port Captain at Noo York said."

Andrew said sharply, "I've my reasons, Mr. Beetle. What's more I'll tolerate no further comment on my decisions."

Of course, he couldn't tell Beetle—Tory that he was—why he didn't dare take the *Evergreen* down the safer, more frequented Windward Passage. British cruisers fairly swarmed there. Still, Caicos Passage held a bad name along New England waterfronts.

Mr. Beetle sniffed, "Yessir. Hope we get a wind. Our passenger ain't a bit pleased over this calm. Mistress Allen's got her tongue going a-plenty."

The good-humored lines usually in evidence about Andrew's mouth faded. It was undiluted hell having a woman aboard at any time—but on *this* of all cruises! She'd been sicker than sick all the way down into the Horse Latitudes, so, thank God, he'd hardly laid eyes on her. Joe Atherton, who was as handy with his hands as with his speech, had been ministering to her wants as well as he could, but the hundred-ton brig offered few comforts.

Not until a week ago, when the brig was crossing the 24° parallel of latitude, had Mistress Allen appeared on deck. Even then she had spoken hardly an unnecessary word, had addressed him with heavy formality.

Though Andrew had striven to smother his resentment at his having her forced upon him and had been polite as pie, Mistress Minga Allen had been colder than a fish caught through the ice. For all of that she was a fine, handsome piece. Only needed to be brought to heel—to be set on the right tack. He had figured it would be fun bringing that about. But it wasn't. Never had he come up against a female so unpredictable, so subtly exasperating, yet so genuinely provocative as Mistress Allen. He was hanged if he knew what to make of this self-contained, supple young woman with the wide gray-green eyes.

Usually the girls, even the well-bred ones who lived along Congress Street back home in Portsmouth, cosied up in short order—especially when he wore the blue and scarlet of a Naval lieutenant. Yet Minga Allen might have been weaned on pickles for all the sweetness she showed him.

The crew, composed of Tories, waterfront idlers, and broken-down British Naval ratings, had growled plenty over her being aboard ship—they'd liefer sail in company with a preacher or "a furry thing" as they cautiously called a rabbit. The boatswain had said, and loudly enough for everyone to hear, that the *Evergreen* wouldn't meet with even a pinch of luck this cruise.

What was really amazing was that this crisp, apparently self-sufficient young lady could keep herself so thoroughly aloof aboard a vessel so small as the *Evergreen*.

Every morning she appeared on deck, offered a polite "Good morning," then crossed to the awning Atherton had rigged amidships to occupy herself with reading or stitching embroidery on a tambour frame. When the sun got really hot, Mistress Allen would vanish below, not to reappear until the late afternoon.

She took her meals on deck whenever possible and made dainty play with an ivory-handled knife and fork. Andrew noted she licked her fingers not even once and even went to the rail briefly to employ the small gold tooth-pick she carried in a little horn case.

When the weather drove her to eating below and sharing his table in the main cabin, she had refused all conversational advances though he was pretty adroit in suggesting topics calculated to draw her out. When their silent meals drew to a close she would incline her head and say, "I wish you good evening, Captain Warren." Then she'd go directly to her hutch of a cabin.

At first this routine had annoyed Andrew. He wasn't used to being rebuffed, but then he got used to it—the devil take her anyway. He could smoke his pipe in peace and continue his painful study of the *Art of Marine Gunnery* by one Captain Sir Guy Holly, R.N., Bart.

Besides, no one could truthfully term Minga Allen a classic beauty—her mouth was a little too wide and her nose was a trifle short with a powdering of tiny freckles across its bridge. Still, her straight carriage, firm bosoms and clear skin weren't unpleasant to behold when she wandered about the *Evergreen's* spotless decks— her chestnut mane of hair bound in a length of azure silk.

The brig rolled heavily, monotonously on the glassy rollers, and the kettle continued to rattle. A line of pelicans came cruising along, gray and shaggy, over the slow surf on a long line of reefs. The more he thought on it, the more Andrew felt sure that if she were not indeed Colonel Saunders' dismissed mistress, something catastrophic had happened to his passenger. Every now and then shadows darkened the depths of Mistress Allen's lively gray-green eyes, such shadows as one noticed on women's faces when a casualty list was first posted. After the *Andrew Doria* and the *Racehorse* fight it had been like that.

As near as he could tell, this curious young woman was quite alone in the world. For all her aloofness he couldn't complain she'd ever been ill-tempered or unreasonable since the voyage had begun. She seemed, rather, to live in a universe divorced from reality.

So far so good. Of the crew only Joe Atherton suspected he wasn't the dyed-in-the-wool Loyalist he let on to be. His two officers didn't seem to possess any particular convictions— probably they trimmed their political sails as the wind blew. Mr. Beetle boasted a family of eleven more or less legitimate offspring.

One night Andrew had heard the passenger singing "Royal Americans" in sweet but untrained voice. This, of course, was an out-and-out Tory song. Before sailing he'd made a few cautious inquiries concerning Colonel Saunders' protégé, had learned that she hailed from somewhere in Putnam County, in New York State.

The one time the Allen girl actually opened conversation she'd voiced such Tory notions he'd got pretty smoking under the collar. This had happened off Charleston, when the *Evergreen* had passed a frigate, H.M.S. *Iris*. She had been the United States Ship *Hancock*—in fact, that patriot's effigy still served as the *Iris'* figurehead; but the wooden effigy lacked its right hand—the one with which Hancock had signed the Declaration of July Fourth 1776. The British, in a burst of ponderous humor, had sawed it off.

"There, sir," Minga Allen had cried in clear confident tones, "sails a vessel captured from the Rebels."

Rebels! He hated her at that moment. Had she any idea what those "Rebels" had suffered, were suffering to gain their right to live and trade as they chose? He hoped she'd never see a naval engagement, see a shrieking, hopelessly wounded sailor lugged to the rail and heaved over. That was only customary.

As he had watched the tall vessel rushing by so swiftly, he'd felt his throat tighten. So much work and care and sacrifice had gone into her construction.

"She is a sweet-sailing vessel," he'd murmured.

"So she is," the Allen girl had admitted. "The Rebels do seem able to build men-o'-war, but to what purpose, since they cannot discover officers fit to command them?"

This was little short of the truth, Andrew had had to admit, once he got his dander down. For a fact, there weren't in the Continental Navy, at present, a full dozen captains who really understood their business, which was to seek the enemy and fight him whenever and wherever possible. Too many were cautious privateersmen at heart, and therein lay one of the greatest, deadliest dangers for the new Union.

This suffocating heat, added to the odors of a none-too-fragrant cargo, must render below decks well-nigh unbearable. Ere long Mistress Allen would surely put in her appearance.

Jerusha! It was stifling enough on deck; the heat had set tar, caulking the decks, to creeping towards the scuppers in glistening rivulets. From the brig's deckload of yellow pine boards came resinous odors poignantly reminiscent of green forests stretching interminably westward from Portsmouth.

Joe Beaver, the half-breed Penobscot, was still observing the islets off to port. Andrew looked carefully, but couldn't observe anything more interesting than clouds of seabirds diving and wheeling over that long breastwork of reefs separating the islets from the becalmed brig.

It was not in Andrew's nature to remain idle; it set a poor example for the crew. Aboard the *Randolph* Captain Biddle had never been still a waking moment. From a locker the brig's captain brought out a leaden ink bottle, the log-book, a chronometer and a battered brass sextant which once had belonged to Uncle Hosea.

Methodically, he took his sights, then perspiring more than ever, struggled to establish his position. Figuring for him had always been like having a tooth pulled.

Amidships, the larboard watch was splicing gear in the scant shadow of the bulwarks.

Andrew dipped a goose quill into the ink bottle, merged straight black brows and wrote:

> Wednesday, ye 23rd of
> April, 1778

> This day again no Wind. Ye Current, however, bares us slow thru Caicos Passage. Sea calm, weather very hott, feer our turnips may spoil. 5:00 a.m. raized Little Inagua to port. Position 12 min. 74°, 9 Minutes, longitude West; 22°, 7 minutes, latitude North. We need a Wind from ye N.E.

Glancing up, Andrew saw Joe Beaver steadying the wheel, but his unblinking attention was still on Little Inagua. What he said was unexpected.

"Wind come."

"When?"

"Sometime, maybe soon."

Andrew felt the sweat meandering down his back under his bleached blue-and-white-striped jersey. It tickled uncomfortably.

"Look quick, Cappee," the Penobscot said suddenly. "See little flash, like sail?"

Lazily, Andrew pulled his spy-glass from a rack beside the binnacle and once more surveyed those islands—the Little Inagua group.

There was nothing there, of course. Still, with so many cruisers from the Jamaica and West Indies Station detached for blockade duty along the coast of America—the picaroons *might* have become daring. When a cruiser was about, the local inhabitants were peaceful boucan makers, but let the men-o'-war's topsails vanish too long—and, well, quite a few small vessels had disappeared forever in Caicos Passage.

Through Andrew's glass the Little Inaguas moved closer. Now he could see a double row of palm-thatch huts fringing a cove where perhaps fifteen or twenty piraguas were drawn up on the beach— very much they suggested a row of alligators sunning themselves.

He fiddled with the focus. Beyond a rank of coconut trees something had glimmered; a sail was being raised. There could be no doubt that Joe Beaver was right; a vessel of some sort *was* lying on the far side of a point which probed like a great, silver-gold forefinger into Caicos Channel.

Andrew sought to read his quartermaster's expression, but the half-breed's blunt features were impassive as he stood steadying the useless wheel with small dark hands. Sweat was drawing bright patterns over his cheekbones and along a jagged scar running down one cheek.

He returned his glass to the strange vessel—she looked like a large island-built schooner. Sure enough, she was getting under way. Um-m. Her captain must have sweeps out; there was no more wind over the Little Inaguas than in the Channel. The use of those sweeps—um-m—the heat—thinking was an effort. Most likely just a—

"Something of absorbing interest lies yonder?"

Andrew was too hot to turn quickly. He put down the glass, stood straighter when he sensed who was there.

Mistress Allen was scarcely band-box dainty today. Her gray callimanca gown hung so straight down her flanks he deduced she'd dispensed with every last petticoat. Well, he couldn't blame her. The heat was slapping like demonic hands. Nor was there any place to seek relief.

"Yes," he said. "I thought I'd sighted a cooling breeze."

For a wonder she smiled. "Indeed, Captain? Humor is like golden guineas on such a day."

Jerusha! Mistress Allen had actually left off those stays under which she'd suffered and squirmed these many torrid days. There was evidently some recompense for every discomfort, since Mistress Allen's figure now had opportunity to betray how pleasantly Nature had fashioned it.

Sensing his awareness, the Allen girl flushed clear down to the limp linen edging her bodice. Hurriedly moving a frayed palm-leaf fan, she made a forlorn effort at jauntiness.

He turned away his eyes. "A bit hot below?" God, what a fool thing to say. He laughed silently at himself.

"Like a baker's oven." Minga sighed. From the start Captain Andrew Warren had presented an unfamiliar pattern of problems. If she'd not been so battered in her heart, so dreadfully worried about what the Brunswickers had done, she might have enjoyed shattering his monumental self-assurance.

She guessed the Captain came from New England, though his speech wasn't just that. He'd some education, too. Once when he'd mentioned Saint Domingue, he'd given it a foreign pronunciation, not "Saint do-min-gew" like an Englishman but "San Do-mang."

He could be dangerous, this Andrew Warren, her instinct warned her. He suggested a ruffler, a trifler of the type who'd get a girl in the family way, then leave her to face the shame—and the heavier problem of providing for a baby.

That first dinner below when she'd mended of the sea-sickness he'd spoken pretty free. She'd never heard such talk. Why, from his bold manner, she might have been some high-priced trollop. Still, there was an open, sun-lit way to his boldness—nothing furtive or false or sly.

Also, he knew how to handle his ship, did Captain Warren. The way the crew jumped when he spoke was something to see. But they hated him; he was so exact. Almost like a Naval officer.

As she stood by his side she noticed his intense black eyes flicker over to the islands again. How full of life he was, fairly overflowing with energy and zest. Yet oddly enough, he lent the impression of having suffered some all-important disappointment. To his jaw at times came a hard, almost cruel tautening.

No, Andrew Warren was not a man to be crossed for sheer deviltry.

An interesting point for consideration was his ability to suggest, all in an instant, a responsible officer and an enthusiastic young man.

"La, sir! By the intensity of your gaze there must be a whole school of mermaids disporting themselves on yonder beaches."

Puzzled by her unexpected affability he shrugged. "No, Madam, I was searching for a remora."

"A—a remora?"

Under the fierce sunlight his black eyes narrowed. "Aye, the remora's a great monster which bears a saw-shaped horn in its snout," he explained perfectly seriously. "This remora swims under a becalmed vessel and in a single night will cut a hole in her bottom. Once the ship founders the monster swims into the wreck and devours all the crew."

"La! Captain Warren, I'm not a-feared. You could most easily slay this remora with the deadly harpoon of your wit."

Today for coolness, Minga Allen had abandoned her azure scarf, had twisted her chestnut hair into a knot on the top of her head and secured it with a single comb of tortoise shell. She was pleasing even with a beading of perspiration dewing her upper lip and temples.

For all his pleasure at this unexpected unbending, Andrew kept an eye on the distant schooner. It was scarcely reassuring to perceive that, slowly but steadily, she was working down a channel dividing two of the larger islets. Still, she might be only a cargo boat setting sail on an inter-island cruise.

"How cool and lovely it looks down there," Minga said leaning far out over the rail.

As so often before, the sea bottom presented a vivid, ever-altering pattern of blue, green and white. Brain corals, branch corals, weeds and bold pinnacles of rock glimmered and wavered before Minga's enchanted eyes. "Such lovely fishes are below."

"Those," Andrew explained, "are scarlet groupers, that's a parrot fish. The striped ones are zebra fish, and the little silvery fellows are mullets."

For him, too, it was always a pleasure to watch the hundreds of fishes go darting about among the sponges and the arbors formed by branch corals. So clear was the water that the shadows of the swimmers could be seen whipping over pure white sand on the bottom.

Languidly, the girl dropped into her accustomed seat beneath the canopy. Sunlight, beating through the old jib's worn texture, lent an effect of gilding on her face and arms.

"I trust Jamaica will not be like this," she sighed. "I am about to suffocate."

Limply, she fanned herself as the brig continued her tedious, endless rolling.

"Pray, Captain, don't consider me with such attention. I know I—I look a fright. When are we to reach Montego Bay?"

"A fair wind, Madam, should give us the landfall of Jamaica in about three days."

"But when shall we have wind?"

"Before tonight," he encouraged her. "Mr. Beetle says the glass is falling—almost too fast."

His eyes flickered over the rail to where a school of flying fish had suddenly broken water. Like the jab of a boarding pike, came realization that that strange sail had cleared the distant channel and now was coming steadily in the brig's direction.

"Masthead! Masthead there!" Andrew bellowed through cupped hands. It was comical to watch the look-out rouse himself. The fellow knew he stood to get docked a day's pay for not having reported the stranger.

"Aye, aye, sir?"

"How does yonder draft sail? What do you make her rig?"

"She heads southwest-by-south, sir. She's a two-masted schooner, sir, with several sweeps out."

Minga roused herself. The intense way that half-Indian

helmsman was watching the islands was disquieting. Captain Warren had lost completely his careless half-mocking air. She got to her
feet and joined him at the rail.

"What is she? A man-of-war?"

"A sponger, most likely," he returned briefly. "Perhaps a
turtler."

"But I have been informed that the natives hereabouts are
uncommon indolent. Why would an honest craft man her sweeps in
the heat of the day?"

He shrugged. Damned if he liked the look of this, not in such a
tiny tub as the *Evergreen*—and with such a hell's delight of a crew.

Through his glass Andrew surveyed the distant vessel. It was
apparent now that her hull was painted black, that her sails were
brown as tobacco leaves. They slatted uselessly when, under the
propulsion of six twelve-foot sweeps, the stranger pulled over the
oily seas towards a long line of reefs raising an irregular barrier
between her and the hopelessly becalmed *Evergreen*.

II

THE BARRIER REEF

LONG GEORGE the brig's gigantic black cook, thrust a bullet-shaped
head out of his galley, considered the vessel beyond the barrier reef.
"Sho' hopes dat reef run all de way to Cuba—"

Captain Andrew Warren reached a decision promptly. Over the
creaking of the yards and the slap-slapping of the useless canvas he
shouted, "Mr. Beetle! All hands on deck and smartly! Atherton. Go
rout out Mr. Tompkins."

Minga Allen felt much as she had when those first Cowboys had
burst out of the birch woods, but only the quickened tempo of her
fan beats betrayed her growing uneasiness.

Down the forecastle hatch the captain of the larboard watch
bawled "A-a-ll hands on deck and stir yer blasted stumps."

The crew got to their feet leaving dark sweat marks on the deck
where they had been sitting.

Sleepily cursing the heat, Eli Tompkins appeared on deck. He dug knuckles into blood injected eyes and stared so stupidly about that Andrew wanted to root him one in the pants. "Wha's wrong?"

"Plenty," Andrew snapped. "Have the larboard watch cast off the gun covers."

"Mr. Beetle," he called through a leather speaking horn, "re-stack that deck-load of lumber. You'll need more room in serving the port battery."

The passenger watched curiously from the shade of the impro-vised awning. Umm. Certainly Captain Warren *had* served aboard a man-o'-war some time; no mistaking that quarterdeck briskness. He wasn't displeasing to look upon as he strode quickly, lightly about.

Captain Warren turned apologetically. "Very likely nothing untoward will chance. But in these latitudes, Ma'am, well, it's best to keep a weather eye out. You'll excuse my absence."

Once he had descended a short ladder to the deck, Minga Allen focused her attention upon the crew of the nearest of the three cannons composing the port battery. Captain Warren, extra rangy in his striped jersey, duroy knee breeches and white thread stockings, alternately was glancing at the distant, but still-advancing schooner and superintending the stacking of a number of roundshot in circlets of rope which kept them in position.

"Smartly now," he rasped. "God in Heaven! Can't you navvies get out of the way of your own feet?"

Now rammers and spongers were being lifted from their racks as training tackles were tested and cast loose. At this sudden activity the brig's supply of livestock, penned in the port long boat, com-menced variously to bleat, to grunt or to cackle.

"Shake a leg there!" Mr. Beetle brought a rope's end smacking down across the shoulders of a bandy-legged seaman, belted him good and hard. The fellow snarled and so earned a swipe across the face.

Minga looked away hurriedly. Spouting obscenities, Mr. Tomp-kins was driving his men. She liked the second mate least of the three officers. He was so dirty—mentally as well as physically, and his breath was nothing if not noxious.

The brig's crew readied the vessel for action with remarkable speed for merchantmen. This was due perhaps to those frequent gun drills upon which the black-browed captain insisted, to the sharp resentment of the crew and Mr. Tompkins no less. They claimed, and with justice, that they were no men-of-war's men; nevertheless the *Evergreen's* tall young captain had, by dint of encouragement and the liberal use of a belaying pin, kept them at it.

Stripped to the waist and scarlet as boiled lobsters, seamen appeared from below lugging bags of grapeshot, bar shot and cylindrical sacks of gunpowder.

Dark eyes alert and bright, Andrew Warren strode back and forth.

Mr. Beetle, in passing, grinned, "Keep your eye peeled, Ma'am. Ain't many a merchant crew can fall to so smart-like. Cap'n Warren handles 'em in true Navy style. *I* can tell. Served in the old *Gladiator* back in the '60's.''

The more she thought on it, the more curious a mixture appeared Captain Warren. At once headstrong, he was also considered in his judgments; for an ex-officer of the Royal Navy the New Englander was amazingly considerate of his crew; on the other hand he could be downright brutal if a situation warranted the use of force.

There were other puzzling aspects of his character, she mused while perspiration coursed down her ribs, thighs, everywhere— drops were even dripping from her fingertips. For the rock-ribbed Tory he professed to be, Captain Warren had acted mighty friendly with a blue-chinned French privateer captain who had ordered the brig hove-to off Hatteras. Not the least astounding of her discoveries was that Andrew Warren could speak excellent French.

The object of Mistress Allen's ponderings climbed back up on the quarterdeck, his gaunt brown face streaked with sweat.

"What of the strange vessel?" She couldn't help asking.

He gave her a quick look then smiled a tight smile.

"She's a big craft. Bigger than I like."

From a locker he produced a heavy cutlass with a scarred brass guard.

When he had buckled it on he caught up his spyglass and once more studied the islander. The black schooner, he found, had turned and was running on a course paralleling the barrier reef. Obviously her skipper was hunting a passage through the barrier as she toiled heavily on over the shimmering bright blue sea.

What most sharpened his anxiety was the discovery that the stranger's foc's'le was fairly a-swarm. For an honest merchantman she was carrying far too numerous a crew. It wasn't especially reassuring either to consider the *Evergreen's* crew—only twenty in all; they were as motley a group as he'd ever seen shipped.

The deck load of pine planking loomed dangerously high and yellow at their backs. God pity the crew if ever a cannon ball went cracking into the lumber; splinters would go a-flying, spreading horrible mutilation in the brig's waist.

Buckets of sand and water now stood ranged about the mast

bases. Eli Tompkins was serving out the brig's scant stock of blunderbusses and boarding pistols.

Already, boarding pikes and a handful of battered old hangers lay in convenient places. But for all of that, Andrew mused, if the schooner indeed turned out to be a picaroon the *Evergreen's* company would not stand the chance of a snowball on a hot skillet. Through his glass he now could count four—six gun-ports let into her starboard side. She'd mount twelve guns in all—twice the brig's armament and her guns would be heavier by a long shot.

Why couldn't even a breath of wind come along to grant his becalmed vessel steerage way? It was a miserably helpless feeling to watch the strange vessel continue her slow rowing along the barrier reef, like a tramp hunting a gap in a hedge row. Well, there was nothing to do but to pray that the reefs marched in unbroken ranks clean down to the horizon.

He admired the Allen girl's gift for keeping quiet, for not asking stupid unanswerable questions. Fanning herself slowly she had gone over to stand quietly beside Joe Beaver, the half-breed quartermaster. Even her white cotton stockings now had become soaked and bright and her silver and enamel bracelet felt hot. This was the worst yet. Sweat was dripping from the quartermaster's elbows.

Creak, crack! Creak, crack! The brig's fabric wearily continued to yield to the oily swells.

Suddenly from the crew arose a murmur, the schooner's sweeps had stopped, then had disappeared inboard.

"Now, Mr. Beetle," Andrew Warren observed, "we'll soon learn what yonder whiskeradoes intend."

III

THE BLACK SCHOONER

HALF a mile distant the black schooner, having lost way, also fell into the trough of the swell and commenced to rock.

"No channel through the reef," muttered Jared Beetle, "that'll call for a boat attack."

"Wish t' God there was a King's cruiser about."

"Now if we'd elected to navigate the Old Bahamas Pas—" A look from Andrew cut the sentence short.

The big, red-haired mate began whistling softly, drummed thick sausage-like fingers on the rail.

"Look! Look! They's a thousand of 'em!" the frightened voice of a youth in the crew penetrated the breathless hot silence.

In scrambling succession a torrent of men were tumbling over the black schooner's side and into five small craft which had been hoisted out in slovenly fashion. Steel sparkled in brief ominous flashes from their midst. She was beyond a doubt a picaroon.

Minga Allen looked hard. So far the situation had come as a welcome relief from the unbearable monotony of this voyage and from the now inescapable realization that that appalling episode beside Hudson's River had not yet done with its consequences. For almost a week she'd expected that, any day, she would "come 'round" as the girls back home put it. But she hadn't. A delay of two weeks wasn't to be shrugged away, no matter how many explanations she took refuge in.

Oh damn! If only it had been Jerry—not some beastly unknown foreigners now hanged higher than Haman himself. One hope remained. She hadn't been ill in the mornings and that, so the Brewster girls claimed, was the only sure-enough proof. She was startled to see Captain Warren stop his anxious parade back and forth across the quarterdeck and to hear him snap:

"Mr. Beetle, order the bosun first to bend a light cable onto the sheet anchor. Then he's to free our starboard anchor."

"Aye, aye, sir." Patently mystified, the big mate swung off down the deck.

"Mr. Tompkins!"

The second mate raised a puffy face framed in ragged gray whiskers.

"Aye, aye, sir."

"Man the gig! Lively now!"

"Be we a-goin' to tow?"

"Damn your eyes, do as I say!"

Under Andrew's immediate supervision the sheet anchor was rowed out a good two hundred yards off the starboard beam before, as covertly as possible, it was eased down among the corals.

Presently the starboard anchor was dropped two hundred yards ahead and somewhat to starboard of the brig's bowsprit.

"You've made out her name?" Andrew demanded of the first mate on regaining the quarterdeck.

Mr. Beetle nodded. "Aye, sir. She's the *Verdugo*, out o' Sant' Jago—leastways, that's what's painted on her."

"*Verdugo?* What's that mean? Below there!" Andrew called. "Any of you know what *Verdugo* means?"

A very thin Negro with restless yellowish eyes knuckled his shiny scalp.

"Dat Spanish, Cappen sar. '*Verdugo*' means executioner man, Cappen sar."

"An apt name it would seem," Minga observed more to herself than to anyone else. "Does this mean, Captain, that we have to deal with pirates?"

"Aye, with pirates—or picaroons as they're named in these latitudes." Andrew nodded, his gaze on the five boats pulling away from the schooner.

Flocks of curious, shrill-voiced seabirds were gliding and rocking above the rowers.

He looked slowly into the gentle oval of her flushed features and said, "Pray accept my compliments, Mistress Allen. There are few females who wouldn't be bawling their eyes out long ere this."

"Then, sir, you seem to have been unfortunate in your acquaintanceship with my sex," she replied with a primness he found exasperating. "And now, pray, what am I to do?"

His sudden warmth for her evaporated. With a bleak grin he said:

"Take what you wish to the cable tier."

"The cable tier?" Her gray-green eyes flew wide open. "Do you intend that I smother to death?"

"You will be safe there. Splinters—"

"Safe. Did I ask to be kept safe? Besides I am confident you will find small difficulty in driving off such a mangy pack of rogues. Why not show your colors? I warrant a view of the British flag will send them scurrying."

"Oh rot!" Andrew said impatiently. "They mean to plunder us and since they outnumber us by three-to-one, we are in for the bloody hell of a time."

Minga didn't like his tone, wasn't accustomed to it. She straightened until her damp hair brushed the old jib. "No gentleman would employ such language—"

Hitherto unseen lights suddenly glinted in the jet depths of Andrew Warren's eyes and his jaw grew long and sharp. "The devil take your finicky ways."

The silly twit; why couldn't she realize that never would the *Evergreen* stand in graver peril? Still, it would accomplish nothing to tell her about the picaroons and their barbarous treatment of

those who fell into their clutches. Sometimes small smoldering
hulks were sighted by passing vessels. Other times half-devoured
bodies came drifting up on beaches—bodies marked also by
knife slashes—the corpses of women lacking ears or breasts or
eyes.

It was part and parcel of the picaroons' way to see that *no*
survivors remained to embroil them with the King's unsympathetic
and implacable men-of-war.

He glanced over the rail. Damn. Those boats were growing larger
momentarily.

"Mistress Allen, time grows short."

Turning aside, Andrew Warren knotted a dark blue handkerchief
about his forehead. It should serve to keep his eyes free of sweat.
Next he eased a pair of heavy brass-mounted pistols into a wide
canvas belt.

In a soft yet curiously ominous tone he said, "Madam, you
astonish me. For the last time—will you go below?"

Color poured into cheeks already fiery with sunburn. "I will
not."

"Quacko!" Andrew beckoned a large Negro rendered hideous
by a double rank of tribal scars running in chevrons down either
cheek.

"Sah?"

"Carry this lady down to the cable tier." He spoke as dispassionately as if ordering a topsail set. "Briskly, now."

"You—you daren't!" Minga raged.

He turned away as he rasped, "Quacko, obey orders!"

Minga looked frantically about. The quartermaster stood like a
statue at the useless wheel, his eyes opaque. Joe Atherton stood
wooden-faced beside the gun he captained.

Grinning nervously the Negro shuffled forward, bare shoulders
shining in the sunlight.

"Don't you dare touch me!" A-quiver with fury Minga whirled
on the figure dominating the tiny quarterdeck. "I have no choice
save to submit, but I warn you, Captain Warren, my uncle is very
highly considered in Jamaica. You will be held severely to account
when we reach Montego Bay."

"*If* we get to Montego Bay, Madam," Andrew Warren corrected
deliberately.

The five picaroon boats having reached extreme range, Andrew
Warren ordered matches lit, then cast a keen glance at the two
anchor lines sloping down until they lost themselves into blue-green
depths. What he had in mind might work—it would, certainly, had
he been commanding a Continental cruiser instead of this stubby
little merchantman.

The pirate flotilla commenced to pick up the beat of their oars until they sent a welter of spray flashing diamond-like in the sun. Backs white, brown and black glistened as the rowers swung back and forth.

Now the *Evergreen's* taut and fearful crew could begin to discern details. Garbed in a brilliant miscellany of garments, the picaroons clutched their weapons and rocked their bodies to the stroke of their rowers. One after another, two big whale boats, a large gig and a pair of dugout canoes, pulled up to the line of reefs which barred the black schooner from her prey. Passed it. Came on.

Jared Beetle, the Long Island Tory, swung up, his hard features eager.

"They'll just about be in range, sir." A ring set in his left ear flashed. "Shall we let 'em have a few rounds?"

"Not yet, Mr. Beetle."

"But, sir,—"

"Get to your station! Blast your soul to hell, I'm commanding here." If only he'd a pair of gun crews out of the *Andrew Doria.*

"Aye, aye, sir." The mate nodded; he was coming to understand Andrew Warren.

Unexpectedly the Indian quartermaster spoke. "Wind come, Cappen, byme by." His eyes, vitreous black in the flat plane of his features, swung over the brig's stern.

Up to the northwest the least dim ghost of a cloud was drifting over the horizon. Though Joe Beaver might be right, there wasn't a chance in the world that a breath of wind could arrive before the black schooner's crew was alongside.

"Mr. Tompkins, show our colors," Andrew flung over his shoulder; sight of the Red Ensign just might give the picaroons pause.

As the signal halyard block began to squeak, Andrew made a careful estimate of the stranger's force; the five crowded and rapidly approaching boats were not two hundred yards distant. A smothered groan arose from the *Evergreen's* crew. Sight of the British flag had given the enemy no pause whatsoever; no reaction at all ensued beyond a brief commotion which caused steel to flicker palely in the boats. Apparently the prolonged absence of Royal patrol ships had lent the islanders courage.

Now the cries of the coxswains, urging on the oarsmen, came clearly over the water.

"*Unos, dos, tres!*—" "*Un, deux, trois!*—" "*Wan, two, t'ree!*"

The cadence was being set in three or more languages. The picaroons were predominately dark-skinned. Andrew recognized pure black Negroes, mustees, sambos. All looked wild, some half-naked in ragged, wide-brimmed straw hats, others wearing a panache of vari-colored macaw, flamingo or parrot feathers.

Now and then one of the raiders would stand up, scream something unintelligible, and flourish an axe or a machete.

As usual, when an action impended, Andrew felt his belly muscles tighten.

It didn't look now as if Dr. Blanchard would ever see those medicines; a great shame, too. Andrew's recollections of that hideous place called the Drydock remained vivid. Curse the ineffective weight of his broadside! They'd have to let the enemy come dangerously close before it would be of use.

To the distant schooner's signal gaff climbed a red banner which hung limp until an errant puff of air stirred it enough to reveal its design. A skeleton crudely executed in white was flanked by two sprawling initials which Andrew made out as a C and a P.

"Means they'll grant us no quarter," grunted the *Evergreen's* gaptoothed gunner.

A sudden fierce clamor arose from the boats.

Swaying easily to his vessel's motion, Andrew cast a quick look down the deck. In patterns repeated thrice his crew fidgeted at battle stations; five men were manning each of the three little guns. At the moment Joe Atherton and the other gun captains were blowing on matches secured from the sand-filled tubs and lashed to wooden linstocks.

He levelled his speaking trumpet. "Make ready!"

"Aye, aye, sir!" Eagerly the gun crews galvanized into motion. The Number Fours leaned far out through the gun ports and soaked their sponges alongside. Number Threes, holding rammers ready, waited while the three little four-pounders were trundled forward by means of block and tackle until their muzzles peered out through the trued-up gun ports.

The crews then stood clear of the recoil path and raised red, black and brown sweaty faces to the tall and erect figure on the quarterdeck.

Joe Beaver, however, kept his attention on that long gray cloud to the northwest. Perceptibly, it had gained in density as well as in size. In his Naval officer's tone, Andrew addressed the crew, told them that no one was to go below in any case, save to fetch ammunition. Mr. Beetle had orders to shoot down anyone who attempted to do so.

Crisply he called his commands. "Number One gun sight on the lead whale boat. Number Two and Three, on the two canoes."

The picaroons began to row faster and so hard that their sweeps bent in flat arcs. In the prow of the leading boat a huge black pirate in a yellow jersey balanced himself and commenced roaring threats in a guttural African dialect as he swung his cutlass in furious glittering arcs.

No use waiting any longer. Andrew drew a deep breath, shouted, "Fire!"

Number One's gun captain, a hairy little fellow, pursed his lips and blew hard on his match. Muscles rippled across his bare back when he leaned to hold his match to the little four pounder's touchhole. Instantly the priming gave a sibilant *huff!* and a small jet of smoke sprang vertically into the air.

The Number One gun belched a great gray blossom of smoke out of the gun port and sprang back like a thing alive. The cannon's breeching cable, snapped taut, checked the recoil.

Compared to the report of a twelve or fourteen pounder these little four pounders certainly didn't make much of a racket.

"God damn it!" Andrew's heart skipped a beat.

A fountain of water had played briefly half-way between the leading boat and the line of reefs.

Worse still, Number Two gun's roundshot also went skipping harmlessly over the sea for all the world like a flat stone flung by a boy. Jerusha! These merchant crews handled their guns like a gang of seamstresses. At such range there was absolutely no excuse for missing.

Number Three gun, Atherton's, did a trifle better, its projectile barely missed the big longboat on the left of the flotilla's line.

"Christ above!" Mr. Beetle was tugging furiously at a training tackle. "You dumb bastards couldn't hit a blind ox on the rump with a scoop shovel."

Andrew standing taut behind the wheel felt aghast. Three clean misses and the time lost was irretrievable.

He tried to inject cool confidence into his command—as a good officer would in a critical moment. This was the hell of most merchant gun crews—the minute things got tight they forgot everything they'd been taught.

"With langrage, re-load. Briskly now. And if you miss this time you'll get no third try." This was obvious. The leading boat was surging up not a hundred yards distant.

"Lay Number Two gun yourself," Andrew flung at Beetle. In two quick leaps he gained the main deck. Should have been there to start with.

From the nearest tub of langrage—odds and ends of scrap iron, nails, broken glass, musket balls and bits of chain—he shovelled three scoopfuls into the muzzle of his cannon, only half aware that the voices beyond the rail were sounding ominously near and had become altered to a more savage pitch.

Bo-om-m! Jed Beetle's piece let go, but Andrew confined his attention to the handspikes as his crew traversed the four pounder. Over the bulwark sang a number of musket balls which cut holes in the main sheet flapping brown and useless over head.

Andrew pierced the powder cartridge in his piece by expertly employing a steel worm through its vent. Next he bit the end of a priming quill filled with fine four F. French powder, spilled its contents down the touchhole and smoothed the black grains in place.

"*Abajo los Ingleses!*" "*Mort!*"

"No quarter, you bloody sea-going grocers."

A regular gale of cries now came ringing over the rail. The clamor of the picaroons put Andrew in mind of a pack of hounds ravening at the foot of a 'coon tree.

IV

CLOSE QUARTERS

WHEN at seventy-five yards' range, Andrew Warren touched off his piece, the little cannon kicked like a curried colt and a cloud of acrid, rotten-smelling heat beat back into his face.

"Hump yourselves," he panted at the gun crew even before the breeching blocks had ceased clattering. Screams, howls and breathless obscenities penetrated the lazy curtain of smoke. When the screen thinned, his gun crew raised a delighted yelp.

Through the gunport they could see that the gun had scored a clean hit which had carried away the starboard oars of the big, dull red-painted whale boat. Deprived of motive power on her starboard side, the whaler was moving now in a slow circle to port with her remaining rowers attempting to switch enough oars over to get their craft back on a straight course. As it was she was effectively blocking the course of the next boat behind and, at the same time, offering an almost unmissable target.

Forward, Joe Atherton's thick voice could be heard cursing his black gun crew.

"Put your backs to it, you club-footed baboons—else you'll smile in hell."

Once Number One gun was reloaded Andrew forced himself to sight carefully at that brilliantly lit tangle of jerseys, shirts and bare bodies in the whale boat. Using a leaded mallet, he gave several taps to one of those quoins which elevated or depressed the four pounder's muzzle.

Setting his teeth, he caught up the linstock and touched off his piece.

"Small arms! Man the rail!" he yelled, well aware that if this time the charge went wide there would be no opportunity to reload.

Snatching out his pistol he looked over the rail. Yonder was a sight he wouldn't readily forget. Where the whaler had been, only pieces of planking, broken oars, several hats and small kegs bobbed about amid a patch of water varying from pale pink to a deep scarlet in color. Half a dozen picaroons struggled in the water and kept up a terrified screaming.

Brushing sweat from his brow Andrew realized that Mr. Beetle's gunnery, too, had been effective. Further out, one of the canoes was down by the stern and filling fast. The three other boats had, by a miracle, stopped in confusion.

"Man the guns! For your lives!"

In frantic haste the brig's crew dropped their pikes and blunderbusses and dashed back to their cannon. Such an undreamt of opportunity wasn't likely to offer itself for long.

Panting, the gunners reached into the langrage tubs set on the lumber piled behind them. Bolts, sections of crow bar, small rocks and even a set of broken-up stove lids went into the *Evergreen's* battery.

The range, Andrew figured, had closed enough for real execution.

Meanwhile the stricken canoe turned lazily onto her beam, spilling into the blue-green water those of her crew who had not already gone overboard.

"Oo, bloody roar!" bellowed one of the crew. "Ain't that clippin' the niggers' combs for 'em?"

"Hold your fire!" At too great a range for langrage the swearing picaroons were backing away, absolutely ignoring the frantic pleas and blasphemies of their comrades struggling in the water.

Snapped Andrew, "Reload with grape."

"Wind come," called the halfbreed, his leather-hued features impassive.

That was true enough. Far off to the northeast the aching blueness of the Caribbean was becoming ruffled. Andrew's thrill of elation faded; beyond a doubt the breeze would reach the schooner first.

Even so there was room for more hope than he had ever dreamed possible. So far no one aboard the *Evergreen* had been hit and his crew were steadying down—even the Negroes.

This was well because the picaroons at last were perceiving the great advantage lent them by the brig's lack of steerage way. Raising hoarse cries, they circled for a second to advance, but this time in line with the *Evergreen's* bow where none of the guns could be brought to bear.

"This passes bearance," Minga Allen decided amid the fetid darkness of the cable tier. "If there is no more cannonading, I'll go on deck. That blackheaded villain has no right to condemn me to stew in this wretched place."

Certainly life was making up in a hurry for those long, placid years in Brewster. Imagine being aboard a vessel attacked by buccaneers! She passed a forefinger over her forehead to scrape away sticky sweat which kept trickling down into her eyes. Suppose the brig were taken. What would happen? She wished she'd thought to stop in her cabin for the little pocket pistol Major de Vaux had pressed upon her.

Merciful Heavens! It was really stifling in this complete darkness. She suppressed a scream when a rat crept over her leg. All along she'd heard the loathsome creatures scuffling and squeaking among the coils of sour-smelling cable. It was miserable, this not knowing what was happening on deck.

She thought she recognized the dull rumble of gun carriage wheels being hauled back and forth. Oaths such as she had never before heard sounded just overhead. A twist of cable kept digging into her thigh, another was chafing her back, and her arms were being continually pricked by hemp fibers. Of course, she *would* have left off her stays today, for the first time.

When a rat nipped at her ankle she couldn't stand it any longer. Bathed in perspiration she commenced to crawl out of the cable hold.

"Man the windlass!" Right over her head Captain Warren was speaking. "Put your backs to it, you misbegotten sons of whores!"

When he saw her, Andrew Warren couldn't for the life of him restrain a broad grin. If Minga Allen had not always been so neat, so crisp, so self-possessed, it wouldn't have been so ludicrous to see her there in the blazing sunlight with her chestnut hair hanging in damp and grimy ringlets, and her pale blue gown smeared with muck and green slime from the cables.

She was so wrathful she had failed to realize that one of her garters had become unfastened, permitting a stocking to sag and wrinkle. Profuse perspiration had caused her clothes to adhere to her figure with treacherous fidelity. Certainly she'd no idea that her up-turned nose was gleaming pink as any carnation.

Rigid, she halted before him. "And on top of everything else you—you d-dare to laugh at me. Oh-h, you infamous b-boor! Oh-h—if only—"

Anticipating his passenger's intention, Andrew intercepted Minga Allen's hand before its palm reached his cheek. They stood an instant glowering at each other while the *Evergreen* continued to roll rhythmically on the glassy swells.

"Why are you on deck?" he demanded, a wicked gleam in the depths of his dark eyes. "I ordered you below."

Her reddened features tightened, then commenced to quiver. "I'll not return to th-that p-pest hole. You m-may as well know that!"

The grim angle to his jaw relaxed. "Please, Mistress Allen, my intent in ordering you below is only—"

"To p-prove your authority, to bully, t-to humiliate me—to—to—"

"—To preserve you from hurt."

"I will *not* go below again." When she wrenched free her hand, he stepped back. "I had rather d-die in the sunlight than s-smother in that revolting darkness."

She had intended to say more, to give this fellow such a tongue-lashing as would release some of the fear and shame and bitterness which had been poisoning her peace of mind ever since Jerry had smiled and drifted away into Eternity. Yet further speech seemed inadvisable. Captain Warren looked distinctly formidable in his battered straw hat and jersey ripped across one shoulder. The brass-mounted butts of the boarding pistols in his belt flashed like angry eyes.

"Very well," said he turning to view the advancing boats. "Stay on deck then, but keep out of the way."

"I will, and be damned to you, Captain Warren," she was amazed to hear her voice sputtering.

Andrew Warren's strategy in running out the two anchors became apparent when he sent a gang up onto the quarterdeck. Grinning, the seamen brushed past the Allen girl. *Phew!* They stank to high Heaven.

"Tail onto the sheet anchor line," Andrew instructed his men while keeping one eye on the three remaining picaroon boats. From this angle, they calculated, never a one of the motionless vessel's guns could be brought to bear because of lack of steerageway.

On his low-pitched command of "Heave away, sheet anchor men!", the brig slowly commenced to swing to. Yard by yard the anchor line was hauled, dripping, in over the starboard quarter, and, one after another, the grim iron mouths of the three little cannons began to bear.

Over the stern rang a bewildered outcry from among the buccaneers. Without wind the becalmed brig should have lain helpless, awaiting her doom like a moose stuck in a snowdrift and ringed by wolves.

"Ay Dios! Qué hay? Vamos aprisa!"

The picaroons, a gaunt, tawdry rabble, garbed in a vivid assortment of ragged silk shirts, tunics, hats and equipment, were too close to flee immediately. The brig's port battery poured grape shot into the biggest canoe, briefly churned the water about it into a white lather. Musket balls peppered the sea just short of the remaining whaler.

Heart in mouth, Minga watched a whole cluster of picaroons knocked spinning into the water. Their weapons flickered wildly through their efforts to maintain balance. She got dazed impressions of Mr. Beetle waving encouragements to his gun crew, of Joe Atherton, his pinched features brightened, standing near the Captain, of Andrew Warren standing in the hot sunshine, hands outflung to check the cable crew at his side.

"Way enough! Quick, Beetle, quick! Give 'em another—no, let be. They're out of range."

Clearly, the boat crews had had enough. They were backing water in a hurry, oblivious of the desperate entreaties of their fellows who remained clinging to the shattered whaler. When safely out of range, the outlaws put about and began pulling back to the black schooner lurking beyond the reefs.

Unforgettably piercing became the screams of the picaroons who remained swimming or clinging to the wrecked whalers and canoes. Several triangular, slate-gray fins had begun cutting the sea's surface in sudden, dreadfully swift maneuvers which brought them successively nearer to the men in the water.

By fives and tens sharks and barracudas congregated. Already the brig's crew commenced to witness chilling sights through the crystalline waters of the Caicos Passage.

Fishes, dazzlingly brilliant in color, were ripping at those bodies or parts of bodies which already reposed on the channel's bottom. Under their tearing assault one of the submerged corpses, that of a Negro, seemed, incredibly, to regain life. Like a marionette, the body began jerking its arms and what the langrage had left of its legs.

A large, black-bearded buccaneer was swimming awkwardly toward the motionless brig.

"Help, mates. The sharks—in Gawd's name don't let—"

The speaker broke off short. One of the deadly fins vanished a few yards distant, and the white of the monster's belly glimmered as it turned over.

"Oh-h! My God!" The swimmer's head vanished under water with magical speed. He reappeared an instant later, yowling amid a crimson bath, then disappeared for good.

The clamor of the remaining picaroons reminded Andrew of such sounds as escaped the *Lexington* after taking a hulling shot. There was nothing to be done. Even had the swimmers deserved the least consideration, the sharks would have completed their massacre of the picaroons before a boat could be manned.

In a futile frenzy of terror some survivors attempted to crawl up on the battered skeleton of their whaler, but all they accomplished was to cause it to roll over. The sea all about appeared to boil with rapid, invisible maneuvers.

Frozen-faced, Minga watched a lemon-featured mestee start swimming desperately towards the *Evergreen*.

In the blue water his scarlet shirt showed bright. Teeth gleamed as he held up an imploring hand and yelled: "*Una linea, Señores! Por piedad, una linea!*"

"Ah-h the 'ell with yer!" shouted Joe Atherton whose bared back revealed a shiny and puckered criss-cross pattern of whitish scars. "Ye'd 'ave slit our bleedin' craws fer us! 'Ere's a preserver fer yer!"

Stooping, he caught up a round shot and hurled it at the swimmer. Before the missile struck the surface, however, a gray and white outline flashed up under the mulatto's bare brown legs. After a brief, furious commotion, the shark sped on leaving the upper half of the mulatto's body to zigzag down, trailed by a dense comet's tail of brilliant scarlet.

Soon there resounded no more shouts. Of the stricken boats and their crews nothing remained save scattered debris, a few oars and, here and there, a handkerchief or a hat floating soddenly.

Thousands of sea birds, aroused from the reefs by the gunfire, still wheeled and darted overhead, their shadows tracing and retracing swift patterns across the *Evergreen's* deck.

"That were a bloody smart trick, if I may say so, sir." The brig's Cockney gunner wagged his head approvingly. "Saving that sheet anchor, them ruddy villains would be aboard o' us this minute."

Andrew was as pleased as he was surprised. Jerusha! Half an hour ago he'd not have wagered a sixpence on the *Evergreen's* chances of escape. Yet here she was, unboarded and whole save for a few musket balls through her canvas.

Minga Allen, stony-faced because of those despairing cries which yet rang in her ears, sought the shade of the mainsheet. Her knees were trembling and she realized, dully, that one of her stockings had sagged down about her ankle. So this was what a sea battle was like? Well, there was no denying that Captain Warren was acquitting himself as should a stout and loyal British subject.

To Joe Beaver and Andrew Warren it became evident that a real breeze was now not far off, but—and therein lay a big "but"—it would almost certainly fill the schooner's sails first. Suppose, with her much heavier battery, the picaroon should sail close up the barrier reefs? There could be no doubt that the *Evergreen* would then be in range. Andrew thought a long minute, then to the starboard watch gave orders to heave in on the bow line as quickly as the sheet anchor was raised.

"I cal'late you aim to tow, sir?" Eli Tompkins possessed a genius for commenting on the obvious.

"To kedge and tow. The whiskeradoes could play hob with us here. Looks like a long eight is mounted amidships."

Since the *Verdugo*—the name was now clearly visible through Andrew's glass—was hoisting her boats inboard and getting out her sweeps it became apparent that the buccaneers intended to continue their attack; at all costs, the brig must be prevented from reporting to Port Royal that the *Verdugo* was looting British merchantmen.

Mr. Beetle in the long boat commenced to tow the *Evergreen* while the gig ran out a light anchor as fast as the men, panting over the capstan bars, could walk in the dripping anchor line.

"They're gaining, sir, closing range fast," Jed Beetle warned from the bows, "and the reefs bow in our direction."

"Starboard your helm!" Andrew directed the half-breed Penobscot.

Under a puff of wind—the first to ruffle the Caicos Passage in three eternal days—the black schooner heeled gently and, in a response to her helm, commenced to bear down on her still becalmed prey.

"Pull her head 'round," Andrew shouted. Presenting his stern to the enemy would offer a smaller target.

"Pull! Pull, you damned jelly backs!" Jed Beetle also foresaw the impending danger.

The boat crews made their oars bow with effort and their blades churned the sea into a welter of flying spray.

Out from the buccaneer's waist spurted a jet of dirty gray smoke; then, a split second later, the *Evergreen* shuddered as if she had struck a rock.

A deadly crackling noise such as Andrew had not heard in almost a year filled the air. He flung up a warning arm as a dense shower of splinters from the deck load went flying in all directions. Like deadly yellow arrows, jagged barbs of wood flew upwards, piercing the limp canvas, littering the deck or falling far out over the sea.

Two, three hands lay motionless in the shadows of the rigging. Forward a man began screaming. Unluckily, the boat crews lost their rhythm, commenced to scramble ineffectually with their oars, whereupon the brig lost headway and, under influence of the current, once more commenced to present her beam to the enemy.

It was a revelation to Minga Allen to witness how surely, how rapidly, the brig's captain met the emergency. His voice was not especially loud, but it carried as he ordered Tompkins' men to cease rowing, to regain their stroke. Next he despatched the carpenter and his mate to estimate the damage.

"Get those bodies overboard!" he flung at the boatswain. The hurt sailor kept on whimpering and rocking back and forth, as Long George the cook, with a red hot poker, cauterized a gaping hollow in the sufferer's thigh.

Captain Warren gave a furious look at his own useless battery— the range was hopeless for four-pounders—then, with Beaver's help, he swung the main boom outboard, ready to catch the first suspicion of wind. In skittish cat's-paws the breeze, with agonizing deliberation, was nearing the *Evergreen*.

Purple-faced, Andrew wheeled, beckoned to the girl crouched round-eyed by the binnacle.

"Bear a hand on the helm," he rasped. "If you're set on staying on deck, you'll work!"

She gave him one startled look, then ran to obey.

"You can steer?"

"A little." Aye, a very little. All she'd ever learned was what the Whittemore boys had taught her on Lake George.

"Take wheel," he panted. "Beaver'll be needed elsewhere."

Already the carpenter's hatchet had begun ringing in the bows. The boat crews were working in unison again so the brig started to swing end on.

Boom-m-m! The *Verdugo* fired again. Making an eerie screech, a round shot whistled up, punched a ragged hole in the main sheet before it raised a brief geyser in the blue water off the starboard bow.

Aware that their prey had regained motion, the outlaws fired a whole broadside and with devastating effect. A chain-shot cut away the main starboard shrouds and two more hit the brig hard under her counter and right at the water-line.

Aware of a nerve pulsing fiercely in his cheek, Andrew ran to the rail and looked over. Hell's roaring bells! The sea was fairly sluicing in through a jagged hole in the side. A heart-chilling litter of broken planks and splinters was floating alongside.

"Hold her steady!" he flung at the girl.

Unexpectedly the picaroons fired a gun a moment after the crack of that disastrous broadside had died away. Minga Allen felt the breath drawn from her lungs, felt an invisible palm smite her across the face. A stay dangling loose was severed not two feet from her nose, its lower end striking the deck with a gentle thump. Death had passed her by just that much. Nor had it missed Captain Warren by any greater margin. He licked his lips but kept on knotting the parted main sheet.

"Clumsy beggars," he grunted, then glanced up. "Steady the wheel! Here's the breeze."

A faint creaking sounded aloft as, simultaneously, the weather-stained canvas lost its lifeless look.

Minga shook the hair out of her eyes, gave the brig's wheel a half turn, just to get the "feel" of the water.

Andrew felt relieved. He guessed she could steer all right. Good stuff, Minga Allen. She might have been churning butter for all the fright she showed standing there with legs braced apart, her long young body tensed.

The carpenter came lumbering aft. "First shot, sir, took us under the cathead 'twixt wind and water."

"Got your sheet lead and oakum to work?"

"Aye, aye, sir—but there's nigh three foot in the forward well a'ready."

"Damnation! Mr. Beetle! Man the forward pump."

It was fine all the same to feel the *Evergreen* stir and go creeping up to overtake the tow boats.

As if to accelerate the crew's efforts, the *Verdugo* fired a second thunderous broadside. The picaroon, having reached the limit of

pursuit, commenced firing at top speed while hovering just inside
the barrier of reefs.

Minga's throat went dry, strange little shivers needled the backs
of her hands and darted down her loins.

Suppose one of those roundshots struck really close? Splinters
were flying everywhere. When a heavy roundshot smashed into the
foc'sle her fingers froze to the wheel handles. It made a noise like
some Titan cutting kindling. Another shot shattered the quarterboat,
released a pig and several chickens and, at the same time, hurled a
javelin-like splinter at Long George. It pierced the cook through the
stomach. Coughing thickly, the Negro tugged at the jagged length
of the splinter with both hands. Slowly his knees buckled and he
swayed violently, staring in white-eyed horror to see his blood
meandering off towards the scuppers. The sand thickened the flow
into dreadful crimson lumps. He fell, squirming slowly.

Another cannonball tore through the port bulwarks, stretched two
seamen quivering on the deck. One of the hens had fallen into the
water, where it flopped desperately about until a shark got it.

Despite her terrific punishment the *Evergreen* began to pick up
speed. Now the tow boats were bumping alongside, disgorging their
sunburned crews.

Through eyes smarting with sweat, Andrew glanced aft. The
Allen girl had given over the wheel to Joe Beaver and now was
crouched under the bulwarks, her features deadly white beneath her
sunburn. Intently, she was studying the battle-torn mainsail. A soft
gurgling sounded alongside as, with painful slowness, the brig
began to lurch away from her antagonist.

From aloft came a series of creaks when the brig's yards swung
about against their parrals. The slick look of the sea had disappeared
and some of the sun's crushing heat was fading.

The picaroons commenced firing furiously but, because of the
diminished proportions of their target and of the increasing range,
their roundshot scored no more hits, only raised tall waterspouts
from among the bubbles drifting lazily in the *Evergreen's* wake.

The carpenter returned, his whiskered, terrier-like face very
grave. "We're hit bad, sir, the hole for'ard is worst."

"Shall I have some guns shifted aft?"

"Aye, aye, sir. The quicker the better."

Andrew raged along the deck, roused his panting crew with fists
and searing language. Some he set to pumping, some to helping the
carpenter. Mr. Beetle and he cast loose those cannons nearest the
forecastle. When their weight was shifted the brig's battered bow
became noticeably elevated.

IV

THE LEE RAIL

JOE ATHERTON, his cheeks filled and bronzed, swung up, knuckled his forelock, man-o'-war style. The salute gave Andrew a poignant, reminiscent twinge. Still, he'd probably never fight in a stiffer engagement aboard a cruiser, than the one the *Evergreen* had fought today. That was some consolation.

"Vittles are ready, sir. I've warned Mistress Allen, sir, and she's waiting in the cabin." The last traces of pallor were gone from the deserter's features, also that pinched look from about his mouth and eyes.

"Lord," thought Andrew, "so it's time to eat." He didn't feel much like it, not when he thought of the five dead men, overboard and doubtless devoured by those sharks which kept dogging the battered brig.

The crew didn't like the way the sharks were keeping the *Evergreen* company; took it as an ill omen. But, as Mr. Beetle unconcernedly put it, "A sailor who's 'feared of gettin' hurt had better bide ashore."

"Very well, Atherton, have the bosun see who can take Long George's place in the galley."

Leaving Tompkins on duty, heavily he swung down the sunsetlighted companionway. Until now, he had scarcely noticed a long, shallow gash in his left forearm; for the life of him he couldn't recall when he had received it. But now it was smarting infernally.

Jet hair tumbling over his eyes and quite unaware that he was smudged black as any Coromantee with burnt powder grains, Andrew paused before the main cabin. Here, perforce, the table had been set. In entering, he bent his head to avoid his cabin lamp rocking rhythmically on its gimbals.

If Mistress Allen was ready so promptly, it argued that she was going to complain about his having sent her to the cable tier, about his having elected to descend Caicos instead of the Leeward Passage. A pity she'd overheard the port captain back in New York advise the latter course.

She was standing looking out of the stern ports, her long slim body yielding gracefully to the brig's revitalized motion. She heard him now and turned, mighty fetching, he thought, in a light green gown.

"Good evening, Captain," she greeted. "I trust the damage is being successfully repaired?"

He bowed low from the waist, in the ceremonious manner Captain Nicholas Biddle demanded of his officers. "The carpenter is working, Madame." He lent the title a French inflection. "But we've been badly hulled and that's a fact! I am sorry if I caused you any inconvenience." Why was she considering him so steadily? Plague take it, it was so dark he couldn't rightly read her expression.

"I regret having earned your displeasure in that matter of the cable tier," he apologized heavily. "I felt that we stood in greater peril than you appreciated."

"'I do not doubt that, sir," she returned evenly. A brief silence fell, disturbed only by dishes clattering gently against the fiddles which kept them from sliding onto the cabin floor.

He reached for the brass doorknob of his cabin. "Pray excuse my appearance, Madame. I will make efforts to repair it."

"Don't go just yet, Captain Warren. I must first—well—I must praise your extremely clever maneuver with—with the anchors." Suddenly Minga's reserve broke. The sweet oval of her face lit and her words came out a-tumbling, like a litter of puppies from a kennel. "Really, Captain—I— You were magnificent throughout! So collected, so shrewd, so—so—commanding!"

He was taken utterly off stride, felt a great warm flood of gratitude well up within him. This was not at all what he'd been expecting—not by a long shot. Here he'd been all braced to meet a furious tirade; instead, she stood there, friendly, a smile curving her wide and vivid mouth.

"'Why, why—" he stammered, "I scarcely deserve such—such—*Nom de Dieu, Madame,* you are much too kind." Damn! He was coloring up like any schoolboy. "Indeed, it is you who deserve unmeasured praise. I shall find it hard to forget your trick at the wheel."

"La, sir, there was no leisure in which to become frightened." Her lashes fell as her gaze flickered to the shattered glass of the stern port. He looked so dreadfully tired she wondered why she'd been so hard on him.

After all, he was a Loyalist and he'd had nothing to do with Jerry's death—or the rest of it. Goodness, if he ever suspected—a ghastly suspicion seized her. Colonel Saunders—what if he'd guessed that she *had* to leave—until she could be sure, at least?

He passed her with the intention of entering his cabin.

She turned to confront him. "Tell me, Captain, why are the Yankees so arrogant as to boast that only *their* women possess fortitude? Why do they protest that Englishwomen are more timorous than mice?"

Unwisely, Andrew interrupted, "But Madame, you are no Englishwoman. That's plain as a pike staff. You're an American— er, Colonial, that is," he added and wondered if he had caught the error in time.

Her smile vanished. "*I am not American!*" she burst out passionately. "I'd die sooner than ever to be called one of those snivelling, mock-heroic hypocrites called 'Patriots.' "

Beside the quarterdeck's lee rail they paused to consider the sea rushing softly, smoothly by. Sudden bursts of phosphorus glowed among waves curling rhythmically away from the brig's side. Now that the sun had gone down at long last, the air was cool and full of balm. The wind set halyards, braces, and shrouds to strumming a gentle obbligato. It whipped Minga Allen's petticoats into a white froth any instant she left them unguarded.

"Have there ever been more stars out at one time?" she demanded, her face tilted to the topmasts and the black rectangles formed by the topsails. "Aren't they like tiny silver lilies stitched onto a purple-black canopy?"

He chuckled. "Puts me more in mind of sugar spilled over a blue china dish. Still it's a fine sight."

He felt all but at ease. The picaroons lay safe leagues astern and his ship was running free again, unleashed from that accursed calm. Why couldn't he be rid of a small, but persistent, worry nagging at his peace of mind?

Most likely 'twas the sound of the pump *clank-clanking* endlessly. If only the carpenter had appeared more certain concerning the damage caused by the *Verdugo's* first broadside. It wasn't pleasant to have to admit that some of the salt fish, vegetables and rice middlings in the forward hold could not have avoided damage. Well, nothing much could be done till the *Evergreen* reached Jamaica and could be hove down.

Reaction from the sharp stress of the afternoon left him mellow, avid of gentleness.

The girl beside him must have guessed his mood. Said she softly, leaning elbows on the rail and staring fixedly out over the great starlit sea, "If I have appeared distant and self-absorbed this voyage, I pray you to forgive me, Captain Warren. My only explanation is—'' she fumbled feverishly a second, ''is that every last farthing I have left in this world is aboard this vessel.''

''Left?''

''My trunks and chests hold all which remains of my father's estate after the Rebel Committee of Public Safety burnt Millwood, my home.'' She spoke less passionately, ''You see, sir, my Mother never recovered from Papa's—murder. The Liberty Boys thought it sport to drag him in a cart through a January night, to half drown him in a horse trough.''

''Not truly!'' He'd heard of such things, had Andrew, but he'd never set much store by them.

''Aye, Captain, truly indeed. Papa was near seventy years and so took the lung fever and died.''

'' 'Twas no sense in such actions,'' Andrew burst out. ''They accomplish nothing.''

''For a loyal officer you employ moderate language,'' Minga observed.

The helmsman, a squat mustee with a bandage glimmering on one wrist, stood, jet eyes fixed on the compass card swaying in the binnacle. Faintly, light from within it gilded his blunt features, lent life to a dirty red shirt he wore open to the belt.

Minga was aware of Andrew Warren's increased proximity, of his interest. Her pulses stirred, commenced to beat a quicker tempo.

''In Jamaica I hope to begin a new life—to dismiss America forever from my memory.'' Her voice gained strength born of a determination slowly conceived. ''I shall live for a while with my Aunt Adelina—the widow of Sir Thomas Moffat of Moffat's Penn. It's situated near Montego Bay.''

''Penn? What in time's a penn?'' Andrew knew very well, but to keep the conversation alive any excuse would serve.

''A penn, I'm told, is Jamaican for a plantation—a stock-raising plantation, that is,'' she explained. ''Oh-h—'' Her hair had at last broken free of its ribbon. She made no effort to control it. Since she had dressed it with French scent, no harm would be done if a tress blew across Captain Warren's lean features.

How badly hurt was his arm? Though he made no to-do over it, he was favoring it the cooler the night grew.

''So, sir, you see me as I am,'' she declared, ''venturing forth with only a scant store of silks, lace, and silverware 'twixt me and a confounded disinterested world.''

He couldn't help but admire her attempt at jauntiness. ''You have not met this aunt?''

"Oh, no. Mama hadn't even heard from Aunt Adelina since— since this trouble."

"Jerusha! Then you aren't certain your Aunt is in Montego Bay?"

Body yielding to the brig's gentle pitching, Minga considered him, round-eyed. "Why, of course, she *must* be there! Uncle Tom left the penn to her attention. Mama said Aunt Adelina was— well,—capable and wasn't afraid of anything and was kind—when she had her way wlth people."

Andrew bit off an acid comment which only a Frenchman would have understood. Well, if Mistress Allen had chosen to voyage so far on a gamble, it was Mistress Allen's lookout. Apparently, she'd no conception of what life in the Sugar Islands was like. Seemed she'd never heard of yellow jack, sunstroke, cholera, or rebellious slaves, either.

She directed a sudden glance at him. "And you, sir, own an interest in this vessel?"

For all the glistening stars, it was too dark to see her well. He struggled to resume an instinctive distrust. "The brig belongs to my uncle."

"And where is his business?"

Andrew remembered his long-rehearsed answer. "On Long Island—at Northport."

"Surely General Clinton will soon whip these rascally Rebels into submission."

Lucky it was dark, else she must have noticed the blood rush into his face. Damn this baggage! If she'd seen the "rascally rebels" aboard the *Enterprise* serving their decrepit guns until they burst, had seen them suffer the surgeon's cold steel—but she hadn't. Let it go.

Calmly, he said, "No doubt you're right, Madame, but I venture Sir Henry will find the matter none so easy."

"Possibly. But, sir, surely God will help to punish such infamous scoundrels."

He stood for the moment astonished clear out of resentment. "Surely you do not deem all Rebels as infamous scoundrels?"

Her voice sounded crisp and cold as the crunch of a snowshoe on a crusted drift. "Never in all the world's history has the name of Liberty been so debased, so perverted by a pack of savage rogues."

Andrew Warren made the evenly spaced seas an object of intense interest. He had to hang on to himself. Dr. Blanchard was counting the days. "Savage rogues." What a term to lay on the men who had followed Montgomery and Arnold up along that tortured trail to

Quebec—and back; who even now were starving and scratching vermin in miserable cantonments outside of Philadelphia. Now he really pitied her—her and her smug, cool attitude. It wasn't to be tolerated.

For the life of him Andrew couldn't help retorting, "Mistress Allen, did you ever hear of the French philosopher who once observed that, 'All broad statements are false—including this one'?"

The girl, standing straight and slim, considered him with new attention. The starlight emphasizing the length of her eye sockets, lent them a suggestion of the Orient. "Indeed, Captain Warren, you are the most perplexing man I have yet encountered."

Mighty stiff, Andrew turned again to face her. "I am flattered, Madame, indeed I am."

"You quote French philosophers, yet during the voyage I have observed how you agonize over your log. I'll warrant you hesitate over the spelling of 'passenger.' "

"Quite correct, Madam, yet I guess I could spell 'vixen' without batting an eye."

He figured Mistress Allen would fire up, but she only threw back her head and laughed, the starlight glinting on her teeth. He couldn't help liking her for it.

"A well-placed shot, Captain," she admitted. Why did she plague him so? If ever she'd needed, craved kindliness, a measure of affection, it was tonight. Her nerves were yet all raw and quivering from that vision of Long George pierced through the stomach.

Her hair, free now, was whipping out in fragile gonfalons. She moved a step closer. The *hush-hushing* of the waves alongside all but hid her soft, "Sir, I had not intended to provoke you. Will you forgive me?"

So the girl *had* some coquetry to her?

"About my schooling, Ma'am, you are in the right." His accent returned to New England. "I spent more time plaguing our poor dominie than in learning from him."

He leaned towards her, suddenly young in his amusement, his dark features alight. "You should have seen the day I varnished the seat of his stool with fish glue. 'Twas in the dead of winter so when Master Thaxter sat himself down, the glue warmed. And—"

"—You provoked him," Minga cut in, "and the schoolmaster jumped up and—"

"—Tore the whole seat out of his breeches! How could you have known that?'' he demanded over the monotonous slobbering of the forward pump. ''You—you didn't do the same?''

Something like a giggle escaped Minga. ''Ruined Mrs. Higginbotham's best 'show' petticoat.''

''I got caned,'' Andrew said.

Minga dropped her voice as the whole scene came back to her ever so vividly. She could even see the Shaw girl's little dog waiting in the dappled sunlight outside the door of Mrs. Higginbotham's Female Academy for Polite Arts. Absently she tested the soft arch of her buttocks. ''I got birched right in front of the whole school. Mrs. Higginbotham even made me kiss the switch.''

''I guess getting a whipping's all right,'' said he, ''but that last, the kissing, was a mean thing to do.''

''It was, very—''

''You puzzle me,'' the girl confessed presently, as Andrew pulled out a sheep's bladder pouch and prepared to pack a short, well-blackened clay pipe. ''You *have* been a Naval officer, haven't you?'' So quickly did she alter her topic, Andrew was caught unprepared.

''Yes,'' he admitted and wished she wouldn't consider him so directly.

''In which of His Majesty's ships?''

What the devil? Had she grown suspicious? ''Aboard the H.M.S. *Racehorse,* and a few other men-o'-war.'' He took refuge in evasion.

''Which others?''

''The *Edward,* sloop, and others so small you would never have heard of them.'' He couldn't suppress a fleeting grin; what he was telling her was literally true. By God, he *had* served aboard His Britannic Majesty's ships of war—as prize master.

''Do you plan to lay long in Montego Bay?'' she demanded, eyes on canvas straining away from the main boom.

''I'll have to careen and refit there.'' His expression hardened. A damned nuisance lying over. Every day ashore meant the additional risk of detection. ''Damned picaroons have blown some sizeable holes through us near our waterline. Chips is clever, yet he can't make sure of the hurt.'' He drew a slow breath, and the pipe glowing emphasized his prominent cheek bones. ''God send we don't encounter heavy weather.''

On impulse he placed his hand over hers as it rested on the rail, murmured, ''Mistress Minga, I—well—I guess I haven't cottoned to you much, but I'd like to state that precious few girls I've met possess so much charm and courage.''

Her lips slipped back from teeth which shone very white in

the half-light as she peered steadily into his deep-set black eyes. "You flatter very convincingly, Captain—and pleasingly." He heard her catch her breath. Lord, how much, how poignantly, he reminded of Jerry! He bent, kissed her hand, then strode over to check the course.

On the foredeck Mr. Beetle grinned. Cap'n Warren, it appeared, wasn't quite the Holy Joe he let on. Well, well! Nor was that nice-Nancy of a passenger the frozen-toes pullet he'd deemed her. Would some attention in that direction bring pleasurable results? Eleven children, to speak of, and God knew how many others scattered from Portsmouth to Norfolk, were ample proof that girls had found reason to remember, if not to love, Jed Beetle.

"When I get to Jamaica," he decided, "I'll get me a whole school o' them mustee girls. By the Great Horn Spoon, I'll have me two, mebbe three at a time—if they ain't too costly. Maybe in Montego Bay they love for nothin'—like in the Sandwich Islands. Hope so. Six weeks at sea is too damned long. I'm sure fit to bust."

VI

THE CAPTAIN'S GIG

A MODERATE and favoring breeze hustled the *Evergreen* southward. Grown more wary than ever, Captain Warren ordered his top canvas clewed up whenever the masthead reported a strange sail. To meet up with a British cruiser at this juncture was the last thing he desired. His condition inescapably would evoke queries, examinations.

During two long days and nights the little brig paralleled the jagged gray-blue outline which was the horizon and the coast of Cuba. On the third day they perforce ran closer in. The island lay green, gold and blue beneath a tattered canopy of cotton-white clouds, until, in the late afternoon, the ship's company saw lead-colored rainstorms weaving restlessly over Cape Maisi's bold headland.

On weathering the Cape, Andrew shifted course for Jamaica. They left Cuba astern.

"Come two sundowns," Andrew informed Mr. Beetle, "we will raise Umbrella Point or Dunn's Hole dead ahead."

The weather remained fair. He thanked the high gods but the forward pump continued to clatter and squelch.

During the night an abrupt drop showed in the glass readings, half a gale arose and kicked up a moderate sea. It wasn't anything to fear; still it was enough to rout Andrew Warren out of his bunk.

When, stuffing nightshirt tails into his waistband, he came on deck a warm, wet wind filled his face with rain, then pounced on him and with playfully rough fingers, tore at his hair. The mates, he guessed, were forward making more secure the *Evergreen's* deckload of lumber.

He came wide awake with a jolt when he noted the lazy ease with which a series of combers leaped the bulwarks, came cascading over the rail. The *Evergreen* shouldered the water off but sluggishly. What the devil? The brig should have risen swiftly and buoyantly.

He ran aft yelling, "Put her before the wind!" at the quartermaster.

Joe Beaver, the bandy-legged half-breed, grunted, "Yessir, Cappen," and ground down the wheel while Andrew himself eased the main sheet.

The main top yards screeched protest in swinging to their new positions under the sudden tension and their braces hummed like harp strings. The *Evergreen* rode more easily as she plunged down wind.

The boatswain, a blue-nosed Tory lobster potter out of East Hampton, growled, "Pump's full o' flour, sir. Bulkhead's givin', shouldn't wonder."

For all her new course, the brig responded to her helm so sluggishly Andrew felt fear lancing his stomach with an icicle. He *had* to bring this ship in, salt, medicines, hard money—all were needed so desperately by the unbreakable survivors of Valley Forge and a dozen other miserable encampments.

Jerusha! It would be a sin and a shame to win through so near to Jamaica and then fail.

"Keep her as she sails," he directed, then made his way forward through the spray-filled dark.

Lord, how black it was! Men, securing the deckload of lumber, were but indistinct blurs against the Stygian background.

"Heave away on the foretop braces." Only faintly did Mr. Tompkins' nasal twang penetrate the dismal droning noise made by the wind in the rigging.

"Why the great leaping Jonah didn't you put this craft with her injured hull before the wind?"

Tompkins' breath reeked of rum when he bellowed. "She only ride bad a mite before you come on deck, sir."

Of course, if Mr. Tompkins had been any smarter, he'd long since have captained a vessel of his own.

"Where's the carpenter?"

"Forward, sir." Mr. Beetle appeared, grinning as if the tumultuous wind and waves were delighting him.

Andrew directed his mates to furl the fore-topsail.

Though the seas were nothing to fear as yet, the *Evergreen's* evident lack of buoyancy rendered him uneasy.

Andrew was preparing to sound the forward well when the brig's whole fabric shuddered and there came a noise like some gigantic branch being broken. This was followed by a series of rending, cracking sounds.

Andrew's first horrified reaction was that, inexplicably, the ship must have struck a reef or some derelict, but he recognized none of the grating and grinding sensations which would have accompanied such a misfortune.

Slowly, so smoothly that Andrew at first was unaware of what impended, the *Evergreen* dipped her bowsprit into the jet black slope of a roller—deeper, deeper.

The carpenter lurched aft, bawling, "Cap'n! Cap'n Warren! Where are you?"

"Here! What's amiss?"

"Stops in the bow's shot holes have give way—hull Goddam' Carribean's pouring into our hold."

There could be no doubt of that. Now the bow was barely clear of the water. The crew came scampering aft, their frightened voices preceding them.

"Stand by to abandon ship! Beetle! Tompkins! man your boats," Andrew yelled, then turned and ran for the companionway. He collided with Joe Atherton.

"Here's yer log and chronometer, sir—figgered yer'd want 'em."

"The passenger. Where's the passenger?"

Atherton nodded over his shoulder. "I pulled her out o' bed. She's right behind."

Ensued a frenzied period of manning the boats—the gig, the cutter and the whaler. Because Andrew had ordered the damaged brig's helm put over and because her headsails still gave her a measure of steerageway, it was not too difficult to lower the small boats.

True, wave tops splashed into the small boats until a foot of water set all manner of gear and floorboards to drifting about and bumping the rowers' ankles. Faintly, the light of storm lanterns lashed into the rigging revealed water smothering the forecastle and making a hurrah's nest of the lumber and foremast rigging.

The second mate's boat got away first and pulled off into the wind without waiting to see what would happen.

A falling spar punched a great hole through his cutter's bottom, so Andrew shifted crew, passenger and all to Mr. Beetle's gig and took command.

The gig had hardly shoved clear when the *Evergreen* heeled lazily to starboard and did not right herself. Minga Allen, drenched and shivering in the night air, was amazed to hear a series of sibilant whistlings and groans fill the night. Air forced up from below was rushing through ports and hatchways.

"Pull! Pull free!" At the steering oar Andrew Warren was throwing his whole weight to port.

The brig's forecastle already had disappeared under a surging flurry of spray; next the foreshrouds began to cut at the black waters. With yards waving crazily, with canvas billowing and slatting, the brig's stern rose. The little merchantman's jet outline swayed and seemed to stand on her nose.

Fumbling at her lucky silver bracelet Minga could only look on in numbed despair, listening to the crack of lumber and loose gear cascading the length of the deck.

This couldn't really be so! Only ten minutes ago she'd been resting peacefully, secure in her berth, relieved in the knowledge that her possessions hadn't been hurt during the action in Caicos Passage. Now, saving this bracelet, she'd lost everything, even the pearls she'd fought for, long ages ago it seemed, on the road to New York town.

One after another, the brig's cannon snapped their lashings and plunged through the sagging forecourse.

"There goes my Sunday go-to-meetin' suit," growled Mr. Beetle tugging at an oar. "Well, always was a mite on the smallish side."

He rowed powerfully, his great shoulders a-swing.

"Damn," he was thinking, "I'll have to beg, borrow or steal money and a suit if ever I'm to sample them mustee girls o' Jamaica."

"Look! T'old sow's fair standing on 'er bleedin' nose," Joe Atherton called. The two other oarsmen who with Mr. Beetle, Andrew and the Allen girl completed the gig's complement, turned dishevelled heads.

Softly, feverishly, Andrew blasted his luck. Into the turbulent blackness of the sea was sinking the last of Hosea Warren's merchantmen, all of the unhappy Allen girl's pitiful possessions, not to mention the last shilling he himself possessed.

There'd be no hope, now, of returning to Boston, deep with Indies goods; there'd be no Jesuit's bark now for those poor tattered devils of Continentals. They'd have to continue to shake with agues and to burn with fevers.

From the *Evergreen* came a deep rumbling. A series of eerie whistles and gigantic sighs became audible as she settled more rapidly.

"Oh-h-h." A muffled groan arose from the gig's crew when, as if loath to disappear forever, the foundering vessel's stern swayed briefly above the waves.

All at once the black loom wasn't there any more, only the empty sea—and wreckage. Of Mr. Tompkins and the whale boat there was no sight. Evidently, despite orders, he had pulled away into the wind-filled gloom.

Until this moment Andrew Warren had never known true hopelessness. When a Captain lost a command he lost with her a big part of his self-respect. He should never have left the *Evergreen's* deck. Yet who could have foretold that a single shot could have caused so much hidden damage?

He clenched his teeth and tried to reason what could have happened. Um-m-m, the cannonball must have entered his brig's hull on an angle, cracking or otherwise weakening several ribs besides the one it had shattered. When these injured ribs had been subjected to strain, they'd given way.

A flirt of spindrift blinded him until, mechanically, he wiped his eyes on a dripping shirt sleeve. He'd met skippers who'd lost their vessels, had been tolerantly understanding of their sullen, defiant attitude.

Small, accusing inner voices bellowed, shouted in his subconscious mind. "You're a bad seaman, Andy Warren. You're not fit for command!"

He swallowed hard. This wouldn't have happened if he'd avoided the Caicos Passage. Oh Lord, if *only* there had been a few cruisers to show the Stars and Stripes, to enforce respect for the United States in these latitudes.

Still and all, with his Naval experience he should have done better—much better. His mind raced on in miserable haste. Of course, the Marine Committee of Congress would hear of this business and then—His big hand closed over the tiller handle.

Would they likely give Andrew Warren an appointment? No. Certainly not. It was obvious that a corner, a big corner, in his career had been turned; in the wrong direction.

On the rower's bench immediately before Andrew Warren crouched Mistress Minga Allen his passenger. She sat vacant-eyed, silent, patently overwhelmed at the magnitude of the disaster.

"Please, Ma'am. Will you put this on?" He struggled out of his sodden pea-jacket, offered it to the girl. She paid not the slightest heed.

He knew that she'd barely had time to struggle half into a dress, and now she sat with one bare shoulder gleaming palely above a blanket with which she was attempting to shelter herself from the chill wind. It was pathetic to notice the elegant Mistress Allen's bare feet immersed in grimy water to their ankles. What would Colonel Saunders think of his leman now?

The picture looked anything but rosy. There hadn't been time to pitch more than a small supply of food, water and some navigating instruments into the gig. Well, he'd best rouse out of this wretched inertia.

The wind was still rising and now the sea thundered ominously up out of the gloom to lick over the gig's thwarts.

"Pick up the stroke, Mr. Beetle," he ordered. "Atherton, you bail. Madame, you'll have to take the tiller. Steer down wind. We're going to try to set sail."

Minga paid no heed but sat huddled as before.

"I said 'Take the tiller!' "

She looked up, cleared her throat of the bitter taste in it. "You bungler! Where do you find the temerity to call yourself a mariner?"

"Will you do as I say?" he demanded. "The sail needs to be raised. We'll broach-to and fill, otherwise."

"I'll see you in hell first." Her features glimmered defiantly in the half light. When he slapped her smartly she emitted a small, startled cry.

"Take the tiller, you vixen—we'll likely founder, else."

She hurried to comply.

Hoping against hope that the canvas would prove sound, Andrew set to work. Once the leg o' mutton sail was set, the gig commenced to answer her tiller. Mr. Beetle, Joe Atherton and a half-grown boy got busy scooping out the water; a difficult task for lack of proper bailers. Andrew and the half-breed Penobscot occupied themselves to secure a water keg which was rolling heavily about the bottom.

It was sobering to reflect that, with the gig possessing a single beaker of water, another calm would mean that, a few days hence, a company of sun-dried corpses might be found a-drifting.

VII

ADRIFT

MINGA ALLEN lay, not very comfortably curled on the gig's starboard locker. Blankly she stared upward, considering more millions of stars than ever she had seen in Brewster. How aloof, how serene seemed those other worlds.

"What can there be left to go wrong?" she demanded wearily of herself.

A button was digging into her ear, so, mechanically, she refolded the coat Captain Warren had insisted on placing under her head.

The world tonight appeared appallingly immense, Minga Allen distressingly small and helpless. Of course, she reassured herself, her occasional sense of nausea was entirely due to the gig's motion.

Cleverly designed, the *Evergreen's* small boat had run before the wind all day. Towards sundown this evening the sea had flattened enough to eliminate the necessity of continued bailing. During the past three days, the gig had shipped water all but incessantly.

It came to her that, for the first time since she could remember, she felt afraid of life. Papa and Mamma, it appeared, hadn't brought her up to cope with such an uncertain, informal and brutish mode of existence.

But Lord above! How could they have foreseen all this? Except for the Rebels she'd still be living at Millwood, probably married and with a couple of babies. Babies! She didn't dare dwell on the subject. If it hadn't been for Hancock, the Adamses and their fellow rabblerousers, there'd have been no Brunswickers in America. A fresh hatred for all Whigs pervaded her.

Restless still, Minga squirmed on the hard bench. From a corner of her eye she now could see Captain Warren's boldly designed head and powerful shoulders. He was scanning the heavens, no doubt searching for Polaris.

Andrew Warren, she had decided, couldn't be called truly handsome—not like Sir Jerry. Essentially, the Loyalist captain's head was that of an alert and aggressive fighter.

Quite clearly silhouetted against the sky, she discerned the slight curve of his rather long nose, the determined thrust of his chin.

Take for instance their second night in the gig. When desperation and hopelessness had suddenly got the better of her she'd blazed up to accuse him of all manner of faults.

"As a sea captain, sir, you are at best a wretched incompetent!" she'd cried. That was, of course, ridiculous, yet perversely she had gone on, "You're not fit to command a herring boat!"

Stony-faced, he had endured her abuse quite a while before filling a bucket with sea water and flinging its contents smack into her face. "Even a good gun can get overheated," he observed.

When she cooled off, Andrew Warren had found some more handsome things to say about her behavior during the fight with the picaroons. Ever since they'd been aboard the gig he had done everything possible for her comfort.

Rough-talking, red-headed Mr. Beetle, too, was so uncommon solicitous Minga debated whether he was furthering some ulterior purpose. Mr. Beetle was very strong, and proud of it, too. Why, with his bare hands he'd straightened the bent shank of the wrought-iron boathook.

Persistently, it lingered in her mind that for Captain Warren to be supporting the King was unusual. Certainly, precious few seafaring men from New England had elected to support the Tory point of view—a fact deeply regretted by the Royal Navy.

When Captain Warren shifted his gig onto the starboard tack, the locker lid dug so mercilessly into Minga's hip that she fetched a sigh and sat up. Now she could see the rest of the company awkwardly curled up on the floor boards, snoring. How young the cabin boy looked—a mere child. Had the war orphaned him? Probably, like so many others.

Andrew Warren's deep voice inquired, "Is there aught I can do for you, Ma'am?"

"No. I—well, I just can't sleep. Tonight the world seems so—so huge, our boat so tiny." Curiously, she regarded him. "Don't you ever tire? Don't you ever sleep?"

His teeth glimmered and the horizontal stripes of his ragged jersey rose in a shrug. "Aye, but tonight I don't dare sleep. Should we miss the landfall of Jamaica it will go very hard for us."

"You don't mind my conversation?"

"Mind? Of course not." He laughed quietly. "Only I confess I'm astonished that you should take any pleasure in it."

Her face swung quickly in his direction and her lips, dark in the starlight, parted slowly. "Please—I, well, I have been unreasonable. But I'll try not to be so any longer."

He grinned, hooked broad bare toes over her bench. "And what shall we talk about?"

"I should like to know what Jamaica is really like," she announced, tucking her chilled and shoeless feet under her. "One sometimes hears that the climate is unhealthy?"

She wondered over the way he hesitated before replying. "Since my ship touched at Port Royal five years ago—only to water and to revictual—I scarce rate as an authority."

"Is it indeed true that the island abounds with all manner of snakes, bats and scorpions and—and other reptiles?"

By the increasingly brilliant starlight he could more certainly make out her clearly chiselled features. Right now, with her hair fallen long and loose about her shoulders, she suggested a girl of sixteen rather than a young woman of maybe twenty or over. Vaguely, he conjectured on why Minga Allen had not married long ago. She was too blamed uppity and independent, most likely. After a day's work most men didn't relish finding an argument waiting at home.

Tonight Mistress Allen had appeared really worn down. Her face was badly swollen with that combination of windburn-sunburn which tormented everyone aboard the gig. Andrew knew that they had better raise Jamaica tomorrow. The food was running short and the water—well, the less said on that subject the better.

With a pretty and well-bred young woman aboard so small a boat, life hadn't been easy. When natural functions could no longer be denied, he'd attempted to rig the sail athwart th' boat, but fatigue soon had put an end to that. Quickly, all hands had accustomed themselves to this irremediable lack of privacy.

That Minga Allen remained such a white-hot Loyalist was a crying shame. After a long cruise a man might like to find someone like her waiting for him.

Suppose he confessed that he'd never been a King's man—and that he'd be boiled in oil before ever he became one? What would she say were she ever to learn that Pa had died in battle against her precious King?

On the other hand, what justification could she offer that, at Brandywine, a big Hessian sergeant should have bayoneted Major

Horatio Warren when he lay helpless and calling for quarter? What might be her reactions to the fact that Cousin Gregory had perished aboard the prison ship, *Jersey*, of nothing else than starvation?

The gig coasted on over an endless succession of rollers, on through a clear, cool darkness lit only by flashes of phosphorescence caused by some fish scurrying away in sudden panic.

Despite Mistress Allen's present mood, he knew it wouldn't do a bit of good to come out with the truth. Even though he had come to admire her courage and good sense, if she so much as uttered another syllable against the United States he knew he'd shut her up so short she'd never address him again.

A small, sad sound returned him to the present. The girl's head was bent, and her shoulders moved in slow irregular jerks. How small she looked, how forlorn. His free arm swept out and, in a single, powerful gesture, he lifted her onto the sheet locker beside him. She started, stiffened, but a half-summoned rebuke remained unspoken.

"It's a big sea, *ma chère*," he murmured. "And the night is so very empty."

When her hand came groping, he took it. Jerusha! *This* was the last tack he'd ever expected to sail! Minga rested her head against his arm and, clinging to it, began to sob softly, sadly, like a winter wind about a nor'east gable.

Though immeasurably embarrassed, he had sense enough to hold his tongue, to let her cry, soberly watched some tears form, then fall from the end of her nose. Charles, his littlest brother, had cried just so when Caesar, his spaniel puppy, had eaten ratbane and died.

When, at length, she quieted and settled against his shoulder, he did not move more than was necessary to guide the gig in her course. Warm wind currents passing over this strange girl's body, protected by a single garment of thin cotton, rendered him aware of an indefinable, yet infinitely harmonious, aura. Odd how contact with her body was at once soothing and strongly stimulating. If only there hadn't been that infernal arrogant Colonel Saunders in her background! He must have been a very common sort to have spoilt so sweet and pleasant a girl.

A strand of her hair commenced to beat against his cheek delicately, like a baby's groping fintertips. The steady lift and sway of the gig set a sleepy rhythm. Once or twice Minga drew closer to him, eyes tight shut. He found it increasingly difficult to remain awake, but he mustn't nod. If he missed sighting Jamaica, they'd all die.

VIII

UMBRELLA POINT

IT WAS Joe Beaver, the Penobscot, who first commented on a faint sour odor brought on the west wind. Andrew Warren heard him talking to Joe Atherton, whose trick it was at the tiller.

"Land soon. Trees, water."

"Garn, yer blinkin' savage, yer carn't see nothink at all," the Englishman was protesting. "Too dark."

"Tomakwe not see—smell land," grunted the halfbreed.

He pointed his thin beak of a nose to port and sniffed audibly several times, like a 'coon dog at the foot of a hollow basswood.

With the first light of dawn a small, desperately weary yellow bird appeared and commenced to circle the gig. At length the warbler settled on the gig's stern and balanced there considering the six unkempt and bleary-eyed humans from a suspicious bright black eye.

Presently, a long slate-color streak made itself visible on a pinkish-gray horizon. Andrew could have felt vastly relieved to be sure that this was, indeed, Jamaica. It could so readily be one of those hundreds of islands which compose the Greater Antilles.

Confidence sprouted when, at sun-up, a range of jagged mountains arose, blue as any Dutchman's breeches, above the rim of the sea. Nearer, though, glinted the flash of a sail. Joe Atherton swallowed hard and Andrew and the rest studied the stranger. Nothing to do but wait—the gig was as defenseless as an egg broken into a saucer.

"I allow yonder's some bulldog's tender. Still maybe she's a coast patroller," Mr. Beetle muttered. "No other craft in these latitudes would show canvas white's a schoolmarm's thigh."

"Pray God she is—I ain't hankerin' to get pressed." The boy sighed. "Yep, that's what she is," he burst out as a huge red ensign was broken out from the gaff of a rakish little cutter.

Joe Atherton wiped sweat from his brow and glanced at the captain. He, too, was looking as if he'd just heard good news. No Navy officer out here, he hoped, would recognize him.

Graceful as a yacht a custom's cutter surged by, a long eight-pounder mounted on her bow. Not a hundred yards astern she came about; the gig's company could distinguish a row of sable heads grinning behind her rail.

Occupying the patrol cutter's cockpit were two mulattos and a long yellow-faced European wearing a uniform coat which, flapping open, exposed a bony, hairy chest.

After surrendering the tiller to one of the mulattos, the white man stood up to survey the gig.

"Boat ahoy!" he hailed through cupped hands. "What do you hear?"

"Castaways from the *Evergreen*, brig, out of New York," Andrew yelled. "Can you take us in tow?"

"You'll damn well row over here and come aboard," bellowed the Englishman. "Don't like the look of you!"

Once the gig pulled alongside, sudden interest animated the customs officer's starved-looking and sallow features. The low-lying early morning sun was striking through Mistress Allen's faded cotton gown. Effectively, it cast her body into silhouette and betrayed that not even a single petticoat protected her long slim legs.

The officer, a lieutenant, so the single tarnished epaulet drooping over his left shoulder ranked him, began to do up his tunic buttons.

"Lieutenant Pollack, Madam, of his Majesty's Customs Service," he mumbled. "Yours to command, Madam."

Minga summoned a wan smile at the awkwardness with which the gaunt individual bowed over her reddened, grimy paw of a hand.

"This is Mistress Allen," Andrew explained with dignity. "She is a niece of Sir Thomas Moffat."

"Eh?" The speaker's pale eyes narrowed. "Did you say the name was Moffat?"

"Why yes." Minga looked sharply at him. "Is there anything odd in that?"

"Why no, Madam," mumbled the customs officer, aware that his black crew stood about grinning. "I fancy not. Indeed not. Were you aware that Sir Thomas, ahem—departed this life last year?"

Minga nodded. "So I heard."

"Indeed, so, Ma'am. Of the putrid fever."

She hesitated. "Does his wife—Mrs. Moffat—still—"

Lieutenant Pollack looked aside. "Oh, yes, Ma'am, Mrs. Moffat remains on the estate and, if I'm well informed, she will never leave it."

"Where is the estate?" Minga demanded, making desperate attempts to keep her sea-stained skirts from blowing.

The customs officer passed a hand over a chin dark from lack of shaving; his dirty fingers quivered incessantly.

"Why, Moffat's Penn is quite remotely situated, near six miles up the Montego River. A rich property, Ma'am, that is, it was, until Sir Thomas died—and—and—well, until rebellion was raised in America."

Wary as seldom before, Andrew wondered at the fellow's uneasy manner, at the wholly unnecessary vigilance with which he superintended the cutter's black crew, the unstepping of the gig's mast, and in other preparations for taking her in.

For all that, and as untidy as he was, the customs officer maintained strict discipline aboard his tiny command. The skinny-legged Negroes of his crew executed their duties with dispatch. All of them went naked save for patched seersucker pantaloons and ragged-edged hats fashioned of rushes.

When Minga came clambering aboard, the crew uncovered, but stared in ivory-eyed wonder on the copper complexioned Penobscot, who boarded the cutter with dignity and a certain grace.

Swaying on legs thin as pipe stems, the Englishman turned, bent over a little companionway.

"Cupid! I say, Cupid!" he roared. "Rouse that lazy black butt of yours. Fetch me up biscuits and Madeira!" He turned to Minga. "Meantime, Madam, I fancy you might wish to go below. You'll discover towels, fresh water and soap."

Aware of, and a trifle alarmed by, the customs officer's obvious admiration, Minga accepted and became lost to sight.

Andrew felt it proper to say, "Mr. Pollack, this is Mr. Beetle, my first officer."

"God no! Beetle? Can't be!" The Englishman burst into a series of crackling laughs. " 'Pon my word when you fetch a beetle to Jamaica, you fetch coals to Newcastle! Beetle! A beetle to Jamaica! Blast me if this ain't rich!"

Scarlet to his brows, the mate surged to his feet, fixed the customs officer with a baleful eye.

"Mister Pollock, a feller who's called after a no-count trash fish hadn't orter make free with names."

The Englishman glared. "Keep a civil tongue in your ugly head!"

Tory or not, Mr. Beetle gathered himself. "One more crack and I'll drive a handful of teeth down yer gullet."

"Silence, you damned insolent dog!"

Andrew barely blocked his mate's lusty swing at the Englishman's sallow jaw. God above! This was a fine way to reach Jamaica!

"Drop it!" he ordered, though he didn't blame Beetle a bit.

"Drop nothin'!" snarled the mate. "Lemme loose, Cap'n, I'll teach that lemon-complected bastard to fun over my name!"

"Sit down"

Lieutenant Pollack's hand had crept to the pocket of his tunic. Mr. Beetle never saw it, yet there was a quality to Andrew's command which exacted obedience.

"Should have known that no common Colonial could be expected to possess a sense of humor," mumbled the customs officer.

There again was that infernal, patronizing manner. Inwardly, Andrew Warren seethed, yet was proud of having actually hung onto his temper. Patronage emanated convincingly from this obscure and distinctly malodorous officer of the Crown.

Joe Atherton, too, was looking grim. Mr. Pollack's manner must be raising a host of grim recollections. Then when the big mate continued to glower and mutter under his breath, Andrew begged a measure of sweet oil and sent him forward to dress his crew's more serious sunburns.

He turned to Lieutenant Pollack, sitting straight as any cattail, a grim twist to his lips.

"Pray, make allowance, sir," Andrew urged, "that for five days we have been adrift in an open boat."

The Englishman nodded slowly. "It's a racking business; was adrift myself once—three weeks in the Bight of Benin. Shouldn't have twitted your mate on his name and that's a fact. Still—" The customs officer's eye sought the distant shore. "Your mate talks uncommon like a Yankee—and so do you."

"Mr. Beetle is from Long Island and is no more a Rebel than you—or I," he had the wit to add. Jerusha! He didn't like this Englishman's air.

"You'll have preserved your ship's papers?" Lieutenant Pollack inquired crisply.

"There was no time. My brig went down like a stone."

"She must have," came the guarded comment. "Well, Cupid, what is it?"

"Misto' Pollack, sar." A shiny buck Negro in glaring yellow came swaying aft, big bare feet softly slapping the deck. "Shall Ah cool dat wine wid sal'petre?"

"No, you confounded idiot, just wrap it in the cooling towel, and be quick about it.

"In the meanwhile"—Lieutenant Pollack delved into a locker and produced a black bottle and poured two tots of rum into well polished half coconut shells.

"There's no denying that Madeira's a capital tipple," quoth the customs officer, wiping his forehead with the free end of a bandanna knotted about his neck, "yet for a long cruise, give me straight Jamaica—To your health, Captain, and the mending of your fortune."

"To *your* health, Mr. Pollack, and to his Majesty's Customs Service—"

They touched dark brown and cleverly carved shells. To Andrew, the amber liquid tasted fine as silk. *Nom de Dieu!* It was French rum out of Martinique and it stirred blood slowed by prolonged inaction. Best go easy on the rum, though, and look alive. This ochre-complexioned individual was nobody's fool. Andrew found it difficult to imagine what might be going on behind the Englishman's haggard, sweat-brightened face.

Lieutenant Pollack put down his helm and, catching a favoring blast of wind, commenced to run westward along a coast lined by tall hills rising boldly from warm fringes of beach, interspersed with swampy entrances where mangroves, plantains and other tropical plants ran riot.

Now and again the palm-thatched roofs of fishermen's huts arose, yellow-brown under the bluish shadows cast by the ragged leaves of coconut palms. Along the beaches canoes, skiffs and tiny little sloops, designed for the capture of turtles, sponges and fish, were drawn up above the water's edge. Very occasionally the outline of some great white house glimmered amid a checkerboard pattern of fields, against lush, blue-green vegetation.

Below, Minga Allen interrupted her ablutions to turn a glistening, sun-reddened face to a nearby port-hole. Yonder lay Jamaica! A sharp excitement invaded her, set her pulses to hammering. This towering island was Jamaica; greatest of Sugar Islands, and by far the most valuable of England's rich West Indian possessions.

Since childhood the word "Jamaica" had aroused in her a lively curiosity. From thence came the sugar, the coffee, the pimentoes, the occasional oranges, lemons and coconuts which once had graced Judge Allen's dinner table.

She'd heard seafarers and ship owners like Obadiah Wright of Norwich and Captain John Cook, Papa's great friend, describe a savage black Jamaican race called Maroons.

Many a Colonial esquire had founded and increased his fortunes in the Jamaica or triangle trade: Jamaica, New England and Africa.

Even as a young girl Minga had explored certain docks along the Eastern River in New York. Whenever a Jamaica ship was in she could recognize it by the sickish-sweet, queer, foreign smell it gave off.

Often she would tell herself, "just think, that ship has seen palm trees, green water and coral reefs." Generally half-naked, wild-eyed black men, wearing gyves, were discharging those vessels.

She half knew other things about the island—the strange social usages, terrible plagues and bloodthirsty repression of uprisings among slaves fresh from steamy jungles of the Ivory Coast.

Well, mighty soon now she'd see for herself. Suddenly she started doubting. Would Aunt Adelina welcome, not the semi-heiress she had invited to visit Moffat's Penn, but a penniless, friendless orphan—who was, it seemed, doomed to bear a bastard child? Resolutely, she returned to her efforts to render herself more presentable.

When she returned to the deck, Lieutenant Pollack was drawling with a coconut shell poised before his lips. "Sighted a boat like yours last week. Three people in it—poor beggars were withered, sun-dried like so many cod-fish on a rack. They never stood a chance of making land."

"No chance? Why?"

Lieutenant Pollack emitted a short, high-pitched cackle of a laugh. "Some picaroons had gouged their eyes out before setting 'em adrift. The whiskeradoes have grown confounded bold of late. Oh! Here's Mistress Allen." His lips flattened slowly as he arose.

Cupid, Pollack's enormous Negro steward, passed, in rapid succession, biscuits, Madeira, star apples, avocados, oranges and even a cold joint of what the cutter's commander referred to as "Jew's mutton."

Forward, Atherton, the boy and the seamen were noisily consuming ackee and salt fish.

"What in the world is 'Jew's mutton'?" Minga demanded.

"Da's goat, Maum," beamed Cupid, waddling about. "For true. Bery young goat."

In the shade of the mainsail, Mr. Beetle and Joe Beaver silently, but liberally, helped themselves from calabashes of vegetables and cold meat.

"This has been a beastly spring," Pollack observed, and steadied the tiller with his knee while employing a tobacco-stained fingernail to dislodge a bit of meat from his teeth. "Up-country estates are becoming deuced hard-hit for supplies." He grinned bleakly. "But from America the planters manage to smuggle in enough salt fish to keep their slaves from starving."

"Starving!" Minga glanced incredulously at the softly green coast slipping so smoothly by. "Why, I can't imagine anyone going hungry in Jamaica. It looks like Paradise over there."

Pollack nodded. "No need to starve, true enough. The planters here have only their own beastly greed to thank for this hunger. Ever since we took over this blasted, plague-ridden island, the Crown has been begging the overseers and attorneys to plant food crops. But the beggars won't do it—every time they'll plant every last square yard with sugar and import food."

"But why?" Minga demanded. "Surely it means only a few guineas more of profit."

"Aye, but it's a profit for owners in England and more commission for their attorneys."

From his pocket, the customs officer produced a yellow bandana which he knotted methodically about a narrow, nearly hairless head. The steadily increasing heat had begun to start sweat trickling down his cheeks. Over this improvised skull-cap the lieutenant replaced a battered tricorn adorned with a limp yellow cockade and braid of tarnished silver.

"Make no mistake about it," he resumed, "the blacks are really starving up in the hill estates. Heard it first-hand that Las Cruces Pern has lost nigh over three hundred niggers. Ought to send you up there, Cupid, eh what?"

A band of little scars running across the steward's forehead wrinkled. "No, sar. Cupid he need stay by de sea." He broke into a nervous cackle and waddled off, enormous buttocks quivering like jelly.

"He'd better, at that." Pollack winked at Andrew, lowering his voice. "Cupid's a man of parts make no mistake. He's got brats strewed along the coast from Rio Bueno to Bloody Bay."

As the *Calypso*, cutter, sailed along, perhaps half a mile off shore, all manner of sea birds glided by—gulls, terns, kestrels and great numbers of lumbering gray pelicans. These last coasted by in lines flying just a foot or so above the surface.

Occasionally the cutter overhauled black slaves working traps. They worked from dug-out canoes equipped with clumsy outriggers. Sometimes they'd only stare sullenly at the trim green and white craft under its huge Red Ensign, but more often they would give halloo and wave strips of blue cloth, or hold up fishes bright as animate rainbows.

Generally their cries were quite unintelligible. *"Ooray busha! Gib nyam!"*

"What tribes are they from?" Andrew queried. "Don't recognize their lingo."

"Guinea birds for the most part," Pollack told him. "Eboes or Mandingos. They make prime haulers and fishermen."

Occasional strips of road became visible and at more frequent intervals one could see brown nets drying, small luggers, sloops and canoes at anchor in the incredibly clear blue-green water of a tiny basin.

"Must be evergreens up on those mountains," Andrew mused. Even as he studied them, clawing at the sky, a billow of woolly clouds came tumbling over the rim of an escarpment and, like milk spilt on a table, commenced to cascade down the mountain side.

"Once we've weathered yonder point," Lieutenant Pollack announced over the steady *swish-swishing* of the waves, "we'll be into Montego Bay."

At the Englishman's mention of the port, Andrew's brown features contracted. Well, certainly he'd never figured on making Montego Bay like this! No money, no cargo, no ship. Somewhere back up there must lie Señor Cardozo's compound—and those drugs and medicines and surgical instruments Dr. Blanchard and his fellows had pled for so fervently. He felt especially low because it was Uncle Hosea's last ship he'd lost; the *Evergreen* also had been the first of the family ships he'd been given to command.

Watching the sparkling rush of rollers over a half-submerged reef, he wondered how in Tunket he was going to get back to America. Before long the *Trumbull* frigate would at last be ready to go to sea? Damnation! This would be no quick turn-around trip. Should it be discovered in Jamaica that he'd served as prize master over three of His Britannic Majesty's men-of-war it would go hard. He'd best look sharp. Some of his former prisoners might have been exchanged.

He shot a sidewise glance at Minga. Now that her chestnut hair had been combed into some pretense of order and she had mended, with a sailmaker's needle, various rips and tears in her gown, she appeared almost well-groomed. He looked at her more attentively, perceived, for the first time, how very gracefully her neck sloped into shoulders which were at once well made, yet capable-looking.

How could such a girl ever have become the protégée of such a crusty old codger as Colonel Saunders? Well, ashore he'd try to find out. Probably she was all-aflame under that composed exterior. It wasn't, he'd found out, the girls who talked with bed springs in their voices or wore provocatively revealing gowns, who were the best fun for a bright moment in a dark corner. No, Lautrec had been right. It was the demure lasses with carry-me-off-to-heaven expressions and downcast eyes who really made it worthwhile to make port.

Gradually, Montego Bay, principal port of the northern coast of

Jamaica, came into view around a small headland. A double tier of white, yellow and brown houses disclosed themselves; some unimportant-appearing wharfs and warehouses were grouped in disorder about a semi-circular bay.

Minga Allen's bright under lip tucked itself between her teeth and her chin quivered just a little. Her eyes were sparkling, however, and if she were experiencing qualms of uncertainty over the future, they manifested themselves not at all.

"So, Captain Warren, we make port?" The subdued excitement in her tone was inescapable. He guessed the reason. He must have felt like that long years ago when, on his first voyage, he'd watched the coast of Brittany begin to move up out of the sea.

"What a queer—what a very pretty harbor!" she murmured.

A surprising number of merchantmen lay at anchor. Quite a few vessels were tied up to a series of rickety, barnacle-riddled docks, but for all that, the port wore a lifeless, sun-dried and definitely down-at-the-heel aspect. On a slimy brown-gray mud bank off to port a number of storm- or battle-broken hulks lay rotting, their gaunt ribs a perch for sea birds.

Promptly, Andrew located the inevitable guardian fort; it proved a small, white-washed battery crowning a hill behind the port. A Union Jack hung lifeless from a flagpole beyond it.

Mr. Beetle's expectant grin was fading. God A'mighty! There wasn't a soul a-stirring, let alone a pretty mustee. Still—maybe when the sun lowered there'd be some fun show up? Money? He'd provoke some bully of the garrison into a prize fight. For all he held to his loyalty, he enjoyed hammering an Englishman whenever the opportunity offered.

Under Lieutenant Pollack's sure piloting through a baffling series of mangrove-covered flats, the cutter shaped a course towards a wharf which betrayed Admiralty design. Spoiled fruit, bits of rind, rubbish and other refuse, drifted by more slowly now that the sea breeze was being shut off by a range of high hills.

"Heavens! Where is everybody?" Minga demanded. "Is there a plague loose?"

"Pray God not!" Pollack burst out. "There's been no yellow jack around for months."

The almost incredible stillness was accentuated by the sound of hammering. It came from aboard a round-bowed brig showing Dutch colors.

Two of the vessels in port captured and held Andrew's attention. First, a large schooner of nearly two hundred tons. A number of fresh yellow shot holes in her black-painted sides marred the smooth sweep of her lines. Her foremast, moreover, was heavily fished and a whole section of her bulwarks had been carried away.

Long before he made out the name, *Enterprise*, Middletown Connecticut, painted across her stern, he guessed the schooner's status. Further on lay the other captive vessel, the *Ranger of Norwich*. She must have been brought into port quite recently, for from her signal gaff hung a depressing sight—a crude representation of the Connecticut State flag and, flapping listlessly above it, the Union Jack.

IX

MR. ALLERDICE

WITH the already sodden end of his yellow bandana Lieutenant Pollack wiped a heavy beading of sweat from faintly greenish features.

"You'd best reserve your report concerning the picaroons for the H.M.S. *Squirrel's* officers," he told Andrew. "She's duty ship on this station and expected in tonight. And now you'll go ashore. I've my patrol to complete. God blast the traitorous merchants smuggling along this coast! In league with the Yankees, some of 'em—or might as well be. Shake a leg there!"

Irritably, the customs officer considered Mr. Beetle as, quite deliberately, he climbed up to the stone wharf.

"Thank you, Mr. Pollack," Minga said. "You have been rarely kind."

"Aye, we're deeply in your debt, sir," Andrew said, offering his hand. The customs officer took it, wrung it listlessly.

Blinking, barefoot, and hatless, the *Evergreen's* survivors stood in the stunning midday sun watching the cutter's lackadaisical black seamen thread the gig's painter through a ring-bolt let into the Admiralty wharf's slimy stone work.

For the first time in many years, Andrew Warren became aware of a sense of helpless confusion. This was enemy territory, he hadn't a penny, only a friendless girl on his hands. He braced a foot on the greasy coping of the government wharf and bent to address the Englishman standing hot and impatient in the cutter's cockpit.

"What do you suggest we had best do? Right away, that is."

"Do? Do? Damme, sir, that is for you to determine. I've done my duty."

A shower of sweat drops sketched circles on the cockpit floor when Pollack wheeled and roared, "Hi, you Jug! You, Punch! You, Jupiter! Cast off, you lazy black bastards, and act alive else I'll see your backsides smoke under a flopper."

Mr. Beetle glowered, observed, "Some day, Mister Fish, I'll dress you down to size."

Atherton grinned broadly, looked relieved to see that tarnished uniform further away. Joe Beaver stood blinking, his vitreous black eyes probing the row of patched and mud-spattered plaster houses beyond the wharf's end. The boy absently rubbed oil over his scarlet sunburns.

When Lieutenant Pollack put over his helm, two Negroes jibed over the cutter's boom.

Her enormous Union Jack stirring lazily, the green and white cutter gathered way. Lieutenant Pollack did not even glance astern, only settled back in the stern sheets and drank thirstily from a coconut, the top of which Cupid had removed with an expert slash from a heavy-bladed machete.

"He—our rescuer—is not over-gallant," murmured Minga.

"Liver's bad, I expect," Andrew hazarded. "Too much rum and salt beef."

Aware of an expectant manner among his companions, Andrew said, "Well, we'd best get out of the sun," and led to a shed beneath which Naval stores were sheltered. He halted among the bluish shadows and fingered his chin.

"I scarce know what to advise," he confessed with a small shrug.

"Hadn't we best fend for ourselves?" Mr. Beetle demanded and rolled his eyes towards some taverns lining the far side of a sunlashed square. Yonder a bright green petticoat had flashed briefly at one of the doorways. The square opposite Admiralty Dock wasn't much, fringed by discouraged-looking palms and adorned by a very ugly statue raised to some obscure celebrity.

"We could meet here tonight—no, say tomorrow morning."

"Ain't no call to worry, sir. We'll not remain stranded long. Crews die off quicker'n usual in these latitudes."

Atherton gathered a straw between calloused toes, exposed several gold teeth in a taut grin.

"Yes. Let us separate. I don't figure to be around when that bulldog makes port—she'll be 'untin' 'ands, she will. They all does.''

This made sense. Nothing was to be gained by keeping together, especially if questions were asked concerning the history of one Andrew Warren. It was agreed, then, to meet on Admiralty wharf at six—in the cool of the morning.

"Keep that temper of yours below hatches," Andrew warned the mate. "Speak out of turn around here, they'll clap you in jail and throw away the key."

"Right you are, sir," Mr. Beetle winked, then more soberly he added, "I sure admired your innards, Ma'am, that day we stood off the whiskeradoes."

A flush leaped into Minga's cheeks. "Why—why thank you, Mr. Beetle. I—we'll see you tomorrow."

"Aye, that you will, Ma'am, barrin' acts of God—"

"—Or of the Devil," Andrew corrected.

On impulse Mr. Beetle asked, "Want to come along, Bub?"

The boy beamed. "Oh, yes, sir."

In company they swung off past a heap of six pound shot and a quartet of dismounted cannon.

"Well, Beaver?"

The Penobscot's jet eyes sought a row of tall green hills rising beyond the port. He hardly moved his lips in saying, "Tomakwe need woods—be lonesome. Three days Tomakwe come back."

The Indian strode lightly on bandy, thin-shanked legs. When he re-entered the sunlight, his long hair glistened like a crow's wing. The sleek dull copper of his skin glowed through a wide tear in his faded blue cotton shirt.

Atherton knuckled his forehead and strode off looking carefully to his left and right.

Alone, Andrew and his companion surveyed each other soberly. Right now, Minga Allen looked surprisingly small and bedraggled —rather like a lost kitten. She had plaited her hair into two long braids and secured them, crown-like, about her head. Because she wore no stays, only a single sea-stained gown, the outlines of high, well-developed breasts, of a gently rounded stomach and straight legs were frankly revealed.

For her part, Minga saw an intense, dark-skinned fellow whose alert eyes were just as black as the powerful mane of hair which should have been clubbed between his shoulders with ribbon.

Certainly he was well and powerfully set up—reminiscent of Mr. Beetle, but on a smaller scale. His blue-and-white striped jersey revealed wide bands of muscle rippling across his shoulders, down nearly hairless arms. His white canvas knee breeches had become so dirtied and stained their original color would be hard to guess. His eyes were tired, hollowed by sleeplessness and long exposure to the sun's pitiless intensity.

Putting hands on hips, Andrew smiled through sun-cracked lips. "D'you suppose, Minga, my dear, that two more destitute persons have ever set foot on Jamaica?"

"Oh, yes. We, at least, are free." She laughed, though the knowledge that they hadn't a farthing between them wasn't a bit amusing. "Free to starve unless you can find us fruit."

Momentarily, Andrew knit heavy brows. "I think we shall look up a Mr. Allerdice."

"Mr. Allerdice?"

"He was my uncle's agent—still is, I hope. Before this war my uncle pursued a great commerce with Winde & Allerdice."

It was sheer torture again to emerge into the pounding sunlight. Minga bit her lip and curled her toes away from the searing heat of the street. This was indeed an unfamiliar world. Not one thing was suggestive of home, neither houses nor shops; trees and plants all were strange. Even the air smelt foreign.

Scarvely a soul was abroad. Ragged Negroes dozed under a line of enormous two-wheeled wains. In the shade of an upturned small boat, some dirty, wan-looking white children were sucking at short lengths of sugar cane.

Uncertainly, Andrew descended the water front, picking an erratic course to avoid the droppings of oxen, mules and other creatures. Before long he sighted a substantial two-storey stone warehouse bearing, in faded brown letters, the legend:

WINDE, ALLERDICE & CO.
Dealers in Sugar, Lumber
Grain, Livestock & American Goods.

Within the warehouse someone could be heard singing off key and in a cracked voice:

"When a' aloud the wind doth blow.
    And coughing drowns the parson's saw,
And birds sit brooding i' the snow
    And Marian's nose looks red and raw,
When roasted crabs hiss in the bowl,
    Then nightly sings the staring owl."

Andrew and his companion halted before a warehouse which had seen better days. No paint protected ponderous iron bars on the

structure's glassless windows, and in great flakes pale blue whitewash applied to its façade was peeling into weeds withering at
the roadside. Nearly all of its clumsy, iron-bound shutters were
warped or broken; some of them hung crookedly from their
hinges.

Andrew's knock reverberated hollowly and, though the discor-
dant singing continued, it evoked no response. In perplexed silence
the unkempt couple regarded each other. Andrew passed a hand
over a jaw black with a week's beard. "Well, I'm damned. You
wait here."

Repeatedly calling the agent's name, the New Englander stepped
boldly into a counting room the air of which was heavy and full of
mouldy smells. Long neglect had permitted invoices, manifests,
inventories and shipping forms of many sorts to drift far and wide
over the dusty floor. Heavy greenish mould had gathered on the
calfskin covers of a series of ledgers; letter books had been stacked
helter-skelter on a chest of a sort in which tea samples were customarily kept.

The only evidence of life was a scrawny cat suckling a litter of
kittens on a wicker armchair's sagging seat; prolonged feline occupancy of the room was pungently unmistakable.

This disorder came as an infinitely disturbing surprise. Uncle
Hosea had pictured Mr. Allerdice as an uncommonly neat and
industrious Scotsman.

> "Death is now the phoenix nest;
>   And the turtle's loyal breast
>   To Eternity doth rest."

Following the sound of the song, Andrew lifted the latch of a
ponderous door, halted on the threshold of a huge room. It was hard
at first to see much in this dim gloom. While he waited for his eyes
to adjust themselves after the intense sunlight, nearby some rats
squeaked and scuttled about.

Gradually he became aware of a galaxy of unpleasant odors. A
stack of cowhides were emitting a faintly nauseous smell; beyond
them hundreds on hundreds of hogsheads of sugar and molasses
climbed in layers towards the roofbeams. Upon them perched
quantities of shrill-voiced sparrows. Arrogantly sure of their
domain, rats by the dozens galloped unconcernedly about the dingy
masses of spoilt sailcloth, chests of china, boxes of hardware, and
over padlocked trunks of Manchester goods.

From a stock, Andrew selected an axehandle, swung it to ward
off the swarming rodents.

"To this urn let those refrain
        That are either true or fair;
        For these dead birds sign a prayer."

The song emanated from beyond a small door to his left so he
rapped sharply with the axehandle, at the same time called, "Mr.
Allerdice?"

The singer broke off, hiccoughed and must have broken something were one to judge by a resounding crash. A dog growled,
sniffed at the door.

"Ye waste yer time, I war-r-n ye, whoever ye are!" quavered an
elderly voice. "I havena' a groat to me name. 'Tis Melhado,
Silveira and Company ye must deal with the noo."

"Mr. Allerdice! This is Andrew Warren."

"What fulishness is this? Go awa', ye bloodsuckers," railed the
thin voice beyond the door. "Get ye gone lest I loose this fearsome
beastie."

Andrew began to get his dander up. Blast this drunken sot!
Sharply he rapped.

"Open up, and be quick about it. I'm from Warren & Whitney of
Boston and Portsmouth, New Hampshire."

"Warren and Whit—Nay, it canna be! Get ye hence and the
Laird's curse lie heavy on ye for making mock o' a puir, unhappy
old mon."

"I'm not mocking you." The New Englander beat down a
sudden flare of resentment. What a time to have to put one's trust in
a rum-soaked old toss-pot. It took quite a tuck in Andrew's pride to
call, "Mr. Allerdice, I—need your help."

One, two, three bolts went *clock!* and then the door creaked back
to disclose a gnome-like figure swaying in the midst of what looked
like a sort of kitchen-dining room.

A three days' beard bristled below bleared blue eyes and above a
filthy, food-stained shirt. The messy little old man was hugging a
dark green bottle in the crook of his left elbow.

Fighting down his repulsion, Andrew inquired, "You are Mr.
Allerdice?"

Unsteadily the merchant's rheumy eyes considered this tall
young man who so nearly filled the doorway, from dusty bare feet to
shock of jet hair brushing the lintel. The old man blinked, rubbed
one eye with a dirty knuckle.

"Aye. I'm a' that remains mortal o' Jamie Allerdice."

"And I'm Hosea Warren's nephew."

"Oh, aye," he cackled. "Ye'll be one o' the Warrens, sure
enough. They're black as auld Clootie's bottom—all o' them."

Belly jiggling loosely under a shirt stained by grease and spilt coffee, Mr. Allerdice stepped backwards. "Come in, Mister Warren, and be welcome tae this abode o' prosperity an' merriment!"

When Mr. Allerdice's wrinkled hand waved his guest into the room, a tired old brown dog lifted his lip at him and growled before retiring beneath a cot. The sheets on it must have been there a long, long time.

Andrew wavered, undecided as to the wisest course. The thought of leaving Minga in her embarrassingly scant costume waiting by the warehouse entrance wasn't attractive, still, it was no more fitting to present her to this decayed old reprobate. Yet, this rum-soaked dotard represented his one real connection in Jamaica with —well, with that secure, orderly past which seemed to have departed forever.

Batting eyes which shone red as brandied cherries, the Scot peered upwards. "So ye'll be Hosea Warren's son?"

In weary patience Andrew corrected him. "No, Mr. Allerdice, I'm his nephew. Horatio Warren was my Pa."

"Ou, aye, that's so, that's so!" He considered his sunburnt guest's apparent destitute condition a long moment, puzzled, but gave up his effort to understand. " 'Tis in a vexsome state ye find me, lad. As in the song, the wur-rld here *is* turned upside down." He held out the bottle, giggling. "Pour yersel' a wee noggin o' this. 'Tis no sae bad. Ne'er tried a drop till '76. 'Twas then Mr. Winde and I lost first the *Anabella,* then the *Tartar* and finally our *Huntress* tae the Yankees."

While Andrew poured out a modest measure, Allerdice smiled an uncertain smile which, somehow, was touching; in it Andrew could glimpse the keen, upright man who must once have been James Allerdice.

"In honor o' the occasion, Captain, I'd gladly offer ye Madeira an I possessed a single drap." Scrawny shoulders sagged and the old man's clouded eyes wavered. "Wi' all shame I own it, Captain Warren, 'tis a beggar ye find."

"A beggar? What? Why that—that's impossible."

"Aye, a beggar. Poor as Christian charity tae a Mahometan!"

"But I saw your warehouse fairly choked, bursting with goods!"

"Foreclosed, lad, a' foreclosed I've been." He sank suddenly onto a stool. " 'Tis mine no more. Melhado, the Jew out of Kingston, will own it come Eastertide. But—" The bent shoulders squared a little and James Allerdice looked Andrew square in the eye, "but I paid my firm's creditors, mark ye, paid 'em off to the last bitter penny and none can say James Allerdice is no' an honest

mon. Aye, I paid off twelve pence tae the shilling—and wrecked a
traffic Johnny Winde and me were twenty year a-building.''

"Uncle Hosea set a deal by you, Mr. Allerdice, and your hon-
esty."

"Did he, lad? Did he, indeed?'' The disreputable figure
straightened. "Ye're a good mon to tell me that. It—it helps.
Though often it has cost us dear, Winde & Allerdice hae been good
o' their pledged wur-rd.''

Never, Andrew thought, would he forget those words. Let who
would lie and cheat, but not one of his people!

"What did ye say yer given name is?''

"Andrew.''

"Andrew? Losh, lad, yon's a braw Scottish name.''

The old merchant, Andrew sensed, was exerting efforts to pull
himself together. Poor devil! He felt an immense pity. He guessed
something of what Allerdice was suffering. He, too, had failed.
Andrew recalled now that right after the *Evergreen* had foundered,
he'd have sold his right arm for a demijohn of rum.

Allerdice swayed to a curtain fashioned of jointed bamboo and
bellowed, "Clorinda! Luk i' the food locker, see if there's aught
there fit to set before a gentleman.''

"—And a—a friend,'' Andrew almost added. There was no
leaving Minga alone any longer. Then he remembered. He needed
to learn, to glean local news, and he couldn't with such a determined
Loyalist as Minga in hearing. In grim amusement he saw that she
would have to suffer for her precious King yet again.

"Here.'' Mr. Allerdice spoke in almost desperate haste, thrust-
ing forward a calabash cup. Into it he splashed a quantity of dark red
rum. "Drink, lad, and remember, the higher we fly our kites o'
ambition why, 'tis the farther they ha'e to fall.''

In despressing eagerness he gulped his drink and made a clacking
noise. "So yer Horatio's son? He was an Army man, an I dinna
mistake meself.''

Andrew explained that Pa had served in the King's Army despite
the slights a Colonial officer had to swallow—up till the fall of '74.
Pa, Andrew elaborated, had fought in seven pitched battles against
the French and their Huron allies, losing a finger at the intaking of
Louisburg. Again he had near perished of yellow-jack during
Admiral Vernon's ill-starred venture against Cartagena.

Mr. Allerdice tugged at a wisp of his greasy gray hair.

"Yer feyther's well?''

"No—he was killed at the battle of Brandywine—damned German ran him through as he lay wounded.''

Briefly, he elaborated on the family's recent ill fortune—Mother dead a month after Pa, Uncle Hosea a bankrupt though he didn't yet know it—and Uncle Isaac a Loyalist. Even now he was thought to be cruising the New England coast, captaining H.M.S. *Scarsborough*, 32 guns.

Bedraggled old Allerdice cast him a sympathetic look, went over to a jar cooler—an affair of porous stone arranged in a wooden frame—and laced his drink with water.

"Ye'll not be disposed tae judge me too harshly? Winde & Allerdice wasn' always like this. Time was when I'd me own polink up in the cool mountains and as fine a kittareen as ye'd see in Kingston. I'd e'en a wee bit o' pleasure boat." The faded craggy features tightened. "Oh, the havoc wrought by yon stubborn, stupid Hanoverian and his hell-bound ministers! E'en a Stuart couldn' be so purblind."

Cautiously, Andrew suggested, "Then His Majesty is not uniformly popular here?"

The Scot glanced mechanically over his shoulder, narrowed bloodshot eyes. "Till last year there were precious few o' us who'd not have tossed our cups tae see the German lout roast i' the nethermost Pit!"

"Till last year?" Andrew was puzzled.

"Now near a' the Jamaica merchants despair o' a Yankee victory." The old man muttered, his lips close to the New Englander's ear. "We've a' lost vessels tae Yankee letters-o'-marque." Mr. Allerdice nodded heavily and the old dog looked up, growled deep in his throat.

"When the Yankee private ships o' war crippled our trade wi' England, most part o' the merchants i' the West Indies turned against the Colonies." Mr. Allerdice rubbed a ruddy button of a nose, looked up quickly. It was clear something had occurred to him.

"Captain—?"

"Well?"

"Ye spoke the now o' yer Uncle Isaac as a King's man. Then o' yer feyther, dead for the Yankee cause." He leaned forward, his breath rank in Andrew's face. "That offers a choice. Are ye—?"

The decision was inevitable, critical—give the wrong answer and disaster would pounce in short order. To give himself time to think he raised the red-brown rum to his mouth.

"I'm Loyal, Mr. Allerdice," then added slowly, "just as loyal as you are."

That ought to give the old man pause. He was surprised at having sensed the right answer. Or was it right?

Mr. Allerdice muttered under his breath and drank deep.

"E'en now many here hold for the King—body and soul."

"Who, for instance?"

"Why, yer Admiralty people, the garrison, the pensioners, the Clergy, the Crown servants and most of all, the Jews."

"The Jews?" This was indeed a surprise.

"Aye, lad, the Jews." In the stale sunlight Mr. Allerdice's shaggy head inclined in drunken gravity.

"Oh, come now—"

James Allerdice flared right up. "Dinna question my wurrd, Andrew Warren, not till ye see what shamefu' prices the Hebrews offer us distressed merchants who *must* sell out to pay our honest debts. I'm no sayin' *some* o' the factors here ain't reaping fortunes."

"But you are a factor yourself?"

"We were," Mr. Allerdice corrected bitterly. " 'Twas our misfortune our trade was wi' North America—not England."

"Cannot you merchants band together? As we—as in New England?"

"We daren't," explained Mr. Allerdice, his shoulders sagging again. "General John Dalling—deputy Governor o'er Jamaica since Sir Basil Keith perished i' June o' the last year—has posted rewards for information 'gainst Yankee sympathizers.

"Still—" Mr. Allerdice winked. "Many's the stand o' muskets, sack o' doubloons and cask o' gunpowder has been shipped north 'twixt Negril Point and Manchioneal."

"If ever the New Englanders get a fleet to sea, much more will be smuggled from this island."

Get a fleet to sea? Aye, there it was again. As he stood in Mr. Allerdice's hot, musty-smelling quarters bitterness boiled within Andrew Warren. Thanks to a deal of pettiness, penny-pinching, backbiting and self-seeking in Philadelphia and Boston, there wasn't much likelihood of the new Confederation's ever getting even a decent-sized fleet to sea. The British could land along the Atlantic Coast almost at will.

Could Mr. Allerdice be trusted? Andrew wondered. The Scots in the Carolinas had proved loyal to the Crown to an astonishing degree. It was impossible to keep Minga waiting any longer, so, after an abbreviated account of the *Evergreen's* loss, Andrew mentioned her presence and suggested that he fetch in the Allen girl.

The old merchant shook his head.

"We'll go greet the lass i' the—the office."

X

AT THE CROWN & DOVE

MR. JAMES ALLERDICE roused himself, even made an effort to button the loose linen waistcoat he wore as he and Andrew neared the office.

Minga Allen had entered, was playing with one of the kittens. When she beheld Andrew's bent and unkempt companion, her clear gray-green eyes opened wide.

The Jamaican bowed so low his head was at a level with her waist. "Yer most humble obedient servant, Ma'am."

"Mr. Allerdice," Andrew explained, "is kind enough to say he can find us clothing of a sort."

"Aye, that I wull, an ye wull excuse me a moment."

When the old man reappeared, he was carrying a simple gown of gray calico, a bundle of blue and white cotton petticoats, some crude sandals, which looked, and were, sizes too large for Minga's feet, and a wide-brimmed leghorn hat. It was no woman's hat at all, yet it would serve to ward off the blinding heat of a tropical sun.

" 'Tis but a puir collection for so fair a lady," he apologized.

Minga laughed, clutched the garments eagerly. "They look fit for a princess. How can I ever thank you, Mr. Allerdice?" La! It would be elegant to get out of the miserable, torn, stained garment in which she had existed this past week.

"Be putting them on and combing yon bonnie hair of yours. Here—" He held out a comb, a length of blue grosgrain ribbon and a yellow kerchief. "Ye'll find privacy i' the storeroom—too much o' it, alas," he sighed. "And noo, Captain Warren, let's see what can be done for you."

In a secluded corner of Mr. Allerdice's vast and shadowy warehouse, Minga prepared to remove her dress. As she stepped out of the ill-smelling affair she noticed a pair of enormous black rats surveying her from between the coils of a hawser piled to one side.

Six months ago she would have screamed, then fainted genteel-ly—as became a lady. But now she merely flapped her discarded dress at them and, when they had rustled off, paused mother-naked behind a rampart of coffee sacks, letting her body breathe. A breeze had sprung up and caressed her damp shoulders, breasts, and thighs with cool, invisible fingers.

A subtle warmth enveloped her. La! What *had* come over Minga Allen? Here she was standing, naked as an egg, with Andrew Warren not a hundred feet distant. The realization, however, was not at all displeasing. If only there wasn't Jerry to remember—

Andrew—how capably, how calmly the wiry New Englander met each new problem. She'd come to notice the vivacity of those black eyes of his—odd, she'd never have believed she'd favor dark eyes.

She slipped Mr. Allerdice's sandals on her dusty feet; they were fashioned from rawhide, tinted a dull, rust-red. All the same, it was indeed good to find something separating her soles from the ground. Her feet, not having had time to develop protective callouses, had grown almighty tender.

Softly she began to hum:

> "We'll rather taste the bright Pomona's store.
>   No fruit shall 'scape
> Our palates, from the damson to the grape.
>   Then, full, we'll seek a shade
>   And hear what music's made."

Thank fortune, the Allens followed the Church of England so were allowed the joys of poetry, music and painting. A pox on the long-faced, tight-lipped Puritans and Dissenters of New England! Their only music was hymns bellowed through their noses.

It was with a rare sense of luxury that she tied about her slender waist a succession of petticoats. They were by no means of a quality with those which now were drifting somewhere about the Caribbean's bottom. Their cleanliness, however, was bliss.

Spirits soaring, she smoothed the calico gown over her hips and flat, softly-rounded stomach, discovered that the garment had been cut for a bosom far more ample and therefore swung dangerously low. A shrewd arrangement of Mr. Allerdice's pale blue neckerchief, however, remedied the exposé. Luckily, the kerchief went agreeably with sandals and dress.

Lips contracted, she considered the great, floppy-brimmed hat. Adorned with a rust-colored ostrich feather, caught up on one side, the leghorn might even acquire a suggestion of modishness.

Meanwhile Mr. Allerdice watched Andrew don long canvas

trousers, a fresh dark red shirt, shoes, and a wide felt set with an enormous brass buckle.

"I've taken these garments out o' stock which ain't no longer mine," said he simply. "Melhado can hail me to jail for it—but be damned to him, I'll no' see good King's people go forlorn. My partner, Johnny Winde, stood the embargo so long as there was hope, then, wi' ruin upon us, he made his will six months back and peeked doon the wrang end o' a horse pistol.

"Let you and the lassie repair tae the Crown & Dove; tell Kendall there ye're a friend o' Jamie Allerdice and I warrant he'll find shelter for ye, savin' when a privateer makes port."

The Jamaican lowered red-rimmed eyes marked with little patches of white at their corners, fumbled in his pocket. "Six shillings, lad, is a miserable pittance, yet 'tis all I can spare now."

Andrew thanked him soberly. He would, he vowed, return the loan within a week and double it out of gratitude.

Who ever had accused the Scots of being niggardly?

The sound of Minga's returning footsteps caused the wizened little man to glance over a knobby shoulder.

Andrew spoke hurriedly, "Mr. Allerdice, Mistress Allen has kinfolk here, but I—well, you must have deduced that I'm on the perch—broke. I must find a ship—immediately. Have you any suggestion?"

Come what might, he intended to get back before the *Trumbull* could be commissioned. He'd make the Marine Committee listen to reason.

"Aiblins ye'll land a berth as second or third mate. 'Tis verra unchancy ye've lost yer ship's papers," he spoke in lowered accents. "Yer speech and your be-damned-to-you way suggests the Yankee more than a true King's man."

Not since she had set out for the Theater Royal had Minga felt such buoyancy—despite the heat, the disconsolate surroundings. Somehow, by sense of touch, she had dressed her hair—eyes shut, as she had used to back in Millwood when she had tried various coiffures up in the attic. Mama would have scolded, called her vain. "The idea! A child of your age dressing hair!" The ribbon was set neatly above her ear, the leghorn pinned up.

"The Laird's mercy!" Mr. Allerdice gasped, when she re-entered the office: "Why, why, 'twas nothing I handed ye."

Andrew hardly heard him. By God, here *was* a beauty! The tension, the responsibility of the voyage removed—no matter how disastrously—left him eager, more than a little reckless. He understood now why Colonel Saunders had taken up with her. Probably she'd been a desperate, penniless Tory refugee—good enough for 'em, too—and her unobtrusive beauty must have captured that red-faced old lecher's eye.

Well, well, and again—well. The French knew how to handle a *poule de luxe* and he'd been around enough to catch on.

The sun was lowering and the terrific heat of day was diminishing. Buzzards—the natives called them John crows—were craning naked, diseased-looking necks. One by one, they fluttered down from lime-whitened perches on roof tops, dead trees and fence posts. Hopping awkwardly, they set about exploring fly-infested mounds of offal.

Negroes of all ages, semi-naked or wearing frayed cotton garments, raised their voices in hawking a variety of wares.

"Cocay watah! Cocay watah!" intoned a shrivelled black crone bent under a burlap sling of fresh coconuts.

"Heah fresh millik!" a bullet-headed child shrilled while she herded a pair of fat-teated nanny goats.

Also offered for sale were glowing baskets of oranges, pawpaws and pots of fammee—a dish of fish ground up with avocados.

All within a few moments the dead streets of Montego Bay became populated with a languidly moving population—predominantly black. Gigs, oxcarts and kittareens—a species of two-wheeled gig peculiar to the island—began to roll by. A Naval officer in blue and gold stared curiously at the tall young couple as he strode along. Now and then a mounted officer would ride by, gold-laced tunic bright in the rich sunlight and his face shinier still with perspiration.

"Trade here certainly appears to be deader than dead," Andrew commented, indicating tall and dusty stacks of logwood and mahogany. Rum casks and hogsheads of sugar cluttered every dock. The strollers lingered over a slat pen erected beside the water's edge. In it dozens of sea-turtles with streamers of moss growing on their shells cruised about in the clear green-blue water or drowsed on the surface, awaiting sale to ships which nowadays put in all too seldom.

Minga allowed her gaze to wander over the harbor—bronze-colored in the late afternoon.

"I fear I don't comprehend, Captain—" She looked at him pleasantly, smiled. "Er—Andrew—if commerce here is at such a desperate pass, why do we find so many ships at anchor? And see, most of them are freighted; they ride deep in water."

It was as Minga pointed out. Above a dozen sizeable British

merchantmen swung to moorings: the *Augustus Caesar,* the *Lady Juliana*, the *Gamecock,* the *Princess Royal* and the *Lady Keith*, and many others. Significantly, the only foreign craft in port were the Dutch schooner and a pair of Spanish sloops, the *Pastoria* and the *Divina.*

"It's small wonder you ask," Andrew replied with a flash of white teeth, "but show me a pink, a snow, a small sloop or a schooner."

"What does size have to do with my question?" Minga queried, brushing a mosquito from her neck.

"Everything," the New Englander told her. "Out there lie only big ocean-going ships. A convoy making up for England."

Minga raised slim, perplexed brows. "Andrew, I must be dense."

"Jamaica, nor any of the other Indies, ever grew rich by trade with England alone."

"Why not?"

"The British market can't use a third of what's grown in Jamaica, the Bahamas, Barbados, St. Kitts, and Grenada." He stopped in the shade of a wide tamarind, turned a suddenly earnest face in her direction. "You see, Parliament and certain self-seeking and absentee landlords now carousing at home won't let a British colony sell *direct to any other nation.*"

Sunlight, glancing off the harbor, struck up under Minga's hat, emphasizing a perplexed V between her brows. "You can't be serious."

"I am serious, my dear; never more so. Mark you, every ship from this island is on its way to a port in Russia, Germany, Spain, Portugal or France—anywhere on the Continent—but *first* she must put in at a British port and lose valuable time in paying duty. This, you'll understand, makes it difficult for local planters to compete with the sugar, rum, and coffee grown in the French, Dutch and Spanish Indies."

She was astonished, hadn't imagined or even thought on such matters, nor held opinions on them. "To require them to pay such a tax don't seem right."

He offered her his arm and kept a sharp lookout. H.M.S. *Squirrel* was in from patrol duty now and her officers had begun to appear on shore. "Yes, that is one of their principal grievances against the Crown."

He enjoyed her obvious interest, continued, "You'll discover, Minga, that it's not generals and admirals that provoke wars—it's a bicker between merchants over commerce and profits." A muscle in his thin brown cheeks worked slowly. "On the other hand, powerful British merchants, through our Parliament—" he had to choke out the "our"—"force enormous quantities of Sheffield and Manchester goods onto the Colonial market."

"Force? How?"

"Well, they don't actually force them, but their factors in the islands tempt planters to over-spend—an easy matter since the banking is done in England—and then hold the poor Colonials in a slavery of perpetual debt. They are very deft at the business."

Minga set her chin and her voice lost some of its softness. "I won't credit that the King or his ministers countenance such wicked practices. Really, Andrew, someone has misled you."

In the shade of a tall warehouse, they paused while she readjusted the straps on her sandals. While she did so a gaunt ginger-complexioned Negro shuffled up, a bundle of placards in one hand and a pot of paste in the other. In no great hurry he attached a broadside to a boarding which was already lumpy with countless notices, posters, and placards. The new one read:

CONVOY NOTICE

Admiral's Penn, May, ye 15, 1778

Application having been made to Me for a CONVOY for the Trade from Port Antonio and the different LADING PORTS on the North side of this ISLAND round to North Negril Point in order to join the CONVOY to Sail from thence the 1st of Next Month.

NOTICE IS HEREBY GIVEN that a MAN-OF-WAR will proceed accordingly from MONTEGO BAY with such SHIPS as may be ready the 24th inst. and made herself known by spreading a blue ENSIGN at the fore-top-gallant-masthead.

Clarke Gayton
Vice-Admiral of the Red

A little to the right fluttered another significant notice:

FOR LONDON

(To sail with June Convoy)

The ship *Spike*, Isaac Laws, Master. Now lying HARBOUR OF PORT ANTONIO, mounting 24 nine pounders under cover on one deck and 6 four pounders on the upper DECK and carrying 70 MEN.

For freight or PASSAGE apply to the said Master.

Geo. Henderson, agent

Still another poster, very faded, attracted their attention.

PRIZE SALE

Prize schooner *Intrepid* of Salem, New England built. 70 tonnes
Burthen and mounting four six pound Cannons. And her CARGO
consisting of

        28 bbls of pickled pork
        17 casks of lard
        47 boxes of oyle
        19 boxes of bacon
        A small copper still
        Some 1000 bricks

The terms are CASH and purchasers to take her away within 2 days.

Dick & Milligan
Agents for the privateer
Schooner GRAYHOUND

Theodosius Kendall, proprietor of the Crown & Dove, proved to
be an enormously obese Jamaican wearing thick, red-gold rings in
his ears. More than a trace of Africa showed in his breeding. Wiping
chubby hands on an apron, he bowed several times.

"Welcome, Ma'am. Welcome, sir. Welcome to the Crown &
Dove."

"I am Captain Warren of—"

"Late of the brig *Evergreen*," he broke in. "Yessir, yessir.
Most unfortunate brush with the picaroons. My sympathy, sir."
Like a grotesque duck in a spotted white apron, the innkeeper
bobbed up and down in the entrance.

In silent surprise Minga noticed a constellation of lavender-hued
freckles scatter'd across the publican's flat nose and almost spheri-
cal cheeks.

Strangely animal-like, soft brown eyes, almost concealed by
folds of fat, were inspecting the newcomers so steadily Andrew felt
uneasy. The world over, many publicans were police spies.

"May I grant myself the privilege of offering ye the best the
Crown & Dove 'as to offer?"

"Alas, we have but little money—" Minga cut in while crushing
a centipede which threatened to crawl into her sandal.

"Oh—" The oleaginous smirk faded.

"My friend, Mr. Allerdice, especially recommended your tavern," Andrew interrupted, at the same time throwing his companion a glance of sharp annoyance. Damn the wench. He was making the arrangements here. "Mr. Allerdice will vouch for my—for our—er—"

"Integrity?" Minga offered meekly.

The name of James Allerdice, it appeared, still carried weight in Montego Bay.

Mr. Kendall mopped his face, looked serious. "A fine, honest man is Mr. Allerdice. In the old days, Ma'am, 'twas many a hundred pounds o' custom he directed to this very door." The Jamaican pursed blubbery lips and fetched a tremendous sigh. "*Kwee!* as the Coromantee niggers say. We are all grieved to see Mr. Allerdice ruined and nearing the grave with drink. Pray come in."

The innkeeper led into a courtyard shaded by a huge tamarind. Beneath had congregated a sad-eyed monkey, a flock of hens, two puppies, and a pair of stark-naked Negro babies. The last considered the intruders from round owl-like eyes; then, when the innkeeper flapped his apron not unkindly at them, waddled across the court, fat little buttocks glistening.

"Twins," Mr. Kendall confided, "And a likely pair. Bred by my second cook to Major Casselman's footman, a veritable giant of a man. Quite an affair, enjoyed by all concerned."

In the tamarind a handful of pigeons and parakeets commenced to chatter. At the entrance to the bay a cannon had boomed; briefly its reverberations caromed off the hills back of town. Andrew, listening hard, felt his heart commence to hammer.

Another shot boomed, then another. Jerusha! Suppose a Continental man-o'-war or a state cruiser like Connecticut's *Oliver Cromwell* was standing in? Such cut-and-run tactics had, in the Bahamas, enabled Captain Rathburne in the Continental ship *Providence* to capture seven British vessels and then to plunder Fort Nassau at his leisure. More recently a bold Yankee privateer, off Savanna la Mar, had sent in his boats and cut out the *Lady Moore,* brigantine, under the muzzles of a battery.

His hope faded when Mr. Kendall paid the gunfire not the least attention.

"Well, sir, as I was saying, on Mr. Allerdice's account I'll let you and your sister have a nice clean room." He tipped Andrew a wink of roguish understanding which sent bright stain cascading down Minga's cheeks.

Suppressing his amusement with difficulty, Andrew said, "You mistake us. Mistress Allen was a passenger aboard my vessel. She desires accommodation until she can pass word to relatives up country."

"So, Ma'am, you have relatives? This way, please." Enormous rear swaying under breeches of unbleached linen, the Jamaican panted up an outside staircase. It led to a gallery which ran across two faces of the courtyard.

"Sir Thomas Moffat is—was my uncle by marriage."

"Sir Thom—! Ahem. Yes, Ma'am, to be sure, to be sure." A change, as subtle as it was definite, took place in the innkeeper's manner. "Sir Thomas was a rare fine gentlemen, Ma'am, most highly esteemed by St. James County sassiety."

Kendall turned a yellowish moon of a face over one shoulder. "You have met Mrs. Moffat?" he queried in a flat, cautious tone.

"Why, no. Is Mrs. Moffat—attractive?" It was dead against Minga's nature thus to discuss a member of the family; yet curiosity would not be denied.

"There are them as thinks so, Ma'am. Very. Now, Ma'am, you can have this 'ere elegant apartment for—well, sixpence—and all the fruit you can eat."

A regular volley of cannon shots thundered among the hills back of Montego Bay.

A spindle-legged Negro youth, disfigured by a big fleur-de-lis-shaped brand on his cheek, came pelting into the court.

"Misto' Kendall! Misto' Kendall, sar! Two privateers standin' in, with three prizes."

"Two privateers. You sure?"

"For sure, sar," gasped the runner. "Dey salutin' de port right now."

Mr. Kendall's air of languid affability departed. Cupping hands, he bawled into the courtyard.

"Shep! Phebba, Cubbenah! Turn out, you lazy black bastards, turn out a-running or you'll taste the flopper!"

From all corners of the tavern, slaves appeared on the run, formed a sable pool at the foot of the steps.

"Phebba, you and Julie and Wimba start killin' roaches and make up beds. Jumbo and Quashie, fetch up limes and fruits. You there, Johnny, pour fresh water into the drip jars.

"Mercury, John, Phillip, hump your backsides down to the waterfront and man my cutter. Bring me the officers, else I'll sell you to Barbados." He paused for breath and mopped at the perspiration beginning to pour down his neck. "Junie, run over to Madame Phelibert's, tell her to wash and scent a dozen o' her prettiest trollops. They're to be here by nine o'clock. And, Julie, tell that old bitch the girls *must* be Mustees. Samboes and Quarteroons won't do!''

Like a covey of quail threatened by a hawk, the slaves pattered off.

Briskly rubbing pink palms, Mr. Kendall turned. ''Under the circumstances it ain't possible to spare more than a single room at the price mentioned. Sorry, but business is business and privateers-men are free spenders. They'll be wanting shore berths tonight.

''Let me see, let me see. Your room is at the end of this row. It ain't too elegant. Still it's better than the beach where the land crabs get you. Here you are.'' It was a tiny dark chamber scarcely ten feet long by eight.

''But—but—Mr. Kendall,'' stammered Minga with a quick look at Andrew. ''As I explained, we're not related, nor are we m-married.''

''I'll make out on the beach,'' Andrew said, though he relished the prospect not at all.

Momentarily Kendall looked concerned. ''Best not; you'll likely wake up aboard a convoy with a split scalp. Some o' the masters are turrible short o' hands.'' The innkeeper was in obvious impatience to be away. ''Again, if the fever's abroad, you'll be bound to take it. Tck! Tck! Well, I must attend my duties.''

XI

ADMIRALTY DOCK

AFTER the slashing heat of the day, to feel the cool vital air beating in from the Caribbean was welcome as a draught of chilled Malaga. Theodosius Kendall in a measure must have repented his churlish attitude, for, shortly after he had hurried away, a gangling mulat-tress had appeared at the door of that small chamber in which Andrew and Minga sat staring blankly at each other. She offered a basket which on examination was found to contain a cold fowl, a dish of hot fammee, some star apples, a great, hairy-husked coconut and a flask of not too terrible smelling rum.

Also in the basket Andrew came across a fold of paper. Scrawled on it was a terse message, "Best stay near Lady, Captain. Privateers ashore aint gents. Yr. Humble obdt. servant, T. Kendall."

Andrew couldn't help laughing when the slave girl pattered off. There was nothing humble or obedient about T. Kendall—unless there was plenty of money in evidence.

Minga smiled, patted her skirt, then picked up the basket and suggested, "I've an idea, Andrew. Why not go down and eat beside the water?"

"Capital! I've noticed that most problems don't appear quite so prodigious after supper."

The returned to the only spot on Montego Bay familiar to them— Admiralty Dock. Slowly they advanced its sturdy stone length and found seats on a pile of decking planks. Sea birds wheeled lazily over them, mewed, cocked yellow eyes, hopeful of waste. Bright-colored land birds frolicked among a tall clump of weeds sprouting from a crevice in the dock's well-worn stone work. Minga sighed, spread her skirts out wide in search of greater coolness and briefly regarded the lights of the harbor. Most were yellow, a few green, a few red.

After they had eaten Andrew wandered over to a stack of cable and settled so comfortably on it that the girl followed. Presently he pulled out a clasp knife, opened it with an expert flick.

"What in the world are you up to?"

"I am about to prepare for you, Minga my dear, the most elegant beverage you've ever tasted."

Thoroughly intrigued, she watched him deftly cut a pair of small holes in the husk of a coconut.

"Try some milk?" He showed her how to tilt the coconut in order to drink.

She wasn't extra clever at it and the pale blue-white fluid dripped over her chin. " 'Nough! 'Nough!"

"Now, *ma petie, regarde-moi.*" He felt so much better he was ready to talk French. With a steady sunburnt hand he tilted a measure of rum into the nut, grinned as he shook it.

"Hark to that pleasant gurgling."

Her straight nose shone faintly, intriguingly in the after-glow as she tilted back her head. "I declare, Andrew, it's hard to believe that you are all New Englander."

He smiled, his dark hair sooty against the starlight. "Neither in body nor spirit. You see, my mother was French—from Quebec."

"Then, indeed I shall have to become doubly wary of you."

"You'd better," he advised, at the same time thinking, "Females are such contrary critters she probably won't heed the advice."

While he continued to jiggle the shell, he studied his companion. Her long slender form had relaxed itself against the thick, dark yellow-stained cable. She remained with arms outstretched, hair stirred by a breeze so balmy it must have lingered all day in some flower-dotted valley high among the Blue Mountains.

For the first time in many weeks Minga was experiencing a sense of well-being. True, barring her silver and green bracelet, she had lost every last penny to her name and was utterly destitute; yet she remained healthy, young, and she figured she possessed courage of a sort.

Another cheering thought: she was sure from the way she felt tonight *there'd be no aftermath* of that ghastly business beside Hudson's River. Whatever could have prevented things happening last month? Belatedly she recalled some old wife's tale about great frights, about the effect of sea voyages. Joyousness born of relief bubbled within her. Life wasn't so rude after all. There'd be no hated, nameless child to suffer for.

Why not evaluate Jamaica on its own worth? There'd be small sense in measuring the island by Brewster standards. One should never try to live one's home life in foreign parts—that was what Papa had always maintained. Besides, what did Brewster matter now?

Suddenly she extended a hand, said lazily, "For heaven's sake, Andy, stop worrying that coconut."

He grinned, nodded, and prepared to sample its contents.

"Please, I'd like a taste."

Andrew was surprised. For all her obvious relationship to Colonel Saunders she'd been so prim, so conservative all along, this was a bit more than he had anticipated. Well, so much the better. A nod from Bacchus was always an encouragement to Eros.

"Careful," he warned. "Jamaica rum isn't Madeira. Even laced with coco milk, it can raise a blister on a doorknob."

At his worldliness impatience seized her, Andy Warren needn't act so confounded superior. What did he think she was? A gangle-legged, whey-faced school girl? Hadn't she travelled, hadn't she attended a theater in New York? Hadn't she lived—well, lived? She wasn't going to stand for any more of this dratted condescension. Minga Allen had learned how to care for herself; besides, she reflected languidly, his profile and that new dark red shirt were strongly appealing.

Lips pursed prettily, Minga took half a mouthful. Not bad. Not bad at all. Quite pleasant, in fact. He must be teasing her. Warm little runlets commenced coursing through her. "You're mean. You told me this was powerful."

Andrew made no immediate reply because he had up-ended the coconut, was drinking readily. Jerusha, this was more like it! Now maybe he could forget for a while the disgrace of having lost his ship, of having been ignored by the Marine Committee.

Eyes wide to the purple-blue heavens, he settled back, let his body slump against the cable, and revelled in the cool night wind which was bringing ashore sounds of the carousal aboard the victorious privateers.

Both vessels had strung up battle lanterns until their yards and hulls were lit up like those Greek churches Andrew remembered seeing along the coasts of the Adriatic Sea. Bursts of strident laughter, concertina and guitar music came drifting over the black, light-speckled harbor water.

High over head some dried palm fronds rustled and a frog whistled softly among the old cannon on the dock. Andrew guessed he was lucky after all. A splinter might have gotten him there in Caicos Passage just as well as not. One of them had near split the brig's colored cook in two. Aye. In the next engagement would he be so lucky?

The fragrant air stirred, set wavelets to *lap-lapping* at the slimy stonework of Admiralty Dock, brushed the girl's hair back and forth across her cheek. Her lips were parted just enough to permit a faint highlight on her front teeth.

When she noticed him looking at her, she made a little grimace. "It is very pleasant here, Andrew," she sighed. "I think I should like a little more of that coconut milk punch." How magically the punch had removed uncertainties, fatigue, and anxieties; wonderful stuff, coco-water and rum.

Because he did not want her to get sick or become noisy, Andrew took the shell away as soon as she'd taken one real swallow, and, so there'd be no room for argument, he finished the last of it.

Clouds of red-gold fireflies kept swirling over a small overgrown point of land nearby. Their light glowed so brilliantly that they even revealed the weather-warped figurehead of some long-captured prize. All along the shore whistling frogs were piping musically if monotonously.

How elegant it was just to lie here, Andrew reflected. Incredible that, last night, he and Minga had been aboard that damned little gig wondering if they were going to die of thirst.

"Content? I am, incredibly so." Minga had laced fingers behind her head after placing Mr. Allerdice's big leghorn hat beside the empty food basket.

Softly she commenced to hum, then to sing:

"Lo, all these trophies of affection hot,
   Of pensiv'd and subdu'd desire the tender,
   Nature hath charg'd me that I hoard them not,
   But yield them up where I myself must render,
   That is, to you, my origin and ender;
   For these, of force, must your oblations be,
   Since I their altar, you enpatron me."

Towards the end of the stanza she let a strength into her voice until it streamed rich and warm like a satin ribbon unrolling.

He thought it was time to take her hand; sure enough, she didn't remove her fingers as he murmured, "Your singing, *ma mignonne,* is all that was needed to make an Hesperides of Jamaica."

"You liked my song?" She leaned towards him slightly, her eyes faintly luminous, and looked down on him as he half reclined.

"I dote on it."

"Then I am pleased, Andrew. Exceedingly glad." Her fingers closed gently on his. "You see, I—up until— Well, I have hardly known what to make of you. You are so—so fierce, so abrupt, so different."

His French blood all at once became predominant. "*Mon Dieu!* That, you should never think of me. Not, at least, with you, *ma mie.*" English, he would always think, was a crippled, inadequate language in which to express subtleties of feeling.

"Oh, please," she said, "continue to talk French. I like it though I cannot understand a word."

"Why, then?"

"Because it sounds so pleasant. Like warm velvet."

So Andrew did. He talked, strangely enough, as never he could in English. Odd, that facility which came to him in his mother's language. In his native tongue he seemed to grope whenever he felt truly moved.

"Oh, Andrew, French is beautiful!"

"*Alors Mingue*—" the name would not go as Minga in French, "*si seulement tu saurais comme bien je t'adore!*"

She recognized that. "Then you really—like me—truly?"

"Like!" There was only one response to that; his arms went about her. *Nom de Dieu!* That old buck, Colonel Saunders, had known what he was about. What a wonderfully firm, soft body was Minga's.

Minga couldn't help thinking, how much stronger Andrew's arms were than Jerry's; and so much less gentle. This was wrong to be letting herself be caressed like this, she kept telling herself. Yet indefinably she did not feel this to be so. Jerry was dead. Poor gay, gallant Jerry! She supposed their love had not more than commenced to blossom? So to let Andrew say his piece couldn't be truly disloyal. After all, she wasn't giving Andrew a thing which had ever belonged to Jerry.

In eager cadences this odd New Englander's voice cascaded fascinating, unfamiliar phrases in her ear. The fragrance of the night, the warmth of the punch prompted her. Her mouth lowered itself as her fingers sought his crisp black hair. Lord knew what would ensue but—plague take it, who knew what would ensue these days?

Andrew met impulse with impulse. *Bigre!* Yes, Colonel Saunders certainly had known what was what. As the fragrant warmth of her mouth met his, he thought, What luck, my lad! What ineffable luck!

Subconsciously, his hands sought the fullness of her loins. But he remembered. Go slow, *André! Doucement. Doucement!* He was surprised, pleased, to find himself so much under control. *Non. Pas ici.* Not here, like a couple of white trash. Later; at the Crown & Dove—decently. There, no drunken mariners or skulking Negro might shadow the iridescence of so priceless a moment.

He heard her voice, soft as the breeze in the palms above. "Andrew, do you truly love me?"

"Aye!" he told her in English. "As surely as the sun rises tomorrow."

"Oh, Andrew, I—I'm so glad! I wanted to be sure of that," Minga told him.

Then she poured out her heart. Told him a thousand things about her dreams, her hopes, her longings that she'd never betrayed to any man. Still, she made no mention of Jerry.

Again and again they embraced, their bodies, fresh, vital and hungry, strained against each other until the lights of Montego Bay harbor wavered like swung torches.

From amid a delicious, unfamiliar haze Minga thought, "What can have come over you, Minga? Is this how the tropics affect people? Does Jamaica thaw out New England nasty-niceness so quickly?" She didn't know; moreover, didn't care. Here was a new and fascinating world; it was fine to discover Andrew Warren's stalwart shoulder ready to interpose.

At long last Andrew uttered an impatient sigh. "My dear, suppose we—well, we can't tarry here much longer."

There was no denying this. Sibilant clouds of mosquitoes were whining in voracious legions which a less amorous couple would have noticed an hour back.

Piqued at having allowed him to take the initiative in the matter of departure, Minga sat up, clung a little to his shoulder. "Oh, Andrew—you are right, we must go. But why—Oh, it has been lovely, so sweetly memorable here on Admiralty Dock."

"Yes—unforgettable." He smiled. *Dieu de Dieu!* Why would so much time have to elapse before in the Crown & Dove—

They arose, a trifle embarrassedly and with elaborate care, brushed the dust from their clothing. Because Minga looked so jaunty with her leghorn tilted 'way back from the provocative outline of her face, Andrew drew her to him, all but crushed the breath out of her.

She hoped he wanted never to relax from the warm substance of her body against him. Voices, the rattle of oars being shipped, put a period to the moment and, hand in hand, they strolled back along Admiralty Dock, so differently from the last time they had walked its length.

"Dame Nature made a great mistake in you, Andrew," she smiled when lights glowed ahead.

"Mistake?"

"She made you a foot too tall."

Of course he knelt and briefly lowered his face to her level. Her fingertips closed over the back of his neck, imparting subtle impulses through his scalp and to his brain.

Jerusha! this girl was one in ten thousand—delicate, refined—and cognizant. When they got back to the Crown & Dove, all these long weeks at sea would remain as a dreary memory.

It was amazing to discover the streets of Montego Bay so crowded. Rendered incautious, Andrew actually smiled at scarlet-coated officers, flourished a cheery brown hand at red-faced officers ashore from H.M.S. *Pegasus*.

Two by two, sambo, quarteroon, and mustee trollops sauntered by, swinging fans and loins in unison. That the port was uncommonly overpopulated tonight was inescapable. News of the new prizes in port must have spread like a mist over the countryside. Browned country gentlemen, fee-hungry magistrates, idle planters, curious merchants, and merchant seamen, restored by the cool air, were making up for the long day's deadening heat.

All at once it happened and so suddenly there was no time for readjustment. About the last thing in the world a body would expect to see on the streets of Montego Bay was an officer wearing the uniform of the Continental Navy. Yet there one came; blue coat, scarlet waistcoat, blue breeches, and white thread stockings.

Arm in arm with a British lieutenant, this incredible apparition drew near. By ill luck the lights of a wine shop shone full on Andrew as he and his gracefully moving companion advanced along an earthen footwalk.

Two yards distant the apparition in the shabby blue, red, and gold halted. "My stars and crown! Why, if it ain't Andy Warren!"

Desperately aware of the critical import of the recognition, Andrew drew himself very straight, bowed formally. "I fear, sir, you are quite mistaken. My name is Whitcomb." He sensed Minga's fingers stiffen as he added, "Joseph Whitcomb."

The stranger swayed forward a step, grabbed at Andrew's forearm. "Oh, go 'way! Don't try to game me. You remember me, George Holcomb? Remember, we served in the old *Providence* together?"

"But, An—" Minga was looking at him in wide-eyed amazement. Why should Andrew deny his identity to an enemy officer? What was this about having served aboard a vessel called the *Providence?* With the warm haze of happiness so close about her it was too much to understand.

The English officer, a jolly, red-faced fellow with reddened eyes, looked on, amused. "Oh, come off it, George. Warned you you'd a bombo too many."

"No. I know Andy—can't fool me." Holcomb held out his hand, looked sober. "Sorry to see you here. When di' they capture the *Boston?*"

"Sir, you mistake me.' I'm not the man you think," Andrew said harshly, "and you are blocking our way."

Over the American lieutenant's flushed features came a look of semi-drunken anger. "I get it. You pups in the *Boston* never were any good—deserted us in the *Hancock*, and now—" His narrow black eyes opened wide. "I know you, Andy Warren. You've deserted! You can't—"

"Come! This fellow's three sheets in the wind!" Andrew snapped and gave Minga's arm a tug.

She followed, but walked stiffly, mechanically, like someone on the verge of exhaustion.

XII

Two Ways

JERUSHA! That *had* been a mighty mischance, Captain Andrew Warren reflected as he strode along with Minga silent by his side. Sweat, he realized, was pouring down his face although it was cooler now than it had been in many hours.

Of all the officers in the Continental Naval service, why would it have to have been Seth Holcomb he'd encounter? Oh, the great lop-eared jackass talking like that. Anyone with a grain of sense would have played mum.

Could Seth have piped up on purpose? It was more than likely, come to think on it. Holcomb had hated his guts when he'd been appointed sailing master to the *Boston*, frigate, whereas Holcomb had only landed a junior lieutenant's berth aboard the *Hancock*, 32 guns.

If ever two ships had been destined to create antagonism, it was they—even though both vessels had been Boston-built and rigged. The Lord alone knew how often Captains McNeill and Manly had bickered and fought. It would be a long time before officers on either ship would stop blaming each other for that crushing disaster off Nova Scotia which had cost the Continental Navy the swift handsome *Hancock* and the *Fox*, 28 guns, a brand new prize frigate taken from the British on June 7, 1777, but a few days earlier.

Damn Seth Holcomb to hell and back! The street had been crowded—had anyone read the situation aright? Andrew's heart, he realized, still was pounding like a prize fighter's fists against a sandbag. Good thing that English lieutenant with Holcomb had been so potted—might have caused a nasty to-do if he'd sensed the true situation.

The streets of Montego Bay at this hour were full of sound. British privateersmen of various ratings were running riot over the luxury of finding themselves ashore, over having taken so rich a pair of prizes. Bickering, wenching, drinking, and all manner of rough games were the order of the evening. Maybe it was their ribald remarks and bold glances which rendered Minga so silent. She walked along as if picking her way through a pestilential forest.

Although Andrew addressed her once or twice, she made no reply. Well, he'd best respect her abstraction. When they got back to the Crown & Dove, they'd recapture that delicious mood discovered on Admiralty Dock. She was a smart girl, was Minga Allen. Near as cute as Julie, back there in Bordeaux, who knew, all too well, how it paid to keep a man at arm's length until sheer craving drove him to all sorts of extravagant promises.

The Crown & Dove resembled not at all the drowsy, silent inn of the afternoon. All but a few of its windows blazed, sketched golden rectangles against the night. Half a dozen privateersmen in gaudy, self-devised uniforms were swilling sangaree on the stoop. They sobered only a little when a relief of sentries swung down Prince Street, with white crossbelts shining and bayonets sloped in sinister pale angles.

Minga halted and filled her lungs when the officer in command of the detail, a brutal-appearing sergeant, marched past only a few feet distant. She said nothing, however.

At the inn's entrance Andrew had literally to force their way past a gang of hairy, heavily sweating officers out of the victorious privateers. The New Englander stood too tall to invite much interference, but one sandy-haired lieutenant stuttered, "Come with me, chickie," and made a snatch at Minga's arm. Andrew landed a well-timed blow, sent the fellow crashing backwards into a tray of glasses.

"Anyone else?" He hoped Minga was being impressed by the quiet way he stood awaiting the next onslaught. Though two or three of the roisterers yelled, "Let's get him, mates," no one moved.

When they got to their room and he had set the gourd lampwick sputtering in its bath of tallow, Minga, instead of seating herself, remained near the door, her lips compressed. She held her body very straight and her fingertips trembled gently. Andrew's sense of elation melted like the first snowflakes on a warm roof. So then, she had grasped the implications of Holcomb's stupidity?

Furiously he fought to clear his mind of the last effects of the rum. He'd better, and in a hurry. When a person was as fanatically Tory as Minga Allen, one couldn't rest easy.

"You seem to expect something," he suggested.

Her words came out in a flat and precise monotone. "What did that man, that—that Rebel prisoner, mean down there?"

"He was drunk," Andrew fenced, sinking onto the edge of the bed. Instantly the gourd lamp dyed his lean features scarlet, emphasized the blackness of his eyes and hair, and projected his shadow in gigantic proportions on the whitewashed wall behind. "What did you fancy he could have meant?"

Minga ignored the question; her gaze never wavered from his face. Above the crash made by a chair overturned below, she demanded, "Why did you tell him that your name was Whitcomb? Why did you deny your own right name?"

Andrew, thinking more clearly now, perceived his danger. Smiling, he got up and, as if to open a window opening onto the street, crossed between the door and her. "I had reasons why I didn't wish to be recognized by Lieutenant Holcomb."

The blue and yellow kerchief covering Minga's breast rose more swiftly. She commenced to breathe faster, resembled not at all the lovely languorous girl who had strained her mouth to his lips not half an hour ago. "And, sir, what were those reasons?" she demanded evenly.

He wanted to say, "None of your confounded business." What right had she, a confounded Loyalist, to be questioning an officer of the United States Navy?

"I don't like the fellow and never have. We grew up together. He hates me because I wouldn't join the Continental Navy."

Minga felt the flush on her face deepen as she stared at him. Insistent devilish voices kept clamoring in her brain, "Andrew is a Rebel! A Rebel officer. A Rebel! A Rebel!"

He was lying—lying clumsily, stupidly. Her voice like a low note on a violoncello, she told him so.

Perspiration began to sting at his temples as he protested, "I'm not lying!" Great God! He couldn't, mustn't, daren't admit his true convictions. This port was swarming with people who'd be ready and eager to hang a Yankee spy.

Minga's body pressed itself to the far wall slowly, as if she was trying to remove herself from him as far as the room would permit. "You *are* lying!" Her lips quivered as they formed her words. "All along, I've wondered about you, Andrew Warren. You, sir, are a damned, disloyal Rebel. You are a perjured Yankee officer! Oh, how I loathe and despise you. I—I— And to think that I—" Slowly, she dragged the back of one hand across her mouth.

The accusations fell like weights from her lips. Stung, he took a couple of steps forward. "Well, and what if I am an American? Who in hell are you to talk—you—you poor, soiled baggage?" She needn't think now that he hadn't understood the nature of her relation with Colonel Saunders,—just what his protection had meant.

From the way Minga winced and gasped, from the way her half-enunciated next words died, from the way her eyes wavered aside, he knew for sure that his suspicions had been accurate. She swallowed painfully. "B-baggage!" She shivered as through her loins and breasts flickered small hot impulses.

"Soiled?" How could he have learned about—about that ghastly night? Merciful heavens! Until now she'd deemed her secret well kept. How hard Mrs. Ashton, Major de Vaux, Colonel Saunders, and the rest had plotted to keep it so.

They were the only ones who knew for sure what had happened—they and the guilty Brunswickers. To keep the affair extra secret the three mercenaries, sniveling, bawling in their terror, had been hanged in the dead of night.

It was amazing that Andrew Warren should have learned, amazing and crushing. What a fool she'd been to dream that she might keep her name clean—despite everything.

"I—I— You don't understand—"

"I understand all too well!" He moved closer, towered over her, his black eyes showering fury. The rum was working again. A damned king-loving Tory! That's what this girl was. When he thought of the suffering of those poor devils rotting in prison hulks like the *Jersey*, of the sick in Dr. Blanchard's "drydock," of Pa pinned to the ground by Hessian bayonets, like a butterfly to a cork—by God, he hated all Tories.

Making a rare effort, he controlled himself. *Nom de Dieu*, he'd come to Jamaica to get those medicines, and get them he would, even though right now he hadn't but two shillings to his name. No, he didn't intend to let this tart of a Loyalist interrupt that chance.

"Steady on, Andy. Steady. Use your head." Suddenly he saw his tack, caught her wrist and said grimly, "Look here, we'll fashion us a deal out of this yet. Your people here in Jamaica don't know you for what you really are, and I guess you ain't over-anxious to have 'em learn." He paused, trying to read her reactions by the uncertain lamp light. "Well, only you and Holcomb know me for what I am."

Minga was aware of his dark Indian-like features dominating the flickering gloom.

"You fail to perceive a distinction," she told him.

"Distinction?"

"Yes. What has happened to me is my own concern. What you have done is the affair of the Crown. My duty to my King—"

"To hell with that stupid, Hanoverian glutton!" he blazed. His hand shot out as she dodged over to the window, but he only knocked her sidewise and she reeled on, put her head out of the window and screamed.

"Help! A spy! The watch! Here, the watch!"

"Damn your sluttish soul! Be still!" Frantically, he dove at her. He caught her, all right, and dealt her such a clip on the side of her face that her head whipped over onto her shoulder. She slipped down onto the floor, and crouched there panting, her skirts about her waist; though her eyes were open, they were for the moment unseeing.

Heart hammering, Andrew looked down into the street, then crossed the room and opened the door onto the courtyard. He felt reassured. The courtyard was full of strident laughter. The privateersmen were playing some rough game, two of them had hoisted mustee wenches onto their backs. The girls were squealing, trying to knock each other off with cushions. Over it all calabash drums were thumping, fifes shrilling.

Infinitely relieved, Andrew turned, grinning. "Go on," he invited, "yell all you please."

Fearfully, she looked up; felt her skin go cold. She would never forget him like this, with his black hair tumbled over his forehead in savage ringlets. When he turned and slammed shut the window, he resembled those Rebels who had come swarming into Millwood to destroy two-generations' accumulation of fine property.

"Help!" she screamed. "A spy! Help me!" He was a traitor and must hang.

"Try E flat," he suggested and tightened his belt. Her terror was somehow fascinating; the rum was running again in his veins. *Nom de Dieu!* this promised to be sport such as he'd never before enjoyed. Along the littoral of the Mediterranean sailors like their wenches to squall and to kick up a fuss.

In a moment now he'd take her. Not gently as he had planned, but furiously, ripping her garments where they interfered. Outside the carouse was growing wilder, bawdy songs were ringing up into the great cottonwood in the courtyard and the music had reverted to the African Coast. Far louder than Ming's cries, an oboe was squealing just below the gallery. There wasn't a chance in the world anybody would notice.

"Now, my pretty pet, you can make yourself pleasing." His hand slipped under her arms, lifted her to her feet. He pulled her, crushed her to him.

"Oh, Andrew, no—please, no!" She should have been revolted —but—but everything was confusion. His arms felt like the coils of a cable, tightened slowly, powerfully.

All at once his head came away from the embrace. Almost subconsciously he had detected a peculiar rhythm in the pattern of noise outside. It sounded familiar—it was. It was the sound of men marching in step. The music, the singing faltered and died away into discords.

Flinging her aside, he rushed to the door, thrust his head out into a glare of torches in time to watch a file of scarlet-clad black soldiers in pointed leather caps come pounding into the courtyard. The officer who had accompanied Holcomb was at their head. The privateersmen were cursing and gaping, but making way.

"Up there!" From among the disordered tables Kendall was pointing with a fat forefinger. "Up there. They're in there."

As from the depths of a bowl of smoky coals, faces were staring up at him. A fierce yell arose when they noticed his head peering out of the room.

Andrew hesitated not even long enough to turn and fling a bitter farewell at the girl, now lying crumpled, weeping, on the bed.

With an expertness born of long years of clambering about rigging, Andrew caught a bougainvillea vine which came cascading down over the roof and swung himself up, up until he felt warm earthenware tiles under his knees. The vine crawled along the apex of the roof a distance.

"There he is!" a voice yelled. "Shoot! Shoot, you black bastards!"

As he went scrambling along the roof, a musket barked and a bullet knocked chips of tile into his face.

"Get him! Quick!"

When he swung into the branches of a tamarind, a staccato volley banged in the courtyard and twigs and leaves fell all about him.

"Spy! 'Ware, spy!" The cry began to be repeated in the street. If ever he was to find Carlos Cardozo, he'd have to have plenty of luck tonight, Andrew realized, as he dropped to earth and commenced to run.

XIII

UP RIVER

THE KITTAREEN rasped the steel tire of one of its two wheels over a rock projecting from the sand. This was no proper road at all, Minga Allen observed, but the dry bed of an old river. At this point the dead stream paralleled the fast-flowing yellow-green Montego.

Mr. Angus Hamilton, bailiff of the Hinton Estates in Westmoreland Parish, leaned forward, clucked at his gray mule, and so set the vehicle to jolting and bouncing faster, until its motion reminded Minga of that of a cornpopper held over the coals.

What a tidy piece of good fortune first to encounter this friend of Mr. Kendall's, then to find him on the eve of returning to the estates he supervised. She had been smart enough to trade transportation with Mr. Kendall for an assurance to the Crown officers that the owner of the Crown & Dove had harbored one Andrew Warren, a Yankee spy, in all innocence. The publican had been desperately anxious when the port commandant had begun barking questions at him.

What in truth had happened to the fugitive? Rumors had circulated that he had been taken, would be tried by court martial; others claimed that the spy had got away scot-free.

Resolutely, Minga diverted her thoughts to the future. It was infinitely stimulating to realize that, at long last, Moffat's Penn lay only a few miles ahead. Here she was riding through a wild, lush countryside which for the moment was quite flat. There had been dense stretches of woods, separating great, heat-brightened vistas of sugar-cane fields.

During the long trip up from Montego Bay the bailiff, garrulous, kindly and wise in the planting of sugar cane, had answered her multitude of eager questions, had explained how the great industry operated. During the late summer months the land, he told her, was manured by the flying pens—movable cattle folds.

"The cuttings, Ma'am, are placed in cane holes three to four feet wide and about eight inches deep—with maize, or corn as ye term it in America, planted in the middle to grow and shade the young cane."

He spoke of the hazards of planting; of the yellow and the black blast, of borers, of hordes of rats, of hurricanes, droughts and, worst of all, of the sudden, fierce fires set by careless or rebellious slaves.

Damaged or tainted cane, Minga learned, was promptly rendered into rum. Mold from river banks was better fertilizer than cattle droppings on trash-tops of sugar canes. Slaves shouldn't be worked much in the rainy season—it was bad for their health.

"When ye get to Moffat's Penn, Ma'am, be sure to view the boiling house. 'Tis there the juice is rendered after the mills have ground it."

"What turns the mills, Mr. Hamilton?"

"Wind, water, oxen, slaves—whatever is most convenient."

"What do they use at Moffat's Penn?"

"Slaves," the bailiff said and looked aside as most everyone did at mention of the estate. There must be something odd about Aunt Adelina's property—of that Minga was entirely aware by now.

Angus Hamilton, it appeared, was in charge of Hinton's Penn, situated some five or six miles further up the Montego from the Moffat property.

Minga was relieved when, suddenly, the road left the old river bed and began to wind in and out through tangles of grenadilla, cordiums, and cottonwoods. In the treetops countless parrakeets, or love birds, chittered and played. Ears canted forward, the mule jogged along more rapidly now that the sun had slipped over the crest of a range of mountains and the air was growing cooler.

The countryside seemed to abound in wild life—if one looked carefully, one could see lizards, quail, ground doves, humming birds brilliant as dabs of paint on a palette, and strange red and black birds with enormous bills. When the road paralleled the Montego flowing with tawny impatience towards the Caribbean, they could see hideous, muddy alligators drowsing on its banks.

"Up above Hinton's, the river's prettier," Hamilton explained. "It's just one wild cataract after another. Over yonder," he pointed across the river to his left, "lies Squire Strudwick's plantation. A main fine chap is Squire Strudwick."

The bailiff gave Minga a sidewise glance. "Bear in mind he's a neighbor, next door, so to speak."

Again Minga wondered, finally made brave to inquire, "And pray, Mr. Hamilton, why do you and everyone else speak so guardedly of Moffat's Penn?"

"Oh, I'd no such intent, Ma'am. Indeed not," the bailiff broke out. "Mrs. Moffat's a very handsome and talented lady. Very capable. Manages the estate herself, now that poor Sir Thomas is gone.

"A great shock to the parish—his going so sudden-like. Now there, Ma'am, was a man who could handle his bookkeepers—keep 'em going the full five years and more, as a rule."

Bookkeepers, Minga soon learned, were young men imported from the British Isles, Englishmen and Scots who, in exchange for passage, sold their services for five years, at the rate of thirty to forty pounds a year. Irishmen, of course, got less.

"Lord, Lord!" Hamilton sighed and cleaned his steel-rimmed spectacles on a grimy handkerchief, "I fancy I'm the last of all of us who came out back in '58."

"Did you find the keeping of books particularly tedious?"

A rasping laugh escaped the dumpy little man at her side. "Lord love ye, Ma'am, bookkeepers don't keep books in Jamaica.

They're slave drivers, that's what they are—nothing more nor less. But we nasty-nice English can't abide to call them that.''

He slapped the reins on the mule's loins. "It's a dog's life, Ma'am, what with sitting up every other night in the boiling house, checking the slaves' thieving, getting the sugar aboard ship, and punishing evil-doers.''

"Then, on the same principle, an attorney isn't an attorney?''

"An attorney,'' Hamilton explained, "is—well, an overseer—of a superior sort, to be sure, who administers the affairs of an estate, be it a penn, a polink, or a coffee mountain. 'Tis he buys the slaves, tends to discipline, hires and discharges bookkeepers. We don't have to discharge many, though,'' Hamilton added, as a drove of wild pigs pattered from a thicket across the road and became lost in a furious tangle of trumpet vines.

Now that the road was smooth Minga was content to settle back on the kittareen's musty-smelling cushions. Merciful heavens, her backside felt as though it had been kicked in a dozen places!

"No need to discharge the poor devils, not when Old Bones tends to it for you. 'Tis at a fearful rate salt food, rum and the sambo wenches carry off your young bookkeepers.''

"Sambo wenches? I don't—can't understand.''

Quite matter-of-fact, Hamilton replied, "Most plantation owners, Ma'am, pay their bookkeepers a bonus—generally a pound—for each mulatto child they sire.''

"*What!*''

"Aye, this is indeed a heartbreaking land, Ma'am—desperate lonesome; these poor devils are poor, poor as the John crows. Mulattoes—girls in particular—fetch high prices in Jamaica.''

"Oh!''

"So it's small wonder, when rum's to be had for the asking and black wenches for the crooking of a finger, that they don't last long.''

"You spoke of a 'sambo'; exactly what is that?''

Mr. Hamilton braced his feet as the kittareen lurched into a set of ruts.

"Why it goes like this. A sambo is born of a black and a mulatto; a mulatto of a white and a black; a quarteroon or quadroon of a white and a mulatto, and a mustee of a quadroon and a white.''

The bailiff sighed. "Aye, like I said, precious few whites ever live out their span. There's the dysentery, the lung fever, and,'' he dropped his voice, "worst of all, the yellow jack. You wouldn't believe, Ma'am, what I have seen. There have been times when a body could ride a-horseback for half a day, and find nothing but empty houses. Corpses lying in the road, in the ditches, in the guinea yards. The John crows—up in America they call them buzzards—were fed so full they couldn't flap off the ground.''

"But, Mr. Hamilton, it isn't right. Jamaica looks so lovely,'' Minga protested. "Look—look yonder. See all those flowers and blossoms; look at that wonderful tree with the scarlet blooms. It's beautiful—''

"Beautiful like paint over a boil,'' Hamilton grunted, steering the mule to one side as a huge oxcart appeared creaking and lurching under a heavy mound of sugar canes. "Now up in the mountains, it's fine and healthful, to be sure. Next year I intend buying a coffee mountain over near Port Antonio. I'll live quiet and—well, maybe, I'll send home for a girl from England.''

The road wound out into the open once more and presently passed a fine, neat-looking residence, almost a mansion it was in proportions. The structure's main floor was elevated perhaps ten feet from the ground by brick pillars, and green shutters screened two sets of galleries which appeared to run all the way round the house itself.

"That's Pondicherry House,'' Hamilton explained. "Built by a Colonel Chandos. Died in a battle in America last year. I expect he never thought—''

"—What a queer fence! What in the world is it made of?''

"You'll be referring to yonder penguin fence?'' Indeed that was what the barrier resembled. Cacti, which had been planted very close together and then trimmed off short, had healed into dumpy rounded figures which suggested rows of tenpins or, more imaginatively, penguins. Covered with long white spines, the barrier looked formidable, indeed.

On rounding a bend in the road, the kittareen advanced upon a crowd of half naked, incredibly ragged Negroes of all ages. In the center of a loose ring two enormous black bucks were backing away from each other; jabbering and snarling, they kept their hands behind them with fingers twisted into their belts.

"Ah make duppy of yo', Benjy!'' one of the two bellowed.

"Hyo, hyo!'' the crowd burst out. "Dey lib for goat.''

Before Minga had opportunity to inquire, the two bucks lowered bullet-shaped heads and dashed furiously for each other. With an audible *t-thunk!* they met head on.

"Oh, *ki-ki!*'' One of them staggered, swayed, then, his eyes half closed, sat down so violently that dust spurted out from under him. But for all that, he held his hands behind him.

"Butting duel,'' the bailiff grunted. "Fool niggers can't hurt themselves much.''

For the life of her, Minga couldn't guess what they were trying to do. Presently the seated Negro man got up, wiped a trickle of blood from his forehead, and backed away.

"Dis time Ah chaw yo' like galli-wasp," panted the other as again the duellists charged each other like sable battering rams.

Hamilton paid only the least of attention. "Damned idiots will keep on like that until one knocks the other out. It's a wonder, Ma'am, they don't bash their stupid heads in, but they never do."

When the kittareen drew nearer, the onlookers scattered, bare-breasted wenches squalling and naked pickaninnies legging it furiously through gaps in the penguin fence. In less than half a minute there remained by the roadside only an old, withered man and a pale young woman hobbling along on a bent, crutch-like stick. She progressed with an odd bobbing gait, one leg dragging. Near the heel showed a purple scar.

At once Minga recognized that the frightened girl was, in a way, lovely. Eyes rolling fearfully, back muscles rippling, she hobbled along towards a break in the fence and guided the old man. Obviously he was sightless. Minga could only think of the halt leading the blind.

When the kittareen came rocking up, the girl dropped her crutch and cringed into the ditch. The old man tottered a few steps, then knelt at the roadside, hands raised in supplication.

Hamilton asked, "Notice that wench?"

"Yes. Poor thing is terribly lame."

With a whalebone whip Hamilton flicked the mule. "An habitual runaway, three times and over," he explained carelessly. "Owner's had her hamstrung. She won't run away again."

"*Hamstrung!*" Incredulous, Minga stared at the handsome Negress. She was peering fearfully out of the crook of her elbow. "You mean her owner ordered her to be lamed—forever?" At the sight of that puckered scar she felt her stomach muscles flutter.

"What else can you do?" the bailiff queried in surprise. "Can't go paying travel money and rewards forever."

The breath departed from Minga's body as the kittareen rolled on leaving a lazy tract of dust to settle over the forlorn figures. "What was it you said, Mr. Hamilton?"

"I said when a slave runs away more than three times, the owner either whips him to death as an example—or cuts the rascal's Achilles tendon. Have to, you know, Ma'am, or every last black would run off to join the Maroons. Now, the Maroons—"

"What are they?"

The bailiff scratched a lean and leathery jaw. "Some say one thing; some say another. General Penn and Admiral Venables drove the Spaniards out of Jamaica back in 1655, you know—chased 'em out so fast the Dons couldn't take their slaves with 'em.'' Mr. Hamilton sobered, glanced towards the mountains now towering like a titanic palisade above the river valley. ''When the Spaniards sailed away, their slaves—called Cimarrons—took a country called 'The Land of Look Behind,' otherwise, the Cockpit Country, which is too near here for my liking.''

''Where is this Cockpit Country?''

''Not thirty miles distant—over that way. Some say the Cockpit is the vent of an old volcano. At any rate, many of the Cimarrons went up in there. Various governors have tried to dislodge them, but they haven't succeeded.

''They've had their own government of a sort for some time, under a black fellow who calls himself 'Colonel.' At first the Royal Government used to fight them, but now—well, the planters pay the Colonel so much a head for each runaway slave returned—so the Maroons bring them back. They're smart as niggers go—country's getting crowded—don't want too many people up in that valley.''

''But are they always content to stay there?''

Under his floppy straw hat Hamilton frowned, then eased the mule's rein because the road had commenced to climb. On the side of a hill some two miles distant glowed a white speck, brilliant against the green background. He indicated it with the whalebone whip.

''That, Ma'am, is where you are bound,'' he explained. ''Hawthorn Hall's the name of the house—as pretty a spot as there is west of St. Jago de la Vega. But, as I was saying, Ma'am, the Maroons behave some years, don't the others. Depends who's Colonel. They've a new one,'' he added. ''Old Papeen died last month.'' Mr. Hamilton fished in his pocket and produced a pouch of tobacco. From it he fished a lump of shreddings which he stowed squirrel-like in his cheek. ''Every time there's a new Colonel, the planters get nervous. Most of 'em ain't followed the law.''

Under the leghorn tied to her head with a topaz-hued kerchief, the girl's sunburned features turned towards him. ''What law, Mr. Hamilton?''

''By law, an owner is required to keep on his property one white man for his first hundred guinea birds, and another buckra—or European—for each seventy-five slaves after that. Ain't one estate out of ten follows the law. Greed, Ma'am, will cause the downfall of Jamaica.''

As the slope increased Mr. Hamilton's gray mule tilted its ears back over its neck, leaned into its breast strap, and put its feet down hard.

"See that milestone?"

Minga turned her eyes aside from the Montego. The river was leaping, vaulting and gurgling over a barrier of great boulders. At a little-travelled crossroads stood a short, moss-covered pillar.

"That's the northwest boundary of Moffat's Penn," the bailiff told her soberly.

Two or three John crows which had been perched, round-shouldered, on a sign post craned scaly, naked necks, and flapped lazily away. The object of their previous attention remained dangling from a bough. Suspended from a cord was a length of meat and bone which continued to revolve in the bluish shadows cast by the mountains.

"What in the world is that?"

"I told you Jamaica's a hard land. Look closer, Ma'am."

To Minga's inexpressible horror, the dangling object proved to be a human leg suspended by its ankle. So recently had the limb been severed that the parched earth beneath showed a scattering of rusty-red splotches.

"Tchk! tchk!" Hamilton grunted, "looks like they've been having trouble at Hawthorn Hall."

"Trouble? What kind of trouble?" Minga fixed her eyes on the mule's dust-flecked rump. "Murder?"

"Oh, scarcely that. I venture some slave raised his hand towards a bookkeeper. When a guinea bird does that, there's nothing for it but hang him. Law says they must be quartered then and a limb exposed at each corner of the property as a warning. A sensible provision, too, I might add."

From the way she went pale and closed her eyes, the bailiff sensed how inexpressibly shocked his passenger was.

"No doubt you deem us Jamaicans hard and merciless people, Ma'am. Well, maybe we are but, as Governor Trelawney used to say, 'When riding a panther, use your club and spurs freely, else the beast will rend you.' "

XIV

ADELINA MOFFAT

MR. HAMILTON was polite, but definite, as he stood adjusting a quarter-strap. "Thank ye kindly, Ma'am, but I've no time to stop in. I'd like to, mind you, but I be late up to Hinton's as it is, and Jeremiah," he nodded at the mule, "is tired. Besides, looks like it's coming on to thunderstorm."

This was no exaggeration—a tremendous black cloud had, with the suddenness of a magician's trick, splashed over the blue-green crest of those not very distant mountains towering above the wide cane fields of Moffat's Penn. On the far side of them, mused Minga, lay the Cockpit Country—savage and untravelled.

" 'Tis but a short distance to the mansion," the bailiff added. "You have only to walk through the black village and then you'll see Hawthorn Hall ahead; and a very elegant residence it is, Ma'am. At least it was when Sir Tom was living."

The bailiff ran a rather greasy, dull brown cuff across his forehead, at the same time considered her seriously. "Pray recall what I say, Mistress Allen—the Strudwicks are *good* neighbors. The Squire—well, he's kept to English ways more than most in these parts."

For all she was bathed in perspiration, Minga smiled her best smile as she alighted. "I vow I don't know whatever I would have done without you, Mr. Hamilton. You have been enormously kind—and instructive." He certainly had been that. Right now her mind was a-boil with all the hints, facts, and conjectures with which he had supplied her during the long ride up the course of the Montego.

She could hear the river rushing and pounding in the distance so clearly there could be no doubt that a storm was brewing. Off the crest of the billowing black clouds glanced dull orange-red reflections cast by a sunset on the far side of the mountains. Over the cane fields fell a hushed stillness in which the moaning of a conch-shell bugle, sounding orders for some slave gang, sounded very clear.

"Well, goodbye, Mistress Allen, and good luck to you." The

bailiff scrambled back up onto the kittareen's shapeless seat, and flapped his reins across the gray mule's rump. The gig's spidery wheels commenced to revolve and, very soon, Minga found herself standing quite alone at the entrance of a dusty drive which, lined with tall royal palms, stretched for an indeterminate distance up a gentle slope.

Never had she felt quite so forlorn or so uncertain. Well, there was nothing for it but to walk on. One small consolation was that she hadn't any luggage to carry, not even a kerchief. Beyond her bracelet and the things Mr. Allerdice had given her, three days back, she hadn't a thing in the world.

Her heated features contracted. If only she'd had opportunity first to communicate with her Aunt, but there was no post, and very little travel went this way. Um. What would Mrs. Moffat think of her niece? Child of her maternal grandmother's second marriage, Aunt Adelina couldn't be so very old.

"Well, I've been through plenty worse than this," she reminded herself. She guessed she should be able to cope with Aunt Adelina. Wasn't it strange how events could pile up all at once? For nineteen years her existence had been so placid, so secure, almost luxurious, and then all in a year—Millwood looted and burnt, Cowboys, Brunswickers, picaroons. The most overwhelming blow of all, though, had been the exposure of Andrew Warren. Think of Andrew as a Rebel and an officer in the enemy service to boot!

To think that she'd all but decided that Andrew, and not Jerry Vaughan, had been destined to play the dominating rôle in the drama of her life. Her suncracked lips tightened. A plague take Andrew Warren! Had they really captured him? If the British did take him, he'd hang, sure enough— She shivered.

She commenced to walk along the drive, avoiding the many ruts and holes. In the mountains a peal of thunder boomed like the opening gun in a salute.

Refusing to develop her present thoughts, Minga quickened her pace until she found herself almost trotting along under the palms, the dried fronds of which had begun to twitch under restless puffs of wind.

To her right appeared what must be the slave village Mr. Hamilton had mentioned. The huts of palm thatch and whitewashed board construction were arranged in four long rows, each with a little garden, or plantain walk, stretching out behind. Pigs and chickens were noticeably scarce, and what few children were about looked gaunt and dull-skinned. All these last went naked, even girls of ten and twelve. So little activity was evident, she deduced that the field gangs must still be at work.

A few aged or pregnant women squatted on their hams about a kettle which apparently contained little of interest. In the depths of the village two or three babies were squalling thinly, drearily. Recent neglect seemed to have overtaken previous care; piles of crushed stone, standing ready for use, had not been used to fill dangerously deep ruts in the drive.

Because the wind began to blow hard enough to send bits of coconut husks and streamers of dried palm fronds scrabbling across the road, she quickened her pace. Soon Minga's nostrils wrinkled to a peculiar sour-sweetish smell which seemed to emanate from a great shed-like structure beyond the slave quarters. It boasted a tall brick chimney from which gray-blue smoke erupted, then sank to cling to the earth and creep off as if ashamed of its existence.

Ever more frequently thunder boomed; flocks of white-winged pigeons began streaking by from the fields on their way to shelter in the forest rising at the foot of the mountains. Vivid streaks of lightning played over the purple-black mountain.

There was more activity in the slave village now; chattering in some West Coast dialect, the slaves ran to secure stray livestock and children. Shutters commenced banging to. Cattle in a crawl, or breeding pen, huddled together, their eyes white and nervous.

All at once Hawthorn Hall loomed white and stately before her. Three tall storeys high stood Adelina Moffat's house of stone and timber. What in New England would be called "welcoming arms" steps of an unusual design led up to the main or second floor. Both wings of the staircase, she observed, were guarded by wrought-iron railings of remarkable beauty.

In crimson splendor heavy bougainvillea vines clambered up stone pillars supporting the upper floors and spouted towards the mansion's pointed roof. A wide gallery, shaded by bamboo lattices, encircled the whole house. Under these porticoes quantities of poultry and peacocks had taken refuge. To either side of the main house extended covered passages or cloisters which connected with smaller buildings, also white-painted.

Again the thunder exploded, this time terrifyingly near and prompt. Then the sky darkened to a livid purple-black so swiftly that, in no time, Minga was hard put to see her way. Another lance of lightning fell, hissing and crackling, into a grove of trees beyond the mansion. The resultant thunder clap was indeed awe-inspiring, made the very ground quiver. Still no rain fell, though the air was overladen with moisture.

Hurriedly, Minga ascended the staircase, looking all the while for a bell-pull; she could find none. To her astonishment, no one was in sight, though Hawthorn Hall's magnificently carved mahogany doors stood ajar. No lights had been lit, but the interior was full of slammings and bangings. Uncertainly, Minga fingered the knocker, a massive affair shaped like a leopard's head and executed in brass.

The wind was fairly booming now, tearing at Minga's skirts and hat, and raising gritty clouds of dust. Half a dozen peacocks appeared flying out of a field, screamed, settled in a formal garden at the left and disappeared under a bank of shrubbery. Next, a string of small gray donkeys galloped by below, ears flat to their backs.

Minga knocked again, more boldly. From inside came no sound beyond the faint tinkle of some stringed instrument, a harp, perhaps.

"Please," she called, "please, is there anybody about?"

Her only answer was a great gust of wind, followed by almost solid sheets of rain that whirled indoors as had spindrift over the *Evergreen's* bow.

Terrifyingly loud was the continued hissing, dry cackle of lightning. One bolt could not have struck very far distant for, instantly, the whole ponderous house trembled and reverberated to a most heart-stilling crack of thunder. Minga had hardly caught her breath when another bolt hissed past. By its brief and unreal light she glimpsed cottonwoods, pawpaws and tamarinds dancing a frenzied minuet before the blast. Like the riffles of an expert drum corps, successive billows of rain lashed at shutters which rattled and slatted.

To avoid getting more drenched than she was, Minga stepped inside and was peering about in the gloom when a draught slammed shut the door. Though she strained her eyes, she couldn't see much beyond the dim outlines of many glassless windows. The house was full of sound, and only faintly now could she hear the faint tinkling of music—serene, despite the rain hurled in fury against the blinds.

When her ears accustomed themselves to the uproar, Minga commenced to recognize the sound of voices, quite a few voices. Down a hallway a light glimmered, glanced off a door of well-polished satinwood, winked cheerfully on its brass door handle, then became multiplied on a floor as smooth and bright as the dining-room table had been at Millwood. The candle advanced.

Mercy! What could she find to say? Involuntarily she stepped back, tried to get back out of doors, to enter properly. Too late.

Above the flame of a candle shielded by a hurricane glass appeared in the humid dark as beautiful a face as Minga Allen had ever beheld—a face rendered in gold, rather than in silver, tints.

"Please don't misunderstand," Minga began. "You see, the door—"

"Oh!" Full lips formed a startled crimson circle. "Who's that?"

Now Minga could observe the apparition more closely. Though not obviously, African blood had lent this lovely creature her color key. Glistening jet hair was drawn into a fascinating arrangement, topped by an enormous tortoise-shell comb tipped with little gold beads. From the girl's delicate ears hung flat earbobs of fine gold filigree. Her dress looked to be of fine yellow lawn looped with little crimson bows.

When the girl saw how damp, dishevelled and bedraggled the stranger was, her manner underwent a change. Her head went back and her eyes narrowed themselves. Haughtily, she demanded, "What are you doing in here? Who are you? Answer up!"

That a person of color should have dared even to address her thus had never occurred to Minga. She was tired and didn't care a rap right now whether school kept or not. She drew herself up, inches taller than the other, and demanded in monumental dignity:

"Are you a servant here?"

By using a similar tone of voice Mamma had been able to check the most obstreperous slave Judge Allen had ever owned.

"What? Why, why I—" The mustee—so Minga judged her—stared, dark eyes suddenly very wide above the candle flame. A terrific crash of thunder held everything breathless. The harp music continued unchecked. From a room down the hall, however, arose frightened whimpering.

"Don't stand there staring like a ninny," Minga snapped. She knew now for sure that this golden girl was what she suspected—a Creole, and not a Spaniard or a Frenchwoman, or an Italian. "Put that light down and go find Mrs. Moffat."

"Excuse me please, Mistress, but—" The girl's bearing returned to her original manner. "I don't think Mrs. Moffat will—"

Because she was wet and hungry and uncertain and angry at this girl's attempt at patronage, she snapped, "Mrs. Moffat is my aunt—I am Mistress Allen of New York. Must I tell you twice to announce me?"

Without warning the front doors blew open and in the sudden inrush of wind a crystal vase of flowers crashed over; but the tinkling music kept on. The golden girl ran to pick up the broken glass, her little feet in scarlet slippers whispering softly over the glossy floor.

Minga was not afraid now, was surer of herself than she had been in a year. Why not? Hadn't she weathered, more or less successfully, some pretty severe tempests?

"Who are you?" she demanded in a milder tone.

"Please, Mistress, I'm Chloë, Mrs. Moffat's confidante."

Confidante? What in mercy's name was a confidante? The two stood there—the golden-brown girl in her full-skirted yellow lawn dress, French lace blouse and vivid scarlet slippers; Minga in the limp blue cotton dress, leghorn hat, and shapeless shoes Mr. Aller-dice had bestowed. She wasn't wearing even a suspicion of stays, stockings, or a decent number of petticoats.

"You may show me to Mrs. Moffat."

"Why, yes, but if Mrs. Moffat is—well—if there's trouble, don't blame me." Chloë dropped the slightest imaginable curtsy, turned to a great circular staircase of glowing, beautifully polished mahogany. The further they mounted the stairs, the louder the sound of harp music grew. "Please, Mistress, don't go in—"

"Nonsense." Minga was amazed at herself. Yet, in its day, Millwood had conceded nothing to this elegant ménage.

"That door." Though Chloë looked downright anxious, a curi-ous half smile sketched pallid teeth between lips sharply etched in crimson. Clearly she admired this stranger's temerity.

Minga knocked. There was no response beyond the harp music. The tune was an old Welch air. She knocked again. The music stopped.

"Come in, Chloë, you damned yellow idiot." The voice was controlled, chilly beautiful, like a hillside spring on an August afternoon. "Why does the least little storm send all you breeds off into tizzies? Why couldn't you find the Malaga sooner?"

Slowly Minga opened the door, was momentarily confused by the light of at least a dozen candles, by a gust of some fascinating perfume which set her nostrils to tingling. In an enormously lofty bedroom a single radiant figure was seated at a small harp. To be freer to play, Adelina Moffat had slipped a gown of pale blue chiffon from her shoulders, and so sat nude to the waist.

She could not have been more than thirty-one or thirty-two, and her hair shone like well-polished old silver, giving off elusive bluish tints. Her face, a trifle too long to be of perfect classic beauty, was not facile, yet not wooden, either. A small, bright mouth showed up sharp as the imprint of a deer's hoof on new fallen snow. Adelina Moffat's eyes were memorable, Minga decided all in an instant—brilliantly blue, large, and set fascinatingly wide apart.

"Well, and who in Tophet are you, my dear?" The woman at the harp made no effort to cover herself, only flexed her arms, slowly, lazily, like a freshly roused feline.

"—Please, are you Mrs. Moffat?"

"For better or for worse—as once I said." Deliberately the figure on the love seat swung slim, stately legs past the bulge of her harp. Minga always had yearned for legs like those—her own were good, but a shade on the muscular side.

Half smiling, half frowning, Adelina Moffat leaned back, her small breasts rising in firm points as she did so. "But pray, Mistress, what business is it of yours?" Her brows, which looked soft as if cut out of mouse skin, rose in fascinating arches. "Who are you? Come, I won't bite your head off."

"I'm Minga Allen, from Brewster, New York, and I believe, your niece."

"My dear!" Adelina Moffat pulled up her gown and her image mocked her in a mirror set above a table laden with vials, pots and powder cells. "My dear, how wonderful! How very wonderful. This is a too delightful surprise!" Her voice suggested the cool perfection of skillfully carved marble. "You're lovely—beautiful. To think we are related! La! I vow I'm flattered—" She swept to her feet and came close. "Your name is—?"

"Minga."

"How fascinating—I don't believe I have ever before heard it." A scent, indescribably subtle and quite alluring, enfolded Minga as her aunt suddenly embraced her and pressed lips to her cheek.

Though the storm boomed and howled louder than ever, it might have been a serene, starlit evening for all the effect it had on the mistress of Hawthorn Hall.

"But you are young—so, so beautiful. I—I can scarce believe that you are my aunt," Minga stammered, feeling a sight more like twelve than like twenty. Quite frankly she peered about, became fascinated by the richness of the draperies, by the amazing luxury of this apartment situated not a few rods from the incredible squalor of the slave village.

The furniture was undoubtedly of French design—green and gold; dominating the whole chamber was the most monumental bed Minga had ever beheld. Raised by two steps from the floor, it occupied most of the opposite wall and its footboard was fashioned like a great gilded dolphin. A mirror formed its headboard.

"I believe," said Mrs. Moffat, carefully, "that you will find Hawthorn Hall somewhat of a change from—what was the name of Judge Allen's—your home? I forget though I did know. Poor Tom used often to speak of it."

"Millwood," Minga told her.

"Please, my dear, sit you down and rest—you must be exhausted."

"Oh, thank you." A warm welcome sense of relief engulfed

Minga. Somehow she had been expecting either a withered harpy of a woman or a fat slug. How lucky, how very fortunate, that Adelina Moffat was young, lovely and dainty as one of those porcelain figures which, off Cape Maisi, had gone plunging to the bottom of the Caribbean.

XV

HAWTHORN HALL

AFTER ONE, TWO weeks had slipped by, Minga wondered how ever she could have been disturbed by those implications half-expressed by Mr. Hamilton and Kendall, the publican.

Reserved, aloof, and disinclined to speak on matters of personal interest, her aunt had proved generous to a fault and, above all, quite devoid of that peculiarly feminine failing—curiosity.

Yet there were times when Aunt Adelina's small red mouth took on curves which defied analysis, and she loved to move about her great house clad in scandalously sheer gowns. On hot afternoons the mistress of Hawthorn Hall thought nothing of lying part, or wholly, nude on her great bed—pale and perfect as a Grecian statue—while Chloë read or sang and a small black boy brushed away chance flies.

To Adelina the black servants evidently were less than human, rather like cats and dogs in human form. She would speak as if they were not in existence.

The impression grew that some sort of invisible barrier restrained her normal impulses. She was too controlled, too detached, too satisfied to do, apparently, one useful thing. Sometimes for a day or two she would become absolutely inaccessible, her apartment a retreat in which much or little might be taking place for all Minga could tell. The next day she would reappear, gracious, smiling and perfect in every detail. She took an extraordinarily great pride and interest in her coiffure—made Chloë spend hours in arranging and rearranging it.

Not one room, but a suite—powder room, robe room, and bedroom—in the far northeast corner of the manor house was assigned to Minga's use. In it tall, drip-stone water jars tinkled day and night, kept abundant drinking water cool by evaporation.

La! Not even Millwood had been like this. Minga grew to love the tall rooms, the wide, glassless windows, the glistening floors of glowing mock orange and mahogany. Mahogany here was a drug on the market; even roof supports had been fashioned of the beautiful wood.

Adelina Moffat took evident pleasure in replacing Minga's wardrobe lost aboard the *Evergreen*. During the cool of the morning she had Chloë fetch dress after dress from cleverly concealed closets, and made Minga, warm and excited, try them on. When one proved unusually becoming, she would say, "It is yours, my dear." Certainly Sir Thomas Moffat had not stinted his wife in the matter of raiment. He must have been as wealthy as old King Midas, Minga decided.

"A pox on so many underclothes," the widow had burst out one afternoon. "I protest. You've a figure Artemis herself might envy—in this Godforsaken climate one or two will do." And so Minga had taken, after a few hot blushes, to wearing just a pair of cambric petticoats.

"How can I ever thank you?" she had exclaimed upon the gift of a vivid blue ball gown. Dishevelled from trying on clothes, her slender figure revealed because perspiration had caused her shift and petticoats to adhere, Minga fairly glowed with excitement.

"Don't try," came the quiet response. "Your presence is reward enough." Then, for the first time, Adelina seemed to notice the silver and green enamel bracelet, had commented on the clever way the dolphins were intertwined. "A pretty bit of work, my dear."

In Hawthorn Hall a normal day began at the unheard-of hour of five in the morning for the household—not for Adelina and herself. Long since she had abandoned the word "aunt." To continue to employ it would have been utterly absurd.

Mercy, but it was fine to be cared for once more, to be waited on. In Hawthorn Hall there was food a-plenty, though Mrs. Moffat's overseer, a handsome, dark-browed Jamaican named Henry Thorne, not once but several times had mentioned to his employer the fact that the estate's stock of salt fish, salt beef was running perilously low. So, too, was the cattle fodder, previously imported from New York and Philadelphia.

One fine morning she and Adelina had gone riding a-horseback and had come upon a bare field. In it two or three oxen lay trembling slowly. It had given Minga an unpleasant turn to see them seek to get up. But they couldn't. From the edge of some tall cane blacks, with eyes sunk preternaturally deep in their heads, looked on furtively.

"What ails them?" Adelina had demanded.

"Hunger, Ma'am. They're dying," Thorne had explained with a slow look at his employer. "We *should* have bought that corn, no matter what the price."

Adelina Moffat's bright blue eyes dropped almost demurely. "Of course, Thorne, I suppose I was headstrong. But we can't be right all the time, can we, Minga?"

Struck by an inspiration, the younger woman suggested, "Since those oxen are practically finished, why not slaughter them and feed your field hands? They're hungry, too; Chloë told me so."

The two burly bookkeepers who always rode as guards grinned. Adelina Moffat's precisely chiseled lips tightened and she shook her head, smart in a tiny emerald-hued tricorn with a jaunty ostrich feather to match.

"Alas, my dear, you don't understand. To feed the slaves meat is to invite disaster, revolt. On a diet of meat our slaves, which are mostly Mandingoes and Senegals, become quarrelsome and get savage ideas.

"When those animals die, Thorne, see that the carcasses are burnt."

The hopeless expressions on the field hands' faces had troubled Minga for quite awhile, but such was the pleasure of living comfortably, securely again, she forgot about it.

It required almost a month of subtle indications to bring home the certainty, the realization that Henry Thorne was more than just the manager of Moffat's Penn. Despite a carefully correct manner with which he invariably addressed the stately blond mistress of Hawthorn Hall, the Jamaican fell off guard every now and then just the least trifle. As, for instance, that time when Minga had returned to retrieve an embroidery frame from her aunt's room. Blended shadows had separated hurriedly and, when, pretending complete unawareness, Minga had entered, Adelina Moffat's primrose-pink complexion had gone a deep rose.

In the evenings it was fascinating to listen to island gossip, to hear accounts of the theater in Kingston, where Mr. Hallam's troupe of American actors had held forth in 1775; of great revels over which presided a notorious Mrs. Williams, of the deadly dull official affairs at Government House. There the ladies were excused at ten o'clock, leaving Lord Balcarres and his ilk to get properly drunk before they called for their horses and went galloping off in search of the warm embraces of some mustee.

There were many Free Mason lodges in the island, Minga learned, and an elaborate system of militia, very necessary in case of slave uprisings such as had threatened Jamaica no further back than 1774. Once a year the slaves made truly merry—on Boxing Day—the day after Christmas. Then the blacks turned out in weird and elaborate costumes to follow their tinsel kings, John Canoe, John Crayfish and Merry Andrew. The Reds and Blues—carnival clubs—vied in adorning themselves.

The island's monetary system proved an involved business, Minga learned. There were not merely pounds, shillings, and pence.

"We have bits worth fourpence, halfpenny," Henry Thorne told her, but his limpid brown eyes clung to Adelina Moffat, lovely in a loose gown of apple-green gauze. " 'Quatties' worth penny ha'penny. 'Gills' of three farthings. 'Macs'—at thruppence. 'Joes' worth five pounds, half joes, 'Macaronis' from the Presidency of Honduras, 'pistoles,' 'ryals,' and 'doubloons' worth two pound' seven and six."

"A simple matter," Minga smiled.

The three of them, one stifling hot twilight, were seated on a broad verandah looking northward towards the distant Caribbean, watching great banks of rounded white clouds go cruising leisurely off in the general direction of Saint Domingue, Puerto Rico, and Turk's Island.

"The rats are bad again," the manager commented, setting down his glass of rum and lime punch. "They're ruining five out of every hundred hogsheads for us."

Minga asked, "Why don't you bring in dogs?"

An ivory fan in Adelina's slim hand barely checked its even rhythm. "It's of no use, dear; always, the slaves either poison the poor brutes or catch them and eat them."

There were other hazards to plantation life, the Jamaican explained. Tom Raffles ants, for instance, which were strong enough to kill poultry and to eat out the eyes of tiny Negro babies. Fire, though, remained the greatest hazard. It was an iron-clad law in the island that when an alarm was sounded on a neighboring penn, every available slave must be rushed to the rescue.

"Oh, Harry, in Heaven's name, give over!"

Minga looked up startled. Never before had Adelina employed the familiar form of her manager's name. This, Minga found, was surprising because, despite his protestations to the contrary, Henry Thorne's fingernails were a shade too blue at their bases, and at the nape of his neck showed a faint ochre pigmentation.

For all of that, though, the Jamaican was uncommonly handsome and carried himself like a young lord.

"Pray don't age poor Minga with all that homely talk," the widow said fanning away an inquisitive fly.

"No, please. This is all new to me," Minga protested. "Mr. Thorne, you were going to tell me how you press the cane?"

Clearly, Thorne was ready to continue. "We have a press powered by oxen, mules, and slaves. Canes are cut in the correct lengths, and fed in between a set of three iron rollers. Compressed, they're returned by a dumb retainer for another passage through the three rollers. The juice, thus extracted, falls into a leaden trough which conducts it to a receiver. Cane juice, Ma'am, is eight parts water to one part sugar, one part essential oil, and one part gross oil."

Alternately fanning himself with a palm leaf and sipping punch, the muscular young Jamaican described how the cane juice followed a second leaden trough into a clarifier, or cauldron, with a capacity of a thousand gallons. Into this, one pint of Bristol lime was added to every hundred gallons of liquor in order to banish acids. Great care, he explained, must be exercised that the liquor did not even come to a boil, that the scum constantly was skimmed off.

"From this cauldron the liquor is ladled by slaves of the boiling house gang into a second copper, from thence to a third. Finally, the syrup is ladled into a cooler where what we call 'striking molasses' takes place. We make what we call the 'touch' by drawing some of the boiling liquor into a thread.

"If your thread hardens and breaks, it's done," Thorne explained, his broad brown features serious. "For muscovado sugar a quarter-inch long is enough. Perhaps you would care to come out to the fields some morning when the big gang is cutting and tying?"

"Big gang?"

"Grown men in their prime. We—er—Mrs. Moffat has ninety-odd—divided into seven gangs. Ten men cut, ten tie, ten haul; then there are fifteen bucks on the top heap squad saving cane tops for the cattle, seven slaves to work in the boiling house, two good ones at the stills, six watchmen, and twelve artisans, two hunters, and eight stock minders.

"The little gang does light work like hoeing, holing and planting. We need the strongest men in the curing house. That's the big shed you will see, Ma'am, where the liquor is cooled and stirred. That's where we add the yeast to make the rum before the brew goes over to the distillers."

"Harry! I said that was enough!"

It was truly a breathless evening. Maybe that accounted for Adelina's impatience, but for all that she looked particularly fetching in her pale green gown. Never a trace of perspiration dewed her cheeks or forehead, to Minga's envious realization.

Adelina spoke crisply, "I expect the wains will soon be in from
the landing. You had better go." Her vivid blue eyes climbed
slowly as the Jamaican heaved a solid, yet lithe, six feet of stature to
its feet. Clad in loose white linen that rendered his face darker than
ever, he crossed to stand beside the long chair upon which she
reclined.

"Yes, Ma'am."

"After supper, Harry, I shall expect your report."

"Thank you, Mrs. Moffat. I shall be punctual." As he bowed the
manager regarded Adelina's slim figure in dumb adoration. God's
blood! To think that this exquisite, fragile, nearly ephemeral god-
dess was his! Brazenly, devotedly, blindly his! He couldn't believe
his luck. Kwanshee made those smelly Fula and Mandingo wenches
look like stupid black cows.

As he turned to quit the verandah, he thought, "Adelina has been
kind never to remind me." He wasn't exactly proud of the fact that
his grandmother had come over from the Grain Coast aboard a
Portuguese slaver.

He felt vastly pleased about being directed to "make a report."
Tonight they'd blend as never before. "Must have been addled to
imagine Adelina's been distant recently," he reflected. "Maybe I
haven't treated her rough enough. What she loves is a paddling and
rough talk. Be gentle and polite, and she's bored.

"Wonder if Old Sir Tom's duppy ever bothers her? I'll ask
Chloë. No, I won't. Chloë is angered at me. A good girl, Chloë—
but where's a fellow get, wasting time on a slave?"

He was striding down the great hall now, his heels clicking
regularly over the wild-orange flooring. "If this crop makes up like
it promises," he reflected, "I can hold out near a thousand pounds
more. Thank God, 'Delina's too damned indolent ever to check
figures. *Kwee!* No, I mustn't use that word—it's slave lingo."

He began smiling. The world wasn't such a bad place tonight.

"Wonder if 'Delina even half guesses how well I've got her
guinea birds feeding out of my hand? Some day it'll strike her, all of
a heap, that she'll do well to marry me. Yellow jack strike that
damned mincing macaroni of a George Kinsman!"

Lightly, Henry Thorne swung down the righthand wing of the
welcoming-arms stair. Darkness was falling and in the row of
bookkeepers' huts lights were beginning to glow.

"So 'Delina wants me to come up tonight? Why was I getting so
worried? She couldn't very well have let on to that pretty niece of
hers about us—not before now. Now take that Allen girl—
Americans are different. She's got muscle and a heart too strong for

her own good, I fancy. *Kwee!* Stab me but I'd hate to have her crack me! All the same, the girl is either confounded innocent—or slow. Why should it take her so long to understand about—us?''

White bills were calling softly in an orange grove, but in the slave village someone was wailing. Another child must be dead of the lockjaw. What a pity nearly every other picanniny took it and perished—a real financial tragedy.

''Wouldn't ever have believed 'Delina could hold off so long— two whole weeks. Must near have killed her, I guess, except— Chloë? Women are funny.

''It will be hard to wait until the house is quiet. Why all this pretense for the sake of that American? When will she leave? It was fine in the old days when 'Delina and me could eat, drink, watch the fun together.''

God's thumb! He guessed he'd never get over that saintly, frozen face of 'Delina's. And what amusing divertissements she could think up. A little on the cruel side. She'd gone a bit too far with that revel, mid-month last.

The manager paused under a huge cottonwood to wipe his face, thoughts flickering like heat lightning. Why did 'Delina intend to celebrate the King's birthday this year—June 4, 1778?

''I told her she oughtn't to buy so much powder,'' he thought. ''Um-m. Whatever chances, King Jack will obey me, but Quarrin? We'll watch that old devil.'' He'd heard about what 'Delina had done to Wimba down there in Wine Cellar Number Two. There were floggings—and floggings.

Once the lattice door had clicked behind the manager's hand-somely proportioned figure, Adelina stopped fanning, turned her almost perfect face. Her breast quivered under the green gauze as she turned to face her guest. ''So far, you have not been bored at Hawthorn Hall?''

''Oh! No, it has been wonderful here.'' Impulsively Minga took the widow's hand. ''Why do you ask? Have I not seemed enchanted? I am, you know.''

Adelina settled back on her cushions. ''Life in Jamaica is so often intolerably tedious—believe me, seven long years here have taught me that.''

She sighed and her gaze shifted to a purplish reflection of the sunset in the east. ''Oh, Minga, do you suppose I shall ever again hear coaches go rumbling down London's streets? I—I— Until Sir Tom's will is probated, I must linger in this accursed dull island.''

She caught her breath and that strange, vitreous quality came to her eyes. ''In America, I hear the Red Indians torment their captives—'', Intently she studied Minga's ruddy features. "Have you ever heard how?''

"Heavens, no!" Minga laughed. "When Sir William Johnson commenced to speak on the subject, Papa sent Mother and me a-packing. Why?''

The widow's fan recommenced its measured beat. "Oh, it's only that tomorrow Sir George Kinsman will be here to dinner. The—the subject is of interest to him. At any rate, my dear, we must see what we can do to amuse him.''

XVI

Soirée

CHLOË was feeling gayer than she had in a long, long while; on the day of the Vodu, she'd been to see the *papaloi*, devoted celebrant of the Legba rites. Nearly all the slaves on the estate, be they cream, coffee or black, secretly worshipped Ougun Bogradis and Damballa, the one great Serpent God, though dutifully they joined palms on Sunday and bent their heads before the Buckra god.

What a great fool was Henry Thorne! Chloë hated him—with the bitter mordant hate of the cast-off, of the deposed. She hated him, clear down to the parings of his finger and toenails.

In the grove above the little savanna at the back of Moffat's Penn the *papaloi* had done some interesting things with those parings. There, the *papaloi* had lit candles, donned a scarlet robe and had consulted the *Gouedé*.

Was it right that Henry Thorne should throw away her affections like the husk of guinea corn when the cob is cooked? No. It was not right. The *papaloi* had said many things—strange, frightening things, for all that Chloë, being nearly white, didn't wholly believe. The witch-doctor had been born and brought up in Dahomey.

Seated in her large and comfortable room, the confidante perceived that, greatly as she hated her ex-lover, she hated Adelina Moffat more. She called her mistress Adelina because the widow had ordered her to—point blank. To begin with, she'd been frightened of such familiarity. Not that 'Delina hadn't been good to her, in a manner at once aloof—and frighteningly intimate.

Sir Thomas had been mightily shocked that time he'd come very quietly to his wife's bedroom to find her pouring out a description of her body's yearnings to a mustee.

"I'll never understand the buckras," Chloë mused. "Whites—the women, I mean—freeze up, like they tell about the rivers in America, until something or someone melts them. Then *whoosh!* from nothing there's too much.

"I wonder why the whites can't live, can't take things more easylike? Not so much unnatural stillness, nor so much boiling over, all at once."

Absently the mustee continued to finger her jewels; some of them were really fine relics of those three gay years spent in Spanish Town where the younger sons of stout English families tried to live a lifetime in a few months—before the dreaded yellow jack or putrid fever carried them off from their ships or regiments.

The *papaloi's wanger* seemed potent, for, if she read the signs aright, Henry was coming back to her, lashed by that scorn of the all-white for the near-white. What would she, Chloë, do then? In the bright sunlight of the late afternoon she threw back her glossy head. She'd watch him gasp, slobber for forgiveness, for everything to be between them as before—and take him back.

In a pier glass the slave stared at herself, bit her lower lip and then winked at her image. In what a fool's paradise did Adelina Moffat dwell! The widow, of course, had never dreamt anybody would ever notice a generous pinch of bamboo gratings, fine as dust, but tough and penetrating as iron needles, concealed in the handle of a certain fan. Only by the sheerest accident had she, Chloë, noticed the lethal dust concealed in a space designed to contain scent or lip rouge.

Adelina's had been a graceful gesture when, with half a dozen people present, she had scattered that fine, but deadly, powder over Sir Tom's curry. He had doted on the dish and liked it strong enough to blister the skin off a bull. Of course, he'd never noticed the little bamboo fibers. Yes. She held Mrs. Moffat like a bird in a snare, only she didn't suspect.

Chloë arose, swung her hips over before a cheval glass, posed there, made pleasant grimaces at herself, then pulled up her dress till it rode about her flat little stomach and inspected her legs. A little plump? Better not eat quite so much rice.

Reseating herself, Chloë pulled out her combs and commenced to do her hair. Expertly she twisted the long, familiar black tresses. She'd just finished doing 'Delina's so it came easy.

At length she stood up and smiled at herself in the mirror, while looping a string of pearls and topazes across the crown of her arrangement.

The *papaloi* had predicted Henry and 'Delina would part forever, so she would enjoy the next two weeks—watch Henry suffer what she had suffered, for as sure as Damballa ruled sky, sea and land, 'Delina was tiring of Henry Thorne.

Sir George Kinsman was one of 'Delina's own kidney, and no deacon; not if even a quarter was true of what the slaves of Lucinea Penn whispered abroad.

Skillfully, the mustee applied lip rouge from a pot which 'Delina would never miss, then real French scent strong enough to drown the day's accumulation of sweat—her fortnightly bath was only a day away now.

Why not—borrow? 'Delina had everything—and would have it for a while longer.

Apparently Sir Tom's exquisite blond widow hadn't learned yet how badly the estate's affairs were going. Some bright day she'd learn how dearly cost were her saddle horses, her brocades, satins, and laces.

The hair-do Chloë almost subconsciously had created was flattering. Like the waves from an obsidian sea her tresses swept upwards in sleek undulations. What a rare joke were she to catch Sir George's eye. He'd a penchant for mustees; the whole island was aware of that.

Chloë giggled. Suppose—*suppose* Sir George were to prefer the lusty, golden-brown of Mistress Allen, to the icicle brilliance of 'Delina!

This American girl was either almighty clever, or so green it wasn't to be believed. Chloë figured, privately, that Minga was far smarter than she was green. A kind sort, though, straightforward and outspoken. She said what she felt, and be damned to you. Americans held that reputation. Queer, though, how it gravelled Mistress Allen when anybody referred to her as "an American."

She could hear Bacchys, the butler, roaring importantly downstairs. Now that the sun was down, the ground doves had begun calling; the tree frogs, too, were commencing to pipe up.

One thing baffled, frightened her a little. From whence did Henry Thorne derive such an amazing influence over the field hands? He passed for white almost everywhere in Jamaica yet the savage Angolos, Whydas and Senegals worshipped him; even Grandy, new Colonel of the Maroons, held Henry in admiration.

Henry was weak in the head not to tell the widow, 'Delina, about the true state of affairs at Moffat's Penn. Why, only yesterday out at

Flying Penn No. 3, not one or two, but fifteen slaves had died not of cocobies, or yaws, or flux, but of sheer starvation.

Cuffee, head boiler, and Crakadill, still watcher, had gone slipping off into the cane again, even though it would mean forty lashes laid on hard when the patrols caught them, brought them back. Bucko, fierce ex-war-chief of the Coromantees, was looking almost pleased these days. That wasn't good. *Kwoy!* He'd a gun hidden away, was the worst rebel on the estate.

Well, enough of that. Chloë wasn't any common field hand; dressed better than ninety out of a hundred white women in the island. Maybe she'd better stay close to 'Delina?— Better than anyone else she knew what Mistress wanted, how—and when. She dabbed rice powder on her throat—rice powder with just a speck of saffron in it.

In the court below a soft voice began to hum a tune. The words were indistinguishable, but Chloë knew them.

> "Young hofficer come home at night,
>   Him give me ring and kisses.
>   Nine months one picaninny white,
>   Him white almost like Missus
>   But Missus lick my back wid a switch.
>   Him say di child for Massa
>   But Massa say him di child for bitch."

A small clock chimed nine times. *Chaw!* She'd best hustle below. The flowers tonight must be particularly well arranged. Sir George, in his drawling fashion, would be sure to comment. She slipped on a saffron-tinted gown with modish paniers bound in pale green ribbon, twisted a necklace of seed pearls around her throat— one young Squire Peters of Port Antonio had given her three years ago, the night before he'd wagered and lost her at pharo to Judge Exelbee Lawford. He in turn had gamed and lost her to Mrs. Moffat.

It was a queer business, this, being owned by a woman. When you belonged to a man you knew straight off how to please him—it was simple enough. Arranging some lace edging to her well-filled bodice, she figured there'd be fun at Hawthorn Hall on the King's birthday. Henry had got 'Delina to promise a real celebration— fireworks and plenty of gunpowder to go *bang!* from those old Spanish pieces salvaged from a wreck off Bloody Bay.

Henry Thorne knew what he was about. Such a display would quiet murmurings for a while at least. Sir Thomas had certainly made a mistake in buying in so many Coromantees, Senegalese, and Whydahs. They were fighting tribes; of the same stock as the Maroons roaming the Land of Look Behind.

Chloë gave her dress a final pat, then fairly galloped downstairs because she could hear horses on the driveway. Already half-naked stable boys were raising shrill cries as they ran to catch the bridles, hopeful that the visiting gentry might toss a few coppers onto the driveway.

The riders, sure enough, were Sir George Kinsman and Dr. Belden, the worst doctor and the best gambler along all the northern coast of Jamaica. The latter existed by peregrinating every few weeks from one great sugar estate to another. His stock of medicines was small, but unlimited was his repertoire of ribald songs and jokes such as made even the most hardened islanders color and laugh nervously. Blotched, swollen with high living, he had difficulty in dismounting from a dusty, fagged-looking cob.

When Chloë appeared at the head of the steps and called, "Good evening and welcome, gentlemen," Sir George stared, paused in the act of easing his tall gelding's curb chain.

"Greetings, O fairest of Ceres' daughters."

Though Chloë had not the least idea of who Ceres was, she spread her skirts, swept a graceful curtsy.

" 'Pon my word!" For all he was dusty as any miller, Dr. Belden whipped out a quizzing glass, peered up his ample red nose. "I say, Sir George, who is this? A Spanish cousin of our hostess?"

"Cousin?" Sir George bellowed. "Gad! The fair Moffat will be flattered if not enormously amused to answer you." The master of Lucinea Penn came swinging up the stone steps, at the same time vigorously slapping the dust from his boots. He used a curious riding crop tipped with a cherub's golden head.

Chloë stayed where she was, well aware that the last glow of sunlight would warm the golden tints in her skin. Squire Peters often had commented on the phenomenon, had made a practice of sending for her at just this hour of the day.

"Welcome, Sir George. And welcome to you, Dr. Belden."

Belden hawked, spat over the guard rail into the dust, then, much like a hound sniffing its quarry, turned his pointed, red-veined nose in Chloë's direction.

"Well, Sir George, you've distractions, praise the Eternal; but as for me, this chick will do. Now then—" The scrofulous old rascal started to slip an arm about her waist, but Chloë spun aside, smiling and not at all ruffled.

"La, sir, you are overhasty." She rolled limpid eyes to mollify him; then, when still he appeared disgruntled, she fell back a step and brushed the back of her hand against his.

"Have you not heard, Doctor, that wine improves—with waiting?"

"And did you hear that? A witty piece. 'Pon my word, yes." Dr. Belden was puffing from the steps. "I say, George, what kind of a place is this? Here we are, perishing of thirst and not a ruddy drink in sight, damme, not a single confounded drop."

"Oh, please, sir, you are mistook. This way, please." Yellow skirts swinging, Chloë indicated a small room to the right; in it Madeira, plunged in wetted saltpetre, should be cooling. Bacchys had done as he should.

Said Sir George, smacking leathery lips, "Pray convey my compliments to Mrs. Moffat, and what time is dinner?"

Chloë said, eyes demurely downcast. "Ten o'clock, a trifle early, I fear." She lowered her voice to a rich, almost husky pitch. "Mrs. Moffat is impatient."

She managed a quick but fetching look at him. La, she had him going, all right! His squarish, deeply lined face was suffused, and she felt his fingers grope briefly at her bodice top when the doctor, in his plum-colored riding coat, plunged his features into a bowl of sangaree.

She'd show Henry Thorne. Maybe there'd be gaming after dinner? Suppose Sir George won her? Being barren, she was worth a lot more than most Creoles and Mrs. Moffat knew it. Moreover, Sir George belonged in the very top drawer of Jamaican society.

She could handle an old boar like Dr. Belden with no trouble at all. Besides, he hadn't a penny.

"I vow, I had no idea Mrs. Moffat possessed such a confidante," Sir George observed, reaching for a box of Cuban segars. "And where were you the last time I visited here?"

"I'd forgot to take my bark and was down of a fever," she explained.

XVII

DISGRACE

ADELINA MOFFAT pushed away her plate, reclined on her settee watching a circlet of moths and mosquitoes play about the candelabra set to attract insects to the far end of the verandah. The mosquitoes weren't so bad tonight, thank goodness. All day a wind had been blowing, rushing down from the mountains.

For some reason Adelina felt irritable, though her gown was a success and the meal was better cooked than usual. Also Henry Thorne should writhe in helpless jealousy when she would flatter and coquette, perhaps, with Sir George.

Critically, she studied Sir George across the candle flame. What a big, masterful brute he looked, all male and fearful of nothing. He was a real devil in a dovecote, too, so the word went. She guessed she'd never be able to dominate, to cow, to bully him as she did Henry Thorne. Maybe that was what she yearned for, a ruling hand and a hot temper that needed watching out for. Under the table she smoothed her new silk stockings. Why should she feel so irritable?

Minga was being her usual charming, forthright self and had captured that odious Dr. Belden's attention.

Who but George Kinsman would dare wear red silk heels? Mm-m—a nasty French touch, and yet—and yet he wore them with masculine forcefulness. He was so sunburned she guessed Sir George must have been working his estate. For all his devotion to pleasure, the proprietor of Lucinea Penn was no wastrel drone.

What was needed at Hawthorn Hall was a man like Sir George. Harry Thorne was competent, in his way, yet he never took the initiative nor came right out and told her what needed to be done, not if it was leastways unpleasant.

A curious character, Harry; but for that taint of Africa he might have risen to a seat on the Governor's assembly beside Hinton East, Digby Dennis, Jamie Crean, Matthew Wallen and the rest. She watched him talking to Minga in that low-pitched, vibrant voice which, for months, had charmed and fascinated her.

An odd creature, Minga, at once soft and feminine, yet she'd good sense; didn't shock too easily. It had come as rather a surprise that the American could become so readily inured to the rather brutal life of the Island. Of course, she hadn't been out to the outlying villages, hadn't seen the gangs working under pressure.

One cause of Adelina's abstraction was the problem of meeting that note of Griggs Barnsby's. Damn! Three thousand pounds sterling was no mean sum. Why ever had Harry let the estate get so deep in debt? A sudden suspicion occurred that the manager's silence might have been deliberate.

She fanned more rapidly. Aware that Dr. Belden was repeating an amazingly salacious bit of gossip about a certain Anne Palmer who lived at Rose Hill on the coast, she listened with care.

"Come rouse yourself," she admonished herself, "you must be extra gracious, charming tonight. I say, George—"

But Sir George did not hear. He was too busy exchanging glances with Chloë.

"Have you heard—?" Adelina began, then, when her neighbor remained absorbed in the mustee's conversation, picked up a fork and playfully, but vigorously, jabbed the master of Lucinea on his elbow.

"Damn me," he roared, rubbing his sleeve. "What's this?"

Adelina's perfect lips parted slowly and her face was quite serene.

"My apologies, Sir George, I fear I mistook your elbow for a joint."

"Impossible."

"No more so than you should mistake Chloë for your hostess."

He stared, then burst out laughing uproariously.

"*Touché*. My apologies, Adelina." How could he so have forgotten the main chance? He felt prompted to kick himself.

Many and many a hundred hogsheads of sugar had been, and would still be, extracted from the rich black soil of Lucinea. But Moffat's Penn—there was a real estate for you. Together, the two penns would constitute the largest holding on the north coast of Jamaica. Yes. Moffat's combined with Lucinea should furnish enough revenue to make possible a return to the pleasures of England, of Paris, and of Sicily.

Adelina should make as good a running mate as any. The woman possessed charm, looks, breeding, plenty of fire beneath that aloof, too perfect exterior and, if he rightly suspected, more than a moderate fortune.

If the wind hadn't been blowing the mustee's perfume and her odd, musky personal aura right into his face, Sir George might have forgotten her. Right in the middle of a sentence he glimpsed her profile, golden in the candlelight—and broke off his conversation with Adelina Moffat.

On the other side of the table Thorne was saying, "Indeed, Mistress Allen, you will find that our mountains are the most beautiful part of Jamaica. Among them it's cool all day long. And such water—you have never seen water like that."

Minga thought of the great clear streams, limpid lakes of America, but said nothing.

"Do those mountains mark the edge of the Cockpit Country?"

The manager's eyes, restless, softly brown like a monkey's, swung quickly in the candlelight. "The Cockpit—yes, it lies on the other side. Why?"

"Oh, coming up from the Coast the man I rode with said that— the—that the Maroons were uneasy. He wasn't right?"

"I hope—"

Everyone started at the sudden smashing of Adelina's glass. Firm, graceful, erect as a caryatid she had risen; her normally pallid features had gone pink and her little mouth had become a crimson cut. She had recognized what had been irritating her all evening.

Said she in accents that fairly tinkled with icy rage, "I fear, Sir George, I cannot hold your attention until—"

Deliberately, Adelina Moffat closed her fan and, reaching out, struck Chloë sharply once, across each cheek. Her mask-like expression never altered. The mustee uttered a bewildered cry, flinched back.

"Apparently it is not enough, you yellow tart, that you steal my perfume nor is it enough that you dare to rob my lip rouge. It's that you would have the supreme effrontery to dare to mimic my coiffure!" The widow's blue eyes shone so coldly menacing that a shiver ran the length of Minga's spine. Sir George choked off some comment.

It was true. To the last curl Chloë had copied her mistress' coiffure, had even duplicated the draping of the strand of topazes and pearls.

" 'Fore God, 'Delina," Chloë burst out, her eyes filling, "I didn't mean—I didn't realize how I—"

"That will do! Sit still, you insolent slut!"

Twice more the Englishwoman's fan impacted against Chloë's cheek. The first two marks took shape, then the second. Never had Minga seen Adelina Moffat stand so tall, so icily beautiful. The Englishwoman's nostrils were pinched, her cheeks drawn in like those of a person long without food, but her breast was full and erect.

"Since my friend Sir George seems to find difficulty in distinguishing us, I propose to remove any possibility of future error. Stand up but stay where you are."

"Yes, 'Delina, dear," Chloë quavered.

Like wax figures in a museum set the guests watched the mustee get to her feet, eyes overflowing and obviously in sheer terror.

"Right here and now," Adelina directed in metallic accents, "you may remove those garments I have been generous—and foolish enough to bestow on you—and return them."

"No! No! You *wouldn't*—" The mustee backed away from the candles.

"Bacchys!" The widow's voice reverberated on the verandah like the crack of a lash. "Call Cudjo and Aneas!"

"Oh, no, please—" Minga experienced at once a sense of revolt, and an overwhelming impulse to witness what might happen.

"Any of you may leave, if you so desire," the widow told her guests, the candles sketching tawny tints amid the silver sheen of her high-dressed hair.

"From this spot," chortled Dr. Belden, "you couldn't budge me with a span of steers. Madame, pray proceed."

Sir George was thinking, "You're a lucky dog, George my lad. You'll see this baggage stripped without buying her so much as a string of brass beads."

Henry Thorne was thinking, "She asked for trouble. You've grown too arrogant, Chloë. Be humble, dear, and some great day we'll make these lords of creation dance to a colored man's tune. Pay for your arrogance, now, though. Haven't seen you bare in months."

At the entrance to the house appeared two towering blacks. Adelina turned deliberately, "Well, Chloë, will you obey my orders?"

Minga felt cold fingers explore the length of her back. She ought to do something, she knew, but still—

Cudjo, a bull-necked, barrel-chested Fula who acted as footman, started in.

"No, I'll do it myself." A new thought struck Chloë. She gripped the hem of her gown in both hands, pulled. The fabric gave with a soft snarling sound. The candles wavered and blinked as piece after piece of cloth ripped and yielded.

"She's too shrewd," thought Adelina Moffat. "The yellow whore is parading herself."

"Stop!" Only the confidante's shift remained.

"Bacchys! Show these gentlemen her brand."

Because he was very black, Bacchys had hated the months and years of taking orders from this mustee. He spun Chloë about, ripped her shift down to her waist. Low below the left shoulderblade shone the smooth white scar the branding iron had left long years ago. It was shaped like a small heart; Dr. Belden recognized it for the brand of Adrien Hart of Kingston. There was an owner who believed in marking his property.

Stately, calm and frigid, Adelina seated herself.

"Chloë, you may serve the dessert."

Completely aghast, Minga could say or do nothing when, sobbing softly, the mustee commenced to clear the table. She hadn't a penny and, if Adelina Moffat cast her out right now, she'd be in a hard case. Since the serene days of Millwood, she'd learned a lot. Yet she felt an immense pity for Chloë tottering about on trembling legs, passing dishes of pineapple, star apple, custard, and sherbet.

Sir George now had no eyes for Chloë, only for the mistress of Hawthorn Hall sitting bolt upright, silverly beautiful.

Henry Thorne sat smiling outwardly, but Dr. Belden viewed Chloë with fat lips loose about a pale and very long segar.

XVIII

Look Behind

FOR A long while Minga lay awake, tense, perspiring heavily on that great four-poster, which at first had awed her. Beyond the mosquito bar a pair of fireflies cruised about. Quite easily, she could see them haloed through the muslin.

Her thoughts weren't on the insects. She was thinking about the expression on Adelina's face when Chloë stood wailing against the verandah wall, a silver tray and a pair of green slippers all that differentiated her by way of garments from any bare-bottomed picaninny in the slave village.

It had been nothing short of devilish so to humilate the confidante; so unfair to elevate a slave to the status of an intimate and then, all in the matter of a few moments, to push her spinning from the heights down to the depths from which she had never really escaped.

Had Adelina always been the way she was tonight? Probably not. How could she? By her own admission, she hailed from a quiet Kentish town where, doubtless, she had learned her catechism and deportment.

Minga turned over. She couldn't remember another evening so terribly hot, an atmosphere so completely devoid of energy. All at once her eyes flew wide open, stared into the dark. Somewhere off in the foothills was sounding a faint, hollow *tunk, tunk-ta-tunk! Tunk!*

Eerily, the rhythm reverberated among various ridges and valleys, but the sound was so far away it presented no immediate concern. How dare any slave—of course, it must have been a slave—defy the law against drumming? Except on a few rare occasions, such as cropover, the beating of drums, even hand drums, was illegal. All too easily did the reverberations of a drum evoke long forgotten emotions, savage memories; worse still, disrespect for the laws of King George III. Thorne had explained in detail, one sultry afternoon, just what drums did to the black exiles.

She wondered what Chloë might be thinking right now—probably not much. The disgrace of having to work before people without a stitch of clothes must have burnt worse than Mr. Hart's hot iron.

"Minga, my dear," she whispered as, from time to time, the drum continued to mutter under that green rampart of mountains dividing the coast from the Cockpit Country, "you'll not sit in judgment on Jamaicans and their ways. Like Massachusettsers, they've their own peculiar way of life. Probably Adelina was right to mortify Chloë so indecently. I expect plenty of owners would have had her whipped for her impudence." Again she turned on the bed, her nightgown clinging stickily. "Still, my dear, we are not Jamaicans and we don't enjoy such scenes."

How could she go away? If only the *Evergreen* hadn't foundered, how different life would have been.

A plague take Andrew Warren! "I wish I—" she started to say, but broke off and lay with eyes shut so tight that little fiery points arched across them under their lids.

Andrew Warren? It was vastly disconcerting that guarded inquiries concerning doings at Montego Bay elicited no information at all. To all intents and purposes the luckless sea captain seemed to have dropped from sight. In a way this was a relief. Had Andrew been caught and hanged, everybody within a hundred miles would have known. Still, he might have been taken, secretly transported for trial at Port Royal, the King's great Naval depot at Kingston. Why, he might this moment once more be fighting against his King, and yet—and yet— Oh dear, why must such persistent memories of him come to torment her? Angrily, she pushed her damp pillow into a new shape.

No, she warned herself, it wouldn't do to dwell any longer on the subject of the New Englander. Certain mannerisms of his clung to her memory. There was that swift, yet graceful, gesture with which he turned his head, always with a little upward movement. When perplexed, his forefingers would pinch his lower lip into a little trough. And his years in France had taught him to use his hands to emphasize his speech.

Had she caused his imprisonment? How awful if her cries had condemned him to moulder in some dreadful island jail! Both Thorne and Chloë had described various Jamaican prisons with harrowing attention to details.

Finally the drums fell silent and the vindictive whining of mosquitoes prying at the muslin cover sounded louder as a result.

Yes, she must leave Hawthorn Hall, Minga decided. There was no other way out; a great pity, because she was lazy enough to love this luxurious way of life. If it had only been beautiful instead of cruel.

All of a sudden her eyelids flew wide apart. Down the hall a door had opened cautiously. Aided by that preternatural keenness of hearing granted to those afflicted with sleeplessness, she detected the quick, soft impact of bare feet.

It flashed across her mind that Chloë might have decided to settle a score. Minga slid out of bed as quietly as possible, ran and opened her door a crack. After all, Adelina was her aunt.

In the hallway on a small side table a single candle, protected by tempest glass, was fluttering. Sir George Kinsman was standing, very tall and disheveled, before the door to his room. He wore a long cambric nightgown and his tawny sunburnt hair tumbled loose over wide shoulders. He was smiling as a golden ray of lamp light marked the closing of Adelina Moffat's door.

Chilled, Minga eased her door shut and was about to climb into bed once more when, beyond her window shutters, there materialized a stealthy shadow. It drifted by, following that gallery which encircled the whole house. The unknown halted before the porch entrance of Mrs. Moffat's room.

Thoroughly alarmed, Minga opened her own lattice door, but as quickly flinched back into the dark. Voices, subdued, yet perfectly audible, came floating along the gallery.

"What is it you want?" demanded Adelina's clipped English voice.

"You," replied the deeper, more vibrant tones of Henry Thorne.

"That is over and done with, pray depart."

"I'll not stand for it," the manager burst out. "I love you, too dearly, can't you understand?"

"What has been has been, and now it is finished. You may go."

Thorne commenced to plead and such a dreadful urgency entered his tone that Minga felt her cheeks go hot. She'd no business eavesdropping like this; she knew it, yet stayed right where she was.

"But, Kwanshee, my own Kwanshee, one doesn't cut off love like a weed. One can't. Kwanshee, please—I—need you."

"Keep your hands away."

Thorne's voice and manner changed. "You are very clever, Kwanshee, almost as clever as you are beautiful."

"Please go."

"No, you had better listen, Kwanshee. Long ago, your very

cleverness served as a warning to me. I have foreseen this and have taken care that you shall not, will not, dare break with me!"

A small silence fell in the gallery and the rush of the distant Montego cascading over a series of miniature falls could distinctly be heard.

"What did you mean by that, Harry?" Adelina was speaking as if she had selected and tested every word before using it.

A soft eagerness returned to the manager's voice. "I hope I shall never have to explain. Come! Kwanshee, let me make—"

"Thorne, I have had enough of this!" Adelina snapped. "Go back to your room and tomorrow—"

Minga saw the overseer's powerful body straighten spasmodically. He was breathing heavily as he snarled, "—And tomorrow you will be what you are now—a chill-hearted murderess!"

The staccato sound of a slap echoed into the dark. "You lying black dog! How *dare* you invent such a falsehood?"

"I dare, because I intend to keep you! If I can't have you, Kwanshee, you may be certain that neither Sir George, or others of his kidney, are going to. We have meant too much to each other."

The feeble wailing of some sick child in the slave quarters assumed importance in the tense quiet.

Presently, in a clear, calm voice Adelina said, "Perhaps you are right, Harry. We *have* been happy together in pleasure—and in pain. I'll chance that it's better that we—that we keep things as they are."

The voices died away on the porch and a lattice door shut. Lord's mercy! Whoever would have dreamed that anyone so lovely, so silver pure-looking, so neat and clean could—

Minga felt a sense of nausea churn at the bottom of her belly. Adelina hadn't really wanted Henry Thorne. Her next reaction was one of fear—of sharp misgiving. Adelina had been frightened into yielding. Why? Murderess? Nonsense, of course. Every year in Jamaica hundreds of people died suddenly and naturally.

Lying there floundering in a mental maëlstrom, Minga commenced to understand many other matters. Henry Thorne was smart, just as Chloë had pointed out. It was he in fact who controlled the finances, who shaped the policies of the estate. It was to him that half a thousand slaves gave obedience, not to the widow, Adelina Moffat.

It now had become imperative that Minga find an excuse and, more difficult still, the means of leaving Hawthorn Hall.

Next morning, on the surface, nothing had been altered. Sir George Kinsman and Dr. Belden slept late, arose and grouchily departed. From a glance exchanged by Adelina and her neighbor,

Minga was ready to wager that their parting would be anything but long.

"Oh, how I hate to see them leave," Adelina sighed as she and her niece stood on the stoop watching the riders trot off down the palm-lined drive. She looked extremely dainty this morning in a pink sacque and pale blue skirt. Her silver-hued hair had been arranged in such precise curls that it resembled chasing on a pitcher. Tiny bluish shadows lurked under her eyes, however.

"Did you not deem Sir George delightful, my dear?"

"Irresistible, but he wasn't in the least interested in me."

"He had best not be," Adelina's laugh tinkled in the hot morning air. "It is I whom Sir George is to admire, as that witless Chloë discovered. Oh, by the bye, I have decided to restore her to grace. Please say nothing when she appears at dinner. She is, after all, without education; just a little animal."

The widow threaded an arm, smooth and cool as silk, through Minga's. "And now, my dear, let us stroll down to the orangery." Adelina commenced to talk more freely than ever before. "On His Majesty's birthday I intend to have a real fête for the Estate. I have sent to Kingston for bunting and masks and gilt paper and all manner of nonsense."

She frowned abstractedly, twirled a tiny parasol edged with lace. "Thorne informs me that this has been a bad year for the cane. Drought in May and many, many rats. He says, too, the blacks need cheering up. Well, we shall feed them well this week, shan't we? But I count on the fireworks display to please them most."

Preparations went forward and Adelina ordered that, on the morrow, dozens of favored slaves be ordered in from the outlying penns to witness the celebration.

"Tonight I have some tedious plantation matters to discuss," the widow announced as they regained the coolness of the great hall and Minga sought a cup of water from the nearest drip jar. "Perhaps you would like your dinner in your room?"

For several reasons Minga accepted the suggestion with readiness.

"I hope, my dear, that you never become mistress of a sugar estate." A trifle searchingly Adelina's bright blue eyes dwelt on Minga and not without affection. She caught her breath, said suddenly, "I have come to the conclusion, Minga, you will do well to visit England." Adelina was in one of her rare moods when once she was considering someone other than herself.

Minga beamed. Glory! If this wasn't a flawless solution to the problems raised last night.

"England! Oh, but that's impossible—you know it is. I'd love—" She spread her hands.

Adelina smiled, taking her hand. "Money will be found. Aren't you my own niece? Sir Thomas set aside a sum for such purposes."

For all her moral lapses, Adelina Moffat couldn't really be so bad. Most likely Sir Thomas *had* died of natural causes. Everyone knew black people were very prone to exaggerate.

In that semi-circular library which had been Sir Thomas' especial pride, Adelina seated herself and picked up a month-old copy of the *Jamaica Royal Gazette*. Lips pressed, she seemed to make hard work of her reading, but at length she smiled.

"There's a packet for London from Liguanea this Wednesday a week," Adelina announced. "I shall book you a cabin. Probably the packet is fast enough to outrun most pirates or privateersmen."

"But Adelina—there's no reason—"

"Hush, hush!" The widow raised a fragile semi-translucent forefinger. "You have demonstrated uncommon good sense, my dear, in understanding us here at Hawthorn. I felt as you when first I came out from England—yes, I, well, I was much like you, but with time and with the heat, I presume we absorb some of the brutishness of the slaves. 'Tis an old saying in the Sugar Islands that, with each passing day, master and slave grow more alike."

XIX

A SOFT WIND CRYING

IN A SILVER and vermilion negligée Adelina Moffat lolled on her chaise longue in the sitting-room of her suite, a slipper dangling from her toe, a slim *cigarro* between slim fingers.

Not in a long time had Henry Thorne appeared quite as appealing as tonight when he had bent to kiss her on the mouth. His well-formed features looked sharpened by his long day of riding about the penn, and that white smile of his almost set her heart to beating as before.

Now the manager had seated himself on a footstool near her feet, and was smoking, studying the amber depths of his brandy glass.

His saffron yellow shirt, open at the neck, revealed a wide, hairless expanse of softly brown skin.

Deftly Adelina flicked the ash of her *cigarro* into a small silver urn. "You are right, Harry, we *do* belong together."

"I am so very happy you feel so," he said quietly. "I have been worried, Kwanshee. Sir George is rich while I—I have only myself to give." He fixed on her intense, spaniel-like eyes. "Oh, my darling, I couldn't live without you and I mean what I say."

"There is no need," she told him softly. "I just wanted to make you jealous, Harry. Come, there's a lamb, and kiss me."

Quivering, he drew away at last.

She lifted her glass, thought hard. "You are very observant, you know, Harry." She smiled. "I wonder when it was you first wondered about Sir Tom?"

He paused, his glass half way to his lips. "The day I found that end of dry bamboo in your boudoir—only a week after I'd told you about the Congo trick." Through the smoke lazily curling about the sitting room, Thorne smiled, a curious angry smile. "I could have stopped you then for I guessed what you intended—"

"Why didn't you, Harry?"

"I wanted you, Kwanshee, more than anything on this earth and—well, Sir Thomas was a barrier."

The hum of insects in the formal garden below sounded very loud. Thorne settled back and put his feet up, eyes fixed on the toes of that little bare foot from which Adelina's slipper had fallen.

"I could have held back your hand that night at dinner so I must be a murderer, too, sweeting, because I let you spill the powder. You were very clever."

"It was for your sake, Harry," she told him, her lips barely moving.

He hesitated on the verge of telling Adelina that Chloë, too, had seen it all. Poor Chloë. Thorne suspected the mustee must still be in love with him. God, how mortified she'd been, scarlet with shame. Sir George and the doctor had enjoyed the affair mightily. He'd better be wary of Chloë, though. She seemed to hate him with an intense, subtle hate.

He ended by saying nothing, only kissing that small mouth which, for near on a year, had been sweet as the hope of Paradise.

The way Kwanshee responded to the caress removed that last doubt which, all evening, had dug at his peace of mind like a broken fingernail.

"Oh, Harry! Harry!" she was breathing. "I'll never be so silly again. No never—" Presently she sighed. "Harry, find me some of the really old cognac."

Light as a leopard, Harry crossed to the wardrobe, checked himself. What if—? No. No, the bottle there was sealed with an old and very dusty wax. He felt angrily ashamed of himself.

When he had finished drawing the cork Adelina was standing before a full-length mirror, luxuriously combing that wonderful silvery hair of hers into glistening gonfalons. They shimmered clear down to her thighs. The reflection lent double enchantment. Some overwhelming power drove him to kneel and kiss her hand as he had in the exquisitely happy days when, in Hawthorn Hall, only two people had mattered.

Looking down and sliding fingers through his glossy hair, Adelina experienced a throb of compassion. Heavens! Harry was actually grovelling for all he was strong enough to break her into a dozen pieces. So handsome—and he passed for white. How could he have kept her secret so long? Well, he had her dead to rights; no mistake about that. The courts wouldn't take a light view of what she had done. Gradually, the realization dawned that she was quite as much at his mercy as any slave on Moffat's Penn was at hers. Probably, to start with, he'd be restrained in the exercise of his hold, but after the first quarrel he'd not resist a reminder. Then, more clearly, he could perceive his advantage.

"Harry," she said, brushing fingertips down his cheek, "I feel like singing. Pour yourself a good measure while I fetch the little guitar." She disappeared through a shimmering white drapery which divided the sitting-room from the bedroom, effortlessly, like a star into a cloud.

Thorne eased his belt, smiled at his reflection, then poured himself a stiff three-fingers of cognac and tossed it off. Whew! This brandy was strong, near twice as potent as Jamaica rum. This kind of rum, he remembered, was made from grapes, not sugar cane.

He felt better, though—a lot better, and extended himself on Kwanshee's chaise longue. The bold course, that was always the best. What a fool he'd been. Here he had been eating out his heart for the last month, and why? Kwanshee had been so quietly terrified while he had recited his knowledge.

Silently Adelina reappeared, held out a restraining hand. "No, sweeting, stay there." Amid a swirl of azure draperies she seated herself on the footstool, delicately, like a thrush on a bough. "Heavens! Harry, you have finished your cognac already? Pour me some."

He obeyed, then refilled his own glass. God's thumb. She'd donned a scent he'd never smelt before—

Adelina struck a chord, sang, *"El Viento Lo Me Dijo,"* a lilting

Spanish song from the nearby island of Cuba. She played not well, nor not badly, either.

Thorne smiled happily when the cognac commenced to "spread out," as the Yankee sea captains had put it before the war changed everything. God above, with New England privateers ravaging the Caribbean like winter wolves, what was going to happen in Jamaica this winter? Stock fish, salt, port, maize, meal, and wheat had gone out of sight in price, or just weren't to be had. To hell with slaves, slave food and such. Kwanshee was singing again—as in the old days. How indescribably lovely Kwanshee was, outwardly. But inside, she became another being—a creature of writhing lips, gorged eyes and sudden fierce ideas.

He raised himself on an elbow, peered adoringly into the pallid perfection of her features. In years not a ray of full sunlight had touched them for more than a few moments.

Every once in a while, when Kwanshee was playing some particularly spirited passage, a small rattling noise was audible, but he was too thoroughly content to conjecture on its origin.

Gradually the candles burned down, and between lingering embraces, Adelina sang, very softly, certain tunes she knew he liked. Every once in a while she would stop, sip from a miniature liqueur glass.

The gold of the candlelight deepened and, as if to render the moments flawless, a breeze off the sea commenced to blow, to flutter the enormous white silk curtains.

Adelina's pet monkey roused in its basket, yawned a ridiculously human yawn, squeaked drowsily, and went back to sleep.

Thorne lay on the chaise longue, his muscled chest bared to the refreshing air currents. Surely life could hold nothing more than this. Plenty of food, good liqueur, a clever, tender mistress—music—

Adelina's fingers fell away from the little guitar strings. She rearranged the garish green and yellow ribbons on its neck. Then, gentle as a kitten's paw, they wandered over his forehead to caress his temples.

"Kwanshee!" Blindly his hands crept upwards, groping. Here, thought Harry Thorne, is peace, for the first time in weeks. It had been a long day on horseback. Must have ridden twenty, maybe thirty miles? His eyelids surrendered to the downward pressure of fatigue. "Shouldn't have spent so much time at Flying Penn Number Three, but I've got to find out who did that drumming, last night. Blewhole Fred has denied knowledge. Leander, too. Don't fancy the situation. Grandy, the new Colonel in the Cockpit acts too

big for his breeches. Don't want Kwanshee's land overrun—
everything's changed.

Mightn't it be wise to send to Montego Bay for a squad of
soldiers? Even a few redcoats will have a sobering effect on rebels
like Blewhole Fred and Leander. God, but this was comfortable.
Kwanshee's breath, fragrant as a mountain breeze, stirred gently
against his forehead.

Thorne's breathing deepened, slowed. Against the pale yellow
upholstery of Adelina's settee, the manager suggested a figure
skillfully wrought of bronze.

Adelina lit a fresh *cigarro*, and in the mirror watched her image
poise it. Harry was relaxed, smiling, eyes closed. If she got to her
feet would Harry waken? He had ever been a light sleeper. On her
stool she sat quite still, five, ten minutes, sketching changing
patterns in cigar smoke, thinking—but not too far. Somewhere in
Hawthorn Hall a clock struck four melodious, shivering notes. He
didn't rouse.

"Harry?" she murmured. Then louder, "Sweeting?" His
eyelids did not stir. The sound of her voice she guessed must be
soothing. Gradually Adelina leaned forward until her fingertips
wavered a scant fraction of an inch from his chest, bare where his
shirt had fallen open.

She leaned forward and, gradually, her lips flattened against her
teeth. Why, one could watch the gentle palpitation of his skin just
below the sternum.

Carefully Adelina Moffat shifted the footstool and her hand
slipped into the guitar between its strings, reached into the interior.

It wasn't a large knife she brought out and, because an Arab had
designed it, its grip was small. The steel blade shone blue-white
even though the candles gave off golden hues. Strange characters
etched in gold glowed on the upper part of the straight, double-
edged blade.

Oddly enough, she wished that Sir Thomas were here; above
everything else, Tom had admired courage. Because Harry wasn't
quite white—well, Tom would understand. Her reflection caught
her attention. She would not be suspected. Sir George would see
that the matter was taken care of. It would be easy enough to prove
there was colored blood in Harry.

Employing great care she placed the guitar on a chair behind her,
then shifted the knife so that its slim, six-inch blade emerged from
the top of her fist. A Cuban had shown her, once, how a real knife
fighter employed his weapon.

How shiny Harry's skin was—down from the nipple and three

inches left—the heart lay much nearer the center of the body than most people supposed. In almost a single gesture Adelina stepped out of the negligée, tossed it well away—no stains to explain—skin washes readily. As an afterthought Adelina tossed her hair back over her bare shoulders.

The widow drew a deep breath, straightened her arm until arm and knife were like a lance, then threw her whole weight behind her shoulder. After a split second's resistance, the blade entered with astonishing ease.

XX

ALARM

IT WAS only after the rapping had been repeated for several moments that Minga roused herself.

"A moment—wait a moment," She struck flint and steel to tinder, lit a taper.

"Minga! Quickly please!" It was Adelina's voice.

"What is it?" Minga flung open her door, guarded the taper's flame against an inrush of wind.

The widow's pale hair was streaming wildly, eddying to her movements.

"A terrible thing has happened!" She entered hurriedly, clutching to her a negligée of vermilion and silver silk.

"Calm yourself, Adelina dear," Minga begged after pushing shut the door. "What's wrong?"

The widow sank onto a chair, covered her face, ignoring the fact that her negligée had fallen apart, to betray that no nightgown covered the white perfection of her figure.

"Tell me, Adelina, what's wrong?"

The widow caught at Minga's arm. "I was restless after checking up accounts, and in walking around the gallery for some air, I saw a light in my sitting-room beating through the lattices of the door. I hadn't noticed it before, because, as you know, I always lock my bedroom door."

The last traces of Minga's drowsiness departed mighty quick.

There was no doubt that something of an appalling nature had happened.

"Oh, Minga, from under that door was creeping blood—a stream of it." Adelina's palms slowly slipped over her face, framing its colorless outline.

"Chloë?" Minga whispered.

"No, Harry—Harry Thorne. He'd stabbed himself."

"Oh, Adelina, how terrible! How perfectly appalling! You're sure he—he's dead?"

"Oh, yes. There can be no doubt of it."

"But why, why should he have done it?"

The Englishwoman shook her head helplessly. "I don't know except that there are some account books scattered about. Before I retired he told me my affairs are at a bad pass—"

This was true enough, Minga knew, from what Chloë had let drop from time to time.

"It's my belief, Harry saw no hope—feared my reproaches. I have trusted him implicitly. I wonder—could he have been stealing?"

Minga couldn't make out Adelina. That she was obviously shaken to the depths of her being was very apparent.

"How needless, how pitiful. Poor, poor Harry," she muttered. "If only this stupid war hadn't cut off our trade with America!"

They sat quite still, holding each other's hands. Finally Minga squared her shoulders. "Well, I suppose we must arouse someone."

"Yes, it would never do for one of the servants to make the discovery. Minga, dear, hurry—fetch Mr. McCabe, the senior bookkeeper," Adelina cried, and flung herself, face down, on the bed. "I am too undone. Tell him quietly, though, and have him fetch two of the younger bookkeepers, O'Brien and Lynch."

Minga twisted her chestnut hair into a knot, then pulled on her slippers. "Keep up your courage, I will be back directly."

At the foot of the worn staircase a shadow materialized. It was Chloë, barefoot and wearing a simple dress of striped seersucker. She carried a small bundle.

"Please, Mistress Allen," the mustee whispered fiercely, "I've something to tell you."

XXI

DISTANT THUNDER

To ANDREW WARREN it seemed somewhat incredible that over two months had passed since he had raced, panting, through the dark and twisted streets of Montego Bay with the clamor of a pursuing mob perilously close behind. Barely in time had he found sanctuary amid the goods spoiling in the depths of Mr. Allerdice's warehouse.

Out of caution, he had made himself known only on the third day when stark starvation was nipping his stomach. No telling what Mr. Allerdice might conceive to be his duty. The old Scot, however, had lent him every possible assistance and then some; this was fortunate because so persistent became the garrison commander's search there was nothing for Andrew to do but to spend two interminably hot weeks among the rats in the warehouse. He employed it reading, studying texts on the art of gunnery.

To set foot outdoors in daylight would have been the rankest folly; at least not until his beard, coming in thick, black and curly, grew long enough to alter the contours of his face. At length Mr. Allerdice deemed it safe for the fugitive to stir abroad, but only during the heat of the day when nearly everyone lay asleep.

"It's in the country districts ye'll run yer greatest risks," the Scot predicted. "A stranger there stands out like a corbie against the cliffs o' Dover."

It was suffocatingly hot this early August evening, and perspiration dripped off Andrew's elbows in runlets as he sat at the table, chewing the old Scot's dish of meagre supper of yams, fish and bammie cakes. Now that events appeared to be shaping into a more hopeful pattern, Andrew ate with better appetite.

Mr. Beetle would be discharged from prison tomorrow, still madder than hops over having been clapped into jail for punching the ears of an insolent seaman out of H.M.S. *Tigress*.

According to Mr. Allerdice, the experience had gone a long way to diminish the brawny mate's affection for the Crown and such officers as represented His Majesty in Jamaica.

Tomorrow, too, Joe Beaver should return from one of his mysterious hunting trips up into the mountains. It was towards the end of Andrew's first week of self-imposed imprisonment that the Indian had appeared, fat and pleased-looking, before Mr. Allerdice's crumbling warehouse. Not much by way of real conversation with the Penobscot was possible, although the half-breed had picked up some French—a language which he believed to be his father's. Through that medium Andrew learned much in few words.

After his initial journey among them, the Penobscot, it seemed, had found Jamaican forests, streams, and game irresistible. In short order he made a bow and manufactured some arrows. The game, high in the mountains, was incredibly tame, Beaver claimed on one of his returns to Montego Bay. It was no trick at all to keep himself well supplied with food.

As time went on Andrew deduced that the little bandy-legged half-breed had, in some inscrutable manner, won the friendship of a clan of Maroon hunters. This was readily understandable, Mr. Allerdice explained, because most of these villains had more than a dash of Indian blood persisting from the days when the Dons had ruled over the island.

Andrew, of course, found time to undertake a deal of thinking, to reappraise himself; also, to make plans. He believed he had arrived on such a plausible scheme, it was hard to wait. But wait, he must, even though up in Connecticut the *Trumbull*, frigate, should be all but ready for commissioning.

It was wearing, galling to his always impatient spirit, to suffer this inactivity. Yet precautions were necessary. The British Crown had a long memory, particularly in the matter of suspected spies. And everywhere were natives eager for a chance to claim the ten pounds' reward money posted for the capture of "One Andrew Warren, Notorious REBEL and SPY. He gives out to hail from Long Island in New York. Very tall, black hair and eyes. Notice of his presence is giv'n to any Magistrate of this Colony."

"Well, lad, I note ye've a better appetite this eve," Allerdice observed, belching softly over the last of his supper.

"And I have reason."

"Aiblins, but ye'd best stay away frae yon prison. Ye've been 'noticed.' "

Andrew considered the old man askance, ended by smiling thanks. "I will heed your advice, Jamie, and stay away. Did you note the prize, a schooner which made port today?"

"Aye. A Yankee-built vessel wi' a dark green streak." The Scot tossed his old dog some scraps, heedless that the grease on them stained the floor.

"That's the one." Ever so clearly Andrew could see her in his mind's eye. She was just what he wanted because a few hands could handle her and in any weather. She looked fast and provided she wasn't tender, just the ship for his purpose. Building for speed, at the cost of sturdiness, was a mistake too many New England shipwrights were making nowadays. In Portsmouth, Salem, Boston and Nantucket they'd design a craft on modified French lines— something faster than a shooting star in a moderate breeze—but come on a real gale any sailing master in his right mind would have to strike canvas or risk turning turtle.

The latter fate had overtaken the *Trident* out of Norwich and the *Pacific*, laid down and built in Ipswich in Massachusetts. Drowned most of their crews. Of course, any vessel with a name like *Pacific* would, indubitably, have met with a sad fate. Any mariner would tell you it was begging for trouble to name a ship after any of King Neptune's oceans. Only superstition, Andrew reflected, yet it was curious how many vessels named for oceans or seas sailed off to remain forever unreported.

Could Jared Beetle be trusted? Andrew wondered. The giant was a consummate sailing master, capable of coaxing every fraction of a knot out of a ship. He could handle men, too. That Mr. Beetle knew little or nothing of gunnery made no difference. A certain officer of the Continental Navy should be able to command that department.

His plan must take shape quickly, though. Montego Bay jail had become so jammed with captive American crews, that the principal keeper had taken to permitting such prisoners as desired to sleep in the courtyard.

The courtyard Andrew had studied, knew that it was surrounded by a twelve-foot stone wall thickly crowned with glistening, razor-sharp shards of broken glass.

Everything depended upon the date a certain prison ship would arrive to convey the captive crews around the island to the dreary Naval prison at Port Royal. She was expected any day now.

Andrew pushed aside his bowl of tea. "Were you able to secure—what I wanted?"

The old merchant, cleaner and with some starch restored to his spine, nodded.

"Aye, I bought twa uniforms off a rogue of a sergeant out o' the mulatto militia from Port Antonio. I'm 'feared the tunics are a wee bit sma' for a mon o' yer inches."

"They'll have to do. And the muskets?"

"Ye'll have the weapons come night." Allerdice sighed, stared mournfully out of the grimy window. "Oh, Andrew, Andrew; 'tis a fearsome bold attempt ye've in mind."

This was true enough. There existed dozens of reasons why a

fatal mischance might befall the attempt. Still, reinforced by a crew from the jail, plus Beetle, Joe Beaver, and Atherton,—the last, so Beaver stated, had found sanctuary in a fishing village near Bloody Point—the schooner might be put out successfully.

Fore-and-aft, that rig was hardier, more efficient in beating to windward, a weak point with most of His Britannic Majesty's cruisers. If the medicines were to be brought to Boston, the job wasn't to be accomplished by sitting around, stewing in this musty old warehouse.

During his concealment Andrew learned in greater detail what the war was meaning to Montego Bay, to Jamaica and to all the British West Indies for that matter. The stagnation in the ports was terrific, despite cargoes unloaded from the captured merchant ships and offered at auction by the King's vendu masters. Now that King Louis XVI's subjects had engaged their ancient enemy yet again, many French prizes commenced to make port.

In the taprooms circulated rumors of French raids at St. Eustatis, on St. Kitts, and on Grenada on the outer Antilles; it was rumored that, from Saint Domingue and Martinique, the French government was putting to sea a swarm of cruisers, privateers with letters-of-marque; swift, graceful vessels so well built, so cleverly conceived that when some of them were taken the Admiralty yard masters would copy the prizes in shameless detail and use them as models for English men-of-war.

At Cape François in Saint Domingue, General Count Charles Hector d'Estaing was said to be collecting a vast armada of nearly thirty ships of the line and God knew how many frigates, razees, brigs, sloops and transports.

Dieu de Dieu! The might His Most Christian Majesty, Louis the Sixteenth, would with the help of the Continental Forces drive the British out of America in jig time.

"Eh, Jock, what is it?"

Mr. Allerdice's dog, fatter, lazier than ever, had raised his battered head.

Andrew's eye flickered to a certain tobacco jar which held no tobacco at all but a pair of fine French pocket pistols. He changed their priming every other day. When the dog only snuffled, failed even to interrupt his asthmatic breathing, Andrew relaxed.

At the door sounded no knock but a faint scratching. So? Joe Beaver, it appeared, had anticipated his promised return by one day. Why? Had the Indian lost count of time? No, it was uncanny how accurately the Penobscot kept track of time, though he could neither read nor write.

Mr. Allerdice, as was the custom, went to the door, shot back its bolts—but kept on a guard chain—and muttered, ''Who's there?''

''Tomakwe—Beaver.''

The dog, who loved the Penobscot's powerful body odor, got up, waddled forward, tail wagging. Joe Beaver entered the room as quietly as a deer entering a windfall. It was remarkable how surprisingly he had reverted to his earlier ways. Gone were his heavy seaman's breeches; his broad, brass buckled belt now supported a long knife and a loin clout of some dull green cloth. He had a single, brilliant blue feather lashed into a plait of hair over his left ear. Because the Penobscot quartermaster no longer wore a shirt, the two white men could see how the red-brown expanse of Beaver's hairless chest glistened with an application of some oil which was anything but fragrant. In his left hand the half-breed was lugging a skin sack of some sort.

''G'night,'' he grunted, but his penetrating jet eyes roved about.

Once Mr. Allerdice shut and re-bolted the door the Penobscot spread his bag on the table and methodically untied a thong.

''Pretty, *hein? Bien jolie?*''

He indicated a pair of copper bracelets, the cleverly cured skins of some birds such as neither Andrew nor the Scot had ever seen. In the candlelight they fairly blazed with color.

Grinning, Beaver spread for inspection the soft brown-and-white-striped pelt of some animal which, for the life of him, Andrew could not identify. Mingled indiscriminately with these was a heel of bread, a greasy chunk of meat, some papayas, two or three bruised bananas, a fishing line, a cake of salt, and a set of long, evil-appearing, hand-fashioned iron arrowheads.

In silence the Penobscot accepted the bowl of food the old merchant offered, commenced to stuff his mouth. Indianlike, he disdained fork or knife, ate with his fingers. In the dim little room a pungent musky, animal-like odor soon began to manifest itself, grew sharper when Joe Beaver commenced to sweat.

''You're a day early, Joe.''

''Ugh. You not sail soon?''

''Don't know,'' Andrew replied. ''Why? You aren't falling in love with some Maroon beauty?''

The Indian's eyes batted once or twice and he licked clean his fingers before replying. ''Maroon chief paint for war soon.'' He wrinkled his nostrils with disdain. ''Black warrior no can shoot bow—quiet, quiet. Chief Maroon promise Tomakwe two pearls, so—'' The impassive bronze figure held up the tip of a little finger.

Mr. Allerdice's rheumy blue eyes became intent upon the savage now fondling the old dog's head.

"Losh, Andy." He shook his untidy gray head. " 'Tis as I fear. Yon new Colonel o' the Maroons is plotting mischief."

"Why?"

Joe Beaver made a gesture to his mouth, all greasy from food. "Slave on plantings hungry—mad—no good work no eat. Many Engee soldiers gone there." He indicated the north. "More go soon, they know."

Apparently news had spread far and wide over the island that a battalion of the 50th Regiment of the Line—a considerable part of the regular establishment—had sailed for America in company with units from the St. Catherine and St. Andrew Regiments of militia.

In the Crown & Dove that very afternoon British officers had been heard roundly cursing Parliament's shortsighted policy in leaving the island so nearly denuded of dependable troops. For months now, Mr. Allerdice had heard various influential planters talk of raising and equipping their own trained bands, but somehow they had not got around to taking action.

Mr. Allerdice shook his head. "I pray yer savage here is mistook, Andy. If he's correct, God help the puir people i' the up-country. Back in '65 I was wi' the militia tae Johnny Carlton's polink the day after a band o' Maroons had sacked it wi' the help o' his ain slaves. Mon, mon! 'Twas a fearful sicht, enough to sicken the stomach o' a Turk."

"Do you suppose the local commandant has been warned?" Andrew demanded.

"I misdoot but he has now," Allerdice replied, frowning at a pair of kittens battling ferociously between his feet. "Alas, Colonel Johnson is too steept i' his rum punches tae heed word from the Archangel himsel'."

The Indian looked so hopefully at the Scot's other tobacco jar that Mr. Allerdice relented, passed it over. In silence the Penobscot selected a plug, drew his hunting knife, a murderous weapon with a heavy eight-inch blade, and commenced to shred the bright Virginia into the bowl of a pipe he produced from the depths of his war bag.

"I suppose, Joe, you've been teaching your Maroon friends in the mountains how to scalp?"

For the first time, Joe Beaver's teeth flashed in the briefest of grins. "No can, Cappen. Try, but no can. Wool too short." That the quartermaster had indeed reverted to type, was attested by the fact that he ignored the chair upon which he would have sat a month ago to squat on his heels, with broad brown toes spread out for balance.

Also smoking, Andrew pushed fingers through the wild black

tangle his hair had become, said thoughtfully, "Joe, the vessel I've been waiting for made port today."

"Uh?"

"What with the garrison here reduced to a skeleton, with both duty frigates at sea next week—well, we'll have the best chance to cut and run we're ever likely to get."

Mr. Allerdice sighed. "I'm of the opinion yer over-optimistic, lad. Ye ne'er can be sure what the Hanoverian's minions will do."

Andrew tugged momentarily at his beard, thought, "Suppose these Maroons do attack? The Commandant in this town of course will send every man he can spare up-country." He slapped his thigh softly. "Yes, by God, an uprising will improve our chances."

The more he questioned Joe Beaver, the lighter his spirits became. The black outlaws, he learned, had been gathering quietly, and, for the past two days, the green-blue peaks above the coastal plain had echoed to muffled drummings. By patient questioning he deduced that the Maroon chiefs had marked two particular estates for attack. Which ones they were, the bandy-legged, half-naked Penobscot had not thought it important to learn. He was positive, however, the new Colonel meant to attack.

In lazy, inverted ringlets, curls of smoke rose from the Penobscot's pipe. He cocked a speculative, narrow black eye at Andrew.

"Yes, Joe?"

"Capen, mebbe Tomakwe bring good news."

"Yes?"

"Remember squaw on brig?"

Andrew's smile faded. Remember? He wasn't likely to forget Minga Allen, not in a month of Sundays; the little slut had come within a particle of costing him his life. Damn her eyes, she needn't have yelled for the watch like that—no matter what her politics.

"Yes. Why do you speak of her?"

Jerusha! Just when he was getting Minga Allen removed to something like a comfortable spot in his memory—and now—

"Tomakwe see—riding horse."

"Come, come, Joseph," Mr. Allerdice broke in. "Whaur is she, mon? She's a friend o' mine, too."

"Big ground, under high mountain," the Indian explained pointing in a southeasterly direction. "Tomakwe no can say name, except 'Hall.' "

Mr. Allerdice swallowed a long draught of lime punch, thought hard. To the southeast were only two estates the names of which ended in the word "Hall." No, there were three, if you counted Pondicherry Hall, but that was 'way down the coast. This left only

Pembroke Hall and Hawthorn Hall, belonging to that extraordinarily cold and beautiful widow of Sir Thomas Moffat.

"Do I understand it is one of these the Maroons intend to ravage?"

Joe Beaver's naked shoulders rose and he looked infuriatingly blank. "Me not know. Cappen—squaw at Hall."

"Which one?" Allerdice demanded. "Pembroke or Hawthorn?"

The bronze figure held up two fingers.

"Mistress Allen must be at Hawthorn."

Andrew shook his head. The devil could take Minga Allen, for all he cared. He wasn't interested.

"If it *is* Hawthorn Hall the Maroons mean to pillage," Allerdice said, "ye'd best send wur-r-rd. Ye canna leave her unwarned. Ye'd not hesitate, Andy, had ye seen the bonny lass we found lying nailed tae puir Johnny Carlton's par-r-lor floor, blinded and split open from belly tae chin."

XXII

THE MAROONS

THERE was a thunderstorm, characteristically Jamaican, rumbling further down the coast. In the late afternoon light the searing brilliance of lightning bolts were to be seen jabbing at the plain. Joe Beaver was confident, however, that it was not going to rain in the direction they were following.

Indefinably, the countryside through which the half-breed had guided Andrew Warren was in an uneasy state. Twice, at crossroads, Andrew and Joe had come upon Europeans and some light mulattoes carrying muskets and looking pretty serious. The drumming kept recurring.

Around five of the afternoon Andrew had reason to figure that, all things considered, they weren't making bad time. He found himself winded time and again, especially when this wild and luxuriantly overgrown terrain sloped upward. The Penobscot, of course, made light going of it, stripped as he was. Besides, he'd had ample opportunity to regain his shore legs.

"Now why the devil am I doing this?" Andrew asked himself as he flung himself, panting, to rest under a clump of logwoods. "Joe Beaver may be mistaken; besides, what in tunket does Minga Allen mean to me?"

She was only a treacherous little baggage, a female Judas who'd tried to condemn him to a gallows, which, if not sixty cubits high, would still certainly have served to choke the life out of him. He wet his lips with his tongue, then rubbed the aching lids of his eyes with his thumbs.

Such slaves as they encountered on the estates he and Joe Beaver traversed were acting sullen and uneasy. Squatting on their hams, they huddled together in patches of shade.

Andrew recognized representatives of various tribes inhabiting the West Coast of Africa from Rio de Oro to the Bight of Benin. There were the fierce Dahomeyans and Coromantees, blue-black Senegalese with filed teeth and rows of cicatrices on cheeks and forehead, apathetic Eboes, brisk Mandingoes. Most were branded in two places, some in only one.

"How far now?" he demanded, sponging his neck with an already sodden bandanna.

Joe Beaver's forefinger indicated the lowering sun. He bent first his second, then his third finger.

"Two hours more, eh?"

Whew! Sweat was prickling at the roots of Andrew's short curly beard. Damn! He'd be rid of it the first moment he dared.

The Penobscot nodded in high good humor. Ever since they had reached the wild foothills his flat, greasy features had become set in a fixed grin. To his drooping blue feather he had added a pair of flaming yellow ones. His copper bracelets shone and he had even run a dab of white lead along his cheek bones. There would be no doubt that Joe Beaver was very familiar with the lay of the land in this direction.

Around midday the voyagers skirted an estate upon which some sort of a fête was in progress. There was the sound of drums and of muskets shooting. From a Negro hunter engaged in netting white wings, Andrew learned that this was the King's birthday. He chuckled, wondered how George III might be feeling on this Fourth of June, 1778? Now that Spain and Holland were growing increasingly hostile the King's name day could not be overly cheery. Fervently, he hoped that His Britannic Majesty would celebrate his next in defeat.

A plague on Minga Allen! What a strange, complex creature. He'd have to be mighty sharp in handling her.

Well she'd had her say that time. He couldn't help admiring her for it. It would be a rare bit of humor if he were to heap coals of fire on her head by appearing two jumps ahead of trouble.

Joe Beaver tapped at his elbow, indicated what seemed a mere game trail.

"Save walk," he muttered, then, his sinewy loins working effortlessly, the Penobscot headed upwards along the course of a brook, away from the sun-baked, deeply rutted highway. They clambered up, up into a cool green woods in which wild pigs jerked their tails and clattered their yellow tusks before running away, followed by their striped and spotted shoats. Dozens of humming birds, gold, green, blue and ruby, darted about; snakes slipped smoothly away under giant ferns.

It felt mighty fine to be off the highroad, to be free of a sneaking suspicion that, at any moment, someone might come along who could, and would, denounce him. Never, until landing in Jamaica, had Andrew suspected what it meant to be hunted. He realized now the uncertainty about how much the pursuers knew, about their numbers and resources. How many thousands of fears had he not suffered in Mr. Allerdice's warehouse?

Twice the Penobscot paused in a small hollow where, days ago, he had made his camp, though how he could have tolerated the swarming insects was a mystery.

Just as twilight was falling the first drums commenced to throb. It came as a muted *thump! thump-thump, thump! Tunk, tunk, a-tunk!* The instant he heard that cadence, Joe Beaver froze in his tracks listening intently. Immediately another drum answered; *blok! blok-blok-blok!*, very quickly. The Penobscot looked increasingly puzzled when, on the mountain side off to their right, still another drum sounded a series of five rapid beats.

His smile vanished; Joe Beaver was listening intently.

"What's wrong?"

"Colonel Grandy this not tell Tomakwe."

Through painful use of French and English Andrew was made to understand the Penobscot's surprise. Apparently, what had been contemplated was a darting raid, a sudden savage descent on the indicated sugar estates. The new Colonel had planned that his barbarous tribesmen would strike, probably at nightfall, kill all whites, then for several hours plunder furiously, and when the dawn came, only buzzards floating down from the sky would occupy the plundered mansions.

From what Andrew was able to gather, the date of the descent had been advanced. Joe Beaver was positive on that point, nodded his head until the feathers fairly squirmed.

"Owoo-eu-ee." Somewhere down on the great hazy blue-green plain stretching away below a conch-shell bugle sounded wailing noises, close to human.

"Ou-ou!" "Ouach-ie-e." Faintly, other conches raised their voices, made an incredibly eerie sound.

"Wagh!" Joe Beaver sounded both angry and definitely disturbed. "Grandy big fool." The Penobscot's dully modelled flat face had thinned and his fingers on his war bag had begun to work like the paws of a nursing kitten. Through the leaves of a palmetto the white striping on his cheeks shone bright in the gathering gloom.

Andrew asked, "Do they intend attacking tonight?"

"Ugh!"

"Which estate?" He had gathered that a place called Lucinea, Hawthorn Hall and Pembroke Hall lay grouped in a loose triangle.

Joe Beaver shrugged. His attention was not on what Andrew was asking but on a multitude of subtle sounds rising from the great green ocean of sugar cane below.

Instinct told him that, beyond a doubt, the Maroons were at this very moment mounting an assault. Damnation! Why wasn't the half-breed more articulate? Trying to get information out of Joe Beaver was like trying to drag a cat by its tail over a rug.

"This trail leads to Hawthorn Hall?" He felt anxious over the drumming. Minga—well, she deserved what she got, but an officer of the Continental Navy couldn't stand by while a lady—even a damned King-loving Tory—stood in peril of a death ghastly beyond imagination.

Joe Beaver nodded. When Andrew commenced to walk more quickly, he shook his plumed head. "No. Bad go fast." Quite vanished was the half-breed's previous gait, his carefree manner.

They presently emerged in a small glade at one end of which the remnants of a campfire described a black circle on the earth, centered with a white powdering of ashes. The Penobscot tossed his war bag onto the ground and ran over to a towering cordium tree. Pushing aside a festoon of grenadilla vines he brought out a bow swathed in some oiled cloth, arrows, and a pair of African made spears.

"Better this," he held up a charred stick and pointed to Andrew's face. Thoroughly, the quartermaster applied charcoal.

Were the threatened estates taking precautions or just arguing as to whether this drumming really meant a raid? The Maroons were far too clever not to drum talk just often enough to accustom people to the hearing of it.

At length the New Englander was darkened satisfactorily. With gratitude he accepted the light spear Joe Beaver offered, added it to the pistol jammed into his belt. He felt better prepared, ready for what might chance.

The lack of light seemed not to bother the Penobscot as he led downwards over a ridge that had seemed tall as a mountain. He travelled at a slow jog, his squat figure twisting and bending readily to avoid those lianas and creepers which dropped tentacle-like loops above the narrow, incredibly crooked path.

Andrew, however, found the going increasingly difficult; uneven stretches of the trail threw him off balance, roots snatched at his low shoes and twigs beat at his face and thorns lacerated his shins and ankles. He hadn't much opportunity to dwell upon his difficulties; more and more conches were moaning and variously pitched drums were banging more insistently.

Joe Beaver halted so abruptly Andrew all but tripped over him. He was close behind when, like a serpent, the Penobscot slipped into the tangle of tall ferns, quickly strung his bow—a short but powerful weapon made of mock orange.

Andrew was glad to lie there beside the trail, sweat-drenched and trying to control his wild breathing. Like a cat gathering itself for a leap, the Penobscot waited, his blunt head outthrust.

A faint noise, like the first drops of a rainstorm, attracted the New Englander's attention. The pattering sound grew louder; then Andrew watched nearly a dozen shadowy outlines speed past his hiding place at a rapid surging run—from the same direction he had come. Though he couldn't rightly see the runners, a rank smell of stale sweat remained in the humid atmosphere. When an owl in a nearby cottonwood raised its ghostly cry, another bird answered further up the ridge.

Punished cruelly by midges and mosquitoes, Andrew started to arise but Joe Beaver's hot hand closed over his elbow.

"No—more coming."

Though the sea captain could hear nothing, another and a larger party of blacks—Maroons, of course—appeared on the path. These weren't running, just moving at a rapid walk. This time Andrew could glimpse the occasional sheen of a spear blade, the dim glint of a gun barrel. The Maroons vanished down the path, their big splay feet patterning the rich black earth of the trail.

Suddenly it became appalling for Andrew to realize that there must be dozens, if not hundreds, of Colonel Grandy's fierce Maroons between him and Hawthorn Hall. Their guttural talk was plainly audible.

"Dat puntop swor'. Whey you get?"

"Weston—las' yeah."

''Man, you mus' a mad, dat tree yeah go. You cuped liard.''

Another towering buck wearing a crown of ostrich feathers announced, ''Ah goin' kill de busha—he whip me. Den Ah tek de young buckra gal—''

''Chaw! Hit's da house fo' me. Hawtawn Hall bery rich.''

Joe Beaver, however, refused to be hurried. Clearly, for the Penobscot the situation held unexpected developments; he wasn't rushing headlong into a possible snare.

Great bats kept swooping, screeching about the travellers' heads when the trees began to thin and more stars to show overhead. The drumming had died away and only a few faraway conch shells sounded now and then.

At the edge of the forest the Penobscot beckoned Andrew off the trail, then led forward through a dense bamboo thicket. In the light of a faint quarter moon lay stretched out that estate Minga had mentioned aboard the lost *Evergreen*. Cane field on cane field, cattle fold on cattle fold, the expansive wealth of Moffat's Penn lay sprawled over a wide, gently undulating terrain. Here and there whitish cart tracks shone, dividing and subdividing the plantation.

Clusters of little white huts grouped themselves under a sheltering grove of trees. Peace immeasurable seemed to rule beneath myriad diamantine stars. The lowing of some thirsty cattle sounded loud out of all proportion.

''Come, there's precious little time,'' Andrew urged, but the quartermaster's feather-garnished head shook violently. He planted his spear in the earth, then, hands braced on knees, peered cautiously downwards from the tall bluff on which they were standing, an eminence rising sheer from a great cane field below. The Penobscot listened intently, his dew-sodden feathers drooping lank over his shoulder.

All at once his breath came in with a hissing rush, and he sprang back into the bamboos when, on the same ridge and not a quarter of a mile distant, a giant drum commenced to roar. The drummers must be pounding with all their strength until the taut bullock's hide bellowed like a Titan in anguish.

''Wagh! See!''

Andrew could scarcely credit his vision. Pinpoints of fire appeared suddenly all over the plain—commenced to move and to converge on a white manor house, standing perhaps a mile and a half distant among its satellite buildings, like an island in the great sea of sugarcane fields.

By fifties and hundreds, more torches sprang into being. Joe Beaver began trembling a little. Sudden gushes of flame shot up in various directions.

"They're firing the cane fields," Andrew thought aloud. Every conch and drum in the vicinity was sounding. Great God! The Allen girl and her Aunt were in the center of that irregular, brilliant circle of death.

"*Hei! Hei!*" voices yelled from the foot of the bluff.

"*Kway! Kway!*" answered Maroons plunging deeper in the cane on their way to the looting of Hawthorn Hall.

"House slaves." Joe Beaver's arm swung to the left.

Apparently some of the outbuildings surrounding the manor had taken fire and quickly began erupting clouds of rose-tinted smoke, sending pinwheels of sparks spiraling dizzily upwards.

Surprisingly late, a musket clanged, then followed a ragged volley. Far distant shouting increased. It was so windless that night that voices, even small voices, carried distinctly.

Quite a large dwelling—the superintendent's quarters, perhaps —next showed fire at its windows. The shooting died away, then recommenced as the defenders—evidently only a handful in number—succeeded in reloading.

What to do? Andrew racked his mind. The obvious course of fighting his way through to the women was hopeless. Now the façade of the manor house, which had appeared white by the starlight, began to reflect flames, and glowed a conch-shell pink.

Andrew turned his smudged countenance to the Indian. "Are we just going to stand here?—Come."

"No! No! Cappen. Too late."

This was indubitably so, for from the plains rose a dreadful, ear-piercing clamor. The firelit area about Hawthorn Hall squirmed with activity as the dull, crashing sound of some heavy object impacting against another suggested the use of a battering ram. A few straggling shots punctuated the uproar.

Andrew could stand inactivity no longer. He couldn't bear the idea of Minga waiting, waiting for that door to splinter and fall.

When Joe Beaver shrugged, Andrew cursed him, then went plunging down the bluff into the canes below, regardless of thorny bushes.

The glare of the fire increased until trees near the Manor House were cast into sharp silhouette. Burning brands were soaring so high it seemed as if, around Hawthorn Hall, a minor volcano was in eruption.

A crashing behind him warned that the Penobscot had decided to follow. Reassured, Andrew ran faster and faster, the broad-bladed spear clutched in his left hand. He didn't properly know how to use such a weapon except that it was like a very light boarding pike; his pistol was another matter.

Now the fire was growing still greater. "*Yoi! yoi! yoi!*" sharp-pitched voices yelled. A series of hideous screams penetrated the clamor.

He became aware that other persons, too, were hurrying through the rows of cane. Without warning, a torch flared just ahead, revealed a cart track, and his heart stopped. Never had he seen such a vision as this—a line of revolted slaves; their features were positively demonic. Fortunately, Joe Beaver stopped instantly, like himself, a few feet short of the track.

The bookkeepers' quarters must have been raided early in the attack, for a giant Negro appeared carrying an armful of bedclothes and a snuff-colored coat. Another was bent under a chest of drawers, and carrying in his free hand a chamberpot, of all things.

"*Heu-dah! Heu-dah!*" A stark-naked buck came prancing along carrying a rum jug and flourishing a pallid head impaled upon the end of a pike.

When Andrew realized that the severed head had long brown hair he started forward, but the Penobscot anticipated his move and held him where he was. It was well he did so. A detachment of Maroons, arriving belatedly, appeared racing down from the bluff. Roughly, they pushed aside the booty-laden plunderers and raced on, swinging heavy cutlasses and howling hideous war cries. In the semi-darkness their sable faces seemed all white-ringed eyes and gleaming teeth.

More half-naked field hands, blacks going berserk with rum looted from the storehouse, went storming by; some were brandishing cane knives, others adzes and hatchets; but the most of them carried great clubs, wicked-looking affairs set with spikes.

"No go nearer." It was clear that Joe Beaver felt none too confident of his own safety. His hunting knife lay free in its sheath and his fingers worked nervously on the handle of his short broad-backed bow. An arrow lay ready, nocked on the rawhide string.

XXIII

THE BRACELET

BEFORE Hawthorn Hall the uproar had become deafening. There was more shooting now. Despairing screams of male and female origin began rising. Andrew shook Beaver off, pushed on towards the fire down seemingly interminable rows of dewy cane stalks. Though sickened and outraged, he retained wit enough to stay off the cart track. Down it the revolted slaves and Maroons were running and capering around.

Not far ahead a horse began screeching in agony. When he reached a clearing, Andrew saw why. Field hands, long famished for meat, had captured a pair of riding horses. After hamstringing the mounts they never bothered to cut the throats of the wretched beasts but used their cane knives to hack gobbets of raw meat off the still living animals. Like wolves they ringed the wretched horses about, slashing and stabbing until at last they lay still.

After veering aside and avoiding the clearing, Andrew emerged on a small garden and so got his first view of the doomed mansion. Up its double doorsteps was eddying a dark swarm of figures, while from its upper stories a continual stream of objects was being hurled to the ground, more often than not hurting those pillagers who were prancing idiotically about.

By now the first buildings to have been set afire were nearly burned down, but the conflagration revived, higher than ever, 'way above branches of the cottonwoods, when Hawthorn Hall's cooking quarters took.

Smudged face or no, there was nothing to be gained by venturing out in the open. The whole clear space around the house was alive with flying sparks, squealing animals, and murderous, drunken blacks.

"Damnation!" Andrew growled. If only he had left Montego Bay just an hour earlier. Still, if any friendly black had chosen to tell Mrs. Moffat that that had been no ordinary drum talk, she and her niece might have escaped.

Off to the eastward where the cane had been set afire, great, soaring sheets of fire, like billows from a flaming ocean, went rolling over the plain with the speed of race horses.

Minga! If only he had a suspicion of where she might be. A hundred visions of her came to torment him. With that awful clear sense of shame which punishes an intelligent person who has played the fool, he stood at the edge of the garden sweating in the hot dark, unconscious of myriad insects lancing at his skin with tiny barbs.

"Don't, in God's name! Don't! Help! Help! Oh-h—don't!" From a patch of cane to Andrew's right the woman's voice cried in an ascending scale; sobbing, gorged with terror.

He wheeled. Despite the gale of sound below the manor house, he sensed it must be Minga. Headlong he plunged back into the humid, sick-sweet-smelling cane. Guided by half-heard cries and pitiful entreaties, he travelled in furious leaps. Dew showered in his face, leaves lashed at his eyes.

"Minga! I'm coming—I'm coming to—" He was too short of breath than more to choke out the words. He lost his hat, but held onto the spear and the pistol. Where Joe was he couldn't tell. He burst into a little clearing before he knew it. It wasn't very big, perhaps fifty feet across. There was another, a larger one opening into it. From there came voices, grunts, squalling sounds, the smell of Africans mingled with the odor of rum.

A squat figure overtook him. "Tomakwe shoot—" Faintly gilded by the flames rippling from the roof of the mansion, the Penobscot drew his short bow into a deep arc. When he loosed, one of the figures forming part of that group busy in the big clearing uttered a rending screech, bounded into the air and fell, legs working spasmodically, arms futilely beating the air.

Seldom had Andrew seen anything so quick, so perfectly articulated as the halfbreed's movements. In the space of twenty seconds the Penobscot had sped half that number of arrows.

"*Ki!* Who da'?" The house slaves, for such they must be by their sodden, ragged uniforms, peered about, bewildered by this silent lethal force.

"Myall man he heah! Oh! Damballa!" They scattered without knowing in which direction to avoid the death raining so silently out of the rustling sugar cane.

A short house-servant with an officer's straight-bladed sword in his hand and a pillowcase full of loot slung over his shoulder, came blundering right at Andrew.

He never saw the New Englander, had time for only a frightened squeak before Andrew's spear caught him full in the throat. The blade struck with such an impact that the haft snapped. Transfixed, the looter described a ludicrous backward half-arc before he fell futilely to scrabble and twist and kick the earthen troughs between the rustling canes.

Andrew was amazed to see the big clearing devoid of erect figures though several garish forms were rolling about, flopping on hands and knees, to collapse and tug at the arrow shafts protruding from their bodies.

"*Abtschiech—goch—gi—hillen!*" Eager as a terrier entering a box stall full of rats, the Penobscot rushed out. His short spear he planted in the nearest raider, then with a grunt of "*Ke-hella!*" Joe Beaver slid out the long knife which normally rode above the crease between his buttocks. Those fallen figures who had groaned made brief whimpering noises; were silent.

Furious at this senseless murder Andrew, too, used his spear head. In his ears reverberated those pitiful cries. Only now he glimpsed what looked like a white puddle in the center of the trampled earth. It was a body lying half in, half out of a ragged mound of white cloth, a pattern of outstretched limbs clear against the black earth. Andrew plunged forward. Minga!

"Take courage," he panted. "Get you out."

Because a headless body cannot speak, he received no answer. His teeth locked as the sea captain stood swaying, outraged, incredulous, above that dreadfully sprawled, pallid outline.

The Penobscot was hopping about, grabbing at items of loot, stuffing them into his war bag.

The fire, soaring ever higher, kindled a deadly glow, drew dull flashes from the wet canes. Andrew stooped, caught up a limp and slippery arm, and peered intently. He didn't have to look twice to recognize the twined dolphins on that luck bracelet.

"Minga!" he gasped. "Minga! This isn't— No sense. You're not—Jamaica!"

Joe Beaver, in jumping over a body, missed his footing, stepped on an arrow projecting from the back of a great fat house-slave. The shaft gave, snapped with a little *crack!*

"Come." The Penobscot, carrying a shirt full of plunder, tugged at his elbow. "Cappen, mus' go quick!"

Go? How could a man go, leave so dear a chalice lying shattered? Never before had he realized Minga's fingers were so slim. Take the bracelet? No. It was a part of her legend. He remembered first seeing it in the Port Commandant's office—that damned Colonel Saunders looking down his long red nose.

"Cappen! Cappen!"

There was no doubt that go they must. Yelping like a pack of beagles in full cry, another party of slaves was rioting down the cart track away from the plundered mansion.

Andrew turned away—yearned to be sick. God's love! What a hideous world. That this should happen! His mind rushed back— saw Minga again on the *Evergreen*'s quarterdeck, serene, supple, and calm. And now. Now!

No sense in staying. The *Trumbull* would be launched some day soon. When Joe Beaver caught up the dead looter's pillowcase, gave it to him, he grabbed it mechanically. Together they shouldered back into the friendly, sheltering sugarcane.

No longer a ruddy glare beat through the tree tops. The animal noises of slaves drunk on the rum their sweat had made possible, lingered as a confused murmur in the distance. But triumphant, ill-timed drums were still muttering.

When they came to a stream, Andrew flung himself flat, drank two or three big gulps, plunged his head under the water until he was all but strangled, then rolled over and lay quite still in the ferns.

Minga. Minga. Why had the counters of life fallen in this order?

He felt somewhat as he had when one of H.M.S. *Racehorse*'s shots had struck Will Hemingway full in the face. That had been the end of Hemingway but he couldn't admit to himself that Will, his sober, cheery companion in many an hour of fight and frolic, wouldn't be on deck tomorrow.

Somehow, he couldn't convince himself either, that Minga Allen no longer lived. Yet she was lying back there, defiled, mutilated, trampled into the black muck of a rural cart track.

Vaguely, Andrew was aware of an increasing tension on his skin. Without looking, he knew the stickiness was caused by the drying of blood which had spurted from the fleeing house-slave he had speared. God above! Why, he still was carrying the fellow's booty.

A fine officer to get into a spin like this! Why, aboard ship, in even a brisk engagement, he had known just what to do, no matter how the battle went. He yearned to go back and kill more of those black hellions who had destroyed so lovely, so irreplaceable a creature as Minga Allen.

Again he doused his head, felt the water drain slowly from his beard and was aware of the taste of charcoal strong in his mouth. Joe Beaver was fishing from his bulging shirt a weird collection of objects—a silver ladle, an amber necklace.

Despite himself, Andrew's curiosity was piqued. What next would the Penobscot produce? A silver snuffer, a fan with an ivory handle, a silver tea box set with jade. The Penobscot kept grunting happily to himself. The white lead on his face had been replaced with a more intricate design. When he had done it, Andrew could not have told, had his life depended upon it.

He simply couldn't reflect on how much he had lost. During the action with the picaroons, in the gig, and penniless ashore. Minga Allen had shone as a fine, rarely courageous woman.

What an utter idiot he had been. Now it was too late. His feeling of impotence was infuriating. A man should be able to do something about such outrages.

"I've got to think on something else," he warned himself. Suppose she *had* been that damned Colonel's leman? He had learned, in the last year, that that which seemed utterly immoral in one person, might be explicable, even admirable, in another.

A mosquito jabbed at his cheekbone. He sat up, studied Joe Beaver across the starlit clearing. Methodically, the Penobscot was packing his loot into a square of cloth, cleverly cramming the ladle into a silver coffeepot, the necklace into a teak and mother-of-pearl tea caddy.

What about his own loot? For the first time he realized that this pillowcase was heavier than lead. Because it was necessary to think about something besides that dreadfully crushed figure down on the plain, he reached into the bag and fumbled about until a case bumped against his fingers.

He drew it out but, before opening it, cast a quick look at Joe Beaver. His ex-quartermaster was fully occupied in packing. Andrew pressed a small steel plunger, was startled that the lid sprang back so readily. Jerusha! Within lay a necklace of stones which gleamed even in this light. Bright stones! The realization sent a hot, jolting current flowing through his weary frame. Diamonds. Jerusha! And again, Jerusha!

Groping deeper into the bag, he encountered a small leather bag. From its shape he guessed it contained coins; from its weight he deduced that the coins were of gold. Inside were lengths of silk and more square boxes. It would appear that the house-slave had known all too well just where Mrs. Moffat had kept her valuables.

Abruptly, the realization came home that the *Evergreen* had been lost, but not in vain. Here, here in this dirty, dew-sodden pillowcase lay power, unexpected, undreamed-of power; gold, a pretty good store of it; diamonds; and those other cases must hold other gems. But Minga now could not benefit—all along he had wanted to replace her losses, though God knew there was no obligation. Every time you went aboard ship, you knew you were exposing yourself to certain risks.

His mind commenced to function once more, but in a species of numbed precision. It wouldn't do, perhaps, to let Joe Beaver suspect, so he slipped the diamond necklace, case and all, into his shirt.

"I can get away now. Why, I can buy a ship if I need to!" He commenced to tug excitedly at his little beard. "And sail it back to Boston, come Lobster backs, hell, or a hurricane!"

In the firefly-lit gloom he smiled in anticipation of his meeting with the drug dealer. Let Senhor Carlos Cardozo ask what he would; what he'd get would be another matter. The whole length of the American Coast the Warrens had a reputation as shrewd bargainers—shrewd but honest.

His imagination took hold, commenced to spread like a grass fire. "Why not be clever, lad? Get yourself over to Saint Domingue where the French are. At Cap François or Port au Prince you can fit yourself out for a privateer. With a regular Naval officer's skill at navigation and gunnery the British can be made to smart."

But no, that wasn't what was wanted back in Boston. His orders read to return with the medicines as swiftly as might be possible. Orders were given to be obeyed. The decision to let privateering go came easier when he remembered Dr. Blanchard's dark tragic eyes and recollected what that hell-hole of mercy called the Drydock had been like.

He got to his feet. "We had better get out of here, Joe."

The woods were swarming with retreating Maroons, some of them still hungry for plunder. It wouldn't do to lose this new lease on hope.

Nor would it do to dwell on Minga Allen's ghastly end.

XXIV

FALMOUTH, THE EVENING TIDE

THE shipper's agent puffed out round little cheeks, folded the invoice, and arose.

"Everything, sir, is now in order. Your chests, boxes and trunks are cleared for Philadelphia." He smiled politely. "Your trunks shall go aboard the *Swan* this very evening, Dr. Pawling. Captain Taplow has declared his intention of setting sail on the morning breeze. You may rely upon it, sir."

Dr. Charles Pawling reset his elegant, Prussian-blue grosgrain waistcoat with a careless tug. "Very well, my man; make sure not a single item is mislaid. I hold you responsible."

"I am conscious of the honor, sir."

"You will see that my retainers get aboard tonight? The Indian, Atherton and Mr. Bird?"

The shipping agent folded plump hands before him, bowed a little. "Drunk or sober, sir, they'll be put aboard." He had a proper respect, had Henry Dawkins, for one of the gentry and if ever he had seen a real nob, it was this elegant physician from Savannah-la-Mar. He made a brave figure did young Dr. Pawling in his sky-blue skirted coat, buff nankeen breeches, and smart, Irish lace jabot. God's truth, for all his unfashionable black beard, he was a gentleman, all right, from the top of his blue-black hair to the soles of his feet.

A bold-looking sort, too—more like a military gent than a physicker. Dr. Pawling's sharp black eyes seemed to see straight into a body; those high cheekbones of his made him look lean and hungry; but of course he couldn't be hungry—not anybody as had so many heavy gold seals a-dangle from his watch fob.

"I claim it's a plagued nuisance to travel like this," drawled Charles Pawling, M.D. "I had been entirely confident of chartering a vessel."

His gaze wandered down the little port's dilapidated but busy waterfront. Several ships, waiting to rendezvous with a convoy for England, rode at anchor in the incredibly clear blue water. "Why I was informed that so wretched a port as Falmouth would be a likely place to find me a vessel, I will never fathom. Should have made for Montego Bay, I fancy."

The shipper's agent clucked commiseration. "A pity, sir, a great pity you found disappointment here. Nonetheless, I venture you will find the *Swan* a comfortable craft. Quite a superior brig, mounts fourteen carriage guns, new and Bristol-built, I might add."

Dr. Charles Pawling tossed a half crown onto the agent's paper-swamped desk. "My friend, you have been helpful. Pray pledge me to a swift and pleasant journey to Philadelphia."

Mr. Dawkins beamed, rubbed his hands, bowed several times. "That I will, sir, and I'll pledge a French cruiser don't come up with you."

He looked suddenly downcast. "The Johnny Crapauds have grown so monstrous bold, sir, insurance rates mount daily—and already the rates run higher than a cat's back. Still, I warrant we'll beat them Froggies again as handily as we did back in '13 and '63."

"I should rather fancy meeting up with a Frenchman of equal metal," the elegant figure remarked and, swinging a gold-headed walking stick, he strolled out into the late afternoon glow.

No, Falmouth certainly wasn't much of a town; just two and a half streets of tumbledown warehouses, sagging docks, and weather-beaten residences. Still, it had seemed small enough to be safe, a good place to sail from, Charles Pawling mused, stroking his brief black beard. Jerusha! He would be almighty glad to shave the thing off—but not for a while yet.

No wind tonight. The *Swan* lay faithfully mirrored beside her dock. The other ships, further out, rode motionless. Andrew Warren felt a vast impatience to be off. The task of playing the part of Dr. Charles Pawling from Savannah-la-Mar was becoming tedious, though he had a real facility at mimicking various accents, especially English intonations.

As he strolled along with a pair of gaunt curs sniffing at his heels, he wondered why it was that most people who were clumsy at mathematics, were able at languages, and the other way around. Yes, it was a nuisance to remember the well-born Britisher's affected drawl, to cultivate a convincingly patronizing and sometimes insulting manner towards underlings.

Two of the ships nearest shore also had been making ready for sea, he noticed. The *Countess of Folkstone* and a larger vessel, the full-rigged ship *Serpentine*. All day gangs of sweating blacks had rowed heavily loaded barges, scows and wherries out of these tall merchantmen. Blocks and tackles had whined protest at the heavy loads of rum, pimento, sugar, and logwood that went swinging up on their decks.

Nor was he the only stranger in town. Far from it. During the past forty-eight hours merchants, insurance brokers, prospective passengers, whores, cut-purses, and estate agents had appeared. Some came sailing along the coast in pinks, cutters and tiny sloops; others rode in on oxcarts, kittareens, or a-horseback. Falmouth teemed with such excitement as would not again prevail for weeks and months.

For all his beard and fine clothes, Andrew grew uneasy at this influx. His inn, the Trident Tavern, had been all but taken over by British and Colonial Army officers ordered to duty in America; army contractors and a scattering of merchants completed the *Swan's* passenger list. The convoy vessels, bound for ports in the British Isles, showed a different sort of passenger—invalid soldiers, gouty sugar planters, wealthy island aristocrats with wives and daughters, gay at the prospect of making a great showing at home.

He encountered Atherton and Joe Beaver—alias John Castor— the latter clad in seamen's clothes again, but, as pre-arranged, gave only the merest nod of recognition. The halfbreed seemed delighted to be returning to America. Now that he was wealthy, according to his standards, the Penobscot's chief amibition was once more to see a buck deer go slipping quietly through a clump of white birches.

Mr. Isaac Bird—otherwise Jared Beetle—also had undergone sharp changes. On his release from jail two weeks back, the big mate had presented a sorry sight; filthy, bearded, and with fetter sores festering on his ankles and wrists. His whole body was lumpy with infected insect bites.

Certainly, his never very positive love for the Crown and its minions had vanished as frost from a sunny windowpane. Andrew figured the mate must be still a-bed after his Homeric carouse of the night before. Beetle had kept half of Falmouth awake until near midnight. Naturally, he hadn't been able to deny poor Beetle a few pounds with which to celebrate his enlargement, though God knew what he could find attractive in the tawdry wenches who in the early evening rolled their hips about Charlotte Square.

The Trident's taproom was fairly overflowing with red-and-blue uniformed officers toasting their luck at leaving such a triple-cursed, dull, sweltering plague-spot as His Majesty's Colony of Jamaica.

A yellow-faced captain with brilliant green revers to his tunic was announcing with bibulous gravity, "Aye, you look on a fortunate fellow. I'm the last of ten line officers in my battalion. We all came out in '73." He raised his cup. "Well, here's to 'em—Smollett, Thompson, Bridges, and all the rest."

A very thin major of artillery nodded. "Can't believe I'm pulling out on me own feet and not pickled in a cask of rum."

"The devil take Jamaica, and all the rest of the West Indies for that matter! Why, in God's name, do we send our best blood out here to rot and die?" The speaker was a mottle-faced, middle-aged naval officer with a loose mouth and hair gone gray years before its time. "Wish we were going home—"

"America ain't so bad, they say—stab me if it is," the artilleryman said. "Collins vows the ladies of Philadelphia are postively prodigal of their affections."

On the tavern's upper floor contractors and officers were cursing their servants, urging them strap up and get the dunnage down to the *Swan*.

"Where are you bound?" the engineer queried of the purple-faced naval officer.

"Lord knows. My orders read for Halifax." Gloomily the officer in blue stared into the bottom of his leathern jack of porter. "I'll damned well freeze to death in those latitudes after my blood's been so thinned out down here."

"Who's for Savannah? You, Mordaunt?" They turned to the yellow-face captain.

"Aye, as a replacement for the 60th—they've had the summer fever bad in Savannah. Well, it's a cheering thought that nothing can be worse than Jamaica." The captain banged his pewter mug on the table. "Host! Host! Fetch us a toddy. I insist, gentlemen." He turned ravaged, jaundiced features, noticed the big doctor from Savannah-la-Mar moodily sipping a glass of Malaga. "I say, Doctor, you must join us," Captain Mordaunt invited.

"A thousand thanks, sir, but I'm on the point of leaving to keep an appointment at the Ram's Head Ordinary." He bowed to the brilliant, heavily perspiring group. "However, I shall hope to join you anon. Perhaps then you will join me in toasting a swift voyage to America?"

Andrew had no appointment, but felt it advisable to remain as aloof as possible. Wouldn't do to have someone question his tale about hailing from Savannah-la-Mar, especially since he had never even laid eyes on the place. So far, he had successfully represented himself as intent now on winning a commission in the Royal Americans, the British Legion, or some other such Loyalist regiment.

He felt disinclined for roistering, at least not until those chests of calomel, ipecac, camphor, spirits, cordials, those boxes of alcohol, benzoin, the chests of surgeon's tools were safely landed in Philadelphia. About getting them through the British lines there, he wasn't particularly concerned—people came and went pretty much as they pleased through Lord Howe's lines.

He chuckled as he sauntered along the waterfront. To think that all those drugs had been bought for only two of the six large diamonds in that breathtaking necklace. Should he have turned the stones in? Possibly. But was this not enemy country? Did not the needs of American sailors take precedence over a parcel of British heirs who probably already had all they needed?

How odd to think that all those friendly chaps at the Trident were, in truth, enemies. Britishers weren't half bad, provided two things: You came to understand their way of thinking, and then refused to be patronized.

Perhaps the Ram's Head might be a quieter place to take supper; his last meal in Jamaica. Jerusha! The three months here had whirled by like a mad rush of leaves on the forest floor under the blast of an autumn gale.

XXV

WATERSIDE

THE Ram's Head Ordinary was a more prepossessing establishment than the Trident, Andrew perceived; less noisy, less busy. A pretty building set right at the harbor's edge, it boasted a wide verandah draped with a flaming vine of some sort. He would relish a final meal of turtle steak and okra, topped off with custard apples and some of that deliciously aromatic coffee such as could only be brewed from beans grown among the Blue Mountains back of Kingston.

Very elegant in his blue coat and waistcoat, the New Englander wandered indoors, nodded to three or four planters in soiled white ducks and a pair of burly young subalterns sitting together in the taproom. He ordered his repast served promptly. Meanwhile, he ordered another Malaga and seated himself on a small terrace sheltered by a canopy of palm leaf thatch.

On the way he paused before a mirror to reset his jabot, to make sure that his curly little beard was in order. His beard, of course, had caused a certain amount of speculation in Falmouth. Almost everyone there had raced to the conclusion that he must be French or Spanish. Whoever had heard of a bearded Englishman in the tropics?

Had England not been at war with France, Andrew readily would have given himself out as French. Now the whole port was smoking mad over an unexpected French descent upon a convoy off St. Kitts. The disaster was even now being discussed in the taproom.

"They'll pay for it, and dearly!" a choleric sea captain was prophesying.

So the French were ambushing British convoys! Andrew's step was light as he went out onto the terrace. Yes, surely the tide of this war had turned. First, Saratoga, and now the French Alliance.

Softly he hummed *"Malbrouck s'en va t'en Guerre."* The French King would dispatch to America battalion after battalion, regiment after regiment of those fine, sturdy troops which had all but beaten the British time and time again. They would have won, the historians claimed, had His Most Christian Majesty's troops been led by real officers instead of a corps of King Louis' dissolute, drunken noblemen. In America, with experienced Continental officers to advise the French Army, a British defeat must follow swiftly, surely.

When he thought of how much sea power now was ranged on the new republic's side, his Malaga tasted like Olympian nectar. In short order the great seventy-five, hundred, and hundred and fifty gun French ships-of-the-line would drive off the dogged British blockade, would free the American men-of-war held prisoner in home ports. Cannons, ammunition, and canvas would again become available to the hard-pressed shipyards building America's swift frigates, brigs and sloops. And, by God, he'd sail on one of them. The Marine Committee couldn't entertain its grudge forever. Verily, the future did look rosy tonight!

With the falling of darkness the Ram's Head Ordinary reverberated with activity. In the kitchen kettle lids clashed pleasantly and out in the inn's rear courtyard a slave was splitting wood. On a street below the terrace heavy-footed oxen were still dragging freight down to the loading jetty. Out on the mirror-like harbor the crew of a barge was singing plaintively as they pulled back for still more merchandise.

It was grand to be going to sea again.

"Supper is sarved, sar." A Negro waiter bowed almost double before him.

Warmed by the Malaga, Andrew set down his glass and went in to his table. To keep himself company, he picked up a tattered copy of the *Jamaica Mercury & Kingston Advertiser*.

Without particular interest he learned that

"Jonathan Swigard, having completed a proper APPARATUS for the purpose of manufacturing tobacco, begs leave to acquaint the public that he has for sale at his house, the corner of White Street and Luke Lane, a quantity of SHAG and SAFFRON CUT prepared from the belt of leaf and equal in quality to any imported from Europe. Retail price 3/9 per lb. boxes.

"Samples in papers of one Ryal each to be had at the Gazette and New Printing Offices.

c.t.f."

Suddenly Andrew's disinterest vanished. It was reported that a force of His Majesty's Loyal American troops, together with a force of Indians, had attacked by surprise and had killed all the settlers in a place called Wyoming in the State of Pennsylvania. That was not good reading. But he took heart when he read:

"It is rumored that a powerful French Fleet under a certain Count d'Estaing hath dropp'd Anchor off Sandy Hook in America with intent of Blockading ye Port of New York."

Jerusha! The British in New York under blockade? Good, let them taste the humiliation of not being free to come and go. It came, clearer than ever, that if ever the new nation were to become strong and prosperous, her ports must be kept open—no privateers could do that, nor any little State navy either—only a powerful national fleet.

A wild impatience set his fingers to drumming. Well, he was on his way back now, back to the *Trumbull*.

A party of Naval men and their military friends came tramping into the dining room, hung their tricornes and sword belts to a series of wooden pegs.

"Dash it all," one of them was rumbling, "what the devil *is* the Parliament thinking of? If the Dutch and Spanish really have come in, we have lost America."

"They won't declare war. Won't dare. Don't believe it."

"Fact, though," grunted the Naval officer. "Shouldn't wonder but we get attacked here 'most any day."

Andrew became so absorbed in the talk that, when a party entered through another door, he didn't even look at them. It was only when a man's voice said, "Pray be seated, Madam," that, mechanically, Andrew's gaze swung in his direction. His scalp tingled and he blinked in utter astonishment. There, slipping into a chair directly opposite to him, was Minga Allen!

His face muscles froze. Too much Malaga, of course. Minga was dead. At the same time he sensed that this was no miracle. Everything had hinged on that bracelet.

He half arose and his lips formed the word, "Minga!" but no sound issued. Lord, but she was lovely! He'd forgotten the rich tints in her chestnut hair, the healthy glow of her complexion.

Her face suddenly gone a brilliant red, she stared at him. Fortunately, her elderly escort had turned aside to greet an acquaintance. She, too, half rose in her chair, smiled. "That beard isn't very becoming, Andrew," was what she said.

Suddenly the warmth went out of her eyes. Andrew knew that she had remembered the barrier. He sat back in his chair, spread his palms above the table, shrugged a little. Should she choose, a rope would be about his neck come daybreak. This time there was no chance of getting away. That knot of sturdy officers was between him and the door.

Minga's wide mouth closed, compressed itself. Twice she drew breath. "I—I must. He isn't in uniform. He's an enemy, a spy. He'll tell all he's seen here when he gets back." For a third time she caught her breath. His dark eyes were very intent, not pleading at all. Andrew wouldn't plead, not even to save himself. A memory returned to her of those miserable hours at Hawthorn Hall, when she had deemed him dead, hunted down and hanged.

Here was a man, a whole stalwart, vital being. In importance what did a phantom crown mean by comparison?

When Andrew saw Minga exhale, he guessed that, sure enough, she wasn't going to turn him in. He smiled, swung eyes to the terrace, and under cover of his napkin held up two fingers. The bright outline of her lips inquired, "In two hours' time?"

When he had nodded, Minga almost couldn't bear the ecstasy of finding him alive and well, despite that horrid black beard which made him look very like the freebooter he must be at heart. Her eyes sought her plate. No. She'd not turn Andrew in. After all, he believed so firmly in the rights of the colonies as to suffer much for them.

But most certainly, Minga Allen would not, could not have more to do with a disloyal subject of His Majesty, the King.

Minga could discover only one real justification for planning to go downstairs to that end of the Ram's Head verandah which was shaded by great festoons of bougainvillea. This would be the very last time she would ever see Andrew Warren.

Of course, she *was* mighty curious to know how he'd come to be so elegantly turned out, but that was beside the point. She knew very well there was no excuse for consorting with an enemy of the Crown. Certainly Papa would never have condoned such a dereliction, even if it was only to say "good-bye."

Was the hand of Providence to be discerned in their meeting like this? She wanted to think so, yet it was entirely logical that they meet. The convoy ships and the *Swan* all were sailing from Falmouth and Falmouth was not exactly a metropolis. A corvette flying the homeward bound pennant would protect the *Serpentine* on her two months' or longer voyage to England.

As from her bedroom window she studied the stars, she wondered what England would be like. Would the island prove as lovely and home-like as she had used to think? Would the English take her unto themselves? Would they? During the past months she had had sound cause to revise, to modify certain expectations.

Poor Aunt Adelina! If only she had credited Mr. Hamilton's urgent warnings. But she hadn't. Sir George had sent word he was returning to discuss a "matter of business." Knowing this, wild horses could not have torn that icily passionate woman away from Hawthorn Hall. If only she had read the profound effect the intelligence of Henry Thorne's so-called suicide had had upon the blacks of the estate. All the day following the tragedy even a blind man could have sensed that undercurrents had begun to run. The house slaves moved slowly, were unprecedentedly silent, almost furtive.

Poor Chloë! She had hardly recognized the confidante that awful dawn of the King's birthday. Gone were the mustee's silks and jewels. In her coarse, seersucker blouse and skirt she resembled a cane field drab, and she had tied her hair up in a handkerchief like any girl of the waterfront.

"Don't cry out!" she had breathed. "I've got things to tell you, Mistress Allen."

"But I don't wish your confidence—"

"Please listen. As God judges us all, you *got* to listen!"

By the foot of the great staircase in Hawthorn Hall Minga had stood, still stunned by Adelina Moffat's ghastly news.

"Mistress Allen," the mustee had cried in a hurried, husky voice. "Don't anybody on Moffat's Penn but me know what happened to Mr. Thorne. He never killed himself."

"Chloë! How dare you—"

"Because it's God's truth, Ma'am," had come the simply effective reply. "First Sir Tom and then poor Harry."

"Chloë, I can't listen to such wicked lies!"

The mustee had taken her hand. "You *know* I ain't lying. You're good and your heart is pure. Mistress Allen, believe me, you've got to leave here right away!"

"But—but, Chloë, why?"

"You always been kind and gentle with me. You hated it when Mrs. Moffat shamed me so—I could see that."

The mustee had shivered and her voice had grown venomous.

"Please leave, *some time today!*"

"Why?"

"I can't tell you, Mistress. Indeed I can't. But you will go?"

In the dim light Minga had nodded. "Yes. I had already planned to leave, but not so soon. You see—I—I, well, I haven't any money."

In the gray light Minga was conscious of the mustee's eyes ringed with white. "If you had money, would you leave today?"

Strangely, the conviction that the manager had not killed himself grew and grew. Who then had murdered him? She had found an answer for that, too.

"Yes. I'll walk off during the midday napping hours."

"Then take this." Chloë had pushed forward a handkerchief heavy with contents.

"But what—?"

"Things I don't want any more—trinkets I don't want to remember—nor how I earned them in Port Royal, Kingston, and Spanish Town."

From the feel of the bundle Minga had swiftly and correctly guessed that it contained the jewelry which, subconsciously, she had envied more than once.

"But, Chloë, you'll need those."

"Not in the Cockpit Country," the mustee muttered. "Please,

Mistress Allen, don't you stay in Jamaica. Go home, or you'll find yourself cruel and dirtied—like 'Delina.

"Folks say 'Delina was just like you when she came out from England, and it wasn't Sir Tom spoilt her. It's doing the same thing, seeing the same people, eating the same food day after day. It drives some people vile, and when they've power—"

Before she had quite realized it, the mustee was gone, swiftly, quietly, like a feather blown through an open doorway.

As Mr. Hamilton had predicted, Mr. Strudwick had proved a good man—and helpful. He asked hardly a question, but supplied her with a riding mule and a mulatto hunter as guide.

When, later, she heard what had happened at Hawthorn Hall, she had felt much as she had the morning after that terrible night beside the Hudson.

Minga pressed a packet in the front of her dress—that same place in which, a lifetime ago it seemed, she had secreted a pearl necklace. The packet still contained an amazing assortment of rings and brooches, most of them devoid of taste, but set with some fine small stones. They should be more than enough to see her comfortably established in England.

From below came a sound of feet slowly pacing. Back and forth, back and forth.

All at once Minga Allen stopped thinking, stopped reasoning, let her feet carry her whither they were so eager to run. Though all this was utterly illogical, disloyal and rash, she went out on the verandah.

He was waiting, arms held wide apart. "My own love—" he cried softly. "Here, my darling, here."

"Yes—Andrew. Yes! Yes! Yes!" His arms closed about her and then the verandah's palm thatched canopy swayed; hundreds of stars came rushing down from the heavens to swim in graceful undulations before her close-shut eyes.

Said he after a while, "You'll order your baggage transferred aboard the *Swan*?"

"A bride's things belong with her husband's, don't they?" she sighed and for quite a while all was rapturous silence.

I

ELLIOTT'S RANGERS

Now that Zubly's Ferry lay behind and that danger of a British ambush had been removed, thanks to Count Pulaski's impetuous lancers, the troops composing General Lincoln's van walked freer. Nevertheless their eyes probed continually each summer-bleached thicket and patch of woods.

Alistair Bryson, Senior Lieutenant of Elliott's Carolina Rangers, didn't ease up after leaving the Ferry. His smallish, dark blue eyes kept lancing deep into the shadows beyond the gray-green tatters of Spanish moss dripping from the giant live oaks on either side of the road.

Under the noonday sun yellow-red dust kept beating up and sifting about. Sweating in heavy, knee-long hunting shirts of undyed homespun the rangers were growing thirsty.

"God damn it," one called, "find us a spring, Lootenant. Got more dirt in my gullet than ye'll find on a New Englander's farm."

Alistair glanced over his shoulder. "What ails ye?" he queried, grinning. "Can you no' walk half a league wi'out bawling for water like a calf for its mother?"

The lean brown-faced men slouching along, with rifles carried any which way, guffawed.

"Ye ain't so fur wrong, Mr. Bryson," snorted the black-bearded man. "Damn me if I'd mind taking a long pull at a well-filled teat right now. Haw! Haw!"

Lieutenant Alistair Bryson deliberated a rebuke but, familiar now with the ways of militia and other irregular troops, he knew it would only evoke more witticisms. Aye, it took more than a wee bit o' managing to handle these lowland riflemen.

Why had the Laird no' seen fit to gi'e him the command over a cadre o' backcountry Scots? Wi' a few more sergeants and men like MacNair, Fitzhugh, Cameron, and Gillis, the Second Company of Colonel Elliott's Carolina Rangers could accomplish a deal.

The fringes of his leggings tapping his calves, he swung along, yearned anew for the kilts he had so unwillingly abandoned on accepting Colonel Elliott's invitation to a commission. Losh! these

311

buckskins were hotter than hot, and plagued a man the way they stiffened when they got wet.

Glancing back at the struggling, dust-covered company, he tried to discover two rangers dressed exactly alike, though he knew it was useless. These free walking, unshaven and hopelessly profane fighters wore linsey-woolsey, homespun, duroy, seersucker, linen, buckskin—anything that would hide their thin and scrawny bodies.

The only hint of uniformity was to be found in their muskets, Brown Besses captured in the *Aeolus*, British supply ship. Their slings, however, had been adjusted as fancy dictated; also their cartridge boxes. He could tell quite distinctly where the royal monogram, "GR" executed in brass, had been ripped away. The shiny black leather traced the outline.

A freckled youth came sidling up and, for a wonder, made a vague gesture intended as a salute. "Say, Mister, how fer is it into Savanny? I'd sho' admire to pick me off a couple of Lobster-backs afore my tail feathers drags in the dust."

Alistair pulled off his rabbit's fur cap and mopped a sunburned forehead. "Ye must ha' patience, lad. We'll no' sight Savannah this day. We have no' yet established contact wi' General MacIntosh. And by the bye, ye'd best stop pulling at yer water bottle."

All afternoon the march continued through a war-ravaged farm land. Everywhere burnt farms and empty fields attested the savagery of the conflict which had scourged the Georgia-South Carolina border for two interminable years. In lazy billows more reddish-yellow dust drifted upwards, settled into the gray beards of moss.

"Where at are them foreigners we heered about, Lootenant?" a gap-toothed ex-blacksmith demanded.

"They'll be landing below Savannah, Leeson, so the Colonel says. We'll no' be meeting them for a day or so maire."

Despite the heat, the swarming flies and the dust, most everybody was in high spirits. Hadn't Augustine Prevost, the British General, been driven back into Savannah? Wasn't the great French fleet and an even greater army sailing up the Savannah, flushed with victories over the enemy at Grenada and St. Vincent?

Alistair wondered. All Charleston had buzzed when the Viscount of Fontanges, all gold orders, lace and fine airs, aide to General Count d'Estaing and Adjutant-General of the Expeditionary Force, had appeared in the trim Frigate *Amazon*.

Great crowds had lined Prince Street, waving and hallooing like lunatics when M. Plombard, King Louis XVI's minister to the new nation, M. Gerand, the French Consul in Charleston, and Governor Rutledge, himself, rode to meet the emissary. They had deemed it an amusing bit of foreign foolishness that the Viscount of Fontanges and Mr. Gerand should kiss each other, first on one cheek and then on the other; and then had shaken hands during a solid five minutes.

There were, of course, plenty of French-speaking people in Charleston, yet the accent of Colonel Dejean, a swaggering dragoon of the Condé regiment, sounded unfamiliar. His perpetual string of blasphemy was as terrifying as it was ample.

The populace, too, had cheered Major-General Benjamin Lincoln, entrusted by the Congress with the defense of the Southern States. He and the Viscount had presented an odd contrast, Alistair recalled. The French nobleman, thin and waspish-looking, in his perfectly curled wig, spotless white uniform and orders and decorations which glistened like a sunlit windowpane after a thunderstorm; General Lincoln heavy and round in the body, face a-gleam with sweat. His dusty, well-worn regimentals were wrinkled and showing white-edged sweat rings under the armpits.

All in all, the American commanding officer hadn't presented too prepossessing a picture when, with hand extended, he came shambling forward, gray eyes restless with uncertainty, to greet King Louis' emissary.

The Continental general had spruced up a bit, though, when the Charleston Artillery's cannon began firing salutes and the people had commenced to cheer Congress and Louis XVI, King of France.

Brass-ankles, artisans, laborers, planters and merchants had cheered more wildly than ever when they learned that the whole British squadron at Tybee—the *Rose, Fowey, Keppel, Germain,* and *Comet*—had been sent pelting back up the Savannah River in search of shelter under British guns mounted on the bluffs before the town. The H.M.S. *Experiment* had been forced to run out to sea—all Charleston remembered the *Experiment,* 54, and the terrible punishment she had endured, back in '76, when brave Colonel Moultrie's batteries had come within an ace of sinking her.

Abruptly, Alistair roused himself from his abstraction. The 2nd Carolina Infantry up ahead had come to a halt. Vaguely their light blue tunics and white crossbelts wove an irregular pattern through the haze of dust.

"Halt and fall oot," Alistair Bryson ordered. "But dinna stray! Sergeants, I'll hold ye responsible."

Gladly, the men sought the side of the road, flung themselves flat among the late fall flowers. As for Alistair, he remained standing, one hand idling with the warm brass hilt of Feyther's claymore; the one the old man had borne so bravely, but so disastrously, at Culloden.

Alistair had vowed never to be parted wi' it. He had come to love the over-heavy, yet well forged weapon he had worn as sergeant o' the Wateree Company o' militia. Sir Henry Clinton's Grenadiers hadna' prevailed against it.

Aye, the claymore should form a part o' the Bryson legend. Hadna' his grandsires wielded it throughout the long and bloody feuds wi' the Fergusons o' Ben Mohr?

"Dinna lie flat i' the ground," he warned his men. "Rest ye against a tree and adjust yer sling straps."

At length the Scot plucked a blade of grass to chew and squatted beside the road, but kept a lively look-out that none of his brown-clad riflemen went slipping off into the underbrush too long. Desertion because of impatience, had long been a fatal and all-too-frequent failing with American militia.

Of sixty-seven men with which the Second Company had quitted Charleston, sixty-five were still in ranks—thanks to Sergeants MacNair, Fitzhugh, Cameron and Gillis. Callously, they had driven back into the column those fainthearted, lazy, or uxorious militiamen who showed signs of losing interest in this campaign.

So the French were about ready to land? Major Rogowski of General Count Pulaski's mess had stated this to be the case. Colonel Laurens, surprisingly grave despite the current optimism of the American forces, had, inexplicably, detailed the senior lieutenant of Elliott's Rangers as aide to the ebullient Pole.

Resplendent in his wine-colored lancer tunic, the Polish Count had drunk a curious toast: "To my Legion, Messieurs! We mus' march fast if we are to defeat *Messieurs les Français* in the winning of glory."

There, thought the backcountry Scot, was one officer he wouldn't have minded serving with. Casimir, Count Pulaski, was all fire, but still an officer well-schooled in warfare.

Aye, Count Pulaski was all soldier, all willingness to fight. The aides gossiped that the Pole was forever plaguing General MacIntosh for permission to ride off on this or that bold exploit. But ruthless General MacIntosh—that dour, practical fighting man—never had given in.

"You're our eyes, Pulaski," Lincoln had explained in his nasal accents. "And I am damned and double-damned if I'll march against Prevost blind as any bat. If the French wish to attack first, let them; God speed, say I."

Actually, the blunt, tough old New Englander was praying that Mounseers d'Estaing, Dillon and de Noailles *would* come up and burr the rough edges off the Redcoats. General Prevost and his men were a plagued, prickly lot; he had discovered that last spring. The poor, weak little Colonies in America had been fighting this war near four starved, anxious years now. Why not let the Johnny-come-lately French make up for lost time? Their metal was white, their braid bright. Maybe a little Georgia rain and red dirt wouldn't do 'em any harm.

"Heyo! Heyo! Three cheers for the General!"

General Lincoln appeared riding at a walk along the column. Behind him his staff officers, French, Polish and Yankee, were sweating and mopping their faces. Carefully, Ben Lincoln looked over his army; it was the biggest he had ever commanded, over two thousand men. Good soldiers, most of them; the best were the 5th South Carolina—sturdy Continentals. Then there were Carolina state troops who only needed "to be shooted over a leetle," as acid, guttural General von Steuben would have put it.

General Lincoln let his charger determine its pace. MacIntosh and Pulaski were up ahead. They'd dispatch gallopers if anything untoward was in the offing.

Yes, the solid blue-and-white clad Continentals were his pride—the troops he was really counting on in this campaign. 'Twas a crying pity that so few South Carolinians had been willing to forego the easy discipline and gay uniforms of the State service for real soldiering.

The General smiled when his tall bay came up with Elliott's lanky riflemen lying flat on their arses or chewing cold rations below the great gray oaks. Crikey! If only this army boasted a few more riflemen such as these. Somehow, the British never had caught on how to cope with sharpshooters.

Alistair Bryson jumped up, saluted. Discipline and the honors of war were the roots of success, so Major Barnard Elliott, Antoinette's doughty cousin, had always said.

Night was falling before the main body of the American Army came up with its advance guard. When they halted, multitudes of mosquitoes descended like minute, whining demons. That this wasn't a good camp site, Alistair could tell at half a glance. Angrily, he strode back and forth, counting his malodorous, caustic-tongued riflemen.

"Take to yon ridge," he ordered. "Sergeant Campbell, build smudges to windward."

The men stacked arms, the Scottish sergeants grimly counting their weapons.

"Sixty-four, sir-r," Sergeant Gillis reported. "We ha' lost yon

ill-savoured cur o' a McCoy. I dinna thocht yon lowlander would be
here come the dark."

Cornmeal, slightly tainted beef—lugged all the way from Charleston—and sweet potatoes appeared from various haversacks.
Campfires commenced to give off acrid blue smoke. Lieutenant
Alistair Bryson commenced his rounds, while keeping one eye out
for a dry hollow in which to sleep.

Men sprawling beneath the trees roused, rolled over and sat up;
the horses of a battery of field guns parked down the road raised
their heads and cocked their ears. The General and his staff reined in
and listened.

Off to the southeast had sounded the very faint, yet clearly
recognizable, report of a cannon. Another followed, then a whole
salvo of dull reverberations. The men in that dusty column stared at
each other, puzzled.

"Oh, God damn!" A subaltern of the 2nd Carolina dashed his hat
in fury to the ground. "Know what that means? *The French have
beat us into Savannah!*" Furiously, he glared about, his over-
sensitive features suffused. "Who'll come with me and get into the
fight before it's too late?"

A number of young sergeants and infantrymen raised a cheer,
began adjusting their knapsacks.

A handsome corporal called out, "Let's go, boys, else old
Granny Lincoln will rob us of our fun. He's too cautious by half!"

A red-faced, beefy captain came running back along the road,
awkwardly, because his sheathed sword kept interfering with his
legs. "What the hell are you up to there?"

"It's the French, sir!" cried the lieutenant excitedly. "We-all
don't aim to let the French beat us into Savannah!"

Other infantrymen promptly sang out, "No, suh, we're goin' on
ahaid! That Yankee gen'ral's slow." "Lead us, Captain, and we'll
twist them Redcoats' tails till they hollers like scalded cats."

"Get back off the road! Don't be crotch-blistered fools!" the
captain panted. "It's above fifteen miles to Savannah and we ain't
sure the French have even landed yet."

"But what's that shootin' then, suh?"

"Ships fighting down river, that's what it is—Colonel Laurens
said so."

Crestfallen and with obvious ill-grace the subaltern saluted.
"Yes, sir, Captain. It's as you say, sir."

Soon the distant cannonading stopped. As stars commenced to
lance through the green-black canopy overhead, the bitter smell of
camp fires stung the soldiers' eyes, set them to coughing as they
tried to cook and to fight mosquitoes at the same time.

Sergeants Cameron and Gillis swung up, heavy Highland clay-mores dragging at the brass-studded baldrics supporting them. The effect of these weapons with the hunting shirts and fur caps bordered on the grotesque. They saluted gravely, then, when Alistair beck-oned them, sank onto the ground beneath a pitch pine. A bivouac fire flickering a few yards away revealed Cameron's bold black brows and craggy features gone peeling scarlet from overexposure.

"Wull, Alistair, and is it yer opeenion the Froggies ha'e stolen a march on us? Could it be that Lachlan MacIntosh and yon sweet-scented macaroni frae Poland ha'e been ambushed?" Gillis was a small, active man with sharp, inquisitive features and a short beard of burnished bronze.

"No, Alan. 'Twas some ships fighting—like the Colonel said."

"I still think the French ha'e done us in."

Alistair remembered something Feyther once had said. "Prince Charlie's greatest mistake was to imagine the French were eager to land in Scotland back in '44, my lad. Old Louis, the grandfeyther o' the present Louis, promised us the world and a', but never did a French soldier set foot i' the British Isles."

"Well, aiblins Louis the XVI is different from Louis the XV?" Cameron ventured.

Alistair nodded, though he didn't know a great deal about the rising for Prince Charles Edward Stuart, Pretender to the Throne of Scotland; Feyther had never waxed talkative on the subject.

One thing seemed sure; a French fleet *was* in the river.

"We'll make anither round, Alistair, afore we set the night watch," Gillis said, arising. "Come, Donald."

On the still warm pine needles which would prevent the earth's chill from striking through and stiffening his muscles, Alistair Bryson relaxed, his Pennsylvania-made rifle primed and ready by his side.

Staring up into the dark tracery of branches, it was easy to conjure up the face of Antoinette Proveaux, she who had become his wife. " 'Tis a lucky dog ye are, lad. What sae sonsie a lass can find tae love in a great clumsy lummox like Alistair Bryson, ye'll never fathom."

It hadn't been pleasant to remain drilling and drawing equipment, nor to send Antoinette, gay, vivacious and adoring as ever, off on a visit with her cousin Théo Habersham. Hesperidée, the Habersham property, he had decided, lay far enough up the Ossabaw and distant enough from the Savannah to deserve no undue attention from the enemy. Losh! Peter Habersham, senior, must have been canny to foresee so much.

'Toinette! His whole solid body craved, yearned, for the fragile softness of his wife. When this campaign was done and the Hanoverian's troops should find themselves crushed and scattered, when the whole of the Southern colonies had been freed of the dreadful fear under which they had dwelt going on four years, then he and 'Toinette might begin searching for that farm they had dreamt of.

Aye, 'twould be a farm, too—nothing so ambitious as a plantation. At least to start with. 'Twas ever best to chase rabbits before hunting for bear, as they said along the Wateree in the back country of South Carolina. Plantation? He had never liked so pretentious a term, never would.

Suddenly Bryson sat up. On the road below had sounded the brisk *clip-clop!* of hooves. An aide, a light cavalryman by his gay yellow tunic and horsehair-crested helmet, came picking his way along the track.

"Is this Elliott's Rangers?"

"Aye." A lantern flashed, showed Sergeant Gillis' bearded face. "What's amiss?"

"Point out your lieutenant—Dyson, or something like that. He's wanted at Colonel Laurens' tent."

II

HESPERIDÉE

OSSABAW CREEK shone like a river of brass. The early autumn sun was so hot that the outlines of trees marching languidly down to the water's edge looked like tired cattle coming to drink.

For all that, it was very pleasant here at Hesperidée, Antoinette Bryson was musing. In many ways the estate was reminiscent of Cousin Elliot Barnard's plantation on the Santee River. Down here, however, the money crop was rice instead of cotton.

Antoinette reckoned the Habershams must be very rich indeed. On all sides in the lowlands near Ossabaw Creek rice fields, only a few inches deep, stretched away for acres and acres. It was yonder bred those vast swarms of mosquitoes which, after sundown, sometimes rendered life a misery.

All afternoon the humidity had increased until now the slightest exertion set perspiration to running in rivulets. She cast a sidewise glance at Théo Habersham. Her cousin was sewing a fichu onto a new gown and sitting under one of those great moss hung live oaks which, by accident, had planted themselves by twos and threes clear down to the water's edge.

"This *is* a lovely spot, *chérie*," murmured Mrs. Bryson. "Look, one may count three, no, four, reaches of Ossabaw Creek before it joins with the Savannah."

"I am pleased you admire our view," Théo Habersham nodded, absently ran fingers through a mass of fine, golden-yellow hair. "I do wish Peter would come. Here it is Saturday and still no word."

"He will return," Antoinette said quietly. "Something must have delayed him."

"Oh, I suppose so, but he's so absent-minded, so vague." Théo bit petulantly at a thread.

Antoinette watched her. *Dieu!* Her cousin was beautiful. The saints must have worked hard to fashion so perfect a face and form.

"It's just like Peter to go wandering off to Charleston at a time like this. Did you hear those cannon again, just now?"

"Yes, Théo." Antoinette's faintly olive-hued features contracted. She had recognized that diapason grumbling noise with a shudder. They reminded her all too vividly of those awful days during which Sir Henry Clinton and Admiral Hyde Parker had come within an ace of capturing Charleston. She reckoned she would always hate thunderstorms.

The cannonade reminded her, also, of poor, learned Lieutenant Nat Coffin, he who had been killed so needlessly after Fort Sullivan had beaten off the British fleet.

Those days during the siege had been exciting, stimulating; what with so many new faces about Charleston, so many new regimentals, so many wild rumors there had come an end to the lovely, lazy life she and all the Proveauxs had always known.

It was cannon which had scattered the family so far and wide. Grand'mère now was living up the Cooper with Uncle Marcel; other cousins, uncles and aunts had become scattered from Beaufort to Cape Fear and as far as Wilmington. Louis Proveaux, her father, however, had elected to remain in Charleston, in an effort to keep at least a fraction of his once-great fortune intact.

Antoinette lay back on the seat, eyes fixed on the glassy river. Incredible that two years now had passed since Desire Harmony Bennett, that strange, gay, brave New England girl, had appeared from nowhere only to vanish so inexplicably during the height of the siege.

Where was Desire now? Was she even still alive? Apparently the earth had swallowed her up, she and her unborn child. No trace of her had ever been discovered. Grand'mère had made the most pertinent observation, *"Ma chère, c'est la guerre."*

Théo reached for her handkerchief, whereupon the little black boy who sat at her feet began guiltily to agitate a fan he had neglected in favor of catching some bluebottle flies.

"I do declare, 'Toinette," drawled Théo Habersham, "it will be very fine to see the British taken, or driven out of Savannah. Peter has been anxious and cross as two sticks ever since the town fell."

Well, everyone along the Coast had been anxious, for that matter, once Major-General Augustine Prevost had captured Savannah, so secure on its bluffs overlooking the yellow-green river. The town itself, of course, had not made much of a prize; the Redcoats had won only a bare four hundred and thirty houses, a single big church—Christ Church—and some warehouses and wharves.

A hot wind began to blow from the rice fields, bringing a stale, rather sour reek. Supplementing the efforts of her slave, Théo fanned herself. If the French ever did land, Peter must invite some of their officers to quarter at Hesperidée. With this exciting prospect she commenced to conjecture.

Speaking French as their mother tongue, she and 'Toinette should cut a wide swathe through the corps of officers. Best part of it was there'd be no grounds to clash on. She, Théo, was as *vive* and blonde and carefree as Antoinette was brunette, *petite* and decorous.

A fine-looking girl, was 'Toinette—even if she was her cousin— as delicate and softly rounded as a painting by Boucher. What 'Toinette found so lovable in that serious, slow-spoken, raw-boned Scottish gawk she's married, the *bon Dieu* alone knew, and He wasn't likely to explain.

Petulantly, she pursed lips, blew from her damp forehead a stray lock of hair. How unnaturally still the afternoon was. Even 'way down here by the creek could be heard a chicken's frantic squawking. Presently, a leggy Negro boy appeared streaking down the driveway in pursuit of a fat white hen. Further away sounded the dull thumping noise of a rice mill at work.

Théo commenced to smile to herself. Oh, la! la! Wouldn't it be fun to hear fresh news, to listen to new tales, to discuss Monsieur Voltaire and that outrageous liberal Rousseau? What regiments would be making this expedition? Peter's uncle, Colonel Joseph Habersham, was very much in the know, but he would only smile, even when Peter tried to find out.

Colonel Cambray, who had been to the Court at Versailles, claimed that the French wore the most gorgeous uniforms imaginable. Privately, Théo hoped they would prove discreet in their *affaires du coeur*.

'Toinette, the silly little goose, would probably play Mademoiselle Ni-touche. All on account of that husband of hers. How desperately in love they were—both of them. Unfashionably so.

The hen's shrieking ended with graphic suddenness.

Théo yawned, disclosing sparkling teeth. Peter, to be sure, was a good man, but so intolerably dull! How unexpected that she and 'Toinette both should have married slow-thinking, slow-moving men—a question of opposites, perhaps?

"Maum? Please look! Look down dere!" The little black boy, round-eyed, was indicating the estuary of Ossabaw Creek.

"*Mon Dieu!*" Théo sat bolt upright. On the Savannah the bowsprit of a very tall vessel was moving slowly into sight at the entrance to the creek.

Théo's heart commenced to thud. Yonder certainly sailed the biggest ship she had ever beheld. Though the hot wind, here, was fitful, it must be blowing strong enough up the Savannah to drive this lumbering man-of-war against the tide.

"Cherub!" she cried so suddenly that Antoinette waked, gave a little "Oh!" and started up, spilling her bright little spools of silk, her scissors, her tambour embroidery onto the ground. "Run! Tell Mr. Pennfeather to ready the barge!"

"*Mon Dieu*, Théo. Why, why, that ship is bigger than St. Michael's Church! Oh, Théo, it is the French! The French!" She jumped up, hugged her larger cousin. "Théo! Théo! The French are here! Oh, Alistair will be *so* pleased!"

From between the four tall white pillars fronting Hesperidée appeared a gray-haired Negro in a chocolate livery with a canary yellow vest. In monumental dignity he advanced. "Maum, de boy he not understand?"

"Oh, damn! I said to order out the barge," Théo snapped. "Immediately, Caesar." She held out her hand to Antoinette. "Come, it can't be much hotter on the creek. Let us examine that vessel."

"But, Théo, suppose she is British?" Antoinette protested. "All big ships in America are British."

"Not this one," Théo burst out and, gathering up her voluminous petticoats, ran like any barmaid down to the landing.

Minutes later, Hesperidée's barge—robin's-egg blue trimmed in white—pushed off from that stout new landing pier Peter Habersham had erected to accommodate rice ships which would be sure to come once the war was over.

Six stocky Negroes, some with rice husks still in their wool, sat at the oars, grinning expectantly. Well pleased to be free of their usual toil, they handled the barge's nine-foot sweeps as easily as walking sticks. Antoinette sensed their pride in the smart fashion in which they shipped the white, scarlet-tipped oars.

The under-overseer, a hollow-eyed young Welshman, silently took his place at the tiller.

"Get on! Pennfeather, get on!"

"Yes, Madam. Where?"

"Mrs. Bryson and I wish to overtake, and to view, a ship ascending the river."

In the shade of a light blue awning, the two young women pushed and prodded the cushions on a stern transom into comfortable positions.

"Ready? Forward, all." With his right hand the under-overseer with a little wooden mallet struck a piece of highly polished wood. The slaves reached forward.

"Row!" *Tock! tock!* went the mallet. The rowers' heads went back, their tendons glistened as they hooked splay toes over braces designed for the purpose. Evenly, six blades sank into the muddy water. The barge commenced to glide away from the shore.

How, with British foraging parties systematically commandeering or destroying every small boat in the countryside, Peter Habersham had been able to retain this barge, was a mystery Antoinette had not yet been able to fathom. The lack of an explanation troubled her. Although many a nearby plantation house— McGillivray's, Urban's, Phoenix—had either gone up in smoke, or had been taken over during the British invasion of December last, Hesperidée had escaped molestation, let alone serious damage.

Of course, there were hardships. Every now and then a shipload of rice, exported from Hesperidée and destined for some neutral port, would be picked off by a British station ship. But, somehow, Peter had never seemed frightfully exercised over his loss, had only shrugged and sighed, "Fortunes of war, y'know."

The barge began slipping along faster, emerged from the grateful shade of the great gray oaks lining the river bank. Reluctantly, some egrets gave up wading and fishing along the shore; taking lazy alarm, they went successively flap-flapping over Ossabaw Creek, to perch like giant cotton blossoms among birds already drowsing in the shade of trees across the stream.

Antoinette, head yielding gently to the dripping, measured

rhythm of the oars, looked back at Hesperidée. What an idyllically beautiful spot Peter Habersham had selected on which to build a home for Théo! Well, so lovely a jewel deserved an adequate setting.

It stood to reason that not for many years could she and Alistair aspire to such a mansion; not that Alistair lacked ability, energy and shrewdness. Like most Scotsmen, he well knew how to make one penny do the work of three.

Antoinette smiled to herself, confidently, serenely. Some day, sure as sure could be, she and Alistair and the children that would come some day, would enjoy wide lawns sloping down to some river's edge. They, too, could afford twenty-five house servants—maybe more.

In a vague way Antoinette resented that Peter hadn't earned one farthing of the fortune which made him the greatest rice planter on the lower Savannah. In Charleston it was well known that, home in England, someone had died intestate. Finally a pair of crabbed old barristers in yellowed wigs, and wearing black suits with dirty cuffs, had appeared to inform Peter Habersham, Senior, that he had fallen heir to a most imposing fortune.

Peter's father had died shortly after—of the shock, so people claimed—and Peter, Junior, hadn't gone to England as everybody had expected; which showed unsuspected good sense. Young Peter wasn't clever, but was bright enough, tacitly, to admit the fact.

Instead, the plump young fellow had gone shopping for the most desirable bride in South Carolina. Théo Proveaux of the candy-colored hair had been his selection—and he, her mother's.

Mr. Pennfeather pressed a thin thigh against the tiller, increased the tempo of his mallet strokes. For all he looked and acted like a heart-broken greyhound, the under-overseer, too, sensed the excitement of the hour.

When a cannon roared downstream, the ladies fluttered, looked at each other.

"I was right," Antoinette said, her brown eyes larger than ever. "What we saw *was* a British ship. The French must be chasing her."

The man-of-war in question, of course, long since had passed from view and the entrance from Ossabaw Creek into the Savannah was empty except for a line of frightened blue peters beating their way upstream in ungainly flight.

"Some Canary, my dear?" As if chilled wine in Georgia weren't rarer than angel's tears, Théo ordered Cherub to open a locker built into the tiny galley's side.

Théo smiled in anticipation. On days like this a cold drink was a luxury above luxury. In the old days, before the war, schooners from time to time had sailed south, laden with great slabs of ice cut up in Massachusetts, Connecticut, and Rhode Island. Wealthy Carolinians bought all they could afford and kept the precious substance under lock and key and packed in sawdust against the blazing summer months.

A reedy point, groping out into the creek, caused the barge to detour and briefly the oar blades made soft snapping noises among shiny reeds. Blissfully Antoinette pressed the chilled wine glass first against her forehead, then against her blue-veined eyelids until she became conscious of the slaves staring in wonderment, not at her, but at the glass. None of them had ever before seen that translucent, mysterious substance known as ice.

Ta-chunk! ta-chunk! the greased leather of the oar guards thumped firmly against the tholepins.

No more cannonading came from down-river or from the direction of Savannah. Théo, sipping the sweet yellow wine, thought, "Isn't Peter exasperating? He *must* have heard about all this.

"Oh, why did God make him so damned literal, so infuriatingly slow-witted? Won't it be wonderful when the French officers come to stay? Imagine having people about who catch a joke immediately, who'll laugh at the right moment!"

Antoinette's breath caught suddenly in her throat. She sat up, pointed frantically downstream. *"Mon Dieu, Théo!"* she gasped, *"regarde là!"*

For once her cousin was startled into an awkward reaction. When Théo glanced down-river, her slender-stemmed glass slipped in her fingers, splashed wine far and wide over her pale green muslin skirt.

Mr. Pennfeather was so astonished he ran the barge smack over a half-submerged snag, to the annoyance of several muddied turtles basking upon it.

It was indeed such a sight as one would never forget. Up the Savannah, in a seemingly interminable line, was ploughing one towering battleship after another. Their sails jaundiced by a sickly sunlight, a great squadron was cruising in from the Atlantic—many-decked ships of the line, transports and frigates; their canvas and yards seemed to scrape the sky.

"Oh, if Alistair could see this!" Antoinette breathed. The slave rowers, fascinated, lay on their oars without command, goggled banjo-eyed at this incredible panorama of power.

Every so often the increasingly uneasy wind flung the French fleet's yards about, caused a great rattling and creaking when spars slewed about against their parrels.

Nearer, nearer sailed the foremost battleship, a veritable Titan among ships of war. The swish of water along her side became audible. *Magnifique* was the name emblazoned in flaming gold leaf above her hawseholes. From her stern floated what seemed, at this distance, to be a pure white flag. But Antoinette saw that sprinkled over it were many golden *fleurs-de-lis*, emblems of the Bourbon Kings of France.

III

THE ALLIES

AT A point where the current formed a convenient eddy, perhaps a hundred yards out from the shore, Mrs. Habersham ordered the trim blue and white barge to be anchored. The point formed a convenient shelter from a wind beating fitfully upstream towards Thunderbolt and Beaulieu plantation which lay some four miles nearer Savannah.

On the shore blacks, whites and Indians appeared by awed tens and twenties to gape incredulously on the mighty spectacle unfolding before their eyes.

Three, five, six great men-of-war now were bowling upstream. Some captains were busily reducing canvas, their sailors laying out on the yards and clewing up while native pilots bellowed for less speed.

In the van sailed *La Chimère*, as dainty a frigate as had ever cleared Toulon breakwater. Proudly she was flying the pennant of Major-General Charles Hector, Comte d'Estaing. She looked quite small, though, by comparison with the towering *Languedoc* 90 guns; *Tonant*, 80; *Robuste*, *César*, and *Annibal*, all mounting 74 carriage guns.

Painted to suit their captains' fancy, the hulls of the various vessels were colored gray, yellow, brown, blue, green, even pink. In stately array the armada ploughed up the river—saucy sloops, stolid brigs, plodding, round-bowed transports. There were a good many of these last.

Supply ships, a few brigs and pinks, a schooner or two, bomb ketches accompanied the more martial craft. Two or three times Antoinette's heart lifted to glimpse, among the tall ships, some smaller vessels flying either the red, white, and blue of the United States, or the bright blue and silver of the South Carolina Navy. The American ships looked like minnows, convoying a school of whales.

One four-decker of 64 guns, the *Sphynxe*, came tacking by at no great distance. Her hairy crew thrust red-capped heads far out over the side to yell indecent invitations at the barge. They were a red-faced lot, by strange contrast with the pallid faces peering over the rail of *La Bricole*, frigate.

The whole river mouth became crowded; too much so. The wind was beginning to give the sailing masters trouble, and to spare.

Théo recalled that the season of the equinox could not be far from due. It was then that mariners in these waters expected the worst of the weather.

For all their majesty, these ships of the line proved clumsy affairs. The wind blew from the barge to them so little could be heard, but on the quarterdeck of *La Truite* shone sparkles of steel; blue, red and white uniforms; white, gold and silver braid.

That handy little frigate, more maneuverable than her sister ships, came slipping by, not a hundred yards distant. In response to cheers from the onlookers ashore, the officers on her quarterdeck removed three-cornered hats, called greetings. When they noticed the barge and the two brilliantly clad ladies reclining under the canopy, two or three of them bowed profoundly. One officer even unsheathed his sword, raised it skyward in salute, and kissed its hilt.

"La, 'Toinette, have you ever beheld a more gallant gesture?" demanded Théo, though Charleston was far from devoid of such cavalier expressions.

For over an hour the French fleet sailed by, ship on ship, their sails tinted first orange, then white, and then gray, depending on the color reflected from a bank of the clouds piling up into formidable ramparts to the northeast.

Only once did the splendor of the pageant pale. That was when a chancy puff of wind blew towards the barge just as the *Provence*, ship of the line, went by, gilded poop aglow with color and her waterline bright green with weeds.

"Phew!" Théo pinched a nose carefully whitened with rice powder; the black oarsmen exchanged glances. They recognized that smell, even those who had made the middle passage twenty years and more ago. The odor was reminiscent of an abattoir out on the edge of Charleston. There, bald-headed buzzards flopped and hopped expectantly about awaiting the inevitable skull and entrails.

"Your pardon, Madam," called Mr. Pennfeather, "a rain squall I believe is approaching. Shall we put back to the landing?"

Across a suddenly leaden, then soot-black sky, darted terrific flares of lightning. The rain delayed, however, until the excursionists were entering a formal garden to the west of Hesperidée; they had only to pick up their skirts and scurry a few yards to shelter.

It was just as well. In gray, lacy torrents a downpour descended until creek and river were lost to sight. Down the lawn, the live oaks were beginning to stir, reluctantly, like gray-bearded giants plagued by insects.

In the old days Antoinette would have fled to her room, muffled her head in a bolster and lain whimpering. But no longer, not when she realized that, somewhere between Charleston and Savannah, Elliott's Rangers were on the march. Alistair, of course, was out in this ever-increasing storm, soaking, drenched.

"*Que Dieu te protège, mon cœur*," she whispered.

Brigadier-General Casimir Count Pulaski, Alistair learned, was still dressed and awake in his quarters near Great Ogeechee Ferry. The Pole was courteous and stood very straight in the center of his tent, calm as if the furious wind were not threatening momentarily to uproot his marquee for good and all. By Alistair Bryson and one Captain Jules Oradon of Heyward's Artillery, the Count was informed of General Lincoln's progress, present bivouac and intentions.

In his gray and scarlet uniform trimmed with gray squirrel's fur and high leather boots of glistening black, the cavalry general offered an odd contrast to the two Americans; Oradon in threadbare blue, a small, stoop-shouldered planter from the upper Ashley, and Bryson big and angular in his buckskin hunting shirt.

"*Bon*. My secretary has made note of what you say." Count Pulaski hesitated, tugged at his spike-sharp mustachios. "One assumes, Messieurs, that you are familiar with this terrain. That is correct?"

"Sure thing, General." Oradon nodded ponderously. "I been here a couple o' times, but Bryson, here, fought down this way all last winter. Why?"

"I am most desirous of learning the present situation of His Excellency le Comte d'Estaing. Capitaine Oradon, Lieutenant Bryson, will you have the goodness to ride at once to Thunderbolt?"

One of the Rutledge boys yawned, but fondled the smooth ivory hilt of the light scimitar as he drawled, "And you all had better warn the Mounseer he better hustle, else the Legion will surely pick Savannah clean.''

Alistair, standing tall and silent among the shadows, recognized at least a dozen of the lancer officers who came trooping into the dimly lighted headquarters tent. Among them appeared the cream of Charleston's fire-eaters, aristocrats and purse-proud young merchants.

Amid the plaudits of their ladies, they had rushed to enroll in Pulaski's Legion of Horse and for months now these lancers, dragoons, and light horse had made a great display on King Street of blue, white, and silver uniforms, of blooded horses and of expensive, imported sidearms.

Was it significant that Count Pulaski should have selected none of these for the highly difficult task of encircling Savannah and evading enemy patrols? No one knew just how far out Major-General Prevost had posted his pickets. Moreover, it was rumored that Sam McGirth's Tory partisans were ranging the back country. Hideous tales of atrocities committed by that guerilla's hellions kept filtering into the American army. Certainly, some dark and bloody pages of history were being written these days along the Georgia-South Carolina border.

Count Pulaski flashed a particularly winning smile which wrinkled an old scar marring his chin. ''On you, M. le Lieutenant Bryson, I repose especial trust that you shall reach Thunderbolt. And you, M. le Capitaine Oradon, please convey to the French officer commanding at the landing that time fights for us now like many fresh squadrons. Haste! Haste!'' His hands gestured rapidly. ''One is informed that the enemy has his earthworks not even half complete.''

One of the small-featured, small-limbed Charleston dandies came forward. The Lieutenant's offer was characteristic of his breed. ''Gentlemen, you ride on a dangerous mission. I pray you, Captain Oradon, to do me the honor, suh, of riding any of my horses you wish. Scorpion!'' he shouted. ''Dammit, Scorpion! where the devil are you?''

A cornet of lancers would have it that Alistair ride his own charger. ''She's nothing to brag on at a race meetin', suh, but she's steady, mighty steady under fire.''

''Ye ken I canna promise tae keep her safe?'' Alistair protested.

''Fie, man! I'd have left the mare at home, were I not ready to risk her.''

''Then, I'll be glad of her use. I'm no' a famous horseman.''

''Scorpion, you black bastard! Come here!''

"Yassuh?" From the shelter of a dripping pine appeared a round-eyed Negro.

"Scorpion, show this gentleman to my mounts."

"I am obleeged, sir, vastly obleeged," Captain Oradon stated. "I shall hope, Mr. Houdon, to pledge you thanks when this is over."

"Within a day or so, suh, we shall surely meet in the long room of Tondee's Tavern—it's situated on Broughton Street," young Houdon smiled. "Take Scorpion with you. He knows how to cool out these beasts of mine."

IV

THUNDERBOLT LANDING

BECAUSE the night remained stormy and black as the inside of any cow, Alistair Bryson and the captain of Heyward's Artillery found themselves a good mile upstream from Thunderbolt Landing when dawn commenced to break. Both rode in grim silence; their faces clawed by branches, their skin pitted by mosquito bites, their clothing wet through.

"A fine show we'll make at the Frenchman's tent," complained Oradon wiping his face on the end of his kerchief. Scorpion, riding bareback, looked even more disreputable.

Alistair said, "I misdoot that the Froggies stayed verra dry, either, an' they were ashore."

Captain Oradon shook his heavy, baldish head. "Mister Bryson, I'll advise ye to forget that habit of referring to our Allies as 'frogs.' After all, aren't they winning this war for us?"

"Aiblins, Captain, aiblins," Alistair admitted. "But I'll no' credit them till they land and this campaign is won."

During the slow ride about Savannah Alistair had gleaned a respectable fund of information. For instance, the British had worked like mad all night to strengthen the environs of the town; also they had withdrawn some of their men-o'-war to an anchorage above the place. Other ships were tied up to docks below the bluff—for what purpose he had no idea. Also he was aware that

General Prevost had withdrawn his scouting parties and had posted his pickets no further than a quarter-mile out of Savannah.

They were quitting the southern limits of Urban's plantation when Alistair reined in so sharply that the cornet's mare sat back on her haunches.

"What's amiss?"

"See?" The Scot was pointing through a screen of palmettoes. Out in a clearing stood a group of soldiers in soiled white uniforms. Their cuffs and epaulets were of bright green and they wore their hair dressed into long, stiff queues.

They must be foreign and very newly arrived to stay bunched like that. "Yon's a French outpost." It lent Alistair a thrill to behold the long-expected Allies on American soil.

Cautious by nature, Alistair had, all along, discounted much of what had been predicted by his father-in-law, Antoinette and the rest of her excitable, yet lovable, family.

"Sweet Jesus, what a target!" grunted Captain Oradon. "Don't them numskulls know *anything*?"

A white-clad grenadier was standing, as no soldier ever should in America, silhouetted against the horizon, his uniform glaring white and the brass buttons on his enormous cuffs winking like miniature beacons. For many moments the picket stood like an image, looked neither right nor left, then commenced tramping back and forth, as if on duty before some barracks in Europe.

"My God, Bryson, will ye look at the damn' fool? He ain't turned his head once in the last minute!"

For various reasons, it would be a long time before Alistair would forget the sight which greeted his eyes when Oradon and he rode out into a field giving a view of the hamlet of Thunderbolt.

Here, on the advice of Colonel Joseph Habersham, Colonel Cambray and Captain Gadsden, the French had elected to make their initial landing. Here the Savannah's estuary took a turn, lapped against a series of magnificent wide sand beaches.

"Well, I never!" Oradon burst out. "Will you *look* at that?"

Anchored off shore were more ships than Alistair had ever dreamed to exist.

Though the storm of the night before seemed done, the wind remained in the east and the sky remained filled with low clouds which scudded by barely above the mast tops. Restlessly, transports, men-of-war, and supply vessels sawed at their anchor lines. Small boats, pulling away from the nearer ships, rowed in a hurry. Even now the big bulk of the fleet lay far out from shore—the river mouth was well over a mile wide here and did not narrow for quite a distance upstream.

From where the two officers and Scorpion sat, they could discern a mound of baggage building up on the two rickety piers which had served Colonel William Stevens' estate. Some troops had kindled fires at the far end of the beach, were attempting to cook with wet wood. A few barges laden with frightened looking horses were pulling slowly inshore. A scattering of tents had been pitched on a little meadow and dominating them was a pavilion, bigger than the average house in Savannah.

"Well," grunted Captain Oradon, "I reckon we better try finding the commander here?"

They rode slowly down off the wooded heights and, gradually, the air became full of strange sounds, sights and smells.

Alistair felt obliged to water the cornet's mare at once. Smiling in friendly fashion at the French, they rode down past a picket who yelled something unintelligible at them, then, uncertainly, presented his musket. Alistair's goal was a fresh water brook which, after meandering across the meadow, emptied into the Savannah.

"Can you tie that?" Oradon demanded incredulously. "Stupid bugger of a picket never even tried to stop us!"

While the Americans were letting their mounts draw deep gulps of water, a barge pulled in.

"Jesus God!" Oradon burst out, staring in astonishment.

From the barge was drifting a sickening odor. As he sat watching, his feet dangling free of the stirrups, Alistair's dark blue eyes widened more and more. That the soldiers in this boat were in a dreadful state he realized with half a glance. Their once white uniforms had turned brown or green or black with filth. These Frenchmen's gaunt faces were dark with lack of shaving, their lacklustre eyes sunk deep in their skulls. Something was wrong with the teeth of most of them; their gums showed withered, and reddish-black. When these scarecrows moved, they moved heavily and their glances were incurious.

Many of the unhappy infantrymen wore no equipment and, unable to sit upright, leaned heavily against their fellows. Their dull and uncomprehending eyes considered dispassionately the greenness all about. Some were completely ragged, their grim gray skin showing through countless rips and tears and parted seams. Losh! They were in worse state than any prisoners Alistair had beheld during the last two years—and he had seen prisoners a-plenty.

When the keel of the barge grated onto the sand below the brook, Oradon commenced to curse in shocked astonishment because in callous haste sailors commenced to push or kick or toss their miserable passengers ashore, or into the water.

Two or three soldiers fell and, too weak to rise, would have drowned had not some of the grenadiers of the Hainault Regiment run in and pulled them, retching and coughing, up on the sand.

"*Ah, les misérables!* Why do they send lousy Provençals to war?" demanded a blond Norman sergeant.

"*Tiens, mon vieux*—you might be lousy, too, or worse, had you not been ashore in three whole months!"

A second barge drew in, discharged a similar cargo of miserable, malodorous humanity. Some of the Auxerre Regiment retained just barely strength to reach the shore. There they collapsed, grabbing handfuls of green weeds, which they crammed into their mouths.

Others threw themselves flat beside the brook and, weeping, drank greedily. Their weapons, Alistair noticed with concern, were in dreadful condition, rusted, damaged, lacking the ramrods and swivels.

"*Vite! Vite! Entrailles de Dieu, depêchez vous!*" Loud curses commenced to come from naval officers being rowed about in small boats; the wind was rising, bumping the clumsy barges against each other.

"Get ashore, you sacred pigs! Hurry!" Officers in spotless uniforms strode about hammering, prodding recalcitrants with tasselled walking sticks.

To Alistair Bryson the whole scene was immensely confusing. Losh! Were these the fine, stout grenadiers who were to strike King George's shackles from America?

His stomach heaved as a pair of light infantrymen dragged ashore a poor wretch whose face and arms were a mass of putrescent ulcers. Another shrivelled, livid scarecrow's hair was so long, so matted it resembled a last year's bird nest. That this soldier had gone more than a little mad, Alistair deduced from the way he lay on the ground and kept pounding at it with skinny fists. "*De l'eau! N'y a pas d'eau! Jamais d'eau douce.*"

Oradon, mighty impressed and sobered, gathered his reins. "My God, Bryson, they *can't* all be like this!"

"Le Comte d'Estaing? He has gone off to reconnoitre. Le Général Dillon commands here," a narrow-faced major of the Auxerre Regiment stated in good English. "The beeg tent—he ees there."

The wind continued to rise, blew so that a labor gang of artillerists found it very hard work to ease their huge pieces over the gunwales of a lighter.

"*Sacré nom de Dieu!*" they cursed. "Hold steady. *Un curé a poile!* Pull, you rabbits! *Nom d'une femme enceinte, tirez! Tirez!*"

Naked to the waist, the matrosses were puffing, cursing, as their craft threatened to be blown offshore.

Sand from the beach commenced to blow about, stung Alistair's cheeks. He remembered, vividly, how the sand had blown that tense afternoon on Long Island when—at long last—Sir Henry Clinton had discovered that the ford between Sullivan's and Long Island was too deep to be crossed.

Ever suspicious of the unfamiliar, Alistair's eyes lanced ahead when a cavalry officer rode by as if the devil were after him. The horse wasn't much; evidently the poor beast had landed but recently and had yet to recover its land legs; a great gall shone orange-scarlet on its flank.

The temptation to rein aside and gallop the four short miles to Peter Habersham's plantation on Ossabaw Creek was all but irresistible. Antoinette! The Scot's whole body felt lighter at the thought of his wife. Losh, what an eternity seemed to have dragged by since last he had held her, petite, fragrant, and wonderfully fragile, in his arms. Yet it was not over three weeks since they had parted. Perhaps, tonight, a way could be found?

The wind kept blowing ever more furiously and to avoid going ashore several vessels were upping their anchors.

"What the devil brings you here?" An officer wearing the blue and buff regimentals of the Continental line emerged from that pavilion before which snapped a most impressive standard. On it the lilies of France had been embroidered in pure gold. In the upper corner a representation of the Virgin and Child had been embroidered with wonderful skill, the haloes of the holy pair formed by small and regular pearls.

"Hello, Gadsden," Oradon called and dismounted heavily. "D'you know Bryson, here?"

The Scot smiled, held out his hand. "Ou, aye. Captain Gadsden danced at my wedding."

The big South Carolinian beckoned a pair of orderlies to lead away the mounts.

Admiringly Alistair gazed upon the big yellow and blue pavilion billowing slowly in the wind. Quite a few officers in blue and white uniforms stood about its entrance talking excitedly or writing orders on portable field desks.

There were present, also, a few Americans on liaison duty; they averaged at least a head taller than their darker-faced and more nervous allies. Beside a group of horses stood a number of express riders, aides, and gallopers awaiting the receipt of orders.

"General Dillon?" Oradon queried. "We bring word from General Pulaski."

The Continental officer's weatherbeaten features hardened. "Ye'd best eat breakfast. General Dillon ain't awake yet."

"Not awake!" The words escaped Alistair before he realized it. "You can't be serious?"

"But I am. The General ate extra well last night; besides he finds the landing of troops a boring business."

Laird above! Alistair thought, and yon Polish cavalry general expects an attack pressed home today!

That the French allies would not attack that day, nor the next, nor for many more days, an imbecile could have foretold.

V

PETER HABERSHAM, JUNIOR

AT ELEVEN o'clock General Charles Dillon's florid features and blood-injected eyes appeared through a flap connecting the pavilion with his private tent. Though the General's tunic was devoid of creases, perspiration had already begun to soak through the fine cambric stock restraining a couple of extra chins. Diagonally across the Irish-Frenchman's ample breast swept the sky blue sash of a Chevalier of the Order of St. Louis; several jewelled decorations, sunbursts and stars winked and blinked bravely. Accompanying him was an Engineer colonel in a blue tunic, red waistcoat, red breeches, and red stockings. He was talking furiously and gesticulating to match.

"*Non*," Dillon was saying. "*Enfin, non!*"

Captain Oradon saluted, advanced and presented Pulaski's dispatches, a somber, dumpy-looking figure. Never had Alistair beheld such human rainbows as these staff officers—not even in Charleston where a set of smart regimentals counted for a good deal. There were Artillery officers all in blue with scarlet cuffs and coat linings, Marines in dark blue turned up in a lighter shade of the same color, and officers of various line regiments in white variously piped with violet, crimson, green or yellow.

Dillon raised bloodshot, brilliant blue eyes; he spoke in English but with a marked Irish accent. "It's thanking you, gentlemen, I

am, for your hardihood in successfully passing around the enemy—
and at night. As soon as I have read General Pulaski's communica-
tion and consulted with my aides, I will prepare a reply.

"Come, Coleau, I'll be needing your opinion. You, too, Der-
neville, de Vizé, let us then consider this plan our excellent brother,
General Lincoln, has in his mind."

Alistair, remembering the uncertain temper and the unpredictable patience of those half-disciplined militia regiments forming the
bulk of Lincoln's forces, started to speak. Right now those levies
were poised, palpitating for action. Tomorrow? No one could tell.
But a warning shake of the head from Gadsden kept him quiet.

Amid a deal of bowing and saluting, General Dillon retired to a
long table at which a trio of military secretaries were busily re-
pointing goose quill pens.

To Gadsden Alistair muttered, "Sir, can you no' press a decision? The enemy troops are in great disorder in Savannah and
though their earthworks are yet in ill repair, they are laboring hard.
Can the French no' be persuaded to order an attack? Generals
MacIntosh and Pulaski are in position, burning to move the instant
General Lincoln comes up—which he will certainly do by Monday—tomorrow."

"No. D'Estaing wishes to land more regiments," Gadsden
growled.

A hussar officer, very impressive in a silver frogged jacket,
pelisse or dolman of sky blue, came forward, bowed politely.
"Please permit that I present myself—I am, for my sins, Baron
Edouard Joseph Marie d'Esperey, Colonel of His Most Christian
Majesty's Hussars of Lauzun."

He had, Alistair realized, sharp brown features dominated by a
long narrow beak of a nose with two shrewdly humorous black eyes
set to either side of it, and pair of carefully pointed mustaches.

As the colonel bowed a second time Alistair noted this fellow's
hair had been plaited into two long pigtails dressed forward of his
ears. These braids were long enough to brush the topmost frogs
upon his remarkably muscular chest.

To both Americans the hussar officer's busby was unfamiliar.
Lacking a visor, the headdress was tall and conical in shape, but flat
at its apex. Affixed to one side of this singular head piece was a
jaunty little plume of close-trimmed white ostrich feathers. Like the
hussar's tunic and dolman, the background of his elaborately mono-
grammed sabretâche was sky blue.

His skin-tight breeches of canary yellow were braided near the
belt into elaborate silver loops which stretched down to meet ele-

gant, tight-fitting black boots adorned at their tops with small silver tassels.

By his side the colonel wore a scimitar rather than a sword. Designed along very graceful lines, the weapon was a light affair with an open guard and sheathed in a black morocco scabbard clasped with what looked like pure gold bands. All in all it was indeed a beautiful piece of armament. Whether such a scimitar would parry the lunge of a sturdy British bayonet was another question. That his claymore could, and had, Alistair knew very well. Subsconsciously, he eased the ponderous weapon forward, crossed his hands on its bright steel guard as he acknowledged the Frenchman's courtesy.

"You will honor my mess with your presence, Messieurs?"

They would and gladly, Captain Oradon assured him.

Colonel d'Esperey said, as he led them to a nearby tent. "Ah, *mes amis*, to feel once more the solid earth is a sublime ecstasy. For two months and over one has not smelt a flower, nor seen anything green except the sea."

His mustaches quivered to the deep breath he drew. "Some among us have been even less fortunate—the Regiments of Auxerre and Augenois have been at sea even longer. *Mon Dieu*, the condition, the very smell of some of their men would turn the stomach of a mule."

Oradon nodded. "How long they been aboard ship, Colonel? Some of them fellows looked pretty well done in."

"Five long months, *Monseiur le Capitaine*. With shame I admit it," d'Esperey replied, and Alistair began to like him for his genuinely unhappy air. "There has been but an incredible stupidity—an inexcusable lack of attention to plans. Some regiments have lost a third of their force and many of those that are left—*faugh!* If ever they fight again, I will burn many candles in honor of Saint Denis."

Apparently depending on what ship transported them, King Louis' soldiers seemed to follow a definite line of cleavage. The majority, however, were lean, brown and well-equipped.

The wind blew harder, tossed General Dillon's blue and yellow-dyed pavilion in restless canvas billows. The business of landing proceeded with increasing difficulty. With this wide river's mouth beginning to show whitecaps it was not easy to unload horses, to complete the always dangerous task of rolling great black siege guns ashore from pontoons and barges. More and more ships were upping anchor and, heeled over by the rising gale, running for the open sea.

"A division assigned to Comte de Noailles will soon debark," d'Esperey remarked through a mouthful of pork and peas, "if the weather will permit. Pierre!" he beckoned his soldier servant. "Some Bordeaux for the gentlemen."

About the weather there was room for considerable doubt. The sky had grown steadily more sombre, blacker; with half an eye Alistair sensed that a gale of serious proportions was making up. Some engineer troops were trying to pitch tents on high land above the river, but the wind was wreaking havoc with their half-raised canvas. A number of small boats were scrambling desperately to make shore. Several, though, appeared to be drifting out into the river. Alistair could see them through the open flap of the mess tent.

Captain Oradon commenced to fidget. "Say, Colonel, d'you think the Commander-in-Chief will attack as soon as he can?"

"Soon?" D'Esperey laughed shortly. "*Mon cher ami*, in the service of Louis XVI time is of little value. *Tiens!* One will learn what chances." Colonel d'Esperey got up, went striding across the sandy ground to an adjacent tent, his long white braids a-swinging, tapping against his chest. "*Monsieur le Capitaine* Foyne?"

"Yes, sir?" A handsome young fellow in a pale green uniform appeared instantly, stood to attention.

"Will you be good enough to see what occupies *Monsieur le Général*?"

"I will, sir," Captain Foyne said, buttoning up his tunic while the wind buffeted his curly, rust-brown hair. "But 'twill be the same answer. General Dillon waits on orders from His Excellency."

"And where is His Excellency to be found?"

"At a place called Beaulieu, sir, on the river above here." Captain Foyne came swinging over, six feet tall, but slight in the body. He had shy greenish-blue eyes and a ready smile.

Beaulieu? Alistair thought fast. The property wasn't two miles from Hesperidée. Of course duty came first, yet if duty coincided with inclination— To Oradon he said, "It may be wise to learn what chances at Beaulieu?"

Oradon, full of belated breakfast, belched and raised tarnished gold epaulets in a prodigious, comfortable sigh. He felt very disinclined to move. "You may as well take a look about. Listen, learn what you can, then report to General Lincoln on the morrow."

"Captain Foyne, Monseiur Bryson will accompany you," the hussar said, giving his mustache an absent-minded tug.

The great tent of Major-General Charles Hector, Comte d'Estaing, had been pitched on a broad and sandy field near Beaulieu plantation. The site enjoyed whatever breeze there was—there was too much wind right now.

Out on the yellow, wind-whipped river the Commander-in-Chief's flagship, the gold, white and blue frigate, *La Chimère*, was swinging to her anchors in restless semicircles.

Observed Captain Foyne as the horses took up a trot, "I'm thinking, Mr. Bryson, 'tis lucky we are to be away from that madhouse at the landing. Faith, and I'm thinking, 'twill soon become a pest-house as well. Holy Mary take pity on them poor devils of the Auxerrois."

Alistair Bryson, getting used to the cornet's sturdy bay mare, felt less sore and tired. "Aye, I counted near thir-rty cadavers by the water's marge."

"Och," the Irishman laughed. "The current will carry them stiffs away pretty as Paddy's pig was stole from a stall at the county fair. 'Tis the fevers, I fear."

On arrival at Beaulieu—or "Bewlie," as the British insisted on calling the place—Alistair surrendered his reins to a wooden-faced French Grenadier with beetling brows and a big jutting jaw. He was readjusting the claymore's brass-studded baldric when a hand clapped him violently on the back.

"The Lord love us if it ain't Alistair Bryson!"

Captain Foyne grinned, his snub nose bright with heat. It was an odd figure which was pumping the Scot's hand.

"Captain Foyne, Mr. Peter Habersham. A neighbor o' mine in better times. Mr. Habersham"—Alistair repeated the name purposely, having always had trouble in recalling names on first hearing—"is related tae my wife by marriage."

"Pleasure, Captain, a pleasure indeed. And may I venture that you are welcome, most welcome to America?" Above an expensive stock of Irish linen Peter Habersham's plump pink features were glistening.

Now a gale commenced to blow in earnest. Trees began juggling their branches. Horses secured to a picket line strung among some willows commenced fidgeting, cocking their ears.

Vastly pleased to find a familiar face, even Peter Habersham's dull countenance, Alistair clapped the civilian on his shoulder. Eagerly, he asked, "My wife—she fares well?"

"Lord love you, man, of course, of course," Habersham boomed. "And growing prettier every day. Ah, 'twas smart fellows we were to marry Proveaux girls—smite me dead if we're not!

"Captain Foyne, you must meet my wife." His heavy features lit momentarily. "Théo will like Captain Foyne, don't you think?"

"But, sir, I—I—" the Irishman smiled.

"Tut, Captain, and again tut! I will not take 'no' for an answer. Alistair will order horses tonight and we will all dine at Hesperidée."

Alistair nodded. He could not find it against even a truly Presbyterian conscience to accept. First though, he'd take a ride about the Count d'Estaing's headquarters, note the condition of his troops, how they fed, and what they were going to do about drinking water and firewood and the midges and mosquitoes.

The headquarters troops appeared in much better case than the unhappy men of Auxerre and Augenois. They were big, stolid, peasant stock soldiers, well turned out; they handled their weapons very smartly. A platoon of the Grenadiers of Armagnac was drawn up before the General's tent, bayonets gleaming, orange cuffs bright despite the lowering sky.

Negro grooms brought forward horses, held stirrups while the men mounted. The track to Hesperidée led a twisting course among towering pines and under streamers of silver-green Spanish moss cascading down from the farflung boughs of hoary gray oaks. For all his hopelessly round thighs and fat behind, Peter Habersham rode well enough.

Alistair sensed that some reason existed why the young rice planter was so anxious to get home—aside from the natural one of wanting to rejoin so beautiful a wife as Théo. For going on two years he had been puzzled, and rendered a little uneasy, by that surprisingly alert mind which inhabited Peter Habersham's clumsy body.

Because his mount was cold-bred, Alistair could not keep up. Foyne, better mounted, had gone pelting after Habersham and the sandy dirt from their hooves had flown into his face. Besides, the big claymore was banging and thumping on his thigh. He really shouldn't have taken the claymore along on this campaign; what could be more absurd than for a ranger to encumber himself with such a ponderous yardstick of a skewer? Still, Feyther once had said half in jest that no harm ever befell any Bryson who wore it.

"Antoinette." He smiled to himself. "It'll be no' sae long now." At the thought of her great brown-black eyes, her lustrous curls, his heart outsped the mare.

It was well that Foyne and Habersham had ridden ahead. He needed this opportunity to study the country, to look for signs of marauding partisans.

His heart gave a great leap when the trail widened and, down a leafy tunnel through woods ahead, he could glimpse a stately brick mansion, bright pink against a background of gray storm clouds.

Losh! The wind was now screaming for fair! Bits of twig, leaves, and the dust of a thousand dried plants beat in his face, tossed the mare's mane about.

He could see Captain Foyne riding, bent forward like a jockey, his light green uniform brilliant in a freak slant of sunshine. Easily, the long-limbed Irishman was outdistancing Peter Habersham in his bottle-green velvet. In a minute Habersham would begin waving greetings to his wife. Alistair was reconciled to arriving last. That was the Bryson way—they made slow, steady runners in the marathon of life—men who generally arrived at the finish, leaving fancier racers foundered and fallen by the track.

VI

THE TEMPEST

IN THE stable court back of Hesperidée furious activity reigned when Lieutenant Alistair Bryson's unemotional mare jogged comfortably into a scene of windy, dusty confusion.

With three slaves obsequious in attendance, Peter Habersham was dismounting. One grinning Negro held the planter's bridle, a second was bracing his knee for the short-legged master of Hesperidée to step on, the third was steadying the stirrup on the off side against Peter Habersham's not inconsiderable weight—he must have balanced the scales at a solid two hundred pounds.

A dozen-odd officer's chargers stood restlessly, hitched to a well-gnawed rail; their saddle cloths of mulberry, blue, emerald, were gay with personal coats of arms or regimental monograms. One of these Alistair thought he recognized—the leopard skin saddle cover of Colonel Baron d'Esperey.

With characteristic courtesy Habersham waited, mopping his eager pink features until the long-legged figure in buckskins could dismount. In his ranger's shirt, even though its thrums and fringes had been dyed a gaudy indigo, Alistair Bryson felt as homely as a cowbird among a flock of tanagers and blue jays.

"I say, Caesar, is Mrs. Habersham well?" the rotund figure in green inquired, his small eyes darting anxiously about. "I had half expected—"

"Why, Mist' Habersham, suh, de Missus she done entertainin'
a—some foreign gen'l'men, suh." The butler looked a trifle disconcerted.

Alistair and Captain Foyne exchanged looks of mutual approval
as, methodically, each one of them took care to ease his mount's
saddle girth.

"Mind ye walk him a long twenty minutes," the Irishman smiled
at the little Negro groom who came running up, his breeches
precariously held in place by a length of frayed twine. "Here's a
penny for you."

"Yassuh, yassuh. Thank you suh!" It was curious how the
restless Irish hunter arched his neck, snuffed at the colored boy,
then perhaps because the picaninny showed not the slightest fear,
consented to be led away.

Said Alistair Bryson to Habersham, "Ye've a houseful already,
Peter, I wonder whether ye'll welcome an extra—"

"Tut, tut, Alistair," the planter puffed. "We've room and to
spare in Hesperidée for everybody." He shot the Scot a particularly
searching glance. "You'll help me make the French welcome?"

"Aye. Are they no' our allies?"

"Well, Captain, what do you think of my humble abode?"
Habersham tried, without success, to speak casually, but a bat could
have seen that he was proud as Punch of his estate.

In honest wonderment the mercenary was gaping at the estate's
wide rice fields, at the orchards, at the house vegetable garden, at
the formal garden with its half-grown maze of privet.

The Irishman nodded. "Faith, Mr. Habersham, I wonder if you
realize yer blessings? So much room, such rich land! There's earls
in Ireland, sir, who can't boast such a foine big manse you have
here."

It was inescapable that up until now Captain Foyne had not been
particularly impressed with young Mr. Habersham. Now he viewed
with envy this lofty handsome red-brick mansion with its neat
vine-grown rows of slave quarters, the bookkeeping offices, the
stables and barns.

If only there were more such homes back in County Clare! The
more he thought on it, the more he determined that, no matter how
this campaign ended, Shaun Foyne would never sail eastward
again. Surely, in this vast silent green continent there must be room
for a man with hot blood, a quick wit, and a sharp blade to carve out
a fortune—and a home?

In lively curiosity the mercenary observed a strange sight. Three
coppery-brown-complexioned figures were squatting on their hams

in the shade of a carriage shed filled with gigs, shays and even a small coach. These strange creatures were sleepy-looking but still swiftly fierce, like caged foxes. Their bright black eyes were restless. Clad only in dirty red loin cloths, they seemed not to suffer from the suddenly overpowering humidity.

In frank amazement Foyne scratched his unruly red hair. "Mr. Bryson—what—what are they?"

Alistair laughed. "Indians, Yamassees. Ye'll see plenty o' the striking brutes ere this campaign is o'er."

"John! Obadiah! Belshazzar!" Peter Habersham shouted as he tramped up a short walk edged with box plants. "Dammit, am I to have no attention?"

"Poor Peter," Alistair thought, "so long as he's wed to Théo he'll strut and brag." He ran his cuff across his forehead. His rabbit's fur cap was unbearably hot, burned like a veritable shirt of Nessus. Where was Antoinette? His blood commenced to surge, to beat in his ears. Losh! What a fortunate lad was Alistair. Still he couldn't believe that gay, clever, rich Antoinette Proveaux had promised to love, honor and obey one Alistair Bryson—an earnest, conscientious Scot. That smell of violets—the scent of her pale little body—soon, soon. So chance then—if in the battle which must be joined sooner or later— Well, no matter!

A door opened and a grizzled majordomo came pattering out.

"Yassuh, Mist' Petuh, yassuh. Welcome home, suh. Did you get to General Pre—"

"Yes, Cato, I saw General Lincoln," Habersham cut in. "Where is Mrs. Habersham?"

"She in de music room, suh."

Habersham thought, "And dishing out my best Madeira with both hands, I'll warrant." It wasn't that he minded Théo's offering the wine, but she might have waited until he could make the gesture. After all, it was *his* wine.

Still, Théo was Théo. She always had been and he expected she always would be taken up with men. From her toddling days up Théo had had but to smile her slow disingenuous smile to command any man.

"Alistair!" A wild flurry of wine red skirts and Antoinette Bryson darted down the wide steps of Hesperidée like the dark, brilliant bird she had always suggested. "*Mon homme*, my love." Passionately she pressed herself to his smoky-smelling hunting shirt, thrilled to feel the pressure of his big hands against her shoulder blades, revelled in the unconscious cruelty of the crushing hardness of his chest against her breasts.

It was an iridescent instant and Alistair held her close then, tightening his arms about her, lifted her clear off the ground. Let Foyne stare all he pleased, let the servants smile. This was his wife, his love—his only love. "Oh, lassie, my own sonsie lass! 'Tis been a wa'esome eternity."

How wonderful it was once more to smell the distinctive scent of violets, again to sense the incredible softness of 'Toinette's jet hair against his cheek. Losh! How soon could they, in all good taste, get away—to love, to bed? His dark blue eyes devoured the sweet triangle her face suggested.

She thrilled quite as much over the familiar odor of wood smoke, gun oil, crude soap, leather and his particular aura. Alistair was sweaty, thick with dust, but she pressed her face to him all the more eagerly.

"*Cœur de mon cœur!*"

"But *mes amis*, is it not wonderful, this conjugal affection in America!" At the doorway of Hesperidée had appeared a trio of French officers. "*Bis! Bis!*" They applauded as if at a theater.

"Mind yer manners, ye niggling macaronis; 'tis better than hugging and squeezing wi' tavern bawds. And if the one of ye that spoke there now wull follow me, I'll teach him—" Bryson swung, muscles tense.

"*Non*—please, *mon mari, non.*" Antoinette's fingers sealed his mouth, held him where he was. "You do not understand. Please, Alistair, please, that was intended as a compliment. These are allies." Then she turned, very dignified, and in French she said, "Messieurs, we are a little more direct here in America than at Versailles."

Alistair struggled to cope with the situation.

"May I present you to my husband? Monsieur Taf, Lieutenant of the Regiment of Dillon. Lieutenant Blandeau of the Regiment of Augenois. And the Monsieur Chevalier d'Anglemont of the Chasseurs of Guadeloupe."

Losh! 'Toinette was presenting those popinjays to him! Not him to them. He felt better, generous in fact. Poor foreigners, they knew no better.

The French came forward, made a bow. Lieutenant Taf said, "I pray you to forgive our astonishment, Monsieur Bryson; in Paris too long it has been utterly *démodé* to demonstrate in public the least affection for one's wife." He sighed. "À silly custom because my Thérèse—"

The two other officers came forward, frosty beaded silver goblets poised, to examine, with disarming curiosity, Alistair's hunting shirt, the great basket guard on his claymore's hilt, the stout dirk at his belt. That same dirk which had first had its use on the eve of the attack on Fort Sullivan against that cursed treacherous Ferguson.

"Mais ça, c'est Ecossais."

"Aye." Alistair, who had picked up a little French from his wife, got the drift of the chasseur's comment when he touched the heavy brass guard of Feyther's claymore.

"Where's my wife?" Habersham demanded, coming impatiently by.

"In there, Peter," Antoinette told him. "She's fascinated our gallant allies. The Adjutant-General already is quite captivated."

"Oh, capital, capital."

A medium-short officer of Engineers came tramping in. "Good evening, nephew." Colonel Joseph Habersham spoke absently. He was far from oblivious of the lowering aspect of the clouds. He had had a strenuous day directing the disposition of the French troops about Beaulieu. Nonetheless, a man was entitled to restore his qualities by getting drunk, at least once a day—a gentleman, that was.

Although not more than a dozen officers were present, the air was heavy with unfamiliar scents of pomatum, perfumes and tobacco of a blend foreign to Georgia and South Carolina.

So absorbed in conversation with the Vicomte de Fontanges and Colonel d'Esperey was Théo Habersham that she failed to notice her husband's presence until Peter caught her in his plump arms and bestowed on her such a resounding kiss that everyone present smiled.

"God bless my soul if you aren't the perfect strategist. I see you have won our allies already." Habersham fairly beamed, his plump features bright with perspiration. "Welcome, welcome, all you gentlemen. Wish I could speak French but I'll have to leave that up to Mrs. Habersham. She can talk for two. Always has. Ha! Ha!"

Egad, wasn't it something to possess a wife so charming, so dazzling, so witty, so exquisitely, beautifully blonde as Théo Jeannette Augustine Proveaux Habersham?

Pink to her ear tips, Théo linked her arm through his, led him over to a lean, wiry figure standing with a certain powerful grace before the fireplace. "Baron d'Esperey, may I present my husband, master of Hesperidée." She added to please Peter—"and of my fortunes."

"Monsieur Habersham one deems the most fortunate man in America," d'Esperey declared, his long white braids swaying forward as he bowed.

Bigre! How could so lovely a creature share the conjugal bed of a sweating fat slug like this? Lightly, he continued, "You are a gentleman of great discernment, Monsieur."

"Why, thank you, Count—er—Baron—didn't rightly take your name—Osprey, ain't it?"

"D'Esperey, Monsieur, the family inhabits Gascony."

Colonel d'Esperey's bold grey eyes flickered to Théo, came away as he declared, "In my lamentable ignorance I would never have dreamed that in this great, savage country dwelt such ravishingly beautiful goddesses."

"Now ain't that interesting. Say what do you think of America? Hey? Well, Colonel, America ain't so savage as you might imagine. You'll get used to it." Habersham took a silver mug of flip from a tray and passed it to Major Dorno. The windows rattled restlessly.

Though Théo had indeed ordered up his very best Madeira, Peter stifled his pique, clapped his hands.

"Caesar," said he loudly, "send down and fetch me up some of the really fine cognac, the '23—no the '19—and mix a juleppe for Baron Osprey." He'd show these foreigners Théo wasn't the only person in Hesperidée who recognized amenities.

The Vicomte de Fontanges, incisive of manner and withered of complexion, interrupted a brief conversation with doughty and short-tempered old Colonel Joseph Habersham.

"Monsieur is most kind," said he hurriedly. "A most excellent wine has been served to us. Do you not think that Cognac might produce—" Unhappily, he sensed Habersham's embarrassment and broke off, then added—"But, of course, in this climate liquors, no doubt, act differently than in France."

In a hurried undertone Théo muttered, "Don't be an idiot, Peter. Don't insist. Heavy liqueurs on wine? Who ever heard of such a thing?"

The objections came as a blow to Peter. In the whole new State of Georgia there weren't five people who owned an ice house. Not even Colonel Pinckney, for all his high opinion of himself and his family, was able to set iced drinks before a guest—let alone a whole roomful of distinguished guests.

"As you say, my dear." In search of surer ground he hunted up Captain Foyne and commenced a labored discussion on the risks of rice planting. Politely the long bodied Irishman listened, but his eyes were on the countryside. Such rare rich soil. Och, this was indeed fine land.

"You may be afflicted with our stupidity, Madame, a little longer." The Vicomte Fontanges smiled at Antoinette like a benevolent wolf. "Tomorrow the Count Pulaski"—he pronounced the name "Pulaffski"—"is to confer with His Excellency. General Dillon has reported many of our men indisposed."

A masterpiece of understatement, Alistair thought. Indisposed! A pretty term to describe men rotting on the edge of the grave with scurvy and God knew how many other terrible diseases. It would be a long while ere he could rid himself of the recollection of those hairy scarecrows stumbling ashore, their regimentals reduced to foul tatters. Colonel d'Esperey thought an attack should be organized at once; so too did the Colonel de Colignon—but the haughty Sieur de O'Dun objected.

Covertly Antoinette's fingers pressed her husband's.

He looked guiltily at her though the whole of his being heaved within him. Her silks whispering softly, he red as fire, they slipped out of a French door and were hurrying down a walk bowered with crimson climbing roses when, with a shriek and a howl, the storm broke in full force.

"Oh, 'Toinnie, dearest!" A supple green branch from one of the climbing rose bushes had flickered suddenly and drew three scratches across the pallor of her forearm.

"It's nothing," she smiled. "but, *hélas, mon cœur,* we swiftly must return. Look there!"

The sky was turning an ominous livid purple-black. Over Ossabaw Creek queer silvery sheet lightning was illumining the landscape. Back of the manor house sounded the frightened trampling of horses, the excited shouts of servants attempting to lead them into the long brick stables.

Regardless of the howling wind Alistair could not turn back but held his tiny wife to him. " 'Toinnie! My white rose. Oh, these lang weeks I've been fair tormented for the love and the lack of you." His hard bronzed hands ran the length of her body, fumbled, caressed her wondrous soft firmness.

Alone with the wind roaring high in the sky they remained very close. Ragged, wind-torn clouds went flashing past. Over the tops of the trees across the creek there came no thunder, no lightning, yet the air was full of sound. Those great live oaks in seeming defiance of gravity thrust their arms out over the wide lawns of Hesperidée, wildly tossed their gonfalons of Spanish moss. In increasing numbers leaves began to whirl by.

In the manor house, slaves were running to close shutters which had commenced to slat and crash back and forth.

"Alistair! I cannot yet trust my senses. So often I have conjured your image." It was incredible, inexplicable, thought Antoinette, this indescribable bond that held her so close to this tall, big-boned country man—farmer, for that was what Alistair Bryson was—and glad of it. Logically, this clumsy Scot should be the last man in the world for her to have found so completely, so blissfully desirable. Tight against the olive-dyed laces at the front of his hunting shirt, she wondered what Mère Bryson would make of a wife who couldn't even churn butter? Still, she reckoned, she might give Mère Bryson a lesson or two on marketing.

She was content to press her face very close against his. What luck that Théo, dear generous cousin, had promised her the principal guest room; it boasted a great, canopied bed which was a monument to some furniture maker's skill and imagination.

The atmosphere suddenly lost its humid quality, turned almost cold. Bushes, shrubs, plants, bowed deeper and deeper in deference to the furious successive impulse. The length of Ossabaw Creek was no longer yellow but white as if gone pale with fright at the ordeal about to be endured. Down near the Savannah the woods were squirming, twisting, threshing their boughs up and down. A scattering of orderlies came pelting in from the servants' quarters, some of them still wearing napkins tied about their necks. Their high-pitched French voices sounded thin.

Steadily the wind gathered force, lashed Alistair's dark hair in a copper-brown froth, flattened Antoinette's clothes until the outline of her whole slim form was betrayed in bold relief.

"Shall we go?" Her hand crept up.

"No, with you I fear nothing. This tempest is like this war," she cried, cheeks flushed and brilliant. "It blows hard now, *mon cœur*, yet soon the wind will die away."

Softly the rain came and laughing they ran to get back to Hesperidée. The first rain had barely drawn smoking puffs from the path when a solid sheet of water descended. In a twinkle they were drenched from head to foot.

"No great loss without some sma' gain," Alistair exulted. "Dinna ye ken? We now have excuse to withdraw."

Antoinette's red lips curved. "Then let us walk very slowly, *mon ange*, let us get very wet indeed."

Only because of their leisurely gait were they destined to see the first of the French fleet go reeling, careening past the entrance to Ossabaw Creek. Tattered topsails streaming wildly from the yards, they fled down stream in headlong rout. A transport, a brig, then a sloop appeared, went racing, reeling out of sight. Through the lashing rain and the haze they watched, in awed silence, a supply vessel roll over, over until her copper bottom became exposed to the infuriated skies.

VII

RECONNAISSANCE

ALL NIGHT long the storm persisted, blew at times with a hurricane's velocity. Along the driveway and back of the slave quarters trees crashed over and just after dawn the dairy shed lost its roof and the pigeon loft of Hesperidée was torn from its mast.

Sleepily, Antoinette felt Alistair stir, then start slipping gently sidewise from out of the covers. Smiling she wound arms about his bare, leather-colored body.

"You are my prisoner," she said, looking up all brown-black eyes and tumbled hair. "There is no escape for you."

He humored her during a delicious few moments, then he tickled his wife until she had to let go.

"Now then, now then," he murmured, patting her near shoulder. "I must be gaeing back to Colonel Laurens and that fancy foreign cavalry general. Dinna tease, sweeting, I ha'e reports to render."

Aye, he had reports, but such reports as would dash hopes soaring in the American bivouac not fifteen miles distant. Reports of shameless incompetence, of disinterest, of jealousy and of arrogant contempt. For every thought the French entertained about the sacred cause of Liberty, they held three of hatred for England and fifty in the interests of personal advancement.

There was, Alistair had noticed, the greatest difference between the elder officers, nearly all of whom were cynical old campaigners or bankrupt rakes or discredited aristocrats—and their juniors. The latter were gay, irresponsible, many of them burning for action and exhilarated over their first commands. Their silken nightshirts edged with Valenciennes lace or even Flemish lace, shocked Alistair's simple soul. All they talked of was women, or how soon could they find women.

There remained, of course, a tried and quite important element in General d'Estaing's Corps of officers—the mercenaries. One and all they were here to win or to recoup a fortune and made no pretense to the contrary. A reckless, hard living lot, all of them—but possessed, when they so chose, of real charm and no lack of cour-

348

age. Their kind of war, Alistair decided, began and ended by the clock, was regulated by such niceties as elaborately polite parleys, field music, fanfares for the General, salutes to the enemy, brave gestures of chivalry. No ambushing, trickery for them; no scalping, no torturing of prisoners.

What a night it had been! In his cups hard-bitten Colonel d'Esperey at first had flirted with his hostess, then, boldly, fondled her. If Peter Habersham had noticed it, it appeared not to concern him for he got drunk with almost undignified haste.

The Chevalier du Romain, a pop-eyed naval officer had suggested cards—a game Alistair had never heard of—*écarté*. To see the heavy *louis d'or* glistening, clinking over the rich mahogany of Habersham's dining room table made his Scottish bowels writhe.

As the tobacco smoke thickened and King Louis' gentlemen pulled off first their tunics and then their wigs and waistcoats, remarks were let fall concerning the voyage, concerning regiments riddled by the King's evil, concerning cavalry horses by the dozens tossed overboard, dead or dying.

Alistair combed his hair thoughtfully. The Laird in Heaven only knew what damage the storm had done. How far out to sea had the French boats been driven?

One never would have guessed that Savannah lay only six leagues distant. Right now not an outpost or picket guarded the approaches to Hesperidée.

"Alistair." Antoinette half sat up, very serious all at once. "I am very silly, but—but I had a dream—such an evil dream!"

"Moonshine! Once proper waked, ye'll not recall it."

Her fragile fingers clung to the fringes of his sleeve. "I fear I shall not forget this dream, *mon adoré*." She bent her head. "It was so horrible! I saw an Indian—an Indian in a red coat. You were on horseback. The Indian rose from—from"—she hesitated, drew her palm slowly across her forehead—"from the ruins of a carriage and—and—"

"Gave me a bunch of marigolds? Tut! Ye'll have me worried mine own sel' and noo more of this, there's a good lass. We'll have yon Lobster-backs caged inside o' a week."

"Don't leave me. Oh, Alistair, that Indian—his face was so cruel. He'd a red fox tail woven into his scalp lock. I saw it ever so clearly." She clung to the shiny leather of his hunting shirt.

"Now gae back to bed, 'Toinette. I'll come riding back within the week. Ye may rely on that." He kissed her soundly, shoved her playfully deep under the coverlet and hurried out. Losh! How he yearned to linger.

None of the French officers, let alone Peter Habersham or the

Vicomte de Fontanges were astir, Alistair discovered as in surprising silence he descended the stair.

He was wrong in one respect. Below, he found Baron Edouard d'Esperey, Colonel of the Hussars of Lauzun, hard at work, bent over a portable military desk. In this uncertain early morning light his long, thin nose looked almost vulpine.

The cavalryman had not yet donned the wig with the long, white braids, and his sky blue jacket was unbuttoned so far down that strong dark hair erupted from between its silver loops and buttons. Colonel d'Esperey's natural hair, a reddish-brown of a shade such as Alistair could not remember having seen before, was cropped very close.

"Yet stirring early, sir."

"If one plays, one must work," laughed the Hussar, "or there is no fun in playing, *hein?*"

D'Esperey must have been writing for quite some time. At his elbow were seated two sleepy-looking orderlies. One was busily sharpening quills, the other copying a set of orders.

The cavalryman got up, stood quite as tall but not as broad in the shoulder as Alistair.

"One observes, *mon ami Américain*, that at least we two hold that devotion to Mars should not wait on the worship of Venus, *hein?*" His thin lips smiled in such a straightforward fashion that Alistair grinned amiably though he had not the vaguest idea of what the Frenchman spoke.

"*Hélas*, there is much work of routine to be done before my regiment is ready for combat."

"Yer regiment, sir?" Alistair had heard no mention of the Hussars of Lauzun. "It must still be aboard ship. I havena seen any troopers about."

The Frenchman frowned. "What you say is but too true, *Monsieur le Lieutenant*. One holds only temporary command, of the *sacré* Chasseurs de Guadeloupe." He sniffed. "*Sang de Dieu!* Those mulattoes assume such airs. Chasseurs? Pah! Chasseurs only of street girls, of wine bottles, and laziness."

He gave to his pointed mustache a thoughtful tug. "*Monsieur le Lieutenant*, I have lost very many horses. I cannot mount even a half-troop. Will you see what you can do to find me some?"

Alistair considered. "And how many do ye need?"

The Frenchman laughed, clapped him on the back. "*Bon!* Had you replied simply 'yes,' I would not have permitted myself to become hopeful. I'll need as near thirty troopers' mounts as can be secured." D'Esperey sighed and looked genuinely downcast. "That rolling off the coast of Carolina broke so many legs."

Edouard d'Esperey, the Scot decided, missed being remarkably handsome by only a small margin. Had those puffy little pouches not lurked beneath his lively dark blue eyes, and had his teeth been a little better . . .

"Colonel, I canna promise ye a single nag, but I will do my best."

"Excellent, you are very good."

"No, 'tis only that I've admiration for har-r-d working men—and officers." Moved to a rare confidential mood, Alistair almost added that Peter Habersham wasn't quite the fat, stupid and purse-proud fool he appeared to be. But he didn't.

Back of the still dripping stables, orderlies, naked to the waist, were grooming horses. With their hair tied, the white-skinned, ribby French cavalrymen more resembled visitors from another world than from another continent. All of them dropped sponges and scrapers and stiffened to ramrod attention when the stolid figure in fringed buckskins strode lightly by with thrums a-swaying and a brass hunting knife handle brightly shining. The rooms eyed him with consuming curiosity, exchanged glances as if to say, "*Voilà, enfin un vrai sauvage Américain.*"

Having no orderly, Alistair strode into the stable and up to the cornet's heavy-boned mare.

"So-o-o girl! So-o-o, so-o-o." He had caught up a handful of rice straw and was commencing to cleanse the animal's saddle place and other bearing surfaces when a sudden brittle stillness descended. The grooms were staring at him like so many owls. It annoyed him.

"Stop yer gawking. What ails ye?"

"But, but Monsieur is an officer, *non*?" demanded a blond young fellow.

Slowly he retrieved a brush Alistair had dropped. "And dinna ever ye doot it," Alistair advised. He would have begun grooming but the blond young fellow hurried forward.

"Monsieur, permit that I do this for you."

Before Alistair could intervene the Frenchman set to work with a peculiar brush which seemed to fetch out every bit of hay, dust and seeds.

Puzzled, Alistair let him have his way. He had hardly begun to inspect the mare's saddle and bridle when other orderlies leaped forward.

"Permit, *mon lieutenant. Pour Monsieur l'ouvrage est indigne.*"

Alistair clung to the bridle. "But I would do this, mon, mine own self."

"No doubt, *Monsieur le Lieutenant*," the English-speaking orderly said, "but should any of our officers pass by and see you cleaning harness, we would suffer punishment of the greatest severity. Grooming is not a work for gentlemen."

Alistair shrugged, scratched his head in bewilderment. In Lincoln's army none of the officers save Colonels and Generals and a few Charleston fops felt above caring for their own mounts. In battle it could make a vital difference whether the gear was in order, whether the animal was clean, well-watered and properly fed. Well, if the foreigners wanted it that way, he'd humor them this once—it could do no harm. Accordingly, he waited until, a little later, the cornet's big bay mare was led out, saddle gleaming and bit shining.

He missed the drag of the claymore when he swung up into the saddle; somehow he felt incomplete. That his great clumsy weapon remained with Antoinette, a tangible part of him, lent him a sense of satisfaction. Hadn't he been wearing it when first they met? When, as a sergeant in Wateree Company of Volunteers he'd gone clumping into her home in Charleston in search of pewter and lead?

After the unfamiliar gaiety, the unusual effort of trying to catch the gist of what was being said by the French, after the imposing luxuries of Hesperidée, Alistair found it sheer delight to follow a trail paralleling the north bank of Ossabaw Creek. He would, he figured, skirt the Savannah clear up to the southern fringe of the town. Maybe he could see something of what the British might have accomplished during the night.

Revelling in the cool stillness, he let the mare pick her way, splashing sturdily through storm puddles reflecting the refreshing green of leaves high overhead. She shied, once, when a great sinuous blacksnake slithered smoothly over the trail, disappeared into a clump of ferns.

Alistair maintained a sharp lookout. He'd no hankering to blunder into the clutches of McGirth's pitiless Tory partisans. Though, as a rule, the British Generals were prone to move sluggishly, Sir Augustine Prevost had, more than once, proved himself a commander of energy and resource.

Again and again the mare had to buck-jump over the trunks of trees blown down during the storm, had to splash belly deep through rivulets flowing angrily down to join the orange-red river.

When the trail crossed an open space he reined in, looked back over his shoulder at Hesperidée—what a fine rich property it was! New, clean and well-planned. By the great Harry, if Antoinette wished a home like it, he would in time win such a domain.

It worried him that no children had come to complete their union. Why? God alone knew. Both he and 'Toinette yearned and had counted on having at least two by now.

He pressed moccasined heels into the mare's sides and lifted her to a slow but space-covering trot. Passing strange that outburst of 'Toinette's. Wasn't like her. 'Twas all moonshine, he assured himself, sheer moonshine.

Presently the trail took and maintained an upward course until he drew rein on the crest of a bluff rising boldly above the low country all about and commanding a view of Beaulieu's landing.

What havoc had the gale not caused? His heart sank. Instead of twenty to thirty vessels lying in the river's mouth, there weren't half a dozen still at their original anchorage. Downstream, two transports had driven ashore after snapping their masts.

Below the mouth of Ossabaw Creek another vessel had turned turtle, the same one he and 'Toinette had seen capsize. Forlornly her broken masts and spars trailed downstream like the shattered limbs of a wounded soldier.

The river this morning, gorged as it was by the downpour, had turned a furious golden-orange. All manner of snags, branches, and even a pitiful Negro shack or two went drifting by at the foot of the bluff.

In the French encampment on the flats below Urban's burnt plantation house was furious activity. Muddied infantry in white coats labored to right upset tents, to bale landing barges, to cook some sort of breakfast with sodden wood.

Gloomily, Alistair rode on. Losh! Through the trees he could see another wrecked transport careened on her side and stranded on a sandbar perhaps half a mile upstream. How she had got there was a mystery. Perhaps a back wind had flung her against the force of the main storm.

Alistair circled General Count d'Estaing's camp with no difficulty whatsoever; in this type of country the exterior guard had been posted dangerously close to the main camp.

Alistair pushed boldly on, riding slowly, making shrewd mental note of any significant fact no matter how trivial.

Skirting the abandoned rice fields of the Phoenix plantation, Alistair found and followed a familiar lane. From its foot he was able to get a clear view of Savannah, sprawling huddled about its lone church like sheep about a protecting dog.

The British, it undoubtedly became clear, must have worked all night, storm or no storm. Nor had they paused to rest even now. If in place of Lord Howe, General Prevost had commanded in New

York, Alistair decided, the year 1778 would have been even less auspicious for the American cause. Parties of brown-skinned enemy sappers were busily constructing lunettes, flêches, and bastions. Even so, their last works were far from complete. In only one out of ten embrasures did the black snout of a field piece peer at the investing army.

Now if General Lincoln, leaving the French out of it, were to order an immediate attack, a really determined assault, nothing could prevent Pulaski's jaunty lancers, the Continentals, the Carolina Regulars, and the raggle-taggle, but momentarily inspired militia, from driving the British into the river.

During the night the British had sunk a number of ships to form an unbroken barrier from shore to shore just above the town. Forlornly, the ruined ships thrust their masts out of the current. They looked like a line of Cyclopean reeds trapping debris. Green branches, logs, and bits of wreckage from upstream tangled with sagging shrouds and stays.

So? General Prevost certainly had made certain that none of the big ships in the French fleet could get upstream to deliver a raking fire on his position. In addition two ships had been sunk in the main channel below Savannah. Of course, they didn't begin to block the channel and there was always another passage beyond the long low-lying bulk of Hutchinson's Island. But they constituted a hazard that any pilot would worry a lot about.

Also he learned that the British were impressing slaves. A big gang of blacks was to be seen marching along and guarded by a band of kilted Highlanders.

Scots. Why had so many Highlanders kept faith with the King who had ruined, beggared and slaughtered them? Slowly Alistair's stout legs tightened about the mare's belly. He guided her carefully back into the shadows of the woods. Once he was well down the lane, he broke off a light branch, trimmed it methodically, then hit the cornet's mare with it.

The sooner he fetched Colonel Laurens, the better. Maybe something could be done. Certainly Savannah would never be more helpless than at the present time.

VIII

The Armies Meet

Colonel Laurens, they told Alistair Bryson, had departed for the headquarters of Major-General Charles Hector, Comte d'Estaing.

To the Lieutenant of Elliott's Rangers the French encampment was a revelation. Familiar with the casual hit-or-miss cantonments, bivouacs, and camps of the South Carolina troops, it was inspiring to behold these neat and orderly rows of white canvas.

The troops of the Commander-in-Chief's, d'Estaing's, own division composing the Regiments of Cambrai, Hainault, Berges, and Gatinois were smartly turned out, their hair carefully dressed and powdered and their long white gaiters comparatively clean.

Sleekly black of face, but rather uncertain in ranks, were the grenadiers of Captain François and the Port au Prince Volunteers. To the Americans present it appeared that these Haitians had been but recently inducted into the service of His Most Christian Majesty.

Everywhere troops were falling into ranks to be dressed by their officers; aides, splendid in their white, pale blue, and yellow uniforms, were riding about bawling commands.

Was an attack contemplated? Everywhere drummers were sounding calls, trumpets wailed. Alistair's mind was still obsessed with a vision of British seamen hard at work hoisting inshore the guns of His Britannic Majesty's Ship, *Rose and Fowey*.

"Colonel Laurens?" Colonel Thomas Pinckney, assigned as aide to the French Commander, shook his long head. "Not come up yet. Must be with General MacIntosh. Any word, Gadsden?"

That thick-bodied captain with the hard blue eyes shook his head savagely. "No. But Pulaski will be along any minute; you can count on that."

That the two Carolinians were mad clean through, Alistair could tell at a glance. At the first opportunity, he drew Captain Gadsden aside.

"What's amiss?"

"This damned macaroni d'Estraing intends to demand that Prevost surrender at once to him, won't wait for our troops to come up," Gadsden fairly hissed. Savagely the Carolinian crumpled a sheet of paper in his hand.

"He wouldn't dare offer us such an affront."

"Wouldn't he? By God, he and his sweet-scented pimps have been drafting a summons this last hour." He pointed to a blue velvet curtain beyond which sounded an indistinct hum of voices. "It's a deliberate, downright slur on national dignity and an insult to our arms!" He unfolded the paper he had been crushing. "Here's a copy Colonel Pinckney was given."

Carefully Alistair smoothed the crumpled foolscap. Because of alterations and erasures it was difficult to decipher, but he read:

"Count d'Estaing summons his Excellency General Prevost to surrender himself to the arms of his Majesty the King of France. He admonishes him that he will be personally answerable for every event and misfortune attending a defence demonstrated to be absolutely impossible and useless from the superiority of the force which attacks him by land and by sea. He also warns him that he will be nominally and personally answerable henceforward for the burning, previous to or at the hour of attack, of any ships or vessels of war or merchant ships in the Savannah River, as well as of magazines in the town.

"The situation of the Morne de l'Hôpital in Grenada, the strength of the three redoubts which defended it, the disproportion betwixt the number of the French troops now before Savannah and the inconsiderable detachment which took Grenada by assault, should be a lesson for the future. Humanity requires that Count d'Estaing should remind you of it. After this he can have nothing with which to reproach himself.

"Lord Macartney had the good fortune to escape in person on the first onset of troops forcing a town sword in hand, but having shut up his valuable efforts in a fort deemed impregnable by all his officers and engineers, it was impossible for Count d'Estaing to be happy enough to prevent the whole town from being pillaged.

"P.S. I apprize your Excellency that *I have not been able to refuse the Army of the United States uniting itself with that of the King*. The junction will probably be effected this day. If I have not an answer therefore immediately, you must confer in future with General Lincoln and me."

To Alistair the tent grew unbearably hot. So the French Commander had not been able to refuse the help of the Army of the United States! Was it to be treated with such contempt that Carolina had endured internal revolution and British assault for three long anguished years?

Colonel Pinckney was having a difficult task in controlling his wrath. He stamped back and forth, so angrily that little puffs of dust spurted from beneath his carefully burnished boots. The silver rowels of his spurs gave off angry little tinkles.

From the camp they all could easily see the roofs of Savannah sprawled along the bluff above the river. It seemed a humble, undistinguished-looking little town to be the object of so much fanfare and commotion.

"While the French dilly-dally," Pinckney burst out in a furious undertone, "look over there. Can you see the redcoats? They're as industrious as ants about a dead mouse."

Gadsden snatched up a stalk of sweet grass, chewed on it viciously, gazed with smouldering eyes upon the long lines of white-clad light infantry, grenadiers, sappers and matrosses.

"Twelve hundred picked troops ready to launch," he growled, "and that God damn' sweet-scented French son of a buzzard sits coolly drawing pretty manifestoes."

To the Scot, a tall dim-colored figure among the brilliant uniforms, the opportunity seemed inescapable, criminal to ignore.

The voices buzzed louder than even from the Comte d'Estaing's tent. A staff officer, in blue with scarlet breeches and stockings and glistening gold gorget flashing, came striding out. In one hand he carried a heavy black tricorn adorned with an ostrich feather. In the other hand, he bore a scroll secured by an elaborate bright blue ribbon.

"Pierre, mon cheval! Gustav, vite, vite!" Out from the Commander-in-Chief's pavilion they came, Generals Dillon, de Stedrig, de Noailles; the Colonels Dejean, de Rouveai, de Calegnon, d'Esperey, de Belize; the Admirals, Count de Broves and La Motte-Picquet and the Chevaliers du Romain and Chesteret de Puysegur, all sparkling with decorations, vari-colored sashes, jewelled swords and splendid regimentals.

"Well, gentlemen, there goes the general's proclamation and our best chance," Pinckney snorted. Savagely he pulled at his long and slightly reddish nose. In his solid boots and dark blue tunic with pale blue revers, the Carolinian seemed to swell with rage.

Escorted by a squad of mulatto Chasseurs of Guadeloupe under Colonel d'Esperey, the aide rode slowly away.

Presently the cavalry escort reined and presented sabres. A detail of infantry from the Auxerre Regiment presented arms, and after their officer had saluted, fell in behind the emissary. To a vibrant beating of drums and a shrilling of pipes, the little column started out across a broad sunbeaten plain separating the French camp from Savannah.

When the distance to the British earthworks was less than a thousand yards, the parley detail halted, made a play with the white flag it marched under. At a walk a pair of mounted trumpeters moved out another two hundred yards, drew rein and raised bugles to their lips, sending a cheerful brazen summons to echo among the dingy-wooded houses of Savannah.

From behind a half-completed battery there presently appeared an officer supported by at least a platoon of scarlet-coated infantry. They also carried a white flag. Their bayonets winking and cross belts flashing, the British marched out over the plain in perfect unison. Some two hundred yards short of the French trumpeters they halted. A pair of little drummer boys beat one, two, three riffles, then fell silent.

The French then presented arms to the enemy. The impact of hands against muskets sounded clear in the sultry air.

Cooks, grooms and valets began running through the camp to get a better view of the proceedings. General d'Estaing and his staff, however, remained under the shade of a wide marquee.

The British party boasted but a single trumpeter; he, however, sounded a mighty flourish. Decorously, the French white flag dipped until it touched the yellow-brown grass; an instant later the British followed suit.

For all his sense of outrage, Alistair remained fascinated as the French officer dismounted gracefully. Accompanied by a pair of gigantic sergeants armed with only halberts, he advanced briskly towards that solid double line of scarlet-clad figures.

As promptly, the British officer set out to meet him. One, two. One, two. Like clockwork toys the distant figures approached one another, their bared swords giving off pale flashes. When separated by perhaps twenty feet, the two officers, halted, saluted each other, bowed formally.

"God!" Gadsden snarled. "Is this a war or a goddamn dancing lesson?"

Alistair laughed and two or three hard-bitten officers in the blue and buff of the Continental service guffawed. The French nearby either looked puzzled or angry.

The parley reached its climax when the Frenchman presented the scroll he carried and the Englishman accepted it. Once more they saluted each other, then about-facing smartly, returned to their own escorts.

The matter was all correct, precise, and very elegant.

Having gulped down a dish of cold meat and black-eyed beans, Lieutenant Alistair Bryson sought Colonel Pinckney's quarters. He found the Carolinian stripped to his shirt sleeves and busily sanding a sheet of foolscap.

"As strongly as I dare," said he, heavily, "I have advised General Lincoln of the situation."

Gadsden added, "By God, Tom, if our army chose to launch an attack, the Britishers are likely to capitulate. Prevost is reported by deserters to have less than eighteen hundred troops in the town and many of them are mercenaries and invalids."

Suddenly drums rolled and thundered. "What the devil?" Colonel Pinckney jumped to his feet, clapped on the wig he had removed for the sake of coolness, and ran to the flap of his tent.

Everywhere officers were bawling at their men. Sergeants and corporals were planting guidons, yelling, *"En ordre! Ici les Gatinois! Ici l'artillérie."*

Gadsden's face lit. "By God, Tom, old Lace Pants is going to attack after all!"

Trumpets brayed throughout the encampment, dust rose in billows as troops ran to their rallying points. While the French army had fallen into impressively perfect ranks, the focus of attention was a tall cloud of dust hanging off to the left over some pitch pines bleached pale green by the fierce suns of the dying summer.

"What in the Laird's name?" A flank attack? No. His heart sank when he realized that the French weren't fixing bayonets, trying flints, priming, or otherwise preparing for battle.

"That," remarked Gadsden, "will be some of General MacIntosh's command in from Augusta."

A perspiring orderly planted General d'Estaing's personal standard in front of the headquarters pavilion.

"Damnation. What new monkeyshines are these?" Colonel Pinckney rasped as he struggled into a faded blue tunic. One of his heavy gold epaulets got twisted and his orderly had quite a job getting it straight.

Gadsden, securing his belt buckle, began cursing under his breath. " 'I have not been able to refuse the Army of the United States uniting itself with that of the King,' " he quoted. "There's a pretty sentiment for an Ally."

A long, rather thin cheer went up as onto the little parade ground before the Comte d'Estaing's headquarters trotted a column of cavalry—lancers gay in gray and silver uniforms.

Captain Gadsden spat, shrugged, "It's the Polack, by God."

When still a hundred yards from the Commander-in-Chief's pavilion, Count Pulaski set spurs to his tall black stallion which reared in protest, beat the air with its forehoofs, then broke into a dead run.

In grudging admiration Alistair realized that the Pole had retained complete control of his mount. He was alternately curbing and spurring his charger, making its leopard-skin saddle housing gleam gold and black.

The Comte d'Estaing appeared, very elegant in a spotless white uniform adorned by the blue ribbon of the Order of St. Louis. Supple, tall, and surprisingly muscular was Charles Hector, Comte d'Estaing. Even his high heels could not make him mince in his gait as did so many of the other French officers.

Pulaski whirled up, long black hair streaming over the silver-braided collar of his tunic. The empty sleeve of the Pole's pelisse fluttered high into the brazen sky as all in one movement he reined in, jumped to the ground, and eagerly hurried forward, steadying a light scimitar in his left hand.

A few feet short of the commanding general, the exile hesitated. *"Soyez le bienvenu, mon Général!"*

"Casimir, mon ami!" d'Estaing called in a powerful rich voice.

"Well, I'm dommed!" Alistair heard his own voice say. Laird in Heaven! It wasna every day ye saw a pair of officers kissing each other like schoolgirls reunited after a holiday.

IX

GENERAL LINCOLN ARRIVES

NOT UNTIL three of that afternoon, Tuesday, September fifteenth, did the first elements of General Benjamin Lincoln's sun-darkened and footsore columns reach McGillivray's Plantation and, thankfully, go into bivouac in a pine forest to the left of the French forces.

More French troops having been landed, the Commander-in-

Chief had disposed his army in a great semi-circle which pinned Savannah and its garrison against the river.

From left to right the Frenchman had divided his army into three ground divisions of roughly a thousand men each. General Baron Noailles had been assigned the regiments of Champagne, Auxerre, Foix, Guadeloupe, and Martinique. D'Estaing had reserved for his immediate command a Corps d'Elite composed of the Regiments of Cambrai and Hainault, Augenois, Gatinois, the Volunteers of Berges, the Cape Legion of Color, and the Port au Prince Regiments. Parked in imposing array before the center of the demi-lune position was such of the artillery as had been hauled up from the landing.

Holding the French right lay General Dillon's division. He commanded the Armagnac and Volunteer Grenadiers, a half regiment charged with the protection of the powder magazine, cattle depot, and hospital.

Forming a sub-corps, whose sector flanked the Savannah River to the extreme southeast of the beleaguered town, was encamped Colonel Count Dejean. His troops consisted of the dragoons of Condé and Belzunce, supported by Colonel de Rouverais' 750 unpredictable volunteer mulatto chasseurs.

Unit after unit of the American force were arriving to reinforce the troops of General MacIntosh's command.

First of Lincoln's troops to appear was the lean, soft-treading irregulars from the backcountry such as Elliott's Rangers; tough fighters, but as ignorant of the meaning of discipline as so many tomcats.

Marching in somewhat better order, the first and second Carolina Regiments next made camp. A South Carolina Artillery battery, when ordered into park on the left of the French, did so with enthusiasm.

"Say, look! Will ya look at them foreign guns?" they cried. "Gawd, ain't they *handsome*?" Immediately they began concocting just how to "adopt" certain items of equipment from these strangers.

The Charleston militia on arrival looked like just what it was—militia. Armed with every kind of piece from ancient Spanish fuzees to fowling pieces, they straggled and slouched into camp making obscene jokes over the conduct of a stallion on scenting the presence of a mare in heat.

"Thank God, we've got *some* honest-to-God soldiers," Colonel Pinckney observed as, marching well together, though their blue uniforms and pale blue cuffs were tinted red with dust, the 5th

Continentals, 1003 strong, came swinging into camp behind their fifers and drummers. They went into the bivouac without the least commotion amid the silent admiration of the militia and the state line regiments.

General Lincoln ordered Pulaski's dragoons to throw out picket lines along the Yamacran Swamp, a morass guarding the extreme left of the American camp. Once this was done the Negro servants of the Charleston blue bloods set about washing down and grooming the lancers' dainty-treading thoroughbreds. Many young gentlemen, inspired by the exiled Pole's promises of danger and glory, had enlisted in the ranks.

Quite a while after the bulk of the American forces had settled down to cooking, washing or smoking, some militia levies from Virginia, hollow-cheeked and worn from their long march, appeared in company with Colonel Twiggs' Georgia militia. The last were a wild, hardy-looking collection of men of all ages. They were garbed in homespun, duroy, osnaburg—any kind of clothing —but hard of eye and, as they announced loudly, always ready for a fight or a frolic whenever the turn was called.

"Heyo Caroliny! Now we're here it's safe to start the battle," yelled one of the Georgians. The Virginians hawked the road dust out of their throats before joining in. "What you chicken cocks waiting for? Want us to lash on yer gaffs fer ye?"

William Jasper, Sergeant of the 2nd Carolina, Georgia born, grinned, waved an amiable paw. "Shucks boys, we ain't aiming to shut you off from glory. You shoulda been to Fort Sullivan."

"Why dad burn my burn! If it ain't Willie. Hey, Jasper," roared a black-bearded trapper, "ain't you wearied of playing around with these here no-account Caroliny pond chickens?"

Heads commenced to turn. The name of Sergeant William Jasper had drifted up many a silent creek, across miles of sandy barren pine lands—that, and legends of his heroic rescue of a battle flag fallen over the bastion.

"Save me some real Gaw'gia chittlin's," he shouted. "I'll be over, come suppertime."

In the American headquarters reigned angry consternation. General Benjamin Lincoln was in a towering rage. The idea of d'Estaing's treating with Prevost without so much as a by-your-leave! The General's round, heavily modelled face was red as any sunset as had ever shone on the Savannah River. Perhaps, if he had not had such a long hot ride that day, perhaps, if the boats at Zubly's Ferry had not nearly all been destroyed by the British, perhaps, if General Count Pulaski had not gone caracoling into the embrace of the

Comte d'Estaing, the Yankee wouldn't have loosed such a blistering stream of profanity.

"So that bum-blistered, lily-scented whoreson of a Frenchman can't prevent the Army of the United States from joining him, hey?" He looked about confusedly. "Split me, gentlemen, here's a pretty pass!"

Savage dark-faced Colonel Twiggs of the Georgia militia fingered the long scalping knife at his belt. "T'hell with them Goddam' foreigners," he snarled. "If we attack tonight"—his shadow was sketched large on the lamp-gilded canvas—"the French are bound to join in or stand disgraced forever."

"Hear, hear! That's the right track!" Major Wise of the 2nd Carolinian militia began to applaud, was supported by Captain Roux and Major Jones, General MacIntosh's own aide.

"Let us at those Lobster-backs! We ain't tired," voices urged from the faded shrubbery. "We'll swaller old Preevo' without even greasin' his ears."

General Lincoln rubbed a pinkish-gray chin. So far he hadn't cottoned to these new allies, but after the tragic campaign which had lost Savannah last spring, he entertained a smart respect for the Britishers.

A pox on the Vicomte de Fontanges, Adjutant-General of the French! He thought things out a sight too quick for any honest soldier.

Heavily, Lincoln turned his distressed gaze on Colonel Cambray, Colonel Twiggs, and General MacIntosh—much like a hostess trying to catch the attention of her guests at the end of a dinner party. However, everyone was aware that Colonel Thomas Pinckney was riding up, with a face like a thunder cloud, his jaw thin beneath the heavy superstructure of his cheeks and forehead.

Promptly he dismounted, came striding forward and saluted the Continental General correctly enough. "Sir, I regret to report that General d'Estaing has just granted the enemy a truce of twenty-four hours' duration."

"Truce! Great God! You can't mean it, Tom?" Captain Gadsden broke out.

"Grant a delay now? I reckon the Frenchman must be daft!" Alistair Bryson heard his own voice saying.

A black-haired major of the Virginia levies, by the name of Alan Maxwell, shook his mane of hair. "He's moonstruck! Look! Look over there, gentlemen. The town but waits our taking."

From the background spoke a smooth voice, "You put it well, Major Maxwell, when you say—*our* taking." Peter Habersham's rotund figure, tight in its modish garments, pushed forward.

"What's your meaning, man?" General MacIntosh mumbled.

"I make bold to say that this is just what the French anticipate by holding back on their part. You are to deliver the great attack and get yourselves blown to bits, then d'Estaing's troops will march over your bodies and claim the prize."

"Yer in error, sir. Quite deluded in fact." Captain Foyne couldn't help speaking up. Detached for service with Pulaski's dragoons, the Irishman had become attracted by the crowd before the American general's tent. "Whatever ye may think o' the French, they are here to fight."

A beetle-browed Scot, the Captain from an up-country Charleston militia regiment, frowned. "Dinna believe the Papist—him what wears a foreign uniform."

Captain Foyne swung about, fumbled at his sword. "Who's the black son-of-a-bitch who said that? Yer naught but a damned turncoat Scot yerself." Stiff-legged like a dog preparing to fight he walked over to the speaker.

"That will do. Gentlemen! Gentlemen, quiet!" Colonel Laurens and some others undertook to placate the mercenary and in the end succeeded.

General Lincoln's stumpy, round-shouldered figure seemed particularly undistinguished by contrast to Colonel Pinckney's erect and muscular stature. "You're sure of this, Tom?"

"Yes, sir," the Carolinian cried. "I argued my best, offered every inducement to bring about an immediate assault, but General d'Estaing is so infatuated with the belief that the enemy is, in any case, undone he will not listen. He wants his heavy artillery in place. In fact, gentlemen, what General d'Estaing and that extraordinary old quiz Dillon, and de Noailles contemplates is a formal siege, a siege with parallels, saps and salients, all of which is to impress us ignorant Americans with the strategic skill of King Louis' General Officers."

"He's right," MacIntosh grunted, " 'tis an object lesson for our benefit and to show off their siege cannon which they brought so far."

Alistair, had he been an officer of field grade, would have made bold to speak. Not for nothing had he fought the Fort Sullivan campaign and had seen how swiftly militia men lost interest, went drifting off by two's and dozens, until suddenly the commanding officer found himself left with a mere cadre of troops. A vast impatience seized him. Why, a regular, formal siege of the town would take days and weeks, perhaps months. It was all so stupid, especially with all those ships lying in a most unprotected roadstead.

But there matters stood, and there they remained. When twilight fell, the troops in bivouac heard that significant sound of hammers, the crunching of spades against good Georgia earth in the direction of Savannah.

Next day the French sappers set to work, skillfully to construct redoubts, redans, and a line of entrenchments out of which parallels would soon start creeping towards the outer perimeter of a great semi-circle of fortifications designed to protect Savannah from the investing force.

X

THE GAZEBO

To Colonel Baron Edouard d'Esperey the commander's decision to undertake a siege came as most welcome. With Violette, his golden bay mare, between his legs, he found, by quick experimentation, that he could cover the six leagues from the siege lines to Hesperidée in just under fifty minutes of hard riding. He found, also, that as the days went by he grew more eager to get away from the dull routine of posting sentries, patrolling the areas in the rear of His Most Christian Majesty's army.

Sang de Dieu! The Chasseurs of Guadeloupe were as sorry a lot of troopers as he'd ever had to command. Nothing seemed to stay in their stupid black heads. This afternoon the mare, delicate in her stride as a deer, seemed to revel in the uncertain footing and unexpected intricacies of a game trail revealed to her master by that curiously deep, though naïve-seeming lieutenant of Elliott's Rangers.

Colonel d'Esperey was puzzled by Alistair Bryson; *un vrai type*. He had thought to fathom the ranger almost at a glance, but the discovery came that he understood the fascinating Antoinette Bryson's husband not even a little.

On reaching a fairly straight stretch of trail he touched Violette with the little silver spurs which were screwed into his boot heels. *Grace à Dieu*, tonight he wanted his arms about Théo more than ever—her charm, her appeal were growing ever greater. How passionately curious she was to hear about France, Versailles,

Gascony; to learn with avid aptitude the many pleasant things he so enjoyed teaching her.

Because certain Charleston pilots had refused to carry the Chevalier de la Motte-Picquet's men-of-war over Port Royal bar early in the month, no attack on Beaufort had been possible. Because of this it was possible for one Lieutenant-Colonel Maitland and some seven hundred tough and unimaginative Scottish troops of His Britannic Majesty's 71st Regiment to make a brilliant, resourceful and courageous march across wood, dune and swamps and finally join General Prevost's garrison. Yes, General d'Estaing had double reason now to regret his delay.

No wonder the crafty British General had begged for a twenty-four hours' truce, the Colonel mused bending his head to avoid a low-sweeping branch. That delay had permitted Colonel Maitland's force to come sneaking into Savannah, most unfairly to be sure, through a forgotten route along an old irrigation ditch.

That had taken place Friday last. Since then there had passed between Major-General Augustine Prevost and Major-General Charles Hector, Comte d'Estaing, many militarily correct demands, counter-demands, ultimatums, defiances, and counter-defiances. Philosophically, Edouard d'Esperey admitted that all this correspondence had accomplished nothing beyond winning an advantage for the English General.

All this seemed to follow the old, disastrous tradition. Whenever Frenchmen and Englishmen fought and died, the English profited.

D'Esperey picked up the bit, and Violette sailed the trunk of a sycamore which had blown over during the great gale. *Dieu de Dieu!* How agreeable to find oneself ashore again, to eat good food, to sleep in a warm and comfortable bed. How fortunate that the sluggish M. Habersham had a really excellent taste in wines.

Théo! The Colonel straightened in his saddle, flicked a bit of bark from the silver lacework of his tunic. Théo, possessed with all the fire, the ardor, the sparkle, imagination—and the restraint—of a truly great *maîtresse*; and, *parbleu*, she was a lady to her fingertips. Her marriage with the gross, unimaginative Peter Habersham, a plodding hackney shod with golden horseshoes, of course, had been one of convenience—quite as it should be.

He set his mare to a slow canter, a gait more appropriate to his mood. *Oh, la la!* What was happening to a certain colonel of the Hussars of Lauzun? Things were so different in this great, empty continent of America, where the food, the water, the very air exuded energy. Whoever would have imagined that Edouard d'Esperey could again become so thoroughly captivated, so truly devoted? He could imagine her already, with honey-colored hair cascading over her shoulders, with great blue eyes raised adoringly to his.

"Dieu de Dieu!" he rapped. "Edouard, *mon vieux*, I fear that like any *gosse* of a schoolboy you are smitten to the heart. Théo is so very sweet, so generous—"

He wanted to sink his small spurs of solid silver deep in the satin of Violette's golden bay flank—quickly, quickly to Théo. The Colonel, however, forced himself to take an interest in the landscape. From the northwest could be heard the dull *bom-m! bom!* of the frigate *La Truite's* cannonading. She now lay just below Savannah and for several days had bombarded Savannah without visible effect.

Had M. Habersham so far entertained suspicion? It seemed hardly possible. Of late he had been away from Hesperidée securing supplies for the besiegers, and curiously enough, everywhere he went he took with him—as a sort of bodyguard—a ruthless-looking sergeant-major from an American regiment, the Charleston Grenadiers. By no stretch of imagination could this Sergeant Curry be termed a gentleman.

"Be more liberal in your views, *mon vieux*," d'Esperey advised himself and, leaning forward, brushed a fly from his mare's withers. "Yes, the protocol of Versailles, of Europe must be forgotten. This is *l'Amérique–autre pays, autres mœurs.*"

In Versailles certainly no one would take either General Lincoln or Colonel Twiggs for gentlemen; let alone that big Scots-American who so thoroughly possessed the unswerving devotion of the beautiful Antoinette Bryson, *née* Proveaux. Several of his comrades in arms, the dashing Marquis du Pont de Vaux in particular, had lavished gallantries upon Mme. Bryson, had offered the subtlest of flatteries, but all in vain. The dark-eyed petite little wife had laughed, teased, and had paid de Vaux no serious attention at all.

His wiry figure yielding easily to the mare's stride, Colonel d'Esperey plucked a bright blue blossom from a creeper dangling over the trail, set it above the false hair dangling before his ear, and commenced to sing: *"Dites moi, petite abeille, Où trouverais-je pareille?"*

"Best ride slowly," he warned himself. "Théo cannot come to the gazebo until six. Besides, one must cool oneself a little—to smell like a stable boy is not desirable."

The American climate he found infinitely trying—so hot, so humid. Still, this served as welcome relief from campaigning in miserably overcrowded countries like the Lowlands, the Rhine, and

Italy. Why, in America even the peasants—or farmers—were permitted to kill and eat all the game they wished. Why not? The forests and rivers teemed with wild life.

In the whole first two weeks of this campaign he had not seen a blind decoy songbird. D'Esperey's long, brown face contracted. For silver-voiced and gorgeous little songbirds to be rendered sightless, merely that they might lure their fellows into the nets and potpies of a stinking peasantry, had always revolted his soul.

Almost before the Colonel realized it, he was riding out onto a slight rise overlooking the wide rice fields and the green lawns beyond Hesperidée. From below sounded the melodic clanging of a bell. He reined in.

Bigre! Le Capitaine Foyne had been right, for all he was Irish. This *was* a great rich country, incredibly idealistic and naïve right now, ripe for the plucking of the first European conqueror ready to conduct a serious war, not a bungling, half-hearted effort like this one of the British King and his ministers.

Deftly, the figure in blue, yellow and silver reined to the left and took a deer trail which circled the plantation. It would emerge, he knew by now, very close to a little knoll overlooking Ossabaw Creek. To tether Violette in the woods, then on foot and quite unseen, to reach the gazebo was of delightful simplicity. Later, one had only to ride back onto the road from Urban's plantation and Savannah, then appear at Hesperidée all hot and tired from a long ride in from camp.

Théo Habersham was waiting, lovely and dainty as a fresh new moon. When she saw him her arms flew apart and in her eyes shone such a light that Edouard d'Esperey experienced a wild upsurge of joy.

"*Ma petite colombe!*" he murmured. "My sweet little pigeon!" He captured one of the two curls which, by design, had escaped Théo's coiffure to tremble over her shoulder. Tenderly the hussar lifted the soft strands to his hard, brown lips. "Théo!" he whispered. "Théo!"

Smiling tenderly, she lifted a monitory forefinger. "*Doucement*, Edouard, softly. Tonight it is so very still one can hear a long way."

D'Esperey removed his tall busby, tossed it on to one of the two benches in the gazebo.

"Is he—?"

Théo sighed, bit her lip. "Yes. He sent word, but—well, we still shall manage somehow, *mon amour*."

I

Thunderbolt Landing

THAT THE VOYAGE down the coast from Charleston and up to
Thunderbolt hadn't been particularly comfortable, Minga Warren
readily admitted. Though his wife had uttered never a word of
complaint, Andrew Warren, Captain in the Navy of South Carolina,
was equally certain that the snow, *Two Sisters*, had not been
designed with an eye to the comfort of a woman some six months
pregnant.

Still and all, the weather had been favorable and the three days
and nights had passed pleasantly enough. Although Andrew and his
wife had been prepared for an impressive spectacle, their anticipation was as nothing to the amazing pageant presented by the anchorage off Thunderbolt.

"La, Andy!" Minga had gasped as the little coaster went skim-
ming under the great, elaborately-carved and gilded counters and
sterns. "I had never dreamed half so many ships even existed!
Why, they're huge! Enormous!"

The young Naval officer, very sober in a handsome new uniform,
had fairly beamed. "You'll credit me now? And I tell you once
more, this is but a small part of King Louis' Navy. *Allo là!*" He
shouted French to some hairy, sick-looking seamen who had found
energy enough to peer over the rail. They only stared in response.

Presently Andrew's enthusiasm waned when he recognized the
dreadful condition of a majority of the transports and men-of-war.
Unerringly, his sailor's eye detected sprung yards, weather-worn
rigging, gaping seams, crudely patched shot holes in the French
ships. Moreover, their bottoms were shamefully foul, regular
marine hayfields.

What really made him think hard was the fact that, in this almost
unprotected roadstead, a really strong east wind, let alone a gale,
would cause terrible and inevitable destruction among this vast
armada.

Of this, of course, he said nothing. No use worrying Minga;
she'd meet with more than her share of problems once the shore was
reached.

And he? He had given up trying to pick out the *Confederation* galley, the command of which he had accepted a week ago. Not anywhere could he spy a galley of any description.

Still, she was known to be in the vicinity. Lord! Wouldn't it be fine to walk the deck of a man-o'-war once more? Even the deck of an insignificant little state galley.

The Warrens' cottage, an ex-overseer's quarters, was small but fortunately removed from that heterogeneous tent village which had sprung up about the landing. The dwelling stood not far from the river upon a knoll shaded by some tremendous pines. Crude, and with no conveniences, it yet offered shelter and might be considered moderately attractive. By their third day of occupancy it had become a bit more livable.

Minga was in bad humor. Ever since reaching Thunderbolt, Andrew had been insufferably cocky and outspokenly contemptuous of General Prevost's brave little garrison. Andy just wasn't playing fair, wasn't living up to the compact they had solemnly entered into aboard the *Swan*.

Clearly, it had been understood that whatever Andrew thought of the King and the men who wore the royal scarlet, his opinions were never to be mentioned in the Warren house; conversely, she was never to repeat those Loyalist sentiments she had voiced so pungently off Caicos Passage.

Many a time it had come hard to honor that compact, but they had, and so their love had grown and grown. But now the Rebel talk, heard on all sides, was having its effect. She must warn him, give him a sharp reminder if necessary, Minga decided. She fanned herself angrily as she sat beneath a graceful mulberry tree, introduced years ago. The tree had thrived, though the silk industry which it had been intended to support, had not.

Late afternoon shadows began to creep over the bluffs. Out in the river the towering line of battleships was swinging to a change in the tide. She was able now to recognize a few of them. The *Robuste*, the *Caesar*, the *Hannibal*.

Heavens, all of them towered higher than the church steeple back home in Brewster. As the vessels swung further to their anchors, the gilded work on their ornate sterns gave off blinding flashes.

Up the river lay smaller ships, frigates—*La Fortune*—36; *Chimère*—26. Every now and then Minga scanned the upper reaches of the river for a flashing of oars which would mean that the French fleet had finished its daily bombardment of Savannah and that Andrew was returning.

Andrew? No. What she had seen was a barge passing from one

ship to another. One thing was truly fortunate: that Dr. Blanchard had had good friends in Charleston, else she and Andrew would never have found Arabia.

A singular creature, Arabia—with her stately carriage, her small hands and feet, and her pathetic conviction that she was no Negro at all, but the kidnapped daughter of a Berber *tchek*. Was this so? Possibly. Her features were coppery-brown and her nose slim and straight. The slave girl had been immensely grateful because Andrew, with his curious tact, had accepted her at her own valuation, yet never had allowed her to become derelict in her duties.

Using a frayed palmetto leaf Arabia had picked up near the landing, Minga fanned herself. Was it right that a young couple should have to live like this? Especially when a child was expected? First she'd had to stay in Philadelphia, frightened to death for fear some British Naval officer might recognize her husband. What a magnificent end for a honeymoon—to see her bridegroom hanged!

How Andrew had ever managed to charter a schooner and get her up the coast to Boston, she would never know. But he'd managed it.

Slowly her fingers locked as she remembered her certainty that Andrew would never return to a wife who, in the depths of her being, still held that the rebellion was "a wicked, unnatural revolt against constituted authority." That was the way Papa always had put it. But Andrew had come back, thinner of face and a little less forward. The Marine Committee, she guessed without his saying it, was still recalling that matter of the *Boston* and the *Hancock*.

A little uncomfortably she recalled how she had fortified her self-confidence, during those weeks in Philadelphia, by encouraging the polite attention and admiration of certain British officers in the garrison. When, incredibly, Sir Henry Clinton had had to evacuate Philadelphia, the temptation to depart with His Majesty's troops had been fearful. But she hadn't yielded, had been glad of it until they'd left Charleston to come to this God-forsaken spot.

Yes, despite pointed remarks from departing Loyalists, she had stayed, waited and had prayed for Andrew's safe return, even if it meant reoccupation of Philadelphia by the Continental Armies. She needed to think about those days now, Minga realized, as surreptitiously she eased her stay laces.

Land sakes! If she kept on at this rate she certainly was going to embarrass Andrew by presenting him with twins. She would have felt dreadfully conspicuous except that in Charleston so many women, and of every social status, were in the same condition. It was curious that, as Andrew pointed out in one of his detestable logical moods, the war brought on so many pregnancies.

"Replacements," he'd chuckled and had patted her swollen abdomen in a gentle fashion, "that's what the Navy needs!"

Never, Minga decided, would she ever forget the night he'd returned from Boston. His somber hair had smelt strong of the sea, his face was hard from the buffeting of the winds.

It might well have been that night that Theophrastus—as they playfully had come to name the unborn child—had been conceived. The rapture of reunion after so hazardous a separation had been exquisite, overwhelming. Could they ever make love so intensely again?

The trip north had wrought changes in Andrew. His Yankee relatives and friends must have gorged him with a certainty that, because of the French Alliance, the war was now as good as won. Stuff and nonsense! Who would expect the British to throw in their hand simply because King Louis' grenadiers, siege guns and line of battleships had appeared on the coasts of America?

Despite all this, she had prayed every night for Andrew to get an appointment to some vessel in the Continental Navy—his return to duty was the principle goal of his present existence. Would the Marine Committee act favorably upon receipt of Dr. Blanchard's report concerning certain drugs and surgical instruments, imported at great risk from Jamaica?

Curiously, she tested her distended abdomen. It was astonishing how the skin there could stretch and stretch. Where she was going to find some new stays Minga didn't know, but she must have some— the old pair were 'way too small.

Minga picked some sweet grasses, idly commenced to plait them into a little bracelet. A faint mutter in the distance suggested that it might be going to storm again. Sure enough, after a bit, orange-hued clouds began to bank up across the mouth of the Savannah.

Blom-m! She listened carefully. No. That wasn't thunder, not this time. The French, in desultory fashion, still were bombarding the British defenses.

Although the redistribution of her body's weight had rendered some of her movements unexpectedly awkward, Minga rose not ungracefully and went indoors to lay out a fresh shirt and other clothes. Andrew would certainly be hot and black with burnt powder.

"Arabia, run down to the spring and fetch me up a pitcher of water. Oh, and a bottle of Canary, too."

"Yes, Mistress." The copper-skinned slave smiled, pattered out on small bare feet.

Minga hoped the wine would be cool enough; Andrew was fussy on that point. What a curious blend her husband was! The heritage of a French mother and traits derived from Horatio Warren and his grim New England forebears made a perpetual battleground of his emotions.

During the past months Minga pretty well had decided that, in Andrew's character, the New England side dominated in the serious problems of life, while the French ruled his lighter moments. La! Andy possessed a real appreciation of the social amenities, of culinary skill, of the beauties of nature and of the opposite sex!

From time to time Andrew had betrayed the existence of some surprising, and distinctly Gallic, notions beneath that heavy black hair of his. Yet, even when she was beginning to be troubled, she had read in the depths of his dark eyes a certain light which was infinitely reassuring.

Thank goodness a breeze had begun to beat up-river! It brought not only a freshness to the air, but the savory odors of cooking under way in the French boat guards' camp.

Arabia came running back from the spring by the big sycamore, skirt looped up high and earthenware pitcher slopping over.

"The Master is coming," she panted. "Mr. Warren has got good news!"

The slave's assumption of knowledge inexpressibly annoyed Minga. "What makes you talk such foolishness? How do you know the Captain has good news? Probably nothing has happened at all."

The Arab girl's smile faded and her narrow jet eyes sought the ground.

"Of course I don't *know*, Mrs. Warren; it's just the way Mr. Warren is coming up from the landing."

"Go in and set the table." Minga got to her feet, gave a flick to the lace edging her bodice. Automatically, she then glanced at her belly. Good. When she stood, she didn't stick out half so much.

After expelling her breath, she set up her stay laces, thus achieved quite a bit of false slenderness. Aside from her swollen figure, she guessed she was looking uncommonly well, because as her pregnancy advanced, her color had become more pronounced, and her gray-green eyes had achieved fresh luster.

Andrew came into sight on the trail winding up from the crowded beach at Thunderbolt Landing; he wasn't exactly running but he was carrying his tunic and moving his long legs very fast.

"Minga! Minga!" he yelled. "She's here! My galley's come down from Beaufort."

"Oh, sweet, I'm so glad," she called. But she wasn't. Soon that galley's guns would be firing upon, killing the King's men, driving law and order from America. She was glad though that, as the lesser of two evils, he had command over an American ship. All along she'd been terrified that Andrew would tire of waiting for an American vessel and, in his impetuous way, take service under Louis XVI. He could converse with those foreigners without the least difficulty and they seemed very prone to like him; worst of all, the French naval officers appreciated his worth to their service.

"Minga, you ought to see her! She's well built and new." He came up beaming, face bright with perspiration, chest tossing with deep breathing, ridiculously like a small boy at that moment.

"That's good, Andrew," she murmured. "How big is she?"

"Confound it, the *Confederation* ain't extra large—only seventy-eight feet at the water line."

He flung both arms around her, kissed her again and again. "No, by some standards I guess she isn't much, darling, but she's American and a man-o'-war, and mounts two eighteen pounders and I haven't learned my gunnery if I don't shoot the backside off old Prevost's goddamned bloody-blacks and hired killers."

"Andrew." Minga twisted herself out of his arms. "How dare you say such things to me?"

"What things?" he demanded in amazement.

"Calling His Majesty's troops 'bloody-blacks' and 'hired killers.' "

The elation faded from his face. "Well," said he slowly, "that's what they are, aren't they?"

"No, they're not!"

"In Old George's Army," he insisted ominously, "a soldier can get the skin flogged off his back for the least sort of a mistake and—"

"That's a lie!" Minga blazed.

He went white. "Don't call me a liar; I don't take that from anybody!"

"You are! You promised never to defame the King, England or the British Army. Yet ever since we came to this—this awful place you've—"

"—I've told you the truth," Andrew growled and violently flung his tunic onto a bench beside the cottage door. "Look here, my lass, it's time we quit this silly business of pretending to be neutral between ourselves. It can't be done and it won't be. I'm fighting the British, and either you'll come over to my side or—"

Minga's lips commenced to quiver not with sorrow but with rage. "Come to *your* side? I, join a pack of cowardly, treacherous, ungrateful savages who call for help from England's greatest enemy—"

"—And tell me, Madam, who was it hired a pack of damned,

murdering German looters to ravage America? Who is it who starves helpless prisoners?''

"Ha! Hark at who's talking about ill-treating prisoners!'' Minga raged. "What about that awful place at Simbury? What about the abominable treatment of Burgoyne's men, of the Convention troops?''

"They refused to obey orders,'' Andrew cried. His fingers clamped down on her elbow.

"Let me go, you coward!''

"I won't!''

"You will! I'll make you mighty sorry!''

"Try it! Anyhow I'll not go on like this—when you reach a decision, Madam, you can send word aboard the galley whether it's *me* you want—or that precious German blockhead in Whitehall Palace!''

He let go. Amid a grim silence, he retrieved his coat, turned on his heel and went striding back towards the landing.

II

THE EIGHTEEN POUNDER

SMOKE from several houses burning in Savannah poured down the face of the bluff on which the town stood, crept out over the river. Bitter-smelling powder smoke from French frigates' guns also hung low and, fog-like, drifted down-stream. As resonant as notes on a kettle drum reverberated the methodical firing of French mortars mounted on salients which, day by day, had been creeping closer towards the British lines.

Once in a while, British matrosses would make reply from the fourteen guns in a bastion erected an an anchor for the extreme left of General Prevost's line. Brief flashes of orange-red flame could be seen through the smoke which now lifted, now closed in, blinding the crew serving a long, eighteen pound gun mounted on the *Confederation*'s short bow deck.

A report heavier than usual beat down through the smoky haze.

"That, sir, were a twenty-five pounder,'' observed Joe Atherton, standing at the side of Captain Andrew Warren, C.S.N.

The crew of the *Confederation* long since had come to recognize the report peculiar to almost every piece in the bastion. Although he did not lower his night glass, Andrew nodded, listening hard. Could the enemy's twenty-five range this position?

Atherton cast an eye to windward, noted the palpitating glare of several new fires. 'S truth, after nigh-on three weeks of near inactivity this siege was beginning to pick up. By straining his eyes the gunner's mate could make out the silhouette of three tall masts protruding from the current. Yonder lay scuttled H.M.S. *Rose*, frigate. Up in Newport, Bristol and Providence in Rhode Island, the people would be glad to hear that this well-bated vessel had been sunk to block a channel—an ignominious end.

"Stand by, there."

Atherton jumped. Captain Warren bent over, was sighting the long eighteen pounder himself. Employing a leaded mallet, he was delivering a series of taps on the quoins which elevated or depressed the piece.

That their captain was a rare fine gunner the whole of the *Confederation*'s company would defend to their last breath. The crew had cheered themselves hoarse when he'd shot out of existence two guns and embrasures on the enemy bastion.

This Monday, the fourth of August, 1779, marked a commencement of the first real bombardment by the allied armies. The thunder of the besiegers' guns swelled in the distance and Andrew's heart lifted to watch the scarlet-gold parabolas described by high-arching mortar shells.

The British—damn their stubborn refusal to submit—couldn't be sleeping extra well tonight. Half a dozen, maybe more, fires were raging in different parts of the town, filling the night with the acrid scent of destruction.

Joe Atherton was grinning a fierce, happy grin. Every time the *Confederation*'s long eighteen went off, he prayed her shell would burst where it would find some officers of His Britannic Majesty's Navy. There must be quite a few of them up in the town, out of the *Rose*, the *Germaine*, the *Keppel*, the *Fowey*, the *Ariel* and the rest.

For the thousandth time the Englishman slipped a hand up under his shirt, tested those cold, too-smooth ridges of scar tissue. Because he'd kept an unmarked handkerchief found aboard H.M.S. *Niger*, he'd bear those scars for life. Such brutality was wrong, wrong! Yet he wondered. Aboard American ships no one got catted, but the discipline aboard such vessels was something to despair over.

Jed Beetle drawled, "There must be something afoot, or them

there sweet-scented frog-eaters wouldn't be wasting all that powder.''

A house in town flared like a giant torch, revealed in silhouette the French frigate lying in the lee of Hutchinson's Island. *La Truite's* gun crews kept on firing methodically, carefully, trying to drop a shell into a powder magazine which everyone knew to be situated to the southeast of Christ Church.

Now Jed Beetle second in command could make out a huddle of British merchantmen anchored close to the King's provisioning houses.

''A hot shot, Gunner!'' the Captain called. ''We'll try one now.''

Volunteer rowers sat tense on their benches, put down a supper of bread and cold meat which they had been sluicing down with beer. A fine sturdy crew they were, for the most part composed of free mulattoes with a sprinkling of poor whites.

''Hey, Cap! What ye going to fetch this time?'' one of them yelled.

Andrew's lips tightened. Again he had to remind himself that this wasn't a Continental vessel, just a state cruiser manned by a volunteer crew.

He wished to God his eighteen-pounder's range included that huddle of vessels lying in the river under the bluff, but it didn't. To see a mast or even a yard come crashing, smashing down, meant something; to bombard a great, inert town like this, was an unexciting as opening a breakfast egg.

If only he could range that magazine!

Delicately, he estimated his galley's swing to the current and laid his sights on the church steeple. When they were in line, he then traversed his piece two degrees to port.

''Fetch me the ball.''

Down in the waist of the galley half a dozen roundshot lay like a phoenix's clutch of eggs, glowing upon a bed of charcoal. The fire had been kindled on a sandbox and concealed from the batteries on the bluff by a canvas dodger. Lazily its smoke drifted astern past a blue flag bearing in its field a slim, silver crescent. Some day, Andrew hoped privately, the Stars and Stripes would supplant all these fancy state flags.

''Heave, ho!'' Atherton and a sergeant of the Carolina State Marines employed an apparatus consisting of a bar, equipped with claws like an ice dealer's tongs, to pluck a cannonball from the heart of the charcoal fire.

''Wad! Wad!'' ordered Andrew; whereupon a freckled-faced mulatto drove a wad of water-soaked oakum deep down the eighteen-pounder's throat.

Everyone watched the forward progress of the red-hot shot. A faint glow from the molten metal lit the faces of Atherton and the sergeant as they heaved the reddish-white globe to the cannon's lip. Sparks flickered from the grip of the claws; the sponger poised his ramrod.

"Release!" Andrew directed in a quiet voice. "Easy does it, lads."

An expert push of the rammer guided the red-hot shot into the bore, then the claws let go. Instantly, a furious hissing sound ensued and from the cannon's mouth gushed a dense column of steam.

"Stand clear!" rapped Jed Beetle.

His weight on the balls of his feet, Andrew poised the linstock and the glowing end of his gunner's match over a teaspoonful of 4F powder, priming the eighteen pounder.

A few of the rowers clapped hands over their ears, turned aside. Joe Atherton stood peering intently at the town. He didn't want to miss the effect of another shot at His Bloody Majesty's Navy.

When a lance of fire started upwards through the dark, the whole galley rocked to starboard and for a brief instant flame illuminated the little craft from stern to stern; the mulattoes' teeth shining, their faces yellower than ever.

Like a thing alive, the eighteen pounder sprang backwards under the recoil, its gun carriage wheels rumbling. The breeching tackle snapped leisurely. The *Confederation* rolled back to port as a great puff of acrid, rotten-smelling smoke set the crew to coughing and rubbing their eyes.

"Swab, and be quick about it," ordered Andrew Warren. Next he beckoned Atherton—the deserter's eyes were astonishing good by night—and went forward to learn whether, presently, a new fire would flicker amid the silhouette of the besieged city.

Smoothly, the galley swung to the current, the water gurgling placidly about her bow. The rowers bet among themselves. The two men poised on the galley's bow strained their eyes.

Billows of smoke from homes already burning continued to sting the eyes of the watchers.

Atherton caught his breath. "You see it, sir."

"Where?"

"Over there, sir, south o' the church—a big storehouse. A main fine shot, sir, if I may say so."

Andrew chuckled. Owing to his clumsiness with figures, the theories of gunnery had come hard, so his satisfaction was the greater, therefore, when they brought results. Quickly, a slender spindle of flame began to spiral skywards, to draw reflection from nearby roofs. Pretty soon the whole of Christ Church glowed with firelight.

"Heh! heh! heh!" chuckled the oarsmen. "Ain't the Cappen *somethin'*?" They slapped each other on the back, reckoned that when next Cappen Warren wanted the beat lifted, plenty of oars would be eager to oblige.

"Cappen, if only dem Frog-eaters shoot half so handy," the free mulatto steersman called, "why, Savannah'd have fell days ago!"

Andrew chuckled.

From the French siege lines several more mortar bombs strewed sparks skywards before plunging into General Prevost's position.

Now that the smoke was driving away those plagues of mosquitoes which made life a hell ashore, it was not uncomfortable out here on the North Branch. Andrew was smiling and still. A neat bit of gunnery that last shot, even if he had done it. It would cost the damned British—damned British? No, they were enduring cruel punishment and jeering at their enemies.

Smart, that's what Prevost was. Trust him to play on d'Estaing's out-moded ideas of chivalry until he had strengthened his defenses. Damned British? Minga! Why couldn't she be made to understand that you could hate a man and yet respect him at the same time?

The French logic in his make-up came to the fore. She loved and admired everything British simply because it *was* British.

The French weren't like that. They liked some Americans, despised others, judged the individual case in its own merits. Minga. Why had she flared up like that? Why? He hadn't wanted to pick a fight, not with her in a strange place—and pregnant.

Just the same there would have to be some head to this business; a family couldn't go on being half American and half English, in sympathy. Unhappily he wondered if, when he got back to the anchorage at Thunderbolt, Minga would be waiting at the landing.

"Only one more shot, sir," Jed Beetle reported. "The powder chest is near empty."

Standing on the galley's blunt bow, Andrew considered his next target. Nothing offered itself. Well, in any case he'd better place his last shot up-wind. A conflagration from that position would spread. He wished to glory he could find that powder house.

Sullenly, British cannon kept growling at the French siege lines, at the ships in the river.

"Sir, the enemy's up to something in the bastion," Atherton reported. Sure enough, voices and undertone of dull, indistinguishable sounds marked some new activity there.

The *Truite* fired again and, faithfully, the flashes of her guns became reflected in the Savannah's slow current. High overhead, a bittern croaked in startled surprise.

After his galley's last shot had flown screaming into the dark, Andrew ordered his crew to their benches. They manned their eighteen foot oars with celerity because the smoke hanging over the river had lifted and the houses in town were burning brighter than ever, lighting up the whole scene.

Hardly had the galley benches been manned, however, than fresh clouds of smoke came beating down from the bluff. Rapidly, they masked the French frigate, the shore line and the *Confederation* in an eye-stinging, blinding smoke.

With Atherton, Andrew remained on the bow, trying to determine whether the galley's last shot had been effective.

"Ready oars?" The coxswain yelled as the galley's anchor came splashing, bumping over the side.

"Forward, all!" Followed a dull thumping and banging of sweeps against greased oar-ports cut into the galley's thwarts.

Sluggishly, the *Confederation* got under way. The wood smoke became so dense that Andrew's eyes smarted and he had to dig knuckles into his eyes.

It must have been a round shot from the twenty-five pounder on the bastion which struck the galley full in the bow. Under the impact splinters flew and the *Confederation* heeled far over to the starboard.

Andrew, jarred loose, fell into the river, but came up in time to hear Mr. Beetle yelling, "Pull! Pull for your lives! We've been struck!" A sweep's heavy oaken blade descended, struck the swimmer's head with such stunning force that fiery serpents writhed before Andrew's eyes. Into his mouth rushed quantities of warm and muddy water.

III

THE DESERTER

JOE ATHERTON swam slowly towards a faint splashing, sensed, rather than saw, a figure making weak struggles. He hooked a hand under the apparition's chin. " 'Ere, mate, 'ang on. They'll be coming back soon's they've found we're gorn."

Treading water, trying to see through the smoke, Joe Atherton listened. Ha! The galley *was* returning; very distinctly he recognized the rhythmic swish and splash of oars.

" 'Ere!" he yelled. " 'Ere! *'Ere!''*

"Who's that?" a voice demanded.

"Joe Atherton, yer bloody idiots. Got some other cove—'e's hurt."

The oars slowed and through the murk loomed a dim outline. It wasn't the galley, but a smaller craft. Winded and weary from supporting the other swimmer's weight, Atherton was glad to grab at a boat hook when someone called, "Grab hold!"

" 'Ere, save me, mate," he called, then hands gripped him under the arms and hauled him over the gunwale of a small boat. A moment later his companion was dumped, dripping and silent, onto the floor boards.

For many moments Atherton was content to lie still, gasping, while the rowboat continued to pull steadily along, her oarsmen puffing with effort. Presently the wind raised the smoke and at the same time fanned flames burning above.

"Why! Wot the—'' Atherton struggled up between the legs of the oarsmen. His breath went out with a rush because the uniforms of the men in the stern sheets were not blue, but of a palpitating scarlet.

"Hullo!" The lieutenant in charge of the British picket boat, also, had made a discovery. "Stab my bowels, Jenkins, these aren't chaps off the *Comet*! It's a couple of bleeding Rebels we've rescued."

Joe Atherton shivered from more than the night wind's rawness. That voice he'd have recognized anywhere as belonging to Hubert Bentley Laughton, a sub-lieutenant of His Britannic Majesty's Regiment of Marines. Laughton who, aboard H.M.S. *Niger*, had presided on that accursed summary court, supremely indifferent that his finding would sentence this poor devil of a seaman to have half the skin lashed from his back.

"Stop him! Stop him, there!" snapped the lieutenant. Atherton had risen, and tried to plunge over the side. With a carbine barrel a marine hit the deserter across the chest so hard that he collapsed, lay on the floor boards again, gasping like a fish stranded on a sandbank.

Without interest Atherton heard the French frigate fire some more shots, heard the mortars boom in the distance. He turned his head and, by the light of the conflagration, tried to see who it was had been knocked overboard with him. Blood, pouring over the limp figure's face, made him hard to recognize, but after a bit

Atherton's jaw tightened. He should have guessed it would be Captain Warren. They hadn't been standing five feet apart when that blooming cannon ball had struck below them.

Oars rattled and presently the boat slid in beside a small wooden jetty.

"Easy there," a voice spoke sharply. "That one's an officer."

"He's a damned rebel," someone else retorted. A musket barrel dug into Atherton's ribs with cruel force. "On yer feet, you!"

A lantern gleamed. "What about the officer?"

"He's senseless, sir."

"Detail two men to carry him then, you stupid ass," the marine lieutenant rasped. "Staff may want to question him."

A dull gleam of braid showed. "Question him? Damme, Laughton, your man's dead—look at his bally head, man. It's stove in."

"Orders were to bring in any prisoners, sir."

"Correct. Well, most likely the surgeons will finish him off, if he don't die before they get at him."

The night was full of sound, smoke, and restless, dancing red lights.

"What about the other? Where's a lantern?"

When the glare lit his features, Joe Atherton knew it was all up.

"Stab me!" Lieutenant Laughton ejaculated, "Why, it's that cockerel who spoke so big aboard the *Niger*. Pinion him!"

A quartet of sailors grabbed Atherton, lashed his arms behind him.

"Who's this?" demanded a hollow-eyed captain of marines.

"A deserter out of the *Niger*, sir, I sat on a summary court over him." Laughton chuckled. "Damme, since the *Fowey's* been scuttled the Old Man's been lower than a tadpole's bottom. This hanging will cheer him up no end."

On the floor of what once had been a blacksmith's shop Joe Atherton lay because his feet had been lashed so tightly together he couldn't stand on them; they felt numb and cold, so very cold.

A pity that his guards were Germans—a queer lot, heavy, doltish fellows out of the Regiment of Wissenbach. Had they been true-blue Englishmen, he might have persuaded one of them to ease these agonizing cords a trifle. But, here, in the face of the enemy the mercenaries were anxious. All too well they were aware of the sentiments towards mercenaries entertained by native Americans. They couldn't stand looting and reprisals and brutality as should a well-regulated peasantry. Whenever a German detachment got cut off there were precious few prisoners taken; in fury over the wanton torture of noncombatants, many a wounded Hessian, Brunswicker, and Wissenbacher had been clubbed to death by farmers and petty merchants or scalped by woodsmen.

Soon it would be broad daylight, Joe Atherton's last daylight in this world. Hot tears welled from under the deserter's eyelids. "Here's the end of it," he admitted. "Gawd help me."

A beautiful morning this, all pink and gray and a little misty. The siege cannon had fallen silent hours ago, the drums had not yet sounded the reveille.

Wearily, Atherton's memory trudged back over the years, back until it paused in lovely, green Devonshire; back, more precisely, to a little seaside hamlet just above Biddeford. A smile twisted the prisoner's dirty features when he saw waves come swishing up to a red-faced lad's short legs. Ever so clearly he could recall that same boy watching the seagulls swoop and cry overhead, snaring those rabbits which, in prodigious warrens, inhabited the cliffs.

His had been a happy childhood and boyhood. The Athertons were a respected family—had been for generations.

Gramper hadn't done badly for a fisherman—he had owned his own cottage and fishing smack, he had; Pa, too, no less had thriven, had paid his taxes, feared God, and had honored his King.

Some of the pain and uncertainty left Joe Atherton. Gawd! There was pretty, red-cheeked Isabel leaving the mossy old church of a Sunday, all trigged out in white; bold, saucy Isabel who had tormented him because his hands and feet were so big—and had kissed him fondly among the cool shadows of Sir Charles Coffin's buttery.

He groaned but not loud enough to earn another kick from his blue-coated guardian. How awful it was to know that he couldn't ever again smell the sea, as it smelt in Devon. Nor would Joe Atherton ever again watch storm waves vault the barricado off Boston harbor.

What was going to be done with Captain Warren—if he had survived? Gawd's truth, last night he'd looked deader than dead—a great shame, for there went a fine officer and a rare brave gentleman.

The mockingbird went on singing, a dog barked, and somewhere a cow mooed. From head to foot Atherton's whole body ached, but not so much as his mind. Captain Reid had had no right to call him "a scoundrel, a hang-dog traitor to his King, a worthless cur of a deserter."

The pain in his wrists was becoming intolerable; the cords gnawed at his flesh like the fangs of some animal. He supposed he had deserted—but what? Injustice, hopelessness, blows, foul food, fouler companions, misery in a service into which he had been forced without any legal right.

His tongue's tip sought a gap left by the teeth knocked out by a boatswain's mate in command of the press gang. February the seventh, 1772, was the date of that terrible night in Bristol. He'd not been treated like a true-born Briton. Before God's throne he could lay to that. Futile revolt wrung his soul.

Was there any justice in hanging a man for quitting a service into which he had been driven by blows and insults and threats? No war was being fought back in '72.

"Oh, God, don't let them hang me," he prayed softly, while sweat rolled down his cheeks and stung his eyes. "I'm feared, dear Lord. I'm terrible feared to hang. What happens after that rope chokes the life out of a man?" He shuddered, ground his teeth to stifle screams of fright. "Oh, Jesus, save me. Please save me. They did You to death, too, didn't they? And for doing nothing wrong." On the floor, lumpy with old hoof parings, Atherton writhed slowly.

How bright the sky was growing. The tears slipped faster down his cheeks. To think he'd never in Boston again know the tender compulsion of Jennie's arms about him! He'd never feel that rare, fine glow of good Jamaica rum warming his bowels.

Somewhere a drum began to rattle briskly. Further away, a horse whinnied. Savannah was awaking. Through the open door of the blacksmith shop he saw a file of Loyalist infantry in dirty orange uniforms march by, heavily, like the dead-tired men they were.

A detail halted at the door of the smithy and voices spoke in German. Atherton shivered. They had come to take him, Joseph Lake Atherton, out to be hanged. He didn't dare look up. But to his intense and delighted surprise the detail marched on almost immediately. A single pair of black gaiters and heavy shoes drew near.

"So? Mine brave spy veeps?" The new guard was a fat red-nosed fellow with a face like a character in one of those broadsides the urchins peddled along Piccadilly. "A fine morning, mine friend, eh? *Ja*, a fine cheerful morning to hang. Rain iss so sad. Ha! Ha!"

Joe shut his eyes, said nothing. He felt the earth tremble under his cheek when a battery of artillery rolled by.

The German propped his musket against the anvil and, reaching into his haversack, brought out a piece of bread and cheese. "Hanging iss not so bad, mine friend," he observed. "Not if der hangman kicks you from the ladder off und you drop.'' The Wissenbacher chuckled, bit off another mouthful. "But ven dey hoist, you choke, you kick, you strangle slow—''

"—Shut up, yer bleedin' swine! Stop it!'' To avoid the fellow's mocking gaze Joe rolled over stiffly onto his other side. This was a mistake because a horseshoe, with two or three broken nails protruding from it, immediately dug into his thigh. He rolled back.

The German roared with laughter and bent over the condemned prisoner. "Did you hear? To strangle slow, slow, iss not good, no.''

"I won't 'ang! God won't let them 'ang me! I ain't done nothing wrong! I—I— Oh, God, don't let them strangle me! I—I *want to live!*''

Suddenly terror-stricken, Atherton began to writhe and squirm over the earthen floor, was still writhing when the measured tread of several men penetrated his consciousness.

"I say, what the devil *is* this?'' demanded a brisk young voice.

The German caught up his musket, froze into ramrod rigidity. "The deserter, *mein Herr*. Condemned to death.''

"Oh. Well, let's get on with it.''

The awful moment, then, was at hand. "Oh, please, sir, don't 'ang me!'' Atherton choked. "You won't— I'm innocent, I am.''

The detail was composed of sailors, a hard-looking lot, under command of a tall young midshipman.

The midshipman frowned, caught his breath. "You're certain this is the prisoner?''

"Yes, sir,'' an English voice replied. "Deserter condemned to death.''

The midshipman said, "Where's the rope?''

A petty officer wearing a big, brass-hilted cutlass knuckled his forelock. "Sorry, sir; didn't bring any along.''

"Why the devil not? How can you hang a man without a rope?''

"We was ordered straight up from the docks, sir.''

"Look about, should be one around here.''

In the distance commenced a furious cannonade, followed by yelling. The noise of troops moving northwards on the double-quick followed rapidly.

"No rope here, sir,'' the petty officer reported, all out of breath.

The midshipman looked about impatiently. "Damn! I must get back to my battery. Peterson, run down to the 60th and borrow a length of rope.''

"Aye, aye, sir.''

Atherton rolled onto his back, stared upwards. "In God's name, kind sir, don't let me 'ang. I'm English—'anging ain't for Englishmen."

His blue eyes round as buttons, the fair-haired young midshipman stood looking down. "You talk south of England. You are from Cornwall?"

"No, sir, I'm a Devon man." A desperate eagerness invaded his voice. "You—you won't let me 'ang? I can see you won't, sir. You've a kind face."

Louder grew the sound of battle. A trumpet began to wail, first correctly, then hurriedly, then imperatively.

The midshipman rubbed his chin, glanced out into the fresh sunlight. "No, I'll not hang you."

"Oh-h, God bless you, sir!"

"Be still and turn over on your face."

"He's going to cut the cords," Atherton thought as, joyously, he obeyed. "The Lord God knows I'm innocent. He has 'eard my prayer."

"No. I won't hang you," the midshipman said quickly and held a boarding pistol to the back of the prisoner's dusty head.

Going white as a new topsail, he squeezed the trigger then turned away to be violently ill.

IV

CONSEIL DE GUERRE

IN THE great withdrawing room of Hesperidée General Charles Hector, Comte d'Estaing, was growing impatient with his generals, admirals, colonels, captains, and aides. Antoinette Bryson, stitching at her petit-point frame upstairs was sure of it. By now she had learned to recognize the nervous, icily clear accents of d'Estaing, General Dillon's deep-throated enunciation, the Count Pulaski's French slightly accented by Polish.

The Naval commanders, the Comte de Broves, de la Motte-Picquet and ambitious young La Perouse, generally could out-shout their army colleagues. Bickering with them were the voices of Captain Gadsden, Colonel Pinckney, General MacIntosh, and saturnine General de Noailles.

"In any case we cannot delay a day longer," de la Motte-Picquet was repeating with profane embellishments.

Restlessly, Théo Habersham shifted upon a love seat; her bright blue eyes flickered to a handsome brass clock, the decoration of which represented Diana, shamelessly nude, leaning happily against a somnolent stag.

"Look here, General, this plan just ain't reasonable." Angrily, General Lincoln's hoarse voice beat out of the open window below. On a night so still as this one could almost hear a bat's wings, let alone every word spoken at the council table.

"I am dead agin this business of a joint attack," Lincoln was insisting. "What with the dark and the differences in our speech, we'll likely get all tangled up. Now *I* say, you hit your part of Prevost's line and we'll hit ours—hard as we can, but let's have plenty of room in between."

"*Mon cher Général*, what you propose is nonsense," cut in de Noailles' clipped accents. "If your Corps will be so good as to do as it is told, everything will proceed smoothly. Eh? What do you say, Gadsden?"

Gadsden, although delighted at any opportunity of bringing the siege to a head, deliberated. At length he drawled, "Well, sir, since you ask me, I'd say there's a lot in what General Lincoln says."

"A lot? Boiling tar and damnation!" it was Twiggs, the Georgian, speaking. "Let these foreign—" he checked himself. "Look here, General, why don't we-all attack from opposite sides of the city at the same time? Let's put some militia at the British center for a diversion."

"No, gentlemen," cut in the Commander-in-Chief. "I shall deliver my main attack along the road to—what do you call it, Fontanges?"

"The road to Augusta, *mon Général.*"

"But, dammit all," MacIntosh cut in, "that's where the earthworks are strongest, that's where Prevost and Maitland seem to expect our effort."

"That's correct!" Lincoln raised his voice over an excited gabble of comment. "No, Count, if we hit the Britishers hard—and we've enough men to do it—we can force Prevost to split his force."

Meaningly, Colonel Twiggs added, "If mistakes are made—well, we'll know who's to blame."

"*Messieurs, messieurs!*" D'Estaing's voice rang with a peculiarly compelling quality. "Please to recall that it is *I* who command here." He hesitated. "A delay of, say, a week would advance our works to a point from—"

"Delay? *Sacré nom de Dieu!*" Antoinette all but dropped her

thimble Admiral de Broves had roared so loud. "Delay? There can
be not a day's further delay."

"Why?" demanded Colonel Twiggs. "Gettin' tired o' the
scenery?"

The Frenchman snorted. "You talk like a clown, *Monsieur*.
Cannot any of you understand? My crews are perishing for lack of
supplies—every day thirty to forty of my marines die of disease.
The autumn gales are to be expected at any hour and what shelter
have my ships? None. Not that much!"

D'Estaing spoke in icy displeasure. "Really, de Broves, you
exaggerate. The siege progresses well—"

"Nom d'un nom!" The Admiral was fairly shouting now.
"Think of the Indies—*our* Indies, *Monsieur le Comte*. If my ships
are lost, the accursed English have the islands for the taking. No!
No! No! In duty to his Majesty I dare not delay here. This estuary is
a death trap. You must attack at once, General. In three days' time I
must put out to sea."

Apparently his arguments were not without effect, for a silence
fell, endured until d'Estaing said, "I bow to your opinion, my dear
colleague. The attack will be delivered with all haste."

"Then what will be the order of this attack?" Dillon queried
angrily.

D'Estaing spoke so quickly it was clear he had thought the whole
matter out in advance. "Let there be a feint from our right. M.
Dejean, you will support Colonel Huger and his militia in delivering
the principal feint from the direction of the Phoenix plantation."

In the depths of the room somebody muttered, "Militia!" and
snickered. "They'll faint all right!"

"Very well, General, but there are a lot of rice fields that way."
Colonel Huger's voice was almost British in its incisiveness. "Do
you imagine our enemies would credit our risking a real advance?"

D'Estaing stared coldly at the weatherbeaten figure in the faded
and patched brown tunic. "You gentlemen of America seem prone
to credit M. le General Prevost with omniscience."

"Suppose we win through into the town?"

"Why then, *Monsieur le Colonel*, you will continue to advance. Monsieur de Sablière with the Saint Dominguais and Martinique regiments will arrange another feint at the enemy center."

Abstractedly, the Commander-in-Chief stroked the fine lace at
his throat, bent over and considered the excellent map one M. Julius
Bien had drawn of the operations. From where he stood Alistair
could see neat black- or red-inked oblongs, triangles, and ruler
marks dotting the map.

"I have determined that the grand attack shall be delivered by our left, simultaneously by four columns—two French, two American.''

Alistair Bryson, standing in the hall outside, saw General Lincoln's plump cheeks fill with color as he turned.

''Say, Habersham, what about the country that way? It's over near McGillivray's, ain't it?''

In his rôle of host Peter Habersham occupied a chair at the council table. He smiled. ''The land that way is rather low, General, all the way to Ogeechee Ferry. There's part of Yamacraw Swamp to either side of that road.''

''Which road?'' demanded MacIntosh in obvious uneasiness.

''Why, there's only one. It goes to Ebenezer and then on to Augusta.''

''These swamps will secure our flanks,'' de Noailles pointed out while fiddling with the bejewelled cross of some order.

Young Habersham shook his head. ''That's true enough, Monsieur, but this causeway's blamed narrow. If 'twas me, I don't believe I'd try that.'' Peter Habersham had at long last arrived at a decision. So far, for not too clever a fellow, he had straddled the fence pretty well. On the one hand hadn't he made it possible for Prevost to pass an occasional messenger through the lines? Little favors were what he had bestowed, nothing flagrant, or downright treasonable. No, certainly not!

Yes. It began to look now as if Prevost was in for a licking—a complete capitulation. That last Loyalist deserter had claimed matters were going hard, mighty hard, with the garrison. For one thing, rations were running low; for another, discord was rampant. The Loyalist troops hated both the British and their mercenary allies, while the steady, unimaginative regulars were making no effort to conceal a fine contempt for the less disciplined, more individualistic men serving in the colonial regiments. The Wissenbachers and Hessians were so brutal, so adept at looting that they were despised and hated by English and Loyalist alike.

In studious carelessness, Peter Habersham's small eyes wandered the length of the withdrawing room until they alighted upon the recklessly handsome features of one James Curry, sergeant-major in the Charleston Regiment of Grenadiers. A useful man, Curry—quite without scruples and able to converse with the most faultless of London inflections; a rogue and a politician at heart—he was also ambitious.

Yes, tonight should tell the story of where his loyalties were to rest, Peter decided in the depths of his cautious being. What incredible fortune to sit in, as it were, on the fate of Savannah.

The Allies couldn't help winning, now that the French had

recruited their strength, now that the big siege guns had hammered hell out of Savannah for so long. He felt justified in backing d'Estaing and Lincoln. What pride Théo would feel once the subtle part he was going to play in trouncing the British came to light.

Of course Peter had not yet dwelt on the truly difficult nature of those swamps; the ground there was treacherous, cat-briars grew thorns like spikes and creepers hampered one's legs like gyves. He would wait, point out those facts later—when the dramatic and strategic importance of his revelations would be better appreciated.

Cautiously, his little eyes circled the table. By the candlelight the dress uniforms of the French staff were especially resplendent. The Count Pulaski, in a claret and silver tunic, represented the quintessence of how a lancer should appear. Lord! By contrast, old Ben Lincoln and the Carolinians looked like a pack of farmers.

Peter Habersham wasn't one to be mistaken by outward appearances. Lincoln's troops might not be impressive on review, but they'd been hardened by three years of almost unrelenting fratricidal combat. The French, though, were good soldiers; he'd learned that from the gay and laughing Captain Foyne. Weeks ashore and the issuing of new equipment had gone far towards restoring those haggard wretches who had come stumbling ashore at Thunderbolt.

"Guess I'm not such a dumb-lock, after all." The more Peter reflected upon his shrewdness in biding his time, the more pleased with himself he felt. He beamed on Alistair Bryson, standing straight and brown, beside a white-painted pillar at the far end of the room.

There was a fellow he understood—and trusted. Bryson's mind worked almost as slowly as his own and he, too, had a beautiful wife.

"The Chasseurs of Guadeloupe go where?" Colonel d'Esperey was inquiring, his lean features mahogany between the white braids of his false hair.

At the sight of the hussar Peter felt a queer emptiness at the bottom of his stomach. To imagine that Théo—well, that Théo made too much of the Baron d'Esperey was absurd. Wasn't Théo a devoted wife? A trifle frivolous, to be sure, but any girl of nineteen was bound to be, especially if she were pretty and a little spoiled. Moodily he watched the hussar working earnestly over the map, his long, thin nose extended like that of a well-bred pointer.

Under cover of disputes between various groups d'Esperey commenced talking to Pulaski. Whatever he said must have been forceful because, presently, the Pole began tugging at a pearl dangling below his left ear; then he began twisting perplexedly at a long black mustache. They made quite a picture—the dragoon in wine-red frogged with silver, and the hussar in his light blue and gray, fur-trimmed pelisse.

When a clock in the hall boomed the hour of nine, the Comte d'Estaing arose, the rows of diamond-set orders on his broad chest flashing like miniature rainbows.

"We grow heated, gentlemen," said he calmly. "We shall recess until my orderly sounds his trumpet."

Slowly, Peter Habersham heaved his plump body to its feet; Sergeant-Major Curry's gaze swung expectantly, but almost imperceptibly the planter shook his head. Wooden-faced, the sergeant-major then stood to attention as the members of the council shoved back their chairs and commenced to file out towards the dining room.

"So?" thought Curry. "Master Willie reckons the British are going to lose this siege? Well, maybe the French *have* too many big guns, too many regulars; besides the Americans are itching to beat the French out. Well, whatever Habersham says is right."

To General MacIntosh, Colonel Huger was murmuring, "Let that pretty French fool have his way. Why not? We'll let the Frog-eaters make the first break. They've come a long way looking for trouble. Let 'em sample what we've tasted."

MacIntosh stared thoughtfully at the cold and empty fireplace. Why not, indeed? Prevost and his confounded Britishers were as full of spines as a hedgehog. Yes, let the Frenchies go in ahead, suffer the first blast from above the abattis. Then it would be "Huzzah! boys!" and up and over the parapet behind Continental and Carolina bayonets.

There'd be plenty of fighting, even so, before the Stars and Stripes were raised above Augustine Prevost's headquarters.

With a gentle snap Colonel Edouard Baron d'Esperey closed a pair of graceful silver dividers, then brushed past Alistair. The Scot was enjoying to the fullest a tumbler of chilled flip. Losh! 'Twasna' often a mon got to drink iced liquors in the Carolinas.

Very softly, the hussar's light patent leather boots tapped on the stone flooring of the piazza. Although a vast majority of the council were heading like brave officers and true gentlemen to that point where port, Madeira, sangaree, bombo, rum, and flip were flowing, the colonel pulled down his jacket, reset his sword belt and sauntered off among the fireflies circling brilliantly in the formal garden. This exception attracted the attention of no one except of Peter Habersham—and that quite by chance.

When the last of the clock's nine silvery notes had sounded, Théo smiled, put aside her embroidery and, her petticoats flowing prettily, wandered over to a mirror. A glance at her reflection was reassuring. To the last lustrous strand, her bright yellow hair was in place; thanks to the use of a hare's foot brush the arch of her brows was both smooth and symmetric; her lips glowed with a bit of rouge applied with discretion and undeniable skill.

Antoinette, too, put down her embroidery, fixed dark eyes upon her cousin.

"Well, Théo, and where are you bound?" She knew very well.

"I believe," her hostess replied, "I shall go below for a little while. I—I must make sure that the gentlemen are well served." Smiling, she opened a small fan bound in mother-of-pearl and edged with lace. "I will be back in a moment, dear. Be a lamb and match this silk, will you?"

Antoinette got up, hurried across the room, and took her cousin's hand. "Théo, when you go below, promise me that you will not—"

"Will not what, *ma mie*?"

"That you won't go—outside?"

Théo smiled, brushed Antoinette's cheek with the fan. "Why, 'Toinette, honey, how you do go on!"

"No, Théo, please—" Antoinette flushed, looked desperately unhappy. "You see, I—I heard you come in night before last."

Théo's laugh became metallic. "*Mon Dieu*, what pretty but very sharp ears. You acquired them perhaps by waiting for Alistair to come home?"

Antoinette flushed. When first they had been married, she had lain awake wondering, wondering many and many a night, when Alistair claimed to be at drill. So many of the young officers made it a practice, after the exercises were done, to stop by certain establishments not too far from the armory. But always Alistair had returned to her bed, dog-tired, reeking of sweat and swamp muck, and lumpy with insect bites.

"Alistair is n-not—not l-like the C-Comte d'Esperey," Antoinette managed to stammer.

Théo's laugh rang rich. "Were Alistair not for you the dearest creature in all the world, I might whisper 'thank God for that!' You must attempt to understand, 'Toinette. Your Alistair is not like Edouard—" her brilliant eyes lit as she spoke his name. "Even less is Peter."

Weary disillusion entered the taller girl's voice. "What a clod! What a dull boor he is. Could you see him in his sleep—sweating, puffing, bloated, sprawled across our bed like a dead pig at an abattoir!"

"Théo! Théo! Be quiet." Antoinette was really scandalized.

"You must never say such things! It's wicked. Can't you see? Why, Peter loves you, adores you?"

"He loves my beauty, not me," came the impatient answer. "Even more he loves the prestige of owning Hesperidée, of having married a Proveaux."

"There are obligations, too, to being a Proveaux," Antoinette reminded with a dignity she had not suspected she possessed.

From below burst a great gust of laughter, a clinking of glass on glass and the tinkle of a harpsichord.

"Fine talk! As if your Uncle Marcel and Uncle Joseph are not the worst rake-hells in Carolina!"

"My uncles are men," Antoinette pointed out simply. "It is absurd to hold that men and women are bound by the same rules. You *know* they are not."

Firmly Théo disengaged her cousin's hand. " 'Toinette, you are a dear, sweet little simpleton; for the first time in years you annoy me. Edouard and I understand what we are about."

She spoke in such a fierce undertone that Antoinette drew back, hardly recognized this fiery young woman. "I have a right to the love—to the real, whole-hearted, headlong love of a brave man. I will tolerate no interference. Do you understand?"

Antoinette fluttered, wanted to remind Théo that, after all, Peter had built this stately house. But she did not. Théo, so tall and majestic, was undoubtedly on the edge of an outburst. Why interfere? *"Chacun à son gout,"* Papa had always observed in such matters.

Of course, her cousin could be trusted to be discreet. She had enough French blood in her to admit that Colonel d'Esperey, in his lean, hard bitten and predatory way was fascinating. No one could question his reputation as a clever and courageous cavalry officer. Many of d'Estaing's immediate staff had spoken with envy of the hussar's distinguished military record.

"Théo, dear, please forgive me. It is only that poor Peter loves you so—"

"Bah! Can a turnip love?" Pausing briefly before a pier glass, Théo reset a curl which had escaped from her coiffure. "La! *Ma mie*, don't look so tragic," she laughed. "Within half an hour I will rejoin you."

Lovely as never before, Théo blew her dark little cousin a kiss, caught up her petticoats and darted out into the corridor. Avoiding the glistening main staircase, she pursued a silent course down a private staircase designed, curiously enough, by Peter himself.

V

The Maze

ABOVE the formal garden of Hesperidée a half moon was, with
some success, attempting to create the impression that it was a full
one. Under its pallid splendor statues glistened white as polished
silver against dark banks of shrubbery.

The grass was wet, but Théo didn't mind. Pulling her skirts
garterhigh, she sped along the rose walk towards a cúnning maze
designed by a wandering, and very hungry, Italian architect. Its
privet walls were so newly planted that the shrubs had barely
achieved shoulder height.

At the center of the design stood Colonel d'Esperey, the silver in
his tunic bright and gay looking. When he saw her, he gave a queer,
choked cry, "Théo! Théo! my adored one. It has been an eternity."

"Edouard, mon chevalier, sans peur, sans reproche!"

When his hard arms closed about her, when the squirrel fur of his
pelisse stroked her cheek and the brutal tenderness of his mouth
crushed hers, she clung dizzily to him. Faintly, the odor of horses,
pomatum and newly-cleaned leather beat in her nostrils.

"Mon ange," he whispered. "You must know—after all these
years, I—*nom de Dieu!* I love you, Théo, incredibly! Demand of
me what you will. I will accomplish it. When we charge the British,
it will be for you I fight—my battle cry shall be 'Théo! Théo!' "

Peter Habersham, half crouched in a loop of the maze a few
yards distant, watched them kiss, stroke each other's hair, heard
their every sigh and protestation. Tears started to slip down
over his plump cheeks, but he choked back his sobs. Bent well
over, he stumbled away, brushing the wet leaves, until he came to
a bench.

For a while he wallowed in a slough of exquisite self-pity and
tears trickled down into the lace at his cuffs. No doubt whatever,
now, that Théo, his wife, his own dear wife, had pinned a fine pair
of horns to his forehead. How many times? That she really loved
this Frenchman even his slow perceptions had to admit. Never for

him had her voice trembled as it had when she'd murmured, *"Mon adoré! Cœur de mon cœur!"*

Peter knew now that even if he spent every last dollar of his fortune he would never have from Théo that which she bestowed so freely upon this confounded *beau-sabreur*. Could he live with her now, craving her in vain?

Slowly, a dull hatred for this Frenchman commenced to glow in Peter's brain. Ye yearned to hurt d'Esperey, to watch him suffer and cry out. If only he possessed the courage to challenge this hussar. But he knew he'd be afraid. For years the boys at school had mocked his timidity. Besides, the hussar was bound to be an excellent shot.

In the lee of a magnolia Peter stood blubbering. His nose began to run, but his eyes were full of a strange, shimmering red glare.

"N-no one thinks you're s-smart, Peter," he consoled himself, "b-but we-we'll show 'em, you and I." He was talking aloud—just as he had at school—but nobody could hear him because some of the officers inside had struck up a song. Somehow, he was going to get even with that damned fox-faced Frenchman! He'd hurt Edouard d'Esperey and watch him suffer. But how? *How?*

Wiping his nose on his cuff, the planter blundered around his house towards its river door. There'd be no one there. But there was.

Standing in a rectangle of brilliant yellow light was an angular figure wearing the green and yellow regimentals of the Charleston Grenadiers.

"A fine evening to you, Mr. Habersham," Sergeant-Major Curry saluted. "And were you looking for me?"

With the awful effectiveness of a lightning bolt impacting upon its objective, a solution to Peter's problem presented itself. As never before, the planter's mind raced ahead. Staying in the shadows to hide his swollen eyes, he said, "Sergeant Curry, when the discussion within is concluded, you had better ride for—er, town."

"Town? Why, I thought ye'd made yer mind up different—"

"I had," came the grim reply, "but I've found reason to alter my opinion."

The sergeant smiled thinly. "Your opinion is your business, sir, but it's risky, crossing the siege lines."

"Fifty pounds?"

"My neck's worth more than that, Mr. Habersham."

"A hundred?"

Sergeant-Major James Curry peered through the gloom. Why? What in the world had come over Mr. Habersham? He was shaking all over, damned if the big lummox hadn't been crying! Well, if he was that unstrung, there'd be no harm in trying. "I want a hundred and fifty, or I don't go."

Habersham nodded. "Very well. You had best wait outside, Curry. We will settle the details later."

VI

D'ESTAING S'EN VA T'EN GUERRE

ALTHOUGH most of the staff officers had ridden, singing and otherwise in very good cheer, back to the siege lines the night before, Alistair Bryson had been fortunate enough to remain as aide to Colonel Huger. That sad-eyed Carolinian had been expecting the arrival at Hesperidée of a party of Yamacraws. They should prove very useful guides, once the allied forces at dawn began feeling their way through swamps and forests.

Once more Antoinette felt her husband peck her sleep-warmed cheek, then slip out of bed. Whereas it was her usual custom to yawn and turn drowsily onto her back to watch him dress, this time, she kept her eyes shut. Alistair, she knew, would not return until after the long-anticipated grand assault had been made. She knew her heart would only half beat until she saw him coming striding back to her and whisper, "My own bonnie lass!"

It was strange that a man of Alistair's inches and seeming awkwardness could move with such an utter lack of sound.

What a glorious, unforgettable night this had been with both of them aware that it might be their last together—for all eternity. Under the compulsion of impending doom they seemed to have rediscovered all that was fine and sweet and lovable in each other.

Methodical as always, Alistair knotted the thongs closing the throat of his hunting shirt, then turned and glanced at the claymore. In its worn and scratched brass-mounted scabbard the great weapon stood in a corner of the room. He hated to leave it behind. In three wars it had preserved his grandsir and Feyther and himself. Hadna' he survived the assault on Fort Sullivan?

On the other hand, there was no gainsaying that such a weapon had never been designed for use a-horseback, or among the thick woods of America. Moreover, the sword weighed nearly nine pounds—a weight which, expressed in powder and ball, would wreak far more havoc among King George's men. Only after some difficulty had he learned how, correctly, to load and fire that fine Pennsylvania rifle which Louis Proveaux, Antoinette's father, had bestowed as a wedding gift—with a gay remark on the subject.

Through eyelids barely parted, Antoinette watched her husband tighten his belt, settle the big hunting knife, then stoop and adjust a thong securing his legging. She even noticed a couple of mosquito bites on his cheek.

How very brown he looked in his hunting shirt, how muscularly dangerous with that war bag slung over his left hip, that powder horn over his right. Beneath his fringed leather shirt he had donned a cotton shirt dyed deep purple.

"I must remember him like this," thought Antoinette, her heart beginning to pound painfully. "I *must* remember every little detail. Oh, *Grand Dieu*, see that my husband comes back safe, to grant me more beautiful memories, but always I will keep perfect this sight of him."

Every instinct prompted Antoinette to leap out of bed, for all that her shift had disappeared, to run over and hold Alistair so fast that no force on earth could sweep him up river into that red volcano of destruction commencing to simmer before Savannah.

Somehow, she forced down the impulse. Alistair would be embarrassed, ashamed—but would go just the same. She sighed and in pretended sleep turned her face away—towards the wall.

Alistair heard, smiled tenderly. Yon was indeed a bonnie wife! Long since he'd known 'Toinette was awake, but he hadn't admitted it for fear his thick tongue could never express the thoughts racking his heart.

"I'll leave yon claymore," he decided, "and I'll come back a' the same. Surely, the Laird will let nothing happen tae a love so great, so perfect as 'Toinette's and mine own."

Stooping, he brushed his lips lightly across the damp little ringlets at the base of her neck. Alistair's moccasins made only a soft *whiss, whiss* over the floor as he caught up the Pennsylvania rifle, hurried to the door and went out.

Antoinette's jaws tightened until they ached. But she would, she *would* imprison the wails tearing at her throat and fighting for release. A sickish-sweet taste entered into her mouth; she had bitten deep into her lower lip.

To Alistair's amazement he discovered Théo Habersham serenely presiding over the breakfast table. Already seated there was Captain Gadsden, his hard, red-brown face looking darker than ever against the pale green of the wall; hard, too, because Colonel d'Esperey was addressing his hostess with such a gaze as no gentleman ever should.

"Ah, it is Mr. Bryson! *Bonjour!*" D'Esperey smiled pleasantly. Théo gave him a lazy, good-natured smile.

Captain Gadsden nodded. "Those damn' Yamacraws ain't showed up yet, Bryson. If they don't come in soon, ye'd best go looking for 'em. I don't fancy that swamp country towards McGillivray's."

Théo measured a spoonful of brown sugar. "La, Alistair, you look like a bridegroom this morning, for all you're an old married man. Will 'Toinette be joining us?"

Red as any apple at his hostess' insinuation, Alistair bit into a persimmon. "She's sound asleep, Cousin. I didna think it wise tae wake her."

"In that case I shall leave you and Captain Gadsden to plot the downfall of General Prevost," she laughed. A splash of early sunlight creeping around a shutter touched her pale hair, set it aflame. "I have flowers to cut ere the sun gets high."

Colonel d'Esperey's chair grated back before one of the footmen could even reach for it. Courteously, he bowed, his wiry body very spare and supple. "Will you permit that I accompany you, Madame? At this hour the garden must be beautiful."

"I should be delighted, Colonel. You may brush the snails off the roses for me— I—I—loathe the creatures."

"*A bientôt*, Messieurs," the hussar murmured and, treading lightly, followed Théo Habersham out of the room.

As the crunch of their feet on the gravel faded, Captain Gadsden stared hard at his quite unoffending pork pie, then tilted more tea into his saucer and drank deeply. Although the artilleryman said never a word, Alistair, spearing a slab of ham on a salver, knew well enough what was in Gadsden's mind.

Captain Gadsden belched delicately, wiped a bit of pie from his lips before demanding, "I say, Bryson, where d'you suppose that sergeant-major was going?"

"Sergeant-major, sir?"

"Aye. That fellow out of the Charleston Grenadiers, Irish-appearing."

"Sergeant Curry?"

"That's the one." The thick-bodied artilleryman stared out at Ossabaw Creek, still veiled and smoking with dawn. "Couldn't sleep, bowels too free, so I sat up. Saw this Curry saddle up and ride away."

"Yes, sir?"

" 'Twas near one of the night," Gadsden amplified worriedly. "Why start on a ride at such a heathenish hour?"

Since Alistair could find no plausible explanation, he said nothing. Sergeant-Major Curry was no part of his responsibility.

In silence they consumed the rest of a breakfast consisting of eggs, rice pudding, fried yams, ham, suet pudding, and spoon bread. Alistair was smiling over the aura of perfume which the Frenchman had left behind when, in the far distance, rumbled a burst of cannonading. It sounded very like thunder.

Gadsden snatched off the napkin loosely knotted about his neck, snapped, "The French have attacked on their own, by God!"

The cannons, however, quickly fell silent.

A bandy-legged young fellow in a striped jersey and seamen's petticoat breeches came tramping along to the terrace calling, "Hey, Cunnel Pinckney! Where at is Cunnel Pinckney?"

Grinning, Gadsden went to the door. "You lost, Bub?"

The youth grinned. "Kinder. This heah place is too big. Cain't find the back do'."

"Who are you, Bub, and what do you want?" the artilleryman demanded, not unkindly.

"Ah'm Jawn Fellows, suh. Ah done fotched in a parcel o' Yamacraw Injuns fo' Cunnel Pinckney."

Gadsden belched again but grinned his relief. "That's capital. Where are they?"

"A few is jest outside, suh, but the most part is down by the crick. They's powerful curious Injuns. You know how them rascals are?"

"Yes, Fellows, I know."

Alistair, pushing away his well-cleaned plate, noticed a pair of flat-eyed Indians, peering over some boxwoods beyond the piazza. These Yamacraws were quite naked save for scarlet breech cloths, moccasins, and some broad copper bands they wore clasped about their upper arms.

Without exception their heads were greased and shaved clean except for a single ridge rising in the position of a Grecian warrior's plume. Across their cheekbones the savages had sketched wide smears of scarlet edged with black. Most of these malodorous apparitions carried bows, but a few possessed old, old fuzees— relics of some disastrous Spanish expedition undertaken long ago.

Methodically, Captain Gadsden buckled on his sword belt, hurried over to a dispatch case and commenced to do it up. To Alistair he snapped, "Take Fellows, bring up the rest of his redskins and find that damn' Frenchman while I collect my equipment. Now the

Yamacraws have come in, we'd best get back to the division in a hurry.''

Some yards in advance of Fellows and his shaggy barbarians, Alistair hurried towards the landing. His moccasined feet made so little sound that, in the lee of a vast live oak, he blundered upon Colonel d'Esperey and Théo Habersham locked in the most passionate of embraces.

Too astonished to make his presence known, the Scot stared. Losh! Antoinette's cousin was hugging yon foreigner like her hope o' Heaven.

Gently, the Frenchman spoke. ''After the battle I shall come for you, my earth-bound queen of Heaven.''

''Yes, Edouard, yes?''

''How shameful that you should waste your days coddling this dull clod of a Pierre. *Peste!* It is as stupid to imprison a butterfly in a chamberpot.''

''Oh, yes, Edouard, of course! I—I shall be ready—after the battle. I—I am not afraid. Life holds no greater treasure than our love, darling.''

Scarlet to his hair, Alistair waved back young Fellows and retreated a few yards. Carefully he trod on a branch felled by the storm. ''Colonel d'Esperey! Where are ye? I've been seekin' ye.''

''Ah, indeed?''

''Aye. The Yamacraws ha'e come in. Hold yer nose, Théo, they're a smelly lot!'' He felt proud over his subtlety in adding that last.

''Mornin', Mum.'' The young sailor who had brought the Indians was quite frank in his admiration of the mistress of Hesperidée.

Colonel d'Esperey, quite undisconcerted, drew himself up, tossed his pelisse back over his shoulder. Gravely the hussar bent and pressed his lips to Théo's hand.

''Be ready, *ma chère*. Once the town has been carried, I will return. Never doubt that.''

''I shall not,'' the golden-haired figure whispered. ''I—I dare not doubt it, Edouard.''

VII

Dawn Mists, October 9, 1779

To THE men of the First and Second Carolina Militia brigades the world at this hour sounded empty as an old bucket. Why, the least sort of noises, like the trickling of water in the sluice boxes, the faint croak of a heron fishing among the rice fields, obtruded themselves.

For all the damp, blinding, woolly white ground fog, Captain Shaun Foyne felt happier than he had in years. Simply to have reached a decision meant much.

"Och, I will discharge me debt to old Louis, fair and true," he thought tightening the cinch of his tall gray hunter. "The old bastard has fed and clothed me, so ye'll fight this battle for him, Shaun. Then, by the black bull, it's back o' yer hand to the French and—win, lose, or draw—ye'll ride north and to the west!"

Though it had come hard, he'd avoided cards—they were ever the devil's handmaidens for the Foynes. It was fine, fine as could be, to feel those ten gold louises sewn tight into a length of linen bound tight about his waist. Here, in America, gold was a magic substance—not mere currency—he had found out. The people acted starved, mad, for the bright metal. Rich and poor, they loved gold with fanatic eagerness never to be approached even in Europe.

Standing among the jet shadows of a pine woods Foyne tried to see the keeper of his stirrup leather but couldn't. Aughrim, his tall gray gelding, was in the pink; his skin loose, but not too loose. The charger kept shuffling and stamping; clearly he was disturbed by the clumsy progress of so many men through the underbrush. Hundreds were groping along a lane leading from Phoenix plantation house towards Savannah.

Aye, he and Aughrim would fight this fight, then, be God and begorra, they'd quit King Louis' service as readily as they had joined it. Gentling the gray's neck, Foyne stood planning while more militia struggled by. Aye, he would send in his resignation, formal-like, later.

Somewhere up to the north of here must be a girl who would fancy a true-born Irishman's ruddy hair and blue eyes.

Aughrim was his own, as were his weapons and saddle, so he'd not be stealing a farthing of old Georgius Tertius' property. Should this battle go well, then the condemned British would have suffered—as they should. But if these strangely assorted allies lost—which wasn't a bit likely—there was precious little Shaun Foyne could do about such a disaster. So, chance what would, he'd ride away.

Craftily, he had seen to it that for near on a week Aughrim had been well baited and rested. In these bulging saddlebags were packed all of Shaun Foyne's meagre possessions.

The Irish officer looked up, saw many thousands of stars blazing through the pine branches. Och! In this America wasn't there room and to spare for any man's ambition and for such freedom as he'd never seen. Sure, and it must be here in America that, on some distant day, Shaun Foyne would lay him down and rest his bones until the Archangel summoned the just and the unjust to stand in judgment before the awful footstool of God.

A fresh unit of troops was coming up, stumbling, cursing the darkness. These weren't good troops. The Irishman now was beginning to realize why only militia—Williamson's Brigade, the Virginia Levies, the Charleston Militia, and God alone knew how many other bobtailed organizations—had been ordered to deliver this feint. Radiant Mary! These omadhauns made more racket in their progress than a train of siege guns; it was characteristic that they cursed so loudly to keep a-glow the faint flame of their courage.

Colonel Isaac Huger, in command of these tatterdemalion columns, was near speechless with a rage as violent as it was impotent. "March there! Pick up your goddam' clumsy feet! Why can't you pull yourselves together and move out?"

"Whut fer? It's too damn' dark. I ain't crackin' my shins fer no Charleston macaroni."

"Arrest that man!" Huger called, but the sergeants couldn't identify the insubordinate one—or wouldn't.

"Hurry up," officers kept saying, "we're near half an hour overdue to our post."

Some soldier made a meowing sound. "Them Lobster-backs ain't going to run away."

"No. They ain't expectin' us," a deep voice said. "Remember, boys, if the British give 'way, we're to keep on—"

"Keep on, hell!" a voice called from the rear of the half-seen column. "Why should we-uns get kilt and leave them foreigners to have their way with our women?"

"Yeh! There's a goddam lot sense in that. Let them Mounseers tangle fer a change."

"Quiet! Quiet!" sergeants bawled in ludicrous contradiction. "Form up there, you club-footed bastards, and keep your bloody musket barrels up!"

"Staff officers, front!" an adjutant called. "The Colonel's set to move out."

"God!" thought Foyne, climbing into the saddle, "if this is an army, then I'm a Protestant bishop!" He found his stirrups, then under cover of the dark pulled a crucifix from the front of his shirt, kissed it. "Holy Mary," he breathed, "in Thy infinite grace guide this poor sinner safe through this business. 'Tis young I am, dear Mother o' God, and there's much I must do here in America before I die."

More confident, now that he had prayed, the soldier of fortune settled himself in the saddle, swung lean and concave thighs back and forth to wipe away the slippery dew.

Somehow, the militia companies formed into three parallel columns, though not without oaths and the banging together of many musket barrels. Continually ducking his head to avoid low-sweeping branches, Captain Foyne skirted the lane until he came up with the colonel's staff.

He hadn't much to do here, save to estimate what degree of success the feint might achieve.

Should the maneuver succeed beyond the Commander-in-Chief's calculation, he was to ride hell-for-leather to make the good news known at headquarters.

When Foyne came up to the knot of officers sitting their horses about Colonel Huger, the Carolinian was railing. "Why in God's name didn't that French pimp detail me some decent troops? What can I accomplish with these insubordinate, blasted, misconceived sons of Belial? Damn it, Parkinson, we were to have marched out at four and now it's after five! Get these cowardly cattle moving!"

There was nothing cowardly about Isaac Huger. He wrenched off his cloak, secured it to his saddle, then turned. "Come on, you mud cats! And when I order a cheer, yell your worthless throats out!"

The disorganization of the militia columns continued, became pathetic. Units kept colliding, demanding to know where the bloody hell they were supposed to go? Men straggled, couldn't find their company or platoon and hallooed to locate them. Some officers,

more than a little drunk, began spouting obscenities in a futile effort
to impress their bewildered men.

Crashing, trampling, the column advanced until the woods
thinned and a dim gray vista of rice fields loomed ahead. Foyne,
riding quietly on the right of the colonel's staff, could see the
Savannah now; a little galley was lying in the lee of a tree-less
island.

Once the staff rode away from the trees, horses commenced to
snort and blow at having to move out over the treacherous mud of
the nearly drained rice paddies.

Foyne kept his head, discovered a broad dike leading straight
towards the enemy lines. Pretty soon he made out the British
earthworks, an irregular horizontal streak showing silver-black in
the starlight. To the left shone a bigger blur; that would be the great
bastion guarding the extreme left of the British position. It was still
too black to see anything of Savannah itself.

The night was full of sound; frightened plovers, piping their
terrors, began circling about the heads of the infantry laboring
knee-deep in the muck of the paddies. Splashing, their boots making
obscene sucking noises, the columns sweated, cursed, toiled out
across the flats.

When only a quarter of a mile was left to traverse, Colonel Huger
drew his sword, was preparing to order the charge when, from the
enemy position, military music piped up, played, "Welcome to the
Maypole, ye Merry Farmers All."

Foyne felt the blood drain out of his cheeks, felt his bowels
pucker. "Me boy," he muttered, "as sure as ould Pontius Pilate is
roating in hell, we've been very handsomely betrayed!"

Appalled, the militia men stopped where they were as, louder and
louder, above them that mocking music swelled.

A Georgian voice hailed from the bastion—it looked mountain
high and everyone could glimpse the outline of the guns, could even
see the glow of the gunners' matches—"Come on, you Rebel
bugtits! We're ready fer you, and waitin'."

The rear of the militia kept on, jamming the forward elements.

A plaintive voice queried, "Say, Cap, I thought we wuz supposed to *surprise* them fellers!"

"Never mind!" Colonel Huger's voice rang out over the music.
"Forward, boys! Forward for the honor of Carolina!"

Beyond a few forward steps in the foul-smelling mud and water,
the militia stayed where it was. The officers raged, beat the clumsy
infantrymen with the sides of their swords. When, in despair, they
ordered a volley, the militia canted muskets to the high heavens and
discharged their weapons into the sky, did no damage whatsoever.

Finally a few of the Virginia levies, encouraged by silence beyond the enemy abattis, started forward and grabbed hold of some *chevaux de frise*. From above a ditch on the other side of the obstacles appeared rows of heads. A ripple of scarlet flame danced along the earthworks.

"Ah-h—God! I'm done fer!" Figures fell splashing, flopping in the mire. Came another discouragingly regular volley. More militia men swayed, dropped their weapons and sank crookedly.

"Come on!" Colonel Huger spurred his charger right up to the wooden defenses, then, imploring his men, galloped back and forth, disdainful of the musket balls sighing all about.

It was no use. The ragged ranks broke, wheeled and pelted back across the rice fields to the woods. A few hardy individuals proved exceptions. In handfuls they rallied and, reloading, sent steel ramrods whining down the smoking muzzles of their pieces. Calmly, a group of Virginians sighted, fired, called obscene reproaches at those who splashed by.

"Come back, you lily-hearted heroes!" Huger rode after the runaways, threatened them with his sword. But they wouldn't stop.

The Britishers' derisive music died away; so did their musketry.

"There aren't many of them," a big staff officer yelled. "Come back! For God's sake, come back and charge—"

"You go to hell, Mister. We-uns aim to go in when them Frenchies do—and not a moment before!"

Savagely, the officer turned his heavy-footed mount and, all alone, rode at the earthworks. A volley spilled him and his horse in a struggling heap.

The militia clamored in their miserable confusion, many of them drunkenly, made hideous caterwaulings and ribald sounds.

Captain Foyne rode forward, saluted respectfully, tried to read the Carolina Colonel's long face. "Sir, will yez be pressing the attack again?"

"No. These yellow bellies won't fight."

"Then what shall I report to His Excellency?"

"Report that we have made a feint. Feint? Ha! There's the right word for you. A feint with faint hearts. Oh, God! What *have* I done that I should be condemned to lead such contemptible poltroons?"

"It's no use," Colonel Huger snarled, then made an effort to recover himself. "My compliments to His Excellency. Tell him our feint has been that, and no more."

It was terrible to read the mortification on the Carolinian's powerful features.

"If I live through this, there'll be an end to militia levies in Carolina, so help me God!"

Killdeers commenced to return, to settle and to run about on the trampled rice fields of Phoenix plantation. Their whistling sounded cheerful in contrast to the groans arising out there.

VIII

BARON D'ESPEREY REFLECTS

"Seigneur Dieu!" rapped Major-General Charles Hector Comte d'Estaing. "What can be withholding the movement of Colonel Huger? Here it is an hour and more since he was ordered to deliver the feint."

Colonel de Calignon said, "The orders were clear, *mon Général.*"

"No doubt. The Americans are not to be depended upon; so much is clear. *Voyons, voyons.*" The Count d'Estaing's uneasiness became reflected in the attitude of his staff.

The air was fresher now with the promise of dawn. D'Estaing ordered a dark lantern brought forward and unhooded. By its yellow-red glare the man's face became revealed under an enormous tricorn bound in gold braid. His large, dark blue eyes were steady behind a pointed, well-formed nose and above a handsome mouth marred by petulant lines.

Dismounted beside their horses stood the staff, perhaps twenty-five or thirty in number. Infantry, artillery, sapper and cavalry officers all looked drawn and anxious. *Peste!* This waiting to deliver an attack was always worse than the attack itself, especially when a frontal assault was contemplated.

Some examined their weapons, looked to the priming of their pistols; some told jokes and laughed a little too hard; others went off among the bushes—it was curious how the thought of action stimulated a man's bowels.

In the darkness beyond the range of the dark lantern troops squatted on the ground, conjectured on the chances of the assault. Somewhere in the rear, the horses of Count Pulaski's dandies—the lancers of his Legion—were pawing the ground, playing with their bits.

A faint mist lay over everything. With pleasure Colonel d'Esperey discovered that, as usual, he could see in the dark better than most. For example, he was able to observe a solid column of grenadiers in white waiting under the pines. Being good troops, they kept their voices down.

Bigre, it was reassuring to hear the slow talk of these sturdy peasants of Cambrai, Hainault, and Gatinois. Today the British would feel the weight of their steel. The soldiers remained in disciplined ranks, as should his Most Christian Majesty's regiments. Captains and lieutenants, their swords already out, were walking briskly back and forth. Perhaps for once their thoughts ran on something beside burgundy and brunettes? Non-commissioned officers carrying pikes or halberts gave last minute advice.

A dull trampling and crashing marked the arrival into position of General de Stedding's force. They marched to the left of the Comte d'Estaing's own column which was under the immediate command of General Dillon.

An aide rode up. "Excellency, the Americans of Colonel Huger moved out three hours ago. They must be in position now."

With his cuff d'Esperey erased a beading of sweat from his chin. A curse on this pig of a humid climate! So. Another battle. His fourteenth? Or was it only the thirteenth? Like the veteran he was, the hussar undertook to refresh the priming of the two heavy horse pistols which, in their embossed leather holsters, flanked his pommel.

Next, he slid his scimitar out an inch or so. One had always to make sure the blade was free in its scabbard. Following a long established routine, he then adjusted the sword knot. In the heat of battle he had no desire to be parted from his weapon.

Bon. Violette was fresh, but not too fresh. Nothing could be more troublesome, or dangerous to a cavalryman in battle than a skittish charger.

He cast a glance at the staff, saw the Comte d'Estaing still bent over his map. An orderly holding the General's horse stood like an effigy a few paces away. The hussar's trained ear detected, away off to the left, more troops advancing through the dim and dew-washed woods.

What incredible good fortune to have met, in this barbarous land, so exquisite a being as Théo. Perplexedly d'Esperey tugged at his mustachios. But yes, the little American had fallen in love with him, truly, recklessly. With the realization he sat straighter in his saddle.

To be loved like this was something new—immensely flattering.

Nom de Dieu! Could it be that, after all this time, he was losing control of his heart? No, it could not be—not after Rosalie, Margaret, Helenka, Gina, Dorothy, Inéz and all the rest. And yet, and yet—Théo meant something he had never before known—not a mere prize in a campaign on the field of love—not a dove to be won, petted, and then freed.

"It must be the food here," he decided, impatiently. Still, the wonder, the deep appeal of Théo's love was disorienting. As never before, he desired her.

Théo—what freshness and healthy simplicity there was to her; a simplicity lacking in any woman he had known elsewhere. A sudden impulse to wheel, to ride out of the array, and to spur back to Hesperidée became all but irresistible.

Let that *petit fonctionnaire* husband step aside when this fight was done! One word, and Peter Habersham would discover himself snuffed out, for the gross, unimaginative insect that he was!

His mare became restless, kept pricking her ears; the woods were full of sound. There was no doubt that, on the extreme left of the Allied line, the two American columns under Colonel Laurens and General MacIntosh were trying to arrive at their positions. Out of the dark rang truly magnificent profanity, in defiance of a strict injunction that no one must make an unnecessary sound. Musket barrels kept clashing together. Canteens banged against bayonets.

Still the Commander-in-Chief, Dillon, de Noailles and de Stedding continued to discuss, gesticulating angrily. D'Esperey tested his saddle cover of leopard's skin, found it drenched with dew and speckled with leaves.

Ahead a long barrier of trees barred sight of the enemy lines. Somewhere, to the rear were drawn up some nine hundred men of Champagne, Auxerre, and Foix under the Vicomte de Noailles, doubtless cursing their fate at being assigned to the reserve.

To support this reserve had been ordered up the Comte's field artillery and such un-mated and badly served guns as the Americans managed to bring to the siege.

"And, I ask, why do we not move?" demanded a thick-bodied captain; he spoke with a Norman's slow accents. "These scared American pigs will never attack—not until we show them the route."

It was growing lighter. D'Esperey discovered that now he could discern some silver braid edging the Vicomte de Fontanges' tricorn.

All at once Violette started violently. Away off near the Savannah, and on the far right of the Allied line, a skirmish rattled and banged. Gradually, it swelled.

At once d'Esperey mounted up. With one hand soothing his charger, he started riding after the staff on a course parallel to this column of suddenly tense and restless troops.

Edouard d'Esperey was experiencing no particular emotion at the prospect of meeting death. For too many generations the d'Espereys had led, if not the Hussars of Lauzun, then other troops of those Louis's who, for hundreds of years, had reigned over France.

The Comte d'Estaing, nervous, staccato and brusque of manner, sat astride of a big dappled gray. He appeared uncommonly tall; perhaps because his tricorn was trimmed with fine ostrich feathers. In perfect alignment his personal guard out of the Foix Regiment moved off, gaitered legs swinging in rhythm.

The most gorgeous of his aides was saturnine Major Ragowski in a black, scarlet and gold dragoon uniform; he would, when the moment came, gallop back to launch at the enemy's works Pulaski's impatient lancers. Once through a breach in the British line, the cavalry were to wheel, charge along the rear of the Ebenezer and Spring Hill batteries, principal objectives in this grand assault, and cut down the grimy gunners.

The Comte d'Estaing reined in, listening intently to Colonel Huger's distant musketry. When it faltered and faded away, he passed his map case to an orderly and gathered his reins.

"Monsieur Dillon, sound the advance!"

His adjutant, the Vicomte de Fontanges, instantly kicked forward his horse. "But, Your Excellency! De Stedding is not yet in position."

"He shall answer for it—let him come as quickly as he may. Du Pont de Naux! Du Lac! Boisseau! To your commands, gentlemen!"

Aides went trotting off, called commands which put the big grenadiers on their feet, ranged them in ranks.

The east now had turned distinctly gray-rose, and a more beautiful morning Colonel d'Esperey could not recall.

Slowly, Dillon's troops took up the march, commenced to move through the woods to the right; General de Stedding's men would deploy to the left of the road.

At once the thick underbrush, little streams and fallen trees began to throw the white clad soldiers into difficulties. They could not understand the advice of the Yamacraw guides, lost them, and floundered on over soft ground which quickly stained their uniforms. Light infantry, grenadiers, regulars, and colonials alike fell, clogged the muzzles of their muskets, suffered so terribly from cat briars that many were as streaked with blood as if they were leaving, not entering, battle.

Somehow the column struggled on though vines and creepers
clutched at their ankles and branches stabbed and lashed their faces.
It was no wonder they made a fearful racket.

When, at length, the woods thinned, sergeants ranged back and
forth, panting and blaspheming, pointing with their halberts and
trying to form the scattered white groups into steady lines.

"Ici les Augenois!" they called, or *"Ici les Berges!"*

A sibilant whisper rippled along the French lines. *"Baionettes au
canon!"* As far as Colonel d'Esperey could see, infantry, hot and
still out of breath, began to lock on their bayonets. Older soldiers
loosened the flaps of their heavy leather cartridge boxes and set up
the screws holding their flints.

"Mon Dieu, are we not to wait for M. de Stedding to come up?"
Colonel d'Esperey heard one of the staff officers grunt. "And the
Americans—*nom de Dieu*, where are *they*? If ever I trust in such
savages again, call me a lunatic!"

A dispatch rider, hatless, his wig snatched off by some bough,
galloped up to report de Stedding's troops to be moving up into
position, but not yet deployed.

"Bon!" Comte d'Estaing's voice was vibrant with excitement.
"Then we shall wait no longer. Let us show M. de Stedding the way
to glory, eh, Fontanges?"

The adjutant looked unhappy. "Can we not wait, your Excellency?"

"And what of the Americans?"

No one seemed to know. It was difficult to tell. The regular
American troops moved so quietly through the woods.

Clouds thinned, parted, revealed, as abruptly as if a curtain had
parted, the British lines some two hundred and fifty yards distant.
Soft, almost marshy ground lay between, with wide but shallow
pools in its surface reflecting the sky.

All the way the ground sloped up towards the Spring Hill redoubt
and its formidable sister to the right—the Ebenezer battery. Fifty
yards short of the entrenchments bristled a series of heavy *chevaux
de frise*, showing raw and yellow in the half light—beyond it a bank
of raw earth more than hinted at the presence of a ditch.

"Bigre!" snapped de Malberbe, a wolfish major of the Champagne regiment's light infantry. "What a position to carry in full
daylight!"

An Irish mercenary officer riding at d'Esperey's elbow crossed
himself, grinned ruefully. "Good cess to ye, Colonel, there'll be
plenty of us smiling in hell this night!"

By dozens, French infantrymen fell to their knees, crossed themselves, and bent their heads.

"Allons!" cried the Comte d'Estaing, passing his cordon and his decorations to an orderly. He saw, as did every experienced officer in the column, that each passing instant was increasing the enemy's advantage. The sun would rise very soon and shine directly in the faces of the Allied troops.

When the Comte d'Estaing ripped off his tight jabot and opened his tunic for greater freedom of action, the troops yelled. Even his American aides were impressed at this amazing transition from fop to fighting man.

Rising in his stirrups, the Commander-in-Chief raised his sword as high as he possibly could; the staff followed suit. *"En avant, mes enfants! Vive le Roi!"*

The drum corps sounded the charge, their brass-mounted sticks drawing a thunderous, blood-speeding summons from the gaudily painted tambours.

"Vive! Vive le Roi!" From nearly a thousand throats the words came shrilling out of the semi-darkness amid a deadly glitter of steel. *"Pour Dieu at Saint Louis!"* swelled that age-old battle cry which, for half a millennium, had defied the English.

First out of the woods ran the light infantry, skipping over bog holes, dodging about low bushes. The tall grenadiers of Berges, Gatinois, and Hainault moved slower, dressed ranks and fixed their eyes on the yellow-gray earthworks ahead and above.

Like a white-headed comber mounting a wide beach, the French swept up the hill. Shouting, brandishing their swords, the colonels, majors, and captains rode out in advance—as was customary with the gentlemen of the corps of officers.

A hundred yards and more the French advanced knee-deep in the lush green grass; like metallic reeds under a wind their burnished bayonets wavered and swung above their white cockaded black tricorns.

Colonel d'Esperey recognized that sudden activity in the Ebenezer battery above; he guessed what portended and to cover his anxiety laughed, patted Violette's arching neck.

Making a vast tearing noise, sketching a dazzling line of yellow-red flame, the British opened fire. All in an instant the gray morning air came alive with moaning, keening musket balls.

Not twenty yards to the left of d'Esperey a whole squad fell in a struggling, shrieking heap. Terrified at the enormity of this uproar, the Colonel's mare reared on hind legs, snorting and lashing out with delicate forelegs.

"Peste! That fat fool Jules has fed her too well," d'Esperey said aloud. When he returned to the lines, he would beat that groom within an inch of his life.

"Tranquille! Tranquille," he called and played with the bit until she settled on all fours.

A pretty mess! Here he was supposed to act as liaison with de Noailles' reserve and Violette kept plunging and swerving in all directions.

Piercing screams were arising, but the white lines went on. Streamers of burnt powder smoke began to drift past his nostrils. It was hard to keep up with the Comte d'Estaing. Quite reckless of self, the commander was putting his tall, dappled gray straight at the abattis.

Now the whole summit of the redoubt sparkled with fire. It had been something like this at Minden. Readily, the hussar recognized that distinctive *thock!* which marks a bullet going home deep into a man's body.

Almost at the mare's shoulder a tall corporal snapped his head back, then plunged forward and lay twisting slowly on the trampled ground. His musket landed bayonet down and impaled the earth, remained butt upwards like some grotesque plant.

The heavy, deadly booming of field pieces mounted on the redoubt momentarily eclipsed the musketry, filled the air with the murderous whining noise of grape shot.

"Ah-h! *Jésus! Au secours! Marie! Aidez moi*." Voices coughed and panted beyond a dense gray roller of smoke descending from the English cannon.

Violette somewhat quieted, d'Esperey spurred to come up with his commander. He couldn't help seeing what a fine target d'Estaing presented in his glistening tunic.

A soldier came running out of the battle smoke, hands tightly clutching his belly, but what looked like a string of pinkish sausages was escaping from between his muddied fingers. Tripping on an abandoned musket, he fell, spilt his entrails under the hoofs of a dispatch rider who, on a lathered horse, came pounding up from the rear.

"De Stedding is near," he yelled. "My God, *why didn't you wait*?"

On climbed the French.

"Steady there, the 60th!" Quite calmly a voice was calling beyond the pungent, rotten smelling smoke. "Hold low, lads— low, I tell you."

Up to the heavy, pointed abattis lumbered the men of Cambrai Regiment; they commenced to haul at it with one hand, then, achieving no results, momentarily dropped their muskets to put both hands and their backs to pulling. The obstacles began to jolt over, but gave only slowly. Swords dangling from the leathern knots securing them to their wrists, the officers pulled with the rest. By threes and fours and dozens the French died, sank forward or tumbled over backwards.

Comte d'Esperey's hat was whipped from his head by a grape shot from the same cannon which tore the head off the Chevalier de Malherbe. The same discharge all but cut Captain de Montaigne in two and also emptied the saddles of Staff Captain du Perron and Lieutenant Boisneuf. Shrilling their agony, a half dozen hurt horses fell or commenced plunging crazily about.

"*Allons!* Advance, soldiers of France! We have them!" shouted the Commander-in-Chief. His shirt was open to the waist now and his wig twisted. Before urging his big gray towards a gap in the defenses, he shouted at an aide, "Bid Monsieur de Stedding and the Americans come up!"

So full of sound was the air that the Frenchman had twice to cry out the order before a subaltern of Pulaski's Legion heard and dashed away, his face gone the color of old cheese.

From a trot Comte d'Estaing's charger took up a canter; the vari-colored uniforms of the staff followed, weaving a changing pattern through the twisting tendrils of smoke.

"Ha! 'Ere come the bloody orficers!" roared a red-headed giant engaged in swabbing a huge twenty-pounder out of some man-o'-war.

Less than fifty yards remained to be covered, Colonel d'Esperey calculated, while struggling to control his mare's frantic fight for her head. *Sacré nom d'un nom!* He'd kill Jules when he got back. The reins were slippery with Violette's frothy sweat, but he simply had to tighten his grip on his scimitar. The instant he relaxed his pressure on her bit the mare surged forward, shouldered aside a shifting, scarlet-faced line of infantry.

Before the hussar could check the beast's maddened plunge he found himself looking squarely into an embrasure. Grouped about the field piece there he recognized the tartans of some Scots who must belong to Lieutenant-Colonel Maitland's troops—those veterans who had come through from Beaufort. Ever so distinctly he made out a crew of tight-faced gunners in scarlet uniforms.

"*Vive le Roi!*" he screamed and dashed spurs into the mare's heaving flanks. Expertly, he aimed his scimitar's point at a square-jawed officer with yellow facings to his lapels. Six more strides and his point would go home.

"*Jesus Marie!*" he burst out.

"Battery, fire!" Incredibly calm sounded the English officer's voice.

A gunner shoved forward his match, but before the priming took fire, a pair of Highlanders rose from behind a fascine and fired point-blank at horse and rider. D'Esperey felt the mare rear up, up until he saw nothing but the sky; expertly he kicked his feet out of the stirrups and fell clear, sprawled flat on the ground just before his charger crashed over backwards.

D'Esperey's instinct kept him from rising. It was well he obeyed his senses; above him erupted such a thunderous blast of fire as he had never known. The very breath was sucked from his lungs and it seemed that he whirled dizzily through leagues and leagues of space while a din as of a hundred thousand kettle drums battered his consciousness almost out of existence.

The bitter reek of burning hair acted as an astringent and his experience rallied his intelligence. For the moment an opportunity presented itself; the English would have to re-load.

He got to his feet, paused swaying, the scimitar dangling from its knot. Some of the Hainault Regiment, bright green cuffs and revers gleaming, were plunging up, their bayonets blue-gray against the rosy sky. The grenadiers seemed all black eyes and blacker mustaches; sweat-streaked brown faces were working with effort.

"Here! This way!" He turned in time to see a row of Scots rise and sight over the entrenchment. Miraculously, their volley never touched him, though his pointed busby was torn from his head.

"*Sauve qui peut!*" yelled a voice and the big Frenchmen—the few that were left of them—turned and ran. Because it was only sensible, d'Esperey followed them back through the abattis. A wounded horse overtook him, went plunging, staggering down the slope on three legs. Pitifully the creature dragged behind it, at the end of what looked like stained pink ribbons, a shapeless object.

"*Le Général!*" voices commenced to shout. "The Commander is killed!"

D'Esperey stared dazedly about. He went back to where that disastrous blast of grape shot had riddled the staff. Like flowers cast in the path of some conqueror, the broken bodies and bright uniforms of dead aides lay on the red earth.

At once, d'Esperey sensed the error of that cry. Though shot through the thigh and with blood tracing bright designs down his breeches, the Comte d'Estaing was waving aside importunate aides, shouting, "Tell de Stedding to press the attack. *Dieu de Dieu!* Where *are* those cowardly dogs of Americans?"

REGIMENTAL COLORS

BETWEEN the French and MacIntosh's troops on the left flank of the Allied armies, Colonel Laurens' column paused, gathered itself before launching itself at the Spring Hill battery. The South Carolina Continentals of MacIntosh's command still were panting after a difficult advance along the margins of Yamacraw Swamp. Yet the expressions on their heated features were satisfactory. Not making any fuss whatever, those veterans were looking to the priming of their muskets and passing coarse jests about the way a Virginia militia company was milling about. Obviously, these thirty-day wonders were ready to break and pull foot at the first scream of a shell.

By comparison, Laurens' Second and the Third Carolina State Line Regiments looked steady as oaks; a bit white about the gills, to be sure, but thoroughly determined to make the good showing expected of them. Had they not the shining defense example of Fort Sullivan to live up to? Their eyes indicated that they'd be double-damned if the Continentals were going to lump them in with the militia.

Most of the State Line wore white crossbelts, white breeches, and light blue tunics faced with a darker blue. But many affected the gaudy regimentals of privately raised units.

With a slight tightening of his throat muscles, Alistair Bryson heard the increasing crash of an engagement being fought off to the right.

A drumming of hoofs drew everyone's attention. Colonel Laurens and his officers heard and commenced to ride towards a French officer who with scarlet blood dripping from a scalp wound was urging his mount up to the American column.

"Attaquez! Attaquez!" he was yelling. *"Vous êtes en retard!"*

"Say, anybody know what that feller's hollerin' about?" one of the Carolina officers inquired.

"It means we're goin' in, boys," replied Lieutenant Bailey of the Second Carolina.

Sergeant William Jasper grinned, unbuttoned his cuffs. "What say, you Caroliny pond chickens?" the Georgian drawled. "Let's plant our banner on yonder battery."

Sergeant Jasper was feeling fine as satin; not the least bit scared. On the glacis of Fort Sullivan he had been frightened, and no mistake. Long as he lived, he reckoned he'd never forget the noise the *Experiment's* cannonballs had made driving *ta-chunk!* into the palmetto logs. Subconsciously, he fingered that handsome sword bestowed upon him in gratitude by the City of Charleston.

Well, seemed as if he'd teach these Carolina fellers all over again that a true Georgian had more sand in his little finger than most of them found in their whole backbone.

Almost as smartly as did the Fifth Continentals, the Second Carolina dressed its ranks. Colonel Laurens appeared, loose in the saddle, his strong, seamed face calm as ever. Precisely he was tapping the dottle from a little pipe he'd been smoking. "Well, boys, reckon we'd better be moving."

Alistair Bryson, riding a couple of horse's lengths in the Colonel's rear, couldn't help marveling. Here indeed was a real, a superb leader.

He could hear the snorting and trampling of many horses off in the rear somewhere, but a line of palmettos and pines concealed the exact position of Count Pulaski's dragoons. Two hundred fifty strong, they were itching to hurl the best blood of the patriot south at Maitland's kilted Scots.

Smartly, MacIntosh's Fifth Continentals deployed to the left, while the South Carolina troops under Colonel Laurens moved off to the right.

Suddenly somebody sang out, "Hey, fellers, don't it sound like the Frenchies hev been flung back?"

"Yep, that's gospel. Well, let's show them pretty, furrin poppets where Carolina colors belong!"

The color guards heard, grinned. "E-e-yah-h!" they screeched in imitation of a Creek's scalp cry. The bearer turned, waved on high an elegantly embroidered standard, worked and presented by Mrs. Barnard Elliott.

"E-e-e-yah-h!" Delightedly, the Second Carolina line and the Third heard and took up the shout.

"Forward! Forward!"

The drums rattled, thumped and banged; in a triple rank, the vari-colored units left the edge of the woods; Continentals, State troops, and militia commenced to move on that battery clearly outlined against the increasing daylight. Away off to the right,

French bugles and drums were sounding a rally. A flight of crows, hopelessly confused, flapped overhead cawing as if the devil were after them.

From the back of the cornet's brown gelding Alistair could see light wink on the long bayonets of the Continentals. Those men were real troops—showed what discipline and drill could do. The Virginia militia following the steady, dark blue ranks looked ridiculously like urchins tagging after a parade.

"Come on up, Virginny," they hooted. "Plenty of room up front."

"I ain't got me a bayonet," shouted a thin old man armed with an ancient Tower musket.

A corporal turned. "Say, gran'paw, you kin have mine. I'll pick it up after you get kilt."

A roar of laughter arose as if the wit had been indeed priceless.

The Stars and Stripes of the Continentals fluttered at the foot of the slope and their fifes shrilled "Yankee Doodle," that derisive British tune which had become so strangely popular.

Bravely, the blue banner of South Carolina, sporting its small silver crescent and its inscription, "Liberty," kept abreast.

"Open up, you men! Open up!" the officers kept crying. "D'you want the Bloody-backs to hit you all?"

Bitterly, Alistair wished for his riflemen. Why weren't they here, instead of scouting for Tory reinforcements reported to be on the way to Prevost's relief?

As the incline grew steeper, the blue clad infantrymen commenced to breathe hard; Alistair's horse set its head lower. Fat, round clouds of burnt powder smoke could be seen curling about the crest of the Ebenezer Battery. Although all the gradient below was littered with motionless figures in white, it was patent that the French were reforming. Alistair guessed that, for all their pretty manners, King Louis' men must be good soldiers; the British fire must have been murderous, yet there they were, preparing to come on again.

Captain Bentalou rode up, his brows merged. "Look! See what's happened to them dumb-lock Frenchmen?"

All too plainly it was to be seen that the troops of d'Estaing, in retreating, had retired across the path of General de Stedding's advancing column. A collision was inevitable. Confusion followed despite orders blared from bugles and frantic drummings.

"Open up! Open up!" Colonel Pinckney of the Third kept yelling, his round face scarlet with the effort. "Front ranks will shoot whenever a target opens; but don't stop—keep on!"

Before they had gone much further, some of the Continentals halted, sighted, and fired quite carefully at the heads moving, popping in and out among the embrasures above that very formidable array of *chevaux de frise*. In separate puffs their muskets' smoke spurted into the air.

The British promptly replied, not in a volley, but each man for himself. The Continentals kept on in three widely-spaced ranks. Here and there a man fell or staggered aside but still they weren't doing badly because the enemy was overshooting for the most part—an error easy to commit when one fires at a target downhill.

From the direction of the river sounded, quite unexpectedly, a loud report. A shell came arching over the edge of the bluff, burst squarely above the second rank and spilled half a dozen Continentals onto the ground. Alistair saw that some of them lay still, but others flopped and squirmed about like beheaded chickens.

"That'll be the *Comet*—that damned galley the British hev posted near the line of sunk ships," wheezed a broad-shouldered infantryman.

The fire from the crest of the Spring Hill battery commenced to grow brisker. The grass stirred mysteriously; little tongues of dust flicked up into the air.

General MacIntosh galloped out in front, waved his hat—when he came to grips he figured to use his pistols. "At the double! Forward, boys!"

Long since sweat had been pouring down Alistair's chest in acid torrents, drenching his hunting shirt. He was feeling unco' foolish like this, armed wi' only a brace of horse pistols; still, a man couldna fire a rifle frae horseback. Losh, he should never ha' left Feyther's claymore behind!

"Take hold!" he yelled at a short-legged infantryman toiling along under a heavy pack.

"Thank ye kindly, sir," the soldier gasped.

Two more Carolina light infantrymen clutched Alistair's either stirrup, so he kicked the cornet's big bay into a jolting trot. When the gelding was forced to hurdle a body, one of the infantrymen slipped, fell, and was left behind. The other two ran along, managing their muskets with difficulty.

All at once the British outer works were right ahead, and in ugly red-brown patches, fresh earth covered the grass. Without the least warning, a battery opened up and it seemed as if a covey of gigantic bees had taken flight. Alistair's coonskin cap was snatched away.

The horse snorted its terror, then the short-legged Continental yelled, "God! My leg!" and clung so heavily on the stirrup leather that Alistair's saddle commenced to turn.

"Let go, ye fool!"

But the soldier whimpered, hung on harder than ever. Reluctantly Alistair put his foot to the fellow's shoulder and shoved him clear.

Another volley. Bullets moaned and sighed about Alistair a sight thicker than they had at Fort Sullivan. The air grew dense with smoke, a ragged pattern through which showed hot, red faces, bayonets, tricorns.

Stung by a bullet, Alistair's mount gave a tremendous bound and sent his rider rolling over and over on the ground with mouth and eyes full of dirt. By the time the Scot had picked himself up the bay was yards away, heading away from the breastworks at a tearing gallop.

To Alistair it was wonderfully reassuring to be on the ground again. By choice he never had been, never would be, a horseman. Happily, from the limp hand of a dead Carolinian he picked up a musket with bayonet fixed.

"Keep going, lads!" he yelled. " 'Tisna much further." Fairly in the front rank of the Third Carolina, he glanced to the left to see how MacIntosh's men were faring.

As was to be expected, there wasn't a militia man in sight—they had run for the woods the instant the *Comet*'s shell had burst. The Continentals had paused to reload. Consequently the Carolina troops were making better time. Whooping and screeching like Creeks, Cherokees, or Yamacraws, the State troops disregarded a stream of musket balls and, like the French, tore at the abattis. On the crest of the redoubt men of the First Grenadier Battalion of His Majesty's 60th Line Regiment and some light companies of the 71st had got to their feet and began firing at their enemies struggling among the pointed stakes below.

The execution they wrought was fearful. Worse still, the breathless Americans were too spent to shoot well and knocked only a handful of mitred grenadiers off the sky line.

Most of the other Carolina officers by now had been unhorsed, so eagerly they joined axemen busy among the defenses. Major Jones, aide to General MacIntosh, fell forward, dead, his body impaled upon the cruelly sharp points of an abattis. When, incredibly, one gap, then another, and another appeared in their defenses, the enemy redoubled their rate of fire. The din became deafening, numbing to the ears.

"Forward the Third! Forward!" called Colonel Pinckney and, in wriggling through a gap, left half of his coat-tails on the jagged point of a *cheval de frise*.

Sergeant Jasper dashed a stream of sweat from his brows, tried to draw breath to his aching lungs an instant before he headed a little swirl of infantry in pouring through a gap after the dancing blue standard now carried by Lieutenant Hume—a lithe young fellow with bright yellow hair. Although his legs seemed motivated by red hot wires rather than muscles, Jasper felt an invigorating tide sweep his being when, through the eddying smoke, he glimpsed Mrs. Elliott's flag. Since Fort Sullivan, flags had been a part of his life.

He took a fresh hold on his sword, the one presented him in '77. Ah-h, that light blue banner was still flapping and tossing just ahead, he could see it whenever the shifting, cough-provoking smoke lifted a little.

When the crest of the battery was almost within reach, the air became alive with savagely whining bullets.

"Now's the time—men—at them!" wheezed Lieutenant Bailey. He was bareheaded, his coat in tatters and his breeches ripped half off.

Jasper understood what he meant. From the French lines again was arising a fierce clamor which argued that Baron de Stedding's column had at last pushed by the commanding general's disorganized troops and, bearing a good number of them along, was launching the second French attack of the day.

By the dozen the Carolinians swarmed across the ditch. A body in a red coat lay on the parapet right before Jasper, but he hadn't time to more than hurdle it. More of the Carolinians were behind, their bayonets glancing beside him. His veins felt fit to burst.

Atop the battery Lieutenant Hume, the flag bearer, was holding onto his banner with one hand and trying to beat aside bayonets lunging up from behind the breastworks. Like savage steel tongues more bayonets lunged upwards, licking at young Hume's knees; a billow of cannon smoke rolled by, blotted him from Jasper's vision.

The shouts, the booming of field pieces, the report of the enemy muskets became thunderous; so did the savage clamor of the attackers. Only dully did he note that all the while bomb shells from the *Comet*, galley, were punishing the support.

"Quick, now!" bellowed Major Wise, shaking a captured British musket on high. "We've got— Oh-h, God—" His body jerked convulsively to the left and he vanished from sight.

"Keep a-goin', Caroliny, yer—d-doin' fine!" Jasper gasped and used the side of his sword to push on a wavering Charleston Grenadier. Now that the sergeant's head and shoulders had reached a level with the parapet, he could look over it. To see Hamilton's green-coated Loyalists and a strong detachment of North Carolina Tories rushing up to the support of the dense red eddies of the men already gathered behind the breastworks, was discouraging.

The French were yelling like jays picked alive as, in long white columns, they again charged for the summit of the Ebenezer Battery.

Sergeant Jasper looked around for a target on which he might use his sword—but found none because the defenders, momentarily, had fallen back to reload.

Lieutenant Hume reeled, but, before he toppled onto his face, he managed somehow to drive the staff of the Second Carolina's colors into soft earth contained by the willow work of a fascine. Under the pelting of musket balls splinters flew from the staff. As it canted drunkenly there on the parapet the colors seemed to twist themselves against what little wind there was.

In the ditch below the crest, the Carolinians waited for more of their fellows to come up, but in dense formations green and white clad Tory troops were reinforcing men of the Sixtieth and Maitland's kilted Scots of the Seventy-first.

X

LES LANCIERS

FOR OVER three-quarters of an hour the battle had been reverberating all along the right end of General Prevost's solid lines and now the sun had swung well above the horizon and was drawing flashes from the dew-wetted roofs of Savannah.

"God damn it all! Ain't we *ever* to join in this business? You'd reckon we were a pack of militia!"

Cornet Paul Jamieson swung his sword, savagely decapitated a stalk of milkweed. Other troopers jabbed at tree trunks with their slender, steel-headed lances.

Standing in a long column beside their mounts, the men of Casimir Pulaski's Legion of Cavalry cursed, fiddled with their equipment, strained their eyes for a galloper who would order them into action.

Now that they had become accustomed to the din—the great battery before d'Estaing's camp was fairly pouring shells into the besieged town—the horses cropped at the nearby bushes, switched flies, or dozed with low held heads. Firing from the French parallels was achieving such a crescendo that the air about the spire of Christ Church was dotted with bursting shells.

Impatiently the lancers had watched the black Martinique troops under de Sabilière make the faintest-hearted kind of demonstration towards the British center. Only a few scattered shots had been required to send them and the Haitian Regiment of Color pelting back to the shelter of the earthworks.

Count Pulaski, in his furious impatience for orders to charge, was riding his black charger into a lather.

"*On nous a oublié,*" he complained to Ragowski in bitter accents. "D'Estaing reserves for himself the principal glory! Is there no word from General Lincoln?" But no message came from either commander.

In their leather helmets and hot, tight uniforms, the lancers continued sweating, fidgeting, conjecturing. In the background under a clump of pines, the black grooms who had saddled and equipped the horses looked on in wide-eyed pride.

"Why don't the General order us in?" demanded young Yancey. "That's the third time those damned Frenchmen have gone in."

By straining his eyes Captain Shaun Foyne could tell that a furious struggle was raging on the summit of the Ebenezer Battery. The same kind of deadly conflict was taking place on the Spring Hill redoubt. The Americans had planted a flag of some sort up there, around which a swarm of men in blue, brown and scarlet uniforms were eddying amid a furious sparkle of steel.

Cra—a—a! Cra—a—a! From beyond the thin line of woods marking the jumping off place of the Allies, a trumpet commenced to sound a short, brazen appeal.

"*Nous voilà, enfin,*" Count Pulaski beamed, jerked his horse about so violently that it reared, with dainty hoofs lashing out.

Gracefully, the Pole held his seat. "Ragowski! Mount up my men." Lancers' shafts wavered and red and white pennons tossed gallantly as the lancers swarmed into their saddles.

"In column of pairs, march!" the captain called. A bugler on a white, stubby-legged horse rode up to Count Pulaski's side. On command, he sounded the forward march.

In a rich, exultant voice Pulaski shouted, "You will follow me, gentlemen. Once through enemy entrenchment you will wheel left and right and cut down the matrosses. Saint Stanislaus preserve me," he added in a lower voice; then called, "You will stay close by me, Captain Foyne. I depend on you, you speak both languages so well."

The lancer column moved out, knee to knee, giving the leather sling straps attached to their upper arms a final readjustment.

Captain Foyne grinned. *Arragh!* What a fine thing this battle was becoming. As he glanced back at these handsome young Americans cracking jokes and readying their weapons, he felt his pulses begin to quicken. All his life he had heard of that wild, unforgettable ecstasy which a cavalry charge lends to the participants.

"Trot! Ho!" Voices anticipated the bugle's command. Spur chains jingled, stirrup irons clinked against one another and dust commenced to rise in columns.

Reaching forward, Foyne felt for and found the cool brazen butts of his horse pistols; there was still a bit of dew on them, he noticed, while casting loose the holster covers.

The pines thinned and now the first of those men wounded during d'Estaing's premature assault appeared limping, staggering or walking swiftly away from the tumult. Some nursed ripped arms or held blood-sodden sides; others used their muskets as crutches. All were black with burnt powder and slashed by the terrible briars in the woods.

A loud cry burst forth from a group of militia lurking uncertainly on the edge of the woods. "Whar ye going with them tobaccker stakes?"

"Spear me some real vittles, will ye? I ain't et good in a month."

The lancers paid these ragged critics not the least attention.

Once the thudding of the cannons grew louder, the more high-spirited horses commenced to become fractious. Aughrim lifted his fine gray head, snorted a little, then steadied down. Foyne felt his heart lift. Yes, after this charge he'd ride off and away, deep into the generous green heart of America. A good thing there was so much weight on his charger's back, it steadied the tall hunter not a little.

The Charleston dandies couldn't seem to comprehend what awaited them, though a few of them had stopped boasting about what they were going to do. The column trotted past a group of wounded who lay writhing in the shade of some trees and lowing like thirsty cattle. Many arms and legs lay at grotesque and impossible angles to their torsos.

Foyne swallowed hard. Better keep his attention on Count Pulaski. The Pole's long dark hair had escaped from its tie ribbon and was streaming free over his gold-braid-covered collar. It shone as glossy black as the cavalry commander's pointed mustache. The Count's square-topped Polish cap was scarlet above and subdivided into four squares by loops of golden braid; Foyne realized it for the first time.

Major Ragowski cantered up. "Our immediate objective, Colonel?"

With his sword Pulaski indicated a small lunette mounting four cannons. "That battery to the left of the Spring Hill redoubt. It is taking His Excellency's men in the flank."

The enemy weren't slow to foresee the peculiar danger presented by the appearance of cavalry. Almost at once round shot screamed just a few feet over the heads of the leading fours. Horses commenced to plunge, disordering the ranks, for all their riders could do.

"*En avant!* Sound the charge!" Pulaski brandished his gracefully curved scimitar and, at the same time, struck his black charger so violently with his spurs that the animal's violent leap would have unseated a less skillful horseman.

A second salvo of shots came screaming down from the entrenchments. One cannon ball neatly removed the trumpeter's head and shoulders but his fat white horse kept right on at Shaun Foyne's knee.

"The British," the Irishman thought, "the damned British are up yonder!" Experimentally, he swung the heavy sabre secured to his wrist, in an off forward moulinet. Just let that blade bite English flesh, good and hard, and he'd feel a new man. He, for one, was damned glad Shaun Foyne was to use a sabre instead of a cumbersome, silly-looking lance.

When the lancer column took up a rattling, jangling canter, a few over-eager troopers prepared to couch their lances.

Once again a trumpet gasped its plea from the depths of these French troops milling about the battery. On the flat ground more cannon balls began to plough up the turf, to throw dirt high into the air as one battery after another joined in an effort to destroy this new danger before it could develop. Faster, faster galloped the column. Swiftly, all pretense of formation was abandoned.

"Hark-away! Yoicks!" The Charleston youths began yelling as on the hunting field, or in a point-to-point race. Those with the swiftest animals overtook the van, raced on.

Leaning forward in his saddle to decrease the target offered by his body, Foyne followed orders and kept his attention on Pulaski. The Count was whooping, punishing his charger; Major Ragowski was riding at his elbow. Then there came a dull, incredibly dreadful impact of flesh being shattered. A hurt trooper's mount commenced to shriek shrilly, horribly, as only a wounded horse can.

Foyne saw Pulaski's cap fly off and the Pole's legs take a tighter grip on the black's belly as he settled his neck deep into the fur on the collar of his pelisse. Magically, the guns ahead grew larger; now they were firing grape shot.

Foyne's horse stumbled over a heap of dead Frenchmen and fell to its knees. The gray staggered so heavily in rising that the Irishman thought, with an anguished sob, that his beast was wounded; but it wasn't. Before he could regain speed, half of the lancer column had pounded past, pennons waving, shoulders hunched. A sea of flame crackled out of the entrenchments ahead as guns, charged to the very muzzle with cannister and grape, blasted full into the lancer formation. At such range the effect was deadly—disastrous.

As in a fevered dream, Foyne watched a whole rank of horses and men tumbling earthwards, the iron shoes of the stricken animals lashing and flashing amid billows of reddish dust. Another battery blazed in enfilade.

The lancers, such as were left, kept on behind their twinkling, futile-looking lance points. Some troopers' horses became terrified, refused to advance and, in trying to turn, were knocked flat by horsemen coming up from behind. To Foyne, hell boiled over amid an indescribable confusion when a third battery, masked until now, suddenly blasted the luckless riders from the opposite flank.

"Pulaski! Where is Count Pulaski?" he began to shout. It was so hard to see anything because of the gray banks of smoke. Something rapped Shaun Foyne sharply on the left arm.

" 'Tis wounded I am," he thought, "but 'tis no matter. I must come up with the Count."

Just before him loomed what seemed an impossible barrier of fallen, kicking horses, and staggering men.

"Up, Aughrim!" Crazy as any loon, the Irishman put his good gray at the obstacle as to a bank back in County Clare.

Bravely, Aughrim cleared that barrier which had checked far too many of Pulaski's men; mercilessly the British guns poured their shot into the struggling crowd.

"Pulaski," he heard himself scream.

Ha! There was the Count riding hard to the left. Suddenly the Pole reeled in his saddle, screamed, "Jesus, Maria and Joseph!" Jerkily, he crumpled forward upon his black charger's mane; a scarlet tide cascaded from his groin, sprayed his canary yellow breeches.

"Courage, Casimir!" Major Ragowski sprang from his horse, was able to catch his commander as, gurgling in his agony, he slipped sidewise.

On the ground, Pulaski made a supreme effort—cried so that everyone who heard him remembered it as long as they lived, "Forward, my lancers, to whom I have given the order to attack!"

Again a battery lashed the stricken column, spilled riders by the dozen. Burnt powder fumes drew an impenetrable curtain between

Foyne and the mortally stricken Pole. The mercenary officer spurred on.

Capriciously, a gentle breeze off the Savannah rolled aside the battle smoke again, disclosed this time a great black gun just in front of him. Beside it a blackened artilleryman, his red coat split 'way down the back, was ramming a sponger down the tube's throat. He'd at least get that man, Foyne decided. But inexplicably the tall gray faltered, slowed and halted, trembling violently.

Foyne realized that Aughrim must have been hit that time he had suspected. He jumped clear as the horse toppled over.

"Kill me good gray, will yez?" Red-eyed with rage, Foyne forgot his pistols and extended his sword. Two, three bounds brought him up to the cannoneer with the torn shirt. Setting his shoulder behind the blade, he drove his sabre point deep into the Englishman's back.

Furiously, he was trying to wrench free his weapon when a grim red face under a Scotch bonnet appeared, lunged far out over the parapet and drove the six-inch blade of an espantoon in under Captain Foyne's right arm.

He fell, face down, under the muzzle of a great twenty-pounder.

XI

THREE WIVES

THE French batteries in the distance rumbled and boomed on and on, but, until they fell silent, Antoinette would kneel at the *prie-Dieu* in her room. Long since her legs had gone numb and trembling from lack of circulation; after all, the first distant ripple of rifle fire had sounded a little after five of the dawn. Ever since she had remained on her knees, the beads of an ivory and jet rosary slipping mechanically, endlessly through her fingers.

Antoinette, of course, knew the rosary so well that her prayers flowed on of themselves, her lips forming the words and her throat expelling them in frightened whispers. Actually her mind was running back to the first time she had seen Alistair—her husband. He had worn the Bryson tartan, kilts, and Highland bonnet adorned by a hawk's wing-feather aggressively upthrust. He and his men had come to Papa's house in search of lead.

How big and rough and red-faced he'd seemed—and how essentially guileless and straightforward. Why, even now she could visualize his clumsy, dust-covered shoes depositing dirt on the glossy mahogany floor of Papa's salon.

Less happily, she remembered his return from the battle on Sullivan's Island with a Highlander's dirk stuck into his stocking beside his own. The name etched on it had read "Ferguson." Never had he told her how, or why, he had come by it. When he chose, nothing could get Alistair to open his mouth.

Outside, some tame turkeys began gobbling, dusting themselves in the driveway. Smiling to herself, Antoinette conjured up a vision of Alistair's face as he had come to her on their wedding night— strong yet tender and burning with an overflowing desire. Then she remembered him asleep beside her, his red-brown hair running in wild rivulets in all directions.

Why hadn't Alistair taken his claymore? Wasn't it considered unlucky to put aside a well-tried weapon? The fixation grew that if she kept praying unbrokenly, he would live through this battle.

A small pathetic figure in her nightrobe and unbound black hair, she remained at her prayers though the bed lay in disorder, an affront to her tidy instincts. So far, no servant had come near; as during the siege of Charleston, the house slaves had frozen into inaction with the first sounds of conflict.

Antoinette was therefore surprised when the door swung quietly back. She remained kneeling, however, eyes fixed on the ebony and ivory crucifix before her. There sounded a furious swirl of petticoats.

"*Mon Dieu!* Are you still babbling?" Théo's voice was harsh, as never before. "Stop it, you weak ninny! You are being absurd."

Antoinette ignored her cousin. "I'll keep on praying," she thought and started yet another Hail Mary, Full of Grace.

The mistress of Hesperidée seemed not to notice the lack of response, strode powerfully into the room. In her dressing sacque of canary yellow she looked unusually muscular and determined.

An extra loud salvo made the river valley throw back the reports.

"Oh, why, *why*, WHY? Why do they have to fight? Why?" Rosepink skirt clutched before her, Theo Habersham ran to a window, peered to the north-west.

Nothing unusual was to be seen except several tall pillars of gray-black smoke twisting up from the direction of Savannah.

"Oh, for pity's sake, stop that sniveling!" Théo snapped. "Stop it or I'll slap you. See if I don't!'' Her fingers entwined themselves, writhed briefly. ''Talk to me! Please talk to me, 'Toinette. Can't you see I—I'm—'' Her voice broke, and suddenly she sank to the floor, her face buried in her hands. ''Oh, I love him so, 'Toinette, do you hear? I can't bear this. That last cannonade! Edouard will be nowhere but in the thick of it!'' She lifted her head in a gesture of pride. ''Were he not, he would not be Edouard d'Esperey. He is like a lion, darling. You should see the scars on his chest where an Austrian lancer slashed him, the burn of a German's musket blast on his hip. A Turk, one time, nearly cut his left arm in two.''

Antoinette couldn't help glancing up, though the beads clicked on through her fingers.

''Don't look at me like a—a damned hurt pigeon.'' Théo stamped her foot. ''Of course we have made love. Such love you and that lump you married wouldn't understand—not in a thousand years!''

Firmly Antoinette continued until Théo suddenly snatched away her rosary. ''Stop that infernal mumbling!''

Slowly, Antoinette turned and slipped into a sitting position—her legs would not have obeyed her enough to permit rising. It wasn't her fault that the prayers had been interrupted. Surely the *bon Dieu* would know? Would forgive?

Théo's hand reached blindly out, caught her cousin's, so piteously avid for reassurance that Antoinette turned, took the pale head between her arms.

''Gently, Théo, all will go well.''

Lustrous with unshed tears, Théo's eyes held the smaller woman's. ''Do you really believe that? Do you? Oh, say you do!''

''Of course, Théo, they will return to us—both of them.''

''God bless you, darling!'' Théo hugged her cousin close, kissed her, then bounded to her feet and ran again to the window. ''Oh, why doesn't somebody come to tell me something? 'Toinette, are the French winning? Are they undone? Oh, they must not lose because—because— Come with me and you will learn why.''

She dragged her guest across the hall into her own bedroom, a spacious chamber done in pale blue. Many small golden stars had been affixed to its softly-rounded ceiling.

''Do you see?'' She made a sweeping gesture. ''Do you see those boxes, those chests? When Edouard returns I—we leave this place, together and forever.''

''*Théo!* You can't be so cruel—so wicked! Why, Peter loves you, adores you.''

''Loves me? Adores me?'' A strident, tearing noise intended to be a laugh escaped Théo. ''Bah. Peter loves only himself—my body and his property!" She ran across the room, gripped her startled cousin by the wrists. "He is a monster! Do you know what he has done?" She turned away sobbing. "Like a slimy serpent he has betrayed not only Edouard—but your precious Alistair, our friends and our cousins—to death!"

"Théo! *What did you say?*" Stiffly, Antoinette's hand crept up about her own throat and her dark eyes became huge. *"Betrayed—?"*

Savagely, Théo nodded. "Not an hour ago he bragged that my lover would 'meet a hotter reception than any I ever gave him'—his exact words! Oh, 'Toinette, you have no conception of how coarse and envious and contemptible Peter is."

The cannonade became louder than ever. "Oh-h!" Théo ran quivering fingers through her pale yellow hair. Angrily, she cried, "How can you be so cold? So—so frozen? Have you ever seen a dead man? Do you know how hideous Alistair would look?"

"Hold your tongue!" Antoinette cried. "If you ever say a thing like that again, I—I will tear your eyes out! Do you hear me?" Then she announced stiffly, "I am going back to my prayers."

"Wait, please wait, 'Toinette. I will come with you. Forgive me, darling, I—I don't know what I say." Théo dashed to a chiffonier, fumbled in the drawer, missed what she was looking for, pulled out a Lincoln green riding cloak which was lined with silk—a hideous, blood-red color. "Oh-h—where is that *sacré* rosary? Save Edouard, *O mon Dieu!* Preserve him for me!"

Side by side they knelt, Théo muttering her prayers in a fierce undertone, Antoinette whispering hers slowly, almost serenely, though the thundering of the faraway batteries had reached a new fury.

Down in the tent village behind Thunderbolt landing there was great excitement among the French. Far, far away a noise like a summer storm could be heard from time to time.

When the sun came up and the river breeze died away, Minga Warren could stand the little house no longer. It seemed as constricting, as stifling as the stays which had grown definitely too small.

"I am going for a walk," she informed Arabia, "and I don't know just when I shall return."

The slave regarded her curiously. "Please, Ma'am, you hadn't ought to walk, not very far, not in your—"

Minga snatched up a splinter broom. "If you say that word again, I—damn your eyes—I'll surely split your head wide open!" Unconsciously she had borrowed a phrase of Andrew's.

"Pardon, Ma'am, I—I was only concerned about you." Arabia commenced to sniffle as she backed away.

Minga was mad clear through. As if she needed reminding of her condition! What she needed was to find quiet, leisure to adjust herself to meet this incredible disaster.

What would become of her? What was to become of the infant which would be born in another three months? This morning Arabia had reported that, at long last, the Allied armies were launching the attack which would end this dismal, hateful siege. Well, what of it—now?

Minga reached for the place where her lucky bracelet had rested for so many years. It was gone of course—poor Adelina! The trinket hadn't brought her any luck, and had bereft its original owner of hers.

Imagine Adelina dead, despoiled and so dreadfully mutilated.

"Oh, Andrew, Andrew!" Minga cried within herself. How hateful life had become! Here she was swelled all out of shape, awkward, helpless in this foreign land. And alone, now. Absolutely alone.

Mr. Beetle and the rest of the crew of the *Confederation* had acted mighty sad and solicitous—Carolinians, Yankees and free mulattoes, alike in their very real grief.

Never again would Andrew come striding home, sweep her off her feet, and kiss her as only he could, then smack her bottom and translate some scandalous, but highly humorous, French jest.

Up river men were dying; in Charleston, in the Sugar Islands and in mysterious, far-off France women would rue this day.

Fiercely, she resented her ungainliness. But for that, she might reach Savannah and so make certain that her husband no longer lived.

Dully, but with care, Minga Warren descended the hot path leading to the beach. A party of French marines cooking breakfast on the shore merely waved politely—because she was so obviously pregnant, she guessed. The battle had interrupted the burial of an extra large number of sailors this day. Usually the burial parties interred the deceased with little ceremony. Time and again, Minga had watched a black-clad priest sprinkle water over the lengths of grayed canvas, mutter a few words, then hurry off to take his breakfast at the Marine Major's table.

Only now was she accustoming her mind to the fact that Andy was dead. Ever so distinctly she could hear Jared Beetle's voice saying, "That damn roundshot, Ma'am—well, it struck just where him and Atherton was standing. We put back, soon as ever we could—all we found was this.'' He held out a soggy, shapeless tricorne all smeared with greenish slime but bearing a red, white and blue cockade she had stitched up in Charleston. She had hung it to a peg inside the door.

Why, why had she ever allowed herself that silly quarrel with Andrew? Ministers would argue that this was God's punishment. She should have understood his mood; should have forgiven a natural obedience to his cause.

Of course, her condi— Oh damn! Feverishly she hated the thought of this horrid little thing bumping about inside of her. If it hadn't been for—for *it*, she knew she would never have sent Andy storming off like that. Oh dear, and up until four days ago she'd been prouder than proud of carrying his child.

When Minga reached the river's edge her shoes became filled with sand, became so uncomfortable that she squatted on a log and pulled them off. In nearly a year she had not been able to afford stockings. In the Navy of South Carolina, an officer's pay was neither lavish—nor certain.

She seated herself on the log and worked her toes through the warm sand, her eyes fixed unseeingly upon a flock of sandpipers. The silly little birds were tipping and twittering along the narrow beach.

What to do? What to do? To be sure Mr. Beetle had taken oath that he'd see her back safe and sound to Charleston even if he had to lick the whole French fleet to do it.

Suppose the mate did fulfill his promise? In Charleston there wasn't a soul she could turn to. Well, come what might, Andy's child was not going to say, ''By your leave,'' to anyone, let alone a parcel of South Carolinians.

An American officer had mentioned the presence in Savannah of Skinner's Loyalist Regiment, of the British Legion, and likeliest of all, the New York Volunteers. Certainly there *must* be family friends among General Prevost's Tory troops! But the King's side wasn't her side now. That notion had cost her Andrew.

If only she could break down and cry, she knew she'd feel a heap better; but she couldn't. Papa's sturdy self-control was too strong in her. To Arabia's dismay, she'd not shed a single tear since that night when the *Confederation* had come pulling in to the landing, favoring her shattered bow. When she'd heard the ill tidings, she'd sat staring out over the starlit river. There hadn't been any affectation about her reactions; it was only that, for a while, that she had lost the power to feel, even to move.

An egret emerged from a little marshy place and, with stately tread, began to stalk along the river's edge. Then, finding nothing palatable, the bird took off, beating its wings in a majestic cadence.

No, whatever happened, she'd not return to the Crown. She was afraid she'd never forget Andrew's saying, "Sooner I'd stew in hell for all eternity than see a child of mine brought up a Tory!"

Strong words, yet had she been temperate either? Had she not, just as readily, branded all Americans as rebel dogs? Traitors of a sort with Judas Iscariot?

Recently, the idea had occurred that, say what the King's people would, some principle, some exalted purpose must be guiding the blundering course of these Rebels.

To the Americans this war meant more than a series of campaigns. They weren't fighting this war like the French—for whom this was only another tilt against an ancient and honorable enemy. Little as she understood politics, Minga had sensed the differentiation. Yes, to Andrew and his kind this struggle meant survival, a future, existence itself.

Of all times to recall such a thing; she remembered something Jerry once had said, "You'll never become English, my dear. You are as typically American as the great forests and the clean rivers here."

Poor Adelina Moffat, destroyed in the web of her own spinning, also had observed much the same thing.

Wearily, Minga turned the sayings over in her mind. Were they right? Possibly. So far, none of the English had ever taken her, wholeheartedly, to their bosom; always, they had acted with faint condescension.

"Mistress Warren? Please, Ma'am," Arabia remained at a safe distance, "they's an officer inquiring for Mr. Andrew!"

A relic of some of the impatience she had seen directed against servants in the tropics seized Minga. "Oh, if only I could catch you, you cruel, stupid fool, I'd—"

Arabia winced. How very strange Mistress had become. Poor soul, it was a wonder the widow wasn't clear out of her mind. As gently as she could, the slave insisted, "Ma'am, please. He says he *got* to see you. He's from up north somewhere, from a place called Boston."

Boston! Minga sat up straight as she could and drew a deep shuddering breath. Andrew had relatives living there, an uncle called Hosea.

"Very well, I'm sorry I spoke so sharply just now, Arabia. I fear I—I am not quite myself." Slowly, she drew on her shoes, then started up the beach, noticing that the distant cannon had diminished to a faint growl.

Who was winning? Would they know up at that great, luxurious plantation house? It had a French name and lay more than two leagues up-stream. Perhaps the folks there, too, were losing friends or relatives in the battle?

The officer proved to be a cheerful young fellow in an unfamiliar uniform; blue and gold tunic, turkey-red waistcoat and blue breeches. Although she had never seen one before, Minga knew by Andrew's description that this must be an officer of the Continental Navy.

The caller whipped off his battered tricorne. "Lieutenant Abner Pollard, at your service, Ma'am," he declared, jerking an awkward bow. "Have I the honor of addressing Mrs. Andrew Warren?"

Minga's chin rose a little. "Mr. Pollard, you are addressing Andrew Warren's widow."

"Eh?" The young fellow's smile vanished in a twinkle. His clear gray eyes filled, then sought the dusty ground. "Andy gone? Can't be! I—I served a whole year under him in the old *Andrew Doria*." On the brim of his hat, the officer's hands tightened until their knuckles glistened.

"Why, Ma'am, we worshipped Andy Warren. We'd have tackled a 74 if he asked it of us." The figure in blue came closer, the picture of concern. "It's hard to credit that he's gone—Andy was always so—*so alive*. I vow I had no idea. Will—you—forgive me?"

"There is nothing to forgive; on the contrary I owe you much for having come, for having spoken as you did just now." Even yet, Minga hadn't realized how much store both officers and men had set by her husband.

"I am a blundering ass, Ma'am." The young officer bit his lip. Apparently he had only now noticed how big she was with Andrew's child. "When—?"

"Four days ago."

The young lieutenant's voice sank until she could hardly hear him. "And here I was all rejoiced over the good news we'd fetched." He pulled himself together, bowed again, slowly, sadly. "I regret, Mrs. Warren, I must return aboard the *Wasp* and report this—this lamentable intelligence. Oh, damn!" He abandoned his precise, painfully correct manner and burst out, "Why in hell did it have to be Andy, when there are so many bastards left in the world?"

Only now did Minga perceive that a new arrival had dropped anchor among the great, gilded line of battleships. She was a small, trim vessel and floating from her signal gaff were the Stars and Stripes.

Minga stared through a blur of tears which would not come. Why, yonder lay a Continental man-of-war! A part of that Navy of which Andrew had been so passionately proud and devoted.

She felt Lieutenant Pollard take her hand and shake it gently— she was glad he didn't kiss it like a Frenchman—or an Englishman.

"Pray accept my earnest sympathy, Ma'am," he murmured. "In a day or so may the *Wasp's* officers appear to pay their respects to the widow of one of the bravest officers who ever trod the deck of a Continental man-o'-war?"

"Please do," Minga cried softly. "It will be fine to talk to friends of Andrew's."

XII

The Morning of October the Ninth, 1779

FOR THE hundredth time, it seemed, infantry was marching by at the double-quick. On this occasion they were marines, Andrew Warren decided. From this cellar window one could only see the legs of passersby, nothing more than their gaiters—yes, they must be marines, because their gaiters were black, not white.

Or were they Germans? Some Hessians and the Regiment of Wissenbach were serving under the sagacious British Commander. Some of the mercenaries wore such leggings. Oh, hell, why worry? Thinking is a terrible effort when one's scalp has been well-nigh split in two.

The bombardment must, this time, be reaching a climax. The whole town was trembling, slates were falling into the streets; the heavy, resonant reports of the defending guns, the more succinct crash of shells bursting among the houses, had never before approached this intensity.

His fellow-prisoners, a miserable subaltern of the British Legion caught stealing mess funds, a Frenchman—a Lieutenant of the Armagnac Regiment, captured during a sortie a week earlier—and a suspected deserter, were coughing, sheltering their noses from bits of dust and dirt loosened by the concussions.

Although his head felt heavy under a casque of malodorous rags,

Andrew heaved himself to his feet, shambled over the straw-littered floor to peer out of a little, iron-barred door. Of course the guard was there, attack or no attack. A natural curiosity, however, had drawn him to a cellar door leading out to the street.

The French lieutenant came over, thrust a supporting arm under his elbow. "Courage, *mon ami*. Within the hour we will be free. Do you not hear our good grenadiers shout, *'Vive le Roi'?*"

Good thing, Andrew thought, that the Allies had decided to assault Savannah today. But for this he'd have been transported to that ghastly prison ship out on the river; strong men, let alone invalids, didn't survive long in her hold.

The embezzler raised an unshaven face. "Don't be bloody fools, you two. The Crapauds and Yankees won't break through. Maitland knows where to post his men, now that he's sober for once. Old beggar's been given the best of the garrison, the 60th Marines and the North Carolina Loyalists."

From a house which had been burning for some time somewhere down the street, blue-gray tendrils of smoke kept curling in through the cellar's heavily barred windows.

The suspected deserter crouched in his corner, head buried in arms, and kept groaning, "Oh God, have pity on us. We shall be killed, killed like them poor Negroes of Mrs. Latham's; killed like that poor woman in her bed."

At last Andrew picked up a plate, flung it at the wretched creature. "Be still. Keep your damned poltroon's fears to yourself!"

To hear, in complete helplessness, the thudding of batteries in the British lines, the level crash of disciplined volleys, was as infuriating as it was discouraging.

If he'd been stronger, he'd have raged at the bars and tried to loosen them. As it was he could only sit here forlorn in muddied and blood-spattered clothes. That knock dealt him by the sweep's blade had been no trifling matter. The English surgeon claimed that, by all the rules, he ought to have drowned straight away, or perished of loss of blood in the patrol boat which brought him in.

Andrew guessed he must have lost a deal of blood—scalp wounds were notoriously bloody affairs—because he felt so confounded weak.

More troops came pelting along towards the earthworks. They were Loyalists, the French lieutenant claimed. The dust of their tread came drifting down through the wooden bars.

"Steady, the 71st!" a deep voice roared over the steadily increasing crash of bursting shells above the besieged town. "Keep ranks, blast your ugly eyes. There'll be a plenty of Frog-eaters left for you.''

Andrew had sunk onto some fagots of firewood behind the door, when a carcass, a hollow shell filled with flaming turpentine, crashed into the house directly opposite a Mr. Kenton's humble abode. The French, Andrew judged, at last had found the range. By fives and tens cannon balls knocked gaping holes in roofs, smashed chimneys and dug craters in the long gardens of Savannah.

"Dear God save me! Save me!" whimpered the deserter. "I— I'm terrible feared.''

The French lieutenant growled *"Canaille!"* and bade him be still; then, when the poltroon continued to whimper, kicked him so artistically under the jaw that the bedraggled wretch toppled side-wise and lay breathing stertorously.

To Andrew the officer of Armagnac suggested pleasantly, "Shall I drag over a piece of firewood, *mon cher capitaine?* It might be amusing to observe the spreading of this conflagration!"

Andrew grinned. Jerusha! He admired this humorous young Frenchman's sense of values. Come to think of it, most of the younger officers were likeable, really interested in the winning of liberty for the new nation.

"Voilà!" With the lieutenant's assistance, he stepped up.

In French, they discussed chances while the bombardment grew more and more severe. One had to admire a garrison under such iron control. No panic, no aimless rushing about. But to the onlookers it was discouraging to observe Prevost's blue-and-orange clad troops of the Wissenbach Regiment march up and begin fighting the fire across the street. They had brought kegs of powder with which to blow up adjacent dwellings if the conflagration threatened to spread over the rest of the town.

"The Britishers aren't so bad, at all. They can endure a hammer-ing as well as administer one," Andrew thought. In the distance the drums began *thump-thumping* again.

"Ha! We advance *pour la troisième fois*," the Frenchman grinned and held up three fingers. "This time we shall, of a certainty, carry the works."

"*Mon Dieu*, let's hope so," was Andrew's grim assent.

"There can be no doubt. Do we not number nearly five thousand men? This *sacré* English general has not half that number, and many are provincial troops."

Andrew wanted to add, "Behind a parapet even militia can be mighty brave." But he didn't.

The fire across the street had commenced showering sparks on neighboring dwellings, but a British naval officer was directing a party of sailors in putting them out.

Some Tories of the New York Volunteer Regiment, their green tunics dark with sweat, appeared through acrid, blue waves of smoke. They were hauling along a ship's cannon. Crazily, the piece lurched in the ruts and dried bog holes of the street when its carriage's clumsy wooden wheels slipped into them.

Suddenly, the Frenchman clapped Andrew on the shoulder. "Listen to that!" Cannon fire was reverberating from a new direction—from the river. "Do you hear? That is *La Truite!*"

Andrew listened intently hoping to recognize the resounding report of his long eighteen. Had his galley returned back upstream? Was it fancy or did he in fact recognize the eighteen's ponderous boom? If it were the *Confederation*, who would be in command? Jared Beetle? He hoped so, for all that, as a gunner, Mr. Beetle left much to be desired.

The embezzler got up, his uniform hanging loose because of the buttons which had been cut away.

Out by the earthworks the fight was raging louder than ever, evoking the cries like those of a crowd witnessing a close horse race, like the yelping of excited fox hounds in full cry.

Shells from Comte d'Estaing's grand battery were *carrumping* and crashing closer and closer. The Wissenbachers took shelter when flaming fragments began to fall into the street. A shower of bricks from a shattered chimney fell, knocked senseless the naval officer.

The embezzler's heavy features lit. "We're holding—by God, we're holding!"

"No! *Nom de Dieu*, do you hear?"

Andrew heard high-pitched voices clamoring, *"Vive le Roi!"*

"By God, you're right! They have—"

Right over head sounded an appalling, stunning report and both officers went hurled flat under a small avalanche of falling brickwork, beams, joists and laths.

An indefinite period elapsed before Andrew was able to collect his senses; it was hard work. His eyes were full of dust from the shattered plaster and a falling board had dealt him such a savage blow on the left shoulder he wondered whether or not it had been broken.

Prompted by some inner consciousness he pushed aside the debris, swayed to his feet and dug knuckles into his eyes until his vision cleared.

Jerusha! That shell exploding in the upper storey had made an unholy mess of Mr. Kenton's house. Of the deserter there was no trace. The Frenchman, too, seemed to have disappeared. But no; the embezzler was staring round-eyed at a hand protruding limp and dust whitened from a heavy mound of bricks; its fingers still trembled a little.

Breathless, Andrew perceived that among the damage inflicted by either the French frigate or the *Confederation*, the shot had knocked out a corner of the cellar, facing the river. Bright morning light was beating through a ragged gap to transfix billowing clouds of dust.

The guard coughed, came stumbling along the passage beyond the cellar door. "Nah, then, anybody 'urt?"

When the door bolts commenced to click, Andrew flattened himself against the wall beside the entrance.

The guard, a Royal marine in a low leather cap with a flat silver plate affixed to its front, stuck his head through the door. Gripping a fagot Andrew struck as hard as he was able—a poor effort, but sufficient because the guard crumpled onto his face.

"No use taking chances," the New Englander warned himself; so, picking up a brick, he kicked off the marine's cap and struck him twice, thrice on the top of the head.

The embezzler must have been partially stunned for, even now, he moved not at all, just crouched looking at the Frenchman with unwinking gaze.

Trying to control fingers become unaccustomedly awkward and inexpert, Andrew tore at the fallen marine's equipment.

Even in the marine's uniform, would not his filthy condition and unshaven cheeks attract attention? He worked less rapidly, but made better progress. The house across the street was really blazing now, thank God. But troops kept marching along the street. At any minute the Wissenbachers might return—a wrecked house in the vicinity of a fire was a menace and would be the first to be blown up.

No one appeared. Andrew slipped on the fallen marine's cross-belt. Though barbs of pain shot through his wounded scalp, the New Englander pulled his hair into some kind of a queue, then he set his teeth and eased off his bandages. Well, if the wound started to bleed, he would pass for wounded.

Although the marine's cap was sizes too large, he pressed the sweaty leather contrivance into place. Jerusha! His scalp stung and burnt like fury. The scab on it must have formed into the fabric of the bandage.

A hasty look through the blown-apart corner of the house disclosed the river flowing smooth and oily-yellow below the bluff.

Andrew figured he had better head that way—unless the Allies broke the British lines and advanced into the town. So far they hadn't. After listening awhile he could tell that no hand-to-hand fighting was taking place and that the opposed batteries were still thundering away.

He felt terribly weak, so dizzy he had frequently to pause. ''Minga—my sweet Minga—'' Could he reach the water's edge? If only he could think! But a blur of ideas was all Andrew could collect.

"Tired. Why are you tired, sailor? You've been loafing in jail. Minga—to come to you I'd swim—swim—all the way to New York— Where are you, Minga? At Thunderbolt Landing, of course— Can you swim, Andrew? Why, of course— Here, this isn't getting me— Pull yourself together, man. You can outwit these Bloody-backs—could all right, if you hadn't lost so damned much— Here comes a sergeant. On your hind legs, Royal Marine, and throw your feet.''

He started down the street at a slow, loose-jointed trot. Most officers figured no soldier, not on a mission, would ever hump his lazy backside out of a walk.

"You'll swim back to Minga—but can you swim? The ground is swaying under you, Andrew.''

XIII

MRS. ELLIOTT'S BANNER

DESPERATELY the Second Carolina clung, scarlet-faced and cursing, to the parapet. Gasping for breath, their light blue uniforms smeared and stained, they thrust and parried with what bayonets they possessed, or flailed about with clubbed muskets.

Lieutenant Bush was supporting the standard, now that Lieutenants Hume and Gray had been literally shot to pieces and lay with their powerful young bodies draining blood over the fascines of Spring Hill redoubt.

With his presentation sword Jasper thrust at a North Carolina Loyalist wearing a brown uniform and a baldric of mottled white

and black calfskin. "There's for ye—damn' king loving traitor!"
he snarled.

He was too fatigued for his aim to be good; his blade, instead of
opening the fellow's throat, merely cut a deep gash across his
cheek. Howling, the Tory dropped his rifle and swung aside,
spraying blood onto his fellows.

For the first time Sergeant Jasper could get a good look into the
British position, could see the men serving batteries further along
the earthworks. Between them and the humble, shell-torn dwellings
on the outskirts of Savannah the whole area seemed alive with
figures in scarlet, brown, and some—they must be those damned
German mercenaries—in blue. He even recognized gun crews from
the ships serving some of the pieces.

In rapid succession bomb shells from batteries posted at the
center of the French lines were bursting among the houses. Magically, the explosions bloomed in the morning sky—it was all of
seven o'clock now.

" 'Ooray! Nah then, lads!" Up over the breeches of the cannon,
silent now in the Spring Hill battery, swirled a ripple of red-faced
British regulars; their green lapels proclaimed them of the Sixtieth
of line.

"Rally to the—" Lieutenant Bush shouted. But there were no
more Carolinians to respond. The nearest supports were still many
yards away.

From among the abattis a drum commenced to rattle imperatively.

"Retreat! It's the retreat!" someone choked.

"Oh, my God, boys! Don't give 'way now," panted a gray-
cheeked captain.

"No. Let's get the hell out of here while there's some of us left,"
a voice croaked.

Sergeant William Jasper saw the dismal truth and was glad of that
drum's command. The ditch below the battery was choked, full of
Carolina men, and more bodies hung on the points of the abattis like
toys abandoned by careless children. The British heard the sound
also.

Lieutenant Bush turned, implored, "For Christ's sake, don't go
back! We've won this bat—" His blond head was snapped violently
sidewise and at the same time the tall young fellow's knees flexed
slowly to his right. Mrs. Elliott's embroidered banner sagged,
began to incline towards the advancing British.

"Save our flag!" a voice shouted from the ditch.

No living Carolinian now remained near the stricken officer;

grenadiers, riflemen and light infantry were legging it down the slope, dodging around, or hurdling, the heaps of wounded and dead. Their retreat was hurried by vicious bursts of grape and canister which raised miniature geysers of dust from the ground.

In the partial safety of the ditch Jasper paused, thought, "I did it last time! Why, by God, I can do it again!"

Locking his jaws, he scrambled back up over the yielding dirt of the berm then went plunging along the top of the parapet though langrage, grape whistled deadly strains about him.

He found Lieutenant Bush crumpled but clinging to the staff, yellow head bowed wearily against his hands.

"Good man—take—away—Carolina!"

From among the abattis arose a breathless cry. "Jasper! It's Sergeant Jasper!"

The big Georgian's hand closed over the shaft, found it splintered and rough. How sweet it would be to hear the plaudits of the troops again. Why, b'God, was it necessary to demonstrate for a second time, that a Georgian was worth half a dozen dandified Charleston lick-spittles? His hat had disappeared long since. Something struck his scabbard a sharp rap as he got a firmer hold on the flag.

"Sorry, sir," he wheezed, but Lieutenant Bush didn't hear him. He was dead.

Jasper set his shoulders, tugged hard at the staff which either Hume or Gray had driven unnecessarily deep into the soft earth of the parapet. Ha! It came free. At the same instant he was rocked on his feet; the panorama beyond the guns tilted crazily. His right side seemed, irresistibly, to be caving in. Paralyzed with shock, the sergeant remained immobile a long moment with the banner's soft fabric fanning his face.

"Flag!" he told himself. "Get it down. Ain't really hit."

A pair of coatless, blackened cannoneers lunged forward but, catching his breath amid a glittering haze of pain, Jasper jabbed one of them in the face with the flagstaff's butt, then kicked aside the other, though the effort sent searing, weakening waves of pain spiraling up into his chest.

"Get down! Get back—to—boys." William Jasper half jumped, half slipped into the ditch and fell onto all fours; the banner drooped among the tumbled dead. Though the earth rocked crazily under him, Jasper got to his feet, crossed the ditch and scrambled up the other side. Each stride required a superhuman effort because flames seemed to be licking at the hole in his side.

It came to Jasper that he hadn't been lightly struck. He didn't dare to look down; the whole length of his right leg felt wet, strangely hot. During a lull in the cannonade he shivered to hear, right under him, a soft pattering noise; it reminded him of a gentle rain dripping into a water barrel.

Clouds must be obscuring the sky; it was dark by the time he passed the abattis.

Voices began booming up out of an indescribable turmoil, crying, "Jasper! God bless you, Jasper!"

For the second time in his career, William Jasper gasped, "Here's your banner, you Goddam Carolina swamp rabbits." On this occasion, however, he had nothing more to add. He hadn't the strength. The earth was rushing up to meet him. Jasper was vaguely aware of hands catching at him, of a great wind booming, roaring in his ears, bearing him up, up, into infinity.

Captain Shaun Foyne lay among the corpses below the Ebenezer Battery. Cold as cold could be, but powerless to move, he studied with dimming eyes the green tops of those pines through which Pulaski's lancers had advanced. They were green, but not as green as the trees of County Clare.

If only someone's horse hadn't fallen across his legs—if only somebody would come and rig a compress over his wound. Still, from the way he felt, they would be too late, now.

Strange, how very lucid his mind was. Foyne knew exactly what had happened and what was taking place. He could view it dispassionately, like a dominie lecturing his pupils—even though he couldn't stir hand or foot, or cry out, for that matter.

Instead of waiting for the other French column and the two American columns to come up and attack simultaneously, as he had planned, the Comte d'Estaing, in impatience or in hope of personal glory, had attacked ahead of them.

Too late, by twenty minutes, the Chevalier de Stedding had gone into action, only to find his advance hampered, then disorganized, by the retreat of the Comte d'Estaing's beaten regiments. These should, of course, have retired to their right, but they hadn't. In their stunned confusion they had committed a fatal blunder by falling back to the left.

The Americans had come on as quickly as they could, but only after the battle had started to go against their allies; as near as Foyne could tell by sense of hearing, not even Colonel Laurens' state troops and General MacIntosh's Continentals had attacked together.

Poor Aughrim. He wished he could see the big gray—a link with home would have been very welcome at this fateful hour.

Well, it appeared that there would be no riding off to the north, no hearty American girl to wife, no green acres. Too early, the soil of this great rich continent was claiming his bones.

The Irishman sighed in an infinite weariness and wished he could close his ears as well as his eyes. Everywhere the wounded were whining, whimpering, beseeching, screeching for water.

Something let go in Shaun Foyne's body, induced a comfortable sense of fatigue, so he closed his eyes against the glaring splendor of the morning sky.

Smiling, the mercenary drifted off into a peace at odds with a hellish racket raging near the Spring Hill battery.

It had been a bad day's work. Everyone in the thirsty, sweat-drenched and dust-choked column knew it—if so disorganized a body might be dignified by being called a column. Feet dragged, muskets canted sloppily, shoulders sagged in the defeated army. Bloodstains were frequent and heavy, their bright surfaces dimmed by specks of dust.

" 'Twas them damn' Frenchies starting ahead," grunted a Continental officer. "We were fools ever to trust 'em. My Pa and Grandpa never did—not after what they done to us in '60 and '63."

"You're right, friend," croaked a cornet out of Pulaski's shattered Legion. The cavalryman was making slow progress, limping along and using his lance to support a hurt leg.

An angry-looking officer of the Third Carolina who had left half his clothes on the *chevaux de frise* waved a fist at the sky. "We'd have done better, by God, if we'd hit the British all by ourselves."

"Yer right," Alistair Bryson assented wearily. "Had we attacked the night o' the eighteenth o' September, we could ha'e walked right through yon English. Aye, I know I'm right. A' their desairters ha'e said so."

That he was yet alive and unharmed seemed to Alistair Bryson a minor miracle. Why, time and time again, soldiers had been stricken before him, to either side and to his rear. Aye, Old Bones had whispered loud i' his ear.

He shifted the musket he had found to his other shoulder. Losh! 'twas heavy. Heavier by three pounds than his own rifle which he hadna been permitted to carry on horseback.

Well, here he was, stinking and scratched by wading through Yamacraw Swamp. There, too many good American soldiers lay dead, drowned in their wounded condition by the malodorous muck.

Crashing in a dense thicket to his left attracted the Scot's attention. Losh! From the way branches snapped, yon must be a stray horse; not even a Frenchman would cause such a racket. Well, since he had lost the cornet's animal, it might be a good idea to replace it.

Accordingly, he left the Augusta road, commenced quietly to part branches and look about. The thrashing noise continued to his left. There had been quite a few stray animals. Langrage and the canister had emptied a multitude of saddles.

Pressing through a tangle of myrtle, Alistair halted. To his ears had come a curious blubbering sound. It was inarticulate, quite unrecognizable. Bending leather-clad shoulders under the branch of a young pine, he halted, rooted in utter horror.

A figure in pale blue and yellow was stumbling blindly about, feeling for obstacles and making more gobbling noises in its throat.

Yon uniform was familiar, Alistair realized dully. Those silver frogs, those thin black boots with the little silver tassels.

The dreadful apparition tripped, sank on one knee, then turned, crimsoned hands outstretched.

"D'Esperey!" Alistair yelled. "D'Esperey!"

In his philosophy Colonel Edouard d'Esperey had thought to have made provision for all situations, for all eventualities—but what of this?

Slowly his mind had rallied from that shattering, stunning impact. Edouard d'Esperey coughed heavily, then thought by thought, he attempted to sum up his situation.

For one thing he was lying prostrate. Men stepped on his arms, his legs. *Bon*. He could feel. So far, so good.

He then sent messages to his legs, felt the obedient muscles tighten. What about the arms? They, too, responded. Fingers closed over blades of grass. He could hear trumpets calling—a retreat. Imagine Edouard d'Esperey recognizing that!

But, but—a blank of sensation existed. Where?

Fluid descending his throat made him cough again. He would look—LOOK?

That was where the blank existed. *Grand Dieu!* he was blind! He wanted to cry out. Tried to. Couldn't—*something had happened to his mouth!* What? The familiar muscles motivating his lips—the ones he used to smile with—what?

Shuddering, he raised his still faithful hands—chin, yes, but how slippery and hot. He coughed harder.

Dieu! Dieu! Dieu! Where lips should have been, his probing fingers found only an unfamiliar pulpy substance. A few hard objects met his fingers. Teeth. In a sudden frenzy he groped upwards over this hot and unfamiliar pattern—up—up until—until—Marie! *He was feeling his eyebrows!*

Only a will as rigid, as determined as his, could have weathered the shock. "I will find a weapon—to live like this is not to be supported." On hands and knees d'Esperey groped about, but by perverse chance no weapon came within reach of his twitching fingers.

"I will call some comrade—surely he will not let me endure like—" but when he tried to call out, blood ran into his throat and all but strangled him.

It was then that panic carried the citadel of Edouard d'Esperey's reason. In a blind and hideous frenzy he found his feet, lurched, tripped, arose and ploughed on, on, on into a maddening and unending blackness.

Shaken to the depths of his being, Alistair could only stare at the incredible horror before him. "Laird above, ye puir de'il!"

At the siege of Fort Sullivan the Scot had beheld some frightening spectacles, but never anything even remotely approaching this. Where a face should have been, remained only a ragged, shapeless scarlet smear devoid of eyes and nose. With whitish bits of bone protruding from purplish furrows of skin and raw, indecently exposed flesh, the stricken hussar's chin sagged loose.

Apparently a piece of langrage, a length of chain or something of the sort had removed the Frenchman's face without inflicting any deep and necessarily fatal wound. In his agony the wounded man had ripped apart the front of his blood-saturated tunic so violently that much of its gay silver braid hung in stained loops and his wiry chest, tufted with black hair, was exposed to the sunlight. The Frenchman's gay white wig was gone, exposing a nearly naked scalp covered with short black bristles.

Colonel d'Esperey struggled up, stood swaying clawing at the branches barring his progress. To have come so far he must have been strong as a panther.

"Colonel? Can you hear me? This is Alistair Bryson, Antoinette's husband."

Colonel d'Esperey's hideous head wavered, inclined ever so slightly, swung blindly in his direction.

For a moment Alistair debated driving his bayonet into the Frenchman's heart, but Feyther's voice was reading from the Book, "Thou shalt not kill."

A French grenadier appeared, gaped in wide-eyed horror. He must have come from the reserve, for his white uniform was unmarked by battle.

"Come here!"

"*Comprendes pas.*"

Because Alistair beckoned imperiously the grenadier
approached. Each hooking one of the blinded hussar's arms over his
shoulders, they half guided, half carried Colonel d'Esperey towards
the road, towards Hesperidée and the women waiting there.

XIV

THE U.S.S. *WASP*

WITH an absurd and quite unnecessary attention to detail, Minga
Warren was folding away her husband's garments, arranging them
in a sea chest which bore his monogram executed in bright brass nail
heads. Slowly, she passed fingertips over the bits of cold metal.
"A. W." Andrew Warren was what they stood for. Only there
wasn't any Andrew Warren any more. She crouched, staring fixedly at the chest; they had bought it the day Andrew had accepted
his captaincy in the Navy of South Carolina.

There seemed small point in packing Andrew's clothes, except
that she would need money, desperately, in another two months,
and a good suit of serge should fetch twenty pounds; stockings, two
pounds, shoes, five or six. Good clothing had become scarce in the
southern colonies. To be practical about such matters came hard,
but—well, every penny must count.

Precisely she folded a neckerchief he'd bought in Jamaica.
Besides her own belongings Arabia's modest bundle, done up in an
old red petticoat, lay ready by the cottage door.

Soon some sailors from the U.S.S. *Wasp* should appear and take
the luggage away. The officers of the brig would not hear of leaving
a brother officer's widow in such a plight and so had arranged a
passage to Charleston for her aboard the *Horatio Gates*, transport.

Where Arabia might be at this moment Minga neither knew nor
cared. Most likely, the slave was down at the landing collecting
further news about the battle. Why? Nothing mattered beyond the
fact that the Allied armies had returned to the assault four separate
times, had littered the ground with their dead, only to be beaten back

by the indomitable, undaunted British. This disastrous, crushing defeat was filling every house within miles with groaning wounded and dying.

A wild-eyed express rider had appeared at the landing croaking out ill tidings that above six hundred Americans of the best regiments had fallen, and double that number of French.

Also he reported that the Comte d'Estaing twice had been wounded, also de Stedding, Dillon, and many other officers. Whatever the faults of King Louis' officers, cowardice was not one of them.

Nor had the American corps of officers suffered in any less proportion. The Count Pulaski was thought to have suffered a mortal wound—a grape shot through the groin—and many and many a handsome house in Charleston would see only black this winter.

Slowly, Minga dropped the sea chest's lid, then rested her weight upon it because the infant's sudden shifting had left her momentarily breathless.

Lieutenant Pollard, at midday, had reported that, magnanimously, General Prevost had granted the Allies a truce in order that whimpering wrecks of men might be removed from the ditch below the Ebenezer and Spring Hill batteries, that sun-blasted wretches impaled on the abattis might be lifted free.

Oh, this horrible, never-ending war! What had this strife not done to Minga Allen Warren? She found only a faint consolation in the fact that Andrew had died as he would have wished—as a Naval officer fighting for his country.

If there was any justice at all, the child would be a boy, a boy who might perhaps inherit the best qualities of both antagonists in this insensate war.

Her legs began to go numb from kneeling, so Minga arose and went over to see if a boat had put out from the *Wasp*. None had, as yet.

Down by the landing there was activity. The French intended to lift the siege with all speed, so Lieutenant Pollard had said. Admiral de Broves was terrified—and quite correctly—lest an equinoctial gale trap his fleet in this open roadstead.

Infinitely weary, Minga slumped back onto the chest, heedless of mosquitoes circling about her perspiration-dewed forehead. She wondered whether, at long last, she had not come to the limit of her endurance?

Successively, the war had robbed her of home, honor, husband— of hope itself. Not badly she had weathered those long, cruel

months in Brewster when, gradually, neighbor had turned on
neighbor; then the Liberty boys and the devilish things they had
done at Millwood. She had held her head high during that fearsome
journey down to New York. She had managed, somehow, to rally
her spirit and integrity after the terrible experience beside the
Hudson. At Hawthorn Hall she hadn't allowed herself to get
mucked by the abnormal life on the plantation. But now? She was
just too tired to fight any longer.

Only during the last two days had she appreciated how much she
had leaned on Andrew's wiry strength, how often she had taken
inspiration from his forthright courage and lack of equivocation.
Always, Andrew had made up his mind about what he was going to
do, and then had set about accomplishing it.

"Andrew," she cried aloud, "I have tried to fight, and I have
fought, dearest—but it's no use, any longer."

Slumping onto the fly-infested table beside her, she buried her
head in her arms.

"I feel I must come to you, darling, soon, soon. Without you, life
is too empty, too purposeless."

The Savannah had taken Andrew, why not let the river take her
also? In its cool depths could be found a peace which would endure
forever and ever.

Gradually, a soft gray curtain seemed to envelop, to blur her
consciousness. Why go on living? She knew now she could never
face the ordeal of childbirth, not with her defenses depleted like
this.

Arabia was coming back from the landing, only it seemed as if
the slave must be walking in another world.

"Andrew!" she breathed. "It's the only way we can be reunited."

When Minga heard the slave's foot dislodge a pebble, she
straightened and hurriedly wiped away those hot drops which had
welled from her eye corners. It wouldn't do to let the servant suspect
that she had had enough.

Bracing herself on one hand, Minga raised her heavy body,
called, "Arabia, fetch me some spring water. When Lieutenant
Pollard comes, let me know; I am going down by the river, it's—it
will be cooler there."

The slave stayed where she was. Minga turned, was definitely
startled. A man's and not a woman's figure was outlined in the
doorway. She batted her eyes, at first failed to identify the apparition. He was covered with mud, wore a week's black beard and the
disordered mane of his hair squirmed down over a scarlet uniform
coat. Only the eyes, boldly black, were familiar.

"Oh, Andrew—is—is it really?"

"Oh—my dearest." He lumbered forward as she swayed to her feet, held her as close as his strength permitted.

For a long time they stood, pressed together, hearts thudding against each other, eyes closed.

"Andrew, darling," she whispered, then raised her face until the glory of her eyes shone steadily into his, until the generous warmth of her lips glowed, pled for his. When Andrew kissed his wife, the essence of their existences flowed freely, blending the one with the other.

At length he held Minga at arm's length, peered intently into her radiant features, then passed a hand over his own grimy features. He smiled, and that beloved boyish twist returned to his lips.

"Well, darling, don't stare so. You've always wondered how I'd look wearing the King's scarlet!"

"Oh, Andrew, I don't care what uniform you wear! You—only you, matter."

Again he held her close and they knew that never again would they have trouble on that score.

It became her turn to smile. "A pretty pair aren't we? Me looking like a badly stuffed sausage, and you all dirty and ragged— Oh, my dear," she had just noticed the little drops of blood amid his hair roots, "what have those devils done to you?"

"Quite a bit," he said, "but not too much. Eh, what's all this?" His eyes took in the obvious preparation for departure.

"Mr. Beetle reported you dead, killed by a cannonball," she said simply. "All the *Confederation's* crew were positive you and poor Atherton were dead. There was nothing left to hold me here—so when Mr. Pollard—"

"Who?"

"Lieutenant Pollard of the *Wasp*—"

"*Ab Pollard?*" His body tensed. "Was his name Ab? Abner Pollard?"

"Why, yes, I believe his first name is Abner." Her voice quivered with an almost unbearable happiness. "He serves in the Continental ship, *Wasp*, and—and, Andrew, he brought you orders from the Marine Committee!"

"Orders? For—for me?"

"Yes, Andrew, you're to command a brig." To her last hour Minga would never forget the radiance which stripped the grime and fatigue from his face. "One of the new ones building at Portsmouth."

"We shall win!" he cried and his voice filled the room. "We shall win—by our own efforts—and then this land will be ours, forever, for us and for—'' He couldn't help a downward glance at her well-filled bodice.

Minga laughed. ''Yes, my darling, and for him, too.''

The stained scarlet coat swelled, lifted to the great breath he drew. His eyes looked far beyond the interior of the stuffy little cottage, saw a vision of a great fleet, line-of-battle ships, frigates, brigs, and ships—ships of designs as yet unheard of, sailing to keep the seas for the United States of America and for the liberties for which they stood.

THE END

The Abortion:
An Historical Romance 1966
was originally published by
Simon and Schuster.

Other books by Richard Brautigan

Novels

Trout Fishing in America
A Confederate General from Big Sur
In Watermelon Sugar

Poetry

*The Galilee Hitch-Hiker
*Lay the Marble Tea
*The Octopus Frontier
*All Watched Over by Machines of Loving Grace
Please Plant This Book
The Pill Versus the Springhill Mine Disaster
Rommel Drives On Deep into Egypt

Short Stories

Revenge of the Lawn

*Out of Print

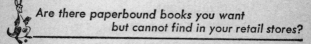

Richard Brautigan

THE
Abortion:

An Historical Romance 1966

PUBLISHED BY POCKET BOOKS NEW YORK

THE ABORTION: An Historical Romance 1966

Simon and Schuster edition published March, 1971
POCKET BOOK edition published March, 1972

Cover photograph by Edmund Shea

A portion of this book
appeared originally in
The Dutton Review, Volume I.

This POCKET BOOK edition includes every word
contained in the original, higher-priced edition. It is printed
from brand-new plates made from completely reset, clear, easy-to-read
type. POCKET BOOK editions are published by POCKET BOOKS, a
division of Simon & Schuster, Inc., 630 Fifth Avenue, New York, N.Y. 10020.
Trademarks registered in the United States and other countries.

L

DEDICATION

Frank:

come on in—
      read novel—
      it's on table
      in front room.
I'll be back
      in about
      2 hours.

                    Richard

Contents

Buffalo Gals, Won't You Come Out Tonight?

The Library

THIS is a beautiful library, timed perfectly, lush and American. The hour is midnight and the library is deep and carried like a dreaming child into the darkness of these pages. Though the library is "closed" I don't have to go home because this is my home and has been for years, and besides, I have to be here all the time. That's part of my position. I don't want to sound like a petty official, but I am afraid to think what would happen if somebody came and I wasn't here.

I have been sitting at this desk for hours, staring into the darkened shelves of books. I love their presence, the way they honor the wood they rest upon.

I know it's going to rain.

Clouds have been playing with the blue style of the sky all day long, moving their heavy black wardrobes in, but so far nothing rain has happened.

I "closed" the library at nine, but if somebody has a book to bring in, there is a bell they can ring by the door that calls me from whatever I am doing in this place: sleeping, cooking, eating or making love to Vida who will be here shortly.

She gets off work at 11:30.

The bell comes from Fort Worth, Texas. The man

who brought us the bell is dead now and no one learned his name. He brought the bell in and put it down on a table. He seemed embarrassed and left, a stranger, many years ago. It is not a large bell, but it travels intimately along a small silver path that knows the map to our hearing.

Often books are brought in during the late evening and the early morning hours. I have to be here to receive them. That's my job.

I "open" the library at nine o'clock in the morning and "close" the library at nine in the evening, but I am here twenty-four hours a day, seven days a week to receive the books.

An old woman brought in a book a couple of days ago at three o'clock in the morning. I heard the bell ringing inside my sleep like a small highway being poured from a great distance into my ear.

It woke up Vida, too.

"What is it?" she said.

"It's the bell," I said.

"No, it's a book," she said.

I told her to stay there in bed, to go back to sleep, that I would take care of it. I got up and dressed myself in the proper attitude for welcoming a new book into the library.

My clothes are not expensive but they are friendly and neat and my human presence is welcoming. People feel better when they look at me.

Vida had gone back to sleep. She looked nice with her long black hair spread out like a fan of dark lakes upon the pillow. I could not resist lifting up the covers to stare at her long sleeping form.

A fragrant odor rose like a garden in the air above the incredibly strange thing that was her body, motionless and dramatic lying there.

I went out and turned on the lights in the library. It looked quite cheerful, even though it was three o'clock in the morning.

The old woman waited behind the heavy glass of the front door. Because the library is very old-fashioned, the door has a religious affection to it.

The woman had a look of great excitement. She was very old, eighty I'd say, and wore the type of clothing that associates itself with the poor.

But no matter . . . rich or poor . . . the service is the same and could never be any different.

"I just finished it," she said through the heavy glass before I could open the door. Her voice, though slowed down a great deal by the glass, was bursting with joy, imagination and almost a kind of youth.

"I'm glad," I said back through the door. I hadn't quite gotten it open yet. We were sharing the same excitement through the glass.

"It's done!" she said, coming into the library, accompanied by an eighty-year-old lady.

"Congratulations," I said. "It's so wonderful to write a book."

"I walked all the way here," she said. "I started at midnight. I would have gotten here sooner if I weren't so old."

"Where do you live?" I said.

"The Kit Carson Hotel," she said. "And I've written a book." Then she handed it proudly to me as if it were the most precious thing in the world. And it was.

It was a loose-leaf notebook of the type that you find everywhere in America. There is no place that does not have them.

There was a heavy label pasted on the cover and written in broad green crayon across the label was the title:

GROWING FLOWERS BY CANDLELIGHT
IN HOTEL ROOMS
BY
MRS. CHARLES FINE ADAMS

"What a wonderful title," I said. "I don't think we have a book like this in the entire library. This is a first."

She had a big smile on her face which had turned old about forty years ago, eroded by the gases and exiles of youth.

"It has taken me five years to write this book," she said. "I live at the Kit Carson Hotel and I've raised many flowers there in my room. My room doesn't have any windows, so I have to use candles. They work the best.

"I've also raised flowers by lanternlight and magnifying glass, but they don't seem to do well, especially tulips and lilies of the valley.

"I've even tried raising flowers by flashlight, but that was very disappointing. I used three or four flashlights on some marigolds, but they didn't amount to much.

"Candles work the best. Flowers seem to like the smell of burning wax, if you know what I mean. Just show a flower a candle and it starts growing."

I looked through the book. That's one of the things I get to do here. Actually, I'm the only person who gets to do it. The book was written in longhand with red, green and blue crayons. There were drawings of her hotel room with the flowers growing in the room.

Her room was very small and there were many flowers in it. The flowers were in tin cans and bottles and jars and they were all surrounded by burning candles.

Her room looked like a cathedral.

There was also a drawing of the former manager of the hotel and a drawing of the hotel elevator. The elevator looked like a very depressing place.

In her drawing of the hotel manager, he appeared to be very unhappy, tired and looked as if he needed a vacation. He also seemed to be looking over his shoulder at something that was about to enter his vision. It was a thing he did not want to see and it was just about there. Under the drawing was written this:

MANAGER OF THE KIT CARSON HOTEL
UNTIL HE GOT FIRED
FOR DRINKING IN THE ELEVATOR
AND FOR STEALING SHEETS

The book was about forty pages long. It looked quite interesting and would be a welcomed addition to our collection.

"You're probably very tired," I said. "Why don't you sit down and I'll make you a cup of instant coffee?"

"That would be wonderful," she said. "It took me five years to write this book about flowers. I've worked very hard on it. I love flowers. Too bad my room doesn't have any windows, but I've done the best I can with candles. Tulips do all right."

Vida was sound asleep when I went back to my room. I turned on the light and it woke her up. She was blinking and her face had that soft marble quality to it that beautiful women have when they are suddenly awakened and are not quite ready for it yet.

"What's happening?" she said. "It's another book," she replied, answering her own question.

"Yes," I said.

"What's it about?" she said automatically like a gentle human phonograph.

"It's about growing flowers in hotel rooms."

I put the water on for the coffee and sat down beside Vida who curled over and put her head on my lap, so that my lap was entirely enveloped in her watery black hair.

I could see one of her breasts. It was fantastic!

"Now what's this about growing flowers in hotel rooms?" Vida said. "It couldn't be that easy. What's the real story?"

"By candlelight," I said.

16

"Uh-huh," Vida said. Even though I couldn't see her face, I knew she was smiling. She has funny ideas about the library.

"It's by an old woman," I said. "She loves flowers but she doesn't have any windows in her hotel room, so she grows them by candlelight."

"Oh, baby," Vida said, in that tone of voice she always uses for the library. She thinks this place is creepy and she doesn't care for it very much.

I didn't answer her. The coffee water was done and I took a spoonful of instant coffee and put it out in a cup.

"Instant coffee?" Vida said.

"Yes," I said. "I'm making it for the woman who just brought the book in. She's very old and she's walked a great distance to get here. I think she needs a cup of instant coffee."

"It sounds like she does. Perhaps even a little amyl nitrate for a chaser. I'm just kidding. Do you need any help? I'll get up."

"No, honey," I said. "I can take care of it. Did we eat all those cookies you baked?"

"No," she said. "The cookies are over there in that sack." She pointed toward the white paper bag on the table. "I think there are a couple of chocolate cookies left."

"What did you put them in the sack for?" I said.

"I don't know," she said. "Why does anyone put cookies in a sack? I just did."

Vida was resting her head on her elbow and watching me. She was unbelievable: her face, her eyes, her . . .

"Strong point," I said.

"Am I right?" she said, sleepily.

"Yup," I said.

I took the cup of coffee and put it on a small wooden tray, along with some canned milk and some sugar and a little plate for the cookies.

Vida had given me the tray as a present. She bought it at Cost Plus Imports and surprised me with it one day. I like surprises.

"See you later," I said. "Go back to sleep."

"OK," and pulled the covers up over her head. Farewell, my lovely.

I took the coffee and cookies out to the old woman. She was sitting at a table with her face resting on her elbow and she was half asleep. There was an expression of dreaming on her face.

I hated to interrupt her. I know how much a dream can be worth, but, alas . . . "Hello," I said.

"Oh, hello," she said, breaking the dream cleanly.

"It's time for some coffee," I said.

"Oh, how nice," she said. "It's just what I need to wake me up. I'm a little tired because I walked so far. I guess I could have waited until tomorrow and taken the bus here, but I wanted to bring the book out right away because I just finished it at midnight and I've been working on it for five years.

"Five Years," she repeated, as if it were the name of a country where she was the President and the flowers growing by candlelight in her hotel room were her cabinet and I was the Secretary of Libraries.

"I think I'll register the book now," I said.

"That sounds wonderful," she said. "These are delicious cookies. Did you bake them yourself?"

I thought that was a rather strange question for her to ask me. I have never been asked that question before. It startled me. It's funny how people can catch you off guard with a question about cookies.

"No," I said. "I didn't bake these cookies. A friend did."

"Well, whoever baked them knows how to bake cookies. The chocolate tastes wonderful. So chocolatey."

"Good," I said.

Now it was time to register the book. We register all the books we receive here in our Library Contents Ledger. It is a record of all the books we get day by day, week by week, month by month, year by year. They all go into the Ledger.

We don't use the Dewey decimal classification or any index system to keep track of our books. We record their entrance into the library in the Library Contents Ledger and then we give the book back to its author who is free to place it anywhere he wants in the library, on whatever shelf catches his fancy.

It doesn't make any difference where a book is placed because nobody ever checks them out and nobody ever comes here to read them. This is not that kind of library. This is another kind of library.

"I just love these cookies," the old woman said, finishing the last cookie. "Such a good chocolate flavor. You can't buy these in a store. Did a friend bake them?"

"Yes," I said. "A very good friend."

"Well, good for them. There isn't enough of that thing going on now, if you know what I mean."

"Yes," I said. "Chocolate cookies are good."

Vida baked them.

By now the old woman had finished the last drops of coffee in her cup, but she drank them again, even though they were gone. She wanted to make sure that she did not leave a drop in the cup, even to the point of drinking the last drop of coffee twice.

I could tell that she was preparing to say good-bye because she was trying to rise from her chair. I knew that she would never return again. This would be her only visit to the library.

"It's been so wonderful writing a book," she said. "Now it's done and I can return to my hotel room and my flowers. I'm very tired."

"Your book," I said, handing it to her. "You are free to put it anywhere you want to in the library, on any shelf you want."

"How exciting," she said.

She took her book very slowly over to a section where a lot of children are guided by a subconscious track of some kind to place their books on that shelf.

I don't remember ever seeing anyone over fifty put a book there before, but she went right there as if guided by the hands of the children and placed her book about growing flowers by candlelight in hotel rooms in between a book about Indians (pro) and an illustrated, highly favorable tract on strawberry jam.

She was very happy as she left the library to walk very slowly back to her room in the Kit Carson Hotel and the flowers that waited for her there.

I turned out the lights in the library and took the tray back to my room. I knew the library so well that I could do it in the dark. The returning path to my room was made comfortable by thoughts of flowers, America and Vida sleeping like a photograph here in the library.

The Automobile Accident

THIS library came into being because of an overwhelming need and desire for such a place. There just simply had to be a library like this. That desire brought into existence this library building which isn't very large and its permanent staffing which happens to be myself at the present time.

The library is old in the San Francisco post-earthquake yellow-brick style and is located at 3150 Sacramento Street, San Francisco, California 94115, though no books are ever accepted by mail. They must be brought in person. That is one of the foundations of this library.

Many people have worked here before me. This

place has a fairly rapid turnover. I believe I am the 35th or 36th librarian. I got the job because I was the only person who could fulfill the requirements and I was available.

I am thirty-one years old and never had any formal library training. I have had a different kind of training which is quite compatible with the running of this library. I have an understanding of people and I love what I am doing.

I believe I am the only person in America who can perform this job right now and that's what I'm doing. After I am through with my job here, I'll find something else to do. I think the future has quite a lot in store for me.

The librarian before me was here for three years and finally had to quit because he was afraid of children. He thought they were up to something. He is now living in an old folks' home. I got a postcard from him last month. It was unintelligible.

The librarian before him was a young man who took a six-months leave of absence from his motorcycle gang to put in his tenure here. Afterward he returned to his gang and never told them where he had been.

"Where have you been the last six months?" they asked him.

"I've been taking care of my mother," he said. "She was sick and needed lots of hot chicken soup. Any more questions?" There were no more questions.

The librarian before him was here for two years, then moved suddenly to the Australian bush. Nothing has been heard from him since. I've heard rumors that he's alive, but I've also heard rumors that he's dead, but whatever he's doing, dead or alive, I'm certain he's still in the Australian bush because he said he wasn't coming back and if he ever saw another book again, he'd cut his throat.

The librarian before him was a young lady who quit because she was pregnant. One day she caught the glint in a young poet's eye. They are now living together in the Mission District and are no longer young. She has a beautiful daughter, though, and he's on unemployment. They want to move to Mexico.

I believe it's a mistake on their part. I have seen too many couples who went to Mexico and then immediately broke up when they returned to America. I believe if they want to stay together they shouldn't go to Mexico.

The librarian before her was here for one year. He was killed in an automobile accident. An automobile went out of control and crashed into the library. Somehow it killed him. I have never been able to figure this out because the library is made of bricks.

The 23

Aн, it feels so good to sit here in the darkness of these books. I'm not tired. This has been an average evening for books being brought in: with 23 finding their welcomed ways onto our shelves.

I wrote their titles and authors and a little about the receiving of each book down in the Library Contents Ledger. I think the first book came in around 6:30.

MY TRIKE by Chuck. The author was five years old and had a face that looked as if it had been struck by a tornado of freckles. There was no title on the book and no words inside, just pictures.

"What's the name of your book?" I said.

The little boy opened the book and showed me the drawing of a tricycle. It looked more like a giraffe standing upside down in an elevator.

"That's my trike," he said.

"Beautiful," I said. "And what's your name?"

"That's my trike."

"Yes," I said. "Very nice, but what's your name?"

"Chuck."

He reached the book up onto the desk and then

headed for the door, saying, "I have to go now. My mother's outside with my sister."

I was going to tell him that he could put the book on any shelf he wanted to, but then he was gone in his small way.

LEATHER CLOTHES AND THE HISTORY OF MAN by S. M. Justice. The author was quite motorcyclish and wearing an awful lot of leather clothes. His book was made entirely of leather. Somehow the book was printed. I had never seen a 290-page book printed on leather before.

When the author turned the book over to the library, he said, "I like a man who likes leather."

LOVE ALWAYS BEAUTIFUL by Charles Green. The author was about fifty years old and said he had been trying to find a publisher for his book since he was seventeen years old when he wrote the book.

"This book has set the world's record for rejections," he said. "It has been rejected 459 times and now I am an old man."

THE STEREO AND GOD by the Reverend Lincoln Lincoln. The author said that God was keeping his eye on our stereophonic phonographs. I don't know what he meant by that but he slammed the book down very hard on the desk.

PANCAKE PRETTY by Barbara Jones. The

author was seven years old and wearing a pretty white dress.

"This book is about a pancake," she said.

SAM SAM SAM by Patricia Evens Summers. "It's a book of literary essays," she said. "I've always admired Alfred Kazin and Edmund Wilson, especially Wilson's theories on *The Turn of the Screw.*" She was a woman in her late fifties who looked a great deal like Edmund Wilson.

A HISTORY OF NEBRASKA by Clinton York. The author was a gentleman about forty-seven who said he had never been to Nebraska but he had always been interested in the state.

"Ever since I was a child it's been Nebraska for me. Other kids listened to the radio or raved on about their bicycles. I read everything I could find on Nebraska. I don't know what got me started on the thing. But, any way, this is the most complete history ever written about Nebraska."

The book was in seven volumes and he had them in a shopping bag when he came into the library.

HE KISSED ALL NIGHT by Susan Margar. The author was a very plain middle-aged woman who looked as if she had never been kissed. You had to look twice to see if she had any lips on her face. It was a surprise to find her mouth almost totally hidden beneath her nose.

"It's about kissing," she said.

I guess she was too old for any subterfuge now.

MOOSE by Richard Brautigan. The author was tall and blond and had a long yellow mustache that gave him an anachronistic appearance. He looked as if he would be more at home in another era.

This was the third or fourth book he had brought to the library. Every time he brought in a new book he looked a little older, a little more tired. He looked quite young when he brought in his first book. I can't remember the title of it, but it seems to me the book had something to do with America.

"What's this one about?" I asked, because he looked as if he wanted me to ask him something.

"Just another book," he said.

I guess I was wrong about him wanting me to ask him something.

IT'S THE QUEEN OF DARKNESS, PAL by Rod Keen. The author was wearing overalls and had on a pair of rubber boots.

"I work in the city sewers," he said, handing the book to me. "It's science-fiction."

YOUR CLOTHES ARE DEAD by Les Steinman. The author looked like an ancient Jewish tailor. He was very old and looked as if he had made some shirts for Don Quixote.

"They are, you know," he said, showing the book to me as if it were a piece of cloth, a leg from a pair of trousers.

JACK, THE STORY OF A CAT by Hilda Simpson. The author was a girl about twelve years old, just entering into puberty. She had lemon-sized breasts against a green sweater. She was awakening to adolescence in a delightful way.

"What do you have with you this evening?" I said. Hilda had brought in five or six books previously.

"It's a book about my cat Jack. He's really a noble animal. I thought I would put him down in a book, bring it here and make him famous," she said, smiling.

THE CULINARY DOSTOEVSKI by James Fallon. The author said the book was a cookbook of recipes he had found in Dostoevski's novels.

"Some of them are very good," he said. "I've eaten everything Dostoevski ever cooked."

MY DOG by Bill Lewis. The author was seven years old and said thank you when he put his book on a shelf.

HOMBRE by Canton Lee. The author was a Chinese gentleman about seventy.

"It's a Western," he said. "About a horse thief. Reading Westerns is my hobby, so I decided to write one myself. Why not? I spent thirty years cooking in a restaurant in Phoenix."

VIETNAM VICTORY by Edward Fox. The author was a very serious young man who said that victory could only be achieved in Vietnam by killing everybody there. He recommended that after we had killed everybody there we turn the country over to

Chiang Kai-shek, so he could attack Red China, then.

"It's only a matter of time," he said.

PRINTER'S INK by Fred Sinkus. The author was a former journalist whose book was almost illegibly written in longhand with his words wrapped around whiskey.

"That's it," he said, handing the book to me. "Twenty years." He left the library unevenly, barely under his own power.

I stood there looking down at twenty years in my hands.

BACON DEATH by Marsha Paterson. The author was a totally nondescript young woman except for a look of anguish on her face. She handed me this fantastically greasy book and fled the library in terror. The book actually looked like a pound of bacon. I was going to open it and see what it was about, but I changed my mind. I didn't know whether to fry the book or put it on the shelf.

Being a librarian here is sometimes a challenge.

UFO VERSUS CBS by Susan DeWitt. The author was an old woman who told me that her book, which was written in Santa Barbara at her sister's house, was about a Martian conspiracy to take over the Columbia Broadcasting System.

"It's all here in my book," she said. "Remember all those flying saucers last summer?"

"I think so," I said.

"They're all in here," she said. The book looked quite handsome and I'm certain they were all in there.

THE EGG LAYED TWICE by Beatrice Quinn Porter. The author said this collection of poetry summed up the wisdom she had found while living twenty-six years on a chicken ranch in San Jose.

"It may not be poetry," she said. "I never went to college, but it's sure as hell about chickens."

BREAKFAST FIRST by Samuel Humber. The author said that breakfast was an absolute requisite for travelling and was overlooked in too many travel books, so he decided that he would write a book about how important breakfast was in travelling.

THE QUICK FOREST by Thomas Funnell. The author was about thirty years old and looked scientific. His hair was thinning and he seemed eager to talk about the book.

"This forest is quicker than an ordinary forest," he said.

"How long did it take you to write it?" I said, knowing that authors seem to like that question.

"I didn't write it," he said. "I stole it from my mother. Serves her right, too. The God-damn bitch."

THE NEED FOR LEGALIZED ABORTION by Doctor O. The author was doctory and very nervous in his late 30s. The book had no title on the cover. The contents were very neatly typed, about 300 pages long.

"It's all I can do," he said.

"Do you want to put it on a shelf yourself?" I said.

"No," he said. "You take care of that yourself. There's nothing else that I can do. It's all a God-damn shame."

It has just started to rain now outside the library. I can hear it splash against the windows and echo among the books. They seem to know it's raining here in the beautiful darkness of lives as I wait for Vida.

Buffalo Gals, Won't
You Come Out Tonight?

I MUST tell you right now that most of the library isn't here. This building is not large and couldn't begin to hold all the books that have been brought in over the years.

The library was in existence before it came to San Francisco in the late 1870s, and the library didn't lose a book during the earthquake and fire of 1906. While everybody else was running around like a bunch of chickens with their heads cut off, we were careful: no panic.

This library rests upon a sloping lot that runs all the way through the block down from Clay to Sacramento Street. We use just a small portion of the lot and the rest of it is overgrown with tall grass and bushes and flowers and wine bottles and lovers' trysts.

There are some old cement stairs that pour through green and busy establishments down from the Clay Street side and there are ancient electric lamps, friends of Thomas Edison, mounted on tall metal asparagus stalks.

They are on what was once the second landing of the stairs. The lights don't work any more and everything is so overgrown that it's hard to tell why anything ever existed in the first place.

The back of the library lies almost disappearing in green at the bottom of the stairs.

The front lawn is neat, though. We don't want this place to look totally like a jungle. It might frighten people away.

A little Negro boy comes and mows the lawn every month or so. I don't have any money to pay him but he doesn't mind. He does it because he likes me and he knows that I have to stay inside here, that I can't mow the lawn myself. I always have to be in here ready to welcome a new book.

Right now the lawn has many dandelions on it and thousands of daisies sprawled here and there together like a Rorschach dress pattern designed by Rudi Gernreich.

The dandelions are loners and pretty much stay

off by themselves, but those daisies! I know all this by looking out the heavy glass door.

This place is constantly bathed in the intermediate barking of dogs from early in the morning when the dogs wake up and continuing until late at night when the dogs go to sleep and sometimes they bark in between.

We are just a few doors down from a pet hospital and, though I can't see the hospital, I am seldom without the barking of dogs and I have grown used to it.

At first I hated their damn barking. It had always been a thing with me: a dislike for dogs. But now in my third year here, I've grown accustomed to their barking and it doesn't bother me any more. Actually, I like it sometimes.

There are high arched windows here in the library above the bookshelves and there are two green trees towering into the windows and they spread their branches like paste against the glass.

I love those trees.

Through the glass door and across the street is a big white garage with cars coming and going all the time in hours of sickness and need. There is a big word in blue on the front of the garage: GULF.

Before the library came to San Francisco, it was in Saint Louis for a while, then in New York for a long time. There are a lot of Dutch books somewhere.

Because this building is so small, we have been forced to store thousands of books at another place. We moved into this little brick building after the

'06 business to be on the safe side, but there just isn't enough room here.

There are so many books being written that end up here, either by design or destiny. We have accepted 114 books on the Model T Ford, fifty-eight books on the history of the banjo and nineteen books on buffalo-skinning since the beginning of this library.

We keep all the ledgers here that we use to record the acceptance of each book in, but most of the books themselves are in hermetically-sealed caves in Northern California.

I have nothing to do with the storing of the books in the caves. That's Foster's job. He also brings me my food because I can't leave the library. Foster hasn't been around for a few months, so I guess he's off on another drunk.

Foster loves to drink and it's always easy for him to find somebody to drink with. Foster is about forty years old and always wears a T-shirt, no matter what the weather is about, rain or shine, hot or cold, it's all the same to his T-shirt because his T-shirt is an eternal garment that only death will rob from his body.

Foster has long buffalo-heavy blond hair and I have never seen Foster when he wasn't sweating. He's very friendly in an overweight sort of style, jolly you might say, and has a way of charming people, total strangers, into buying him drinks. He goes off on month-long drunks in the logging towns near the caves, raises hell with the loggers and chases the Indian girls through the woods.

I imagine he'll be down here one of these days, red-faced and hung-over, full of excuses and driving his big green van and all ready to fill it up with another load of books for the caves.

BOOK 2:

Vida

Vida

WHEN I first met Vida she had been born inside the wrong body and was barely able to look at people, wanting to crawl off and hide from the thing that she was contained within.

This was late last year in San Francisco.

She came to the library one evening after she got off work. The library was "closed" and I was in my room making some coffee and thinking about the books that had come into the library that day.

One of the books was about a great octopus that had leather wings and flew through abandoned school yards at night, demanding entrance into the classrooms.

I was putting some sugar into my coffee when I heard the bell ring ever so slightly, but always just enough to alert me and to summon me.

I went out and turned on the light in the library and there was a young girl at the door, waiting behind the heavy religious glass.

She startled me.

Besides having an incredibly delicate face, beautiful, with long black hair that hung about her shoulders like bat lightning, there was something very unusual about her, but I could not quite tell what that thing was because her face was like a perfect labyrinth that led me momentarily away from a very disturbing thing.

She did not look directly at me as she waited for me to unlock the door and let her in. She was holding something under her arm. It was in a brown paper bag and looked like a book.

Another one for the caves.

"Hello," I said. "Please come in."

"Thank you," she said, coming very awkwardly into the library. I was surprised that she was so awkward. She did not look directly at me and she did not look at the library either. She seemed to be looking at something else. The thing that she was looking at was not in front of me nor behind me nor at the side of me.

"What do you have there? A book?" I said, wanting to sound like a pleasant librarian and make her feel at ease.

Her face was so delicate: the mouth, the eyes, the nose, the chin, the curve of her cheeks all beautiful. She was almost painful to gaze upon.

"Yes," she said. "I hope I didn't disturb you. It's late."

"No," I said. "Not at all. No. Please come over here to the desk and we'll register your book in the Library Contents Ledger. That's how we do it here."

"I was wondering how you were going to do it," she said.

"Did you come far?" I said.

"No," she said. "I just got off work."

She wasn't looking at herself either. I do not know

what she was looking at, but she was looking at something very intently. I believe the thing that she was looking at was inside of herself. It had a shape that only she could see.

She moved very awkwardly over to the desk, stunningly awkward, but again the almost tide-pool delicacy of her face led me away from the source of her awkwardness.

"I hope I'm not disturbing you. I know it's late," she said, kind of hopelessly, and then broke away from the thing that she was looking at, to glance lightspeed at me.

She *was* disturbing me, but not in the way she thought. There was a dynamically incongruous thing about her, but I still couldn't find it. Her face, like a circle of mirrors, led me away from it.

"No, not at all," I said. "This is my job and I love doing it. There's no place I would rather be than where I am now."

"What?" she said.

"I love my work," I said.

"It's good you're happy," she said. She said the word happy as if she were looking at it from a great distance through a telescope. The word sounded celestial upon her mouth, stark and Galilean.

Then I noticed what was so extraordinarily strange about her. Her face was so delicate, perfect, but her body was fantastically developed for the fragility of her face.

She had very large fully realized breasts and an incredibly tiny waist and large full hips that tapered down into long majestic legs.

41

Her body was very sensual, inciting one to think of lust, while her face was Botticellian and set your mind to voyaging upon the ethereal.

Suddenly she sensed my recognition of her body. She blushed bitterly and reached into the paper bag and took out her book.

"This is my book," she said.

She put it down on the desk and almost stepped back when she did it. She was going to step back but then she changed her mind. She glanced at me again and I could feel somebody inside of her looking out as if her body were a castle and a princess lived inside.

The book had a plain brown wrapper on it and there was no title. The book looked like a stark piece of ground burning with frozen heat.

"What's it about?" I said, holding the book in my hand, feeling almost a hatred coming from within the book.

"It's about this," she said and suddenly, almost hysterically, she unbuttoned her coat and flung it open as if it were a door to some horrible dungeon filled with torture instruments, pain and dynamic confession.

She was wearing a blue sweater and skirt and a pair of black leather boots in the style of this time. She had a fantastically full and developed body under her clothes that would have made the movie stars and beauty queens and showgirls bitterly ooze dead make-up in envy.

She was developed to the most extreme of Western man's desire in this century for women to look:

the large breasts, the tiny waist, the large hips, the long *Playboy* furniture legs.

She was so beautiful that the advertising people would have made her into a national park if they would have gotten their hands on her.

Then her blue eyes swirled like a tide pool and she started crying.

"This book is about my body," she said. "I hate it. It's too big for me. It's somebody else's body. It's not mine."

I reached into my pocket and took out a handkerchief and a candy bar. When people are troubled or worried, I always tell them that it will be all right and give them a candy bar. It surprises them and it's good for them.

"Everything's going to be all right," I said.

I gave her a Milky Way. She held it in her startled hand, staring at it. And I gave her the handkerchief.

"Wipe your eyes," I said. "And eat the candy bar while I get you a glass of sherry."

She fumbled abstractedly with the candy bar wrapper as if it were a tool from a distant and future century while I went and got some sherry for us. I figured that we would both need it.

When I came back she was eating the candy bar. "Now isn't that good," I said, smiling.

The ludicrousness of me giving her a candy bar made her smile, ever so slightly, and almost look directly at me.

"Please sit down over here," I said, motioning toward a table and some chairs. She sat down as if her body were six inches larger than she was. After she had sat down, her body was still sitting down.

I poured us each a glass of Gallo sherry, all the library could afford, and then there was a kind of awkward silence as we sat there sipping our sherry.

I was going to tell her that she was a beautiful girl and she shouldn't feel bad about it, that she was all wrong in denouncing herself, but then I changed my mind instantly.

That was not what she wanted to hear and that wasn't really what I wanted to say. After all, I have a little more sense than that. We both didn't want to hear what I first thought of telling her.

"What's your name?" I said.

"Vida. Vida Kramar."

"Do you like to be called V-(ee)-da or V-(eye)-da?"

That made her smile.

"V-(eye)-da."

"How old are you?"

"Nineteen. Soon I'll be twenty. On the tenth."

"Do you go to school?"

"No, I work at night. I went to State for a while, then UC, but I don't know. Now I'm working at night. It's OK."

She was almost looking at me.

"Did you just finish your book?" I said.

"Yes, I finished it yesterday. I wanted to tell how it is to be like me. I figured it was the only thing left for me to do. When I was eleven years old, I had a thirty-six-inch bust. I was in the sixth grade.

"For the last eight years I've been the object,

veneration and butt of at least a million dirty jokes. In the seventh grade they called me 'points.' Isn't that cute? It never got any better.

"My book is about my body, about how horrible it is to have people creeping, crawling, sucking at something I am not. My older sister looks the way I really am.

"It's horrible.

"For years I had a recurrent dream that I got up in the middle of the night and went into my sister's bedroom and changed bodies with her. I took off my body and put on her body. It fit perfectly.

"When I woke up in the morning, I had on my own true body and she had this terrible thing I'm wearing now. I know it's not a nice dream, but I had it all during my early teens.

"You'll never know how it is to be like I am. I can't go anywhere without promoting whistles, grunts, howls, minor and major obscenities and every man I meet wants to go to bed instantly with me. I have the wrong body."

She was staring directly at me now. Her vision was unbroken and constant as a building with many windows standing fully here in this world.

She continued: "My whole life has just been one torment. I, I don't know. I wrote this book to tell how horrible physical beauty is, the full terror of it.

"Three years ago a man was killed in an automobile accident because of my body. I was walking along a highway. I had gone to the beach with my family, but I couldn't stand it any longer.

"They demanded that I put on a bathing suit. 'Don't be bashful, just relax and enjoy yourself.' I was miserable with all the attention I was getting. When an eighty-year-old man dropped his ice-cream cone on his foot, I put my clothes back on and went for a walk along the highway up from the beach. I had to go somewhere.

"A man came driving by in his car. He slowed down and was gawking at me. I tried to ignore him but he was very persistent. He forgot all about where he was and what he was doing and drove his car right into a train.

"I ran over and he was still alive. He died in my arms, still staring at me. It was horrible. There was blood all over both of us and he wouldn't take his eyes off me. Part of the bone was sticking out of his arm. His back felt funny. When he died, he said, 'You're beautiful.' That's just what I needed to make me feel perfect forever.

"When I was fifteen a student in a high-school chemistry class drank hydrochloric acid because I wouldn't go out with him. He was a little crazy, anyway, but that didn't make me feel any better. The principal prohibited me from wearing a sweater to school.

"It's this," Vida said, gesturing rain-like toward her body. "It's not me. I can't be responsible for what it does. I don't attempt to use my body to get anything from anyone and I never have.

"I spend all my time hiding from it. Can you imagine spending your whole life hiding from your own body as if it were a monster in a Grade B

46

movie, but still every day having to use it to eat, sleep and get from one place to another?

"Whenever I take a bath I always feel as if I'm going to vomit. I'm in the wrong skin."

All the time she told me these things she did not take her eyes off me. I felt like a statue in a park. I poured her another glass of sherry and one for myself. I had a feeling that we were going to need a lot of sherry before the night was over.

"I don't know what to say," I said. "I'm just a librarian. I can't pretend that you are not beautiful. That would be like pretending that you are someplace else in the world, say China or Africa, or that you are some other kind of matter, a plant or a tire or some frozen peas or a bus transfer. Do you understand?"

"I don't know," she said.

"It's the truth. You're a very pretty girl and you're not going to change, so you might as well settle down and get used to it."

She sighed and then awkwardly slipped her coat off and let it hang on the chair behind her like a vegetable skin.

"I once tried wearing very baggy formless clothes, muu muus, but that didn't work because I got tired of looking like a slob. It's one thing to have this fleshy thing covering me but it's another thing to be called a beatnik at the same time."

Then she gave me a great big smile and said, "Anyway, that's my problem. Where do we go from here? What's next? Got any more candy bars?"

I pretended to get one from my pocket and she laughed out loud. It was a pleasing thing.

Suddenly she turned her attention upon me in a very strong way. "Why are you here in this funny library?" she said. "This place where losers bring their books. I'm curious about you now. What's your story, Mr. Candyman Librarian?"

She was smiling as she said these things.

"I work here," I said.

"That's too easy. Where did you come from? Where are you going?"

"Well, I've done all sorts of things," I said, sounding falsely old. "I worked in canneries, sawmills, factories, and now I'm here."

"Where do you live?"

"Here," I said.

"You live here in the library?" she said.

"Yes. I have a large room in the back with a small kitchen and toilet."

"Let me see it," she said. "I'm suddenly curious about you. A young-old man like yourself working in a creepy place like this doesn't show that you've come out too far ahead of the game either."

"You're really laying it on the line," I said, because she had really gotten to me.

"I'm that way," she said. "I may be sick, but I'm not stupid. Show me your room."

"Well," I said, dogging a little. "That's a little irregular."

"You're kidding," she said. "You mean there's something irregular for this place? I don't know how to break it to you, but you've got a pretty far-out

48

operation going on here. This library is a little on the whacky side."

She stood up and stretched awkwardly, but it's hard to describe the rest of it. I had never in my life seen a woman graced with such a perfect body whose spell was now working on me. As certain as the tides in the sea rush to the shore, I showed her my room.

"I'd better get my coat," she said. She folded her coat over her arm. "After you, Mr. Librarian."

"I've never done this before," I said, faraway-like as if to no one.

"Neither have I," she said. "It will be a different thing for both of us."

I started to say something else, but abstraction clouded my tongue and made it distant and useless.

"The library isn't really open now, is it?" she said. "I mean, it's after midnight and it's only open for special books, latecomers like myself, right?"

"Yes, it's 'closed' but—"

"But what?" she said.

I don't know where that "but" came from but it vanished just as fast, returning to some conjunctional oblivion.

"But nothing," I said.

"You had better turn out the lights, then," she said. "You don't want to waste electricity."

"Yes," I said, feeling a door close behind me, knowing that somehow this at first-appearing shy unhappy girl was turning, turning into something strong that I did not know how to deal with.

"I'd better turn the lights out," I said.

"Yes," she said.

I turned the lights out in the library and turned the light on in my room. That was not all I was turning on as a door closed behind us and a door opened in front of us.

"Your room is very simple," she said, putting her coat down on my bed. "I like that. You must live a very lonely life with all the losers and dingalings, myself included, that bring their books in here."

"I call it home," I said.

"That's sad," she said. "How long have you been here?"

"Years," I said. What the hell.

"You're too young to have been here that long," she said. "How old are you?"

"Thirty-one."

"That's a good age."

She had her back to me and was staring at the cupboard in my kitchen.

"It's all right to look at me," she said, without turning her head the slightest. "For some strange reason I don't mind your looking at me. Actually, it makes me feel good, but stop acting like a bandit when you do it."

I laughed at that.

Suddenly she turned around and looked half at me, then directly at me and smiled gently. "I really have had a hard time of it."

"I think I can almost understand," I said.

"That's nice," she said. She reached up and brushed her long black hair, causing a storm of bat lightning to flash past her ears.

"I'd like some coffee," she said, looking at me.

"I'll put it on," I said.

"No, let me," she said. "I know how to make good coffee. It's my specialty. Just call me Queen Caffeine."

"Well, damn," I said, a little embarrassed. "I'm sorry but I only have instant."

"Then instant it is," she said. "That's the name of the game. Perhaps I have a way with instant coffee, too. You never can tell," smiling.

"I'll get the stuff for you," I said.

"Oh, no," she said. "Let me do it. I'm a little curious about this kitchen of yours. I want to find out more about you, and this little kitchen is a good place to start. I can see at a glance, though, that you are something like me. You're not at home in the world."

"At least let me get the coffee for you," I said. "It's—"

"Sit down," she said. "You make me nervous. Only one person can make instant coffee at a time. I'll find everything."

I sat down on the bed next to her coat.

She found everything and made the coffee as if she were preparing a grand meal. I have never seen such care and eloquence applied to a cup of instant coffee. It was almost as if making a cup of instant coffee were a ballet and she were a ballerina pirouetting between the spoon, the cups, the jar, and the pan full of boiling water.

She cleared the clutter from my table, but then

decided that we should have our coffee on the bed, because it was more comfortable.

We sat there on the bed, cozy as two bugs in a rug, drinking coffee and talking about our lives. She worked as a laboratory technician for a small institute that was studying the effects of various experiments on dogs in an attempt to solve some of the more puzzling questions of science.

"How did you get the job?" I said.

"Through an ad in the *Chronicle*."

"What happened at San Francisco State?"

"I got tired of it. One of my English teachers fell in love with me. I told him to buzz off, so he failed me. That made me mad, so I transferred to UC."

"And UC?"

"The same story. I don't know what it is about English teachers and me, but they fall like guillotines when they see me coming."

"Where were you born?"

"Santa Clara. All right, I've answered enough of your questions. Now tell me how you got this job. What's your story, Mr. Librarian?"

"I assumed possession of it."

"I take it then that there was no ad in the paper."

"Nope."

"How did you assume possession of it?"

"The fellow who was here before me couldn't stand children. He thought they were going to steal his shoes. I came in here with a book I had written and while he was writing it down in the Library Contents Ledger, a couple of children came in and he flipped, so I told him that I had better take over the library and he had better do something that didn't involve children. He told me he thought he was cracking up, too, and that's how I got this job."

"What did you do before you started working here?"

"I kicked around a lot: canneries, sawmills, factories. A woman supported me for a couple of years, then she got tired of it and kicked my ass out. I don't know," I said. "It was all pretty complicated before I started working here."

"What are you going to do after you quit here or do you plan on quitting?"

"I don't know," I said. "Something will come up. Maybe I'll get another job or find a woman to support me again or maybe I'll write a novel and sell it to the movies."

That amused her.

We had finished our coffee. It was funny because suddenly we both noticed that we did not have any more coffee to drink and we were sitting together on the bed.

"What are we going to do now?" she said. "We can't drink any more coffee and it's late."

"I don't know," I said.

"I guess it would be too corny for us to go to bed together," she said. "But I can't think of anything else that would be better to do. I don't want to go home and sleep by myself. I like you. I want to stay here with you tonight."

"It's a puzzler," I said.

"Do you want to sleep with me?" she said, not

looking at me, but not looking away either. Her eyes were somewhere in between half-looking at me and half-thinking about something else.

"We don't have any place else to go," I said. "I'd feel like a criminal if you left tonight. It's hard to sleep with strangers. I gave it up years ago, but I don't think we are really strangers. Do you?"

She turned her eyes 3/4 towards me.

"No, we're not strangers."

"Do you want to sleep with me?" I asked.

"I don't know what it is about you," she said. "But you make me feel nice."

"It's my clothes. They're relaxing. They've always been this way. I know how to get clothes that make people feel better when they're with me."

"I don't want to sleep with your clothes," she said, smiling.

"Do you want to sleep with me?" I said.

"I've never slept with a librarian before," she said, 99% toward me. The other 1% was waiting to turn. I saw it starting to turn.

"I brought a book in here tonight denouncing my own body as grotesque and elephant-like, but now I want to take this awkward machine and lie down beside you here in this strange library."

Counting toward Tijuana

WHAT an abstract thing it is to take your clothes off in front of a stranger for the very first time. It isn't really what we planned on doing. Your body almost looks away from itself and is a stranger to this world.

We live most of our lives privately under our clothes, except in a case like Vida whose body lived outside of herself like a lost continent, complete with dinosaurs of her own choosing.

"I'll turn the lights out," she said, sitting next to me on the bed.

I was startled to hear her panic. She seemed almost relaxed a few seconds before. My, how fast she could move the furniture about in her mind. I responded to this by firmly saying, "No, please don't."

Her eyes stopped moving for a few seconds. They came to a crashing halt like blue airplanes.

"Yes," she said. "That's a good idea. It will be very hard, but I have no other choice. I can't go on like this forever."

She gestured toward her body as if it were far away in some lonesome valley and she, on top of a mountain, looking down. Tears came suddenly to her eyes. There was now rain on the blue wings of the airplanes.

Then she stopped crying without a tear having left her eyes. I looked again and all the tears had vanished. "We have to leave the lights on," she said. "I won't cry. I promise."

I reached out and, for the first time in two billion years, I touched her. I touched her hand. My fingers went carefully over her fingers. Her hand was almost cold.

"You're cold," I said.

"No," she said. "It's only my hand."

She moved slightly, awkwardly toward me and rested her head on my shoulder. When her head touched me, I could feel my blood leap forward, my nerves and muscles stretch like phantoms toward the future.

My shoulder was drenched in smooth white skin and long bat-flashing hair. I let go of her hand and touched her face. It was tropical.

"See," she said, smiling faintly. "It was only my hand."

It was fantastic trying to work around her body, not wanting to startle her like a deer and have her go running off into the woods.

I poetically shifted my shoulder like the last lines of a Shakespearean sonnet (Love is a babe; then might I not say so, / To give full growth to that which still doth grow.) and at the same time lowered her back onto the bed.

She lay there looking up at me as I crouched forward, descending slowly, and kissed her upon the mouth as gently as I could. I did not want that first kiss to have attached to it the slightest gesture or flower of the meat market.

The Decision

IT'S a hard decision whether to start at the top or the bottom of a girl. With Vida I just didn't know where to begin. It was really a problem.

After she reached up awkwardly and put my face in a small container which was her hands and kissed me quietly again and again, I had to start somewhere.

She stared up at me all the time, her eyes never leaving me as if I were an airfield.

I changed the container and her face became a flower in my hands. I slowly let my hands drift down her face while I kissed her and then further down her neck to her shoulders.

I could see the future being moved in her mind while I arrived at the boundaries of her bosom. Her breasts were so large, so perfectly formed under her sweater that my stomach was standing on a step-ladder when I touched them for the first time.

Her eyes never left me and I could see in her eyes the act of my touching her breasts. It was like brief blue lightning.

I was almost hesitant in a librarian sort of way.

"I promise," she said, reaching up and awkwardly pressing my hands harder against her breasts. She of course had no idea what that did to me. The step-ladder started swirling.

She kissed me again, but this time with her tongue. Her tongue slid past my tongue like a piece of hot glass.

A Continuing Decision

WELL, it had been my decision to start at the top and I was going to have to carry it out and soon we arrived at the time to take off her clothes.

I could tell that she didn't want to have any-thing to do with it. She wasn't going to help. It was all up to me.

Damn it.

It wasn't exactly what I had planned on doing when I started working at the library. I just wanted to take care of the books because the other librarian couldn't do it any more. He was afraid of children, but of course it was too late now to think about his fears. I had my own problems.

I had gone further than taking this strange awk-ward beautiful girl's book. I was now faced with taking her body which lay before me and had to

58

have its clothes taken off, so we could join our bodies together like a bridge across the abyss.

"I need your help," I said.

She didn't say anything. She just continued staring at me. That brief blue lightning flashed again in her eyes, but it was relaxed at the edges.

"What can I do?" she said.

"Sit up, please," I said.

"All right."

She sat up awkwardly.

"Please put your arms up," I said.

"It's that simple, isn't it?" she said.

Whatever was happening I was certainly getting down to it. It would have been much simpler just to have kindly taken her book for the library and sent her on her way but that was history now or like the grammar of a forgotten language.

"How's this?" she said and then smiled. "I feel like a San Francisco bank teller."

"That's right," I said. "Just do what the note says," and I started her sweater gently off. It slid up her stomach and went on over her breasts, getting briefly caught on one of them, so I had to reach down and help it over the breast, and then her neck and face disappeared in the sweater and came out again when the sweater went off her fingers.

It was really fantastic the way she looked. I could have been hung up for a long time there, but I kept moving on, had to. It was my mission in life to take her bra off.

"I feel like a child," she said. She turned sideways from me, so I could get at the brassiere clasp in the back. I fumbled at the clasp for a few moments. I've never had much luck with brassieres.

"Want me to help?" she said.

"No, I can get it," I said. "It may take me a few days but I'll get it. Don't dishearten. There . . . *AH!*"

That made Vida laugh.

She did not need a bra at all. Her breasts stayed right up there after the bra left them like an extra roof on a house and joined her sweater. It was a difficult pile of clothes. Each garment was won in a strange war.

Her nipples were small and delicately colored in relationship to the large full expansion of her breasts. Her nipples were very gentle. They were another incongruity fastened like a door to Vida.

Then at the same time we both looked down at her boots, long and black and leather like a cloud of animals gathered about her feet.

"I'll take your boots off," I said.

I had finished with the top of her and now it was time to start on the bottom. There certainly are a lot of parts to girls.

I took off her boots and then I took off her socks. I liked the way my hands ran along her feet like water over a creek. Her toes were the cutest pebbles I have ever seen.

"Stand up, please," I said. We were really moving along now. She got awkwardly to her feet and I unzipped her skirt. I brought it down her hips to the floor and she stepped out of it and I put it on the pile of other battles.

I looked into her face before I took her panties off. Her features were composed and though there still flashed bolts of brief blue lightning in her eyes, her eyes remained gentle at the edges and the edges were growing.

I took her panties off and the deed was done. Vida was without clothes, naked, there.

"See?" she said. "This isn't me. I'm not here." She reached out and put her arms about my neck. "But I'll try to be here for you, Mr. Librarian."

Two (37-19-36) Soliloquies

"I just don't understand why women want bodies like this. The grotesqueness of them and they try so very hard to get these bodies, moving hell and high water with dieting, operations, injections, obscene undergarments to arrive at one of these damn things and then if they try everything and still can't get one, the dumb cunts fake it. Well, here's one they can have for free. Come and get it, you bitches.

"They don't know what they're getting into or maybe they like it. Maybe they're all pigs like the women who use these bodies to turn the tides of money: the movie stars, models, whores.

"Oh, Christ!

"I just can't see the fatal attraction that bodies

like this hold for men and women. My sister has my body: tall and skinny. All these layers are beyond me. These aren't my breasts. These aren't my hips. This isn't my ass. I'm inside of all this junk. Can you see me? Look hard. I'm in here, Mr. Librarian."

She reached out and put her arms about my neck and I put my hands upon her hips. We stood there looking at each other.

"I think you're wrong," I said. "Whether you like it or not, you're a very beautiful woman and you've got a grand container. It may not be what you want, but this body is in your keeping and you should take good care of it and with pride, too. I know it's hard but don't worry about what other people want and what they get. You've got something that's beautiful and try to live with it.

"Beauty is the hardest damn thing in the world to understand. Don't buy the rest of the world's juvenile sexual thirsts. You're a smart young lady and you'd better start using your head instead of your body because that's what you're doing.

"Don't be a fatalist winner. Life's a little too short to haul that one around. This body is you and you'd better get used to it because this is all she wrote for this world and you can't hide from yourself.

"This is you.

"Let your sister have her own body and start learning how to appreciate and use this one. I think you might enjoy it if you let yourself relax and get your mind out of other people's sewers.

"If you get hung up on everybody else's hang-ups, then the whole world's going to be nothing more than one huge gallows."

We kissed.

BOOK 3:

Calling the Caves

Calling the Caves

FORTUNATELY, I was able to get in touch with Foster up at the caves when Vida discovered that she was pregnant. Vida and I talked it over. The decision to have the abortion was arrived at without bitterness and was calmly guided by gentle necessity.

"I'm not ready to have a child yet," Vida said. "And neither are you, working in a kooky place like this. Maybe another time, perhaps for certain another time, but not now. I love children, but this isn't the time. If you can't give them the maximum of yourself, then it's best to wait. There are too many children in the world and not enough love. An abortion is the only answer."

"I think you're right," I said. "I don't know about this library being a kooky place, but we're not ready for a child yet. Perhaps in a few years. I think you should use the pill after we have the abortion."

"Yes," she said. "It's the pill from now on."

Then she smiled and said, "It looks like our bodies got us."

"It happens sometimes," I said.

"Do you know anything about this kind of business?" Vida said. "I know a little bit. My sister had an abortion last year in Sacramento, but before she had the abortion, she went to a doctor in Marin County who gave her some hormone shots, but they didn't work because it was too late. The shots work if you take them soon enough and they're quite a bit cheaper than an abortion."

"I think I'd better call Foster," I said. "He got into a thing like this last year and had to go down to Tijuana with one of his Indian girls."

"Who's Foster?" Vida said.

"He takes care of the caves," I said.

"What caves?"

"This building is too small," I said.

"What caves?" she said.

I guess I was rattled by the events in Vida's stomach. I hadn't realized it. I calmed myself down a little bit and said, "Yes, we have some caves up in Northern California where we store most of our books because this building is too small for our collection.

"This library is very old. Foster takes care of the caves. He comes down here every few months and loads his van up with books and stores them in the caves.

"He also brings me food and the little things that I need. The rest of the time he stays drunk and chases the local women, mostly Indians. He's quite a guy. A regular explosion of a man.

"He had to go down to Tijuana last year. He told me all about it. He knows a very good doctor there. There's a telephone at the caves. I'll give him a ring. I've never done it before. Never had to. Things are usually pretty calm down here. We might as well get

68

this thing going. Would you watch the library while I do it?"

"Yes," Vida said. "Of course. It would be a privilege. I never thought that I would end up being the librarian of this place, but I guess I should have had an inkling when I came in here with my book under my arm."

She was smiling and wearing a short green dress. Her smile was on top of the dress. It looked like a flower.

"It will only take a few minutes," I said. "I think there's a pay telephone down at the corner. That is, if it's still there. I haven't been out of here in so long that they may have moved it."

"No, it's still there," Vida said, smiling. "I'll take care of everything. Don't worry. Your library is in good hands."

She held her hands out to me and I kissed them.

"See?" she said.

"You know how to put the books down in the Library Contents Ledger?" I said.

"Yes," she said. "I know how to do it and I'll give anyone who brings in a book the royal carpet treatment. Don't worry. Everything's going to be all right. Stop worrying, Mr. Librarian. I think you have been in here too long. I think I'll kidnap you soon."

"You could ask them to wait," I said. "I'll only be gone for a few minutes."

"Come on now!" Vida said. "Let your granny gland relax a little and slow down those rocking chair secretions."

Outside (Briefly)

GEE, it had been a long time. I hadn't realized that being in that library for so many years was almost like being in some kind of timeless thing. Maybe an eternity.

Actually being outside was quite different from looking out the window or the door. I walked down the street, feeling strangely awkward on the sidewalk. The concrete was too hard, aggressive or perhaps I was too light, passive.

It was something to think about.

I had a lot of trouble opening the telephone booth door but finally I got inside and started to call Foster up at the caves when suddenly I realized that I didn't have any money with me. I searched all my pockets but, alas, not a cent. I didn't need money in the library.

"Back already?" Vida said. She looked very pretty behind the counter in her green dress with her flower-like head.

"I don't have any money," I said.

After she stopped laughing, which took about five minutes, very funny, she went and got her purse and gave me a handful of change.

"You're too much," she said. "Are you sure you

haven't forgotten how to use money? You hold it like this." She held an imaginary coin between her fingers and started laughing all over again.

I left. I had my dime.

Foster's Coming

I CALLED Foster up at the caves. I could hear his telephone ringing. It rang seven or eight times and then Foster answered it.

"What's happening?" Foster said. "Who is this? What are you up to, you son-of-a-bitch? Don't you know it's one o'clock in the afternoon. What are you? A vampire?"

"It's me," I said. "You old drunk!"

"Oh," he said. "The kid. Hell, why didn't you say so? What's up down there? Somebody bring in an elephant with a book written on it? Well, feed it some hay and I'll be down with the van."

"Very funny, Foster," I said.

"Not bad," he said. "Nothing's impossible at that loony bin you've got down there. What's up, kid?"

"I've got a problem."

"You?" he said. "How in the hell can you have a problem? You're inside all the time. Is that prison pallor of yours beginning to flake?"

"No," I said. "My girlfriend is pregnant."

"DINGALING CUCKOO!" Foster said and the conversation stopped for a moment while Foster laughed so hard it almost shook the telephone booth hundreds of miles away.

Finally he stopped laughing and said, "It sounds like you've really been working hard at the library, but when did fornication become one of its services? Girlfriend, huh? Pregnant, huh? Cuckoo, kid!"

He started to laugh all over again. It was everybody's day to laugh except mine.

"Well, what do you need?" he said. "A little trip down to Tijuana? A short visit with my abortionist buddy, Dr. Garcia?"

"Something like that," I said.

"Well, I'll have a few drinks for breakfast," he said. "And get in the van and be in sometime late this evening."

"Good," I said. "That's what I need."

Then there was a slight pause at the cave end of the telephone.

"You don't have any money, do you, kid?" Foster said.

"Are you kidding?" I said. "Where would I get any money? This is the lowest-paying job in the world because it doesn't. I had to borrow this dime from my girlfriend to call you collect."

"I guess I'm still gorgonized," he said. "I don't know what I was thinking. I was probably thinking that I spent all my money last night on drink or was it last week? and I haven't got a cent. Cuckoo, have I been out of it!"

"What about my food?" I said, realizing that he had spent my food money, too.

"Is she good-looking?" Foster said. "Will she do in a dust storm at midnight with a candle?"

"What?" I said.

"I'll bring the money, then," he said. "It costs a couple of hundred if you make the good doctor toe the line. He likes to speculate sometimes—it's the businessman in him—but you can hold him down by putting the two hundred in his hand.

"Let's see: You'll need airplane tickets and walking around money and you might need a hotel room for her to rest up after she sees Dr. Garcia.

"I'll go down to the bar and turn a couple of the patrons upside down and see what I can shake out of their pockets, so you hang on, kid, and I'll be in late this evening and we'll get this show on the road.

"I never thought you had it in you, kid. Tell your young lady hello for me and that everything will be all right. Foster's coming."

Masturbation

THAT Foster! I went back to the library. Somebody was just leaving as I arrived. It was a young boy, maybe sixteen. He looked awfully tired and nervous. He hurried past me.

"Thank God, darling, you didn't get lost," Vida said. "I was worried that you wouldn't be able to find your way back up the block. It's great to see you, honey."

She came out from behind the desk and moved breathlessly to where I was given a great big lingering kiss. She had lost about 80% of her awkwardness since she had come to the library that evening late last year. The 20% she had left was very intriguing.

"How did it go?" she said.

"Fine," I said. "Here's your dime. Foster's on his way down. He'll be in late this evening."

"Good," she said. "I'll be glad when this thing is over. I wouldn't like to wait for an abortion. I'm glad we're doing it right now."

"So am I. Foster knows a great doctor," I said. "Everything will be all right. Foster's going to take care of everything."

"Fine, just fine," she said. "What about money? I have—"

"No, no," I said. "Foster will get the money."

"You're sure, because—"

"No, I'm sure," I said. "Who was that boy who was leaving?"

"Some kid who brought in a book," she said. "I welcomed it in my most pleasing manner and recorded it in my best handwriting in the Library Contents Ledger."

"Gee," I said. "This is the first time I haven't received a book in years."

"Oh, honey," she said. "You aren't that old, even

though you try to be, but that kind of thinking is going to make you an old man if you work at it hard enough."

She kissed me again.

"I'll take a look at it," I said.

"Your old age?" she said.

"No, the book."

She stood there and smiled after me as I walked over behind the desk and opened the Library Contents Ledger and read:

THE OTHER SIDE OF MY HAND by Harlow Blade, Jr. The author was about sixteen and seemed a little sadder than he should have been for his age. He was very shy around me. The poor dear. He kept looking at me out of the corner of his eye.

Finally he said, "Are *you* the librarian?"

"Yes," I said.

"I expected a man."

"He's out," I said. "So I'll just have to do. I don't bite."

"You're not a man," he said.

"What's your name?"

"What?"

"Your name, please? I have to write it down here in the ledger before we can take your book. You do have a name, don't you?"

"Yes. Harlow Blade, Jr."

"Now what's your book about? I have to have that, too. Just tell me what it's about and I'll write it down here in the ledger."

"I was expecting a man," he said.

"What's your book about? The subject, please?"

"Masturbation. I'd better be going now."

I started to thank him for bringing his book in and tell him that he could put it anywhere he wanted to in the library, but he left without saying anything else. Poor kid.

What a strange place this library is, but I guess it's the only place you can bring a book in the end. I brought mine here and I'm still here.

Vida trailed over to the desk and moved behind it with me and put her arm around me and read the entry over my shoulder after I finished reading it.

"I think it sounds pretty good," she said.

Gee, the handwriting of a different librarian lay before me on the desk. It was the first book I hadn't welcomed and recorded there myself in years.

I looked over at Vida for a moment. I must have looked at her kind of strangely because she said, "Oh, no. No, no, no."

Foster

FOSTER arrived at midnight. We were in my room, sitting around drinking coffee and talking about small casual things that are never remembered afterward, except perhaps in the twilight of our lives.

Foster never bothered to ring the bell on the front door. He said it made him think he was going into some kind of church and he'd had enough of that to last him forever.

BANG! BANG! BANG! he just slugged the door with his fist and I could always hear him and was afraid that he would break the glass. Foster couldn't be overlooked nor forgotten.

"What's that?" Vida said, jumping up startled from the bed.

"That's Foster," I said.

"It sounds like an elephant," she said.

"He never touches the stuff," I said.

We went out into the library and turned on the lights and there was Foster on the other side of the door, still banging away with that big fist of his.

There was a large smile on his face and he was wearing his traditional T-shirt. He never wore a

77

shirt or a coat or a sweater. It didn't make any difference what the weather did. Cold, wind or rain, Foster always wore his T-shirt. He was of course sweating like a dam and his buffalo-heavy blond hair hung almost down to his shoulders.

"Hello!" he said. His voice came booming through as if the glass door were made of tissue paper. "What's going on in there?"

I opened the door for him and could see the van parked out in front. The van was big and strange and looked like a prehistoric animal asleep in front of the library.

"Well, here I am," he said and threw an arm around me and gave me a big hug. There was a bottle of whiskey in his other hand and half the whiskey was gone.

"How's it going, kid? Cheer up. Foster's here. Hey, *hello* there!" he said to Vida. "My, aren't you a pretty girl! Damn, am I glad I drove down here! Every mile was worth it. My God, ma'am, you're so pretty I'd walk ten miles barefooted on a freezing morning to stand in your shit."

Vida broke up. There was a big smile on her face. I could tell that she liked him instantly.

My, how her body had relaxed these few months we'd been going together. She was still a little awkward, but now instead of treating it as a handicap, she treated it as a form of poetry and it was fantastically charming.

Vida came over and put her arm around Foster. He gave her a great big hug, too, and offered her a drink from his bottle of whiskey.

78

"It's good for you," he said.

"All right, I'll give it a try," she said.

He wiped the mouth of the bottle off with his hand in the grand manner and offered her the bottle and she took a delicate nip.

"Hey, kid. You try some of this stuff, too. It'll grow hair on your books."

I took a drink.

Wow!

"Where did you get this whiskey?" I said.

"I bought it from a dead Indian."

The A D Standoff

"LEAD the way," Foster said.

He had his arm around Vida. They were like two peas in a pod. I was very pleased that they were getting along so well together. We went back to my room to relax and make our plans for Tijuana.

"Where have you been all my life?" Foster said.

"Not on the reservation," Vida said.

"Wonderful!" Foster said. "Where did you find this girl?"

"She came along," I said.

"I should be working down here at the library," Foster said. "Not up at the caves. I got up on the wrong side of the map. Hey, hey, you're the prettiest thing I've ever seen in my life. My God, you're even prettier than my mother's picture."

"It's the whiskey," Vida said. "I always look better through amber-colored fluid."

"Damn, it's the whiskey. You're pulling my 86 proof. I think I'll take over this library for a while and you kids can go up and dust off those God-damn books and live at the caves. It's real nice up there. But don't mention to anyone that you know me. Jesus Christ and old Foster wore out their welcome at the same time. I only survive on my good looks these days."

The Plan for Tijuana

WE went back to my room and we all sat down on the bed together and drank a little whiskey and made plans for Tijuana. I usually don't drink but I figured the present condition of our lives merited a little drink.

"Well, it's a little abortion, huh?" Foster said. "You're sure now?"

"Yeah," I said. "We talked it over. That's what we want."

Foster looked over at Vida.

80

"Yes," she said. "We're too immature right now to have a child. It would only confuse us and this confusion would not be good for a child. It's hard enough being born into this world without having immature and confused parents. Yes, I want the abortion."

"OK, then," Foster said. "There's nothing to be afraid of. I know a good doctor: Dr. Garcia. He won't hurt you and there will be no complications. Everything will be just fine."

"I trust you," she said.

Vida reached over and took my hand.

"The arrangements are very simple," Foster said. "You'll take a plane down there. There's one that leaves at 8:15 tomorrow morning for San Diego. I've got you both round-trip tickets. I called the doctor and he'll be waiting for you. You'll be in TJ before noon and the thing will be over in a short while.

"You can come back in the evening on the plane if you feel up to it, but it you want to stay over in San Diego, I've got a reservation for you at the Green Hotel. I know the guy who runs the place. He's a good guy. You'll feel a little weak after the abortion, so it's up to you if you want to stay. It just depends on how you feel, but don't push it if you feel too woozy, just stay over at the hotel.

"Sometimes Dr. Garcia tries to speculate on the price of the abortion, but I told him you were coming and you only had 200 dollars and there was no more and he said, 'OK, Foster, will do.' He doesn't speak very good English but he's very kind and very good. He's a regular doctor. He did me a good turn with that Indian girl last year. Any questions or anything? Damn! you're a pretty girl."

He gave Vida a nice hug.

"I think you've probably covered it all," I said.

"Vida?" he said.

"No, I can't think of anything."

"What about the library?" I said.

"*Whatabout* the library?" Foster said.

"Who's going to watch it? There has to be somebody here. That's a big part of this library. Somebody has to be here twenty-four hours a day to receive and welcome books. It's the very foundation of this library. We can't close it. It has to remain open."

"You mean me?" Foster said. "Oh, no. I'm strictly a caveman. You'll have to get another boy."

"But there has to be somebody here," I said, looking hard at him.

"Oh, no," Foster said.

"But," I said.

Vida was awfully amused by the whole thing. I was fully aware that Vida did not share the intensity of my feeling toward the library. I could understand that it was a rather strange calling that I had answered, but it was a thing I had to do.

"I'm a caveman," Foster said.

"This is our job," I said. "This is what we were hired to do. We have to take care of this library and the people that need its services."

"I was meaning to bring that up," Foster said.

"This is a kind of slow-paying operation. I haven't been paid in two years. I'm supposed to make $295.50 a month."

"Foster!" I said.

"I was just joking," Foster said. "Just a little joke. Here, have some more whiskey."

"Thanks."

"Vida?" Foster said.

"Yes," she said. "Another sip would be just wonderful. It's relaxing."

"It's the old Indian tranquilizer," Foster said.

"You can take care of this place for a day or so while we're down in Mexico getting the abortion," I said. "It won't kill you to actually put in a day's work. It's been years since you've turned a wheel."

"I have my work up at the caves," he said. "It's quite a responsibility lugging books up there and putting them away, guarding them and making sure cave seepage doesn't get to them."

"Cave seepage!" I said, horrified.

"Forget I said that," Foster said. "I don't want to go into it right now, but OK, I'll stay here and take care of the library until you get back. I don't like it but I'll do it."

"Cave seepage?" I repeated.

"What do I have to do around here?" Foster said. "How do I deal with the nuts that bring their books in? What do you do here, anyway? Have some whiskey. Tell me all about it."

Vida was very amused by what was going on. She certainly was pretty. We were all very relaxed lying

83

there on the bed. The whiskey had made us mud-puddly at the edges of our bodies and the edges of our minds.

"This is delightful," Vida said.

Foster's Girl #1

"WHAT'S that?" Foster said, almost moving on the bed.

"That's the bell," I said. "Somebody is out there with a new book for the library. I'll show you how we honor a book into the library. 'Welcome it' is the phrase I use."

"Sounds like a funeral parlor," Foster said. "Damn, what time is it?" Foster looked around the room. "I can hear it ticking."

I looked over at the clock. Foster couldn't see it because of the way he was lying on the bed.

"After midnight."

"That's kind of late to bring a book in, isn't it? Midnight? That's twelve."

"We're open twenty-four hours a day, seven days a week. We never close," I said.

"Good God!" Foster said.

"See what I mean?" Vida said.

"Do I," Foster said. "This boy needs a rest."

Then he looked over at Vida. He appraised her

in a classic computerized masculine manner without being obvious or sensual and he liked what he saw.

Vida looked at him smiling gently without disturbing her mouth. It remained unchanged by her smile. I believe this thing has been gone into before.

She was not the same girl who had brought her book in a few months before. She had become somebody else with her body.

"Yes," Foster said, finally. "Yes, maybe we had better go out and see who's bringing in a book. We don't want to keep her, I mean, them waiting. It's cold outside."

Foster had never been aware of cold in his entire just gone into full gallop.

"What do you do out there?" Foster said. "Maybe life, so he was a little drunk and his imagination had I'll just go out there and take care of it myself. You kids can sit here and relax. No reason to stop being comfortable when old Foster's around. I'll take care of that book myself. Besides, I have to find out what's going on here if I'm going to run this asylum while you're in TJ."

Vida's smile had opened until now you could see the immaculate boundaries of her teeth. Her eyes had small friendly lightning walking across them.

I was smiling, too.

"What do you do out there? You write down the title of the book and the name of the writer and a little something about the book into that big black ledger, huh?"

"That's right," I said. "And you have to be friendly, too. That's important. To make the person and

85

the book feel wanted because that's the main purpose of the library and to gather pleasantly together the unwanted, the lyrical and haunted volumes of American writing."

"You're kidding," Foster said. "You have to be kidding."

"Come on, Foster," I said. "Or I'll bring up 'cave seepage' again. You know 'cave seepage.'"

"All right. All right. All right, cuckoo," Foster said. "I'll be on my best and besides, who knows: I might want to be on my best. I'm not such a bad guy. Come to think of it, I've got a lot of friends. They may not admit it, but I'm a big place in their hearts."

The bell was still ringing but it was growing weak and needed immediate attention. Foster was by now off the bed. He ran his hand through his buffalo-heavy blond hair as if to comb it before going out to the library.

Blank like Snow

WHILE Foster went into the library to welcome his first book, Vida and I continued lying there on the bed taking little nips from the bottle of whiskey he had graciously left behind. After a while Vida and I were so relaxed that we both could have been rented out as fields of daisies.

Suddenly, we had lost track of time, Foster came slamming into the room. He was very angry in his overweight T-shirt sweating kind of way.

"I think we'd better close this nuthouse while you're south," he said, demanding whiskey with his right hand. "Come to think of it, we should close this God-damn place forever. Everybody go home. Pick up their marbles. That is, if they have any left."

Foster gobbled down a big turkey slug of whiskey. He grimaced and shook when it hit his stomach. "That's better," he said, wiping his hand across his mouth.

"What happened?" Vida said. "It looks like your library vaccination didn't take."

"You're telling me. More whiskey!" Foster said, addressing the bottle as if it were a healing hand of balm.

"I hope you didn't frighten them," I said. "That's not the purpose of this library. It's a service, not a demand that we perform here."

"Frighten them? Are you kidding, kid? It was the other God-damn way around. Hell, I usually get along with people."

"What happened?" Vida repeated.

"Well, I went out there and it wasn't exactly who I expected would be there. I mean, they were standing outside and—"

"Who was it?" Vida said.

"A woman?" I said, a little mercilessly.

"It's not important," Foster said. "Let me continue, damn it! Yes, there was a woman out there and I use the word woman with serious reservation. She

87

was ringing the bell and she had a book under her arm, so I opened the door. That was a mistake."

"What did she look like?" I said.

"It's not important," Foster said.

"Come on," Vida said. "Tell us."

Ignoring us, Foster continued telling the story in his own manner, "When I opened the door she opened her mouth at the same time. 'Who are you?' she demanded to know in a voice just like a car wreck. What the hell!

" 'I'm Foster,' I said.

" 'You don't look like any Foster I've ever seen,' she said. 'I think you're somebody else because you're no Foster.'

" 'That's my name,' I said. 'I've always been Foster.'

" 'Haa! but enough of you. Where's my mother?' she demanded.

" 'What do you mean, your mother? You're too old to have a mother,' I said. I was tired of humoring the bag.

" 'What do you want done with that book?' I said.

" 'That's none of your God-damn business, you impostor Foster. Where's she at?"

" 'Good night,' I said.

" 'What do you mean, good night? I'm not going anywhere. I'm staying right here until you tell me about my mother.'

" 'I don't know where your mother is and frankly, to quote Clark Gable in *Gone with the Wind*, "I don't give a damn." ' "

" 'Call my mother Clark Gable!' she said, and then she tried to slap me. Well, that was quite enough out of her, so I grabbed her hand in mid-flight and spun her around and gave her a big shove out the door. She went flying out that door like a garbage can on the wing.

" 'Let my mother go free!' she yelled. 'My mother! My mother!'

"I started to close the door. It was getting kind of dreamlike about this time. I didn't know whether to wake up or slug the bitch.

"She made a threatening motion toward the glass, so I went outside and escorted her down the stairs. We had a little struggle along the way, but I laid a little muscle on her arm and she cooled it and at the same time I gentlemanly offered to break her chicken neck if she didn't take out down the street as fast as her clotheshanger legs would take her.

"The last I saw of her she was yelling, 'It isn't right that I should end up like this, doing these crazy things that I do, feeling the way I do, saying these things,' and she was tearing pages out of the book and throwing them over her head like a bride at a wedding reception."

"Like a bride at a wedding?" Vida said.

"The flowers," Foster said.

"Oh, I didn't understand," she said.

"I don't understand either," Foster said. "I went down and picked up some of the pages to see what kind of book they came from, but the pages didn't have any writing on them. They were blank like snow."

"That's how it goes here sometimes," I said. "We get some disturbed authors, but most of the time it's quiet. All you have to do is be patient with them and write down the author of the book, its title and a little description in the Library Contents Ledger, and let them put the book any place they want in the library."

"That's easy enough with this one," Foster said.

I started to say something—

"The description," Foster said.

I started to say something—

"Blank like snow," Foster said.

The Van

"I'LL sleep in my van," Foster said.

"No, there's room in here for you," I said.

"Please stay," Vida said.

"No, no," Foster said. "I'm more comfortable in my van. I always sleep there. I got a little mattress and a sleeping bag and it makes me cozy as a bug in a rug.

"No, it's already settled. It's the van for old Foster. You kids get a good night's sleep because you have to leave early on the plane. I'll take you down to the airfield."

"No, you can't do that," I said. "We'll have to

take the bus because you have to stay here and watch the library. Remember? It has to remain open all the time we're gone. You'll have to stay until we get back."

"I don't know about that," Foster said. "After that experience I had a little while ago, I don't know. You couldn't get somebody to come in from one of those temporary employment agencies to handle it, a Kelly Girl or something like that, huh? Hell, I'd pay for it out of my own pocket. They can take care of the library while I go down to North Beach and take in a few topless shows while I'm here."

"No, Foster," I said. "We can't trust this library to just anyone. You'll have to stay here while we're gone. We're not going to be gone long."

"Humor him, Foster," Vida said.

"OK. I wonder what the next nut will be about who brings a book in."

"Don't worry," I said. "That was an exception. Things will run smoothly while we're gone."

"I'll bet."

Foster got ready to go outside. "Here, have another drink of whiskey," Foster said. "I'm going to take the bottle with me."

"When does the plane leave?" Vida said.

"8:15," Foster said. "Our pal here can't drive, so I guess you'll have to take the bus because the Library Kid here wants me to stay and tend his garden of nuts."

"I can drive," Vida said, looking smoothly-beautiful and young.

"Can you drive a van?" Foster said.

"I think so," she said. "I used to drive trucks and pickups one summer when I was on a ranch in Montana. I've always been able to drive anything that's got four wheels, sports cars, anything. I even drove a school bus once, taking some kids on a picnic."

"A van's different," Foster said.

"I've driven a horse van," Vida said.

"This isn't a horse van," Foster said, now somewhat outraged. "There's never been a horse in my van!"

"Foster," Vida said. "Don't get mad, dear. I was just telling you that I can drive it. I can drive anything. I've never been in an accident. I'm a good driver. That's all. You have a beautiful van."

"It is a good one," Foster said, now placated. "Well, I guess I don't see any harm in it and it would get you out there a lot faster than the bus and you could get back here faster. It would be a lot smoother ride. Buses are horrible, and you can park it right out there at the airfield. I guess I won't need the van while I'm working at this God-damn madhouse. Sure, you can take it, but drive carefully. There's only one van like that in the whole world and she's mine and I love her."

"Don't worry," Vida said. "I'll love it, too."

"Good deal," Foster said. "Well, I guess I'd better go out and get to bed. Any more whiskey here?"

"No, I think we've had enough," I said.

"OK."

"Do you want us to wake you?" Vida said.

"No, I'll be up," Foster said. "I can get up when I want to, down to the minute. I've got an alarm clock in my head. It always gets me up. Oh, I almost forgot to tell you something. Don't eat anything for breakfast tomorrow. It's against the rules."

Johnny Cash

AFTER Foster left to go out and spend the night in his van, we started getting ready for tomorrow. We wouldn't have much time in the morning when we woke up.

Vida had enough clothes there at the library, so she wouldn't have to go home. Even though she only lived a block from the library, I of course had never been there. Sometimes in the past I had been curious about her place and she told me about it.

"It's very simple," she told me. "I don't have much. All I have is a few books on a shelf, a white rug, a little marble table on the floor, and some records for my stereo: Beatles, Bach, Rolling Stones, Byrds, Vivaldi, Wanda Landowska, Johnny Cash. I'm not a beatnik. It's just that I always considered my body to be more possessions than I ever needed and so everything else had to be simple."

She packed a few clothes for us in an old KLM

bag and our toothbrushes and my razor in case we had to stay overnight in San Diego.

"I've never had an abortion before," Vida said. "I hope we don't have to stay overnight in San Diego. I was there once and I didn't like it. There are too many unlaid sailors there and everything is either stone stark or neon cheap. It's not a good town."

"Don't worry about it," I said. "We'll just play it by ear and if everything's all right, we'll come back tomorrow evening."

"That sounds reasonable," Vida said, finishing with our simple packing.

"Well, let's have a kiss, honey, and go to bed. We need some sleep," I said. "We're both tired and we have to get up early in the morning."

"I'll have to take a bath and a douche," Vida said. "And put a little dab of perfume behind my ears."

I took Vida in my arms and gathered the leaves and blossoms of her close, a thing she returned to me, delicate and bouquet-like.

Then we took off our clothes and got into bed. I put out the light and she said, "Did you set the clock, honey?"

"Oh, I forgot," I said. "I'll get up."

"I'm sorry," she said.

"No," I said. "I should have remembered to set the clock. What time do you want to wake up? Six?"

"No, I think you'd better make it 5:30. I want to take care of my 'female complaints' before Foster wakes up, so I can cook a good breakfast for all of us. It'll be a long day and we'll need a solid start."

94

"The lady is not for breakfast," I said. "Remember what Foster said?"

"Oh. Oh, that's right. I forgot," Vida said.

It was hard for a minute and then we both smiled across the darkness at what we were doing. Though we could not see our smiles, we knew they were there and it comforted us as dark-night smiles have been doing for thousands of years for the problemed people of the earth.

I got up and turned the light on. Vida was still smiling softly as I set the clock for 5:30. It was absolutely too late for remorse now or to cry against the Fates. We were firmly in the surgical hands of Mexico.

"Genius"

VIDA did not look at all pregnant as she got into her bath. Her stomach was still so unbelievably thin that it was genius and I wondered how there could be enough intestines in there to digest any food larger than cookies or berries.

Her breasts were powerful but delicate and wet at the nipples.

She had put a pot of coffee on before she had gotten into the tub and I was standing there watching it perk and watching her bathe at the same time through the open door of the bathroom.

She had her hair piled and pinned on top of her head. It looked beautiful resting on the calm of her neck.

We were both tired, but not as nervous as we could have been facing the prospects of the day, because we had gone into a gentle form of shock that makes it easier to do one little thing after another, fragile step by fragile step, until you've done the big difficult thing waiting at the end, no matter what it is.

I think we have the power to transform our lives into brand-new instantaneous rituals that we calmly act out when something hard comes up that we must do.

We become like theaters.

I was taking turns watching the coffee perk and watching Vida at her bath. It was going to be a long day but fortunately we would get there only moment by moment.

"Is the coffee done yet?" Vida said.

I smelled the coffee fumes that were rising like weather from the spout. They were dark and heavy with coffee. Vida had taught me how to smell coffee. That was the way she made it.

I had always been an instant man, but she had taught me how to make real coffee and it was a good thing to learn. Where had I been all those years, thinking in terms of coffee as dust?

I thought about making coffee for a little while as

I watched it perk. It's strange how the simple things in life go on while we become difficult.

"Honey, did you hear me?" Vida said. "The coffee. Stop daydreaming and get on the coffee, dear. Is it done?"

"I was thinking about something else," I said.

Foster's Bell

VIDA put on a simple but quite attractive white blouse with a short blue skirt—you could see easily above her knees—and a little half-sweater thing on over the blouse. I've never been able to describe clothes so that anyone knows what I am talking about.

She did not have any make-up on except for her eyes. They looked dark and blue in the way that we like eyes to look in these last years of the seventh decade of the Twentieth Century.

I heard the silver bell ringing on the library door. The bell was ringing rapidly in a kind of shocked manner. The bell seemed almost frightened and crying for help.

It was Foster.

Foster had never really taken to that bell. He had always insisted that it was a sissy bell and always offered to put a bell up himself. He continued the thing as I let him in. I opened the door but he stood there with his hand on the bell rope, though he was not ringing the bell any more.

It was still dark and Foster was wearing his eternal T-shirt and his buffalo-heavy blond hair hung about his shoulders.

"You should take my advice," he said. "Get rid of this damn bell and let me put a real bell up for you."

"We don't want a bell that will frighten people," I said.

"What do you mean frighten people? How in the hell can a bell frighten people?"

"We need a bell that fits the service we offer, that blends in with the library. We need a gentle bell here."

"No roughneck bells, huh?" Foster said.

"I wouldn't put it that way," I said.

"Hell," Foster said. "This bell rings like a God-damn queer down on Market Street. What are you running here?"

"Don't worry about it," I said.

"Well, I'm just trying to look out for your best interests. That's all, kid." He reached over and gave the bell a little tap on its butt.

"Foster!" I said.

"Hell, kid, a tin can and a spoon make a great bell."

"What about a fork and a knife and a bowl of soup to go with it, Foster? A little mashed potatoes and gravy and maybe a turkey leg? What about that? Wouldn't that make a good bell?"

"Forget it," Foster said. He reached over and gave the bell another little tap on its silver butt and said, "Good-bye, sweetie."

The TJ Briefing

VIDA cooked Foster and me a good breakfast, though she didn't have anything with us except some coffee.

"You certainly look pretty this morning," Foster said. "You look like a dream I've never had before."

"I bet you tell that to all the girls," Vida said. "I can see that you're a flirt from way back."

"I've had a girlfriend or two," Foster said.

"Some more coffee?" Vida said.

"Yeah, another cup of coffee would be fine. Sure is good coffee. Somebody here knows their way around coffee beans."

"What about you, honey?" Vida said.

"Sure."

"There you go."

"Thank you."

Vida sat back down.

"Well, you know what you're supposed to do,"

Foster said after breakfast. "There's nothing to worry about. Dr. Garcia is a wonderful doctor. There will be no pain or fuss. Everything will go just beautifully. You know how to get there. It's just a few blocks off the Main Street of town.

"The doc may want to try and get a few extra bucks out of you, but hold the line and say, "Well, Doctor Garcia, Foster said that it was 200 dollars and that's all we brought and here it is,' and take it out of your pocket.

"He'll look a little nervous and then he'll take it and put it in his pocket without counting it and then he's just like the best doctor in the whole wide world. Have faith in him and do what he says and relax and everything will be all right.

"He's a wonderful doctor. He saves a lot of people a lot of trouble."

The Library Briefing

". . . ," I said.

"I promise I won't take down that swishy little bell of yours with the silver pants and put up a tin can with a spoon, which would be the best bell for this asylum. Have you ever heard one?" Foster said.

". . . ," I said.

"I'm sorry about that. It's an awfully pretty sound.

So beautiful to the spirit and so soothing to the nerves."

". . . ," I said.

"That's a real shame," Foster said.

". . . ," I said.

"I didn't know you felt that way about it," Foster said.

". . . ," I said.

"Don't worry, I won't harm a brick on this library's head. I'll treat your library like a child's birthday cake in a little yellow box that I'm carrying home in my arms from the bakery because carrying it by the string would be too risky.

"I've got to be careful of that dog up ahead. He might bite me and I'd drop the cake. There, I'm past him. Good dog.

"Oh, oh, there's a little lady coming toward me. Got to be careful. She might have a heart attack and collapse in front of me and I might trip over her body. I won't take my eyes off her. There, she's passing me. Everything's going to be all right. Your library is safe," Foster said.

". . . ," Vida said, laughing.

"Thank you, honey," Foster said.

". . . ," I said.

"I love this place," Foster said.

". . . ," I said.

"I'll treat your patrons like saintly eggshells. I won't break one of them," Foster said.

". . . ," Vida said, laughing.

"Oh, honey, you're too nice," Foster said.

". . . ," I said.

"Stop worrying, kid. I know what I'm supposed to do and I'll do it the best I can and that's all I can say," Foster said.

". . . ," Vida said.

"Isn't it the truth and he's not old either. He's just a kid," Foster said.

". . . ," I said.

"I don't think I ever really appreciated the peace and quiet, the downhomeness of the caves until now. You've opened up a whole new world for me, kid. I should get down on my hands and knees and thank you with all my heart for what you've done."

". . . ," I said.

"Ah, California!" Foster said.

Foster's Heart

FOSTER insisted on carrying our bag out to the van. It was light and halfway through the dawn. Foster was busy sweating away in his T-shirt, even though we found the morning to be a little chilly.

During the years that I had known Foster, I'd never seen him when he wasn't sweating. It was probably brought about by the size of his heart. I was always certain that his heart was as big as a cantaloupe and sometimes I went to sleep thinking about the size of Foster's heart.

Once Foster's heart appeared to me in a dream. It was on the back of a horse and the horse was going into a bank and the bank was being pushed off a cloud. I couldn't see what was pushing the bank off, but it's strange to think *what* would push a bank off a cloud with Foster's heart in it, falling past the sky.

"What do you have in this bag?" Foster said. "It's so light I don't think there's anything in it."

He was following after Vida who led the way with a delightful awkwardness, looking so perfect and beautiful as not to be with us, as to be alone in some different contemplation of the spirit or an animal stepladder to religion.

"Never you mind our secrets," Vida said, not turning back.

"How would you like to visit my rabbit trap someday?" Foster said.

"And be your Bunny girl?" Vida said.

"I guess you've heard that one," Foster said.

"I've heard them all."

"I'll bet you have," Foster said, falling cleanly past the sky.

Vida Meets the Van

THERE were leftover pieces of blank white paper on the sidewalk from the woman last night. They looked terribly alone. Foster put our little bag in the van.

"There's your bag in the van. Now you're sure you know how to drive this thing?" Foster said. "It's a van."

"Yes, I know how to drive a van. I know how to drive anything that has wheels. I've even flown an airplane," Vida said.

"An airplane?" Foster said.

"I flew one up in Montana a few summers ago. It was fun," Vida said.

"You don't look like the airplane-flying type," Foster said. "Hell, a few summers ago you were in the cradle. Are you sure you weren't flying a stuffed toy?"

"Don't worry about your van," Vida said, returning the conversation from the sky to the ground.

"You've got to drive carefully," Foster said. "This van has its own personality."

"It's in good hands," Vida said. "My God, you're almost as bad with your van as he is with his library."

"Damn! all right," Foster said. "Well, I've told

you what to do and now I guess you'd better go and do it. I'll stay here and take care of the asylum while you're gone. I imagine it won't be dull if that lady I met last night is any example of what's going on here."

There were pieces of white paper on the ground.

Foster put his arms around both of us and gave us a very friendly, consoling hug as if to say with his arms that everything was going to be all right and he would see us in the evening.

"Well, kids, good luck."

"Thank you very much," Vida said, turning and giving Foster a kiss on the cheek. They looked heroically like father and daughter around each other's arms and cheek to cheek in the classic style that has brought us to these years.

"In you go," Foster said.

We got into the van. It suddenly felt awfully strange for me to be in a vehicle again. The metallic egg-like quality of the van was very surprising and in some ways I had to discover the Twentieth Century all over again.

Foster stood there on the curb carefully watching Vida at the controls of the van.

"Ready?" she said, turning toward me with a little smile on her face.

"Yeah, it's been a long time," I said. "I feel as if I'm in a time machine."

"I know," she said. "Just relax. I know what I'm doing."

"All right," I said. "Let's go."

Vida started the van as if she had been born to

the instrument panel, to the wheel and to the pedals.

"Sounds good," Vida said.

Foster was pleased with her performance, nodding at her as if she were an equal. Then he gave her the go signal and she took it and we were off to visit Dr. Garcia who was waiting for us that very day in Tijuana, Mexico.

BOOK 4:

Tijuana

The Freewayers

I HAD forgotten how the streets in San Francisco go to get to the freeway. Actually, I had forgotten how San Francisco went.

It was really a surprise to be outside again, travelling in a vehicle again. It had been almost three years. My God, I was twenty-eight when I went into the library and now I was thirty-one years old.

"What street is this?" I said.

"Divisadero," Vida said.

"Oh, yeah," I said. "It's Divisadero all right."

Vida looked over at me very sympathetically. We were stopped at a red light, next to a place that sold flying chickens and spaghetti. I had forgotten that there were places like that.

Vida took one hand off the wheel and gave me a little pat on the knee. "My poor dear hermit," she said.

We drove down Divisadero and saw a man washing the windows of a funeral parlor with a garden hose. He was spraying the hose against the second-floor windows. It was not a normal thing to see, so early in the morning.

Then Vida made a turn off Divisadero and went around the block. "Oak Street," she said. "You remember Oak Street? It'll take us to the freeway and down to the airport. You remember the airport, don't you?"

"Yes," I said. "But I've never been on an airplane. I've gone out there with friends who were going on airplanes, but that was years ago. Have the airplanes changed any?"

"Oh, honey," she said. "When we're through with all this, I've got to get you out of that library. I think you've been there long enough. They'll have to get somebody else."

"I don't know," I said, trying to drop the subject. I saw a Negro woman pushing an empty Safeway grocery cart on Oak Street. The traffic was very good all around us. It frightened me and excited me at the same time. We were headed for the freeway.

"By the way," Vida said. "Who do you work for?"

"What do you mean?" I said.

"I mean, who pays the bills for your library?" she said. "The money that it takes to run the place? The tab."

"We don't know," I said, pretending that was the answer to the question.

"What do you mean, you don't know?" Vida said. It hadn't worked.

"They send Foster a check from time to time. He never knows when it's coming or how much it will be. Sometimes they don't send us enough."

"They?" she said, keeping right on it.

We stopped for a red light. I tried to find something to look at. I didn't like talking about the financial structure of the library. I didn't like to think in terms of the library and money together. All I saw was a Negro man delivering papers from still another cart.

"Who are you talking about?" Vida said. "Who picks up the tab?"

"It's a foundation. We don't know who's behind it."

"What's the name of the foundation?" Vida said.

I guess that wasn't enough.

"The American Forever, Etc."

"The American Forever, Etc.," Vida said. "Wow! That sounds like a tax dodge. I think your library is a tax write-off."

Vida was now smiling.

"I don't know," I said. "All I know is that I have to be there. It's my job. I have to be there."

"Honey, I think you've got to get some new work. There must be something else that you can do."

"There are a lot of things I can do," I said, a little defensively.

Just then we slammed onto the freeway and my stomach flew into birds with snakes curling at their wings and we joined the mainstream of American motor thought.

It was frightening after so many years. I felt like a dinosaur plucked from my grave and thrust into competition with the freeway and its metallic fruit.

"If you don't want to work, honey," Vida said, "I think I can take care of us until you feel like it, but you've got to get out of that library as soon as possible. It's not the right place for you any more."

I looked out the window and saw a sign with a chicken holding a gigantic egg.

"I've got other things on my mind right now," I said, trying to get away. "Let's talk about it in a few days."

"You're not worried about the abortion, are you, honey?" Vida said. "Please don't be. I have perfect faith in Foster and his doctor. Besides, my sister had an abortion last year in Sacramento and she went to work the next day. She felt a little tired but that was all, so don't worry. An abortion is a rather simple thing."

I turned and looked at Vida. She was staring straight ahead after saying that, watching the traffic in front of us as we roared out of San Francisco down the freeway past Potrero Hill and toward the airplane that waited to fly us at 8:15 down California to land in San Diego at 9:45.

"Maybe when we get back we can go live at the caves for a while," Vida said. "It'll be spring soon. They should be pretty."

"Seepage," I said.

"What?" Vida said. "I didn't hear you. I was watching that Chevrolet up there to see what it was going to do. What did you say now, honey?"

"Nothing," I said.

"Anyway," she said. "We've got to get you out of that library. Maybe the best thing would be just to give the whole thing up, forget the caves and start someplace new together. Maybe we can go to New York or we'll move to Mill Valley or get an apartment on Bernal Heights or I'll go back to UC and get my degree and we'll get a little place in Berkeley. It's nice over there. You'd be a hero."

Vida seemed to be more interested in getting me out of the library than worrying about the abortion.

"The library is my life," I said. "I don't know what I'd do without it."

"We're going to fix you up with a new life," Vida said.

I looked down the freeway to where the San Francisco International Airport waited, looking almost medieval in the early morning like a castle of speed on the entrails of space.

The San Francisco
International Airport

VIDA parked the van near the Benny Bufano statue of Peace that waited for us towering above the cars like a giant bullet. The statue looked at rest in that sea of metal. It is a steel thing with gentle mosaic and marble people on it. They were trying to tell us something. Unfortunately, we didn't have time to listen.

"Well, here we are," Vida said.

"Yeah."

I got our bag and we left the van there quite early

in the morning, planning, if everything went well, to pick it up that evening. The van looked kind of lonesome like a buffalo next to the other cars.

We walked over to the terminal. It was filled with hundreds of people coming and going on airplanes. The air was hung with nets of travelling excitement and people were entangled within them and we became a part of the catch.

The San Francisco International Airport Terminal is gigantic, escalator-like, marble-like, cybernetic-like and wants to perform a thing for us that we don't know if we're quite ready for yet. It is also very *Playboy*.

We went over—over being very large—and got our tickets from the Pacific Southwest Airlines booth. There was a young man and woman there. They were beautiful and efficient. The girl looked as if she would look good without any clothes on. She did not like Vida. They both had pins with half-wings on their chests like amputated hawks. I put our tickets in my pocket.

Then I had to go to the toilet.

"Wait here for me, honey," I said.

The toilet was so elegant that I felt as if I should have been wearing a tuxedo to take a leak.

Three men made passes at Vida while I was gone. One of them wanted to marry her.

We had forty-five minutes or so before our airplane left for San Diego, so we went and got a cup of coffee. It was so strange to be among people again. I had forgotten how complex they were in large units.

Everybody was of course looking at Vida. I had never seen a girl attract so much attention before. It was just as she said it would be: plus so.

A young handsome man in a yellow coat like a God-damn maître d' showed us to a table that was next to a plant with large green leaves. He was extremely interested in Vida, though he tried not to be obvious about it.

The basic theme of the restaurant was red and yellow with a surprising number of young people and the loud clatter of dishes. I had forgotten that dishes could be that noisy.

I looked at the menu, even though I wasn't hungry. It had been years since I had looked at a menu. The menu said good morning to me and I said good morning back to the menu. We could actually end our lives talking to menus.

Every man in the restaurant had been instantly alerted to Vida's beauty and the women, too, in a jealous sort of way. There was a green aura about the women.

A waitress wearing a yellow dress with a cute white apron took our order for a couple cups of coffee and then went off to get them. She was pretty but Vida made her pale.

We looked out the window to see airplanes coming and going, joining San Francisco to the world and then taking it away again at 600 miles an hour.

There were Negro men in white uniforms doing the cooking while wearing tall white hats, but there were no Negroes in the restaurant eating. I guess Negroes don't take airplanes early in the morning.

The waitress came back with our coffee. She put the coffee on the table and left. She had lovely blond hair but it was to no avail. She took the menu with her: good-bye, good morning.

Vida knew what I was thinking because she said, "You're seeing it for the first time. It really used to bother me until I met you. Well, you know all about that."

"Have you ever thought about going into the movies or working here at the airport?" I said.

That made Vida laugh which caused a boy about twenty-one years old to spill his coffee all over himself and the pretty waitress to rush a towel over to him. He was cooking in his own coffee.

It was time now to catch our airplane, so we left the restaurant. I paid a very pretty cashier at the front of the cafe. She smiled at me as she took the money. Then she looked at Vida and she stopped smiling.

There was much beauty among the women working in the terminal, but Vida was chopping it down almost as if it weren't even there. Her beauty, like a creature unto itself, was quite ruthless in its own way.

We walked to catch our plane causing people in pairs to jab each other with their elbows to bring the other's attention to Vida. Vida's beauty had probably caused a million black and blue marks: Ah, de Sade, thy honeycomb of such delights.

Two four-year-old boys walking with their mother suddenly became paralyzed from the neck up as they passed us. They did not take their eyes off Vida. They couldn't.

We walked down to the PSA pre-flight lounge stimulating pandemonium among the males our path chanced to cross. I had my arm around Vida, but it wasn't necessary. She had almost totally overcome the dread of her own body.

I had never seen anything like it. A middle-aged man, perhaps a salesman, was smoking a cigarette as we came upon him. He took one look at Vida and missed his mouth with the cigarette.

He stood there staring on like a fool, not taking his eyes off Vida, even though her beauty had caused him to lose control of the world.

PSA

THE jet was squat and leering and shark-like with its tail. It was the first time I had ever been on an airplane. It was a strange experience climbing into that thing.

Vida caused her usual panic among the male passengers as we got into our seats. We immediately fastened our seat belts. Everybody who got on the airplane joined the same brotherhood of nervousness.

I looked out the window and we were sitting over

the wing. Then I was surprised to find a rug on the floor of the airplane.

The walls of the airplane had little California scenes on them: cable cars, Hollywood, Coit Tower, the Mount Palomar telescope, a California mission, the Golden Gate Bridge, a zoo, a sailboat, etc. and a building that I couldn't recognize. I looked very hard at the building. Perhaps it was built while I was in the library.

The men continued to stare at Vida, though the airplane was filled with attractive stewardesses. Vida made the stewardesses invisible, which was probably a rare thing for them.

"I really can't believe it," I said.

"They can have it all if they want it. I'm not trying to do anything," Vida said.

"You're really a prize," I said.

"Only because I'm with you," she said.

Before taking off a man talked to us over the plane's PA system. He welcomed us aboard and told us too much about the weather, the temperature, clouds, the sun and the wind and what weather waited for us down California. We didn't want to hear that much about the weather. I hoped he was the pilot.

It was gray and cold outside without any hope for the sun. We were now taking off. We started moving down the runway, slow at first, then faster, faster, faster: my God!

I looked at the wing below me. The rivets in the wing looked awfully gentle as if they were not able to hold anything up. The wing trembled from time to time ever so gently, but just enough to put the subtle point across.

"How does it feel?" Vida said. "You look a little green around the edges."

"It's different," I said.

A medieval flap was hanging down from the wing as we took off. It was the metal intestine of some kind of bird, retractable and visionary.

We flew above the fog clouds and right into the sun. It was fantastic. The clouds were white and beautiful and grew like flowers to the hills and mountains below, hiding with blossoms the valleys from our sight.

I looked down on my wing and saw what looked like a coffee stain as if somebody had put a cup of coffee down on the wing. You could see the ring stain of the cup and then a big splashy sound stain to show that the cup had fallen over.

I was holding Vida's hand.

From time to time we hit invisible things in the air that made the plane buck like a phantom horse.

I looked down at the coffee stain again and I liked it with the world far below. We were going to land at Burbank in Los Angeles in less than an hour to let off and pick up more passengers, then on to San Diego.

We were travelling so fast that it only took a few moments before we were gone.

The Coffee Stain

I WAS beginning to love the coffee stain on my wing.
Somehow it was perfect for the day: like a talisman.
I started to think about Tijuana, but then I changed
my mind and went back to the coffee stain.

Things were going on in the airplane with the
stewardesses. They were taking tickets and offering
coffee inside the plane, and making themselves generally liked.

The stewardesses were like beautiful *Playboy* nuns
coming and going through the corridors of the
airplane as if the airplane were a nunnery. They
wore short skirts to show off lovely knees, beautiful
legs, but their knees and legs became invisible in
front of Vida, who sat quietly in her seat next to
me, holding my hand, thinking about her body's
Tijuana destination.

There was a perfect green pocket in the mountains. It was perhaps a ranch or a field or a pasture.
I could have loved that pocket of green forever.

The speed of the airplane made me feel affec-
tionate.

After a while the clouds reluctantly gave up the
valleys, but it was a very desolate land we were
travelling over, not even the clouds wanted it. There

was nothing human kind below, except a few roads that ran like long dry angleworms in the mountains.

Vida remained quiet, beautiful.

The sun kept swinging back and forth on my wing. I looked down beyond my coffee stain to see that we were flying now above a half-desolate valley that showed the agricultural designs of man in yellow and in green. But the mountains had no trees in them and were barren and sloped like ancient surgical instruments.

I looked at the medieval intestinal flap of the wing, rising to digest hundreds of miles an hour, beside my coffee stain talisman.

Vida was perfect, though her eyes were dreaming south.

The people on the other side of the airplane were looking down below at something. I wondered what it was and looked down my side to see a small town and land that looked gentler and there were more towns. The towns began magnifying one another. The gentleness of the land became more and more towns and grew sprawling into Los Angeles and I was looking for a freeway.

The man I hoped was the pilot or involved in some official capacity with the airplane told us that we were going to land in two minutes. We suddenly flew into a cloudy haze that became the Burbank airport. The sun was not shining and everything was murky. It was a yellow murk whereas back in San Francisco it was a gray murk.

The airplane grew empty and then became full again. Vida got a lot of visual action while this was going on. One of the stewardesses lingered for a minute a few seats away and stared at Vida as if to make sure she were really there.

"How do you feel?" I said.

"Fine," Vida said.

A small airliner about the size of a P-38 with rusty-looking propellers taxied by to take off. Its windows were filled with terrified passengers.

Some businessmen were now sitting in front of us. They were talking about a girl. They all wanted to go to bed with her. She was a secretary in a branch office in Phoenix. They were talking about her, using business language. "I'd like to get her account! Ha-ha! Ha-ha! Ha-ha! Ha-ha-ha-ha!"

The "pilot" welcomed the new people aboard and told us too much about the weather again. Nobody wanted to hear what he had to say.

"We'll be landing in San Diego in twenty-one minutes," he said, finishing his weather report.

As we took off from Burbank, a train was running parallel with us across from the airport. We left it behind as if it weren't there and the same with Los Angeles.

We climbed through the heavy yellow haze and then suddenly the sun was shining calmly away on the wing and my coffee stain looked happy like a surfer, but it was only a passing thing.

Bing-Bonging to San Diego

BING-BONG!

The trip to San Diego was done mostly in the clouds. From time to time a bell tone was heard in the airplane. I didn't know what it was about.

Bing-bong!

The stewardesses wanted more tickets and people to like them. The smiles never left their faces. They were smiling even when they weren't smiling.

Bing-bong!

I thought about Foster and the library, then I very rapidly changed the subject in my mind. I didn't want to think about Foster and the library: *grimace.*

Bing-bong!

Then we flew into heavy fog and the plane made funny noises. The noises were fairly solid. I almost thought that we had landed in San Diego and were moving along the runway when a stewardess told us that we *were* going to land shortly, so we were still in the air.

Hmmmmmmmm . . .

Bing-bong!

Hot Water

FROM San Francisco our speed had been amazing. We had gathered hundreds of miles effortlessly, as if guided by lyrical poetry. Suddenly we broke out into the clear to find that we had been over the ocean. I saw white waves below breaking against the shore and there was San Diego. I saw a thing that looked like a melting park and my ears were popping and we were going down.

The airplane stopped and there were many warships anchored across from the airport and they were in a low gray mist that was the color of their bodies.

"You can stop being green now," Vida said.

"Thank you," I said. "I'm new at the tree game. Perhaps it's not my calling."

We got off the airplane with Vida causing her customary confusion among the male passengers and resentment among the female passengers.

Two sailors looked as if their eyes had been jammed with pinball machines and we went on into the terminal. It was small and old-fashioned.

And I had to go to the toilet.

The difference between the San Francisco International Airport and the San Diego International Airport is the men's toilet.

In the San Francisco International Airport the hot water stays on by itself when you wash your hands, but in the San Diego International Airport, it doesn't. You have to hold the spigot all the time you want hot water.

While I was making hot water observations, Vida had five passes made at her. She brushed them off like flies.

I felt like having a drink, a very unusual thing for me, but the bar was small, dark and filled with sailors. I didn't like the looks of the bartender. It didn't look like a good bar.

There was more confusion and distraction among the men in the terminal. One man actually fell down. I don't know how he did it, but he did it. He was lying there on the floor staring up at Vida just as I decided not to have a drink in the bar but a cup of coffee in the cafe instead.

"I think you've affected his inner ear," I said.

"Poor man," Vida said.

Flying Backwards

THE basic theme of the San Diego airport cafe was small and casual with a great many young people and boxes full of wax flowers.

The cafe was also filled with a lot of airplane

folks: stewardesses and pilots and people talking about airplanes and flight.

Vida had her effect on them while I ordered two cups of coffee from a waitress in a white uniform. She was not young or pretty and she was not quite awake either.

The cafe windows were covered with heavy green curtains that held the light out and you couldn't see anything outside, not even a wing.

"Well, here we are," I said.

"That's for certain," Vida said.

"How do you feel?" I said.

"I wish it were over," Vida said.

"Yeah."

There were two men sitting next to us talking about airplanes and the wind and the number eighty kept coming up again and again. They were talking about miles per hour.

"Eighty," one of them said.

I lost track of what they were saying because I was thinking about the abortion in Tijuana and then I heard one of them say, "At eighty you'd actually be flying the plane backwards."

Downtown

It was an overcast nothing day in San Diego. We took a Yellow Cab downtown. The driver was drinking coffee. We got in and he took a long good look at Vida while he finished with his coffee.

"Where to?" he said, more to Vida than to me.

"The Green Hotel," I said. "It's—"

"I know where it's at," he said to Vida.

He drove us onto a freeway.

"Do you think the sun will come out?" I said, not knowing what else to say. Of course I didn't have to say anything, but he was really staring at Vida in his rear-view mirror.

"It will pop out around twelve or so, but I like it this way," he said to Vida.

So I took a good look at his face in the mirror. He looked as if he had been beaten to death with a wine bottle, but by doing it with the contents of the bottle.

"Here we are," he said to Vida, finally pulling up in front of the Green Hotel.

The fare was one dollar and ten cents, so I gave him a twenty-cent tip. This made him very unhappy. He was staring at the money in his hand as we walked away from the cab and into the Green Hotel.

He didn't even say good-bye to Vida.

The Green Hotel

THE Green Hotel was a four-story red brick hotel across the street from a parking lot and next to a bookstore. I couldn't help but look at the books in the window. They were different from the books that we had in the library.

The desk clerk looked up as we came into the hotel. The hotel had a big green plant in the window with enormous leaves.

"Hello, there!" he said. He was very friendly with a lot of false teeth in his mouth.

"Hello," I said.

Vida smiled.

That really pleased him because he became twice as friendly, which was hard to do.

"Foster sent us," I said.

"Oh, Foster!" he said. "Yes. Yes. Foster. He called and said you were coming and here you are! Mr. and Mrs. Smith. Foster. Wonderful person! Foster, yes."

He was really smiling up a storm now. Maybe he was the father of an airline stewardess.

"I have a lovely room with a bath and view," he said. "It's just like home. You'll adore it," he said to Vida. "It's not like a hotel room."

128

For some reason he did not like the idea of Vida staying in a hotel room, though he ran a hotel, and that was only the beginning.

"Yeah, it's a beautiful room," he said. "Very lovely. It'll help you enjoy your stay in San Diego. How long will you be here? Foster didn't say much over the telephone. He just said you were coming and here you are!"

"Just a day or so," I said.

"Business or pleasure?" he said.

"We're visiting her sister," I said.

"Oh, that sounds nice. She has a small place, huh?"

"I snore," I said.

"Oh," the desk clerk said.

I signed Mr. and Mrs. Smith of San Francisco on the hotel register. Vida watched me as I signed our new instant married name. She was smiling. My! how beautiful she looked.

"I'll show you to your room," the desk clerk said. "It's a beautiful room. You'll be happy in it. The walls are thick, too. You'll be at home."

"Good to hear," I said. "My affliction has caused me a lot of embarrassment in the past."

"Really a loud snorer?" he said.

"Yes," I said. "Like a sawmill."

"If you'll please wait a minute," he said. "I'll ring my brother and have him come down and watch the desk while I'm taking you upstairs to the room."

He pushed a silent buzzer that summoned his brother down the elevator a few moments later.

"Some nice people here. Mr. and Mrs. Smith.

Friends of Foster," the desk clerk said. "I'm going to give them Mother's room."

The brother clerk gave Vida a solid once-over as he went behind the desk to take over the wheel from his brother who stepped out and he stepped in.

They were both middle-aged.

"That's good," the brother desk clerk said, satisfied. "They'll love Mother's room."

"Your mother lives here?" I said, now a little confused.

"No, she's dead," the desk clerk said. "But it was her room before she died. This hotel has been in the family for over fifty years. Mother's room is just the way it was when she died. God bless her. We haven't touched a thing. We only rent it out to nice people like yourselves."

We got into an ancient dinosaur elevator that took us up to the fourth floor and Mother's room. It was a nice room in a dead mother kind of way.

"Beautiful, isn't it?" the desk clerk said.

"Very comfortable," I said.

"Lovely," Vida said.

"You'll enjoy San Diego even more with this room," he said.

He pulled up the window shade to show us an excellent view of the parking lot, which was fairly exciting if you'd never seen a parking lot before.

"I'm sure we will," I said.

"If there's anything you want, just let me know and we'll take care of it: a call in the morning, anything, just let us know. We're here to make your stay in San Diego enjoyable, even if you can't stay at your sister's because you snore."

"Thank you," I said.

He left and we were alone in the room.

"What's the snoring thing you told him about?" Vida said, sitting down on the bed.

She was smiling.

"I don't know," I said. "It just seemed like the proper thing to do."

"You are a caution," Vida said. Then she freshened herself up a little, washed the air travel off and we were ready to go visit Dr. Garcia in Tijuana.

"Well, I guess we'd better go," I said.

"I'm ready," Vida said.

The ghost of the dead mother watched us as we left. She was sitting on the bed knitting a ghost thing.

The Bus to Tijuana

I DON'T like San Diego. We walked the few blocks to the Greyhound bus depot. There were baskets of flowers hanging from the light posts.

There was almost a small town flavor to San Diego that morning except for the up-all-night tired sailors or just-starting-out sailors walking along the streets.

The Greyhound bus depot was jammed with people and games of amusement and vending machines and there were more Mexicans in the bus depot than on the streets of San Diego. It was almost as if the bus depot were the Mexican part of town.

Vida's body, perfect face and long lightning hair performed their customary deeds among the men in the bus depot, causing a thing that was just short of panic.

"Well," I said.

Vida replied with a silence.

The bus to Tijuana left every fifteen minutes and cost sixty cents. There were a lot of Mexican men in the line wearing straw and cowboy hats in sprawled laziness to Tijuana.

A jukebox was playing square pop tunes from the time that I had gone into the library. It was strange to hear those old songs again.

There was a young couple waiting for the bus in front of us. They were very conservative in dress and manner and seemed to be awfully nervous and bothered and trying hard to hold on to their composure.

There was a man standing in the line, holding a racing form under his arm. He was old with dandruff on the lapels and shoulders of his coat and on his racing form.

I had never been to Tijuana before but I had been to a couple of other border towns: Nogales and Juarez. I didn't look forward to Tijuana.

Border towns are not very pleasant places. They bring out the worst in both countries, and everything that is American stands out like a neon sore in border towns.

I noticed the middle-aged people, growing old, that you always see in crowded bus depots but never in empty ones. They exist only in numbers and seem to live in crowded bus depots. They all looked as if they were enjoying the old records on the jukebox.

One Mexican man was carrying a whole mess of stuff in a Hunt's tomato sauce box and in a plastic bread wrapper. They seemed to be his possessions and he was going home with them to Tijuana.

Slides

As we drove the short distance to Tijuana it was not a very pleasant trip. I looked out the window to see that there was no wing on the bus, no coffee stain out there. I missed it.

San Diego grew very poor and then we were on a freeway. The country down that way is pretty nothing and not worth describing.

Vida and I were holding hands. Our hands were together in our hands as our real fate moved closer to us. Vida's stomach was flat and perfect and it was going to remain that way.

Vida looked out the window at what is not worth

describing, but even more so and done in cold cement freeway language. She didn't say anything.

The young conservative couple sat like frozen beans in their seats in front of us. They were really having a bad time of it. I pretty much guessed why they were going to Tijuana.

The man whispered something to the woman. She nodded without saying anything. I thought she was going to start crying. She bit her lower lip.

I looked down from the bus into cars and saw things in the back seats. I tried hard not to look at the people but instead to look at the things in the back seats. I saw a paper bag, three coat hangers, some flowers, a sweater, a coat, an orange, a paper bag, a box, a dog.

"We're on a conveyer belt," Vida said.

"It's easier this way," I said. "It will be all right. Don't worry."

"I know it will be all right," she said. "But I wish we were there. Those people in front of us are worse than the idea of the abortion."

The man started to whisper something to the woman, who continued staring straight ahead, and Vida turned and looked out the window at the nothing leading to Tijuana.

The Man from Guadalajara

THE border was a mass of cars coming and going in excitement and confusion to pass under an heroic arch into Mexico. There was a sign that said something like: WELCOME TO TIJUANA THE MOST VISITED CITY IN THE WORLD.

I had a little trouble with that one.

We just walked across the border into Mexico. The Americans didn't even say good-bye and we were suddenly in a different way of doing things.

First there were Mexican guards wearing those .45 caliber automatic pistols that Mexicans love, checking the cars going into Mexico.

Then there were other men who looked like detectives standing along the pedestrian path to Mexico. They didn't say a word to us, but they stopped two people behind us, a young man and woman, and asked them what nationality they were and they said Italian.

"We're Italians."

I guess Vida and I looked like Americans.

The arch, besides being heroic, was beautiful and modern and had a nice garden with many fine river rocks in the garden, but we were more interested in getting a taxi and went to a place where there were many taxis.

I noticed that famous sweet acrid dust that covers Northern Mexico. It was like meeting a strange old friend again.

"TAXI!"

"TAXI!"

"TAXI!"

The drivers were yelling and motioning a new supply of gringos toward them.

"TAXI!"

"TAXI!"

"TAXI!"

The taxis were typically Mexican and the drivers were shoving them like pieces of meat. I don't like people to try and use the hard sell on me. I'm not made for it.

The conservative young couple came along, looking very frightened, and got into a taxi and disappeared toward Tijuana that lay flat before us and then sloped up into some hazy yellow poor-looking hills with a great many houses on them.

The air was beginning electric with the hustle for the Yankee dollar and its biblical message. The taxi drivers seemed to be endless like flies trying to get you into their meat for Tijuana and its joys.

"Hey, beau-ti-ful girl and BE-atle! Get in!" a driver yelled at us.

"Beatle?" I said to Vida. "Is my hair that long?"

"It is a little long," Vida said, smiling.

"Hey, BE-atle and hey, beauty!" another driver yelled.

There was a constant buzzing of TAXI! TAXI! TAXI! Suddenly everything had become speeded up for us in Mexico. We were now in a different country, a country that just wanted to see our money.

"TAXI!"

"TAXI!"

(Wolf whistle.)

"BE-atle!"

"TAXI!"

"HEY! THERE!"

"TAXI!"

"TIJUANA!"

"SHE'S GOOD-LOOKING!"

"TAXI!"

(Wolf whistle.)

"TAXI!"

"TAXI!"

"SENORITA! SENORITA! SENORITA!"

"HEY, BEATLE! TAXI!"

And then a Mexican man walked quietly up to us. He seemed a little embarrassed. He was wearing a business suit and was about forty years old.

"I have a car," he said. "Would you like a ride downtown? It's right over there."

It was a ten-year-old Buick, dusty, but well kept up and seemed to want us to get into it.

"Thank you," I said. "That would be very nice."

The man looked all right, just wanting to be helpful, so it seemed. He didn't look as if he were selling anything.

"It's right over here," he repeated, to show that the car was something that he took pride in owning.

"Thank you," I said.

We walked over to his car. He opened the door for us and then went around and got in himself.

"It's noisy here," he said, as we started driving the mile or less to Tijuana. "Too much noise."

"It is a little noisy," I said.

After we left the border he kind of relaxed and turned toward us and said, "Did you come across for the afternoon?"

"Yes, we thought we'd take a look at Tijuana while we're visiting her sister in San Diego," I said.

"It's something to look at all right," he said. He didn't look too happy when he said that.

"Do you live here?" I said.

"I was born in Guadalajara," he said. "That's a beautiful city. That's my home. Have you ever been there? It's beautiful."

"Yes," I said. "I was there five or six years ago. It is a lovely city."

I looked out the window to see a small carnival lying abandoned by the road. The carnival was flat and stagnant like a mud puddle.

"Have you ever been to Mexico before, Señora?" he said, fatherly.

"No," Vida said. "This is my first visit."

"Don't judge Mexico by this," he said. "Mexico is different from Tijuana. I've been working here for a year and in a few months I'll go back home to Guadalajara, and I'm going to stay there this time. I was a fool to leave."

"What do you do?" I said.

"I work for the government," he said. "I'm taking

a survey among the Mexican people who come and go across the border into your country."

"Are you finding out anything interesting?" Vida said.

"No," he said. "It's all the same. Nothing is different."

A Telephone Call
from Woolworth's

THE government man, whose name we never got, left us on the Main Street of Tijuana and pointed out the Government Tourist Building as a place that could tell us things to do while we were in Tijuana.

The Government Tourist Building was small and glass and very modern and had a statue in front of it. The statue was a gray stone statue and did not look at peace. It was taller than the building. The statue was a pre-Columbian god or fella doing something that did not make him happy.

Though the building was quite attractive, there was nothing the people in that little building could do for us. We needed another service from the Mexican people.

Everybody was shoving us for dollars, trying to sell us things that we didn't want: kids with gum, people wanting us to buy border junk from them, more taxicab drivers shouting that they wanted to take us back to the border, even though we had just gotten there, or to other places where we would have some fun.

"TAXI!"

"BEAUTIFUL GIRL!"

"TAXI!"

"BEATLE!"

　　(Wolf whistle.)

The taxicab drivers of Tijuana remained constant in their devotion to us. I had no idea my hair was so long and of course Vida had her thing going.

We went over to the big modern Woolworth's on the Main Street of Tijuana to find a telephone. It was a pastel building with a big red Woolworth's sign and a red brick front and big display windows all filled up with Easter stuff: lots and lots and lots of bunnies and yellow chicks bursting happily out of huge eggs.

The Woolworth's was so antiseptic and clean and orderly compared to the outside which was just a few feet away or not away at all if you looked past the bunnies in the front window.

There were very attractive girls working as sales girls, dark and young and doing lots of nice things with their eyes. They all looked as if they should work in a bank instead of Woolworth's.

I asked one of the girls where the telephone was and she pointed out the direction to me.

"It's over there," she said in good-looking English.

I went over to the telephone with Vida spreading erotic confusion like missile jam among the men in the store. The Mexican women, though very pretty, were no match for Vida. She shot them down without even thinking about it.

The telephone was beside an information booth, next to the toilet, near a display of leather belts and a display of yarn and the women's blouse section.

What a bunch of junk to remember, but that's what I remember and look forward to the time I forget it.

The telephone operated on American money: a nickel like it used to be in the good old days of my childhood.

A man answered the telephone.

He sounded like a doctor.

"Hello, Dr. Garcia?" I said.

"Yes."

"A man named Foster called you yesterday about our problem. Well, we're here," I said.

"Good. Where are you?"

"We're at Woolworth's," I said.

"Please excuse my English. Isn't so good. I'll get the girl. Her English is . . . better. She'll tell you how to get here. I'll be waiting. Everything is all right."

A girl took over the telephone. She sounded very young and said, "You're at Woolworth's."

"Yes," I said.

"You're not very far away," she said.

That seemed awfully strange to me.

"When you leave Woolworth's, turn right and walk down three blocks and then turn left on Fourth Street, walk four blocks and then turn left again off Fourth Street," she said. "We are in a green building in the middle of the block. You can't miss it. Did you get that?"

"Yes," I said. "When we leave Woolworth's, we turn right and walk three blocks down to Fourth Street, then we turn left on Fourth Street, and walk four blocks and then turn left again off Fourth Street, and there's a green building in the middle of the block, and that's where you're at."

Vida was listening.

"Your wife hasn't eaten, has she?"

"No," I said.

"Good, we'll be waiting for you. If you should get lost, telephone again."

We left Woolworth's and followed the girl's directions amid being hustled by souvenir junk salesmen, the taxi drivers and gum kids of Tijuana, surrounded by wolf whistles, cars cars cars, and cries of animal consternation and HEY, BEATLE!

Fourth Street had waited eternally for us to come as we were always destined to come, Vida and me, and now we'd come, having started out that morning in San Francisco and our lives many years before.

The streets were filled with cars and people and a fantastic feeling of excitement. The houses did not have any lawns, only that famous dust. They were our guides to Dr. Garcia.

There was a brand-new American car parked in front of the green building. The car had California license plates. I didn't have to think about that one too much to come up with an answer. I looked in the back seat. There was a girl's sweater lying there. It looked helpless.

Some children were playing in front of the doctor's office. The children were poor and wore unhappy clothes. They stopped playing and watched us as we went in.

We were no doubt a common sight for them. They had probably seen many gringos in this part of town, going into this green adobe-like building, gringos who did not look very happy. We did not disappoint them.

BOOK 5:

My Three Abortions

Furniture Studies

THERE was a small bell to ring on the door. It was not like the silver bell of my library, so far away from this place. You rang this bell by pressing your finger against it. That's what I did.

We had to wait a moment for someone to answer. The children stayed away from their play to watch us. The children were small, ill-dressed and dirty. They had those strange undernourished bodies and faces that make it so hard to tell how old children are in Mexico.

A child that looks five will turn out to be eight. A child that looks seven will actually be ten. It's horrible.

Some Mexican mother women came by. They looked at us, too. Their eyes were expressionless, but showed in this way that they knew we were *abortionistas*.

Then the door to the doctor's office opened effortlessly as if it had always planned to open at that time and it was Dr. Garcia himself who opened the door for us. I didn't know what he looked like, but I knew it was him.

"Please," he said, gesturing us in.

"Thank you," I said. "I just called you on the telephone. I'm Foster's friend."

"I know," he said, quietly. "Follow, please."

The doctor was small, middle-aged and dressed perfectly like a doctor. His office was large and cool and had many rooms that led like a labyrinth far into the back and places that we knew nothing about.

He took us to a small reception room. It was clean with modern linoleum on the floor and modern doctor furniture: an uncomfortable couch and three chairs that you could never really fit into.

The furniture was the same as the furniture you see in the offices of American doctors. There was a tall plant in the corner with large flat cold green leaves. The leaves didn't do anything.

There were some other people already in the room: a father, a mother and a young teen-age daughter. She obviously belonged to the brand-new car parked in front.

"Please," the doctor said, gesturing us toward the two empty chairs in the room. "Soon," he said, smiling gently. "Wait, please. Soon."

He went away across the corridor and into another room that we could not see, leaving us with the three people. They were not talking and it was strangely quiet all through the building.

Everybody looked at everybody else in a nervous kind of way that comes when time and circumstance reduce us to seeking illegal operations in Mexico.

The father looked like a small town banker in the San Joaquin Valley and the mother looked like a woman who participated in a lot of social activities.

The daughter was pretty and obviously intelligent and didn't know what to do with her face as she waited for her abortion, so she kept smiling in a rapid knife-like way at nothing.

The father looked very stern as if he were going to refuse a loan and the mother looked vaguely shocked as if somebody had said something a little risqué at a social tea for the Friends of the DeMolay.

The daughter, though she possessed a narrow budding female body, looked as if she were too young to have an abortion. She should have been doing something else.

I looked over at Vida. She also looked as if she were too young to have an abortion. What were we all doing there? Her face was growing pale.

Alas, the innocence of love was merely an escalating physical condition and not a thing shaped like our kisses.

My First Abortion

ABOUT forever or ten minutes passed and then the doctor came back and motioned toward Vida and me to come with him, though the other people had been waiting when we came in. Perhaps it had something to do with Foster.

"Please," Dr. Garcia said, quietly.

We followed after him across the hall and into a small office. There was a desk in the office and a typewriter. The office was dark and cool, the shades were down, with a leather chair and photographs of the doctor and his family upon the walls and the desk.

There were various certificates showing the medical degrees the doctor had obtained and what schools he had graduated from.

There was a door that opened directly into an operating room. A teen-age girl was in the room cleaning up and a young boy, another teen-ager, was helping her.

A big blue flash of fire jumped across a tray full of surgical instruments. The boy was sterilizing the instruments with fire. It startled Vida and me. There was a table in the operating room that had metal things to hold your legs and there were leather straps that went with them.

"No pain," the doctor said to Vida and then to me. "No pain and clean, all clean, no pain. Don't worry. No pain and clean. Nothing left. I'm a doctor," he said.

I didn't know what to say. I was so nervous that I was almost in shock. All the color had drained from Vida's face and her eyes looked as if they could not see any more.

"250 dollars," the doctor said. "Please."

"Foster said it would be 200 dollars. That's all we have," I heard my own voice saying. "200. That's what you told Foster."

"200. That's all you have?" the doctor said.

Vida stood there listening to us arbitrate the price of her stomach. Vida's face was like a pale summer cloud.

"Yes," I said. "That's all we have."

I took the money out of my pocket and gave it to the doctor. I held the money out and he took it from my hand. He put it in his pocket, without counting it, and then he became a doctor again, and that's the way he stayed all the rest of the time we were there.

He had only stopped being a doctor for a moment. It was a little strange. I don't know what I expected. It was very good that he stayed a doctor for the rest of the time.

Foster was of course right.

He became a doctor by turning to Vida and smiling and saying, "I won't hurt you and it will be clean. Nothing left after and no pain, honey. Believe me. I'm a doctor."

Vida smiled 1/2: ly.

"How long has she been?" the doctor said to me and starting to point at her stomach but not following through with it, so his hand was a gesture that didn't do anything.

"About five or six weeks," I said.

Vida was now smiling 1/4: ly.

The doctor paused and looked at a calendar in his mind and then he nodded affectionately at the calendar. It was probably a very familiar calendar to him. They were old friends.

"No breakfast?" he said, starting to point again at Vida's stomach but again he failed to do so.

"No breakfast," I said.

"Good girl," the doctor said.

Vida was now smiling 1/37: ly.

After the boy finished sterilizing the surgical instruments, he took a small bucket back through another large room that was fastened to the operating room.

The other room looked as if it had beds in it. I moved my head a different way and I could see a bed in it and there was a girl lying on the bed asleep and there was a man sitting in a chair beside the bed. It looked very quiet in the room.

A moment after the boy left the operating room, I heard a toilet flush and water running from a tap and then the sound of water being poured in the toilet and the toilet was flushed again and the boy came back with the bucket.

The bucket was empty.

The boy had a large gold wristwatch on his hand.

"Everything's all right," the doctor said.

The teen-age girl, who was dark and pretty and also had a nice wristwatch, came into the doctor's office and smiled at Vida. It was that kind of smile that said: It's time now; please come with me.

"No pain, no pain, no pain," the doctor repeated like a nervous nursery rime.

No pain, I thought, how strange.

"Do you want to watch?" the doctor asked me, gesturing toward an examination bed in the operating room where I could sit if I wanted to watch the abortion.

I looked over at Vida. She didn't want me to watch and I didn't want to watch either.

"No," I said. "I'll stay in here."

"Please come, honey," the doctor said.

The girl touched Vida's arm and Vida went into the operating room with her and the doctor closed the door, but it didn't really close. It was still open an inch or so.

"This won't hurt," the girl said to Vida. She was giving Vida a shot.

Then the doctor said something in Spanish to the boy who said OK and did something.

"Take off your clothes," the girl said. "And put this on."

Then the doctor said something in Spanish and the boy answered him in Spanish and the girl said, "Please. Now put your legs up. That's it. Good. Thank you."

"That's right, honey," the doctor said. "That didn't hurt, did it? Everything's going to be all right. You're a good girl."

Then he said something to the boy in Spanish and then the girl said something in Spanish to the doctor who said something in Spanish to both of them.

Everything was very quiet for a moment or so in the operating room. I felt the dark cool of the doctor's office on my body like the hand of some other kind of doctor.

"Honey?" the doctor said. "Honey?"

There was no reply.

Then the doctor said something in Spanish to the boy and the boy answered him in something metallic, surgical. The doctor used the thing that was metallic and surgical and gave it back to the boy who gave him something else that was metallic and surgical.

Everything was either quiet or metallic and surgical in there for a while.

Then the girl said something in Spanish to the boy who replied to her in English. "I know," he said.

The doctor said something in Spanish.

The girl answered him in Spanish.

A few moments passed during which there were no more surgical sounds in the room. There was now the sound of cleaning up and the doctor and the girl and the boy talked in Spanish as they finished up.

Their Spanish was not surgical any more. It was just casual cleaning-up Spanish.

"What time is it?" the girl said. She didn't want to look at her watch.

"Around one," the boy said.

The doctor joined them in English. "How many more?" he said.

"Two," the girl said.

"¿Dos?" the doctor said in Spanish.

"There's one coming," the girl said.

The doctor said something in Spanish.

The girl answered him in Spanish.

"I wish it was three," the boy said in English.

"Stop thinking about girls," the doctor said, jokingly.

Then the doctor and the girl were involved in a brief very rapid conversation in Spanish.

This was followed by a noisy silence and then the sound of the doctor carrying something heavy and unconscious out of the operating room. He put the thing down in the other room and came back a moment later.

The girl walked over to the door of the room I was in and finished opening it. My dark cool office was suddenly flooded with operating room light. The boy was cleaning up.

"Hello," the girl said, smiling. "Please come with me."

She casually beckoned me through the operating room as if it were a garden of roses. The doctor was sterilizing his surgical instruments with the blue flame.

He looked up at me from the burning instruments and said, "Everything went OK. I promised no pain, all clean. The usual." He smiled. "Perfect."

The girl took me into the other room where Vida was lying unconscious on the bed. She had warm covers over her. She looked as if she were dreaming in another century.

"It was an excellent operation," the girl said. "There were no complications and it went as smoothly as possible. She'll wake up in a little while. She's beautiful, isn't she?"

"Yes."

The girl got me a chair and put it down beside Vida. I sat down in the chair and looked at Vida. She was so alone there in the bed. I reached over and touched her cheek. It felt as if it had just come unconscious from an operating room.

The room had a small gas heater that was burning quietly away in its own time. The room had two

155

beds in it and the other bed where the girl had lain a short while before was now empty and there was an empty chair beside the bed, as this bed would be empty soon and the chair I was now sitting in: to be empty.

The door to the operating room was open, but I couldn't see the operating table from where I was sitting.

My Second Abortion

THE door to the operating room was open, but I couldn't see the operating table from where I was sitting. A moment later they brought in the teen-age girl from the waiting room.

"Everything's going to be all right, honey," the doctor said. "This won't hurt." He gave her the shot himself.

"Please take off your clothes," the girl said.

There was a stunned silence for a few seconds that bled into the awkward embarrassed sound of the teenage girl taking her clothes off.

After she took off her clothes, the girl assistant who was no older than the girl herself said, "Put this on."

The girl put it on.

156

I looked down at the sleeping form of Vida. She was wearing one, too.

Vida's clothes were folded over a chair and her shoes were on the floor beside the chair. They looked very sad because she had no power over them any more. She lay unconscious before them.

"Now put your legs up, honey," the doctor was saying. "A little higher, please. That's a good girl."

Then he said something in Spanish to the Mexican girl and she answered him in Spanish.

"I've had six months of Spanish I in high school," the teen-age girl said with her legs apart and strapped to the metal stirrups of this horse of no children.

The doctor said something in Spanish to the Mexican girl and she replied in Spanish to him.

"Oh," he said, a little absentmindedly to nobody in particular. I guess he had performed a lot of abortions that day and then he said to the teen-age girl, "That's nice. Learn some more."

The boy said something very rapidly in Spanish.

The Mexican girl said something very rapidly in Spanish.

The doctor said something very rapidly in Spanish and then he said to the teen-age girl, "How do you feel, honey?"

"Nothing," she said, smiling. "I don't feel anything. Should I feel something right now?"

The doctor said something very rapidly to the boy in Spanish. The boy did not reply.

"I want you to relax," the doctor said to the teen-age girl. "Please take it easy."

All three of them had a very rapid go at it in

Spanish. There seemed to be some trouble and then the doctor said something very rapidly in Spanish to the Mexican girl. He finished it by saying, "¿Como se dice treinta?"

"Thirty," the Mexican girl said.

"Honey," the doctor said. He was leaning over the teen-age girl. "I want you to count to, to thirty for us, please, honey."

"All right," she said, smiling, but for the first time her voice sounded a little tired.

It was starting to work.

"1, 2, 3, 4, 5, 6 . . ." There was a pause here. "7, 8, 9 . . ." There was another pause here, but it was a little longer than the first pause.

"Count to, to thirty, honey," the doctor said.

"10, 11, 12."

There was a total stop.

"Count to thirty, honey," the boy said. His voice sounded soft and gentle just like the doctor's. Their voices were the sides of the same coin.

"What comes after 12?" the teen-age girl giggled. "I know! 13." She was very happy that 13 came after 12. "14, 15, 15, 15."

"You said 15," the doctor said.

"15," the teen-age girl said.

"What's next, honey?" the boy said.

"15," the teen-age girl said very slowly and triumphantly.

"What's next, honey?" the doctor said.

"15," the girl said. "15."

"Come on, honey," the doctor said.

"What's next?" the boy said.

"What's next?" the doctor said.

The girl didn't say anything.

They didn't say anything either. It was very quiet in the room. I looked down at Vida. She was very quiet, too.

Suddenly the silence in the operating room was broken by the Mexican girl saying, "16."

"What?" the doctor said.

"Nothing," the Mexican girl said, and then the language and silences of the abortion began.

Chalkboard Studies

VIDA lay there gentle and still like marble dust on the bed. She had not shown the slightest sign of consciousness, but I wasn't worried because her breathing was normal.

So I just sat there listening to the abortion going on in the other room and looking at Vida and where I was at: this house in Mexico, so far away from my San Francisco library.

The small gas heater was doing its thing because it was cool within the adobe walls of the doctor's office.

Our room was in the center of a labyrinth.

There was a little hall on one side of the room,

running back past the open door of the toilet and ending at a kitchen.

The kitchen was about twenty feet away from where Vida lay unconscious with her stomach vacant like a chalkboard. I could see the refrigerator and a sink in the kitchen and a stove with some pans on it.

On the other side of our room was a door that led into a huge room, almost like a small gym, and I could see still another room off the gym.

The door was open and there was the dark abstraction of another bed in the room like a large flat sleeping animal.

I looked down at Vida still submerged in a vacuum of anesthesia and listened to the abortion ending in the operating room.

Suddenly there was a gentle symphonic crash of surgical instruments and then I could hear the sounds of cleaning up joined to another chalkboard.

My Third Abortion

THE doctor came through the room carrying the teenage girl in his arms. Though the doctor was a small man, he was very strong and carried the girl without difficulty.

She looked very silent and unconscious. Her hair hung strangely over his arm in a blond confusion. He took the girl through the small gym and into the adjoining room where he lay her upon the dark animal-like bed.

Then he came over and closed the door to our room and went into the forward reaches of the labyrinth and came back with the girl's parents.

"It went perfect," he said. "No pain, all clean."

They didn't say anything to him and he came back to our room. As he passed through the door, the people were watching him and they saw Vida lying there and me sitting beside her.

I looked at them and they looked at me before the door was closed. Their faces were a stark and frozen landscape.

The boy came into the room carrying the bucket and he went into the toilet and flushed the fetus and the abortion leftovers down the toilet.

Just after the toilet flushed, I heard the flash of the instruments being sterilized by fire.

It was the ancient ritual of fire and water all over again to be all over again and again in Mexico today.

Vida still lay there unconscious. The Mexican girl came in and looked at Vida. "She's sleeping," the girl said. "It went fine."

She went back into the operating room and then the next woman came into the operating room. She was the "one" coming the Mexican girl had mentioned earlier. I didn't know what she looked like because she had come since we'd been there.

"Has she eaten today?" the doctor said.

"No," a man said sternly, as if he were talking about dropping a hydrogen bomb on somebody he didn't like.

The man was her husband. He had come into the operating room. He had decided that he wanted to watch the abortion. They were awfully tense people and the woman said only three words all the time she was there. After she had her shot, he helped her off with her clothes.

He sat down while her legs were strapped apart on the operating table. She was unconscious just about the time they finished putting her in position for the abortion because they started almost immediately.

This abortion was done automatically like a machine. There was very little conversation between the doctor and his helpers.

I could feel the presence of the man in the operating room. He was like some kind of statue sitting there looking on, waiting for a museum to snatch him and his wife up. I never saw the woman.

After the abortion the doctor was tired and Vida was still lying there unconscious. The doctor came into the room. He looked down at Vida.

"Not yet," he said, answering his own question.

I said no because I didn't have anything else to do with my mouth.

"It's OK," he said. "Sometimes it's like this."

The doctor looked like an awfully tired man. God only knows how many abortions he had performed that day.

He came over and sat down on the bed. He took Vida's hand and he felt her pulse. He reached down and opened one of her eyes. Her eye looked back at him from a thousand miles away.

"It's all right," he said. "She'll be back in a few moments."

He went into the toilet and washed his hands. After he finished washing his hands, the boy came in with the bucket and took care of that.

The girl was cleaning up in the operating room. The doctor had put the woman on the examination bed in the operating room.

He had quite a thing going just taking care of the bodies.

"OHHHHHHHHHH!" I heard a voice come from behind the gym door where the doctor had taken the teen-age girl. "OHHHHHHHHHHH!" It was a sentimental drunken voice. It was the girl. "OHHHHHHHHHH!

"16!" she said. "I-OHHHHHHHHHH!"

Her parents were talking to her in serious, hushed tones. They were awfully respectable.

"OHHHHHHHHHHHHHHHHHHHHHHHH!"

They were acting as if she had gotten drunk at a family reunion and they were trying to cover up her drunkenness.

"OHHHHHHHHHH! I feel funny!"

There was total silence from the couple in the operating room. The only sound was the Mexican girl. The boy had come back through our room and had gone somewhere else in the building. He never came back.

After the girl finished cleaning up the operating room, she went into the kitchen and started cooking a big steak for the doctor.

She got a bottle of Miller's beer out of the refrigerator and poured the doctor a big glass of it. He sat down in the kitchen. I could barely see him drinking the beer.

Then Vida started stirring in her sleep. She opened her eyes. They didn't see anything for a moment or so and then they saw me.

"Hi," she said in a distant voice.

"Hi," I said, smiling.

"I feel dizzy," she said, coming in closer.

"Don't worry about it," I said. "Everything is fine."

"Oh, that's good," she said. There.

"Just lie quietly and take it easy," I said.

The doctor got up from the table in the kitchen and came in. He was holding the glass of beer in his hand.

"She's coming back," he said.

"Yes," I said.

"Good," he said. "Good."

He took his glass of beer and went back into the kitchen and sat down again. He was very tired.

Then I heard the people in the outside gym room dressing their daughter. They were in a hurry to leave. They sounded as if they were dressing a drunk.

"I can't get my hands up," the girl said.

Her parents said something stern to her and she got her hands up in the air, but they had so much trouble putting her little brassiere on that they finally abandoned trying and the mother put the brassiere in her purse.

"OHHHHHHHHHH! I'm so dizzy," the girl said as her parents half-carried her, half-dragged her out of the place.

I heard a couple of doors close and then everything was silent, except for the doctor's lunch cooking in the kitchen. The steak was being fried in a very hot pan and it made a lot of noise.

"What's that?" Vida said. I didn't know if she was talking about the noise of the girl leaving or the sound of the steak cooking.

"It's the doctor having lunch," I said.

"Is it that late?" she said.

"Yes," I said.

"I've been out a long time," she said.

"Yes," I said. "We're going to have to leave soon but we won't leave until you feel like it."

"I'll see what I can do," Vida said.

The doctor came back into the room. He was nervous because he was hungry and tired and wanted to close the place up for a while, so he could take it easy, rest some.

Vida looked up at him and he smiled and said, "See, no pain, honey. Everything wonderful. Good girl."

Vida smiled very weakly and the doctor returned to the kitchen and his steak that was ready now.

While the doctor had his lunch, Vida slowly sat up and I helped her get dressed. She tried standing up but it was too hard, so I had her sit back down for a few moments.

While she sat there, she combed her hair and then she tried standing up again but she still didn't have it and sat back down on the bed again.

"I'm still a little rocky," Vida said.

"That's all right."

The woman in the other room had come to and her husband was dressing her almost instantly, saying, "Here. Here. Here. Here," in a painful Okie accent.

"I'm tired," the woman said, using up 2/3 of her vocabulary.

"Here," the man said, helping her put something else on.

After he got her dressed he came into our room and stood there looking for the doctor. He was very embarrassed when he saw Vida sitting on the bed, combing her hair.

"Doctor?" he said.

The doctor got up from his steak and stood in the doorway of the kitchen. The man started to walk toward the door, but then stopped after taking only a few steps.

The doctor came into our room.

"Yes," he said.

"I can't remember where I parked my car," the man said. "Can you call me a taxi?"

"You lost your auto?" the doctor said.

"I parked it next to Woolworth's, but I can't remember where Woolworth's is," the man said. "I can find Woolworth's if I can get downtown. I don't know where to go."

"The boy's coming back," the doctor said. "He'll take you there in his auto."

"Thank you," the man said, returning to his wife in the other room. "Did you hear that?" he said to her.

"Yes," she said, using it all up.

"We'll wait," he said.

Vida looked over at me and I smiled at her and took her hand to my mouth and kissed it.

"Let's try again," she said.

"All right," I said.

She tried it again and this time it was all right. She stood there for a few moments and then said, "I've got it. Let's go."

"Are you sure you have it?" I said.

"Yes."

I helped Vida on with her sweater. The doctor looked at us from the kitchen. He smiled but he didn't say anything. He had done what he was supposed to do and now we did what we were supposed to do. We left.

We wandered out of the room into the gym and worked our way to the front of the place, passing through layers of coolness to the door.

Even though it had remained a gray overcast day, we were stunned by the light and everything was instantly noisy, car-like, confused, poor, rundown and Mexican.

It was as if we had been in a time capsule and now were released again to be in the world.

The children were still playing in front of the doctor's office and again they stopped their games of life to watch two squint-eyed gringos holding, cling-ing, holding to each other walk up the street and into a world without them.

BOOK 6:

The Hero

Woolworth's Again

WE slowly, carefully and abortively made our way back to downtown Tijuana surrounded and bombarded by people trying to sell us things that we did not want to buy.

We had already gotten what we'd come to Tijuana for. I had my arm around Vida. She was all right but she was a little weak.

"How do you feel, honey?" I said.

"I feel all right," she said. "But I'm a little weak."

We saw an old man crouching like a small gum-like piece of death beside an old dilapidated filling station.

"HEY, a pretty, pretty girl!"

Mexican men kept reacting to Vida's now pale beauty.

Vida smiled faintly at me as a taxicab driver dramatically stopped his cab in front of us and leaned out the window and gave a gigantic wolf whistle and said, "WOW! You need a taxi, honey!"

We made our way to the Main Street of Tijuana and found ourselves in front of Woolworth's again and the bunnies in the window.

"I'm hungry," Vida said. She was tired. "So hungry."

"You need something to eat," I said. "Let's go inside and see if we can get you some soup."

"That would be good," she said. "I need something."

We went off the confused dirty Main Street of Tijuana into the clean modern incongruity of Woolworth's. A very pretty Mexican girl took our order at the counter. She asked us what we wanted.

"What would you like?" she said.

"She'd like some soup," I said. "Some clam chowder."

"Yes," Vida said.

"What would you like?" the waitress said in very good Woolworth's English.

"I guess a banana split," I said.

I held Vida's hand while the waitress got our orders. She leaned her head against my shoulder. Then she smiled and said, "You're looking at the future biggest fan The Pill ever had."

"How do you feel?" I said.

"Just like I've had an abortion."

Then the waitress brought us our food. While Vida slowly worked her soup, I worked my banana split. It was the first banana split I'd had in years.

It was unusual fare for the day, but it was no different from anything else that had happened since we'd come to the Kingdom of Tijuana to avail ourselves of the local recreational facilities.

The taxicab driver never took his eyes off Vida as we drove back to America. His eyes looked at us from the rear-view mirror as if he had another face and it was a mirror.

"Did you have a good time in Tijuana?" he said.

"Lovely," I said.

"What did you do?" he said.

"We had an abortion," I said.

"HAHAHAHAHAHAHAHAVERYFUNNYJOKE!"

the driver laughed.

Vida smiled.

Farewell, Tijuana.

Kingdom of Fire and Water.

The Green Hotel Again

OUR desk clerk was waiting for us, agog with smiles and questions. I had an idea that he drank on the job. There was something about how friendly he was.

"Did you see your sister?" he asked Vida with a big falseteeth smile.

"What?" Vida said. She was tired.

"Yes, we saw her," I said. "She was just as we remembered her."

"Even more so," Vida said, catching the game by the tail.

"That's good," the clerk said. "People should never change. They should always be the same. They are happier that way."

I tried that one on for size and was able to hold a straight face. It had been a long day.

"My wife's a little tired," I said. "I think we'll go up to our room."

"Relatives can be tiring. The excitement of it all. Renewing family ties," the desk clerk said.

"Yes," I said.

He gave us the key to his mother's room.

"I can take you up to the room if you don't remember the way," he said.

"No, that's not necessary," I said. "I remember the way." I headed him off by saying, "It's such a beautiful room."

"Isn't it?" he said.

"Very lovely room," Vida said.

"My mother was so happy there," he said.

We took the old elevator upstairs and I opened the door with the key. "Get off the bed," I said as we went into the room. "Off," I repeated.

"What?" Vida said.

"The Mother Ghost," I said.

"Oh."

Vida lay down on the bed and closed her eyes. I took her shoes off, so she could be more comfortable.

"How do you feel?" I said.

"A little tired."

"Let's take a nap," I said, putting her under the covers and joining her.

We slept for an hour or so and then I woke up. The Mother Ghost was brushing her teeth and I told her to get into the closet until we were gone. She got into the closet and closed the door after her.

"Hey, baby," I said. Vida stirred in her sleep and then opened her eyes.

"What time is it?" she said.

"About the middle of the afternoon," I said.

"What time does our plane leave?" she said.

"6:25," I said. "Do you feel you can make it? If you don't, we'll spend the night here."

"No, I'm all right," she said. "Let's go back to San Francisco. I don't like San Diego. I want to get out of here and leave all this behind."

We got up and Vida washed her face and straightened herself up and felt a lot better, though she was still a little weak.

I told the hotel ghost mother good-bye in the closet and Vida joined me. "Good-bye, ghost," she said.

We went down the elevator to the waiting desk clerk whom I suspected of drinking on the job.

He was startled to see me standing there holding the KLM bag in my hand and returning the room key to him.

"You're not spending the night?" he said.

"No," I said. "We've decided to stay with her sister."

"What about your snoring?" he said.

"I'm going to see a doctor about it," I said. "I can't hide from this all my life. I can't go on living like this forever. I've decided to face it like a man."

Vida gave me a little nudge with her eyes to tell me that I was carrying it a little too far, so I retreated by saying, "You have a lovely hotel here and I'll recommend it to all my friends when they visit San Diego. What do I owe you?"

"Thank you," he said. "Nothing. You're Foster's friend. But you didn't even spend the night."

"That's all right," I said. "You've been very friendly. Thank you and good-bye."

"Good-bye," the desk clerk said. "Come again when you can spend the night."

"We will," I said.

"Good-bye," Vida said.

Suddenly he got a little desperate and paranoid. "There was nothing wrong with the room, was there?" he said. "It was my mother's room."

"Nothing," I said. "It was perfect."

"A wonderful hotel," Vida said. "A beautiful room. A truly beautiful room."

Vida seemed to have calmed him down because he said to us as we were going out the door, "Say hello to your sister for me."

That gave us something to think about as we drove out to the San Diego airport sitting very close together in the back seat of a cab where the driver, American this time, did not take his eyes off Vida in the mirror.

When we first got into the cab, the driver said, "Where to?"

I thought it would be fairly simple just to say, "The International Airport, please."

It wasn't.

"That's the San Diego International Airport, isn't it? That's where you want to go, huh?"

"Yes," I said, knowing that something was wrong.

"I just wanted to be sure," he said. "Because I had a fare yesterday that wanted to go to the Inter-

176

national Airport, but it was the Los Angeles International Airport he wanted to go to. That's why I was checking."

Oh, yeah.

"Did you take him?" I said. I didn't have anything else to do and my relationship with the cab driver was obviously out of control.

"Yes," he said.

"He was probably afraid of flying," I said.

The cab driver didn't get the joke because he was watching Vida in the rear-view mirror and Vida was watching me after that one.

The driver continued staring at Vida. He paid very little attention to his driving. It was obviously dangerous to ride in a cab with Vida.

I made a mental note of it for the future, not to have Vida's beauty risk our lives.

The San Diego
(Not Los Angeles)
International Tipping Abyss

UNFORTUNATELY, the cab driver was very unhappy with the tip I gave him. The fare was again one dollar and ten cents and remindful of the experience we'd had earlier in the day with that first cab driver, I raised the tip-ante to thirty cents.

He was startled by the thirty-cent tip and didn't want to have anything else to do with us. Even Vida didn't make any difference when he saw that thirty cents.

What *is* the tip to the San Diego airport?

Our plane didn't leave for an hour. Vida was quite hungry, so we had something to eat in the cafe. It was about 5:30.

We had hamburgers. It was the first time I'd had a hamburger in years, but it turned out not to be very good. It was flat.

Vida said her hamburger was good, though.

"You've forgotten how a hamburger is supposed to taste," Vida said. "Too many years in the monastery have destroyed your better judgment."

There were two women sitting nearby. One of them had platinum hair and a mink coat. She was middle-aged and talking to a young, blandly pretty girl who was talking in turn about her wedding and the little caps that were being designed for the bridesmaids.

The girl was nice in the leg department but a little short in the titty line or was I spoiled? They departed their table without leaving a tip.

This made the waitress mad.

She was probably a close relative to the two cab drivers I'd met that day in San Diego.

She stared at the tipless table as if it were a sex criminal. Perhaps she was their mother.

Farewell, San Diego

I TOOK a closer look at the San Diego airport. It was petite, uncomplicated with no *Playboy* stuff at all. The people were there to work, not to look pretty.

There was a sign that said something like: Animals arriving as baggage may be claimed in the airline air freight areas in the rear of bldg.

You can bet your life that you don't see signs like that in the San Francisco International Airport.

A young man with crutches, accompanied by three old men, came along as we were going out to wait for our airplane. They all stared at Vida and the young man stared the hardest.

It was a long way from the beautiful PSA pre-flight lounge in San Francisco to just standing outside, beside a wire fence in San Diego, waiting to get on our airplane that was shark-like and making a high whistling steam sound, wanting very much to fly.

The evening was cold and gray coming down upon us with some palm trees, nearby, by the highway. The palm trees somehow made it seem colder than it actually was. They seemed out of place in the cold.

There was a military band playing beside one of the airplanes parked on the field, but it was too far away to see why they were playing. Maybe some big wig was coming or going. They sounded like my hamburger.

My Secret Talisman Forever

WE got our old seats back over the wing and I was sitting again next to the window. Suddenly it was dark in twelve seconds. Vida was quiet, tired. There was a little light on the end of the wing. I became quite fond of it out there in the dark like a lighthouse burning twenty-three miles away and I made it my secret talisman forever.

A young priest was sitting across the aisle from us. He was quite smitten by Vida for the short distance to Los Angeles.

At first he tried not to be obvious about it, but after a while he surrendered himself to it and one time he leaned across the aisle and was going to say something to Vida. He was actually going to say something to her, but then he changed his mind.

I will probably go on for a long time wondering what he would have said to my poor aborted darling who, though weak and tired from the ways of Tijuana, was the prettiest thing going in the sky above California, the rapidly moving sky to Los Angeles.

I went from the priest's interest in Vida to wondering about Foster at the library, how he was handling the books that were coming in that day.

I hoped he was welcoming them the right way and making the authors feel comfortable and wanted as I made them feel.

"Well, we'll be home soon," Vida said to me after a long silence that was noisy with thought. The priest's composure vibrated with tension when Vida spoke.

"Yes," I said. "I was just thinking about that."

"I know," she said. "I could hear the noise in your mind. I think everything's all right at the library. Foster's doing a good job."

"You're doing a good job yourself," I said.

"Thank you," she said. "It will be good to get home. Back to the library and some sleep."

I was very pleased that she considered the library her home. I looked out the window at my talisman. I loved it as much as the coffee stain flying down.

Perhaps and Eleven

THINGS are different at night. The houses and towns far below demand their beauty and get it in distant lights twinkling with incredible passion. Landing at Los Angeles was like landing inside a diamond ring.

The priest didn't want to get off the plane at Los

Angeles, but he had to because that's where he was going. Perhaps Vida reminded him of somebody. Perhaps his mother was very beautiful and he didn't know how to handle it and that's what drove him to the Cloth and now to see that beauty again in Vida was like swirling back through the mirrors of time.

Perhaps he was thinking about something completely different from what I have ever thought about in my life and his thoughts were of the highest nature and should have been made into a statue ... perhaps. To quote Foster, "Too many perhapses in the world and not enough people."

I was suddenly wondering about my library again and missed the actual departure of the priest to become part of Los Angeles, to add his share to its size and to take memories of Vida into whatever.

"Did you see that?" Vida said.

"Yes," I said.

"This has been happening ever since I was eleven," she said.

Fresno, Then 3½ Minutes to Salinas

THE stewardesses on this flight were fantastically shallow and had been born from half a woman into a world that possessed absolutely no character except chrome smiles. All of them were of course beautiful.

One of them was pushing a little cart down the aisle, trying to sell us cocktails. She had a singsong inhuman voice that I'm positive was prerecorded by a computer.

"Purchase a cocktail.

"Purchase a cocktail.

"Purchase a cocktail."

While pushing her little cart down the sky.

"Purchase a cocktail.

"Purchase a cocktail.

"Purchase a cocktail."

There were no lights below.

Shine on, O talisman!

I pushed my face against the window and looked very hard and saw a star and I made a wish but I won't tell. Why should I? Purchase a cocktail from pretty Miss Zero and find your own star. There's one for everyone in the evening sky.

There were two women behind us talking about nail polish for the thirty-nine minute way to San Francisco. One of them thought that fingernails without polish should be put under rocks.

Vida had no polish on her fingernails but she didn't care and gave the women's conversation no attention.

From time to time the airplane was bucked by an invisible horse in the sky but it didn't bother me because I was falling in love with the 727 jet, my sky home, my air love.

The pilot or some male voice told us that if we looked out the window, we could see the lights of

Fresno and were 3½ minutes away from the lights of Salinas.

I was already looking for Salinas, but something happened on the plane. One of the women spilt her fingernail polish on a cat ten years ago and I looked away for a moment to wonder about that and missed Salinas, so I pretended my talisman was Salinas.

The Saint of Abortion

WE were about to land at San Francisco when the women behind us finished their conversation about fingernail polish.

"I wouldn't be caught dead without fingernail polish," one of them said.

"You're right," the other one said.

We were only three miles away from landing and I couldn't see the wing that led like a black highway to my talisman. It seemed as if we were going to land without a wing, only a talisman.

Ah, the wing appeared magically just as we touched the ground.

There were soldiers everywhere in the terminal. It was as if an army were encamped there. They flipped when they saw Vida. She was increasing the United States Army sperm count by about three tons as we walked through the place, heading toward the van in the parking lot.

Vida also affected the civilian population by causing a man who looked like a banker to walk directly into an Oriental woman, knocking the woman down. She was rather surprised because she had just flown in from Saigon and didn't expect this to happen on her first visit to America.

Alas, another victim of Vida's thing.

"Do you think you can take it?" Vida said.

"We ought to bottle what you've got," I said.

"Vida Pop," Vida said.

"How do you feel?" I said with my arm around her.

"Glad to be home," she said.

Even though the San Francisco International Airport acted like a *Playboy* cybernetic palace wanting to do things for us that we were not quite ready to have done, at that moment I felt that the International Airport was our first home back from Tijuana.

I was also anxious to get back to the library and see Foster.

The Bufano statue waited for us with a peace that we couldn't understand with its strange people fastened projectile-like upon a huge bullet.

As we got into the van, I thought there should be a statue for the Saint of Abortion, whoever that was, somewhere in the parking lot for the thousands of women who had made the same trip Vida and I had just finished, flying into the Kingdom of Fire and Water, the waiting and counting hands of Dr. Garcia and his associates in Mexico.

Thank God, the van had an intimate, relaxed human feeling to it. The van reflected Foster in its smells and ways of life. It felt very good to be in the van after having travelled the story of California.

I put my hand on Vida's lap and that's where it stayed following the red lights of cars in front of us shining back like roses into San Francisco.

A New Life

WHEN we arrived back at the library the first thing we saw was Foster sitting out on the steps in his traditional T-shirt, even though it was now dark and cold.

The lights were on in the library and I wondered what Foster was doing sitting outside on the steps. That didn't seem to be the correct way to run a library.

Foster stood up and waved that big friendly wave of his.

"Hello, there, strangers," he said. "How did it go?"

"Fine," I said, getting out of the van. "What are you doing out here?"

"How's my baby?" Foster said to Vida.

"Great," she said.

"Why aren't you inside?" I said.

186

"Tired, honey?" Foster said to Vida. He put his arm gently around her.

"A little," she said.

"Well, that's the way it should be, but it won't last long."

"The library?" I said.

"Good girl," Foster said to Vida. "Am I glad to see you! You look like a million dollars in small change. What a sight!" giving her a kiss on the cheek.

"The library?" I said.

Foster turned toward me. "I'm sorry about that," he said, then turning to Vida, "Oh, what a girl!"

"You're sorry about what?" I said.

"Don't worry," Foster said. "It's for the best. You need a rest, a change of scene. You'll be a lot happier now."

"Happier, what? What's going on?"

"Well," Foster said. He had his arm around Vida and she was looking up at him as he tried to explain what was going on.

There was a slight smile on her face that grew larger and larger as Foster continued, "Well, it happened this way. I was sitting there minding your asylum when this lady came in with a book and she—"

I looked away from Foster toward the library where its friendly light was shining out and I looked inside the glass door and I could see a woman sitting behind the desk.

I couldn't see her face but I could see that it was a woman and her form looked quite at home. My heart and my stomach started doing funny things in my body.

"You mean?" I said, unable to find the words.

"That's right," Foster said. "She said the way that I was handling the library was a disgrace and I was a slob and she would take it over now: thank you.

"I told her that you'd been here for years and that you were great with the library and I was just watching it during an emergency. She said that didn't make any difference, that if you had turned the library over to me, even for a day, you didn't deserve to be in charge of the library any more.

"I told her that I worked at the caves and she said that I didn't work there any more, that her brother would take care of it from now on, that I should think of doing something else like getting a job.

"Then she asked me where the living quarters were and I pointed out the way and she went in and packed all your stuff. When she found Vida's things there, she said, 'I got here just in time!' Then she had me take it all out here and I've been sitting here ever since."

I looked down at my meager possessions piled on the steps. I hadn't even noticed them.

"I can't believe it," I said. "I'll go tell her that it's all a mistake, that—"

Just then the woman got up from behind the desk and strolled very aggressively to the front door and opened the door without stepping outside and she yelled at me, "Get your God-damn stuff out of here right now and never come back, not unless you've got a book under your arm!"

"There's been a mistake," I said.

"Yes," she said. "I know and you are it. Farewell, creep!"

She turned and the front door closed behind her as if it were obeying her.

I stood there like Lot's wife on one of her bad days.

Vida was laughing like hell and Foster was, too. They started doing a little dance on the sidewalk around me.

"There must be a mistake," I cried in the wilderness.

"You heard the lady," Foster said. "Damn! Damn! Damn! am I glad to be out of the cave business. I thought I was going to get TB."

"Oh, darling," Vida said, breaking the dance to throw her arms around me while Foster started loading our stuff into the van. "You've just been fired. You're going to have to live like a normal human being."

"I can't believe it," I sighed. Then they loaded me into the van.

"Well, what are we going to do?" Foster said.

"Let's go to my place," Vida said. "It's just around the block on Lyon Street."

"I can always sleep in the van," Foster said.

"No, there's plenty of room in my place for all of us," Vida said.

Somehow Vida had ended up driving the van and she parked it in front of a big red shingled house that had an ancient iron fence in front of it. The fench looked quite harmless. Time had removed its ferocity and Vida lived in the attic.

Her place was nice and simple. There was practically no furniture and the walls were painted white and there was nothing on them.

We sat on the floor on a thick white rug that had a low marble table in the center of it.

"Do you want a drink?" Vida said. "I think we all need a drink."

Foster smiled.

She made us some very dry vodka martinis in glasses full of ice. She didn't put any vermouth in them. The drinks were done off with twists of lemon peel. The lemon lay there like flowers in the ice.

"I'll put something on the stereo," Vida said. "Then I'll start some dinner."

I was shocked by losing my library and surprised at being inside a real house again. Both feelings were passing like ships in the night.

"Damn, does that vodka taste good!" Foster said.

"No, honey," I said. "I think you'd better rest. I'll cook up something."

"No," Foster said. "A little logger breakfast is what we all need now. Some fried potatoes and onions and eggs all cooked together with a gallon of catsup on top. Do you have the makings?"

"No," Vida said. "But there's a store open down at California and Divisadero."

"OK," Foster said.

He put some more vodka in his mouth.

"Ah, do you kids have any money left? I'm flat."

I gave Foster a couple of dollars that I had left and he went to the store.

Vida put a record on the phonograph. It was the Beatles' album *Rubber Soul*. I had never heard the Beatles before. That's how long I was in the library.

"I want you to hear this one first," Vida said.

We sat there quietly listening to the record.

"Who sang that?" I said.

"John Lennon," she said.

Foster came back with the food and started cooking our dinnerbreakfast thing. Soon the whole attic was filled with the smell of onions.

That was months ago.

It's now the last of May and we're all living together in a little house in Berkeley. It has a small back yard. Vida's working at a topless place over in North Beach, so she'll have some money to go back to school next fall. She's going to give English another try. Foster has a girlfriend who is an exchange student from Pakistan. She's twenty and majoring in sociology.

She's in the other room now cooking up a big Pakistani dinner and Foster is watching her with a can of beer in his hand. He's got a job at Bethlehem Steel over in San Francisco at night working on an aircraft carrier that's in dry dock being fixed. Today is Foster's day off.

Vida is off doing something or other and will be home soon. She doesn't work tonight either. I've spent the afternoon at a table across from Sproul Hall where they took all those hundreds of Free

Speech kids off to jail in 1964. I've been gathering contributions for The American Forever, Etc.

I like to set my table up around lunch time near the fountain, so I can see the students when they come pouring through Sather Gate like the petals of a thousand-colored flowers. I love the joy of their intellectual perfume and the political rallies they hold at noon on the steps of Sproul Hall.

It's nice near the fountain with green trees all around and bricks and people that need me. There are even a lot of dogs that hang around the plaza. They are of all shapes and colors. I think it's important that you find things like this at the University of California.

Vida was right when she said that I would be a hero in Berkeley.